2

THE KELLYS AND THE O'KELLYS

ANTHONY TROLLOPE, the fourth of six surviving children, was born on 24 April 1815 in London. As he describes in his *Autobiography*, poverty and debt made his childhood acutely unhappy and disrupted his education: his school fees at Harrow and Winchester were frequently unpaid. His family attempted to restore their fortunes by going to America, leaving the young Anthony alone in England, but it was not until his mother, Frances, began to write that there was any improvement in the family's finances. Her success came too late for her husband, who died in exile in Belgium in 1835. Trollope was unable to afford a university education, and in 1834 he became a junior clerk in the Post Office. He achieved little until he was appointed Surveyor's Clerk in Ireland in 1841. There he worked hard, travelled widely, took up hunting and still found time for his literary career. He married Rose Heseltine, the daughter of a bank manager, in 1844; they had two sons, one of whom emigrated to Australia. Trollope frequently went abroad for the Post Office and did not settle in England again until 1859. He is still remembered as the inventor of the letter-box. In 1867 he resigned from the Post Office and became the editor of *St Paul's Magazine* for the next three years. He failed in his attempt to enter Parliament as a Liberal in 1868. Trollope took his place among London literary society and counted William Thackeray, George Eliot and G. H. Lewes among his friends. He died on 6 December 1882 as the result of a stroke.

Anthony Trollope wrote forty-seven novels and five volumes of short stories as well as travel books, biographies and collections of sketches. The Barsetshire series and the six Palliser or 'political' books were the first novel-sequences to be written in English. His works offer an unsurpassed portrait of the professional and landed classes of Victorian England. In his *Autobiography* (published posthumously in 1883) Trollope describes the self-discipline that enabled his prolific output: he would produce a given number of words per hour in the early morning, before work; he always wrote while travelling by rail or sea, and as soon as he finished one novel he began another. His efforts resulted in his becoming one of England's most successful and popular writers.

The Kellys and the O'Kellys: Or Landlords and Tenants (1848) is Trollope's second novel and is set in Ireland like its predecessor, *The Macdermots of Ballycloran* (1847). The author describes it in his *Autobiography* as 'a good Irish story ... superior in the mode of telling' to *The Macdermots*. A contemporary review praised it as 'free from that outrageous exaggeration which is so common in sketches of Irish life and character. That the author knows well the subject on which he writes, is evident enough, even to those who have never been in Dublin ... he has the power of putting his readers in possession of his knowledge and experience ...'

THE KELLYS AND THE O'KELLYS

OR LANDLORDS AND TENANTS

ANTHONY TROLLOPE

PENGUIN BOOKS

PENGUIN BOOKS

Published by the Penguin Group
Penguin Books Ltd, 27 Wrights Lane, London W8 5TZ, England
Penguin Books USA Inc., 375 Hudson Street, New York, New York 10014, USA
Penguin Books Australia Ltd, Ringwood, Victoria, Australia
Penguin Books Canada Ltd, 10 Alcorn Avenue, Toronto, Ontario, Canada M4V 3B2
Penguin Books (NZ) Ltd, 182–190 Wairau Road, Auckland 10, New Zealand

Penguin Books Ltd, Registered Offices: Harmondsworth, Middlesex, England

First published 1848
Published in Penguin Books 1993
1 3 5 7 9 10 8 6 4 2

Printed in England by Clays Ltd, St Ives plc

CONTENTS

I.	THE TRIAL	1
II.	THE TWO HEIRESSES	18
III.	MORRISON'S HOTEL	29
IV.	THE DUNMORE INN	47
V.	A LOVING BROTHER	57
VI.	THE ESCAPE	68
VII.	MR. BARRY LYNCH MAKES A MORNING CALL	81
VIII.	MR. MARTIN KELLY RETURNS TO DUNMORE	95
IX.	MR. DALY, THE ATTORNEY	105
X.	DOT BLAKE'S ADVICE	117
XI.	THE EARL OF CASHEL	129
XII.	FANNY WYNDHAM	142
XIII.	FATHER AND SON	154
XIV.	THE COUNTESS	168
XV.	HANDICAP LODGE	179
XVI.	BRIEN BORU	189
XVII.	MARTIN KELLY'S COURTSHIP	207
XVIII.	AN ATTORNEY'S OFFICE IN CONNAUGHT	221
XIX.	MR. DALY VISITS THE DUNMORE INN	232
XX.	VERY LIBERAL	248
XXI.	LORD BALLINDINE AT HOME	263
XXII.	THE HUNT	279
XXIII.	DR. COLLIGAN	291
XXIV.	ANTY LYNCH'S BED-SIDE; SCENE THE FIRST	300
XXV.	ANTY LYNCH'S BED-SIDE; SCENE THE SECOND	309

XXVI. LOVE'S AMBASSADOR . . . 317

XXVII. MR. LYNCH'S LAST RESOURCE . . 329

XXVIII. FANNY WYNDHAM REBELS . . 348

XXIX. THE COUNTESS OF CASHEL IN TROUBLE 363

XXX. LORD KILCULLEN OBEYS HIS FATHER 377

XXXI. THE TWO FRIENDS 396

XXXII. HOW LORD KILCULLEN FARES IN HIS WOOING 409

XXXIII. LORD KILCULLEN MAKES ANOTHER VISIT TO THE BOOK-ROOM . . 425

XXXIV. THE DOCTOR MAKES A CLEAN BREAST OF IT 439

XXXV. MR. LYNCH BIDS FAREWELL TO DUNMORE 451

XXXVI. MR. ARMSTRONG VISITS GREY ABBEY ON A DELICATE MISSION . . 468

XXXVII. VENI; VIDI; VICI 479

XXXVIII. WAIT TILL I TELL YOU . . . 484

XXXIX. IT NEVER RAINS BUT IT POURS . 495

XL. CONCLUSION 510

THE
KELLYS AND THE O'KELLYS

I

THE TRIAL

DURING the first two months of the year 1844, the greatest possible excitement existed in Dublin respecting the State Trials, in which Mr. O'Connell, his son, the Editors of three different repeal newspapers, Tom Steele, the Rev. Mr. Tierney—a priest who had taken a somewhat prominent part in the Repeal Movement—and Mr. Ray, the Secretary to the Repeal Association, were indicted for conspiracy. Those who only read of the proceedings in papers, which gave them as a mere portion of the news of the day, or learned what was going on in Dublin by chance conversation, can have no idea of the absorbing interest which the whole affair created in Ireland, but more especially in the metropolis. Every one felt strongly, on one side or on the other. Every one had brought the matter home to his own bosom, and looked to the result of the trial with individual interest and suspense.

Even at this short interval Irishmen can now see how completely they put judgment aside, and allowed feeling and passion to predominate in the matter. Many of the hottest protestants, of the staunchest foes to O'Connell, now believe that his absolute imprisonment was not to be desired, and that whether he were acquitted or convicted, the Government would have sufficiently shown, by instituting his trial, its determination to put down proceedings of which they did not approve. On the other hand, that class of men who then styled themselves Repealers are now aware that the continued imprisonment of their leader—the persecution, as they believed it to be, of 'the Liberator'—would have been the one thing most certain to have sustained his influence, and to have given fresh force to their agitation. Nothing ever so strengthened the love of the Irish for, and the obedience of the Irish to O'Connell, as his imprisonment; nothing ever so weakened his power over them as his unexpected enfranchisement. The country shouted for joy when he was set free, and expended all its enthusiasm in the effort.

At the time, however, to which I am now referring, each party felt the most intense interest in the struggle, and the most eager desire for success. Every Repealer, and every Anti-Repealer in Dublin felt that it was a contest, in which he himself was, to a certain extent, individually engaged. All the tactics of the opposed armies, down to the minutest legal details, were eagerly and passionately canvassed in every circle. Ladies, who had before probably never heard of 'panels' in forensic phraseology, now spoke enthusiastically on the subject; and those on one side expressed themselves indignant at the fraudulent omission of certain names from the lists of jurors; while those on the other were capable of proving the legality of choosing the jury from the names which were given, and stated most positively that the omissions were accidental.

'The traversers' were in everybody's mouth—a term heretofore confined to law courts, and lawyers' rooms. The Attorney-General, the Commander-in-Chief of the Government forces, was most virulently assailed; every legal step which he took was scrutinised and abused ; every measure which he used was base enough of itself to hand down his name to everlasting infamy. Such were the tenets of the Repealers. And O'Connell and his counsel, their base artifices, falsehoods, delays, and unprofessional proceedings, were declared by the Saxon party to be equally abominable.

The whole Irish bar seemed, for the time, to have laid aside the habitual *sang froid* and indifference of lawyers, and to have employed their hearts as well as their heads on behalf of the different parties by whom they were engaged. The very jurors themselves for a time became famous or infamous, according to the opinions of those by whom their position was discussed. Their names and additions were published and republished; they were declared to be men who would stand by their country and do their duty without fear or favour—so said the Protestants. By the Roman Catholics, they were looked on as perjurors determined to stick to the Government with blind indifference to their oaths. Their names are now, for the most part, forgotten, though so little time has elapsed since they appeared so frequently before the public.

Every day's proceedings gave rise to new hopes and fears. The evidence rested chiefly on the reports of certain short-hand writers, who had been employed to attend Repeal meetings, and their examinations and cross-examinations were read, re-read, and scanned with the minutest care. Then, the various and long speeches of the different counsel, who, day after day, continued to address the jury; the heat of one, the weary legal technicalities of another, the perspicuity of a third, and the splendid forensic eloquence of a fourth, were criticised, depreciated and admired. It seemed as though the chief lawyers of the day were standing an examination, and were candidates for some high honour, which each was striving to secure.

The Dublin papers were full of the trial; no other subject, could, at the time, either interest or amuse. I doubt whether any affair of the kind was ever, to use the phrase of the trade, so well and perfectly reported. The speeches appeared word for word the same in the columns of newspapers of different politics. For four-fifths of the contents of the paper it would have been the same to you whether you were reading the Evening Mail, or the Freeman. Every word that was uttered in the Court was of importance to every one in Dublin; and half-an-hour's delay in ascertaining, to the minutest shade, what had taken place in Court during any period, was accounted a sad misfortune.

The press round the Four Courts, every morning before the doors were open, was very great: and except by the favoured few who were able to obtain seats, it was only with extreme difficulty and perseverance, that an entrance into the body of the Court could be obtained.

It was on the eleventh morning of the proceedings, on the day on which the defence of the traversers was to be commenced, that two young men, who had been standing for a couple of hours in front of the doors of the Court, were still waiting there, with what patience was left to them, after having been pressed and jostled for so long a time. Richard Lalor Sheil, however, was to address the jury on behalf of Mr. John O'Connell—and every one in Dublin knew that that was a treat not to be lost. The two young men, too, were violent Repealers. The elder of them was a three-year-old denizen of Dublin, who knew the names of the contributors to the 'Nation', who had constantly listened to the indignation and enthusiasm of O'Connell, Smith O'Brien, and O'Neill Daunt, in their addresses from the rostrum of the Conciliation Hall; who had drank much porter at Jude's, who had eaten many oysters at Burton Bindon's, who had seen and contributed to many rows in the Abbey Street Theatre; who, during his life in Dublin, had done many things which he ought not to have done, and had probably made as many omissions of things which it had behoved him to do. He had that knowledge of the persons of his fellow-citizens, which appears to be so much more general in Dublin than in any other large town; he could tell you the name and trade of every one he met in the streets, and was a judge of the character and talents of all whose employments partook, in any degree, of a public nature. His name was Kelly; and, as his calling was that of an attorney's clerk, his knowledge of character would be peculiarly valuable in the scene at which he and his companion were so anxious to be present.

The younger of the two brothers, for such they were, was a somewhat different character. Though perhaps a more enthusiastic Repealer than his brother, he was not so well versed in the details of Repeal tactics, or in the strength and weakness of the Repeal ranks. He was a young farmer, of the better class, from the County Mayo, where he held three or four hundred wretchedly bad acres under Lord Ballindine, and one or two other small farms, under different landlords. He was a good-looking young fellow, about twenty-five years of age, with that mixture of cunning and frankness in his bright eye, which is so common among those of his class in Ireland, but more especially so in Connaught.

The mother of these two young men kept an inn in the small town of Dunmore, and though from the appearance of the place, one would be led to suppose that there could not be in Dunmore much of that kind of traffic which innkeepers love, Mrs. Kelly was accounted a warm, comfortable woman. Her husband had left her for a better world some ten years since, with six children; and the widow, instead of making continual use, as her chief support, of that common wail of being a poor, lone woman, had put her shoulders to the wheel, and had earned comfortably, by sheer industry, that which so many of her class, when similarly situated, are willing to owe to compassion.

She held on the farm, which her husband rented from Lord Ballindine, till her eldest son was able to take it. He, however, was now a gauger in the north of Ireland. Her second son was the attorney's clerk; and the farm had descended to Martin, the younger, whom we have left jostling and jostled at one of the great doors of the Four Courts, and whom we must still leave there for a short time, while a few more of the circumstances of his family are narrated.

Mrs. Kelly had, after her husband's death, added a small grocer's establishment to her inn. People

wondered where she had found the means of supply-
ing her shop: some said that old Mick Kelly must
have had money when he died, though it was odd
how a man who drank so much could ever have kept
a shilling by him. Others remarked how easy it was
to get credit in these days, and expressed a hope that
the wholesale dealer in Pill Lane might be none the
worse. However this might be, the widow Kelly
kept her station firmly and constantly behind her
counter, wore her weeds and her warm, black, stuff
dress decently and becomingly, and never asked anything of anybody.

At the time of which we are writing, her two elder
sons had left her, and gone forth to make their own
way, and take the burden of the world on their own
shoulders. Martin still lived with his mother, though
his farm lay four miles distant, on the road to
Ballindine, and in another county—for Dunmore is
in County Galway, and the lands of Toneroe, as
Martin's farm was called, were in the County Mayo.
One of her three daughters had lately been married
to a shop-keeper in Tuam, and rumour said that he
had got £500 with her; and Pat Daly was not the
man to have taken a wife for nothing. The other two
girls, Meg and Jane, still remained under their
mother's wing, and though it was to be presumed
that they would soon fly abroad, with the same comfortable plumage which had enabled their sister to
find so warm a nest, they were obliged, while sharing
their mother's home, to share also her labours, and were
not allowed to be too proud to cut off pennyworths
of tobacco, and mix dandies of punch for such of
their customers as still preferred the indulgence of
their throats to the blessing of Father Mathew.

Mrs. Kelly kept two ordinary in-door servants to
assist in the work of the house; one, an antiquated
female named Sally, who was more devoted to her
tea-pot than ever was any bacchanalian to his glass.
Were there four different teas in the inn in one evening, she would have drained the pot after each,

though she burst in the effort. Sally was, in all, an honest woman, and certainly a religious one—she never neglected her devotional duties, confessed with most scrupulous accuracy the various peccadillos of which she might consider herself guilty; and it was thought, with reason, by those who knew her best, that all the extra prayers she said—and they were very many—were in atonement for commissions of continual petty larceny with regard to sugar. On this subject did her old mistress quarrel with her, her young mistress ridicule her; of this sin did her fellow-servant accuse her; and, doubtless, for this sin did her Priest continually reprove her; but in vain. Though she would not own it, there was always sugar in her pocket, and though she declared that she usually drank her tea unsweetened, those who had come upon her unawares had seen her extracting the pinches of moist brown saccharine from the huge slit in her petticoat, and could not believe her.

Kate, the other servant, was a red-legged lass, who washed the potatoes, fed the pigs, and ate her food nobody knew when or where. Kates, particularly Irish Kates, are pretty by prescription; but Mrs. Kelly's Kate had been excepted, and was certainly a most positive exception. Poor Kate was very ugly. Her hair had that appearance of having been dressed by the turkey-cock, which is sometimes presented by the heads of young women in her situation; her mouth extended nearly from ear to ear; her neck and throat, which were always nearly bare, presented no feminine charms to view; and her short coarse petticoat showed her red legs nearly to the knee; for, except on Sundays, she knew not the use of shoes and stockings. But though Kate was ungainly and ugly, she was useful, and grateful—very fond of the whole family, and particularly attached to the two young ladies, in whose behalf she doubtless performed many a service, acceptable enough to them, but of which, had she known of them, the widow would have been but little likely to approve.

Such was Mrs. Kelly's household at the time that
her son Martin left Connaught to pay a short visit to
the metropolis, during the period of O'Connell's trial.
But, although Martin was a staunch Repealer, and
had gone as far as Galway, and Athlone, to be present
at the Monster Repeal Meetings which had been held
there, it was not political anxiety alone which led
him to Dublin. His landlord, the young Lord Ballindine, was there; and, though Martin could not
exactly be said to act as his lordship's agent—for
Lord Ballindine had, unfortunately, a legal agent,
with whose services his pecuniary embarrassments did
not allow him to dispense—he was a kind of confidential tenant, and his attendance had been requested. Martin, moreover, had a somewhat important piece of business of his own in hand, which
he expected would tend greatly to his own advantage;
and, although he had fully made up his mind to
carry it out if possible, he wanted, in conducting it,
a little of his brother's legal advice, and, above all,
his landlord's sanction.

This business was nothing less than an intended
elopement with an heiress belonging to a rank somewhat higher than that in which Martin Kelly might
be supposed to look, with propriety, for his bride;
but Martin was a handsome fellow, not much burdened with natural modesty, and he had, as he supposed, managed to engage the affections of Anastasia
Lynch, a lady resident near Dunmore.

All particulars respecting Martin's intended—the
amount of her fortune—her birth and parentage—
her age and attractions—shall, in due time, be made
known; or rather, perhaps, be suffered to make themselves known. In the mean time we will return to the
two brothers, who are still anxiously waiting to effect
an entrance into the august presence of the Law.

Martin had already told his brother of his matrimonial speculations, and had received certain hints
from that learned youth as to the proper means of
getting correct information as to the amount of the

lady's wealth—her power to dispose of it by her own deed,—and certain other particulars always interesting to gentlemen who seek money and love at the same time. John did not quite approve of the plan; there might have been a shade of envy at his brother's good fortune; there might be some doubt as to his brother's power of carrying the affair through successfully; but, though he had not encouraged him, he gave him the information he wanted, and was as willing to talk over the matter as Martin could desire.

As they were standing in the crowd, their conversation ran partly on Repeal and O'Connell, and partly on matrimony and Anty Lynch, as the lady was usually called by those who knew her best.

'Tear and 'ouns Misther Lord Chief Justice!' exclaimed Martin, 'and are ye niver going to opin them big doors?'

'And what'd be the good of his opening them yet,' answered John, 'when a bigger man than himself an't there? Dan and the other boys isn't in it yet, and sure all the twelve judges couldn't get on a peg without them.'

'Well, Dan, my darling!' said the other, 'you're thought more of here this day than the lot of 'em, though the place in a manner belongs to them, and you're only a prisoner.'

'Faix and that's what he's not, Martin; no more than yourself, nor so likely, may-be. He's the traverser, as I told you before, and that's not being a prisoner. If he were a prisoner, how did he manage to tell us all what he did at the Hall yesterday?'

'Av' he's not a prisoner, he's the next-door to it; it's not of his own free will and pleasure he'd come here to listen to all the lies them thundhering Saxon ruffians choose to say about him.'

'And why not? Why wouldn't he come here and vindicate himself? When you hear Sheil by and by, you'll see then whether they think themselves likely to be prisoners! No—no; they never will be, av' there's a ghost of a conscience left in one of them Protesthant raps, that they've picked so carefully out of all Dublin to make jurors of. They can't convict 'em! I heard Ford, the night before last, offer four to one that they didn't find the lot guilty; and he knows what he's about, and isn't the man to thrust a Protesthant half as far as he'd see him.'

'Isn't Tom Steele a Protesthant himself, John?'

'Well, I believe he is. So's Gray, and more of 'em too; but there's a difference between them and the downright murdhering Tory set. Poor Tom doesn't throuble the Church much; but you'll be all for Protesthants now, Martin, when you've your new brother-in-law. Barry used to be one of your raal out-and-outers!'

'It's little, I'm thinking, I and Barry'll be having to do together, unless it be about the brads; and the law about them now, thank God, makes no differ for Roman and Protesthant. Anty's as good a Catholic as ever breathed, and so was her mother before her; and when she's Mrs. Kelly, as I mane to make her, Master Barry may shell out the cash and go to heaven his own way for me.'

'It ain't the family then, you're fond of, Martin! And I wondher at that, considering how old Sim loved us all.'

'Niver mind Sim, John! he's dead and gone; and av' he niver did a good deed before, he did one when he didn't lave all his cash to that precious son of his, Barry Lynch.'

'You're prepared for squalls with Barry, I suppose?'

'He'll have all the squalling on his own side, I'm thinking, John. I don't mane to squall, for one. I don't see why I need, with £400 a-year in my pocket, and a good wife to the fore.'

'The £400 a-year's good enough, av' you touch it, certainly,' said the man of law, thinking of his own insufficient guinea a-week, 'and you must look to have some throuble yet before you do that. But as to the wife—why, the less said the better—eh, Martin?

'Av' it's not asking too much, might I throuble you, sir, to set anywhere else but on my shouldher?' This was addressed to a very fat citizen, who was wheezing behind Martin, and who, to escape suffocation in the crowd, was endeavouring to raise himself on his neighbour's shoulders. 'And why the less said the better?—I wish yourself may never have a worse.'

'I wish I mayn't, Martin, as far as the cash goes; and a man like me might look a long time in Dublin before he got a quarter of the money. But you must own Anty's no great beauty, and she's not over young, either.'

'Av' she's no beauty, she's not downright ugly, like many a girl that gets a good husband; and av' she's not over young, she's not over old. She's not so much older than myself, after all. It's only because her own people have always made nothing of her; that's what has made everybody else do the same.'

'Why, Martin, I know she's ten years older than Barry, and Barry's older than you!'

'One year; and Anty's *not* full ten years older than him. Besides, what's ten years between man and wife?'

'Not much, when it's on the right side. But it's the wrong side with you, Martin!'

'Well, John, now, by virtue of your oath, as you chaps say, wouldn't you marry a woman twice her age, av' she'd half the money?—Begad you would, and leap at it!'

'Perhaps I would. I'd a deal sooner have a woman eighty than forty. There'd be some chance then of having the money after the throuble was over! Anty's neither ould enough nor young enough.'

'She's not forty, any way; and won't be yet for five years and more; and, as I hope for glory, John— though I know you won't believe me—I wouldn't marry her av' she'd all Sim Lynch's ill-gotten

property, instead of only half, av' I wasn't really
fond of her, and av' I didn't think I'd make her a
good husband.'

'You didn't tell mother what you're afther, did
you?'

'Sorrow a word! But she's so 'cute she partly
guesses; and I think Meg let slip something. The
girls and Anty are thick as thiefs since old Sim died;
though they couldn't be at the house much since
Barry came home, and Anty daren't for her life come
down to the shop.'

'Did mother say anything about the schame?'

'Faix, not much; but what she did say, didn't
show she'd much mind for it. Since Sim Lynch tried
to get Toneroe from her, when father died, she'd
never a good word for any of them. Not but what
she's always a civil look for Anty, when she sees her.'

'There's not much fear she'll look black on the
wife, when you bring the money home with her. But
where'll you live, Martin? The little shop at Dunmore'll be no place for Mrs. Kelly, when there's a
lady of the name with £400 a-year of her own.'

''Deed then, John, and that's what I don't know.
Maybe I'll build up the ould house at Toneroe;
some of the O'Kellys themselves lived there, years
ago.'

'I believe they did; but it *was* years ago, and very
many years ago, too, since they lived there. Why
you'd have to pull it all down, before you began to
build it up!'

'Maybe I'd build a new house, out and out. Av' I
got three new lifes in the laise, I'd do that; and the
lord wouldn't be refusing me, av' I asked him.'

'Bother the lord, Martin; why you'd be asking
anything of any lord, and you with £400 a-year of
your own? Give up Toneroe, and go and live at
Dunmore House at once.'

'What! along with Barry—when I and Anty's
married? The biggest house in county Galway
wouldn't hould the three of us.'

'You don't think Barry Lynch'll stay at Dunmore afther you've married his sisther?'

'And why not?'

'Why not! Don't you know Barry thinks himself one of the raal gentry now? Any ways, he wishes others to think so. Why, he'd even himself to Lord Ballindine av' he could! Didn't old Sim send him to the same English school with the lord on purpose? —tho' little he got by it, by all accounts! And d'you think he'll remain in Dunmore, to be brother-in-law to the son of the woman that keeps the little grocer's shop in the village?—Not he! He'll soon be out of Dunmore when he hears what his sister's afther doing, and you'll have Dunmore House to yourselves then, av' you like it.'

'I'd sooner live at Toneroe, and that's the truth; and I'd not give up the farm av' she'd double the money! But, John, faith, here's the judges at last. Hark, to the boys screeching!'

'They'd not screech that way for the judges, my boy. It's the traversers—that's Dan and the rest of 'em. They're coming into court. Thank God, they'll soon be at work now!'

'And will they come through this way? Faith, av' they do, they'll have as hard work to get in, as they'll have to get out by and by.'

'They'll not come this way—there's another way in for them: tho' they are traversers now, they didn't dare but let them go in at the same door as the judges themselves.'

'Hurrah, Dan! More power to you! Three cheers for the traversers, and Repale for ever! Success to every mother's son of you, my darlings! You'll be free yet, in spite of John Jason Rigby and the rest of 'em! The prison isn't yet built that'd hould ye, nor won't be! Long life to you, Sheil—sure you're a Right Honourable Repaler now, in spite of Greenwich Hospital and the Board of Trade! More power, Gavan Duffy; you're the boy that'll settle 'em at last! Three cheers more for the Lord Mayor, God

bless him! Well, yer reverence, Mr. Tierney!—never
mind, they could come to no good when they'd be
parsecuting the likes of you! Bravo, Tom!—Hurrah
for Tom Steele!'

Such, and such like, were the exclamations which
greeted the traversers, and their *cortège*, as they
drew up to the front of the Four Courts. Dan
O'Connell was in the Lord Mayor's state carriage,
accompanied by that high official; and came up to
stand his trial for conspiracy and sedition, in just
such a manner as he might be presumed to proceed
to take the chair at some popular municipal assembly;
and this was just the thing qualified to please those
who were on his own side, and mortify the feelings
of the party so bitterly opposed to him. There was
a bravado in it, and an apparent contempt, not of the
law so much as of the existing authorities of the law,
which was well qualified to have this double effect.

And now the outer doors of the Court were
opened, and the crowd—at least as many as were
able to effect an entrance—rushed in. Martin and
John Kelly were among those nearest to the door,
and, in reward of their long patience, got sufficiently
into the body of the Court to be in a position to see,
when standing on tiptoe, the noses of three of the
four judges, and the wigs of four of the numerous
counsel employed. The Court was so filled by those
who had a place there by right, or influence enough to
assume that they had so, that it was impossible to
obtain a more favourable situation. But this of
itself was a great deal—quite sufficient to justify
Martin in detailing to his Connaught friends every
particular of the whole trial. They would probably
be able to hear everything; they could positively see
three of the judges, and if those two big policemen,
with high hats, could by any possibility be got to
remove themselves, it was very probable that they
would be able to see Sheil's back, when he stood up.

John soon began to show off his forensic knowledge. He gave a near guess at the names of the four

counsel whose heads were visible, merely from the different shades and shapes of their wigs. Then he particularised the inferior angels of that busy Elysium.

'That's Ford—that's Gartlan—that's Peirce Mahony,' he exclaimed, as the different attorneys for the traversers, furiously busy with their huge bags, fidgetted about rapidly, or stood up in their seats, telegraphing others in different parts of the Court.

'There's old Kemmis,' as they caught a glimpse of the Crown agent; 'he's the boy that doctored the jury list. Fancy, a jury chosen out of all Dublin, and not one Catholic! As if that could be fair!' And then he named the different judges. 'Look at that big-headed, pig-faced fellow on the right—that's Pennefather! He's the blackest sheep of the lot—and the head of them! He's a thoroughbred Tory, and as fit to be a judge as I am to be a general. That queer little fellow, with the long chin, he's Burton—he's a hundred if he's a day—he was fifty when he was called, seventy when they benchcd him, and I'm sure he's a judge thirty years! But he's the sharpest chap of the whole twelve, and no end of a boy afther the girls. If you only saw him walking in his robes—I'm sure he's not three feet high! That next, with the skinny neck, he's Crampton—he's one of Father Mathew's lads, an out and out tee-totaller, and he looks it; he's a desperate cross fellow, sometimes! The other one, you can't see, he's Perrin. There, he's leaning over—you can just catch the side of his face—he's Perrin. It's he'll acquit the traversers av' anything does—he's a fair fellow, is Perrin, and not a red-hot thorough-going Tory like the rest of 'em.'

Here John was obliged to give over the instruction of his brother, being enjoined so to do by one of the heavy-hatted policemen in his front, who enforced his commands for silence, with a backward shove of his wooden truncheon, which came with rather unnecessary violence against the pit of John's stomach.

The fear of being turned out made him for the nonce refrain from that vengeance of abuse which his education as a Dublin Jackeen well qualified him to inflict. But he put down the man's face in his retentive memory, and made up his mind to pay him off.

And now the business of the day commenced. After some official delays and arrangements Sheil arose, and began his speech in defence of John O'Connell. It would be out of place here to give either his words or his arguments; besides, they have probably before this been read by all who would care to read them. When he commenced, his voice appeared, to those who were not accustomed to hear him, weak, piping, and most unfit for a popular orator; but this effect was soon lost in the elegance of his language and the energy of his manner; and, before he had been ten minutes on his legs, the disagreeable tone was forgotten, though it was sounding in the eager ears of every one in the Court.

His speech was certainly brilliant, effective, and eloquent; but it satisfied none that heard him, though it pleased all. It was neither a defence of the general conduct and politics of the party, such as O'Connell himself attempted in his own case, nor did it contain a chain of legal arguments to prove that John O'Connell, individually, had not been guilty of conspiracy, such as others of the counsel employed subsequently in favour of their own clients.

Sheil's speech was one of those numerous anomalies with which this singular trial was crowded; and which, together, showed the great difficulty of coming to a legal decision on a political question, in a criminal court. Of this, the present day gave two specimens, which will not be forgotten; when a Privy Councillor, a member of a former government, whilst defending his client as a barrister, proposed in Court a new form of legislation for Ireland, equally distant from that adopted by Government, and that sought to be established by him whom he was defending;

and when the traverser on his trial rejected the defence of his counsel, and declared aloud in Court, that he would not, by his silence, appear to agree in the suggestions then made.

This spirit of turning the Court into a political debating arena extended to all present. In spite of the vast efforts made by them all, only one of the barristers employed has added much to his legal reputation by the occasion. Imputations were made, such as I presume were never before uttered by one lawyer against another in a court of law. An Attorney-General sent a challenge from his very seat of office; and though that challenge was read in Court, it was passed over by four judges with hardly a reprimand. If any seditious speech was ever made by O'Connell, that which he made in his defence was especially so, and he was, without check, allowed to use his position as a traverser at the bar, as a rostrum from which to fulminate more thoroughly and publicly than ever, those doctrines for uttering which he was then being tried; and, to crown it all, even the silent dignity of the bench was forgotten, and the lawyers pleading against the Crown were unhappily alluded to by the Chief Justice as the 'gentlemen on the *other* side.'

Martin and John patiently and enduringly remained standing the whole day, till four o'clock; and then the latter had to effect his escape, in order to keep an appointment which he had made to meet Lord Ballindine.

As they walked along the quays they both discussed the proceedings of the day, and both expressed themselves positively certain of the result of the trial, and of the complete triumph of O'Connell and his party. To these pleasant certainties Martin added his conviction, that Repeal must soon follow so decided a victory, and that the hopes of Ireland would be realised before the close of 1844. John was neither so sanguine nor so enthusiastic; it was the battle, rather than the thing battled for, that was dear to him; the strife, rather than the result. He felt that it would be dull times in Dublin, when they should have no usurping Government to abuse, no Saxon Parliament to upbraid, no English laws to ridicule, and no Established Church to curse.

The only thing which could reconcile him to immediate Repeal, would be the probability of having then to contend for the election of an Irish Sovereign, and the possible dear delight which might follow, of Ireland going to war with England, in a national and becoming manner.

Discussing these important measures, they reached the Dublin brother's lodgings, and Martin turned in to wash his face and hands, and put on clean boots, before he presented himself to his landlord and patron, the young Lord Ballindine.

II

THE TWO HEIRESSES

FRANCIS John Mountmorris O'Kelly, Lord Viscount Ballindine, was twenty-four years of age when he came into possession of the Ballindine property, and succeeded to an Irish peerage as the third viscount; and he is now twenty-six, at this time of O'Connell's trial. The head of the family had for many years back been styled 'The O'Kelly', and had enjoyed much more local influence under that denomination than their descendants had possessed, since they had obtained a more substantial though not a more respected title. The O'Kellys had possessed large tracts of not very good land, chiefly in County Roscommon, but partly in Mayo and Galway. Their property had extended from Dunmore nearly to Roscommon, and again on the other side to Castlerea and Ballyhaunis. But this had been in their palmy days, long, long ago. When the government, in consideration of past services, in the year 1800, converted 'the O'Kelly' into Viscount Ballindine, the family property consisted of the greater portion of the land lying between the villages of Dunmore and Ballindine. Their old residence, which the peer still kept up, was called Kelly's Court, and is situated in that corner of County Roscommon which runs up between Mayo and Galway.

The first lord lived long enough to regret his change of title, and to lament the increased expenditure with which he had thought it necessary to accompany his more elevated rank. His son succeeded, and showed in his character much more of the new-fangled viscount than of the ancient O'Kelly. His whole long life was passed in hovering about the English Court. From the time of his father's death, he never once put his foot in Ireland. He had been appointed, at different times from his youth upwards, Page, Gentleman in Waiting, Usher of the Black Rod, Deputy Groom of the Stole, Chief Equerry to the Princess Royal, (which appointment only lasted till the princess was five years old), Lord Gold Stick, Keeper of the Royal Robes; till, at last, he had culminated for ten halcyon years in a Lord of the Bedchamber. In the latter portion of his life he had grown too old for this, and it was reported at Ballindine, Dunmore, and Kelly's Court,—with how much truth I don't know,—that, since her Majesty's accession, he had been joined with the spinster sister of a Scotch Marquis, and an antiquated English Countess, in the custody of the laces belonging to the Queen Dowager.

This nobleman, publicly useful as his life had no doubt been, had done little for his own tenants, or his own property. On his father's death, he had succeeded to about three thousand a-year, and he left about one; and he would have spent or mortgaged this, had he not, on his marriage, put it beyond his own power to do so. It was not only by thriftless extravagance that he thus destroyed a property which, with care, and without extortion, would have doubled its value in the thirty-five years during which it was in his hands; but he had been afraid to come to Ireland, and had been duped by his agent. When he came to the title, Simeon Lynch had been recommended to him as a fit person to manage his property, and look after his interests; and Simeon had managed it well in that manner most conducive to the prosperity of the person he loved best in the world; and that was himself. When large tracts of land fell out of lease, Sim had represented that tenants could not be found—that the land was not worth cultivating—that the country was in a state which prevented the possibility of letting; and, ultimately put himself into possession, with a lease for ever, at a rent varying from half a crown to five shillings an acre.

The courtier lord had one son, of whom he made a soldier, but who never rose to a higher rank than that of Captain. About a dozen years before the date of my story, the Honourable Captain O'Kelly, after numerous quarrels with the Right Honourable Lord of the Bedchamber, had, at last, come to some family settlement with him; and, having obtained the power of managing the property himself, came over to live at his paternal residence of Kelly's Court.

A very sorry kind of Court he found it,—neglected, dirty, and out of repair. One of the first retainers whom he met was Jack Kelly, the family fool. Jack was not such a fool as those who, of yore, were valued appendages to noble English establishments. He resembled them in nothing but his occasional wit. He was a dirty, barefooted, unshorn, ragged ruffian, who ate potatoes in the kitchen of the Court, and had never done a day's work in his life. Such as he was, however, he was presented to Captain O'Kelly, as 'his honor the masther's fool.'

'So, you're my fool, Jack, are ye?' said the Captain.

'Faix, I war the lord's fool ance; but I'll no be anybody's fool but Sim Lynch's, now. I and the lord are both Sim's fools now. Not but I'm the first of the two, for I'd never be fool enough to give away all my land, av' my father'd been wise enough to lave me any.'

Captain O'Kelly soon found out the manner in which the agent had managed his father's affairs. Simeon Lynch was dismissed, and proceedings at common law were taken against him, to break such of the leases as were thought, by clever attorneys, to have the ghost of a flaw in them. Money was borrowed from a Dublin house, for the purpose of carrying on the suit, paying off debts, and making Kelly's Court habitable; and the estate was put into their hands. Simeon Lynch built himself a large staring house at Dunmore, defended his leases, set up for a country gentleman on his own account, and sent his only son, Barry, to Eton;—merely because young O'Kelly was also there, and he was determined to show, that he was as rich and ambitious as the lord's family, whom he had done so much to ruin.

Kelly's Court was restored to such respectability as could ever belong to so ugly a place. It was a large red stone mansion, standing in a demesne of very poor ground, ungifted by nature with any beauty, and but little assisted by cultivation or improvement. A belt of bald-looking firs ran round the demesne inside the dilapidated wall; but this was hardly sufficient to relieve the barren aspect of the locality. Fine trees there were none, and the race of O'Kellys had never been great gardeners.

Captain O'Kelly was a man of more practical sense, or of better education, than most of his family, and he did do a good deal to humanise the place. He planted, tilled, manured, and improved; he imported rose-trees and strawberry-plants, and civilised Kelly's Court a little. But his reign was not long. He died about five years after he had begun his career as a country gentleman, leaving a widow and two daughters in Ireland; a son at school at Eton; and an expensive lawsuit, with numerous ramifications, all unsettled.

Francis, the son, went to Eton and Oxford, was

presented at Court by his grandfather, and came back to Ireland at twenty-two, to idle away his time till the old lord should die. Till this occurred, he could neither call himself the master of the place, nor touch the rents. In the meantime, the lawsuits were dropped, both parties having seriously injured their resources, without either of them obtaining any benefit. Barry Lynch was recalled from his English education, where he had not shown off to any great credit; and both he and his father were obliged to sit down prepared to make the best show they could on eight hundred pounds a-year, and to wage an underhand internecine war with the O'Kellys.

Simeon and his son, however, did not live altogether alone. Anastasia Lynch was Barry's sister, and older than him by about ten years. Their mother had been a Roman Catholic, whereas Sim was a Protestant; and, in consequence, the daughter had been brought up in the mother's, and the son in the father's religion. When this mother died, Simeon, no doubt out of respect to the memory of the departed, tried hard to induce his daughter to prove her religious zeal, and enter a nunnery; but this, Anty, though in most things a docile creature, absolutely refused to do. Her father advised, implored, and threatened; but in vain; and the poor girl became a great thorn in the side of both father and son. She had neither beauty, talent, nor attraction, to get her a husband; and her father was determined not to encumber his already diminished property with such a fortune as would make her on that ground acceptable to any respectable suitor.

Poor Anty led a miserable life, associating neither with superiors nor inferiors, and her own position was not sufficiently declared to enable her to have any equals. She was slighted by her father and the servants, and bullied by her brother; and was only just enabled, by humble, unpresuming disposition, to carry on her tedious life from year to year without grumbling.

In the meantime, the *ci-devant* Black Rod, Gold Stick, Royal Equerry, and Lord of the Bedchamber, was called away from his robes and his finery, to give an account of the manner in which he had renounced the pomps and vanities of this wicked world; and Frank became Lord Ballindine, with, as I have before said, an honourable mother, two sisters, a large red house, and a thousand a-year. He was not at all a man after the pattern of his grandfather, but he appeared as little likely to redeem the old family acres. He seemed to be a reviving chip of the old block of the O'Kellys. During the two years he had been living at Kelly's Court as Frank O'Kelly, he had won the hearts of all the tenants—of all those who would have been tenants if the property had not been sold, and who still looked up to him as their 'raal young masther'—and of the whole country round. The 'thrue dhrop of the ould blood', was in his veins; and, whatever faults he might have, he wasn't likely to waste his time and his cash with furs, laces, and hangings.

This was a great comfort to the neighbourhood, which had learned heartily to despise the name of 'Lord Ballindine'; and Frank was encouraged in shooting, hunting, racing—in preparing to be a thorough Irish gentleman, and in determining to make good the prophecies of his friends, that he would be, at last, one more 'raal O'Kelly to brighten the counthry.'

And if he could have continued to be Frank O'Kelly, or even 'the O'Kelly', he would probably have done well enough, for he was fond of his mother and sisters, and he might have continued to hunt, shoot, and farm on his remaining property without further encroaching on it. But the title was sure to be his ruin. When he felt himself to be a lord, he could not be content with the simple life of a country gentleman; or, at any rate, without taking the lead in the country. So, as soon as the old man was buried, he bought a pack of harriers, and despatched a couple of race-horses to the skilful hands of old Jack Igoe, the Curragh trainer.

Frank was a very handsome fellow, full six feet high, with black hair, and jet-black silky whiskers, meeting under his chin—the men said he dyed them, and the women declared he did not. I am inclined, myself, to think he must have done so, they were so very black. He had an eye like a hawk, round, bright, and bold; a mouth and chin almost too well formed for a man; and that kind of broad forehead which conveys rather the idea of a generous, kind, open-hearted disposition, than of a deep mind or a commanding intellect.

Frank was a very handsome fellow, and he knew it; and when he commenced so many ill-authorised expenses immediately on his grandfather's death, he consoled himself with the idea, that with his person and rank, he would soon be able, by some happy matrimonial speculation, to make up for what he wanted in wealth. And he had not been long his own master, before he met with the lady to whom he destined the honour of doing so.

He had, however, not properly considered his own disposition, when he determined upon looking out for great wealth; and on disregarding other qualifications in his bride, so that he obtained that in sufficient quantity. He absolutely fell in love with Fanny Wyndham, though her twenty thousand pounds was felt by him to be hardly enough to excuse him in doing so,—certainly not enough to make his doing so an accomplishment of his prudential resolutions. What would twenty thousand pounds do towards clearing the O'Kelly property, and establishing himself in a manner and style fitting for a Lord Ballindine! However, he did propose to her, was accepted, and the match, after many difficulties, was acceded to by the lady's guardian, the Earl of Cashel. It was stipulated, however, that the marriage should not take place till the lady was of age; and at the time of the bargain, she wanted twelve months of that

period of universal discretion. Lord Cashel had
added, in his prosy, sensible, aristocratic lecture on
the subject to Lord Ballindine, that he trusted that,
during the interval, considering their united limited
income, his lordship would see the wisdom of giving
up his hounds, or at any rate of withdrawing from
the turf.

Frank pooh-poohed at the hounds, said that horses
cost nothing in Connaught, and dogs less, and that
he could not well do there without them; but promised to turn in his mind what Lord Cashel had said
about the turf; and, at last, went so far as to say
that when a good opportunity offered of backing out,
he would part with Finn M'Coul and Granuell—as
the two nags at Igoe's were patriotically denominated.

They continued, however, appearing in the Curragh
lists in Lord Ballindine's name, as a part of Igoe's
string; and running for Queen's whips, Wellingtons
and Madrids, sometimes with good and sometimes
with indifferent success. While their noble owner,
when staying at Grey Abbey, Lord Cashel's magnificent seat near Kilcullen, spent too much of his time
(at least so thought the earl and Fanny Wyndham)
in seeing them get their gallops, and in lecturing the
grooms, and being lectured by Mr. Igoe. Nothing
more, however, could be done; and it was trusted
that when the day of the wedding should come, he
would be found minus the animals. What, however,
was Lord Cashel's surprise, when, after an absence of
two months from Grey Abbey, Lord Ballindine
declared, in the earl's presence, with an air of ill-
assumed carelessness, that he had been elected one
of the stewards of the Curragh, in the room of Walter
Blake, Esq., who had retired in rotation from that
honourable office! The next morning the earl's
chagrin was woefully increased by his hearing that
that very valuable and promising Derby colt, Brien
Boru, now two years old, by Sir Hercules out of
Eloisa, had been added to his lordship's lot.

Lord Cashel felt that he could not interfere,

further than by remarking that it appeared his young
friend was determined to leave the turf with *éclat*;
and Fanny Wyndham could only be silent and
reserved for one evening. This occurred about four
months before the commencement of my tale, and
about five before the period fixed for the marriage;
but, at the time at which Lord Ballindine will be
introduced in person to the reader, he had certainly
made no improvement in his manner of going on.
He had, during this period, received from Lord
Cashel a letter intimating to him that his lordship
thought some further postponement advisable; that
it was as well not to fix any day; and that, though
his lordship would always be welcome at Grey Abbey,
when his personal attendance was not required at
the Curragh, it was better that no correspondence
by letter should at present be carried on between
him and Miss Wyndham; and that Miss Wyndham
herself perfectly agreed in the propriety of these
suggestions.

Now Grey Abbey was only about eight miles
distant from the Curragh, and Lord Ballindine had
at one time been in the habit of staying at his friend's
mansion, during the period of his attendance at the
race-course; but since Lord Cashel had shown an
entire absence of interest in the doings of Finn
M'Coul, and Fanny had ceased to ask after Granuell's
cough, he had discontinued doing so, and had spent
much of his time at his friend Walter Blake's residence at the Curragh. Now, Handicap Lodge offered
much more dangerous quarters for him than did
Grey Abbey.

In the meantime, his friends in Connaught were
delighted at the prospect of his bringing home a
bride. Fanny's twenty thousand were magnified to
fifty, and the capabilities even of fifty were greatly
exaggerated; besides, the connection was so good a
one, so exactly the thing for the O'Kellys! Lord
Cashel was one of the first resident noblemen in
Ireland, a representative peer, a wealthy man, and

possessed of great influence; not unlikely to be a
cabinet minister if the Whigs came in, and able to
shower down into Connaught a degree of patronage,
such as had never yet warmed that poor unfriended
region. And Fanny Wyndham was not only his
lordship's ward, but his favourite niece also! The
match was, in every way, a good one, and greatly
pleasing to all the Kellys, whether with an O or
without, for 'shure they were all the one family.'

Old Simeon Lynch and his son Barry did not
participate in the general joy. They had calculated
that their neighbour was on the high road to ruin,
and that he would soon have nothing but his coronet
left. They could not, therefore, bear the idea of his
making so eligible a match. They had, moreover,
had domestic dissensions to disturb the peace of
Dunmore House. Simeon had insisted on Barry's
taking a farm into his own hands, and looking after
it. Barry had declared his inability to do so, and had
nearly petrified the old man by expressing a wish to
go to Paris. Then, Barry's debts had showered in,
and Simeon had pledged himself not to pay them.
Simeon had threatened to disinherit Barry; and
Barry had called his father a d—d obstinate old
fool.

These quarrels had got to the ears of the neighbours, and it was being calculated that, in the end,
Barry would get the best of the battle; when, one
morning, the war was brought to an end by a fit of
apoplexy, and the old man was found dead in his
chair. And then a terrible blow fell upon the son; for
a recent will was found in the old man's desk, dividing his property equally, and without any other
specification, between Barry and Anty.

This was a dreadful blow to Barry. He consulted
with his friend Molloy, the attorney of Tuam, as to
the validity of the document and the power of breaking it; but in vain. It was properly attested, though
drawn up in the old man's own hand-writing; and
his sister, whom he looked upon but as little better

than a head maid-servant, had not only an equal right
to all the property, but was equally mistress of the
house, the money at the bank, the wine in the cellar,
and the very horses in the stable!

This was a hard blow; but Barry was obliged to
bear it. At first, he showed his ill-humour plainly
enough in his treatment of his sister; but he soon saw
that this was folly, and that, though her quiet disposition prevented her from resenting it, such conduct would drive her to marry some needy man.
Then he began, with an ill grace, to try what coaxing
would do. He kept, however, a sharp watch on all
her actions; and on once hearing that, in his absence,
the two Kelly girls from the hotel had been seen
walking with her, he gave her a long lecture on what
was due to her own dignity, and the memory of her
departed parents.

He made many overtures to her as to the division
of the property; but, easy and humble as Anty was,
she was careful enough to put her name to nothing
that could injure her rights. They had divided the
money at the banker's, and she had once rather
startled Barry by asking him for his moiety towards
paying the butcher's bill; and his dismay was completed shortly afterwards by being informed, by a
steady old gentleman in Dunmore, whom he did not
like a bit too well, that he had been appointed by
Miss Lynch to manage her business and receive
her rents.

As soon as it could be decently done, after his
father's burial, Barry took himself off to Dublin, to
consult his friends there as to what he should do;
but he soon returned, determined to put a bold face
on it, and come to some understanding with his sister.

He first proposed to her to go and live in Dublin,
but she said she preferred Dunmore. He then talked
of selling the house, and to this she agreed. He next
tried to borrow money for the payment of his debts;
on which she referred him to the steady old man.
Though apparently docile and obedient, she would

not put herself in his hands, nor would her agent allow him to take any unfair advantage of her.

Whilst this was going on, our friend Martin Kelly had set his eye upon the prize, and, by means of his sister's intimacy with Anty, and his own good looks, had succeeded in obtaining from her half a promise to become his wife. Anty had but little innate respect for gentry; and, though she feared her brother's displeasure, she felt no degradation at the idea of uniting herself to a man in Martin Kelly's rank. She could not, however, be brought to tell her brother openly, and declare her determination; and Martin had, at length, come to the conclusion that he must carry her off, before delay and unforeseen changes might either alter her mind, or enable her brother to entice her out of the country.

Thus matters stood at Dunmore when Martin Kelly started for Dublin, and at the time when he was about to wait on his patron at Morrison's hotel.

Both Martin and Lord Ballindine (and they were related in some distant degree, at least so always said the Kellys, and I never knew that the O'Kellys denied it)—both the young men were, at the time, anxious to get married, and both with the same somewhat mercenary views; and I have fatigued the reader with the long history of past affairs, in order to imbue him, if possible, with some interest in the ways and means which they both adopted to accomplish their objects.

III

MORRISON'S HOTEL

AT about five o'clock on the evening of the day of Sheil's speech, Lord Ballindine and his friend, Walter Blake, were lounging on different sofas in a room at Morrison's Hotel, before they went up to dress for dinner. Walter Blake was an effeminate-looking, slight-made man, about thirty or thirty-three years of age; good looking, and gentlemanlike,

but presenting quite a contrast in his appearance to
his friend Lord Ballindine. He had a cold quiet grey
eye, and a thin lip; and, though he was in reality
a much cleverer, he was a much less engaging man.
Yet Blake could be very amusing; but he rather
laughed *at* people than with them, and when there
were more than two in company, he would usually
be found making a butt of one. Nevertheless, his
society was greatly sought after. On matters connected with racing, his word was infallible. He rode
boldly, and always rode good horses; and, though he
was anything but rich, he managed to keep up a comfortable snuggery at the Curragh, and to drink the
very best claret that Dublin could procure.

Walter Blake was a finished gambler, and thus it
was, that with about six hundred a year, he managed
to live on equal terms with the richest around him.
His father, Laurence Blake of Castleblakeney, in
County Galway, was a very embarrassed man, of
good property, strictly entailed, and, when Walter
came of age, he and his father, who could never be
happy in the same house, though possessing in most
things similar tastes, had made such a disposition of
the estate, as gave the father a clear though narrowed
income, and enabled the son at once to start into the
world, without waiting for his father's death; though,
by so doing, he greatly lessened the property which
he must otherwise have inherited.

Blake was a thorough gambler, and knew well how
to make the most of the numerous chances which the
turf afforded him. He had a large stud of horses, to
the training and working of which he attended almost
as closely as the person whom he paid for doing so.
But it was in the betting-ring that he was most formidable. It was said, in Kildare Street, that no one at
Tattersall's could beat him at a book. He had latterly
been trying a wider field than the Curragh supplied
him, and had, on one or two occasions, run a horse in
England with such success, as had placed him, at any
rate, quite at the top of the Irish sporting tree.

He was commonly called 'Dot Blake', in consequence of his having told one of his friends that the
cause of his, the friend's, losing so much money on
the turf, was, that he did not mind 'the dot and
carry on' part of the business; meaning thereby,
that he did not attend to the necessary calculations.
For a short time after giving this piece of friendly
caution, he had been nick-named, 'Dot and carry
on'; but that was too long to last, and he had now
for some years been known to every sporting man in
Ireland as 'Dot' Blake.

This man was at present Lord Ballindine's most
intimate friend, and he could hardly have selected a
more dangerous one. They were now going down
together to Handicap Lodge, though there was nothing to be done in the way of racing for months to
come. Yet Blake knew his business too well to suppose that his presence was necessary only when the
horses were running; and he easily persuaded his
friend that it was equally important that he should
go and see that it was all right with the Derby
colt.

They were talking almost in the dark, on these
all-absorbing topics, when the waiter knocked at the
door and informed them that a young man named
Kelly wished to see Lord Ballindine.

'Show him up,' said Frank. 'A tenant of mine,
Dot; one of the respectable few of that cattle, indeed,
almost the only one that I've got; a sort of sub-
agent, and a fifteenth cousin, to boot, I believe. I am
going to put him to the best use I know for such
respectable fellows, and that is, to get him to borrow
money for me.'

'And he'll charge you twice as much for it, and
make three times as much bother about it, as the
fellows in the next street who have your title-deeds.
When I want lawyer's business done, I go to a lawyer;
and when I want to borrow money, I go to my own
man of business; he makes it his business to find
money, and he daren't rob me more than is decent,

fitting, and customary, because he has a character
to lose.'

'Those fellows at Guinness's make such a fuss
about everything; and I don't put my nose into that
little back room, but what every word I say, by some
means or other, finds its way down to Grey Abbey.'

'Well, Frank, you know your own affairs best; but
I don't think you'll make money by being afraid of
your agent; or your wife's guardian, if she is to be
your wife.'

'Afraid, man? I'm as much afraid of Lord Cashel
as you are. I don't think I've shown myself much
afraid; but I don't choose to make him my guardian,
just when he's ceasing to be hers; nor do I wish, just
now, to break with Grey Abbey altogether.'

'Do you mean to go over there from the Curragh
next week?'

'I don't think I shall. They don't like me a bit too
well, when I've the smell of the stables on me.'

'There it is, again, Frank! What is it to you what
Lord Cashel likes? If you wish to see Miss Wyndham, and if the heavy-pated old Don doesn't mean
to close his doors against you, what business has he
to inquire where you came from? I suppose he
doesn't like me a bit too well; but you're not weak
enough to be afraid to say that you've been at
Handicap Lodge?'

'The truth is, Dot, I don't think I'll go to Grey
Abbey at all, till Fanny's of age. She only wants a
month of it now; and then I can meet Lord Cashel in
a business way, as one man should meet another.'

'I can't for the life of me,' said Blake, 'make out
what it is that has set that old fellow so strong against
horses. He won the Oaks twice himself, and that not
so very long ago; and his own son, Kilcullen, is
deeper a good deal on the turf than I am, and, by a
long chalk less likely to pull through, as I take it.
But here's the Connaught man on the stairs,—I
could swear to Galway by the tread of his foot!'—
and Martin knocked at the door, and walked in.

'Well, Kelly,' said Lord Ballindine, 'how does Dublin agree with you?' And, 'I hope I see your lordship well, my lord?' said Martin.

'How are they all at Dunmore and Kelly's Court?'

'Why thin, they're all well, my lord, except Sim Lynch—and he's dead. But your lordship'll have heard that.'

'What, old Simeon Lynch dead!' said Blake, 'well then, there's promotion. Peter Mahon, that was the agent at Castleblakeney, is now the biggest rogue alive in Connaught.'

'Don't swear to that,' said Lord Ballindine. 'There's some of Sim's breed still left at Dunmore. It wouldn't be easy to beat Barry, would it, Kelly?'

'Why then, I don't know; I wouldn't like to be saying against the gentleman's friend that he spoke of; and doubtless his honor knows him well, or he wouldn't say so much of him.'

'Indeed I do,' said Blake. 'I never give a man a good character till I know he deserves it. Well, Frank, I'll go and dress, and leave you and Mr. Kelly to your business,' and he left the room.

'I'm sorry to hear you speak so hard agin Mr. Barry, my lord,' began Martin. 'May-be he mayn't be so bad. Not but that he's a cross-grained piece of timber to dale with.'

'And why should you be sorry I'd speak against him? There's not more friendship, I suppose, between you and Barry Lynch now, than there used to be?'

'Why, not exactly frindship, my lord; but I've my rasons why I'd wish you not to belittle the Lynches. Your lordship might forgive them all, now the old man's dead.'

'Forgive them!—indeed I can, and easily. I don't know I ever did any of them an injury, except when I thrashed Barry at Eton, for calling himself the son of a gentleman. But what makes you stick up for them? You're not going to marry the daughter, are you?'

Martin blushed up to his forehead as his landlord thus hit the nail on the head; but, as it was dark, his blushes couldn't be seen. So, after dangling his hat about for a minute, and standing first on one foot, and then on the other, he took courage, and answered.

'Well, Mr. Frank, that is, your lordship, I mane— I b'lieve I might do worse.'

'Body and soul, man!' exclaimed the other, jumping from his recumbent position on the sofa, 'You don't mean to tell me you're going to marry Anty Lynch?'

'In course not,' answered Martin; 'av' your lordship objects.'

'Object, man!—How the devil can I object? Why, she's six hundred a year, hasn't she?'

'About four, my lord, I think 's nearest the mark.'

'Four hundred a year! And I don't suppose you owe a penny in the world!'

'Not much—unless the last gale to your lordship— and we never pay that till next May.'

'And so you're going to marry Anty Lynch!' again repeated Frank, as though he couldn't bring himself to realise the idea; 'and now, Martin, tell me all about it,—how the devil you managed it—when it's to come off—and how you and Barry mean to hit it off together when you're brothers. I suppose I'll lose a good tenant any way?'

'Not av' I'm a good one, you won't, with my consent, my lord.'

'Ah! but it'll be Anty's consent, now, you know. She mayn't like Toneroe. But tell me all about it. What put it into your head?'

'Why, my lord, you run away so fast; one can't tell you anything. I didn't say I was going to marry her—at laist, not for certain—I only said I might do worse.'

'Well then; are you going to marry her, or rather, is she going to marry you, or is she not?'

'Why, I don't know. I'll tell your lordship just how it is. You know when old Sim died, my lord?'

'Of course I do. Why, I was at Kelly's Court at the time.'

'So you were, my lord; I was forgetting. But you went away again immediately, and didn't hear how Barry tried to come round his sisther, when he heard how the will went; and how he tried to break the will and to chouse her out of the money.'

'Why, this is the very man you wouldn't let me call a rogue, a minute or two ago!'

'Ah, my lord! that was just before sthrangers; besides, it's no use calling one's own people bad names. Not that he belongs to me yet, and maybe never will. But, between you and I, he is a rogue, and his father's son every inch of him.'

'Well, Martin, I'll remember. I'll not abuse him when he's your brother-in-law. But how did you get round the sister?—That's the question.'

'Well, my lord, I'll tell you. You know there was always a kind of frindship between Anty and the girls at home, and they set her up to going to old Moylan—he that receives the rents on young Barron's property, away at Strype. Moylan's uncle to Flaherty, that married mother's sister. Well, she went to him—he's a kind of office at Dunmore, my lord.'

'Oh, I know him and his office! He knows the value of a name at the back of a bit of paper, as well as any one.'

'May-be he does, my lord; but he's an honest old fellow, is Moylan, and manages a little for mother.'

'Oh, of course he's honest, Martin, because he belongs to you. You know Barry's to be an honest chap, then.'

'And that's what he niver will be the longest day he lives! But, however, Moylan got her to sign all the papers; and, when Barry was out, he went and took an inventhory to the house, and made out everything square and right, and you may be sure Barry'd have to get up very 'arly before he'd come round him. Well, after a little, the ould chap came

to me one morning, and asked me all manner of
questions—whether I knew Anty Lynch? whether
we didn't used to be great friends? and a lot more.
I never minded him much; for though I and Anty
used to speak, and she'd dhrank tay on the sly with
us two or three times before her father's death, I'd
never thought much about her.'

'Nor wouldn't now, Martin, eh? if it wasn't for
the old man's will.'

'In course I wouldn't, my lord. I won't be denying
it. But, on the other hand, I wouldn't marry her now
for all her money, av' I didn't mane to trate her well.
Well, my lord, after beating about the bush for a long
time, the ould thief popped it out, and told me that
he thought Anty'd be all the betther for a husband;
and that, av' I was wanting a wife, he b'lieved I
might suit myself now. Well, I thought of it a little,
and tould him I'd take the hint. The next day he
comes to me again, all the way down to Toneroe,
where I was walking the big grass-field by myself,
and began saying that, as he was Anty's agent, of
course he wouldn't see her wronged. "Quite right,
Mr. Moylan," says I; "and, as I mane to be her
husband, I won't see her wronged neither." "Ah!
but," says he, "I mane that I must see her property
properly settled." "Why not?" says I, "and isn't
the best way for her to marry? and then, you know,
no one can schame her out of it. There's lots of them
schamers about now," says I. "That's thrue for
you," says he, "and they're not far to look for,"—
and that was thrue, too, my lord, for he and I were
both schaming about poor Anty's money at that
moment. "Well," says he, afther walking on a little,
quite quiet, "av' you war to marry her."—"Oh, I've
made up my mind about that, Mr. Moylan," says I.
"Well, av' it should come to pass that you *do* marry
her—of course you'd expect to have the money settled
on herself?" "In course I would, when I die," says I.
"No, but," says he, "at once: wouldn't it be enough
for you to have a warm roof over your head, and a

leg of mutton on the table every day, and no work to do for it?'' and so, my lord, it came out that the money was to be settled on herself, and that he was to be her agent.'

'Well, Martin, after that, I think you needn't go to Sim Lynch, or Barry, for the biggest rogues in Connaught—to be settling the poor girl's money between you that way!'

'Well, but listen, my lord. I gave in to the ould man; that is, I made no objection to his schame. But I was determined, av' I ever did marry Anty Lynch, that I would be agent and owner too, myself, as long as I lived; though in course it was but right that they should settle it so that av' I died first, the poor crature shouldn't be out of her money. But I didn't let on to him about all that; for, av' he was angered, the ould fool might perhaps spoil the game; and I knew av' Anty married me at all, it'd be for liking; and av' iver I got on the soft side of her, I'd soon be able to manage matthers as I plazed, and ould Moylan'd soon find his best game'd be to go asy.'

'Upon my soul, Martin, I think you seem to have been the sharpest rogue of the two! Is there an honest man in Connaught at all, I wonder?'

'I can't say rightly, just at present, my lord; but there'll be two, plaze God, when I and your lordship are there.'

'Thank ye, Kelly, for the compliment, and especially for the good company. But let me hear how on earth you ever got face enough to go up and ask Anty Lynch to marry you.'

'Oh!—a little soft sawther did it! I wasn't long in putting my com'ether on her when I once began. Well, my lord, from that day out—from afther Moylan's visit, you know—I began really to think of it. I'm sure the ould robber meant to have asked for a wapping sum of money down, for his good will in the bargain; but when he saw me he got afeard.'

'He was another honest man, just now!'

'Only among sthrangers, my lord. I b'lieve he 's

a far-off cousin of your own, and I wouldn't like to
spake ill of the blood.'

'God forbid! But go on, Kelly.'

'Well, so, from that out, I began to think of it in
arnest. The Lord forgive me! but my first thoughts
was how I'd like to pull down Barry Lynch; and my
second that I'd not demane myself by marrying the
sisther of such an out-and-out ruffian, and that it
wouldn't become me to live on the money that'd
been got by chating your lordship's grandfather.'

'My lordship's grandfather ought to have looked
after that himself. If those are all your scruples they
needn't stick in your throat much.'

'I said as much as that to myself, too. So I soon
went to work. I was rather shy about it at first; but
the girls helped me. They put it into her head, I
think, before I mentioned it at all. However, by
degrees, I asked her plump, whether she'd any mind
to be Mrs. Kelly? and, though she didn't say "yes,"
she didn't say "no."'

'But how the devil, man, did you manage to get
at her? I'm told Barry watches her like a dragon,
ever since he read his father's will.'

'He couldn't watch her so close, but what she could
make her way down to mother's shop now and again.
Or, for the matter of that, but what I could make my
way up to the house.'

'That 's true, for what need she mind Barry, now?
She may marry whom she pleases, and needn't tell
him, unless she likes, until the priest has his book
ready.'

'Ah, my lord! but there 's the rub. She is afraid of
Barry; and though she didn't say so, she won't agree
to tell him, or to let me tell him, or just to let the
priest walk into the house without telling him. She 's
fond of Barry, though, for the life of me, I can't see
what there is in him for anybody to be fond of. He
and his father led her the divil's own life mewed up
there, because she wouldn't be a nun. But still is
both fond and afraid of him; and, though I don't

think she'll marry anybody else—at laist not yet
awhile, I don't think she'll ever get courage to marry
me—at any rate, not in the ordinary way.'

'Why then, Martin, you must do something extraordinary, I suppose.'

'That's just it, my lord; and what I wanted was,
to ask your lordship's advice and sanction, like.'

'Sanction! Why I shouldn't think you'd want anybody's sanction for marrying a wife with four hundred a-year. But, if that's anything to you, I can
assure you I approve of it.'

'Thank you, my lord. That's kind.'

'To tell the truth,' continued Lord Ballindine,
'I've a little of your own first feeling. I'd be glad of
it, if it were only for the rise it would take out of my
schoolfellow, Barry. Not but that I think you're a
deal too good to be his brother-in-law. And you
know, Kelly, or ought to know, that I'd be heartily
glad of anything for your own welfare. So, I'd advise
you to hammer away while the iron's hot, as the saying is.'

'That's just what I'm coming to. What'd your
lordship advise me to do?'

'Advise you? Why, you must know best yourself
how the matter stands. Talk her over, and make her
tell Barry.'

'Divil a tell, my lord, in her. She wouldn't do it
in a month of Sundays.'

'Then do you tell him, at once. I suppose you're
not afraid of him?'

'She'd niver come to the scratch, av' I did. He'd
bully the life out of her, or get her out of the counthry
some way.'

'Then wait till his back's turned for a month or so.
When he's out, let the priest walk in, and do the
matter quietly that way.'

'Well, I thought of that myself, my lord; but he's
as wary as a weazel, and I'm afeard he smells something in the wind. There's that blackguard Moylan,
too, he'd be telling Barry—and would, when he

came to find things weren't to be settled as he
intended.'

'Then you must carry her off, and marry her up
here, or in Galway or down in Connemara, or over at
Liverpool, or any where you please.'

'Now you've hit it, my lord. That's just what I'm
thinking myself. Unless I take her off Gretna Green
fashion, I'll never get her.'

'Then why do you want my advice, if you've made
up your mind to that? I think you're quite right;
and what's more, I think you ought to lose no time in
doing it. Will she go, do you think?'

'Why, with a little talking, I think she will.'

'Then what are you losing your time for, man?
Hurry down, and off with her! I think Dublin's
probably your best ground.'

'Then you think, my lord, I'd betther do it at
once?'

'Of course, I do! What is there to delay you?'

'Why, you see, my lord, the poor girl's as good as
got no friends, and I wouldn't like it to be thought in
the counthry, I'd taken her at a disadvantage. It's
thrue enough in one way, I'm marrying her for the
money; that is, in course, I wouldn't marry her
without it. And I tould her, out open, before her
face, and before the girls, that, av' she'd ten times
as much, I wouldn't marry her unless I was to be
masther, as long as I lived, of everything in my own
house, like another man; and I think she liked me
the betther for it. But, for all that, I wouldn't like
to catch her up without having something fair done
by the property.'

'The lawyers, Martin, can manage that, afterwards.
When she's once Mrs. Kelly, you can do what you
like about the fortune.'

'That's thrue, my lord. But I wouldn't like the
bad name I'd get through the counthry av' I whisked
her off without letting her settle anything. They'd
be saying I robbed her, whether I did or no: and
when a thing's once said, it's difficult to unsay it.

The like of me, my lord, can't do things like you noblemen and gentry. Besides, mother'd never forgive me. They think, down there, that poor Anty's simple like; tho' she's cute enough, av' they knew her. I wouldn't, for all the money, wish it should be said that Martin Kelly ran off with a fool, and robbed her. Barry'd be making her out a dale more simple than she is; and, altogether, my lord, I wouldn't like it.'

'Well, Martin, perhaps you're right. At any rate you're on the right side. What is it then you think of doing?'

'Why, I was thinking, my lord, av' I could get some lawyer here to draw up a deed, just settling all Anty's property on herself when I die, and on her children, av' she has any,—so that I couldn't spend it you know; she could sign it, and so could I, before we started; and then I'd feel she'd been traited as well as tho' she'd all the friends in Connaught to her back.'

'And a great deal better, probably. Well, Martin, I'm no lawyer, but I should think there'd not be much difficulty about that. Any attorney could do it.'

'But I'd look so quare, my lord, walking into a sthranger's room and explaining what I wanted—all about the running away and everything. To be sure there's my brother John's people; they're attorneys; but it's about robberies, and hanging, and such things they're most engaged; and I was thinking, av' your lordship wouldn't think it too much throuble to give me a line to your own people; or, may-be, you'd say a word to them explaining what I want. It'd be the greatest favour in life.'

'I'll tell you what I'll do, Kelly. I'll go with you, to-morrow, to Mr. Blake's lawyers—that's my friend that was sitting here—and I've no doubt we'll get the matter settled. The Guinnesses, you know, do all my business, and they're not lawyers.'

'Long life to your lordship, and that's just like yourself! I knew you'd stick by me. And shall I call on you to-morrow, my lord? and at what time?'

'Wait! here's Mr. Blake. I'll ask him, and you might as well meet me there. Grey and Forrest's the name; it's in Clare Street, I think.' Here Mr. Blake again entered the room.

'What!' said he; 'isn't your business over yet, Ballindine? I suppose I'm *de trop* then. Only mind, dinner's ordered for half past six, and it's that now, and you're not dressed yet!'

'You're not *de trop*, and I was just wanting you. We're all friends here, Kelly, you know; and you needn't mind my telling Mr. Blake. Here's this fellow going to elope with an heiress from Connaught, and he wants a decently honest lawyer first.'

'I should have thought,' said Blake, 'that an indecently dishonest clergyman would have suited him better under those circumstances.'

'May-be he'll want that, too, and I've no doubt you can recommend one. But at present he wants a lawyer; and, as I have none of my own, I think Forrest would serve his turn.'

'I've always found Mr. Forrest ready to do anything in the way of his profession—for money.'

'No, but—he'd draw up a deed, wouldn't he, Blake? It's a sort of a marriage settlement.'

'Oh, he's quite at home at that work! He drew up five, for my five sisters, and thereby ruined my father's property, and my prospects.'

'Well, he'd see me to-morrow, wouldn't he?' said Lord Ballindine.

'Of course he would. But mind, we're to be off early. We ought to be at the Curragh, by three.'

'I suppose I could see him at ten?' said his lordship.

It was then settled that Blake should write a line to the lawyer, informing him that Lord Ballindine wished to see him, at his office, at ten o'clock the next morning; it was also agreed that Martin should meet him there at that hour; and Kelly took his leave, much relieved on the subject nearest his heart.

'Well, Frank,' said Blake, as soon as the door was closed, 'and have you got the money you wanted?'

'Indeed I've not, then.'

'And why not? If your protégé is going to elope with an heiress, he ought to have money at command.'

'And so he will, and it'll be a great temptation to me to know where I can get it so easily. But he was telling me all about this woman before I thought of my own concerns—and I didn't like to be talking to him of what I wanted myself, when he'd been asking a favour of me. It would be too much like looking for payment.'

'There, you're wrong; fair barter is the truest and honestest system, all the world over.—"Ca me, ca thee," as the Scotch call it, is the best system to go by. I never do, or ask, *a favour*; that is, for whatever I do, I expect a return; and for whatever I get, I intend to make one.'

'I'll get the money from Guinness. After all, that'll be the best, and as you say, the cheapest.'

'There you're right. His business is to lend money, and he'll lend it you as long as you've means to repay it; and I'm sure no Connaught man will do more—that is, if I know them.'

'I suppose he will, but heaven only knows how long that'll be!' and the young lord threw himself back on the sofa, as if he thought a little meditation would do him good. However, very little seemed to do for him, for he soon roused himself, and said, 'I wonder how the devil, Dot, you do without borrowing? My income's larger than yours, bad as it is; I've only three horses in training, and you've, I suppose, above a dozen; and, take the year through, I don't entertain half the fellows at Kelly's Court that you do at Handicap Lodge; and yet, I never hear of your borrowing money.'

'There's many reasons for that. In the first place, I haven't an estate; in the second, I haven't a mother; in the third, I haven't a pack of hounds; in the fourth, I haven't a title; and, in the fifth, no one would lend me money, if I asked it.'

'As for the estate, it's devilish little I spend on it;

as for my mother, she has her own jóinture; as for
the hounds, they eat my own potatoes; and as for
the title, I don't support it. But I haven't your luck,
Dot. You'd never want for money, though the mint
broke.'

'Very likely I mayn't when it does; but I'm likely
to be poor enough till that happy accident occurs.
But, as far as luck goes, you've had more than me;
you won nearly as much, in stakes, as I did, last
autumn, and your stable expenses weren't much
above a quarter what mine were. But, the truth is,
I manage better; I know where my money goes to,
and you don't; I work hard, and you don't; I spend
my money on what's necessary to my style of living,
you spend yours on what's not necessary. What the
deuce have the fellows in Mayo and Roscommon
done for you, that you should mount two or three
rascals, twice a-week, to show them sport, when
you're not there yourself two months in the season?
I suppose you don't keep the horses and men for
nothing, if you do the dogs; and I much doubt
whether they're not the dearest part of the bargain.'

'Of course they cost something; but it's the only
thing I can do for the country; and there were always
hounds at Kelly's Court till my grandfather got the
property, and they looked upon him as no better
than an old woman, because he gave them up.
Besides, I suppose I shall be living at Kelly's Court
soon, altogether, and I could never get on then without hounds. It's bad enough, as it is.'

'I haven't a doubt in the world it's bad enough.
I know what Castleblakeney is. But I doubt your
living there. I've no doubt you'll try; that is, if you
do marry Miss Wyndham; but she'll be sick of it in
three months, and you in six, and you'll go and live
at Paris, Florence, or Naples, and there'll be another
end of the O'Kellys, for thirty or forty years, as far as
Ireland's concerned. You'll never do for a poor
country lord; you're not sufficiently proud, or stingy.
You'd do very well as a country gentleman, and

you'd make a decent nobleman with such a fortune as Lord Cashel's. But your game, if you lived on your own property, would be a very difficult one, and one for which you've neither tact nor temper.'

'Well, I hope I'll never live out of Ireland. Though I mayn't have tact to make one thousand go as far as five, I've sense enough to see that a poor absentee landlord is a great curse to his country; and that's what I hope I never shall be.'

'My dear Lord Ballindine; all poor men are curses, to themselves or some one else.'

'A poor absentee's the worst of all. He leaves nothing behind, and can leave nothing. He wants all he has for himself; and, if he doesn't give his neighbours the profit which must arise somewhere, from his own consumption, he can give nothing. A rich man can afford to leave three or four thousand a year behind him, in the way of wages for labour.'

'My gracious, Frank! You should put all that in a pamphlet, and not inflict it on a poor devil waiting for his dinner. At present, give your profit to Morrison, and come and consume some mock-turtle; and I'll tell you what Sheil's going to do for us all.'

Lord Ballindine did as he was bid, and left the room to prepare for dinner. By the time that he had eaten his soup, and drank a glass of wine, he had got rid of the fit of blue devils which the thoughts of his poverty had brought on, and he spent the rest of the evening comfortably enough, listening to his friend's comical version of Sheil's speech; receiving instruction from that great master of the art as to the manner in which he should treat his Derby colt, and being flattered into the belief that he would be a prominent favourite for that great race.

When they had finished their wine, they sauntered into the Kildare Street Club.

Blake was soon busy with his little betting-book, and Lord Ballindine followed his example. Brien Boru was, before long, in great demand. Blake took fifty to one, and then talked the horse up till he ended by giving twenty-five. He was soon ranked the first of the Irish lot; and the success of the Hibernians had made them very sanguine of late. Lord Ballindine found himself the centre of a little sporting circle, as being the man with the crack nag of the day. He was talked of, courted, and appealed to; and, I regret to say, that before he left the club he was again nearly forgetting Kelly's Court and Miss Wyndham, had altogether got rid of his patriotic notions as to the propriety of living on his own estate, had determined forthwith to send Brien Boru over to Scott's English stables; and then, went to bed, and dreamed that he was a winner of the Derby, and was preparing for the glories of Newmarket with five or six thousand pounds in his pocket.

Martin Kelly dined with his brother at Jude's, and spent his evening equally unreasonably; at least, it may be supposed so from the fact that at one o'clock in the morning he was to be seen standing on one of the tables at Burton Bindon's oyster-house, with a pewter pot, full of porter, in his hand, and insisting that every one in the room should drink the health of Anty Lynch, whom, on that occasion, he swore to be the prettiest and the youngest girl in Connaught.

It was lucky he was so intoxicated, that no one could understand him; and that his hearers were so drunk that they could understand nothing; as, otherwise, the publicity of his admiration might have had the effect of preventing the accomplishment of his design.

He managed, however, to meet his patron the next morning at the lawyer's, though his eyes were very red, and his cheeks pale; and, after being there for some half hour, left the office, with the assurance that, whenever he and the lady might please to call there, they should find a deed prepared for their signature, which would adjust the property in the manner required.

That afternoon Lord Ballindine left Dublin, with his friend, to make instant arrangements for the exportation of Brien Boru; and, at two o'clock the next day, Martin left, by the boat, for Ballinaslie, having evinced his patriotism by paying a year's subscription in advance to the 'Nation' newspaper, and with his mind fully made up to bring Anty away to Dublin with as little delay as possible.

IV

THE DUNMORE INN

ANTY LYNCH was *not* the prettiest, or the youngest girl in Connaught; nor would Martin have affirmed her to be so, unless he had been very much inebriated indeed. However young she might have been once, she was never pretty; but, in all Ireland, there was not a more single-hearted, simple-minded young woman. I do not use the word simple as foolish; for, though uneducated, she was not foolish. But she was unaffected, honest, humble, and true, entertaining a very lowly idea of her own value, and unelated by her newly acquired wealth.

She had been so little thought of all her life by others, that she had never learned to think much of herself; she had had but few acquaintances, and no friends, and had spent her life, hitherto, so quietly and silently, that her apparent apathy was attributable rather to want of subjects of excitement, than to any sluggishness of disposition. Her mother had died early; and, since then, the only case in which Anty had been called on to exercise her own judgment, was in refusing to comply with her father's wish that she should become a nun. On this subject, though often pressed, she had remained positive, always pleading that she felt no call to the sacred duties which would be required, and innocently assuring her father, that, if allowed to remain at home, she would cause him no trouble, and but little expense.

So she had remained at home, and had inured herself to bear without grumbling, or thinking that

she had cause for grumbling, the petulance of her
father, and the more cruel harshness and ill-humour
of her brother. In all the family schemes of aggran-
disement she had been set aside, and Barry had been
intended by the father as the scion on whom all the
family honours were to fall. His education had been
expensive, his allowance liberal, and his whims permitted; while Anty was never better dressed than a
decent English servant, and had been taught nothing
save the lessons she had learnt from her mother, who
died when she was but thirteen.

Mrs. Lynch had died before the commencement of
Sim's palmy days. They had seen no company in her
time—for they were then only rising people; and,
since that, the great friends to whom Sim, in his
wealth, had attached himself, and with whom alone
he intended that Barry should associate, were all of
the masculine gender. He gave bachelor dinner-
parties to hard-drinking young men, for whom Anty
was well contented to cook; and when they—as·they
often, from the effect of their potations, were per-
force obliged to do—stayed the night at Dunmore
House, Anty never showed herself in the breakfast-
parlour, but boiled the eggs, made the tea, and took
her own breakfast in the kitchen.

It was not wonderful, therefore, that no one proposed for Anty; and, though all who knew the
Lynches, knew that Sim had a daughter, it was very
generally given out that she was not so wise as her
neighbours; and the father and brother took no pains
to deny the rumour. The inhabitants of the village
knew better; the Lynches were very generally disliked, and the shameful way 'Miss Anty was trated,'
was often discussed in the little shops; and many of
the townspeople were ready to aver that, 'simple or
no, Anty Lynch was the best of the breed, out-and-
out.'

Matters stood thus at Dunmore, when the quarrel
before alluded to, occurred, and when Sim made his
will, dividing his property,—and died before destroy-

ing it, as he doubtless would have done, when his passion was over.

Great was the surprise of every one concerned, and of many who were not at all concerned, when it was ascertained that Anty Lynch was an heiress, and that she was now possessed of four hundred pounds a-year in her own right; but the passion of her brother, it would be impossible to describe. He soon, however, found that it was too literally true, and that no direct means were at hand, by which he could deprive his sister of her patrimony. The lawyer, when he informed Anty of her fortune and present station, made her understand that she had an equal right with her brother in everything in the house; and though, at first, she tacitly acquiesced in his management, she was not at all simple enough to be ignorant of the rights of possession, or weak enough to relinquish them.

Barry soon made up his mind that, as she had and must have the property, all he could now do was to take care that it should revert to him as her heir; and the measure of most importance in effecting this, would be to take care that she did not marry. In his first passion, after his father's death, he had been rough and cruel to her; but he soon changed his conduct, and endeavoured to flatter her into docility at one moment, and to frighten her into obedience in the next.

He soon received another blow which was also a severe one. Moylan, the old man who proposed the match to Martin, called on him, and showed him that Anty had appointed him her agent, and had executed the necessary legal documents for the purpose. Upon this subject he argued for a long time with his sister— pointing out to her that the old man would surely rob her—offering to act as her agent himself— recommending others as more honest and fitting— and, lastly, telling her that she was an obstinate fool, who would soon be robbed of every penny she had, and that she would die in a workhouse at last.

But Anty, though she dreaded her brother, was

firm. Wonderful as it may appear, she even loved
him. She begged him not to quarrel with her—
promised to do everything to oblige him, and
answered his wrath with gentleness; but it was of no
avail. Barry knew that her agent was a plotter—
that he would plot against his influence—though he
little guessed then what would be the first step
Moylan would take, or how likely it would be, if
really acted on, to lead to his sister's comfort and
happiness. After this, Barry passed two months of
great misery and vexation. He could not make up
his mind what to do, or what final steps to take,
either about the property, his sister, or himself. At
first, he thought of frightening Moylan and his sister,
by pretending that he would prove Anty to be of
weak mind, and not fit to manage her own affairs,
and that he would indict the old man for conspiracy;
but he felt that Moylan was not a man to be frightened by such bugbears. Then, he made up his mind
to turn all he had into money, to leave his sister to
the dogs, or any one who might choose to rob her,
and go and live abroad. Then he thought, if his sister
should die, what a pity it would be, he should lose it
all, and how he should blame himself, if she were to
die soon after having married some low adventurer;
and he reflected, how probable such a thing would be
—how likely that such a man would soon get rid of
her; and then his mind began to dwell on her death,
and to wish for it. He found himself constantly
thinking of it, and ruminating on it, and determining
that it was the only event which could set him right.
His own debts would swallow up half his present
property; and how could he bring himself to live
on the pitiful remainder, when that stupid idiot, as
he called her to himself, had three times more than
she could possibly want? Morning after morning,
he walked about the small grounds round the house,
with his hat over his eyes, and his hands tossing
about the money in his pockets, thinking of this—
cursing his father, and longing—almost praying for

his sister's death. Then he would have his horse, and
flog the poor beast along the roads without going
anywhere, or having any object in view, but always
turning the same thing over and over in his mind.
And, after dinner, he would sit, by the hour, over
the fire, drinking, longing for his sister's money, and
calculating the probabilities of his ever possessing it.
He began to imagine all the circumstances which
might lead to her death; he thought of all the ways in
which persons situated as she was, might, and often
did, die. He reflected, without knowing that he was
doing so, on the probability of robbers breaking into
the house, if she were left alone in it, and of their
murdering her; he thought of silly women setting
their own clothes on fire—of their falling out of
window—drowning themselves—of their perishing in
a hundred possible but improbable ways. It was
after he had been drinking a while, that these ideas
became most vivid before his eyes, and seemed like
golden dreams, the accomplishment of which he could
hardly wish for. And, at last, as the fumes of the
spirit gave him courage, other and more horrible
images would rise to his imagination, and the drops
of sweat would stand on his brow as he would invent
schemes by which, were he so inclined, he could
accelerate, without detection, the event for which he
so ardently longed. With such thoughts would he
turn into bed; and though in the morning he would
try to dispel the ideas in which he had indulged overnight, they still left their impression on his mind—
they added bitterness to his hatred—and made him
look on himself as a man injured by his father and
sister, and think that he owed it to himself to redress
his injuries by some extraordinary means.

It was whilst Barry Lynch was giving way to such
thoughts as these, and vainly endeavouring to make
up his mind as to what he would do, that Martin
made his offer to Anty. To tell the truth, it was
Martin's sister Meg who had made the first overture;
and, as Anty had not rejected it with any great dis-

dain, but had rather shown a disposition to talk
about it as a thing just possible, Martin had repeated
it in person, and had reiterated it, till Anty had at
last taught herself to look upon it as a likely and
desirable circumstance. Martin had behaved openly
and honourably with regard to the money part of the
business; telling his contemplated bride that it was,
of course, her fortune which had first induced him to
think of her; but adding, that he would also value
her and love her for herself, if she would allow him.
He described to her the sort of settlement he should
propose, and ended by recommending an early day
for the wedding.

Anty had sense enough to be pleased at his
straightforward and honest manner; and, though
she did not say much to himself, she said a great
deal in his praise to Meg, which all found its way to
Martin's ears. But still, he could not get over the
difficulty which he had described to Lord Ballindine.
Anty wanted to wait till her brother should go out of
the country, and Martin was afraid that he would not
go; and things were in this state when he started for
Dublin.

The village of Dunmore has nothing about it which
can especially recommend it to the reader. It has
none of those beauties of nature which have taught
Irishmen to consider their country as the 'first flower
of the earth, and first gem of the sea'. It is a dirty,
ragged little town, standing in a very poor part of
the country, with nothing about it to induce the
traveller to go out of his beaten track. It is on no
high road, and is blessed with no adventitious circumstances to add to its prosperity.

It was once the property of the O'Kellys; but, in
those times the landed proprietors thought but little
of the towns; and now it is parcelled out among
different owners, some of whom would think it folly
to throw away a penny on the place, and others of
whom have not a penny to throw away. It consists
of a big street, two little streets, and a few very little

lanes. There is a Court-house, where the barrister sits twice a year; a Barrack, once inhabited by soldiers, but now given up to the police; a large slated chapel, not quite finished; a few shops for soft goods; half a dozen shebeen-houses, ruined by Father Mathew; a score of dirty cabins offering 'lodging and enthertainment', as announced on the window-shutters; Mrs. Kelly's inn and grocery-shop; and, last though not least, Simeon Lynch's new, staring house, built just at the edge of the town, on the road to Roscommon, which is dignified with the name of Dunmore House. The people of most influence in the village were Mrs. Kelly of the inn, and her two sworn friends, the parish priest and his curate. The former, Father Geoghegan, lived about three miles out of Dunmore, near Toneroe; and his curate, Father Pat Connel, inhabited one of the small houses in the place, very little better in appearance than those which offered accommodation to travellers and trampers.

Such was, and is, the town of Dunmore in the county of Galway; and I must beg the reader to presume himself to be present there with me on the morning on which the two young Kellys went to hear Sheil's speech. At about ten o'clock, the widow Kelly and her daughters were busy in the shop, which occupied the most important part of the ground-floor of the inn. It was a long, scrambling, ugly-looking house. Next to the shop, and opening out of it, was a large drinking-room, furnished with narrow benches and rickety tables; and here the more humble of Mrs. Kelly's guests regaled themselves. On the other side of this, was the hall, or passage of the house; and, next to that again, a large, dingy, dark kitchen, over which Sally reigned with her teapot dynasty, and in which were always congregated a parcel of ragged old men, boys, and noisy women, pretending to be busy, but usually doing but little good, and attracted by the warmth of the big fire, and the hopes of some scraps of food and drink.

'For the widow Kelly—God bless her! was a thrue
Christhian, and didn't begrudge the poor—more
power to her—like some upstarts who might live to
be in want yet, glory be to the Almighty!'

The difference of the English and Irish character
is nowhere more plainly discerned than in their
respective kitchens. With the former, this apartment
is probably the cleanest, and certainly the most
orderly, in the house. It is rarely intruded into by
those unconnected, in some way, with its business.
Everything it contains is under the vigilant eye of
its chief occupant, who would imagine it quite impossible to carry on her business, whether of an
humble or important nature, if her apparatus was
subjected to the hands of the unauthorised. An Irish
kitchen is devoted to hospitality in every sense of the
word. Its doors are open to almost all loungers and
idlers; and the chances are that Billy Bawn, the
cripple, or Judy Molloy, the deaf old hag, are more
likely to know where to find the required utensil than
the cook herself. It is usually a temple dedicated to
the goddess of disorder; and, too often joined with
her, is the potent deity of dirt. It is not that things
are out of their place, for they have no place. It isn't
that the floor is not scoured, for you cannot scour dry
mud into anything but wet mud. It isn't that the
chairs and tables look filthy, for there are none. It
isn't that the pots, and plates, and pans don't shine,
for you see none to shine. All you see is a grimy,
black ceiling, an uneven clay floor, a small darkened
window, one or two unearthly-looking recesses, a heap
of potatoes in the corner, a pile of turf against the
wall, two pigs and a dog under the single dresser,
three or four chickens on the window-sill, an old
cock moaning on the top of a rickety press, and a
crowd of ragged garments, squatting, standing,
kneeling, and crouching, round the fire, from which
issues a babel of strange tongues, not one word of
which is at first intelligible to ears unaccustomed to
such eloquence.

And yet, out of these unfathomable, unintelligible dens, proceed in due time dinners, of which the appearance of them gives no promise. Such a kitchen was Mrs. Kelly's; and yet, it was well known and attested by those who had often tried the experiment, that a man need think it no misfortune to have to get his dinner, his punch, and his bed, at the widow's.

Above stairs were two sitting-rooms and a colony of bed-rooms, occupied indiscriminately by the family, or by such customers as might require them. If you came back to dine at the inn, after a day's shooting on the bogs, you would probably find Miss Jane's work-box on the table, or Miss Meg's album on the sofa ; and, when a little accustomed to sojourn at such places, you would feel no surprise at discovering their dresses turned inside out, and hanging on the pegs in your bed-room ; or at seeing their side-combs and black pins in the drawer of your dressing-table.

On the morning in question, the widow and her daughters were engaged in the shop, putting up pen'norths of sugar, cutting bits of tobacco, tying bundles of dip candles, attending to chance customers, and preparing for the more busy hours of the day. It was evident that something had occurred at the inn, which had ruffled the even tenor of its way. The widow was peculiarly gloomy. Though fond of her children, she was an autocrat in her house, and accustomed, as autocrats usually are, to scold a good deal ; and now she was using her tongue pretty freely. It wasn't the girls, however, she was rating, for they could answer for themselves; and did, when they thought it necessary. But now, they were demure, conscious, and quiet. Mrs. Kelly was denouncing one of the reputed sins of the province to which she belonged, and describing the horrors of ' schaming.'

' Them underhand ways,' she declared, ' niver come to no good. Av' it 's thrue what Father Connel's afther telling me, there'll harum come of it before it 's done and over. Schaming, schaming, and schaming for iver ! The back of my hand to such doings ! I wish

the tongue had been out of Moylan's mouth, the ould
rogue, before he put the thing in his head. Av' he
wanted the young woman, and she was willing, why
not take her in a dacent way, and have done with it.
I'm sure she's ould enough. But what does he want
with a wife like her?—making innimies for himself. I
suppose he'll be sitting up for a gentleman now—bad
cess to them for gentry; not but that he's as good a
right as some, and a dale more than others, who are
ashamed to put their hand to a turn of work. I hate
such huggery muggery work up in a corner. It's half
your own doing; and a nice piece of work it'll be,
when he's got an ould wife and a dozen lawsuits!—
when he finds his farm gone, and his pockets empty;
for it'll be a dale asier for him to be getting the wife
than the money—when he's got every body's abuse,
and nothing else, by his bargain!'

It was very apparent that Martin's secret had not
been well kept, and that the fact of his intended
marriage with Anty Lynch was soon likely to be
known to all Dunmore. The truth was, that Moylan
had begun to think himself overreached in the matter
—to be afraid that, by the very measure he had himself proposed, he would lose all share in the great
prize he had put in Martin's way, and that he should
himself be the means of excluding his own finger from
the pie. It appeared to him that if he allowed this,
his own folly would only be equalled by the young
man's ingratitude; and he determined therefore, if
possible, to prevent the match. Whereupon he told
the matter as a secret, to those whom he knew would
set it moving. In a very short space of time it
reached the ears of Father Connel; and he lost none
in stepping down to learn the truth of so important
a piece of luck to one of his parishioners, and to
congratulate the widow. Here, however, he was out
in his reckoning, for she declared she did not believe
it—that it wasn't, and couldn't be true; and it was
only after his departure that she succeeded in extracting the truth from her daughters.

The news, however, quickly reached the kitchen and its lazy crowd; and the inn door and its constant loungers; and was readily and gladly credited in both places.

Crone after crone, and cripple after cripple, hurried into the shop, to congratulate the angry widow on 'masther Martin's luck; and warn't he worthy of it, the handsome jewel—and wouldn't he look the gintleman, every inch of him?' and Sally expatiated greatly on it in the kitchen, and drank both their healths in an extra pot of tea, and Kate grinned her delight, and Jack the ostler, who took care of Martin's horse, boasted loudly of it in the street, declaring that 'it was a good thing enough for Anty Lynch, with all her money, to get a husband at all out of the Kellys, for the divil a know any one knowed in the counthry where the Lynchs come from; but every one knowed who the Kellys wor—and Martin wasn't that far from the lord himself.'

There was great commotion, during the whole day, at the inn. Some said Martin had gone to town to buy furniture; others, that he had done so to prove the will. One suggested that he'd surely have to fight Barry, and another prayed that 'if he did, he might kill the blackguard, and have all the fortin to himself, out and out, God bless him!'

V

A LOVING BROTHER

THE great news was not long before it reached the ears of one not disposed to receive the information with much satisfaction, and this was Barry Lynch, the proposed bride's amiable brother. The medium through which he first heard it was not one likely to add to his good humour. Jacky, the fool, had for many years been attached to the Kelly's Court family; that is to say, he had attached himself to it, by getting his food in the kitchen, and calling himself the lord's fool. But, latterly, he had quarrelled with

Kelly's Court, and had insisted on being Sim Lynch's fool, much to the chagrin of that old man; and, since his death, he had nearly maddened Barry by following him through the street, and being continually found at the house-door when he went out. Jack's attendance was certainly dictated by affection rather than any mercenary views, for he never got a scrap out of the Dunmore House kitchen, or a halfpenny from his new patron. But still, he was Barry's fool; and, like other fools, a desperate annoyance to his master.

On the day in question, as young Mr. Lynch was riding out of the gate, about three in the afternoon, there, as usual, was Jack.

'Now yer honor, Mr. Barry, darling, shure you won't forget Jacky to-day. You'll not forget your own fool, Mr. Barry?'

Barry did not condescend to answer this customary appeal, but only looked at the poor ragged fellow as though he'd like to flog the life out of him.

'Shure your honor, Mr. Barry, isn't this the time then to open yer honor's hand, when Miss Anty, God bless her, is afther making sich a great match for the family?—Glory be to God!'

'What d'ye mean, you ruffian?'

'Isn't the Kellys great people intirely, Mr. Barry? and won't it be a great thing for Miss Anty, to be sib to a lord? Shure yer honor'd not be refusing me this blessed day.'

'What the d—— are you saying about Miss Lynch?' said Barry, his attention somewhat arrested by the mention of his sister's name.

'Isn't she going to be married then, to the dacentest fellow in Dunmore? Martin Kelly, God bless him! Ah! there'll be fine times at Dunmore, then. He's not the boy to rattle a poor divil out of the kitchen into the cold winther night! The Kellys was always the right sort for the poor.'

Barry was frightened in earnest, now. It struck him at once that Jack couldn't have made the story

out of his own head; and the idea that there was any
truth in it, nearly knocked him off his horse. He
rode on, however, trying to appear to be regardless
of what had been said to him, and, as he trotted off,
he heard the fool's parting salutation.

'And will yer honor be forgething me afther the
news I've brought yer? Well, hard as ye are, Misther
Barry, I've hot yer now, any way.'

And, in truth, Jack had hit him hard. Of all
things that could happen to him, this would be about
the worst. He had often thought, with dread, of
his sister's marrying, and of his thus being forced
to divide everything—all his spoil, with some confounded stranger. But for her to marry a shop-
keeper's son, in the very village in which he lived,
was more than he could bear. He could never hold
up his head in the county again. And then, he
thought of his debts, and tried to calculate whether
he might get over to France without paying them,
and be able to carry his share of the property with
him; and so he went on, pursuing his wretched,
uneasy, solitary ride, sometimes sauntering along at
a snail's pace, and then again spurring the poor brute,
and endeavouring to bring his mind to some settled
plan. But, whenever he did so, the idea of his sister's
death was the only one which seemed to present either
comfort or happiness.

He made up his mind, at last, to put a bold face on
the matter; to find out from Anty herself whether
there was any truth in the story; and, if there should
be,—for he felt confident she would not be able to
deceive him,—to frighten her and the whole party
of the Kellys out of what he considered a damnable
conspiracy to rob him of his father's property.

He got off his horse, and stalked into the house.
On inquiry, he found that Anty was in her own room.
He was sorry she was not out; for, to tell the truth,
he was rather anxious to put off the meeting, as he
did not feel himself quite up to the mark, and was
ashamed of seeming afraid of her. He went into the

stable, and abused the groom; into the kitchen, and
swore at the maid; and then into the garden. It was
a nasty, cold, February day, and he walked up and
down the damp muddy walks till he was too tired
and cold to walk longer, and then turned into the
parlour, and remained with his back to the fire, till
the man came in to lay the cloth, thinking on the one
subject that occupied all his mind—occasionally
grinding his teeth, and heaping curses on his father
and sister, who, together, had inflicted such grievous,
such unexpected injuries upon him.

If, at this moment, there was a soul in all Ireland
over whom Satan had full dominion—if there was a
breast unoccupied by one good thought—if there was
a heart wishing, a brain conceiving, and organs ready
to execute all that was evil, from the worst motives,
they were to be found in that miserable creature, as
he stood there urging himself on to hate those whom
he should have loved—cursing those who were
nearest to him—fearing her, whom he had ill-treated
all his life—and striving to pluck up courage to take
such measures as might entirely quell her. Money
was to him the only source of gratification. He had
looked forward, when a boy, to his manhood, as a
period when he might indulge, unrestrained, in
pleasures which money would buy; and, when a man,
to his father's death, as a time when those means
would be at his full command. He had neither ambition, nor affection, in his nature; his father had
taught him nothing but the excellence of money, and,
having fully imbued him with· this, had cut him off
from the use of it.

He was glad when he found that dinner was at
hand, and that he could not now see his sister until
after he had fortified himself with drink. Anty
rarely, if ever, dined with him; so he sat down, and
swallowed his solitary meal. He did not eat much,
but he gulped down three or four glasses of wine; and,
immediately on having done so, he desired the servant, with a curse, to bring him hot water and sugar,

and not to keep him waiting all night for a tumbler
of punch, as he did usually. Before the man had got
into the kitchen, he rang the bell again; and when
the servant returned breathless, with the steaming
jug, he threatened to turn him out of the house at
once, if he was not quicker in obeying the orders
given him. He then made a tumbler of punch, filling
the glass half full of spirits, and drinking it so hot as
to scald his throat; and when that was done he again
rang the bell, and desired the servant to tell Miss
Anty that he wanted to speak to her. When the door
was shut, he mixed more drink, to support his
courage during the interview, and made up his mind
that nothing should daunt him from preventing the
marriage, in one way or another. When Anty opened
the door, he was again standing with his back to the
fire, his hands in his pockets, the flaps of his coat
hanging over his arms, his shoulders against the
mantel-piece, and his foot on the chair on which he
had been sitting. His face was red, and his eyes were
somewhat blood-shot; he had always a surly look,
though, from his black hair, and large bushy whiskers,
many people would have called him good looking;
but now there was a scowl in his restless eyes, which
frightened Anty when she saw it; and the thick drops
of perspiration on his forehead did not add benignity
to his face.

'Were you wanting me, Barry?' said Anty, who
was the first to speak.

'What do you stand there for, with the door open?'
replied her brother, 'd' you think I want the servants
to hear what I've got to say?'

''Deed I don't know,' said Anty, shutting the
door; 'but they'll hear just as well now av' they wish,
for they'll come to the kay-hole.'

'Will they, by G——!' said Barry, and he rushed to
the door, which he banged open; finding no victim
outside on whom to exercise his wrath—'let me
catch 'em!' and he returned to his position by
the fire.

Anty had sat down on a sofa that stood by the wall opposite the fireplace, and Barry remained for a minute, thinking how he'd open the campaign. At last he began:

'Anty, look you here, now. What scheme have you got in your head?—You'd better let me know, at once.'

'What schame, Barry?'

'Well—what schame, if you like that better.'

'I've no schame in my head, that I know of—at laist—' and then Anty blushed. It would evidently be easy enough to make the poor girl tell her own secret.

'Well, go on—at laist—'

'I don't know what you mane, Barry. Av' you're going to be badgering me again, I'll go away.'

'It's evident you're going to do something you're ashamed of, when you're afraid to sit still, and answer a common question. But you must answer me. I'm your brother, and have a right to know. What's this you're going to do?' He didn't like to ask her at once whether she was going to get married. It might not be true, and then he would only be putting the idea into her head. 'Well—why don't you answer me? What is it you're going to do?'

'Is it about the property you mane, Barry?'

'What a d—d hypocrite you are! As if you didn't know what I mean! As for the property, I tell you there'll be little left the way you're going on. And as to that, I'll tell you what I'm going to do; so, mind, I warn you beforehand. You're not able—that is, you're too foolish and weak-headed to manage it yourself; and I mean, as your guardian, to put it into the hands of those that shall manage it for you. I'm not going to see you robbed and duped, and myself destroyed by such fellows as Moylan, and a crew of huxtering blackguards down in Dunmore. And now, tell me at once, what's this I hear about you and the Kellys?'

'What Kellys?' said Anty, blushing deeply, and

half beside herself with fear—for Barry's face was very red, and full of fierce anger, and his rough words frightened her.

'What Kellys!—Did you ever hear of Martin Kelly?—d—d young robber that he is!' Anty blushed still deeper—rose a little way from the sofa, and then sat down again. 'Look you here, Anty—I'll have the truth out of you. I'm not going to be bamboozled by such an idiot as you. You got an old man, when he was dying, to make a will that has robbed me of what was my own, and now you think you'll play your own low game; but you're mistaken! You've lived long enough without a husband to do without one now; and I can tell you I'm not going to see my property carried off by such a low, paltry blackguard as Martin Kelly.'

'How can he take your property, Barry?' sobbed forth the poor creature, who was, by this time, far gone in tears.

'Then the long and the short of it is, he shan't have what you call yours. Tell me, at once, will you—is it true, that you've promised to marry him?'

Anty replied nothing, but continued sobbing violently.

'Cease your nonsense, you blubbering fool! A precious creature you are to take on yourself to marry any man! Are you going to answer me, Anty?' And he walked away from the fire, and came and stood opposite to her as she sat upon the sofa. 'Are you going to answer me or not?' he continued, stamping on the floor.

'I'll not stop here—and be trated this way—Barry —I'm sure—I do all I—I can for you—and you're always—bullying me because father divided the property.' And Anty continued sobbing more violently than ever. 'I won't stop in the room any more,' and she got up to go to the door.

Barry, however, rushed before her, and prevented her. He turned the lock, and put the key in his pocket; and then he caught her arm, as she attempted

to get to the bell, and dragged her back to the
sofa.

'You're not off so easy as that, I can tell you.
Why, d' you think you're to marry whom you please,
without even telling me of it? What d'you think the
world would say of me, if I were to let such an idiot
as you be caught up by the first sharper that tried to
rob you of your money? Now, look here,' and he sat
down beside her, and laid his hand violently on her
arm, as he spoke, 'you don't go out of this room,
alive, until you've given me your solemn promise,
and sworn on the cross, that you'll never marry without my consent; and you'll give me that in writing,
too.'

Anty at first turned very pale when she felt his
heavy hand on her arm, and saw his red, glaring
eyes so near her own. But when he said she shouldn't
leave the room alive, she jumped from the sofa, and
shrieked, at the top of her shrill voice—'Oh, Barry!
you'll not murdher me! shure you wouldn't murdher
your own sisther!'

Barry was rather frightened at the noise, and,
moreover, the word 'murder' quelled him. But when
he found, after a moment's pause, that the servants
had not heard, or had not heeded his sister, he determined to carry on his game, now that he had proceeded so far. He took, however, a long drink out of
his tumbler, to give him fresh courage, and then
returned to the charge.

'Who talked of murdering you? But, if you
bellow in that way, I'll gag you. It's a great deal I'm
asking, indeed—that, when I'm your only guardian,
my advice should be asked for before you throw
away your money on a low ruffian. You're more fit
for a mad-house than to be any man's wife; and, by
Heaven, that's where I'll put you, if you don't give
me the promise I ask! Will you swear you'll marry
no one without my leave?'

Poor Anty shook with fear as she sate, with her
eyes fixed on her brother's face. He was nearly drunk

now, and she felt that he was so,—and he looked so
hot and so fierce—so red and cruel, that she was all
but paralysed. Nevertheless, she mustered strength
to say,

'Let me go, now, Barry, and, to-morrow, I'll tell
you everything—indeed I will—and I'll thry to do
all you'd have me; indeed, and indeed, I will! Only
do let me go now, for you've frighted me.'

'You're likely to be more frighted yet, as you call
it! And be tramping along the roads, I suppose, with
Martin Kelly, before the morning. No! I'll have an
answer from you, any way. I've a right to that!'

'Oh, Barry!—What is it you want?—Pray let me
go—pray, pray, for the love of the blessed Jesus, let
me go.'

'I'll tell you where you'll go, and that's into
Ballinasloe mad-house! Now, mark me—so help
me——I'll set off with you this night, and have you
there in the morning—as an idiot as you are, if you
won't make the promise I'm telling you!'

By this time Anty's presence of mind had clean
left her. Indeed, all the faculties of her reason had
vanished; and, as she saw her brother's scowling face
so near her own, and heard him threatening to drag
her to a mad-house, she put her hands before her
eyes, and made one rush to escape from him—to the
door—to the window—anywhere to get out of his
reach.

Barry was quite drunk now. Had he not been so,
even he would hardly have done what he then did.
As she endeavoured to rush by him, he raised his
fist, and struck her on the face, with all his force.
The blow fell upon her hands, as they were crossed
over her face; but the force of the blow knocked her
down, and she fell upon the floor, senseless, striking
the back of her head against the table.

'Confound her,' muttered the brute, between his
teeth, as she fell, 'for an obstinate, pig-headed fool!
What the d—l shall I do now? Anty, get up!—get
up, will you!—What ails you?'—and then again to

himself, 'the d—l seize her! What am I to do now?'
and he succeeded in dragging her on to the sofa.

The man-servant and the cook although up to this
point, they had considered it would be ill manners to
interrupt the brother and sister in their family interview, were nevertheless at the door; and though they
could see nothing, and did not succeed in hearing
much, were not the less fully aware that the conversation was of a somewhat stormy nature on the part of
the brother. When they heard the noise which
followed the blow, though not exactly knowing what
had happened, they became frightened, and began
to think something terrible was being done.

'Go in, Terry, avich,' whispered the woman—
'Knock, man, and go in—shure he's murdhering her!'

'What 'ud he do to me thin, av' he'd strick a
woman, and she his own flesh and blood! He'll not
murdher her—but, faix, he's afther doing something
now! Knock, Biddy, knock, I say, and screech out
that you're afther wanting Miss Anty.'

The woman had more courage than the man—or
else more compassion, for, without further parleying,
she rapped her knuckles loudly against the door, and,
as she did so, Terry sneaked away to the kitchen.

Barry had just succeeded in raising his sister to the
sofa as he heard the knock.

'Who's that?' he called out loudly; 'what do
you want?'

'Plaze yer honer, Miss Anty's wanting in the
kitchen.'

'She's busy, and can't come at present; she'll be
there directly.'

'Is she ill at all, Mr. Barry? God bless you, spake,
Miss Anty; in God's name, spake thin. Ah! Mr.
Barry, thin, shure she'd spake av' she were able.'

'Go away, you fool! Your mistress'll be out in a
minute.' Then, after a moment's consideration, he
went and unlocked the door, 'or—go in, and see
what she wants. She's fainted, I think.'

Barry Lynch walked out of the room, and into the

garden before the house, to think over what he had done, and what he'd better do for the future, leaving Anty to the care of the frightened woman.

She soon came to herself, and, excepting that her head was bruised in the fall, was not much hurt. The blow, falling on her hands, had neither cut nor marked her; but she was for a long time so flurried that she did not know where she was, and, in answer to all Biddy's tender inquiries as to the cause of her fall, and anathemas as to the master's bad temper, merely said that 'she'd get to bed, for her head ached so, she didn't know where she was.'

To bed accordingly she went; and glad she was to have escaped alive from that drunken face, which had glared on her for the last half hour.

After wandering about round the house and through the grounds, for above an hour, Barry returned, half sobered, to the room; but, in his present state of mind, he could not go to bed sober. He ordered more hot water, and again sat down alone to drink, and drown the remorse he was beginning to feel for what he had done—or rather, not remorse, but the feeling of fear that every one would know how he had treated Anty, and that they would side with her against him. Whichever way he looked, all was misery and disappointment to him, and his only hope, for the present, was in drink. There he sat, for a long time, with his eyes fixed on the turf, till it was all burnt out, trying to get fresh courage from the spirits he swallowed, and swearing to himself that he would not be beat by a woman.

About one o'clock he seized one of the candles, and staggered up to bed. As he passed his sister's door, he opened it and went in. She was fast asleep; her shoes were off, and the bed-clothes were thrown over her, but she was not undressed. He slowly shut the door, and stood, for some moments, looking at her; then, walking to the bed, he took her shoulder, and shook it as gently as his drunkenness would let him. This did not wake her, so he put the candle down on the

table, close beside the bed, and, steadying himself
against the bedstead, he shook her again and again.
'Anty', he whispered, 'Anty'; and, at last, she
opened her eyes. Directly she saw his face, she closed
them again, and buried her own in the clothes; however, he saw that she was awake, and, bending his
head, he muttered, loud enough for her to hear, but
in a thick, harsh, hurried, drunken voice, 'Anty—
d'ye hear? If you marry that man, I'll have your
life!' and then, leaving the candle behind him, he
staggered off into his own room in the dark.

VI

THE ESCAPE

IN vain, after that, did Anty try to sleep; turn
which way she would, she saw the bloodshot eyes
and horrid drunken face of her cruel brother. For
a long time she lay, trembling and anxious; fearing
she knew not what, and trying to compose herself—
trying to make herself think that she had no present
cause for fear; but in vain. If she heard a noise, she
thought it was her brother's footstep, and when the
house was perfectly silent and still, she feared the
very silence itself. At last, she crept out of bed, and,
taking the candle left by her brother, which had now
burned down to the socket, stepped softly down the
stairs, to the place where the two maid-servants
slept, and, having awakened them, she made Biddy
return with her and keep her company for the remainder of the night. She did not quite tell the good-
natured girl all that had passed; she did not own that
her brother had threatened to send her to a mad-
house, or that he had sworn to have her life; but
she said enough to show that he had shamefully ill-
treated her, and to convince Biddy that wherever
her mistress might find a home, it would be very
unadvisable that she and Barry should continue to
live under the same roof.

Early in the morning, 'Long afore the break o' day,' as the song says, Biddy got up from her hard bed on the floor of her mistress' room, and, seeing that Anty was at last asleep, started to carry into immediate execution the counsels she had given during the night. As she passed the head of the stairs, she heard the loud snore of Barry, in his drunken slumber; and, wishing that he might sleep as sound for ever and ever, she crept down to her own domicile, and awakened her comrade.

'Whist, Judy—whist, darlint! Up wid ye, and let me out.'

'And what'd you be doing out now?' yawned Judy.

'An arrand of the misthress—shure, he used her disperate. Faix, it's a wondher he didn't murther her outright!'

'And where are ye going now?'

'Jist down to Dunmore—to the Kellys then, avich. Asy now; I'll be telling you all bye and bye. She must be out of this intirely.'

'Is't Miss Anty? Where'd she be going thin out of this?'

'Divil a matther where! He'd murther her, the ruffian 'av he cotched her another night in his dhrunkenness. We must git her out before he sleeps hisself right. But hurry now, I'll be telling you all when I'm back again.'

The two crept off to the back door together, and, Judy having opened it, Biddy sallied out, on her important and good-natured mission. It was still dark, though the morning was beginning to break, as she stood, panting, at the front door of the inn. She tried to get in at the back, but the yard gates were fastened; and Jack, the ostler, did not seem to be about yet. So she gave a timid, modest knock, with the iron knocker, on the front door. A pause, and then a second knock, a little louder; another pause, and then a third; and then, as no one came, she remembered the importance of her message, and

gave such a rap as a man might do, who badly
wanted a glass of hot drink after travelling the whole
night.

The servants had good or hardy consciences, for
they slept soundly; but the widow Kelly, in her little
bed-room behind the shop, well knew the sound of
that knocker, and, hurrying on her slippers and her
gown, she got to the door, and asked who was there.

'Is that Sally, ma'am?' said Biddy, well knowing
the widow's voice.

'No, it's not. What is it you're wanting?'

'Is it Kate thin, ma'am?'

'No, it's not Kate. Who are you, I say; and what
d'you want?'

'I'm Biddy, plaze ma'am—from Lynch's, and I'm
wanting to spake to yerself, ma'am—about Miss
Anty. She's very bad intirely, ma'am.'

'What ails her—and why d'you come here? Why
don't you go to Doctor Colligan, av' she's ill; and
not come knocking here?'

'It ain't bad that way, Miss Anty is, ma'am. Av'
you'd just be good enough to open the door, I'd tell
you in no time.'

It would, I am sure, be doing injustice to Mrs.
Kelly to say that her curiosity was stronger than her
charity; they both, however, no doubt had their
effect, and the door was speedily opened.

'Oh, ma'am!' commenced Biddy, 'sich terrible
doings up at the house! Miss Anty's almost kilt!'

'Come out of the cowld, girl, in to the kitchen fire,'
said the widow, who didn't like the February blast,
to which Biddy, in her anxiety, had been quite indifferent; and the careful widow again bolted the
door, and followed the woman into certainly the
warmest place in Dunmore, for the turf fire in the
inn kitchen was burning day and night. 'And now,
tell me what is it ails Miss Anty? She war well
enough yesterday, I think, and I heard more of her
then than I wished.'

Biddy now pulled her cloak from off her head,

settled it over her shoulders, and prepared for telling a good substantial story.

'Oh, Misthress Kelly, ma'am, there's been disperate doings last night up at the house. We were all hearing, in the morn yesterday, as how Miss Anty and Mr. Martin, God bless him!—were to make a match of it,—as why wouldn't they, ma'am? for wouldn't Mr. Martin make her a tidy, dacent, good husband?'

'Well, well, Biddy—don't mind Mr. Martin; he'll be betther without a wife for one while, and he needn't be quarrelling for one when he wants her. What ails Miss Anty?'

'Shure I'm telling you, ma'am; howsomever, whether its thrue or no about Mr. Martin, we were all hearing it yestherday; and the masther, he war afther hearing it too, for he come into his dinner as black as tunder; and Terry says he dhrunk the whole of a bottle of wine, and then he called for the sperrits, and swilled away at them till he was nigh dhrunk. Well, wid that, ma'am, he sent for Miss Anty, and the moment she comes in, he locks to the door, and pulls her to the sofa, and swears outright that he'll murdher her av' she don't swear, by the blessed Mary and the cross, that she'll niver dhrame of marrying no one.'

'Who tould you all this, Biddy? was it herself?'

'Why, thin, partly herself it war who tould me, ma'am, and partly—; you see, when Mr. Barry war in his tantrums and dhrunken like, I didn't like to be laving Miss Anty alone wid him, and nobody nigh, so I and Terry betook ourselves nigh the door, and, partly heard what was going on; that's the thruth on it, Mrs. Kelly; and, afther a dale of rampaging and scolding, may I niver see glory av' he didn't up wid his clenched fist, strik her in the face, and knock her down—all for one as 'av she wor a dhrunken blackguard at a fair!'

'You didn't see that, Biddy?'

'No, ma'am—I didn't see it; how could I, through

the door?—but I heerd it, plain enough. I heerd the
poor cratur fall for dead amongst the tables and
chairs—I did, Mrs. Kelly—and I heerd the big blow
smash agin her poor head, and down she wint—why
wouldn't she? and he, the born ruffian, her own
brother, the big blackguard, stricking at her wid all
his force! Well, wid that ma'am, I rushed into the
room—at laist, I didn't rush in—for how could I, and
the door locked?—but I knocked agin and agin, for
I war afeard he would be murthering her out and out.
So, I calls out, as loud as I could, as how Miss Anty
war wanting in the kitchen: and wid that he come
to the door, and unlocks it as bould as brass, and
rushes out into the garden, saying as how Miss Anty
war afther fainting. Well, in course I goes in to her,
where he had dragged her upon the sofa, and, thrue
enough, she war faint indeed.'

'And, did she tell you, Biddy, that her own brother
had trated her that way?'

'Wait, Mrs. Kelly, ma'am, till I tell yer how it all
happened. When she comed to herself—and she
warn't long coming round—she didn't say much, nor
did I; for I didn't just like then to be saying much
agin the masther, for who could know where his ears
were?—perish his sowl, the blackguard!'

'Don't be cursing, Biddy.'

'No, ma'am; only he must be cursed, sooner or
later. Well, when she comed to herself, she begged
av' me to help her to bed, and she went up to her
room, and laid herself down, and I thought to myself
that at any rate it was all over for that night. When
she war gone, the masther he soon come back into the
house, and begun calling for the sperrits again, like
mad; and Terry said that when he tuk the biling wather
into the room, Mr. Barry war just like the divil—
as he's painted, only for his ears. After that Terry
wint to bed; and I and Judy weren't long afther him,
for we didn't care to be sitting up alone wid him, and
he mad dhrunk. So we turned in, and we were in
bed maybe two hours or so, and fast enough, when

down come the misthress—as pale as a sheet, wid
a candle in her hand, and begged me, for dear life, to
come up into her room to her, and so I did, in coorse.
And then she tould me all and, not contint with
what he'd done down stairs, but the dhrunken ruffian
must come up into her bed-room and swear the most
dreadfullest things to her you iver heerd, Mrs. Kelly.
The words he war afther using, and the things he
said, war most horrid; and Miss Anty wouldn't for
her dear life, nor for all the money in Dunmore, stop
another night, nor another day in the house wid him.'

'But, is she much hurt, Biddy?'

'Oh! her head's cut, dreadful, where she fell,
ma'am: and he shuck the very life out of her poor
carcase; so he did, Mrs. Kelly, the ruffian!'

'Don't be cursing, I tell you, girl. And what is it
your misthress is wishing to do now? Did she tell
you to come to me?'

'No, ma'am; she didn't exactly tell me—only as
she war saying that she wouldn't for anything be
staying in the house with Mr. Barry; and as she
didn't seem to be knowing where she'd be going, and
av' she be raally going to be married to Mr. Martin—'

'Drat Mr. Martin, you fool! Did she tell you she
wanted to come here?'

'She didn't quite say as much as that. To tell the
thruth, thin, it wor I that said it, and she didn't
unsay it; so, wid that, I thought I'd come down here
the first thing, and av' you, Mrs. Kelly, wor thinking
it right, we'd get her out of the house before the
masther's stirring.'

The widow was a prudent woman, and she stood,
for some time, considering; for she felt that, if she
held out her hand to Anty now, she must stick to her
through and through in the battle which there would
be between her and her brother; and there might be
more plague than profit in that. But then, again, she
was not at all so indifferent as she had appeared to be,
to her favourite son's marrying four hundred a-year.
She was angry at his thinking of such a thing without

consulting her; she feared the legal difficulties he
must encounter; and she didn't like the thoughts of
its being said that her son had married an old fool,
and cozened her out of her money. But still, four
hundred a-year was a great thing; and Anty was a
good-tempered tractable young woman, of the right
religion, and would not make a bad wife; and, on
reconsideration, Mrs. Kelly thought the thing wasn't
to be sneezed at. Then, again, she hated Barry, and,
having a high spirit, felt indignant that he should
think of preventing her son from marrying his sister,
if the two of them chose to do it; and she knew she'd
be able, and willing enough, too, to tell him a bit of
her mind, if there should be occasion. And lastly,
and most powerfully of all, the woman's feeling came
in to overcome her prudential scruples, and to open
her heart and her house to a poor, kindly, innocent
creature, ill-treated as Anty Lynch had been. She
was making up her mind what to do, and determining
to give battle royal to Barry and all his satellites, on
behalf of Anty, when Biddy interrupted her by
saying—

'I hope I warn't wrong, ma'am, in coming down
and throubling you so arly? I thought maybe you'd
be glad to befrind Miss Anty—seeing she and Miss
Meg, and Miss Jane, is so frindly.'

'No, Biddy—for a wondher, you're right, this morning. Mr. Barry won't be stirring yet?'

'Divil a stir, ma'am! The dhrunkenness won't be
off him yet this long while. And will I go up, and be
bringing Miss Anty down, ma'am?'

'Wait a while. Sit to the fire there, and warm your
shins. You're a good girl. I'll go and get on my shoes
and stockings, and my cloak, and bonnet. I must go
up wid you myself, and ask yer misthress down, as
she should be asked. They'll be telling lies on her 'av
she don't lave the house dacently, as she ought.'

'More power to you thin, Mrs. Kelly, this blessed
morning, for a kind good woman as you are, God
bless you!' whimpered forth Biddy, who, now that

she had obtained her request, began to cry, and to stuff the corner of her petticoat into her eyes.

'Whist, you fool—whist,' said the widow. 'Go and get up Sally—you know where she sleeps—and tell her to put down a fire in the little parlour upstairs, and to get a cup of tay ready, and to have Miss Meg up. Your misthress'll be the better of a quiet sleep afther the night she's had, and it'll be betther for her jist popping into Miss Meg's bed than getting between a pair of cowld sheets.'

These preparations met with Biddy's entire approval, for she reiterated her blessings on the widow, as she went to announce all the news to Sally and Kate, while Mrs. Kelly made such preparations as were fitting for a walk, at that early hour, up to Dunmore House.

They were not long before they were under weigh, but they did not reach the house quite so quickly as Biddy had left it. Mrs. Kelly had to pick her way in the half light, and observed that 'she'd never been up to the house since old Simeon Lynch built it, and when the stones were laying for it, she didn't think she ever would; but one never knowed what changes might happen in this world.'

They were soon in the house, for Judy was up to let them in; and though she stared when she saw Mrs. Kelly, she merely curtsied, and said nothing.

The girl went upstairs first, with the candle, and Mrs. Kelly followed, very gently, on tiptoe. She need not have been so careful to avoid waking Barry, for, had a drove of oxen been driven upstairs, it would not have roused him. However, up she crept—her thick shoes creaking on every stair—and stood outside the door, while Biddy went in to break the news of her arrival.

Anty was still asleep, but it did not take much to rouse her; and she trembled in her bed, when, on her asking what was the matter, Mrs. Kelly popped her bonnet inside the door, and said,

'It's only me, my dear. Mrs. Kelly, you know, from the inn,' and then she very cautiously insinuated the rest of her body into the room, as though she thought that Barry was asleep under the bed, and she was afraid of treading on one of his stray fingers. ' It's only me, my dear. Biddy's been down to me, like a good girl; and I tell you what—this is no place for you, just at present, Miss Anty; not till such time as things is settled a little. So I'm thinking you'd betther be slipping down wid me to the inn there, before your brother's up. There's nobody in it, not a sowl, only Meg, and Jane, and me, and we'll make you snug enough between us, never fear.'

' Do, Miss Anty, dear—do, darling,' added Biddy. ' It'll be a dale betther for you than waiting here to be batthered and bruised, and, perhaps, murthered out and out.'

' Hush, Biddy—don't be saying such things,' said the widow, who had a great idea of carrying on the war on her own premises, but who felt seriously afraid of Barry now that she was in his house, 'don't be saying such things, to frighthen her. But you'll be asier there than here,' she continued, to Anty; 'and there's nothin like having things asy. So, get up alanna, and we'll have you warm and snug down there in no time.'

Anty did not want much persuading. She was soon induced to get up and dress herself, to put on her cloak and bonnet, and hurry off with the widow, before the people of Dunmore should be up to look at her going through the town to the inn; while Biddy was left to pack up such things as were necessary for her mistress' use, and enjoined to hurry down with them to the inn as quick as she could; for, as the widow said, 'there war no use in letting every idle bosthoon in the place see her crossing with a lot of baggage, and set them all asking the where and the why and the wherefore; though, for the matther of that, they'd all hear it soon enough.'

To tell the truth, Mrs. Kelly's courage waned from the moment of her leaving her own door, and it did not return till she felt herself within it again. Indeed, as she was leaving the gate of Dunmore House, with Anty on her arm, she was already beginning to repent what she was doing; for there were idlers about, and she felt ashamed of carrying off the young heiress. But these feelings vanished the moment she had crossed her own sill. When she had once got Anty home, it was all right. The widow Kelly seldom went out into the world; she seldom went anywhere except to mass; and, when out, she was a very modest and retiring old lady; but she could face the devil, if necessary, across her own counter.

And so Anty was rescued, for a while, from her brother's persecution. This happened on the morning on which Martin and Lord Ballindine met together at the lawyer's, when the deeds were prepared which young Kelly's genuine honesty made him think necessary before he eloped with old Sim Lynch's heiress. He would have been rather surprised to hear, at that moment, that his mother had been before him, and carried off his bride elect to the inn!

Anty was soon domesticated. The widow, very properly, wouldn't let her friends, Meg and Jane, ask her any questions at present. Sally had made, on the occasion, a pot of tea sufficient to supply the morning wants of half a regiment, and had fully determined that it should not be wasted. The Kelly girls were both up, and ready to do anything for their friend; so they got her to take a little of Sally's specific, and put her into a warm bed to sleep, quiet and secure from any interruption.

While her guest was sleeping, the widow made up her mind that her best and safest course, for the present, would be, as she expressed it to her daughter, Meg, 'to keep her toe in her pump, and say nothing to nobody.'

'Anty can just stay quiet and asy,' she continued, 'till we see what Master Barry manes to be afther; he'll find it difficult enough to move her out of this, I'm thinking, and I doubt his trying. As to money matthers, I'll neither meddle nor make, nor will you,

mind; so listen to that, girls; and as to Moylan, he's
a dacent quiet poor man—but it's bad thrusting any
one. Av' he's her agent, however, I s'pose he'll look
afther the estate; only, Barry'll be smashing the
things up there at the house yonder in his anger and
dhrunken fits, and it's a pity the poor girl's property
should go to rack. But he's such a born divil, she's
lucky to be out of his clutches alive; though, thank
the Almighty, that put a good roof over the lone
widow this day, he can't clutch her here. Wouldn't
I like to see him come to the door and ax for her!
And he can't smash the acres, nor the money they
say Mulholland has, at Tuam; and faix, av' he does
any harm up there at the house, shure enough Anty
can make him pay for it—every pot and pan of it—
out of his share, and she'll do it, too—av' she's said
by me. But mind, I'll neither meddle nor make;
neither do you, and then we're safe, and Anty too.
And Martin'll be here soon—I wondher what good
Dublin'll do him?—They might have the Repale
without him, I suppose?—And when he's here, why,
av' he's minded to marry her, and she's plased, why,
Father Geoghegan may come down, and do it before
the whole counthry, and who's ashamed? But
there'll be no huggery-muggery, and schaming; that
is, av' they're said by me. Faix, I'd like to know
who she's to be afeared of, and she undher this roof!
I s'pose Martin ain't fool enough to care for what such
a fellow as Barry Lynch can do or say—and he with
all the Kellys to back him; as shure they would, and
why not, from the lord down? Not that I recommend the match; I think Martin a dale betther off as
he is, for he's wanting nothing, and he's his own
industhry—and, maybe, a handful of money besides.
But, as for being afeard—I niver heard yet that
a Kelly need be afeard of a Lynch in Dunmore.'

   In this manner did Mrs. Kelly express the various
thoughts that ran through her head, as she considered Anty's affairs; and if we could analyse the
good lady's mind, we should probably find that the

result of her reflections was a pleasing assurance that
she could exercise the Christian virtues of charity
and hospitality towards Anty, and, at the same time,
secure her son's wishes and welfare, without subjecting her own name to any obloquy, or putting
herself to any loss or inconvenience. She determined
to put no questions to Anty, nor even to allude to
her brother, unless spoken to on the subject; but, at
the same time, she stoutly resolved to come to no
terms with Barry, and to defy him to the utmost,
should he attempt to invade her in her own territories.

After a sound sleep Anty got up, much strengthened and refreshed, and found the two Kelly girls
ready to condole with, or congratulate her, according
to her mood and spirits. In spite of their mother's
caution, they were quite prepared for gossiping, as
soon as Anty showed the slightest inclination that
way; and, though she at first was afraid to talk about
her brother, and was even, from kindly feeling, unwilling to do so, the luxury of such an opportunity
of unrestrained confidence overcame her; and, before
the three had been sitting together for a couple of
hours, she had described the whole interview, as well
as the last drunken midnight visit of Barry's to her
own bed-room, which, to her imagination, was the
most horrible of all the horrors of the night.

Poor Anty. She cried vehemently that morning—
more in sorrow for her brother, than in remembrance
of her own fears, as she told her friends how he had
threatened to shut her up in a mad-house, and then
to murder her, unless she promised him not to marry;
and when she described how brutally he had struck
her, and how, afterwards, he had crept to her room,
with his red eyes and swollen face, in the dead of the
night, and, placing his hot mouth close to her ears,
had dreadfully sworn that she should die, if she
thought of Martin Kelly as her husband, she trembled
as though she was in an ague fit.

The girls said all they could to comfort her, and
they succeeded in a great degree; but they could not

bring her to talk of Martin. She shuddered whenever his name was mentioned, and they began to fear that Barry's threat would have the intended effect, and frighten her from the match. However, they kindly talked of other things—of how impossible it was that she should go back to Dunmore House, and how comfortable and snug they would make her at the inn, till she got a home for herself; of what she should do, and of all their little household plans together; till Anty, when she could forget her brother's threats for a time, seemed to be more comfortable and happy than she had been for years.

In vain did the widow that morning repeatedly invoke Meg and Jane, first one and then the other, to assist in her commercial labours. In vain were Sally and Kate commissioned to bring them down. If, on some urgent behest, one of them darted down to mix a dandy of punch, or weigh a pound of sugar, when the widow was imperatively employed elsewhere, she was upstairs again, before her mother could look about her; and, at last, Mrs. Kelly was obliged to content herself with the reflection that girls would be girls, and that it was 'nathural and right they shouldn't wish to lave Anty alone the first morning, and she sthrange to the place.'

At five o'clock, the widow, as was her custom, went up to her dinner; and Meg was then obliged to come down and mind the shop, till her sister, having dined, should come down and relieve guard. She had only just ensconced herself behind the counter, when who should walk into the shop but Barry Lynch.

Had Meg seen an ogre, or the enemy of all mankind himself, she could not, at the moment, have been more frightened; and she stood staring at him, as if the sudden loss of the power of motion alone prevented her from running away.

'I want to see Mrs. Kelly,' said Barry; 'd'ye hear? I want to see your mother; go and tell her.'

But we must go back, and see how Mr. Lynch had managed to get up, and pass his morning.

VII

MR. DARRY LYNCH MAKES A MORNING CALL

IT was noon before Barry first opened his eyes, and discovered the reality of the headache which the night's miserable and solitary debauch had entailed on him. For, in spite of the oft-repeated assurance that there is not a headache in a hogshead of it, whiskey punch will sicken one, as well as more expensive and more fashionable potent drinks. Barry was very sick when he first awoke; and very miserable, too; for vague recollections of what he had done, and doubtful fears of what he might have done, crowded on him. A drunken man always feels more anxiety about what he has not done in his drunkenness, than about what he has; and so it was with Barry. He remembered having used rough language with his sister, but he could not remember how far he had gone. He remembered striking her, and he knew that the servant had come in; but he could not remember how, or with what he had struck her, or whether he had done so more than once, or whether she had been much hurt. He could not even think whether he had seen her since or not; he remembered being in the garden after she had fallen, and drinking again after that, but nothing further. Surely, he could not have killed her? he could not even have hurt her very much, or he would have heard of it before this. If anything serious had happened, the servants would have taken care that he should have heard enough about it ere now. Then he began to think what o'clock it could be, and that it must be late, for his watch was run down; the general fate of drunkards, who are doomed to utter ignorance of the hour at which they wake to the consciousness of their miserable disgrace. He feared to ring the bell for the servant; he was afraid to ask the particulars of last night's work; so he turned on his pillow, and tried to sleep again. But in vain. If he closed his eyes, Anty was before them, and he was dreaming, half awake, that he was trying to stifle her, and that she was escaping, to tell all the world of his brutality and cruelty. This happened over and over again; for when he dozed but for a minute, the same thing re-occurred, as vividly as before, and made even his waking consciousness preferable to the visions of his disturbed slumbers. So, at last, he roused himself, and endeavoured to think what he should do.

Whilst he was sitting up in his bed, and reflecting that he must undress himself before he could dress himself—for he had tumbled into bed with most of his clothes on—Terry's red head appeared at the door, showing an anxiety, on the part of its owner, to see if 'the masther' was awake, but to take no step to bring about such a state, if, luckily, he still slept.

'What's the time, Terry?' said Lynch, frightened, by his own state, into rather more courtesy than he usually displayed to those dependent on him.

'Well then, I b'lieve it's past one, yer honer.'

'The d—l it is! I've such a headache. I was screwed last night; eh, Terry?'

'I b'lieve yer war, yer honer.'

'What o'clock was it when I went to bed?'

'Well then, I don't rightly know, Mr. Barry; it wasn't only about ten when I tuk in the last hot wather, and I didn't see yer honer afther that.'

'Well; tell Miss Anty to make me a cup of tea, and do you bring it up here.' This was a feeler. If anything was the matter with Anty, Terry would be sure to tell him now; but he only said, 'Yis, yer honer,' and retreated.

Barry now comforted himself with the reflection that there was no great harm done, and that though, certainly, there had been some row between him and Anty, it would probably blow over; and then, also, he began to reflect that, perhaps, what he had said and done, would frighten her out of her match with Kelly.

In the meantime, Terry went into the kitchen, with the news that 'masther was awake, and axing for tay.' Biddy had considered herself entitled to remain all the morning at the inn, having, in a manner, earned a right to be idle for that day, by her activity during the night; and the other girl had endeavoured to enjoy the same luxury, for she had been found once or twice during the morning, en-sconced in the kitchen, under Sally's wing; but Mrs. Kelly had hunted her back, to go and wait on her master, giving her to understand that she would not receive the whole household.

'And ye're afther telling him where Miss Anty's gone, Terry?' inquired the injured fair one.

'Divil a tell for me thin,—shure, he may find it out hisself, widout my telling him '

'Faix, it's he'll be mad thin, when he finds she's taken up with the likes of the widdy Kelly!'

'And ain't she betther there, nor being mur-thered up here? He'd be killing her out and out some night.'

'Well, but Terry, he's not so bad as all that; there's worse than him, and ain't it rasonable he shouldn't be quiet and asy, and she taking up with the likes of Martin Kelly?'

'May be so; but wouldn't she be a dale happier with Martin than up here wid him? Any ways it don't do angering him, so, get him the tay, Judy.'

It was soon found that this was easier said than done, for Anty, in her confusion, had taken away the keys in her pocket, and there was no tea to be had.

The bell was now rung, and, as Barry had gradually re-assured himself, rung violently; and Terry, when he arrived distracted at the bed-room door, was angrily asked by his thirsty master why the tea didn't appear? The truth was now obliged to come out, or at any rate, part of it: so Terry answered, that Miss Anty was out, and had the keys with her.

Miss Anty was so rarely out, that Barry instantly trembled again. Had she gone to a magistrate, to

swear against him? Had she run away from him?
Had she gone off with Martin?

'Where the d—l's she gone, Terry?' said he, in
his extremity.

'Faix, yer honer, thin, I'm not rightly knowing;
but I hear tell she's down at the widow Kelly's.'

'Who told you, you fool?'

'Well thin, yer honer, it war Judy.'

'And where's Judy?'

And it ended in Judy's being produced, and the
two of them, at length, explained to their master,
that the widow had come up early in the morning
and fetched her away; and Judy swore 'that not a
know she knowed how it had come about, or what
had induced the widow to come, or Miss Anty to go,
or anything about it; only, for shure, Miss Anty was
down there, snug enough, with Miss Jane and Miss
Meg; and the widdy war in her tantrums, and
wouldn't let ony dacent person inside the house-
door—barring Biddy. And that wor all she knowed
av' she wor on the book.'

The secret was now out. Anty had left him, and
put herself under the protection of Martin Kelly's
mother; had absolutely defied him, after all his
threats of the preceding night. What should he do
now! All his hatred for her returned again, all his
anxious wishes that she might be somehow removed
from his path, as an obnoxious stumbling-block. A
few minutes ago, he was afraid he had murdered her,
and he now almost wished that he had done so. He
finished dressing himself, and then sat down in the
parlour, which had been the scene of his last night's
brutality, to concoct fresh schemes for the persecution of his sister.

In the meantime, Terry rushed down to the inn,
demanding the keys, and giving Mrs. Kelly a fearful
history of his master's anger. This she very wisely
refrained from retailing, but, having procured the
keys, gave them to the messenger, merely informing
him, that 'thanks to God's kind protection, Miss

Anty was tolerably well over the last night's work, and he might tell his master so.'

This message Terry thought it wisest to suppress, so he took the breakfast up in silence, and his master asked no more questions. He was very sick and pale, and could eat nothing; but he drank a quantity of tea, and a couple of glasses of brandy-and-water, and then he felt better, and again began to think what measures he should take, what scheme he could concoct, for stopping this horrid marriage, and making his sister obedient to his wishes. 'Confound her,' he said, almost aloud, as he thought, with bitter vexation of spirit, of her unincumbered moiety of the property, 'confound them all!' grinding his teeth, and meaning by the 'all' to include with Anty his father, and every one who might have assisted his father in making the odious will, as well as his own attorney in Tuam, who wouldn't find out some legal expedient by which he could set it aside. And then, as he thought of the shameful persecution of which he was the victim, he kicked the fender with impotent violence, and, as the noise of the falling fire irons added to his passion, he reiterated his kicks till the unoffending piece of furniture was smashed; and then with manly indignation he turned away to the window.

But breaking the furniture, though it was what the widow predicted of him, wouldn't in any way mend matters, or assist him in getting out of his difficulties. What was he to do? He couldn't live on £200 a-year; he couldn't remain in Dunmore, to be known by every one as Martin Kelly's brother-in-law; he couldn't endure the thoughts of dividing the property with such 'a low-born huxtering blackguard', as he called him over and over again. He couldn't stay there, to be beaten by him in the course of legal proceedings, or to give him up amicable possession of what ought to have been—what should have been his—what he looked upon as his own. He came back, and sat down again over the fire, contemplating the débris of the fender, and turning all these miserable circumstances over in his mind. After remaining there till five o'clock, and having fortified himself with sundry glasses of wine, he formed his resolution. He would make one struggle more; he would first go down to the widow, and claim his sister, as a poor simple young woman, inveigled away from her natural guardian; and, if this were unsuccessful, as he felt pretty sure it would be, he would take proceedings to prove her a lunatic. If he failed, he might still delay, and finally put off the marriage; and he was sure he could get some attorney to put him in the way of doing it, and to undertake the work for him. His late father's attorney had been a fool, in not breaking the will, or at any rate trying it, and he would go to Daly. Young Daly, he knew, was a sharp fellow, and wanted practice, and this would just suit him. And then, if at last he found that nothing could be done by this means, if his sister and the property *must* go from him, he would compromise the matter with the bridegroom, he would meet him half way, and, raising what money he could on his share of the estate, give leg bail to his creditors, and go to some place abroad, where tidings of Dunmore would never reach him. What did it matter what people said? he should never hear it. He would make over the whole property to Kelly, on getting a good life income out of it. Martin was a prudent fellow, and would jump at such a plan. As he thought of this, he even began to wish that it was done; he pictured to himself the easy pleasures, the card-tables, the billiard-rooms, and cafés of some Calais or Boulogne; pleasures which he had never known, but which had been so glowingly described to him; and he got almost cheerful again as he felt that, in any way, there might be bright days yet in store for him.

He would, however, still make the last effort for the whole stake. It would be time enough to give in, and make the best of a *pis aller*, when he was forced to do so. If beaten, he would make use of Martin

Kelly; but he would first try if he couldn't prove him to be a swindling adventurer, and his sister to be an idiot.

Much satisfied at having come to this salutary resolution, he took up his hat, and set out for the widow's, in order to put into operation the first part of the scheme. He rather wished it over, as he knew that Mrs. Kelly was no coward, and had a strong tongue in her head. However, it must be done, and the sooner the better. He first of all looked at himself in his glass, to see that his appearance was sufficiently haughty and indignant, and, as he flattered himself, like that of a gentleman singularly out of his element in such a village as Dunmore; and then, having ordered his dinner to be ready on his return, he proceeded on his voyage for the recovery of his dear sister.

Entering the shop, he communicated his wishes to Meg, in the manner before described; and, while she was gone on her errand, he remained alone there, lashing his boot, in the most approved, but still, in a very common-place manner.

'Oh, mother!' said Meg, rushing into the room where her mother, and Jane, and Anty, were at dinner, 'there's Barry Lynch down in the shop, wanting you.'

'Oh my!' said Jane. 'Now sit still, Anty dear, and he can't come near you. Shure, he'll niver be afther coming upstairs, will he, Meg?'

Anty, who had begun to feel quite happy in her new quarters, and among her kind friends, turned pale, and dropped her knife and fork. 'What'll I do, Mrs. Kelly?' she said, as she saw the old lady complacently get up. 'You're not going to give me up? You'll not go to him?'

'Faith I will thin, my dear,' replied the widow; 'never fear else—I'll go to him, or any one else that sends to me in a dacent manner. May-be it's wanting tay in the shop he is. I'll go to him immediately. But, as for giving you up, I mane you to stay here,

till you've a proper home of your own; and Barry
Lynch has more in him than I think, av' he makes me
alter my mind. Set down quiet, Meg, and get your
dinner.' And the widow got up, and proceeded to the
shop.

The girls were all in commotion. One went to the
door at the top of the stairs, to overhear as much as
possible of what was to take place; and the other
clasped Anty's hand, to re-assure her, having first
thrown open the door of one of the bed-rooms, that
she might have a place of retreat in the event of the
enemy succeeding in pushing his way upstairs.

'Your humble sarvant, Mr. Lynch,' said the widow,
entering the shop and immediately taking up a position of strength in her accustomed place behind the
counter. 'Were you wanting me, this evening?' and
she took up the knife with which she cut penn'orths
of tobacco for her customers, and hitting the counter
with its wooden handle looked as hard as copper, and
as bold as brass.

'Yes, Mrs. Kelly,' said Barry, with as much dignity
as he could muster, 'I do want to speak to you. My
sister has foolishly left her home this morning, and my
servants tell me she is under your roof. Is this true?'

'Is it Anty? Indeed she is thin: ating her dinner,
upstairs, this very moment;' and she rapped the
counter again, and looked her foe in the face.

'Then, with your leave, Mrs. Kelly, I'll step up,
and speak to her. I suppose she's alone?'

'Indeed she ain't thin, for she's the two girls ating
wid her, and myself too, barring that I'm just come
down at your bidding. No; we're not so bad as that,
to lave her all alone; and as for your seeing her, Mr.
Lynch, I don't think she's exactly wishing it at
present; so, av' you've a message, I'll take it.'

'You don't mean to say that Miss Lynch—my
sister—is in this inn, and that you intend to prevent
my seeing her? You'd better take care what you're
doing, Mrs. Kelly. I don't want to say anything
harsh at present, but you'd better take care what

you're about with me and my family, or you'll find
yourself in a scrape that you little bargain for.'

'I'll take care of myself, Mr. Barry; never fear for
me, darling; and, what's more, I'll take care of your
sister, too. And, to give you a bit of my mind—
she'll want my care, I'm thinking, while you're in
the counthry.'

'I've not come here to listen to impertinence, Mrs.
Kelly, and I will not do so. In fact, it is very unwillingly that I came into this house at all.'

'Oh, pray lave it thin, pray lave it! We can do
without you.'

'Perhaps you will have the civility to listen to me.
It is very unwillingly, I say, that I have come here
at all; but my sister, who is, unfortunately, not able
to judge for herself, is here. How she came here I
don't pretend to say—'

'Oh, she walked,' said the widow, interrupting
him; 'she walked, quiet and asy, out of your door,
and into mine. But that's a lie, for it was out of her
own. She didn't come through the kay-hole, nor
yet out of the window.'

'I'm saying nothing about how she came here, but
here she is, poor creature!'

'Poor crature, indeed! She was like to be a poor
crature, av' she stayed up there much longer.'

'Here she is, I say, and I consider it my duty to
look after her. You cannot but be aware, Mrs. Kelly,
that this is not a fit place for Miss Lynch. You must
be aware that a road-side public-house, however
decent, or a village shop, however respectable, is not
the proper place for my sister; and, though I may
not yet be legally her guardian, I am her brother, and
am in charge of her property, and I insist on seeing
her. It will be at your peril if you prevent me.'

'Have you done, now, Misther Barry?'

'That's what I've got to say; and I think you've
sense enough to see the folly—not to speak of the
danger, of preventing me from seeing my sister.'

'That's your say, Misther Lynch; and now, listen

to mine. Av' Miss Anty was wishing to see you, you'd be welcome upstairs, for her sake; but she ain't, so there's an end of that; for not a foot will you put inside this, unless you're intending to force your way, and I don't think you'll be for trying that. And as to bearing the danger, why, I'll do my best; and, for all the harm you're likely to do me—that's by fair manes,—I don't think I'll be axing any one to help me out of it. So, good bye t' ye, av' you've no further commands, for I didn't yet well finish the bit I was ating.'

'And you mean to say, Mrs. Kelly, you'll take upon yourself to prevent my seeing my sister?'

'Indeed I do; unless she was wishing it, as well as yourself; and no mistake.'

'And you'll do that, knowing, as you do, that the unfortunate young woman is of weak mind, and unable to judge for herself, and that I'm her brother, and her only living relative and guardian?'

'All blathershin, Masther Barry,' said the uncourteous widow, dropping the knife from her hand, and smacking her fingers: 'as for wake mind, it's sthrong enough to take good care of herself and her money too, now she's once out of Dunmore House. There's many waker than Anty Lynch, though few have had worse tratement to make them so. As for guardian, I'm thinking it's long since she was of age, and, av' her father didn't think she wanted one, when he made his will, you needn't bother yourself about it, now she's no one to plaze only herself. And as for brother, Masther Barry, why didn't you think of that before you struck her, like a brute, as you are —before you got dhrunk, like a baste, and then threatened to murdher her? Why didn't you think about brother and sisther before you thried to rob the poor *wake* crature, as you call her; and when you found she wasn't quite wake enough, as you call it, swore to have her life, av' she wouldn't act at your bidding? That's being a brother and a guardian, is it, Masther Barry? Talk to me of danger, you ruffian,' continued the widow, with her back now thoroughly up; 'you'd betther look to yourself, or I know who'll be in most danger. Av' it wasn't the throuble it'd be to Anty,—and, God knows, she's had throubles enough, I'd have had her before the magisthrates before this, to tell of what was done last night up at the house, yonder. But mind, she can do it yet, and, av' you don't take yourself very asy, she shall. Danger, indeed! a robber and ruffian like you, to talk of danger to me—and his *dear* sisther, too, and afther trying his best, last night, to murdher her!'

These last words, with a long drawl on the word *dear*, were addressed rather to the crowd, whom the widow's loud voice had attracted into the open shop, than to Barry, who stood, during this tirade, half stupefied with rage, and half frightened, at the open attack made on him with reference to his ill-treatment of Anty. However, he couldn't pull in his horns now, and he was obliged, in self-defence, to brazen it out.

'Very well, Mrs. Kelly—you shall pay for this impudence, and that dearly. You've invented these lies, as a pretext for getting my sister and her property into your hands!'

'Lies!' screamed the widow; 'av' you say lies to me agin, in this house, I'll smash the bones of ye myself, with the broom-handle. Lies, indeed! and from you, Barry Lynch, the biggest liar in all Connaught—not to talk of robber and ruffian! You'd betther take yourself out of that, fair and asy, while you're let. You'll find you'll have the worst of it, av' you come rampaging here wid me, my man;' and she turned round to the listening crowd for sympathy, which those who dared were not slow in giving her.

'And that's thrue for you, Mrs. Kelly, Ma'am,' exclaimed one.

'It's a shame for him to come storming here, agin a lone widdy, so it is,' said a virago, who seemed well able, like the widow herself, to take her own part.

'Who iver knew any good of a Lynch—barring Miss Anty herself?' argued a third.

'The Kellys is always too good for the likes of them,' put in a fourth, presuming that the intended marriage was the subject immediately in discourse.

'Faix, Mr. Martin's too good for the best of 'em,' declared another.

'Niver mind Mr. Martin, boys,' said the widow, who wasn't well pleased to have her son's name mentioned in the affair—'it's no business of his, one way or another; he ain't in Dunmore, nor yet nigh it. Miss Anty Lynch has come to me for protection; and, by the Blessed Virgin, she shall have it, as long as my name's Mary Kelly, and I ain't like to change it; so that's the long and short of it, Barry Lynch. So you may go and get dhrunk agin as soon as you plaze, and bate and bang Terry Rooney, or Judy Smith; only I think either on 'em's more than a match for you.'

'Then I tell you, Mrs. Kelly,' replied Barry, who was hardly able to get in a word, 'that you'll hear more about it. Steps are now being taken to prove Miss Lynch a lunatic, as every one here knows she unfortunately is; and, as sure as you stand there, you'll have to answer for detaining her; and you're much mistaken if you think you'll get hold of her property, even though she were to marry your son, for, I warn you, she's not her own mistress, or able to be so.'

'Drat your impudence, you low-born ruffian,' answered his opponent; 'who cares for her money? It's not come to that yet, that a Kelly is wanting to schame money out of a Lynch.'

'I've nothing more to say, since you insist on keeping possession of my sister,' and Barry turned to the door. 'But you'll be indicted for conspiracy, so you'd better be prepared.'

'Conspiracy, is it?' said one of Mrs. Kelly's admirers; 'maybe, Ma'am, he'll get you put in along with Dan and Father Tierney, God bless them! It's conspiracy they're afore the judges for.'

Barry now took himself off, before hearing the last of the widow's final peal of thunder.

'Get out wid you! You're no good, and never will bo. An' it waɛn't for the young woman upstairs, I'd have the coat off your back, and your face well mauled, before I let you out of the shop!' And so ended the interview, in which the anxious brother can hardly be said to have been triumphant, or successful.

The widow, on the other hand, seemed to feel that she had acquitted herself well, and that she had taken the orphan's part, like a woman, a Christian, and a mother; and merely saying, with a kind of inward chuckle, 'Come to me, indeed, with his roguery! he's got the wrong pig by the ear!' she walked off, to join the more timid trio upstairs, one of whom was speedily sent down, to see that business did not go astray.

And then she gave a long account of the interview to Anty and Meg, which was hardly necessary, as they had heard most of what had passed. The widow however was not to know that, and she was very voluble in her description of Barry's insolence, and of the dreadfully abusive things he had said to her— how he had given her the lie, and called her out of her name. She did not, however, seem to be aware that she had, herself, said a word which was more than necessarily violent; and assured Anty over and over again, that, out of respect to her feelings, and because the man was, after all, her brother, she had refrained from doing and saying what she would have done and said, had she been treated in such a manner by anybody else. She seemed, however, in spite of the ill-treatment which she had undergone, to be in a serene and happy state of mind. She shook Anty's two hands in hers, and told her to make herself 'snug and asy where she was, like a dear girl, and to fret for nothing, for no one could hurt or harum her, and she undher Mary Kelly's roof.' Then she wiped her face in her apron, set to at her dinner; and even went

so far as to drink a glass of porter, a thing she hadn't
done, except on a Sunday, since her eldest daughter's
marriage.

Barry Lynch sneaked up the town, like a beaten
dog. He felt that the widow had had the best of it,
and he also felt that every one in Dunmore was
against him. It was however only what he had
expected, and calculated upon; and what should he
care for the Dunmore people? They wouldn't rise
up and kill him, nor would they be likely even to
injure him. Let them hate on, he would follow his
own plan. As he came near the house gate, there was
sitting, as usual, Jacky, the fool.

'Well, yer honer, Masther Barry,' said Jacky,
'don't forget your poor fool this blessed morning!'

'Away with you! If I see you there again, I'll
have you in Bridewell, you blackguard.'

'Ah, you're joking, Masther Barry. You wouldn't
like to be afther doing that. So yer honer's been
down to the widdy's? That's well; it's a fine thing
to see you on good terms, since you're soon like to be
so sib. Well, there an't no betther fellow, from this
to Galway, than Martin Kelly, that's one comfort,
Masther Barry.'

Barry looked round for something wherewith to
avenge himself for this, but Jacky was out of his
reach; so he merely muttered some customary but
inaudible curses, and turned into the house.

He immediately took pen, ink, and paper, and,
writing the following note dispatched it to Tuam, by
Terry, mounted for the occasion, and directed on no
account to return without an answer. If Mr. Daly
wasn't at home, he was to wait for his return; that is,
if he was expected home that night.

Dunmore House, Feb. 1844.

My dear Sir,

I wish to consult you on legal business, which will
bear no delay. The subject is of considerable importance, and I am induced to think it will be more ably

handled by you than by Mr. Blake, my father's man of business. There is a bed at your service at Dunmore House, and I shall be glad to see you to dinner to-morrow.

> I am, dear Sir, Your faithful servant,
>   BARRY LYNCH.

P.S.—You had better not mention in Tuam that you are coming to me,—not that my business is one that I intend to keep secret.

J. Daly, Esq., Solicitor, Tuam.

In about two hours' time, Terry had put the above into the hands of the person for whom it was intended, and in two more he had brought back an answer, saying that Mr. Daly would be at Dunmore House to dinner on the following day. And Terry, on his journey there and back, did not forget to tell everyone he saw, from whom he came, and to whom he was going.

VIII

MR. MARTIN KELLY RETURNS TO DUNMORE

WE will now return to Martin Kelly. I have before said that as soon as he had completed his legal business,—namely, his instructions for the settlement of Anty Lynch's property, respecting which he and Lord Ballindine had been together to the lawyer's in Clare Street,—he started for home, by the Ballinasloe canal-boat, and reached that famous depôt of the fleecy tribe without adventure. I will not attempt to describe the tedium of that horrid voyage, for it has been often described before; and to Martin, who was in no ways fastidious, it was not so unendurable as it must always be to those who have been accustomed to more rapid movement. Nor yet will I attempt to put on record the miserable resources of those, who, doomed to a twenty hours' sojourn in one of these floating prisons, vainly endeavour to occupy or amuse their minds. But I will advise any, who from ill-contrived arrangements, or unforeseen misfortune,[1] may find themselves on board the Ballinasloe canal-boat, to entertain no such vain dream. The *vis inertiæ* of patient endurance, is the only weapon of any use in attempting to overcome the lengthened ennui of this most tedious transit. Reading is out of the question. I have tried it myself, and seen others try it, but in vain. The sense of the motion, almost imperceptible, but still perceptible; the noises above you; the smells around you; the diversified crowd, of which you are a part; at one moment the heat this crowd creates; at the next, the draught which a window just opened behind your ears lets in on you; the fumes of punch; the snores of the man under the table; the noisy anger of his neighbour, who reviles the attendant sylph; the would-be witticisms of a third, who makes continual amorous overtures to the same overtasked damsel, notwithstanding the publicity of his situation; the loud complaints of the old lady near the door, who cannot obtain the gratuitous kindness of a glass of water; and the baby-soothing lullabies of the young one, who is suckling her infant under your elbow. These things alike prevent one from reading, sleeping, or thinking. All one can do is to wait till the long night gradually wears itself away, and reflect that,

Time and the hour run through the longest day.

I hardly know why a journey in one of these boats should be much more intolerable than travelling either outside or inside a coach; for, either in or on the coach, one has less room for motion, and less opportunity of employment. I believe the misery of the canal-boat chiefly consists in a pre-conceived and erroneous idea of its capabilities. One prepares oneself for occupation—an attempt is made to achieve actual comfort—and both end in disappointment;

[1] Of course it will be remembered that this was written before railways in Ireland had been constructed.

the limbs become weary with endeavouring to fix themselves in a position of repose, and the mind is fatigued more by the search after, than the want of, occupation.

Martin, however, made no complaints, and felt no misery. He made great play at the eternal half-boiled leg of mutton, floating in a bloody sea of grease and gravy, which always comes on the table three hours after the departure from Porto Bello. He, and others equally gifted with the *dura ilia messorum*, swallowed huge collops of the raw animal, and vast heaps of yellow turnips, till the pity with which a stranger would at first be inclined to contemplate the consumer of such unsavoury food, is transferred to the victim who has to provide the meal at two shillings a head. Neither love nor drink—and Martin had, on the previous day, been much troubled with both —had affected his appetite; and he ate out his money with the true persevering prudence of a Connaught man, who firmly determines not to be done.

He was equally diligent at breakfast; and, at last, reached Ballinasloe, at ten o'clock the morning after he had left Dublin, in a flourishing condition. From thence he travelled, by Bianconi's car, as far as Tuam, and when there he went at once to the hotel, to get a hack car to take him home to Dunmore.

In the hotel yard he found a car already prepared for a journey; and, on giving his order for a similar vehicle for his own use, was informed, by the dis-interested ostler, that the horse then being harnessed, was to take Mr. Daly, the attorney, to Tuam, and that probably that gentleman would not object to join him, Martin, in the conveyance. Martin, think-ing it preferable to pay fourpence rather than six-pence a mile for his jaunt, acquiesced in this arrange-ment; and, as he had a sort of speaking acquaintance with Mr. Daly, whom he rightly imagined would not despise the economy which actuated himself, he had his carpet-bag put into the well of the car, and, plac-ing himself on it, he proceeded to the attorney's door.

He soon made the necessary explanation to Mr. Daly, who made no objection to the proposal; and he also throwing a somewhat diminutive carpet-bag into the same well, placed himself alongside of our friend, and they proceeded on their journey, with the most amicable feelings towards each other.

They little guessed, either the one or the other, as they commenced talking on the now all-absorbing subject of the great trial, that they were going to Dunmore for the express object—though not with the expressed purpose, of opposing each other—that Daly was to be employed to suggest any legal means for robbing Martin of a wife, and Anty of her property; and that Martin was going home with the fixed determination of effecting a wedding, to prevent which his companion was, in consideration of liberal payment, to use all his ingenuity and energy.

When they had discussed O'Connel and his companions, and their chances of liberation for four or five miles, and when Martin had warmly expressed his assurance that no jury could convict the saviours of their country, and Daly had given utterance to his legal opinion that saltpetre couldn't save them from two years in Newgate, Martin asked his companion whether he was going beyond Dunmore that night?

'No, indeed, then,' replied Daly; 'I have a client there now—a thing I never had in that part of the country before yesterday.'

'We'll have you at the inn, then, I suppose, Mr. Daly?'

'Faith, you won't, for I shall dine on velvet. My new client is one of the right sort, that can feed as well as fee a lawyer. I've got my dinner, and bed to-night, whatever else I may get.'

'There's not many of that sort in Dunmore thin; any way, there weren't when I left it, a week since. Whose house are you going to, Mr. Daly, av' it's not impertinent asking?'

'Barry Lynch's.'

'Barry Lynch's!' re-echoed Martin; 'the divil you are! I wonder what's in the wind with him now. I thought Blake always did his business?'

'The devil a know I know, so I can't tell you; and if I did, I shouldn't, you may be sure. But a man that's just come to his property always wants a lawyer; and many a one, besides Barry Lynch, ain't satisfied without two.'

'Well, any way, I wish you joy of your new client. I'm not over fond of him myself, I'll own; but then there were always rasons why he and I shouldn't pull well together. Barry's always been a dale too high for me, since he was at school with the young lord. Well, good evening, Mr. Daly. Never mind the car coming down the street, as you're at your friend's gate,' and Martin took his bag on his arm, and walked down to the inn.

Though Martin couldn't guess, as he walked quickly down the street, what Barry Lynch could want with young Daly, who was beginning to be known as a clever, though not over-scrupulous practitioner, he felt a presentiment that it must have some reference to Anty and himself, and this made him rather uncomfortable. Could Barry have heard of his engagement? Had Anty repented of her bargain, during his short absence? Had that old reptile Moylan, played him false, and spoilt his game? 'That must be it,' said Martin to himself, 'and it's odd but I'll be even with the schamer, yet; only she's so asy frightened!—Av' she'd the laist pluck in life, it's little I'd care for Moylan or Barry either.'

This little soliloquy brought him to the inn door. Some of the tribe of loungers who were always hanging about the door, and whom in her hatred of idleness the widow would one day rout from the place, and, in her charity, feed the next, had seen Martin coming down the street, and had given intelligence in the kitchen. As he walked in, therefore, at the open door, Meg and Jane were ready to receive him in the passage. Their looks were big with some important news. Martin soon saw that they had something to tell.

'Well, girls,' he said, as he chucked his bag and coat to Sally, 'for heaven's sake get me something to ate, for I'm starved. What's the news at Dunmore?'

'It's you should have the news thin,' said one, 'and you just from Dublin.'

'There's lots of news there, then; I'll tell you when I've got my dinner. How's the ould lady?' and he stepped on, as if to pass by them, upstairs.

'Stop a moment, Martin,' said Meg; 'don't be in a hurry; there's some one there.'

'Who's there? is it a stranger?'

'Why, then, it is, and it isn't,' said Jane.

'But you don't ask afther the young lady!' said her sister.

'May I be hanged thin, av' I know what the two of ye are afther! Is there people in both the rooms? Come, girls, av' ye've anything to tell, why don't you out wid it and have done? I suppose I can go into the bed-room, at any rate?'

'Aisy, Martin, and I'll tell you. Anty's in the parlour.'

'In the parlour upstairs?' said he; 'the deuce she is! And what brought her here? Did she quarrel with Barry, Meg?' added he, in a whisper.

'Indeed she did, out and out,' said Meg.

'Oh, he used her horrible!' said Jane.

'He'll hear all about that by and by,' said Meg. 'Come up and see her now, Martin.'

'But does mother know she's here?'

'Why, it was she brought her here! She fetched her down from the house, yesterday, before we was up.'

Thus assured that Anty had not been smuggled upstairs, her lover, or suitor as he might perhaps be more confidently called, proceeded to visit her. If he wished her to believe that his first impulse, on hearing of her being in the house, had been to throw himself at her feet, it would have been well that this conversation should have been carried on out of her hearing. But Anty was not an exigent mistress, and was perfectly contented that as much of her recent history as possible should be explained before Martin presented himself.

Martin went slowly upstairs, and paused a moment at the door, as if he was a little afraid of commencing the interview; he looked round to his sisters, and made a sign to them to come in with him, and then, quickly pushing open the unfastened door, walked briskly up to Anty and shook hands with her.

'I hope you're very well, Anty,' said he; 'seeing you here is what I didn't expect, but I'm very glad you've come down.'

'Thank ye, Martin,' replied she; 'it was very good of your mother, fetching me. She's been the best friend I've had many a day.'

'Begad, it's a fine thing to see you and the ould lady pull so well together. It was yesterday you came here?'

'Yesterday morning. I was so glad to come! I don't know what they'd been saying to Barry; but the night before last he got drinking, and then he was very bad to me, and tried to frighten me, and so, you see, I come down to your mother till we could be friends again.'

Anty's apology for being at the inn, was perhaps unnecessary; but, with the feeling so natural to a woman, she was half afraid that Martin would fancy she had run after him, and she therefore thought it as well to tell him that it was only a temporary measure. Poor Anty! At the moment she said so, she trembled at the very idea of putting herself again in her brother's power.

'Frinds, indeed!' said Meg; 'how can you iver be frinds with the like of him? What nonsense you talk, Anty! Why, Martin, he was like to murdher her!—he raised his fist to her, and knocked her down —and, afther that, swore to her he'd kill her outright av' she wouldn't sware that she'd niver—'

'Whist, Meg! How can you go on that way?' said Anty, interrupting her, and blushing. 'I'll not stop in the room; don't you know he was dhrunk when he done all that?'

'And won't he be dhrunk again, Anty?' suggested Jane.

'Shure he will: he'll be dhrunk always, now he's once begun,' replied Meg, who, of all the family was the most anxious to push her brother's suit; and who, though really fond of her friend, thought the present opportunity a great deal too good to be thrown away, and could not bear the idea of Anty's even thinking of being reconciled to her brother. 'Won't he be always dhrunk now?' she continued; 'and ain't we all frinds here? and why shouldn't you let me tell Martin all? Afther all's said and done, isn't he the best frind you've got?'—Here Anty blushed very red, and to tell the truth, so did Martin too—'well so he is, and unless you tell him what's happened, how's he to know what to advise; and, to tell the truth, wouldn't you sooner do what he says than any one else?'

'I'm sure I'm very much obliged to Mr. Martin'— it had been plain Martin before Meg's appeal; 'but your mother knows what's best for me, and I'll do whatever she says. Av' it hadn't been for her, I don't know where I'd be now.'

'But you needn't quarrel with Martin because you're frinds with mother,' answered Meg.

'Nonsense Meg,' said Jane, 'Anty's not going to quarrel with him. You hurry her too much.'

Martin looked rather stupid all this time, but he plucked up courage and said, 'Who's going to quarrel? I'm shure, Anty, you and I won't; but, whatever it is Barry did to you, I hope you won't go back there again, now you're once here. But did he railly sthrike you in arnest?'

'He did, and knocked her down,' said Jane.

'But won't you get your brother his dinner?' said Anty; 'he must be very hungry, afther his ride—and won't you see your mother afther your journey, Mr. Martin? I'm shure she's expecting you.'

This, for the present, put an end to the conversation; the girls went to get something for their brother to eat, and he descended into the lower regions to pay his filial respects to his mother.

A considerable time passed before Martin returned to the meal the three young women had provided for him, during which he was in close consultation with the widow. In the first place, she began upbraiding him for his folly in wishing to marry an old maid for her money; she then taxed him with villany, for trying to cheat Anty out of her property; and when he defended himself from that charge by telling her what he had done about the settlement, she asked him how much he had to pay the rogue of a lawyer for that 'gander's job'. She then proceeded to point out all the difficulties which lay in the way of a marriage between him, Martin, and her, Anty; and showed how mad it was for either of them to think about it. From that, she got into a narrative of Barry's conduct, and Anty's sufferings, neither of which lost anything in the telling; and having by this time gossiped herself into a good humour, she proceeded to show how, through her means and assistance, the marriage might take place if he was still bent upon it. She eschewed all running away, and would hear of no clandestine proceedings. They should be married in the face of day, as the Kellys ought, with all their friends round them. 'They'd have no huggery-muggery work, up in a corner; not they indeed! why should they?—for fear of Barry Lynch? —who cared for a dhrunken blackguard like that?— not she indeed!—who ever heard of a Kelly being afraid of a Lynch?—They'd ax him to come and see his sister married, and av' he didn't like it, he might do the other thing.'

And so, the widow got quite eloquent on the glories of the wedding, and the enormities of her son's future brother-in-law, who had, she assured Martin,

come down and abused her horribly, in her own shop,
before all the town, because she allowed Anty to stay
in the house. She then proceeded to the consequences
of the marriage, and expressed her hope that when
Martin got all that ready money he would 'do something for his poor sisthers—for Heaven knew they
war like to be bad enough off, for all she'd be able to
do for them!' From this she got to Martin's own
future mode of life, suggesting a 'small snug cottage
on the farm, just big enough for them two, and, may-
be, a slip of a girl servant, and not to be taring and
tatthering away, as av' money had no eend; and,
afther all,' she added, 'there war nothing like industhry; and who know'd whether that born villain,
Barry, mightn't yet get sich a hoult of the money,
that there'd be no getting it out of his fist?' and she
then depicted, in most pathetic language, what would
be the misery of herself and all the Kellys if Martin,
flushed with his prosperity, were to give up the farm
at Toneroe, and afterwards find that he had been
robbed of his expected property, and that he had no
support for himself and his young bride.

On this subject Martin considerably comforted her
by assuring her that he had no thoughts of abandon-
ing Toneroe, although he did not go so far as to
acquiesce in the very small cottage; and he moreover
expressed his thorough confidence that he would
neither be led himself, nor lead Anty, into the
imprudence of a marriage, until he had well satisfied
himself that the property was safe.

The widow was well pleased to find, from Martin's
prudent resolves, that he was her own son, and that
she needn't blush for him; and then they parted, she
to her shop, and he to his dinner: not however, before
he had promised her to give up all ideas of a clandestine marriage, and to permit himself to be united to
his wife in the face of day, as became a Kelly.

The evening passed over quietly and snugly at the
inn. Martin had not much difficulty in persuading
his three companions to take a glass of punch each

out of his tumbler, and less in getting them to take a second, and, before they went to bed, he and Anty were again intimate. And, as he was sitting next her for a couple of hours on the little sofa opposite the fire, it is more than probable that he got his arm round her waist—a comfortable position, which seemed in no way to shock the decorum of either Meg or Jane.

IX

MR. DALY, THE ATTORNEY

WE must now see how things went on in the enemy's camp.

The attorney drove up to the door of Dunmore House on his car, and was shown into the drawing-room, where he met Barry Lynch. The two young men were acquainted, though not intimate with each other, and they bowed, and then shook hands; and Barry told the attorney that he was welcome to Dunmore House, and the attorney made another bow, rubbed his hands before the fire and said it was a very cold evening; and Barry said it was 'nation cold for that time of the year; which, considering that they were now in the middle of February, showed that Barry was rather abroad, and didn't exactly know what to say. He remained for about a minute, silent before the fire, and then asked Daly if he'd like to see his room; and, the attorney acquiescing, he led him up to it, and left him there.

The truth was, that, as the time of the man's visit had drawn nearer, Barry had become more and more embarrassed; and now that the attorney had absolutely come, his employer felt himself unable to explain the business before dinner. 'These fellows are so confoundedly sharp—I shall never be up to him till I get a tumbler of punch on board,' said he to himself, comforting himself with the reflection; 'besides, I'm never well able for anything till I get a little warmed. We'll get along like a house on fire

when we've got the hot water between us.' The true
meaning of all which was, that he hadn't the courage
to make known his villanous schemes respecting his
sister till he was half drunk; and, in order the earlier
to bring about this necessary and now daily consummation, he sneaked downstairs and took a solitary
glass of brandy to fortify himself for entertaining the
attorney.

The dinner was dull enough; for, of course, as long
as the man was in the room there was no talking on
business, and, in his present frame of mind Barry was
not likely to be an agreeable companion. The attorney ate his dinner as if it was a part of the fee,
received in payment of the work he was to do, and
with a determination to make the most of it.

At last, the dishes disappeared, and with them
Terry Rooney; who, however, like a faithful servant,
felt too strong an interest in his master's affairs to be
very far absent when matters of importance were
likely to be discussed.

'And now, Mr. Daly,' said Lynch, 'we can be snug
here, without interruption, for an hour or two.
You'll find that whiskey old and good, I think; but,
if you prefer wine, that port on the table came from
Barton's, in Sackville Street.'

'Thank ye; if I take anything, it'll be a glass of
punch. But as we've business to talk of, may-be I'd
better keep my head clear.'

'My head's never so clear then, as when I've done
my second tumbler. I'm never so sure of what I'm
about as when I'm a little warmed; "but," says you,
"because my head's strong, it's no reason another's
shouldn't be weak:" but do as you like; liberty hall
here now, Mr. Daly; that is, as far as I'm concerned.
You knew my father, I believe, Mr. Daly?'

'Well then, Mr. Lynch, I didn't exactly know him;
but living so near him, and he having so much business in the county, and myself having a little, I
believe I've been in company with him, odd times.'

'He was a queer man: wasn't he, Mr. Daly?'

'Was he, then? I dare say. I didn't know much about him. I'll take the sugar from you, Mr. Lynch; I believe I might as well mix a drop, as the night's cold.'

'That's right. I thought you weren't the fellow to sit with an empty glass before you. But, as I was saying before, the old boy was a queer hand; that is, latterly—for the last year or so. Of course you know all about his will?'

'Faith then, not much. I heard he left a will, dividing the property between you and Miss Lynch.'

'He did! Just at the last moment, when the breath wasn't much more than left in him, he signed a will, making away half the estate, just as you say, to my sister. Blake could have broke the will, only he was so d—— pig-headed and stupid. It's too late now, I suppose?'

'Why, I could hardly answer that, you know, as I never heard the circumstances; but I was given to understand that Blake consulted McMahon; and that McMahon wouldn't take up the case, as there was nothing he could put before the Chancellor. Mind I'm only repeating what people said in Tuam, and about there. Of course, I couldn't think of advising till I knew the particulars. Was it on this subject, Mr. Lynch, you were good enough to send for me?'

'Not at all, Mr. Daly. I look upon that as done and gone; bad luck to Blake and McMahon, both. The truth is, between you and me, Daly—I don't mind telling you; as I hope now you will become my man of business, and it's only fair you should know all about it—the truth is, Blake was more interested on the other side, and he was determined the case shouldn't go before the Chancellor. But, when my father signed that will, it was just after one of those fits he had lately; that could be proved, and he didn't know what he was doing, from Adam! He didn't know what was in the will, nor, that he was signing a will at all; so help me, he didn't. However,

that's over. It wasn't to talk about that that I sent
for you; only, sorrow seize the rogue that made the
old man rob me! It wasn't Anty herself, poor
creature; she knew nothing about it; it was those
who meant to get hold of my money, through her,
that did it. Poor Anty! Heaven knows she wasn't
up to such a dodge as that!'

'Well, Mr. Lynch, of course I know nothing of the
absolute facts; but from what I hear, I think it's as
well to let the will alone. The Chancellor won't put
a will aside in a hurry; it's always a difficult job—
would cost an immense sum of money, which should,
any way, come out of the property; and, after all,
the chances are ten to one you'd be beat.'

'Perhaps you're right, now; though I'm sure, had
the matter been properly taken up at first—had you
seen the whole case at the first start, the thing could
have been done. I'm sure you would have said so;
but that's over now; it's another business I want you
for. But you don't drink your punch!—and it's dry
work talking, without wetting one's whistle,' and
Barry carried out his own recommendation.

'I'm doing very well, thank ye, Mr. Lynch. And
what is it I can do for you?'

'That's what I'm coming to. You know that, by
the will, my sister Anty gets from four to five hundred a year?'

'I didn't know the amount; but I believe she has
half whatever there is.'

'Exactly: half the land, half the cash, half the
house, half everything, except the debts! and those
were contracted in my name, and I must pay them
all. Isn't that hard, Mr. Daly?'

'I didn't know your father had debts.'

'Oh, but he had—debts which ought to have been
his; though, as I said, they stand in my name, and
I must pay them.'

'And, I suppose, what you now want is to saddle
the debts on the entire property? If you can really
prove that the debts were incurred for your father's

benefit, I should think you might do that. But has your sister refused to pay the half? They can't be heavy. Won't Miss Lynch agree to pay the half herself?'

This last lie of Barry's—for, to give the devil his due, old Sim hadn't owed one penny for the last twenty years—was only a bright invention of the moment, thrown off by our injured hero to aggravate the hardships of his case; but he was determined to make the most of it.

'Not heavy?—faith, they *are* heavy, and d—d heavy too, Mr. Daly!—what'll take two hundred a-year out of my miserable share of the property; divil a less. Oh! there's never any knowing how a man'll cut up till he's gone.'

'That's true; but how could your father owe such a sum as that, and no one know it? Why, that must be four or five thousand pounds?'

'About five, I believe.'

'And you've put your name to them, isn't that it?'

'Something like it. You know, he and Lord Ballindine, years ago, were fighting about the leases we held under the old Lord; and then, the old man wanted ready money, and borrowed it in Dublin; and, some years since—that is, about three years ago,—sooner than see any of the property sold, I took up the debt myself. You know, it was all as good as my own then; and now, confound it! I must pay the whole out of the miserable thing that's left me under this infernal will. But it wasn't even about that I sent for you; only, I must explain exactly how matters are, before I come to the real point.'

'But your father's name must be joined with yours in the debt; and, if so, you can come upon the entire property for the payment. There's no difficulty about that; your sister, of course, must pay the half.'

'It's not so, my dear fellow. I can't explain the thing exactly, but it's I that owe the money, and I must pay it. But it's no good talking of that. Well, you see, Anty—that's my sister, has this property all in her own hands. But you don't drink your punch,' and Barry mixed his third tumbler.

'Of course she has; and, surely she won't refuse to pay half the claims on the estate?'

'Never mind the claims!' answered Barry, who began to fear that he had pushed his little invention a thought too far. 'I tell you, I must stand to them; you don't suppose I'd ask her to pay a penny as a favour? No; I'm a little too proud for that. Besides, it'd be no use, not the least; and that's what I'm coming to. You see, Anty's got this money, and—. You know, don't you, Mr. Daly, poor Anty's not just like other people?'

'No,' said Mr. Daly—'I didn't. I can't say I know much about Miss Lynch. I never had the pleasure of seeing her.'

'But did you never hear she wasn't quite right?'

'Indeed, I never did, then.'

'Well that's odd; but we never had it much talked about, poor creature. Indeed, there was no necessity for people to know much about it, for she never gave any trouble; and, to tell the truth, as long as she was kept quiet, she never gave us occasion to think much about it. But, confound them for rogues —those who have got hold of her now, have quite upset her.'

'But what is it ails your sister, Mr. Lynch?'

'To have it out, at once, then—she's not right in her upper story. Mind, I don't mean she's a downright lunatic; but she's cracked, poor thing, and quite unable to judge for herself, in money-matters, and such like; and, though she might have done very well, poor thing, and passed without notice, if she'd been left quiet, as was always intended, I'm afraid now, unless she's well managed, she'd end her life in the Ballinasloe Asylum.'

The attorney made no answer to this, although Barry paused, to allow him to do so. Daly was too sharp, and knew his employer's character too well to believe all he said, and he now began to fancy

that he saw what the affectionate brother was after.
'Well, Daly,' continued Barry, after a minute's
pause; 'after the old man died, we went on quiet
enough for some time. I was up in Dublin mostly,
about that confounded loan, and poor Anty was left
here by herself; and what should she do, but take
up with a low huxter's family in the town here.'

'That's bad,' said the attorney. 'Was there an
unmarried young man among them at all?'

'Faith there was so; as great a blackguard as there
is in Connaught.'

'And Miss Lynch is going to marry him?'

'That's just it, Daly; that's what we must prevent.
You know, for the sake of the family, I couldn't let
it go on. Then, poor creature, she'd be plundered
and ill-treated—she'd be a downright idiot in no
time; and, you know, Daly, the property'd go to the
devil; and where'd I be then?'

Daly couldn't help thinking that, in all probability,
his kind host would not be long in following the
property; but he did not say so. He merely asked the
name of the 'blackguard' whom Miss Anty meant
to marry?

'Wait till I tell you the whole of it. The first thing
I heard was, that Anty had made a low ruffian,
named Moylan, her agent.'

'I know him; she couldn't have done much worse.
Well?'

'She made him her agent without speaking to me,
or telling me a word about it; and I couldn't make
out what had put it into her head, till I heard that
this old rogue was a kind of cousin to some people
living here, named Kelly.'

'What, the widow, that keeps the inn?'

'The very same! confound her, for an impertinent
scheming old hag, as she is. Well; that's the house
that Anty was always going to; drinking tea with
the daughters, and walking with the son—an infernal
young farmer, that lives with them, the worst of the
whole set.'

'What, Martin Kelly?—There's worse fellows than him, Mr. Lynch.'

'I'll be hanged if I know them, then; but if there are, I don't choose my poor sister—only one remove from an idiot, and hardly that—to be carried off from her mother's house, and married to such a fellow as that. Why, it's all the same infernal plot; it's the same people that got the old man to sign the will, when he was past his senses!'

'Begad, they must have been clever to do that! How the deuce could they have got the will drawn?'

'I tell you, they *did* do it!' answered Barry, whose courage was now somewhat raised by the whiskey. 'That's neither here nor there, but they did it; and, when the old fool was dead, they got this Moylan made Anty's agent: and then, the hag of a mother comes up here, before daylight, and bribes the servant, and carries her off down to her filthy den, which she calls an inn; and when I call to see my sister, I get nothing but insolence and abuse.'

'And when did this happen? When did Miss Lynch leave the house?'

'Yesterday morning, about four o'clock.'

'She went down of her own accord, though?'

'D—l a bit. The old hag came up here, and filched her out of her bed.'

'But she couldn't have taken your sister away, unless she had wished to go.'

'Of course she wished it; but a silly creature like her can't be let to do all she wishes. She wishes to get a husband, and doesn't care what sort of a one she gets; but you don't suppose an old maid—forty years old, who has always been too stupid and foolish ever to be seen or spoken to, should be allowed to throw away four hundred a-year, on the first robber that tries to cheat her? You don't mean to say there isn't a law to prevent that?'

'I don't know how you'll prevent it, Mr. Lynch. She's her own mistress.'

'What the d—l!—Do you mean to say there's nothing to prevent an idiot like that from marrying?'

'If she *was* an idiot! But I think you'll find your sister has sense enough to marry whom she pleases.'

'I tell you she *is* an idiot; not raving, mind; but everybody knows she was never fit to manage anything.'

'Who'd prove it!'

'Why, I would. Divil a doubt of it! I could prove that she never could, all her life.'

'Ah, my dear Sir! you couldn't do it; nor could I advise you to try—that is, unless there were plenty more who could swear positively that she was out of her mind. Would the servants swear that? Could you yourself, now, positively swear that she was out of her mind?'

'Why—she never had any mind to be out of.'

'Unless you are very sure she is, and, for a considerable time back, has been, a confirmed lunatic, you'd be very wrong—very ill-advised, I mean, Mr. Lynch, to try that game at all. Things would come out which you wouldn't like; and your motives would be—would be—' seen through at once, the attorney was on the point of saying, but he stopped himself, and finished by the words 'called in question'.

'And I'm to sit here, then, and see that young blackguard Kelly, run off with what ought to be my own, and my sister into the bargain? I'm blessed if I do! If you can't put me in the way of stopping it, I'll find those that can.'

'You're getting too much in a hurry, Mr. Lynch. Is your sister at the inn now?'

'To be sure she is.'

'And she is engaged to this young man?'

'She is.'

'Why, then, she might be married to him to-morrow, for anything you know.'

'She might, if he was here. But they tell me he's away, in Dublin.'

'If they told you so to-day, they told you wrong:

he came into Dunmore, from Tuam, on the same car
with myself, this very afternoon.'

'What, Martin Kelly? Then he'll be off with her
this night, while we're sitting here!' and Barry
jumped up, as if to rush out, and prevent the immediate consummation of his worst fears.

'Stop a moment, Mr. Lynch,' said the more prudent and more sober lawyer. 'If they were off, you
couldn't follow them; and, if you did follow and find
them, you couldn't prevent their being married, if
such were their wish, and they had a priest ready to
do it. Take my advice; remain quiet where you are,
and let's talk the matter over. As for taking out
a commission "de lunatico", as we call it, you'll find
you couldn't do it. Miss Lynch may be a little weak
or so in the upper story, but she's not a lunatic; and
you couldn't make her so, if you had half Dunmore to
back you, because she'd be brought before the Com-
missioners herself, and that, you know, would soon
settle the question. But you might still prevent the
marriage, for a time, at any rate—at least, I think
so; and, after that, you must trust to the chapter of
accidents.'

'So help me, that's all I want! If I got her once up
here again, and was sure the thing was off, for a month
or so, let me alone, then, for bringing her to reason!'

As Daly watched his comrade's reddening face,
and saw the malicious gleam of his eyes as he declared how easily he'd manage the affair, if poor
Anty was once more in the house, his heart misgave
him, even though he was a sharp attorney, at the
idea of assisting such a cruel brute in his cruelty; and,
for a moment, he had determined to throw up the
matter. Barry was so unprincipled, and so wickedly
malicious in his want of principle, that he disgusted
even Daly. But, on second thoughts, the lawyer
remembered that if he didn't do the job, another
would; and, quieting his not very violent qualms of
conscience with the idea that, though employed by
the brother, he might also, to a certain extent, pro-

tect the sister, he proceeded to give his advice as to the course which would be most likely to keep the property out of the hands of the Kellys.

He explained to Barry that, as Anty had left her own home in company with Martin's mother, and as she now was a guest at the widow's, it was unlikely that any immediate clandestine marriage should be resorted to; that their most likely course would be to brazen the matter out, and have the wedding solemnised without any secrecy, and without any especial notice to him, Barry. That, on the next morning, a legal notice should be prepared in Tuam, and served on the widow, informing her that it was his intention to indict her for conspiracy, in enticing away from her own home his sister Anty, for the purpose of obtaining possession of her property, she being of weak mind, and not able properly to manage her own affairs; that a copy of this notice should also be sent to Martin, warning him that he would be included in the indictment if he took any proceedings with regard to Miss Lynch; and that a further copy should, if possible, be put into the hands of Miss Lynch herself.

'You may be sure that'll frighten them,' continued Daly; 'and then, you know, when we see what sort of fight they make, we'll be able to judge whether we ought to go on and prosecute or not. I think the widow'll be very shy of meddling, when she finds you're in earnest. And you see, Mr. Lynch,' he went on, dropping his voice, 'if you *do* go into court, as I don't think you will, you'll go with clean hands, as you ought to do. Nobody can say anything against you for trying to prevent your sister from marrying a man so much younger than herself, and so much inferior in station and fortune; you won't seem to gain anything by it, and that's everything with a jury; and then, you know, if it comes out that Miss Lynch's mind is rather touched, it's an additional reason why you should protect her from intriguing and interested schemers. Don't you see?'

Barry did see, or fancied he saw, that he had now
got the Kellys in a dead fix, and Anty back into his
own hands again; and his self-confidence having been
fully roused by his potations, he was tolerably happy,
and talked very loudly of the manner in which he
would punish those low-bred huxters, who had presumed to interfere with him in the management of his
family.

Towards the latter end of the evening, he became
even more confidential, and showed the cloven foot,
if possible, more undisguisedly than he had hitherto
done. He spoke of the impossibility of allowing four
hundred a year to be carried off from him, and suggested to Daly that his sister would soon drop off,—
that there would then be a nice thing left, and that
he, Daly, should have the agency, and if he pleased,
the use of Dunmore House. As for himself, he had no
idea of mewing himself up in such a hole as that; but,
before he went, he'd take care to drive that villain,
Moylan, out of the place. 'The cursed villany of
those Kellys, to go and palm such a robber as that
off on his sister, by way of an agent!'

To all this, Daly paid but little attention, for he
saw that his host was drunk. But when Moylan's
name was mentioned, he began to think that it might
be as well either to include him in the threatened
indictment, or else, which would be better still, to
buy him over to their side, as they might probably
learn from him what Martin's plans really were.
Barry was, however, too tipsy to pay much attention
to this, or to understand any deep-laid plans. So
the two retired to their beds, Barry determined, as he
declared to the attorney in his drunken friendship,
to have it out of Anty, when he caught her; and
Daly promising to go to Tuam early in the morning,
have the notices prepared and served, and come back
in the evening to dine and sleep, and have, if possible,
an interview with Mr. Moylan. As he undressed, he
reflected that, during his short professional career,
he had been thrown into the society of many un-

mitigated rogues of every description; but that his new friend, Barry Lynch, though he might not equal them in energy of villany and courage to do serious evil, beat them all hollow in selfishness, and utter brutal want of feeling, conscience, and principle.

X

DOT BLAKE'S ADVICE

AN hour or two after Martin Kelly had left Porto Bello in the Ballinasloe fly-boat, our other hero, Lord Ballindine, and his friend Dot Blake, started from Morrison's hotel, with post horses, for Handicap Lodge; and, as they travelled in Blake's very comfortable barouche, they reached their destination in time for a late dinner, without either adventure or discomfort. Here they remained for some days, fully occupied with the education of their horses, the attention necessary to the engagements for which they were to run, and with their betting-books.

Lord Ballindine's horse, Brien Boru, was destined to give the Saxons a dressing at Epsom, and put no one knows how many thousands into his owner's hands, by winning the Derby; and arrangements had already been made for sending him over to John Scott, the English trainer, at an expense, which, if the horse should by chance fail to be successful, would be of very serious consequence to his lordship. But Lord Ballindine had made up his mind, or rather, Blake had made it up for him, and the thing was to be done; the risk was to be run, and the preparations —the sweats and the gallops, the physicking, feeding, and coddling, kept Frank tolerably well employed; though the whole process would have gone on quite as well, had he been absent.

It was not so, however, with Dot Blake. The turf, to him, was not an expensive pleasure, but a very serious business, and one which, to give him his due, he well understood. He himself, regulated the work, both of his horses and his men, and saw that both did what was allotted to them. He took very good care that he was never charged a guinea, where a guinea was not necessary; and that he got a guinea's worth for every guinea he laid out. In fact, he trained his own horses, and was thus able to assure himself that his interests were never made subservient to those of others who kept horses in the same stables. Dot was in his glory, and in his element on the Curragh, and he was never quite happy anywhere else.

This, however, was not the case with his companion. For a couple of days the excitement attending Brien Boru was sufficient to fill Lord Ballindine's mind; but after that, he could not help recurring to other things. He was much in want of money, and had been civilly told by his agent's managing clerk, before he left town, that there was some difficulty in the way of his immediately getting the sum required. This annoyed him, for he could not carry on the game without money. And then, again, he was unhappy to be so near Fanny Wyndham, from day to day, without seeing her. He was truly and earnestly attached to her, and miserable at the threat which had been all but made by her guardian, that the match should be broken off.

It was true that he had made up his mind not to go to Grey Abbey, as long as he remained at Handicap Lodge, and, having made the resolution, he thought he was wise in keeping it; but still, he continually felt that she must be aware that he was in the neighbourhood, and could not but be hurt at his apparent indifference. And then he knew that her guardian would make use of his present employment—his sojourn at such a den of sporting characters as his friend Blake's habitation—and his continued absence from Grey Abbey though known to be in its vicinity, as additional arguments for inducing his ward to declare the engagement at an end.

These troubles annoyed him, and though he daily

stood by and saw Brien Boru go through his man-
œuvres, he was discontented and fidgety.

He had been at Handicap Lodge about a fortnight,
and was beginning to feel anything but happy. His
horse was to go over in another week, money was not
plentiful with him, and tradesmen were becoming
obdurate and persevering. His host, Blake, was not
a soothing or a comfortable friend, under these
circumstances: he gave him a good deal of practical
advice, but he could not sympathise with him.
Blake was a sharp, hard, sensible man, who reduced
everything to pounds shillings and pence. Lord
Ballindine was a man of feeling, and for the time,
at least, a man of pleasure; and, though they were,
or thought themselves friends, they did not pull well
together; in fact, they bored each other terribly.

One morning, Lord Ballindine was riding out from
the training-ground, when he met, if not an old, at
any rate an intimate acquaintance, named Tierney.
Mr. or, as he was commonly called, Mat Tierney, was
a bachelor, about sixty years of age, who usually
inhabited a lodge near the Curragh; and who kept
a horse or two on the turf, more for the sake of the
standing which it gave him in the society he liked
best, than from any intense love of the sport. He
was a fat, jolly fellow, always laughing, and usually
in a good humour; he was very fond of what he
considered the world; and the world, at least that
part of it which knew him, returned the compliment.

'Well, my lord,' said he, after a few minutes of
got-up enthusiasm respecting Brien Boru, 'I congratulate you, sincerely.'

'What about?' said Lord Ballindine.

'Why, I find you've got a first-rate horse, and I hear
you've got rid of a first-rate lady. You're very
lucky, no doubt, in both; but I think fortune has
stood to you most in the latter.'

Lord Ballindine was petrified: he did not know
what to reply. He was aware that his engagement
with Miss Wyndham was so public that Tierney could

allude to no other lady; but he could not conceive how any one could have heard that his intended marriage was broken off—at any rate how he could have heard it spoken of so publicly, as to induce him to mention it in that sort of way, to himself. His first impulse was to be very indignant; but he felt that no one would dream of quarrelling with Mat Tierney; so he said, as soon as he was able to collect his thoughts sufficiently,

'I was not aware of the second piece of luck, Mr. Tierney. Pray who is the lady?'

'Why, Miss Wyndham,' said Mat, himself a little astonished at Lord Ballindine's tone.

'I'm sure, Mr. Tierney,' said Frank, 'you would say nothing, particularly in connection with a lady's name, which you intended either to be impertinent, or injurious. Were it not that I am quite certain of this, I must own that what you have just said would appear to be both.'

'My dear lord,' said the other, surprised and grieved, 'I beg ten thousand pardons, if I have unintentionally said anything, which you feel to be either. But, surely, if I am not wrong in asking, the match between you and Miss Wyndham is broken off?'

'May I ask you, Mr. Tierney, who told you so?'

'Certainly—Lord Kilcullen; and, as he is Miss Wyndham's cousin, and Lord Cashel's son, I could not but think the report authentic.'

This overset Frank still more thoroughly. Lord Kilcullen would never have spread the report publicly unless he had been authorised to do so by Lord Cashel. Frank and Lord Kilcullen had never been intimate; and the former was aware that the other had always been averse to the proposed marriage; but still, he would never have openly declared that the marriage was broken off, had he not had some authority for saying so.

'As you seem somewhat surprised,' continued Mat, seeing that Lord Ballindine remained silent, and apparently at a loss for what he ought to say, 'perhaps I ought to tell you, that Lord Kilcullen mentioned it last night very publicly—at a dinner-party, as an absolute fact. Indeed, from his manner, I thought he wished it to be generally made known. I presumed, therefore, that it had been mutually agreed between you, that the event was not to come off—that the match was not to be run; and, with my peculiar views, you know, on the subject of matrimony, I thought it a fair point for congratulation. If Lord Kilcullen had misled me, I heartily beg to apologise; and at the same time, by giving you my authority, to show you that I could not intend anything impertinent. If it suits you, you are quite at liberty to tell Lord Kilcullen all I have told you; and, if you wish me to contradict the report, which I must own I have spread, I will do so.'

Frank felt that he could not be angry with Mat Tierney; he therefore thanked him for his open explanation, and, merely muttering something about private affairs not being worthy of public interest, rode off towards Handicap Lodge.

It appeared very plain to him that the Grey Abbey family must have discarded him—that Fanny Wyndham, Lord and Lady Cashel, and the whole set, must have made up their minds to drop him altogether; otherwise, one of the family would not have openly declared the match at an end. And yet he was at a loss to conceive how they could have done so—how even Lord Cashel could have reconciled it to himself to do so, without the common-place courtesy of writing to him on the subject. And then, when he thought of her, 'his own Fanny,' as he had so often called her, he was still more bewildered: she, with whom he had sat for so many sweet hours talking of the impossibility of their ever forgetting, deserting, or even slighting each other; she, who had been so entirely devoted to him—so much more than engaged to him—could she have lent her name to such a heartless mode of breaking her faith?

'If I had merely proposed for her through her

guardian,' thought Frank, to himself—'if I had got
Lord Cashel to make the engagement, as many men
do, I should not be surprised; but after all that has
passed between us—after all her vows, and all her
——' and then Lord Ballindine struck his horse with
his heel, and made a cut at the air with his whip, as
he remembered certain passages more binding even
than promises, warmer even than vows, which
seemed to make him as miserable now as they had
made him happy at the time of their occurrence.
'I would not believe it,' he continued, meditating,
'if twenty Kilcullens said it, or if fifty Mat Tierneys
swore to it!' and then he rode on towards the lodge,
in a state of mind for which I am quite unable to
account, if his disbelief in Fanny Wyndham's constancy was really as strong as he had declared it to
be. And, as he rode, many unusual thoughts—for,
hitherto, Frank had not been a very deep-thinking
man—crowded his mind, as to the baseness, falsehood, and iniquity of the human race, especially of
rich cautious old peers who had beautiful wards in
their power.

By the time he had reached the lodge, he had
determined that he must now do something, and that,
as he was quite unable to come to any satisfactory
conclusion on his own unassisted judgment, he must
consult Blake, who, by the bye, was nearly as sick of
Fanny Wyndham as he would have been had he
himself been the person engaged to marry her.

As he rode round to the yard, he saw his friend
standing at the door of one of the stables, with a
cigar in his mouth.

'Well, Frank, how does Brien go to-day? Not that
he'll ever be the thing till he gets to the other side of
the water. They'll never be able to bring a horse out
as he should be, on the Curragh, till they've regular
trained gallops. The slightest frost in spring, or sun
in summer, and the ground's so hard, you might as
well gallop your horse down the pavement of Grafton
Street.'

'Confound the horse,' answered Frank; 'come here, Dot, a minute. I want to speak to you.'

'What the d—l's the matter?—he's not lame, is he?'

'Who?—what?—Brien Boru? Not that I know of. I wish the brute had never been foaled.'

'And why so? What crotchet have you got in your head now? Something wrong about Fanny, I suppose?'

'Why, did you hear anything?'

'Nothing but what you've told me.'

'I've just seen Mat Tierney, and he told me that Kilcullen had declared, at a large dinner-party, yesterday, that the match between me and his cousin was finally broken off.'

'You wouldn't believe what Mat Tierney would say? Mat was only taking a rise out of you.'

'Not at all: he was not only speaking seriously, but he told me what I'm very sure was the truth, as far as Lord Kilcullen was concerned. I mean, I'm sure Kilcullen said it, and in the most public manner he could; and now, the question is, what had I better do?'

'There's no doubt as to what you'd better do; the question is what you'd rather do?'

'But what had I *better* do?—call on Kilcullen for an explanation?'

'That's the last thing to think of. No; but declare what he reports to be the truth; return Miss Wyndham the lock of hair you have in your desk, and next your heart, or wherever you keep it; write her a pretty note, and conclude by saying that the "Adriatic's free to wed another". That's what I should do.'

'It's very odd, Blake, that you won't speak seriously to a man for a moment. You've as much heart in you as one of your own horses. I wish I'd never come to this cursed lodge of yours. I'd be all right then.'

'As for my heart, Frank, if I have as much as my horses, I ought to be contented—for race-horses are usually considered to have a good deal; as for my cursed lodge, I can assure you I have endeavoured, and, if you will allow me, I will still endeavour, to make it as agreeable to you as I am able; and as to my speaking seriously, upon my word, I never spoke more so. You asked me what I thought you had better do—and I began by telling you there would be a great difference between that and what you'd rather do.'

'But, in heaven's name, why would you have me break off with Miss Wyndham, when every one knows I'm engaged to her; and when you know that I wish to marry her?'

'Firstly, to prevent her breaking off with you—though I fear there's hardly time for that; and secondly, in consequence—as the newspapers say, of incompatibility of temper.'

'Why, you don't even know her!'

'But I know you, and I know what your joint income would be, and I know that there would be great incompatibility between you, as Lord Ballin-dine, with a wife and family—and fifteen hundred a year, or so. But mind, I'm only telling you what I think you'd better do.'

'Well, I shan't do that. If I was once settled down, I could live as well on fifteen hundred a year as any country gentleman in Ireland. It's only the inter-ference of Lord Cashel that makes me determined not to pull in till I am married. If he had let me have my own way, I shouldn't, by this time, have had a horse in the world, except one or two hunters or so, down in the country.'

'Well, Frank, if you're determined to get yourself married, I'll give you the best advice in my power as to the means of doing it. Isn't that what you want?'

'I want to know what you think I ought to do, just at this minute.'

'With matrimony as the winning-post?'

'You know I wish to marry Fanny Wyndham.'

'And the sooner the better—is that it?'

'Of course. She'll be of age now, in a few days,' replied Lord Ballindine.

'Then I advise you to order a new blue coat, and to buy a wedding-ring.'

'Confusion!' cried Frank, stamping his foot, and turning away in a passion; and then he took up his hat, to rush out of the room, in which the latter part of the conversation had taken place.

'Stop a minute, Frank,' said Blake, 'and don't be in a passion. What I said was only meant to show you how easy I think it is for you to marry Miss Wyndham if you choose.'

'Easy! and every soul at Grey Abbey turned against me, in consequence of my owning that brute of a horse! I'll go over there at once, and I'll show Lord Cashel that at any rate he shall not treat me like a child. As for Kilcullen, if he interferes with me or my name in any way, I'll——'

'You'll what?—thrash him?'

'Indeed, I'd like nothing better!'

'And then shoot him—be tried by your peers—and perhaps hung; is that it?'

'Oh, that's nonsense. I don't wish to fight any one, but I am not going to be insulted.'

'I don't think you are: I don't think there's the least chance of Kilcullen insulting you; he has too much worldly wisdom. But to come back to Miss Wyndham: if you really mean to marry her, and if, as I believe, she is really fond of you, Lord Cashel and all the family can't prevent it. She is probably angry that you have not been over there; he is probably irate at your staying here, and, not unlikely, has made use of her own anger to make her think that she has quarrelled with you; and hence Kilcullen's report.'

'And what shall I do now?'

'Nothing to-day, but eat your dinner, and drink your wine. Ride over to-morrow, see Lord Cashel, and tell him—but do it quite coolly, if you can— exactly what you have heard, and how you have

heard it, and beg him to assure Lord Kilcullen that
he is mistaken in his notion that the match is off;
and beg also that the report may not be repeated.
Do this; and do it as if you were Lord Cashel's equal,
not as if you were his son, or his servant. If you are
collected and steady with him for ten minutes, you'll
soon find that he will become bothered and un-
steady.'

'That's very easy to say here, but it's not so easy
to do there. You don't know him as I do: he's so
sedate, and so slow, and so dull—especially sitting
alone, as he does of a morning, in that large, dingy,
uncomfortable, dusty-looking book-room of his. He
measures his words like senna and salts, and their
tone is as disagreeable.'

'Then do you drop out yours like prussic acid, and
you'll beat him at his own game. Those are all ex-
ternals, my dear fellow. When a man knows he has
nothing within his head to trust to,—when he has
neither sense nor genius, he puts on a wig, ties up his
neck in a white choker, sits in a big chair, and
frightens the world with his silence. Remember, if
you were not a baby, he would not be a bugbear.'

'And should I not ask to see Fanny?'

'By all means. Don't leave Grey Abbey without
seeing and making your peace with Miss Wyndham.
That'll be easy with you, because it's your *métier*.
I own that with myself it would be the most difficult
part of the morning's work. But don't ask to see her
as a favour. When you've done with the lord (and
don't let your conference be very long)—when you've
done with the lord, tell him you'll say a word to
the lady; and, whatever may have been his pre-
determination, you'll find that, if you're cool, he'll be
bothered, and he won't know how to refuse; and if he
doesn't prevent you, I'm sure Miss Wyndham won't.'

'And if he asks about these wretched horses of
mine?'

'Don't let him talk more about your affairs than
you can help; but, if he presses you—and he won't if

you play your game well—tell him that you're quite aware your income won't allow you to keep up an establishment at the Curragh after you're married.'

'But about Brien Boru, and the Derby?'

'Brien Boru! You might as well talk to him about your washing-bills! Don't go into particulars—stick to generals. He'll never ask you those questions unless he sees you shiver and shake like a half-whipped school-boy.'

After a great deal of confabulation, in which Dot Blake often repeated his opinion of Lord Ballindine's folly in not rejoicing at an opportunity of breaking off the match, it was determined that Frank should ride over the next morning, and do exactly what his friend proposed. If, however, one might judge from his apparent dread of the interview with Lord Cashel, there was but little chance of his conducting it with the coolness or assurance insisted on by Dot. The probability was, that when the time did come, he would, as Blake said, shiver and shake like a half-whipped school-boy.

'And what will you do when you're married, Frank?' said Blake; 'for I'm beginning to think the symptoms are strong, and you'll hardly get out of it now.'

'Do! why, I suppose I'll do much the same as others—have two children, and live happy ever afterwards.'

'I dare say you're right about the two children, only you might say two dozen; but as to the living happy, that's more problematical. What do you mean to eat and drink?'

'Eggs—potatoes and bacon—buttermilk, and potheen. It's odd if I can't get plenty of them in Mayo, if I've nothing better.'

'I suppose you will, Frank; but bacon won't go down well after venison; and a course of claret is a bad preparative for potheen punch. You're not the man to live, with a family, on a small income, and what the d——l you'll do I don't know. You'll fortify Kelly's Court—that'll be the first step.'

'Is it against the Repealers?'

'Faith, no; you'll join them, of course: but against the sub-sheriff, and his officers,—an army much more likely to crown their enterprises with success.'

'You seem to forget, Dot, that, after all, I'm marrying a girl with quite as large a fortune as I had any right to expect.'

'The limit to your expectations was only in your own modesty; the less you had a right—in the common parlance—to expect, the more you wanted, and the more you ought to have looked for. Say that Miss Wyndham's fortune clears a thousand a year of your property, you would never be able to get along on what you'd have. No; I'll tell you what you'll do. You'll shut up Kelly's Court, raise the rents, take a moderate house in London; and Lord Cashel, when his party are in, will get you made a court stick of, and you'll lead just such a life as your grandfather. If it's not very glorious, at any rate it's a useful kind of life. I hope Miss Wyndham will like it. You'll have to christen your children Ernest and Albert, and that sort of thing; that's the worst of it; and you'll never be let to sit down, and that's a bore. But you've strong legs. It would never do for me. I could never stand out a long tragedy in Drury Lane, with my neck in a stiff white choker, and my toes screwed into tight dress boots. I'd sooner be a porter myself, for he can go to bed when the day's over.'

'You're very witty, Dot; but you know I'm the last man in Ireland, not excepting yourself, to put up with that kind of thing. Whatever I may have to live on, I shall live in my own country, and on my own property.'

'Very well; if you won't be a gold stick, there's the other alternative: fortify Kelly's Court, and prepare for the sheriff's officers. Of the two, there's certainly more fun in it; and you can go out with the harriers on a Sunday afternoon, and live like a "ra'al O'Kelly of the ould times";—only the punch'll kill you in about ten years.'

'Go on, Dot, go on. You want to provoke me, but you won't. I wonder whether you'd bear it as well, if I told you you'd die a broken-down black-leg, without a friend or a shilling to bless you.'

'I don't think I should, because I should know that you were threatening me with a fate which my conduct and line of life would not warrant any one in expecting.'

'Upon my word, then, I think there's quite as much chance of that as there is of my getting shut up by bailiffs in Kelly's Court, and dying drunk. I'll bet you fifty pounds I've a better account at my bankers than you have in ten years.'

'Faith, I'll not take it. It'll be hard work getting fifty pounds out of you, then! In the meantime, come and play a game of billiards before dinner.'

To this Lord Ballindine consented, and they adjourned to the billiard-room; but, before they commenced playing, Blake declared that if the names of Lord Cashel or Miss Wyndham were mentioned again that evening, he should retreat to his own room, and spend the hours by himself; so, for the rest of that day, Lord Ballindine was again driven back upon Brien Boru and the Derby for conversation, as Dot was too close about his own stable to talk much of his own horses and their performances, except when he was doing so with an eye to business.

XI

THE EARL OF CASHEL

ABOUT two o'clock on the following morning, Lord Ballindine set off for Grey Abbey, on horseback, dressed with something more than ordinary care, and with a considerable palpitation about his heart. He hardly knew, himself, what or whom he feared, but he knew that he was afraid of something. He had a cold, sinking sensation within him, and he felt absolutely certain that he should be signally defeated in his present mission. He had

plenty of what is usually called courage; had his
friend recommended him instantly to call out Lord
Kilcullen and shoot him, and afterwards any number
of other young men who might express a thought in
opposition to his claim on Miss Wyndham's hand, he
would have set about it with the greatest readiness
and aptitude; but he knew he could not baffle the
appalling solemnity of Lord Cashel, in his own study.

Frank was not so very weak a man as he would
appear to be when in the society of Blake. He unfortunately allowed Blake to think for him in many
things, and he found a convenience in having some
one to tell him what to do; but he was, in most
respects, a better, and in some, even a wiser man
than his friend. He often felt that the kind of life he
was leading—contracting debts which he could not
pay, and spending his time in pursuits which were
not really congenial to him, was unsatisfactory and
discreditable: and it was this very feeling, and the
inability to defend that which he knew to be wrong
and foolish, which made him so certain that he would
not be able successfully to persist in his claim to
Miss Wyndham's hand in opposition to the trite and
well-weighed objections, which he knew her guardian
would put forward. He consoled himself, however,
with thinking that, at any rate, they could not
prevent his seeing her; and he was quite sanguine as
to her forgiveness, if he but got a fair opportunity of
asking it. And when that was obtained, why should
he care for any one? Fanny would be of age, and
her own mistress, in a few days, and all the solemn
earls in England, and Ireland too, could not then
prevent her marrying whom and when she liked.

He thought a great deal on all his friend had said
of his future poverty; but then, his ideas and Blake's
were very different about life. Blake's idea of happiness was, the concentrating of every thing into a
focus for his own enjoyment; whereas he, Frank, had
only had recourse to dissipation and extravagance,
because he had nothing to make home pleasant to

him. If he once had Fanny Wyndham installed as
Lady Ballindine, at Kelly's Court, he was sure he
could do his duty as a country gentleman, and live
on his income, be it what it might, not only without
grumbling, but without wishing for anything more.
He was fond of his country, his name, and his
countrymen: he was fully convinced of his folly in
buying race-horses, and in allowing himself to be
dragged on the turf: he would sell Brien Boru, and
the other two Irish chieftains, for what they would
fetch, and show Fanny and her guardian that he was
in earnest in his intention of reforming. Blake might
laugh at him if he liked; but he would not stay to be
laughed at. He felt that Handicap Lodge was no
place for him; and besides, why should he bear Dot's
disagreeable sarcasms? It was not the part of a real
friend to say such cutting things as he continually
did. After all, Lord Cashel would be a safer friend,
or, at any rate, adviser; and, instead of trying to
defeat him by coolness or insolence, he would at
once tell him of all his intentions, explain to him
exactly how matters stood, and prove his good
resolutions by offering to take whatever steps the
earl might recommend about the horses. This final
determination made him easier in his mind, and, as
he entered the gates of Grey Abbey Park, he was
tolerably comfortable, trusting to his own good
resolutions, and the effect which he felt certain the
expression of them must have on Lord Cashel.

Grey Abbey is one of the largest but by no means
one of the most picturesque demesnes in Ireland.
It is situated in the county of Kildare, about two
miles from the little town of Kilcullen, in a flat, uninteresting, and not very fertile country. The park
itself is extensive and tolerably well wooded, but it
wants water and undulation, and is deficient of any
object of attraction, except that of size and not very
magnificent timber. I suppose, years ago, there was
an Abbey here, or near the spot, but there is now no
vestige of it remaining. In a corner of the demesne

there are standing the remains of one of those strong, square, ugly castles, which, two centuries since, were the general habitations of the landed proprietors of the country, and many of which have been inhabited even to a much later date. They now afford the strongest record of the apparently miserable state of life, which even the favoured of the land then endured, and of the numberless domestic comforts which years and skill have given us, apt as we are to look back with fond regret to the happy, by-gone days of past periods.

This old castle, now used as a cow-shed, is the only record of antiquity at Grey Abbey; and yet the ancient family of the Greys have lived there for centuries. The first of them who possessed property in Ireland, obtained in the reign of Henry II, grants of immense tracts of land, stretching through Wicklow, Kildare, and the Queen's and King's Counties; and, although his descendants have been unable to retain, through the various successive convulsions which have taken place in the interior of Ireland since that time, anything like an eighth of what the family once pretended to claim, the Earl of Cashel, their present representative, has enough left to enable him to consider himself a very great man.

The present mansion, built on the site of that in which the family had lived till about seventy years since, is, like the grounds, large, commodious, and uninteresting. It is built of stone, which appears as if it had been plastered over, is three stories high, and the windows are all of the same size, and at regular intervals. The body of the house looks like a huge, square, Dutch old lady, and the two wings might be taken for her two equally fat, square, Dutch daughters. Inside, the furniture is good, strong, and plain. There are plenty of drawing-rooms, sitting-rooms, bed-rooms, and offices; a small gallery of very indifferent paintings, and a kitchen, with an excellent kitchen-range, and patent boilers of every shape.

Considering the nature of the attractions, it is somewhat strange that Lord Cashel should have considered it necessary to make it generally known that the park might be seen any day between the hours of nine and six, and the house, on Tuesdays and Fridays between the hours of eleven and four. Yet such is the case, and the strangeness of this proceeding on his part is a good deal diminished by the fact that persons, either induced by Lord Cashel's good nature, or thinking that any big house must be worth seeing, very frequently pay half-a-crown to the housekeeper for the privilege of being dragged through every room in the mansion.

There is a bed there, in which the Regent slept when in Ireland, and a room which was tenanted by Lord Normanby, when Lord Lieutenant. There is, moreover, a satin counterpane, which was made by the lord's aunt, and a snuff-box which was given to the lord's grandfather by Frederick the Great. These are the lions of the place, and the gratification experienced by those who see them is, no doubt, great; but I doubt if it equals the annoyance and misery to which they are subjected in being obliged to pass one unopened door—that of the private room of Lady Selina, the only daughter of the earl at present unmarried.

It contains only a bed, and the usual instruments of a lady's toilet; but Lady Selina does not choose to have it shown, and it has become invested, in the eyes of the visitors, with no ordinary mystery. Many a petitionary whisper is addressed to the housekeeper on the subject, but in vain; and, consequently, the public too often leave Grey Abbey dissatisfied.

As Lord Ballindine rode through the gates, and up the long approach to the house, he was so satisfied of the wisdom of his own final resolution, and of the successful termination of his embassy under such circumstances, that he felt relieved of the uncomfortable sensation of fear which had oppressed him; and it was only when the six-foot high, powdered servant told him, with a very solemn face, that the earl was alone, in the book-room—the odious room he hated so much—that he began again to feel a little misgiving. However, there was nothing left for him now, so he gave up his horse to the groom, and followed the sober-faced servant into the book-room.

Lord Cashel was a man about sixty-three, with considerable external dignity of appearance, though without any personal advantage, either in face, figure, or manner. He had been an earl, with a large income, for thirty years; and in that time he had learned to look collected, even when his ideas were confused; to keep his eye steady, and to make a few words go a long way. He had never been intemperate, and was, therefore, strong and hale for his years,—he had not done many glaringly foolish things, and, therefore, had a character for wisdom and judgment. He had run away with no man's wife, and, since his marriage, had seduced no man's daughter; he was, therefore, considered a moral man. He was not so deeply in debt as to have his affairs known to every one; and hence was thought prudent. And, as he lived in his own house, with his own wife, paid his servants and labourers their wages regularly, and nodded in church for two hours every Sunday, he was thought a good man. Such were his virtues; and by these negative qualities—this *vis inertiæ*, he had acquired, and maintained, a considerable influence in the country.

When Lord Ballindine's name was announced, he slowly rose, and, just touching the tip of Frank's fingers, by way of shaking hands with him, hoped he had the pleasure of seeing him well.

The viscount hoped the same of the earl—and of the ladies. This included the countess and Lady Selina, as well as Fanny, and was, therefore, not a particular question; but, having hoped this, and the earl remaining silent, he got confused, turned red, hummed and hawed a little, sat down, and then, endeavouring to drown his confusion in volubility, began talking quickly about his anxiety to make final arrangements concerning matters, which, of course, he had most deeply at heart; and, at last, ran himself fairly aground, from not knowing whether, under the present circumstances, he ought to speak of his affianced to her guardian as 'Fanny', or 'Miss Wyndham'.

When he had quite done, and was dead silent, and had paused sufficiently long to assure the earl that he was going to say nothing further just at present, the great man commenced his answer.

'This is a painful subject, my lord—most peculiarly painful at the present time; but, surely, after all that has passed—but especially after what has *not* passed'— Lord Cashel thought this was a dead hit—'you cannot consider your engagement with Miss Wyndham to be still in force?'

'Good gracious!—and why not, my lord? I am ready to do anything her friends—in fact I came solely, this morning, to consult yourself, about—I'm sure Fanny herself can't conceive the engagement to be broken off. Of course, if Miss Wyndham wishes it—but I can't believe—I can't believe—if it's about the horses, Lord Cashel, upon my word, I'm ready to sell them to-day.'

This was not very dignified in poor Frank, and to tell the truth, he was completely bothered. Lord Cashel looked so more than ordinarily glum; had he been going to put on a black cap and pass sentence of death, or disinherit his eldest son, he could not have looked more stern or more important. Frank's lack of dignity added to his, and made him feel immeasurably superior to any little difficulty which another person might have felt in making the communication he was going to make. He was really quite in a solemn good humour. Lord Ballindine's confusion was so flattering.

'I can assure you, my lord, Miss Wyndham calls for no such sacrifice, nor do I. There was a time when, as her guardian, I ventured to hint—and I

own I was taking a liberty, a fruitless liberty, in
doing so—that I thought your remaining on the turf
was hardly prudent. But I can assure you, with all
kindly feeling—with no approach to animosity—
that I will not offend in a similar way again. I hear,
by mere rumour, that you have extended your
operations to the other kingdom. I hope I have not
been the means of inducing you to do so ; but, advice,
if not complied with, often gives a bias in an opposite
direction. With regard to Miss Wyndham, I must
express—and I really had thought it was unnecessary to do so, though it was certainly my intention,
as it was Miss Wyndham's wish, that I should have
written to you formally on the subject—but your
own conduct—excuse me, Lord Ballindine—your
own evident indifference, and continued, I fear
I must call it, dissipation—and your, as I considered,
unfortunate selection of acquaintance, combined
with the necessary diminution of that attachment
which I presume Miss Wyndham once felt for you—
necessary, inasmuch as it was, as far as I understand,
never of a sufficiently ardent nature to outlive the
slights—indeed, my lord, I don't wish to offend you,
or hurt your feelings—but, I must say, the slights
which it encountered——.' Here the earl felt that
his sentence was a little confused, but the viscount
looked more so ; and, therefore, not at all abashed
by the want of a finish to his original proposition, he
continued glibly enough :

' In short, in considering all the features of the case,
I thought the proposed marriage a most imprudent
one ; and, on questioning Miss Wyndham as to her
feelings, I was, I must own, gratified to learn that
she agreed with me ; indeed, she conceived that your
conduct gave ample proof, my lord, of your readiness
to be absolved from your engagement ; pardon me
a moment, my lord—as I said before, I still deemed
it incumbent on me, and on my ward, that I, as her
guardian, should give you an absolute and written
explanation of her feelings:—that would have been

done yesterday, and this most unpleasant meeting would have been spared to both of us, but for the unexpected—Did you hear of the occurrence which has happened in Miss Wyndham's family, my lord?'

'Occurrence? No, Lord Cashel; I did not hear of any especial occurrence.'

There had been a peculiarly solemn air about Lord Cashel during the whole of the interview, which deepened into quite funereal gloom as he asked the last question; but he was so uniformly solemn, that this had not struck Lord Ballindine. Besides, an appearance of solemnity agreed so well with Lord Cashel's cast of features and tone of voice, that a visage more lengthened, and a speech somewhat slower than usual, served only to show him off as so much the more clearly identified by his own characteristics. Thus a man who always wears a green coat does not become remarkable by a new green coat; he is only so much the more than ever, the man in the green coat.

Lord Ballindine, therefore, answered the question without the appearance of that surprise which Lord Cashel expected he would feel, if he had really not yet heard of the occurrence about to be related to him. The earl, therefore, made up his mind, as indeed he had nearly done before, that Frank knew well what was going to be told him, though it suited his purpose to conceal his knowledge. He could not, however, give his young brother nobleman the lie; and he was, therefore, constrained to tell his tale, as if to one to whom it was unknown. He was determined, however, though he could not speak out plainly, to let Frank see that he was not deceived by his hypocrisy, and that he, Lord Cashel, was well aware, not only that the event about to be told had been known at Handicap Lodge, but that the viscount's present visit to Grey Abbey had arisen out of that knowledge.

Lord Ballindine, up to this moment, was perfectly ignorant of this event, and it is only doing justice to

him to say that, had he heard of it, it would at least
have induced him to postpone his visit for some time.
Lord Cashel paused for a few moments, looking at
Frank in a most diplomatic manner, and then proceeded to unfold his budget.

'I am much surprised that you should not have
heard of it. The distressing news reached Grey
Abbey yesterday, and must have been well known
in different circles in Dublin yesterday morning.
Considering the great intercourse between Dublin
and the Curragh, I wonder you can have been left
so long in ignorance of a circumstance so likely to be
widely discussed, and which at one time might have
so strongly affected your own interests.' Lord Cashel
again paused, and looked hard at Frank. He flattered
himself that he was reading his thoughts; but he
looked as if he had detected a spot on the other's
collar, and wanted to see whether it was ink or
soot.

Lord Ballindine was, however, confounded. When
the earl spoke of 'a circumstance so likely to be
widely discussed', Mat Tierney's conversation recurred to him, and Lord Kilcullen's public declaration that Fanny Wyndham's match was off.—It was
certainly odd for Lord Cashel to call this an occurrence in Miss Wyndham's family, but then, he had
a round-about way of saying everything.

'I say,' continued the earl, after a short pause,
'that I cannot but be surprised that an event of so
much importance, of so painful a nature, and, doubtless, already so publicly known, should not before
this have reached the ears of one to whom, I presume, Miss Wyndham's name was not always wholly
indifferent. But, as you have not heard it, my lord,
I will communicate it to you,' and again he paused,
as though expecting another assurance of Lord Ballindine's ignorance.

'Why, my lord,' said Frank, 'I did hear a rumour,
which surprised me very much, but I could not
suppose it to be true. To tell the truth, it was very

much in consequence of what I heard that I came
to Grey Abbey to-day.'

It was now Lord Cashel's turn to be confounded.
First, to deny that he had heard anything about it—
and then immediately to own that he had heard it,
and had been induced to renew his visits to Grey
Abbey in consequence! Just what he, in his wisdom,
had suspected was the case. But how could Lord
Ballindine have the face to own it?

I must, however, tell the reader the event of which
Frank was ignorant, and which, it appears, Lord
Cashel is determined not to communicate to him.

Fanny Wyndham's father had held a governor-
ship, or some golden appointment in the golden days
of India, and consequently had died rich. He left
eighty thousand pounds to his son, who was younger
than Fanny, and twenty to his daughter. His son
had lately been put into the Guards, but he was not
long spared to enjoy his sword and his uniform.
He died, and his death had put his sister in possession
of his money; and Lord Cashel thought that, though
Frank might slight twenty thousand pounds, he
would be too glad to be allowed to remain the accepted admirer of a hundred thousand.

'I thought you must have heard it, my lord,' re-
sumed the senior, as soon as he had collected his
shreds of dignity, which Frank's open avowal had
somewhat scattered, 'I felt certain you must have
heard it, and you will, I am sure, perceive that this is
no time for you—excuse me if I use a word which
may appear harsh—it is no time for any one, not
intimately connected with Miss Wyndham by ties
of family, to intrude upon her sorrow.'

Frank was completely bothered. He thought that
if she were so sorrowful, if she grieved so deeply at
the match being broken off, that was just the reason
why he should see her. After all, it was rather
flattering to himself to hear of her sorrows; dear
Fanny! was she so grieved that she was forced to
part from him?

'But, Lord Cashel,' he said, 'I am ready to do whatever you please. I'll take any steps you'll advise. But I really cannot see why I'm to be told that the engagement between me and Miss Wyndham is off, without hearing any reason from herself. I'll make any sacrifice you please, or she requires; I'm sure she was attached to me, and she cannot have overcome that affection so soon.'

'I have already said that we require—Miss Wyndham requires—no sacrifice from you. The time for sacrifice is past; and I do not think her affection was of such a nature as will long prey on her spirits.'

'My affection for her is, I can assure you—'

'Pray excuse me—but I think this is hardly the time either to talk of, or to show, your affection. Had it been proved to be of a lasting, I fear I must say, a sincere nature, it would now have been most valued. I will leave yourself to say whether this was the case.'

'And so you mean to say, Lord Cashel, that I cannot see Miss Wyndham?'

'Assuredly, Lord Ballindine. And I must own, that I hardly appreciate your delicacy in asking to do so at the present moment.'

There was something very hard in this. The match was to be broken off without any notice to him; and when he requested, at any rate, to hear this decision from the mouth of the only person competent to make it, he was told that it was indelicate for him to wish to do so. This put his back up.

'Well, my lord,' he said with some spirit, 'Miss Wyndham is at present your ward, and in your house, and I am obliged to postpone the exercise of the right, to which, at least, I am entitled, of hearing her decision from her own mouth. I cannot think that she expects I should be satisfied with such an answer as I have now received. I shall write to her this evening, and shall expect at any rate the courtesy of an answer from herself.'

'My advice to my ward will be, not to write to

you; at any rate for the present. I presume, my
lord, you cannot doubt my word that Miss Wyndham
chooses to be released from an engagement, which
I must say your own conduct renders it highly in-
expedient for her to keep.'

'I don't doubt your word, of course, Lord Cashel;
but such being the case, I think Miss Wyndham
might at least tell me so herself.'

'I should have thought, Lord Ballindine, that you
would have felt that the sudden news of a dearly
loved brother's death, was more than sufficient to
excuse Miss Wyndham from undergoing an interview
which, even under ordinary circumstances, would be
of very doubtful expediency.'

'Her brother's death! Good gracious! Is Harry
Wyndham dead!'

Frank was so truly surprised—so effectually
startled by the news, which he now for the first time
heard, that, had his companion possessed any real
knowledge of human nature, he would at once have
seen that his astonishment was not affected. But he
had none, and, therefore, went on blundering in his
own pompous manner.

'Yes, my lord, he is dead. I understood you to
say that you had already heard it; and, unless my
ears deceived me, you explained that his demise was
the immediate cause of your present visit. I cannot,
however, go so far as to say that I think you have
exercised a sound discretion in the matter. In expressing such an opinion, however, I am far from
wishing to utter anything which may be irritating or
offensive to your feelings.'

'Upon my word then, I never heard a word about
it till this moment! Poor Harry! And is Fanny
much cut up?'

'Miss Wyndham is much afflicted.'

'I wouldn't for worlds annoy her, or press on her
at such a moment. Pray tell her, Lord Cashel, how
deeply I feel her sorrows: pray tell her this, with my
kindest—best compliments.'

This termination was very cold—but so was Lord
Cashel's face. His lordship had also risen from his
chair, and Frank saw it was intended that the interview should end. But he would now have been glad
to stay. He wanted to ask a hundred questions;
—how the poor lad had died? whether he had been
long ill?—whether it had been expected? But he
saw that he must go; so he rose and putting out his
hand, which Lord Cashel just touched, he said,

'Good bye, my lord. I trust, after a few months
are gone by, you may see reason to alter the opinion
you have expressed respecting your ward. Should
I not hear from you before then, I shall again do
myself the honour of calling at Grey Abbey; but
I will write to Miss Wyndham before I do so.'

Lord Cashel had the honour of wishing Lord Ballindine a very good morning, and of bowing him to
the door; and so the interview ended.

XII

FANNY WYNDHAM

WHEN Lord Cashel had seen Frank over the
mat which lay outside his study door, and that
there was a six foot servitor to open any other door
through which he might have to pass, he returned
to his seat, and, drawing his chair close to the fire,
began to speculate on Fanny and her discarded lover.

He was very well satisfied with himself, and with
his own judgment and firmness in the late conversation. It was very evident that Frank had heard of
Harry Wyndham's death, and of Fanny's great accession of wealth; that he had immediately determined that the heiress was no longer to be neglected,
and that he ought to strike while the iron was hot:
hence his visit to Grey Abbey. His pretended ignorance of the young man's death, when he found he
could not see Miss Wyndham, was a ruse; but an old
bird like Lord Cashel was not to be caught with chaff.
And then, how indelicate of him to come and press

his suit immediately after news of so distressing a nature had reached Miss Wyndham! How very impolitic, thought Lord Cashel, to show such a hurry to take possession of the fortune! How completely he had destroyed his own game. And then, other thoughts passed through his mind. His ward had now one hundred thousand pounds clear, which was, certainly, a great deal of ready money. Lord Cashel had no younger sons; but his heir, Lord Kilcullen, was an expensive man, and owed, he did not exactly know, and was always afraid to ask, how much. He must marry soon, or he would be sure to go to the devil. He had been living with actresses and opera-dancers quite long enough for his own respectability; and, if he ever intended to be such a pattern to the country as his father, it was now time for him to settle down. And Lord Cashel bethought himself that if he could persuade his son to marry Fanny Wyndham and pay his debts with her fortune—(surely he couldn't owe more than a hundred thousand pounds?)—he would be able to give them a very handsome allowance to live on.

To do Lord Cashel justice, we must say that he had fully determined that it was his duty to break off the match between Frank and his ward, before he heard of the accident which had so enriched her. And Fanny herself, feeling slighted and neglected—knowing how near to her her lover was, and that nevertheless he never came to see her—hearing his name constantly mentioned in connection merely with horses and jockeys—had been induced to express her acquiescence in her guardian's views, and to throw poor Frank overboard. In all this the earl had been actuated by no mercenary views, as far as his own immediate family was concerned. He had truly and justly thought that Lord Ballindine, with his limited fortune and dissipated habits, was a bad match for his ward; and he had, consequently, done his best to break the engagement. There could, therefore, he thought, be nothing unfair in his taking advantage of the pru-

dence which he had exercised on her behalf. He did
not know, when he was persuading her to renounce
Lord Ballindine, that, at that moment, her young,
rich, and only brother, was lying at the point of
death. He had not done it for his own sake, or Lord
Kilcullen's; there could, therefore, be nothing unjust
or ungenerous in their turning to their own account the
two losses, that of her lover and her brother, which
had fallen on Miss Wyndham at the same time. If he,
as her guardian, would have been wrong to allow
Lord Ballindine to squander her twenty thousands,
he would be so much the more wrong to let him
make ducks and drakes of five times as much. In
this manner he quieted his conscience as to his premeditated absorption of his ward's fortune. It was
true that Lord Kilcullen was a heartless *roué*, whereas
Lord Ballindine was only a thoughtless rake; but
then, Lord Kilcullen would be an earl, and a peer of
parliament, and Lord Ballindine was only an Irish
viscount. It was true that, in spite of her present
anger, Fanny dearly loved Lord Ballindine, and was
dearly loved by him; and that Lord Kilcullen was
not a man to love or be loved; but then, the Kelly's
Court rents—what were they to the Grey Abbey
rents? Not a twentieth part of them! And, above
all, Lord Kilcullen's vices were filtered through the
cleansing medium of his father's partiality, and Lord
Ballindine's faults were magnified by the cautious
scruples of Fanny's guardian.

The old man settled, therefore, in his own mind,
that Fanny should be his dear daughter, and the
only difficulty he expected to encounter was with his
hopeful son. It did not occur to him that Fanny
might object, or that she could be other than pleased
with the arrangement. He determined, however, to
wait a little before the tidings of her future destiny
should be conveyed to her, although no time was to
be lost in talking over the matter with Lord Kilcullen. In the meantime, it would be necessary for
him to tell Fanny of Lord Ballindine's visit; and the

wily peer was glad to think that she could not but be
further disgusted at the hurry which her former
lover had shown to renew his protestations of affection, as soon as the tidings of her wealth had reached
him. However, he would say nothing on that head:
he would merely tell her that Lord Ballindine had
called, had asked to see her, and had been informed
of her determination to see him no more.

He sat, for a considerable time, musing over the
fire, and strengthening his resolution; and then he
stalked and strutted into the drawing-room, where
the ladies were sitting, to make his communication
to Miss Wyndham.

Miss Wyndham, and her cousin, Lady Selina Grey,
the only unmarried daughter left on the earl's hands,
were together. Lady Selina was not in her *première
jeunesse*, and, in manner, face, and disposition, was
something like her father: she was not, therefore,
very charming; but his faults were softened down
in her; and what was pretence in him, was, to a
certain degree, real in her. She had a most exaggerated conception of her own station and dignity,
and of what was due to her, and expected from
her. Because her rank enabled her to walk out of
a room before other women, she fancied herself
better than them, and entitled to be thought better.
She was plain, red-haired, and in no ways attractive;
but she had refused the offer of a respectable country
gentleman, because he was only a country gentleman, and then flattered herself that she owned the
continuance of her maiden condition to her high
station, which made her a fit match only for the most
exalted magnates of the land. But she was true,
industrious, and charitable; she worked hard to
bring her acquirements to that pitch which she considered necessary to render her fit for her position;
she truly loved her family, and tried hard to love her
neighbours, in which she might have succeeded but
for the immeasurable height from which she looked
down on them. She listened, complacently, to all

those serious cautions against pride, which her religion taught her, and considered that she was obeying its warnings, when she spoke condescendingly to those around her. She thought that condescension was humility, and that her self-exaltation was not pride, but a proper feeling of her own and her family's dignity.

Fanny Wyndham was a very different creature. She, too, was proud, but her pride was of another, if not of a less innocent cast; she was proud of her own position; but it was as Fanny Wyndham, not as Lord Cashel's niece, or anybody's daughter. She had been brought out in the fashionable world, and liked, and was liked by, it; but she felt that she owed the character which three years had given her, to herself, and not to those around her. She stood as high as Lady Selina, though on very different grounds. Any undue familiarity would have been quite as impossible with one as with the other. Lady Selina chilled intruders to a distance; Fanny Wyndham's light burned with so warm a flame, that butterflies were afraid to trust their wings within its reach. She was neither so well read, nor so thoughtful on what she did read, as her friend; but she could turn what she learned to more account, for the benefit of others. The one, in fact, could please, and the other could not.

Fanny Wyndham was above the usual height; but she did not look tall, for her figure was well-formed and round, and her bust full. She had dark-brown hair, which was never curled, but worn in plain braids, fastened at the back of her head, together with the long rich folds which were collected there under a simple comb. Her forehead was high, and beautifully formed, and when she spoke, showed the animation of her character. Her eyes were full and round, of a hazel colour, bright and soft when she was pleased, but full of pride and displeasure when her temper was ruffled, or her dignity offended. Her nose was slightly *retroussé*, but not so much so as to give to her that pertness, of which it is usually the index. The line of her cheeks and chin was very lovely: it was this which encouraged her to comb back that luxuriant hair, and which gave the greatest charm to her face. Her mouth was large, too large for a beauty, and therefore she was not a regular beauty; but, were she talking to you, and willing to please you, you could hardly wish it to be less. I cannot describe the shade of her complexion, but it was rich and glowing; and, though she was not a brunette, I believe that in painting her portrait, an artist would have mixed more brown than other colours.

At the time of which I am now speaking, she was sitting, or rather lying, on a sofa, with her face turned towards her cousin, but her eyes fixed on vacancy. As might have been expected, she was thinking of her brother, and his sudden death; but other subjects crowded with that into her mind, and another figure shared with him her thoughts. She had been induced to give her guardian an unqualified permission to reject, in her name, any further intercourse with Frank; and though she had doubtless been induced to do so by the distressing consciousness that she had been slighted by him, she had cheated herself into the belief that prudence had induced her to do so. She felt that she was not fitted to be a poor man's wife, and that Lord Ballindine was as ill suited for matrimonial poverty. She had, therefore, induced herself to give him up; may-be she was afraid that if she delayed doing so, she might herself be given up. Now, however, the case was altered; though she sincerely grieved for her brother, she could not but recollect the difference which his death made in her own position; she was now a great heiress, and, were she to marry Lord Ballindine, if she did not make him a rich man, she would, at any rate, free him from all embarrassment.

·Besides, could she give him up now?—now that she was rich? He would first hear of her brother's death and her wealth, and then would immediately be told that she had resolved to reject him. Could she bear

that she should be subjected to the construction
which would fairly be put upon her conduct, if she
acted in this manner? And then, again, she felt
that she loved him; and she did love him, more
dearly than she was herself aware. She began to
repent of her easy submission to her guardian's advice, and to think how she could best unsay what she
had already said. She had lost her brother; could she
afford also to lose her lover? She had had none she
could really love but those two. And the tears again
came to her eyes, and Lady Selina saw her, for the
twentieth time that morning, turn her face to the
back of the sofa, and heard her sob.

Lady Selina was sitting at one of the windows,
over her carpet-work frame. She had talked a great
deal of sound sense to Fanny that morning, about
her brother, and now prepared to talk some more.
Preparatory to this, she threw back her long red
curls from her face, and wiped her red nose, for it
was February.

'Fanny, you should occupy yourself, indeed you
should, my dear. It's no use your attempting your
embroidery, for your mind would still wander to him
that is no more. You should read; indeed you should.
Do go on with Gibbon. I'll fetch it for you, only tell
me where you were.'

'I could not read, Selina; I could not think about
what I read, more than about the work.'

'But you should try, Fanny,—the very attempt
would be work to your mind: besides, you would be
doing your duty. Could all your tears bring him back
to you? Can all your sorrow again restore him to his
friends? No! and you have great consolation, Fanny,
in reflecting that your remembrance of your brother
is mixed with no alloy. He had not lived to be
contaminated by the heartless vices of that portion
of the world into which he would probably have been
thrown; he had not become dissipated—extravagant
—and sensual. This should be a great consolation
to you.'

It might be thought that Lady Selina was making sarcastic allusions to her own brother and to Fanny's lover; but she meant nothing of the kind. Her remarks were intended to be sensible, true, and consolatory; and they at any rate did no harm, for Fanny was thinking of something else before she had half finished her speech.

They had both again been silent for a short time, when the door opened, and in came the earl. His usual pomposity of demeanour was somewhat softened by a lachrymose air, which, in respect to his ward's grief, he put on as he turned the handle of the door; and he walked somewhat more gently than usual into the room.

'Well, Fanny, how are you now?' he said, as he crept up to her. 'You shouldn't brood over these sad thoughts. Your poor brother has gone to a better world; we shall always think of him as one who had felt no sorrow, and been guilty of but few faults. He died before he had wasted his fortune and health, as he might have done:—this will always be a consolation.'

It was singular how nearly alike were the platitudes of the daughter and the father. The young man had not injured his name, or character, in the world, and had left his money behind him: and, therefore, his death was less grievous!

Fanny did not answer, but she sat upright on the sofa as he came up to her—and he then sat down beside her.

'Perhaps I'm wrong, Fanny, to speak to you on other subjects so soon after the sad event of which we heard last night; but, on the whole, I think it better to do so. It is good for you to rouse yourself, to exert yourself to think of other things; besides it will be a comfort to you to know that I have already done, what I am sure you strongly wished to have executed at once.'

It was not necessary for the guardian to say anything further to induce his ward to listen. She knew that he was going to speak about Lord Ballindine, and she was all attention.

'I shall not trouble you, Fanny, by speaking to you now, I hope?'

'No;' said Fanny, with her heart palpitating. 'If it's anything I ought to hear, it will be no trouble to me.'

'Why, my dear, I do think you ought to know, without loss of time that Lord Ballindine has been with me this morning.'

Fanny blushed up to her hair—not with shame, but with emotion as to what was coming next.

'I have had a long conversation with him,' continued the earl, 'in the book-room, and I think I have convinced him that it is for your mutual happiness' —he paused, for he couldn't condescend to tell a lie; but in his glib, speechifying manner, he was nearly falling into one—'mutual happiness' was such an appropriate prudential phrase that he could not resist the temptation; but he corrected himself—'at least, I think I have convinced him that it is impossible that he should any longer look upon Miss Wyndham as his future wife.'

Lord Cashel paused for some mark of approbation. Fanny saw that she was expected to speak, and, therefore, asked whether Lord Ballindine was still in the house. She listened tremulously for his answer; for she felt that if her lover were to be rejected, he had a right, after what had passed between them, to expect that she should, in person, express her resolution to him. And yet, if she had to see him now, could she reject him? could she tell him that all the vows that had been made between them were to be as nothing? No! she could only fall on his shoulder, and weep in his arms. But Lord Cashel had managed better than that.

'No, Fanny; neither he nor I, at the present moment, could expect you—could reasonably expect you, to subject yourself to anything so painful as an interview must now have been. Lord Ballindine has left the house—I hope, for the last time—at least, for many months.'

These words fell cold upon Fanny's ears, 'Did he leave any—any message for me?'

'Nothing of any moment; nothing which it can avail to communicate to you: he expressed his grief for your brother's death, and desired I should tell you how grieved he was that you should be so afflicted.'

'Poor Harry!' sobbed Fanny, for it was a relief to cry again, though her tears were more for her lover than her brother. 'Poor Harry! they were very fond of each other. I'm sure he must have been sorry— I'm sure he'd feel it'—and she paused, and sobbed again—'He had heard of Harry's death, then?'

When she said this, she had in her mind none of the dirty suspicion that had actuated Lord Cashel; but he guessed at her feelings by his own, and answered accordingly.

'At first I understood him to say he had; but then, he seemed to wish to express that he had not. My impression, I own, is, that he must have heard of it; the sad news must have reached him.'

Fanny still did not understand the earl. The idea of her lover coming after her money immediately on her obtaining possession of it, never entered her mind; she thought of her wealth as far as it might have affected him, but did not dream of its altering his conduct towards her.

'And did he seem unhappy about it?' she continued. 'I am sure it would make him very unhappy. He could not have loved Harry better if he had been his brother,' and then she blushed again through her tears, as she remembered that she had intended that they should be brothers.

Lord Cashel did not say anything more on this head; he was fully convinced that Lord Ballindine only looked on the young man's death as a windfall which he might turn to his own advantage; but he thought it would be a little too strong to say so outright, just at present.

'It will be a comfort for you to know that this matter is now settled,' continued the earl, 'and that no one can attach the slightest blame to you in the matter. Lord Ballindine has shown himself so very imprudent, so very unfit, in every way, for the honour you once intended him, that no other line of conduct was open to you than that which you have wisely pursued.'

This treading on the fallen was too much for Fanny. 'I have no right either to speak or to think ill of him,' said she, through her tears; 'and if any one is ill-treated in the matter it is he. But did he not ask to see me?'

'Surely, Fanny, you would not, at the present moment, have wished to see him!'

'Oh, no; it is a great relief, under all the circumstances, not having to do so. But was he contented? I should be glad that he were satisfied—that he shouldn't think I had treated him harshly, or rudely. Did he appear as if he wished to see me again?'

'Why, he certainly did ask for a last interview— which, anticipating your wishes, I have refused.'

'But was he satisfied? Did he appear to think that he had been badly treated?'

'Rejected lovers,' answered the earl with a stately smile, 'seldom express much satisfaction with the terms of their rejection; but I cannot say that Lord Ballindine testified any strong emotion.' He rose from the sofa as he said this, and then, intending to clinch the nail, added as he went to the door—'to tell the truth, Fanny, I think Lord Ballindine is much more eager for an alliance with your fair self now, than he was a few days back, when he could never find a moment's time to leave his horses, and his friend Mr. Blake, either to see his intended wife, or to pay Lady Cashel the usual courtesy of a morning visit.' He then opened the door, and, again closing it, added—'I think, however, Fanny, that what has now passed between us will secure you from any further annoyance from him.'

Lord Cashel, in this last speech, had greatly over-shot his mark; his object had been to make the separation between his ward and her lover permanent; and, hitherto, he had successfully appealed to her pride and her judgment. Fanny had felt Lord Cashel to be right, when he told her that she was neglected, and that Frank was dissipated, and in debt. She knew she should be unhappy as the wife of a poor nobleman, and she felt that it would break her proud heart to be jilted herself. She had, therefore, though unwillingly, still entirely agreed with her guardian as to the expediency of breaking off the match; and, had Lord Cashel been judicious, he might have confirmed her in this resolution; but his last thunderbolt, which had been intended to crush Lord Ballindine, had completely recoiled upon himself. Fanny now instantly understood the allusion, and, raising her face, which was again resting on her hands, looked at him with an indignant glance through her tears.

Lord Cashel, however, had left the room without observing the indignation expressed in Fanny's eyes; but she was indignant; she knew Frank well enough to be sure that he had come to Grey Abbey that morning with no such base motives as those ascribed to him. He might have heard of Harry's death, and come there to express his sorrow, and offer that consolation which she felt she could accept from him sooner than from any living creature:—or, he might have been ignorant of it altogether; but that he should come there to press his suit because her brother was dead—immediately after his death—was not only impossible; but the person who could say it was possible, must be false and untrue to her. Her uncle could not have believed it himself: he had basely pretended to believe it, that he might widen the breach which he had made.

Fanny was alone, in the drawing-room—for her cousin had left it as soon as her father began to talk about Lord Ballindine, and she sat there glowering

through her tears for a long time. Had Lord Ballindine been able to know all her thoughts at this
moment, he would have felt little doubt as to the
ultimate success of his suit.

XIII

FATHER AND SON

LORD CASHEL firmly believed, when he left the
room, that he had shown great tact in discovering Frank's mercenary schemes, and in laying them
open before Fanny; and that she had firmly and
finally made up her mind to have nothing more to do
with him. He had not long been re-seated in his
customary chair in the book-room, before he began
to feel a certain degree of horror at the young lord's
baseness, and to think how worthily he had executed
his duty as a guardian, in saving Miss Wyndham
from so sordid a suitor. From thinking of his duties
as a guardian, his mind, not unnaturally, recurred to
those which were incumbent on him as a father, and
here nothing disturbed his serenity. It is true that,
from an appreciation of the lustre which would reflect
back upon himself from allowing his son to become
a decidedly fashionable young man, he had encouraged him in extravagance, dissipation, and heartless worldliness; he had brought him up to be super-
cilious, expensive, unprincipled, and useless. But
then, he was gentlemanlike, dignified, and sought
after; and now, the father reflected, with satisfaction, that, if he could accomplish his well-conceived
scheme, he would pay his son's debts with his ward's
fortune, and, at the same time, tie him down to some
degree of propriety and decorum, by a wife. Lord
Kilcullen, when about to marry, would be obliged to
cashier his opera-dancers and their expensive crews;
and, though he might not leave the turf altogether,
when married he would gradually be drawn out of
turf society, and would doubtless become a good
steady family nobleman, like his father. Why, he—

Lord Cashel himself—wise, prudent, and respectable
as he was—example as he knew himself to be to
all peers, English, Irish, and Scotch,—had had his
horses, and his indiscretions, when he was young.
And then he stroked the calves of his legs, and smiled
grimly; for the memory of his juvenile vices was
pleasant to him.

Lord Cashel thought, as he continued to reflect on
the matter, that Lord Ballindine was certainly a
sordid schemer; but that his son was a young man
of whom he had just reason to be proud, and who was
worthy of a wife in the shape of a hundred thousand
pounds. And then, he congratulated himself on
being the most anxious of guardians and the best of
fathers; and, with these comfortable reflections, the
worthy peer strutted off, through his ample doors,
up his lofty stairs, and away through his long
corridors, to dress for dinner. You might have heard
his boots creaking till he got inside his dressing-room,
but you must have owned that they did so with a
most dignified cadence.

It was pleasant enough, certainly, planning all these
things; but there would be some little trouble in
executing them. In the first place, Lord Kilcullen—
though a very good son, on the whole, as the father
frequently remarked to himself—was a little fond of
having a will of his own, and may-be, might object
to dispense with his dancing-girls. And though there
was, unfortunately, but little doubt that the money
was indispensably necessary to him, it was just
possible that he might insist on having the cash without his cousin. However, the proposal must be made,
and, as the operations necessary to perfect the marriage would cause some delay, and the money would
certainly be wanted as soon as possible, no time was
to be lost. Lord Kilcullen was, accordingly, summoned to Grey Abbey; and, as he presumed his
attendance was required for the purpose of talking
over some method of raising the wind, he obeyed the
summons.—I should rather have said of raising a

storm, for no gentle puff would serve to waft him through his present necessities.

Down he came, to the great delight of his mother, who thought him by far the finest young man of the day, though he usually slighted, snubbed, and ridiculed her—and of his sister, who always hailed with dignified joy the return of the eldest scion of her proud family to the ancestral roof. The earl was also glad to find that no previous engagement detained him; that is, that he so far sacrificed his own comfort as to leave Tattersall's and the *Figuranti* of the Opera-House, to come all the way to Grey Abbey, in the county of Kildare. But, though the earl was glad to see his son, he was still a little consternated: the business interview could not be postponed, as it was not to be supposed that Lord Kilcullen would stay long at Grey Abbey during the London season; and the father had yet hardly sufficiently crammed himself for the occasion. Besides, the pressure from without must have been very strong to have produced so immediate a compliance with a behest not uttered in a very peremptory manner, or, generally speaking, to a very obedient child.

On the morning after his arrival, the earl was a little uneasy in his chair during breakfast. It was rather a sombre meal, for Fanny had by no means recovered her spirits, nor did she appear to be in the way to do so. The countess tried to chat a little to her son, but he hardly answered her; and Lady Selina, though she was often profound, was never amusing. Lord Cashel made sundry attempts at general conversation, but as often failed. It was, at last, however, over; and the father requested the son to come with him into the book-room.

When the fire was poked, and the chairs were drawn together over the rug, there were no further preliminaries which could be decently introduced, and the earl was therefore forced to commence.

'Well, Kilcullen, I'm glad you're come to Grey Abbey. I'm afraid, however, we shan't induce you to stay with us long, so it's as well perhaps to settle our business at once. You would, however, greatly oblige your mother, and I'm sure I need not add, myself, if you could make your arrangements so as to stay with us till after Easter. We could then return together.'

'Till after Easter, my lord! I should be in the Hue and Cry before that time, if I was so long absent from my accustomed haunts. Besides I should only put out your own arrangements, or rather, those of Lady Cashel. There would probably be no room for me in the family coach.'

'The family coach won't go, Lord Kilcullen. I am sorry to say, that the state of my affairs at present renders it advisable that the family should remain at Grey Abbey this season. I shall attend my parliamentary duties alone.'

This was intended as a hit the first at the prodigal son, but Kilcullen was too crafty to allow it to tell. He merely bowed his head, and opened his eyes, to betoken his surprise at such a decision, and remained quiet.

'Indeed,' continued Lord Cashel, 'I did not even intend to have gone myself, but the unexpected death of Harry Wyndham renders it necessary. I must put Fanny's affairs in a right train. Poor Harry!—did you see much of him during his illness?'

'Why, no—I can't say I did. I'm not a very good hand at doctoring or nursing. I saw him once since he got his commission, glittering with his gold lace like a new weather-cock on a Town Hall. He hadn't time to polish the shine off.'

'His death will make a great difference, as far as Fanny is concerned—eh?'

'Indeed it will: her fortune now is considerable;— a deuced pretty thing, remembering that it's all ready money, and that she can touch it the moment she's of age. She's entirely off with Ballindine, isn't she?'

'Oh, entirely,' said the earl, with considerable self-complacency; 'that affair is entirely over.'

'I've stated so everywhere publicly; but I dare say, she'll give him her money, nevertheless. She's not the girl to give over a man, if she's really fond of him.'

'But, my dear Kilcullen, she has authorised me to give him a final answer, and I have done so. After that, you know, it would be quite impossible for her to—to—'

'You'll see—she'll marry Lord Ballindine. Had Harry lived, it might have been different; but now she's got all her brother's money, she'll think it a point of honour to marry her poor lover. Besides, her staying this year in the country will be in his favour: she'll see no one here—and she'll want something to think of. I understand he has altogether thrown himself into Blake's hands—the keenest fellow in Ireland, with as much mercy as a foxhound. He's a positive fool, is Ballindine.'

'I'm afraid he is—I'm afraid he is. And you may be sure I'm too fond of Fanny—that is, I have too much regard for the trust reposed in me, to allow her to throw herself away upon him.'

'That's all very well; but what can you do?'

'Why, not allow him to see her; and I've another plan in my head for her.'

'Ah!—but the thing is to put the plan into *her* head. I'd be sorry to hear of a fine girl like Fanny Wyndham breaking her heart in a half-ruined barrack in Connaught, without money to pay a schoolmaster to teach her children to spell. But I've too many troubles of my own to think of just at present, to care much about hers;' and the son and heir got up, and stood with his back to the fire, and put his arms under his coat-laps. 'Upon my soul, my lord, I never was so hard up in my life!'

Lord Cashel now prepared himself for action. The first shot was fired, and he must go on with the battle.

'So I hear, Kilcullen; and yet, during the last four years, you've had nearly double your allowance; and, before that, I paid every farthing you owed. Within the last five years, you've had nearly forty thousand pounds! Supposing you'd had younger brothers, Lord Kilcullen—supposing that I had had six or eight sons instead of only one; what would you have done? How then would you have paid your debts?'

'Fate having exempted me and your lordship from so severe a curse, I have never turned my mind to reflect what I might have done under such an infliction.'

'Or, supposing I had chosen, myself, to indulge in those expensive habits, which would have absorbed my income, and left me unable to do more for you, than many other noblemen in my position do for their sons—do you ever reflect how impossible it would then have been for me to have helped you out of your difficulties?'

'I feel as truly grateful for your self-denial in this respect, as I do in that of my non-begotten brethren.'

Lord Cashel saw that he was laughed at, and he looked angry; but he did not want to quarrel with his son, so he continued:

'Jervis writes me word that it is absolutely necessary that thirty thousand pounds should be paid for you at once; or, that your remaining in London—or, in fact, in the country at all, is quite out of the question.'

'Indeed, my lord, I'm afraid Jervis is right.'

'Thirty thousand pounds! Are you aware what your income is?'

'Why, hardly. I know Jervis takes care that I never see much of it.'

'Do you mean that you don't receive it?'

'Oh! I do not at all doubt its accurate payment. I mean to say, that I don't often have the satisfaction of seeing much of it at the right side of my banker's book.'

'Thirty thousand pounds! And will that sum set you completely free in the world?'

'I am sorry to say it will not—nor nearly.'

'Then, Lord Kilcullen,' said the earl, with most

severe, but still most courteous dignity, 'may I
trouble you to be good enough to tell me what, at
the present moment, you do owe?'

'I'm afraid I could not do so with any accuracy;
but it is more than double the sum you have named.'

'Do you mean, that you have no schedule of your
debts?—no means of acquainting me with the
amount? How can you expect that I can assist you,
when you think it too much trouble to make yourself thoroughly acquainted with the state of your
own affairs?'

'A list could certainly be made out, if I had any
prospect of being able to settle the amount. If your
lordship can undertake to do so at once, I will undertake to hand you a correct list of the sums due, before
I leave Grey Abbey. I presume you would not require to know exactly to whom all the items were
owing.'

This effrontery was too much, and Lord Cashel
was very near to losing his temper.

'Upon my honour, Kilcullen, you're cool, very
cool. You come upon me to pay, Heaven knows how
many thousands—more money, I know, than I'm
able to raise; and you condescendingly tell me that
you will trouble yourself so far as to let me know
how much money I am to give you—but that I am
not to know what is done with it! No; if I am to pay
your debts again, I will do it through Jervis.'

'Pray remember,' replied Lord Kilcullen, not at
all disturbed from his equanimity, 'that I have not
proposed that you should pay my debts without
knowing where the money went; and also that I
have not yet asked you to pay them at all.'

'Who, then, do you expect will pay them? I can
assure you I should be glad to be relieved from the
honour.'

'I merely said that I had not yet made any proposition respecting them. Of course, I expect your
assistance. Failing you, I have no resource but the
Jews. I should regret to put the property into their

hands; especially as, hitherto, I have not raised money on post obits.'

'At any rate, I'm glad of that,' said the father, willing to admit any excuse for returning to his good humour. 'That would be ruin; and I hope that anything short of that may be—may be—may be done something with.'

The expression was not dignified, and it pained the earl to make it; but it was expressive, and he didn't wish at once to say that he had a proposal for paying off his son's debts. 'But now, Kilcullen, tell me fairly, in round figures, what do you think you owe?—as near as you can guess, without going to pen and paper, you know?'

'Well, my lord, if you will allow me, I will make a proposition to you. If you will hand over to Mr. Jervis fifty thousand pounds, for him to pay such claims as have already been made upon him as your agent, and such other debts as I may have sent in to him: and if you will give myself thirty thousand, to pay such debts as I do not choose to have paid by an agent, I will undertake to have everything settled.'

'Eighty thousand pounds in four years! Why, Kilcullen, what have you done with it?—where has it gone? You have five thousand a-year, no house to keep up, no property to support, no tenants to satisfy, no rates to pay—five thousand a-year for your own personal expenses—and, in four years, you have got eighty thousand in debt! The property never can stand that, you know. It never can stand at that rate. Why, Kilcullen, what have you done with it?'

'Mr. Crockford has a portion of it, and John Scott has some of it. A great deal of it is scattered rather widely—so widely that it would be difficult now to trace it. But, my lord, it has gone. I won't deny that the greater portion of it has been lost at play, or on the turf. I trust I may, in future, be more fortunate and more cautious.'

'I trust so. I trust so, indeed. Eighty thousand pounds! And do you think I can raise such a sum as that at a week's warning?'

'Indeed, I have no doubt as to your being able to do so: it may be another question whether you are willing.'

'I am not—I am not able,' said the libelled father. 'As you know well enough, the incumbrances on the property take more than a quarter of my income.'

'There can, nevertheless, be no doubt of your being able to have the money, and that at once, if you chose to go into the market for it. I have no doubt but that Mr. Jervis could get it for you at once at five per cent.'

'Four thousand a-year gone for ever from the property!—and what security am I to have that the same sacrifice will not be again incurred, after another lapse of four years?'

'You can have no security, my lord, against my being in debt. You can, however, have every security that you will not again pay my debts, in your own resolution. I trust, however, that I have some experience to prevent my again falling into so disagreeable a predicament. I think I have heard your lordship say that you incurred some unnecessary expenses yourself in London, before your marriage!'

'I wish, Kilcullen, that you had never exceeded your income more than I did mine. But it is no use talking any further on this subject. I cannot, and I will not—I cannot in justice either to myself or to you, borrow this money for you; nor, if I could, should I think it right to do so.'

'Then what the devil's the use of talking about it so long?' said the dutiful son, hastily jumping up from the chair in which he had again sat down. 'Did you bring me down to Grey Abbey merely to tell me that you knew of my difficulties, and that you could do nothing to assist me?'

'Now, don't put yourself into a passion—pray don't!' said the father, a little frightened by the sudden ebullition. 'If you'll sit down, and listen to me, I'll tell you what I propose. I did not send for you here without intending to point out to you some method of extricating yourself from your present pecuniary embarrassment; and, if you have any wish to give up your course, of—I must say, reckless profusion, and commence that upright and distinguished career, which I still hope to see you take, you will, I think, own that my plan is both a safer and a more expedient one than that which you have proposed. It is quite time for you now to abandon the expensive follies of youth; and,' Lord Cashel was getting into a delightfully dignified tone, and felt himself prepared for a good burst of common-place eloquence; but his son looked impatient, and as he could not take such liberty with him as he could with Lord Ballindine, he came to the point at once, and ended abruptly by saying, 'and get married.'

'For the purpose of allowing my wife to pay my debts?'

'Why, not exactly that; but as, of course, you could not marry any woman but a woman with a large fortune, that would follow as a matter of consequence.'

'Your lordship proposes the fortune not as the first object of my affection, but merely as a corollary. But, perhaps, it will be as well that you should finish your proposition, before I make any remarks on the subject.' And Lord Kilcullen, sat down, with a well-feigned look of listless indifference.

'Well, Kilcullen, I have latterly been thinking much about you, and so has your poor mother. She is very uneasy that you should still—still be unmarried; and Jervis has written to me very strongly. You see it is quite necessary that something should be done—or we shall both be ruined. Now, if I did raise this sum—and I really could not do it—I don't think I could manage it, just at present; but, even if I did, it would only be encouraging you to go on just in the same way again. Now, if you were to

marry, your whole course of life would be altered, and
you would become, at the same time, more respectable and more happy.'

'That would depend a good deal upon circumstances, I should think.'

'Oh! I am sure you would. You are just the same
sort of fellow I was when at your age, and I was much
happier after I was married, so I know it. Now, you
see, your cousin has a hundred thousand pounds; in
fact something more than that.'

'What?—Fanny! Poor Ballindine! So that's the
way with him is it! When I was contradicting the
rumour of his marriage with Fanny, I little thought
that I was to be his rival! At any rate, I shall have
to shoot him first.'

'You might, at any rate, confine yourself to sense,
Lord Kilcullen, when I am taking so much pains to
talk sensibly to you, on a subject which, I presume,
cannot but interest you.'

'Indeed, my lord, I'm all attention; and I do
intend to talk sensibly when I say that I think you
are proposing to treat Ballindine very ill. The world
will think well of your turning him adrift on the
score of the match being an imprudent one; but it
won't speak so leniently of you if you expel him, as
soon as your ward becomes an heiress, to make way
for your own son.'

'You know that I'm not thinking of doing so. I've
long seen that Lord Ballindine would not make a
fitting husband for Fanny—long before Harry died.'

'And you think that I shall?'

'Indeed I do. I think she will be lucky to get you.'

'I'm flattered into silence: pray go on.'

'You will be an earl a peer—and a man of
property. What would she become if she married
Lord Ballindine?'

'Oh, you are quite right! Go on. I wonder it never
occurred to her before to set her cap at me.'

'Now do be serious. I wonder how you can joke
on such a subject, with all your debts. I'm sure I

feel them heavy enough, if you don't. You see Lord
Ballindine was refused—I may say he was refused—
before we heard about that poor boy's unfortunate
death. It was the very morning we heard of it, three
or four hours before the messenger came, that Fanny
had expressed her resolution to declare it off, and
commissioned me to tell him so. And, therefore,
of course, the two things can't have the remotest
reference to each other.'

'I see. There are, or have been, two Fanny
Wyndhams—separate persons, though both wards
of your lordship. Lord Ballindine was engaged to the
girl who had a brother; but he can have no possible
concern with Fanny Wyndham, the heiress, who has
no brother.'

'How can you be so unfeeling?—but you may pay
your debts in your own way. You won't ever listen
to what I have to say! I should have thought that,
as your father, I might have considered myself entitled to more respect from you.'

'Indeed, my lord, I'm all respect and attention,
and I won't say one more word till you've finished.'

'Well—you must see, there can be no objection on
the score of Lord Ballindine?'

'Oh, none at all.'

'And then, where could Fanny wish for a better
match than yourself? It would be a great thing for
her, and the match would be, in all things, so—so
respectable, and just what it ought to be; and your
mother would be so delighted, and so should I, and—'

'Her fortune would so nicely pay all my debts.'

'Exactly. Of course, I should take care to have
your present income—five thousand a year—settled
on her, in the shape of jointure; and I'm sure that
would be treating her handsomely. The interest of
her fortune would not be more than that.'

'And what should we live on?'

'Why, of course, I should continue your present
allowance.'

'And you think that that which I have found so

insufficient for myself, would be enough for both of us?'

'You must make it enough, Kilcullen—in order that there may be something left to enable you to keep up your title when I am gone.'

By this time, Lord Kilcullen appeared to be as serious, and nearly as solemn, as his father, and he sat, for a considerable time, musing, till his father said, 'Well, Kilcullen, will you take my advice?'

'It's impracticable, my lord. In the first place, the money must be paid immediately, and considerable delay must occur before I could even offer to Miss Wyndham; and, in the next place, were I to do so, I am sure she would refuse me.'

'Why; there must be some delay, of course. But I suppose, if I passed my word, through Jervis, for so much of the debts as are immediate, that a settlement might be made whereby they might stand over for twelve months, with interest, of course. As to refusing you, it's not at all likely: where would she look for a better offer?'

'I don't know much of my cousin; but I don't think she's exactly the girl to take a man because he's a good match for her.'

'Perhaps not. But then, you know, you understand women so well, and would have such opportunities; you would be sure to make yourself agreeable to her, with very little effort on your part.'

'Yes, poor thing—she would be delivered over, ready bound, into the lion's den.' And then the young man sat silent again, for some time, turning the matter over in his mind. At last, he said,—

'Well, my lord; I am a considerate and a dutiful son, and I will agree to your proposition: but I must saddle it with conditions. I have no doubt that the sum which I suggested should be paid through your agent, could be arranged to be paid in a year, or eighteen months, by your making yourself responsible for it, and I would undertake to indemnify you. But the thirty thousand pounds I must have at once. I

must return to London, with the power of raising it
there, without delay. This, also, I would repay you
out of Fanny's fortune. I would then undertake to use
my best endeavours to effect a union with your ward.
But I must positively will not agree to this—nor have
any hand in the matter, unless I am put in immediate
possession of the sum I have named, and unless you will
agree to double my income as soon as I am married.'

To both these propositions the earl, at first, refused
to accede; but his son was firm. Then, Lord Cashel
agreed to put him in immediate possession of the
sum of money he required, but would not hear of
increasing his income. They argued, discussed, and
quarrelled over the matter, for a long time; till, at
last, the anxious father, in his passion, told his son
that he might go his own way, and that he would
take no further trouble to help so unconscionable a
child. Lord Kilcullen rejoined by threatening immediately to throw the whole of the property, which
was entailed on himself, into the hands of the Jews.

Long they argued and bargained, till each was
surprised at the obstinacy of the other. They ended,
however, by splitting the difference, and it was
agreed, that Lord Cashel was at once to hand over
thirty thousand pounds, and to take his son's bond
for the amount; that the other debts were to stand
over till Fanny's money was forthcoming; and that
the income of the newly married pair was to be seven
thousand five hundred a-year.

'At least,' thought Lord Kilcullen to himself, as he
good-humouredly shook hands with his father, at the
termination of the interview—'I have not done so
badly, for those infernal dogs will be silenced, and I
shall get the money. I could not have gone back
without that. I can go on with the marriage, or not,
as I may choose, hereafter. It won't be a bad
speculation, however.'

To do Lord Cashel justice, he did not intend cheat-
ing his son, not did he suspect his son of an intention
to cheat him. But the generation was deteriorating.

XIV

THE COUNTESS

IT was delightful to see on what good terms the earl and his son met that evening at dinner. The latter even went so far as to be decently civil to his mother, and was quite attentive to Fanny. She, however, did not seem to appreciate the compliment. It was now a fortnight since she had heard of her brother's death, and during the whole of that time she had been silent, unhappy, and fretful. Not a word more had been said to her about Lord Ballindine, nor had she, as yet, spoken about him to any one; but she had been thinking about little else, and had ascertained,—at least, so she thought,—that she could never be happy, unless she were reconciled to him.

The more she brooded over the subject, the more she felt convinced that such was the case; she could not think how she had ever been induced to sanction, by her name, such an unwarrantable proceeding as the unceremonious dismissal of a man to whom her troth had been plighted, merely because he had not called to see her. As for his not writing, she was aware that Lord Cashel had recommended that, till she was of age, they should not correspond. As she thought the matter over in her own room, long hour after hour, she became angry with herself for having been talked into a feeling of anger for him. What right had she to be angry because he kept horses? She could not expect him to put himself into Lord Cashel's leading-strings. Indeed, she thought she would have liked him less if he had done so. And now, to reject him just when circumstances put it in her power to enable her to free him from his embarrassments, and live a manner becoming his station! What must Frank think of her?—For he could not but suppose that her rejection had been caused by her unexpected inheritance.

In the course of the fortnight, she made up her mind that all Lord Cashel had said to Lord Ballindine should be unsaid;—but who was to do it? It would be a most unpleasant task to perform ; and one which, she was aware, her guardian would be most unwilling to undertake. She fully resolved that she would do it herself, if she could find no fitting ambassador to undertake the task, though that would be a step to which she would fain not be driven. At one time, she absolutely thought of asking her cousin, Kilcullen, about it:—this was just before his leaving Grey Abbey; he seemed so much more civil and kind than usual. But then, she knew so little of him, and so little liked what she did know: that scheme, therefore, was given up. Lady Selina was so cold, and prudent—would talk to her so much about propriety, self-respect, and self-control, that she could not make a confidante of her. No one could talk to Selina on any subject more immediately interesting than a Roman Emperor, or a pattern for worsted-work. Fanny felt that she would not be equal, herself, to going boldly to Lord Cashel, and desiring him to inform Lord Ballindine that he had been mistaken in the view he had taken of his ward's wishes: no— that was impossible ; such a proceeding would probably bring on a fit of apoplexy.

There was no one else to whom she could apply, but her aunt. Lady Cashel was a very good-natured old woman, who slept the greatest portion of her time, and knitted through the rest of her existence. She did not take a prominent part in any of the important doings of Grey Abbey; and, though Lord Cashel constantly referred to her, for he thought it respectable to do so, no one regarded her much. Fanny felt, however, that she would neither scold her, ridicule her, nor refuse to listen: to Lady Cashel, therefore, at last, she went for assistance.

Her ladyship always passed the morning, after breakfast, in a room adjoining her own bed-room, in which she daily held deep debate with Griffiths, her factotum, respecting household affairs, knitting-needles, and her own little ailments and cossetings. Griffiths, luckily, was a woman of much the same tastes as her ladyship, only somewhat of a more active temperament; and they were most stedfast friends. It was such a comfort to Lady Cashel to have some one to whom she could twaddle!

The morning after Lord Kilcullen's departure Fanny knocked at her door, and was asked to come in. The countess, as usual, was in her easy chair, with the knitting-apparatus in her lap, and Griffiths was seated at the table, pulling about threads, and keeping her ladyship awake by small talk.

'I'm afraid I'm disturbing you, aunt,' said Fanny, 'but I wanted to speak to you for a minute or two. Good morning, Mrs. Griffiths.'

'Oh, no! you won't disturb me, Fanny. I was a little busy this morning, for I wanted to finish this side of the—You see what a deal I've done,'—and the countess lugged up a whole heap of miscellaneous worsted from a basket just under her arm—'and I must finish it by lady-day, or I shan't get the other done, I don't know when. But still, I've plenty of time to attend to you.'

'Then I'll go down, my lady, and see about getting the syrup boiled,' said Griffiths. 'Good morning, Miss Wyndham.'

'Do; but mind you come up again immediately— I'll ring the bell when Miss Wyndham is going; and pray don't leave me alone, now.'

'No, my lady—not a moment,' and Griffiths escaped to the syrup.

Fanny's heart beat quick and hard, as she sat down on the sofa, opposite to her aunt. It was impossible for any one to be afraid of Lady Cashel, there was so very little about her that could inspire awe; but then, what she had to say was so very disagreeable to say! If she had had to tell her tale out loud, merely to the empty easy chair, it would have been a dreadful undertaking.

'Well, Fanny, what can I do for you? I'm sure you look very nice in your bombazine; and it's very nicely made up. Who was it made it for you?'

'I got it down from Dublin, aunt; from Foley's.'

'Oh, I remember; so you told me. Griffiths has a niece makes those things up very well; but then she lives at Namptwich, and one couldn't send to England for it. I had such a quantity of mourning by me, I didn't get any made up new; else, I think I must have sent for her.'

'My dear aunt, I am very unhappy about something, and I want you to help me. I'm afraid, though, it will give you a great deal of trouble.'

'Good gracious, Fanny!—what is it? Is it about poor Harry? I'm sure I grieved about him more than I can tell.'

'No, aunt: he's gone now, and time is the only cure for that grief. I know I must bear that without complaining. But, aunt, I feel—I think, that is, that I've used Lord Ballindine very ill.'

'Good gracious me, my love! I thought Lord Cashel had managed all that—I thought that was all settled. You know, he would keep those horrid horses, and all that kind of thing; and what more could you do than just let Lord Cashel settle it?'

'Yes, but aunt—you see, I had engaged myself to Lord Ballindine, and I don't think—in fact—oh, aunt! I did not wish to break my word to Lord Ballindine, and I am very very sorry for what has been done,' and Fanny was again in tears.

'But, my dear Fanny,' said the countess, so far excited as to commence rising from her seat—the attempt, however, was abandoned, when she felt the ill effects of the labour to which she was exposing herself—'but, my dear Fanny—what would you have? It's done, now, you know; and, really, it's for the best.'

'Oh, but, dear aunt, I must get somebody to see him. I've been thinking about it ever since he was here with my uncle. I wouldn't let him think that

I broke it all off, merely because—because of poor Harry's money,' and Fanny sobbed away dreadfully.

'But you don't want to marry him!' said the naïve countess.

Now, Fanny did want to marry him, though she hardly liked saying so, even to Lady Cashel.

'You know, I promised him I would,' said she; 'and what will he think of me?—what must he think of me, to throw him off so cruelly, so harshly, after all that's past?—Oh, aunt! I must see him again.'

'I know something of human nature,' replied the aunt, 'and if you do, I tell you, it will end in your being engaged to him again. You know it's off now. Come, my dear; don't think so much about it: I'm sure Lord Cashel wouldn't do anything cruel or harsh.'

'Oh, I must see him again, whatever comes of it;' and then she paused for a considerable time, during which the bewildered old lady was thinking what she could do to relieve her sensitive niece. 'Dear, dear aunt, I don't want to deceive you!' and Fanny, springing up, knelt at her aunt's feet, and looked up into her face. 'I do love him—I always loved him, and I cannot, cannot quarrel with him.' And then she burst out crying vehemently, hiding her face in the countess's lap.

Lady Cashel was quite overwhelmed. Fanny was usually so much more collected than herself, that her present prostration, both of feeling and body, was dreadful to see. Suppose she was to go into hysterics —there they would be alone, and Lady Cashel felt that she had not strength to ring the bell.

'But, my dear Fanny! oh dear, oh dear, this is very dreadful!—but, Fanny—he's gone away now. Lift up your face, Fanny, for you frighten me. Well, I'm sure I'll do anything for you. Perhaps he wouldn't mind coming back again,—he always was very good-natured. I'm sure I always liked Lord Ballindine very much,—only he would have all those horses. But I'm sure, if you wish it, I should be very glad to see him marry you; only, you know, you must wait

some time, because of poor Harry; and I'm sure I
don't know how you'll manage with Lord Cashel.'

'Dear aunt—I want you to speak to Lord Cashel.
When I was angry because I thought Frank didn't
come here as he might have done, I consented that
my uncle should break off the match: besides, then,
you know, we should have had so little between us.
But I didn't know then how well I loved him. Indeed, indeed, aunt, I cannot bring my heart to
quarrel with him; and I am quite, *quite* sure he would
never wish to quarrel with me. Will you go to my
uncle—tell him that I've changed my mind; tell him
that I was a foolish girl, and did not know my mind.
But tell him I *must* be friends with Frank again.'

'Well, of course I'll do what you wish me,—indeed,
I would do anything for you, Fanny, as if you were
one of my own; but really, I don't know—Good
gracious! What am I to say to him? Wouldn't
it be better, Fanny, if you were to go to him
yourself?'

'Oh, no, aunt; pray do you tell him first. I
couldn't go to him; besides, he would do anything
for you, you know. I want you to go to him—do,
now, dear aunt—and tell him—not from me, but
from yourself—how very, very much I—that is, how
very very—but you will know what to say; only
Frank must, *must* come back again.'

'Well, Fanny, dear, I'll go to Lord Cashel; or,
perhaps, he wouldn't mind coming here. Ring the
bell for me, dear. But I'm sure he'll be very angry.
I'd just write a line and ask Lord Ballindine to come
and dine here, and let him settle it all himself, only
I don't think Lord Cashel would like it.'

Griffiths answered the summons, and was despatched to the book-room to tell his lordship that her
ladyship would be greatly obliged if he would step
up-stairs to her for a minute or two; and, as soon as
Griffiths was gone on her errand, Fanny fled to her
own apartment, leaving her aunt in a very bewildered
and pitiable state of mind: and there she waited, with

palpitating heart and weeping eyes, the effects of the interview.

She was dreadfully nervous, for she felt certain that she would be summoned before her uncle. Hitherto, she alone, in all the house, had held him in no kind of awe; indeed, her respect for her uncle had not been of the most exalted kind; but now she felt she was afraid of him.

She remained in her room much longer than she thought it would have taken her aunt to explain what she had to say. At last, however, she heard footsteps in the corridor, and Griffiths knocked at the door. Her aunt would be obliged by her stepping into her room. She tried not to look disconcerted, and asked if Lord Cashel were still there. She was told that he was; and she felt that she had to muster up all her courage to encounter him.

When she went into the room, Lady Cashel was still in her easy-chair, but the chair seemed to lend none of its easiness to its owner. She was sitting upright, with her hands on her two knees, and she looked perplexed, distressed, and unhappy. Lord Cashel was standing with his back to the fire-place, and Fanny had never seen his face look so black. He really seemed, for the time, to have given over acting, to have thrown aside his dignity, and to be natural and in earnest.

Lady Cashel began the conversation.

'Oh, Fanny,' she said, 'you must really overcome all this sensitiveness; you really must. I've spoken to your uncle, and it's quite impossible, and very unwise; and, indeed, it can't be done at all. In fact, Lord Ballindine isn't, by any means, the sort of person I supposed.'

Fanny knit her brows a little at this, and felt somewhat less humble than she did before. She knew she should get indignant if her uncle abused her lover, and that, if she did, her courage would rise in proportion. Her aunt continued—

'Your uncle's very kind about it, and says he

can, of course, forgive your feeling a little out of sorts just at present; and, I'm sure, so can I, and I'm sure I'd do anything to make you happy; but as for making it all up with Lord Ballindine again, indeed it cannot be thought of, Fanny; and so your uncle will tell you.'

And then Lord Cashel opened his oracular mouth, for the purpose of doing so.

'Really, Fanny, this is the most unaccountable thing I ever heard of. But you'd better sit down, while I speak to you,' and Fanny sat down on the sofa. 'I think I understood you rightly, when you desired me, less than a month ago, to inform Lord Ballindine that circumstances—that is, his own conduct—obliged you to decline the honour of his alliance. Did you not do so spontaneously, and of your own accord?'

'Certainly, uncle, I agreed to take your advice; though I did so most unwillingly.'

'Had I not your authority for desiring him—I won't say to discontinue his visits, for that he had long done—but to give up his pretensions to your hand? Did you not authorise me to do so?'

'I believe I did. But, uncle—'

'And I have done as you desired me; and now, Fanny, that I have done so—now that I have fully explained to him what you taught me to believe were your wishes on the subject, will you tell me—for I really think your aunt must have misunderstood you —what it is that you wish me to do?'

'Why, uncle, you pointed out—and it was very true then, that my fortune was not sufficient to enable Lord Ballindine to keep up his rank. It is different now, and I am very, very sorry that it is so; but it is different now, and I feel that I ought not to reject Lord Ballindine, because I am so much richer than I was when he—when he proposed to me.'

'Then it's merely a matter of feeling with you, and not of affection? If I understand you, you are afraid that you should be thought to have treated Lord Ballindine badly?'

'It's not only that—' And then she paused for a few moments, and added, 'I thought I could have parted with him, when you made me believe that I ought to do so, but I find I cannot.'

'You mean that you love him?' and the earl looked very black at his niece. He intended to frighten her out of her resolution, but she quietly answered,

'Yes, uncle, I do.'

'And you want me to tell him so, after having banished him from my house?'

Fanny's eyes again shot fire at the word 'banished', but she answered, very quietly, and even with a smile,

'No, uncle; but I want you to ask him here again. I might tell him the rest myself.'

'But, Fanny, dear,' said the countess, 'your uncle couldn't do it: you know, he told him to go away before. Besides, I really don't think he'd come; he's so taken up with those horrid horses, and that Mr. Blake, who is worse than any of 'em. Really, Fanny, Kilcullen says that he and Mr. Blake are quite notorious.'

'I think, aunt, Lord Kilcullen might be satisfied with looking after himself. If it depended on him, he never had a kind word to say for Lord Ballindine.'

'But you know, Fanny,' continued the aunt, 'he knows everybody; and if he says Lord Ballindine is that sort of person, why, it must be so, though I'm sure I'm very sorry to hear it.'

Lord Cashel saw that he could not trust any more to his wife: that last hit about Kilcullen had been very unfortunate; so he determined to put an end to all Fanny's yearnings after her lover with a strong hand, and said,

'If you mean, Fanny, after what has passed, that I should go to Lord Ballindine, and give him to understand that he is again welcome to Grey Abbey, I must at once tell you that it is absolutely—abso-

lutely impossible. If I had no personal objection to
the young man on any prudential score, the very fact
of my having already, at your request, desired his
absence from my house, would be sufficient to render
it impossible. I owe too much to my own dignity,
and am too anxious for your reputation, to think of
doing such a thing. But when I also remember that
Lord Ballindine is a reckless, dissipated gambler—
I much fear, with no fixed principle, I should consider
any step towards renewing the acquaintance between
you a most wicked and unpardonable proceeding.'

When Fanny heard her lover designated as a reckless gambler, she lost all remaining feelings of fear at
her uncle's anger, and, standing up, looked him full
in the face through her tears.

'It's not so, my lord!' she said, when he had
finished. 'He is not what you have said. I know him
too well to believe such things of him, and I will not
submit to hear him abused.'

'Oh, Fanny, my dear!' said the frightened countess; 'don't speak in that way. Surely, your uncle
means to act for your own happiness; and don't you
know Lord Ballindine has those horrid horses?'

'If I don't mind his horses, aunt, no one else need;
but he's no gambler, and he's not dissipated—I'm
sure not half so much so as Lord Kilcullen.'

'In that, Fanny, you're mistaken,' said the earl;
'but I don't wish to discuss the matter with you.
You must, however, fully understand this: Lord
Ballindine cannot be received under this roof. If
you regret him, you must remember that his rejection was your own act. I think you then acted most
prudently, and I trust it will not be long before you
are of the same opinion yourself,' and Lord Cashel
moved to the door as though he had accomplished
his part in the interview.

'Stop one moment, uncle,' said Fanny, striving
hard to be calm, and hardly succeeding. 'I did not
ask my aunt to speak to you on this subject, till I
had turned it over and over in my mind, and resolved

that I would not make myself and another miserable for ever, because I had been foolish enough not to know my mind. You best know whether you can ask Lord Ballindine to Grey Abbey or not; but I am determined, if I cannot see him here, that I will see him somewhere else,' and she turned towards the door, and then, thinking of her aunt, she turned back and kissed her, and immediately left the room.

The countess looked up at her husband, quite dumbfounded, and he seemed rather distressed himself. However, he muttered something about her being a hot-headed simpleton and soon thinking better about it, and then betook himself to his private retreat, to hold sweet converse with his own thoughts—having first rung the bell for Griffiths, to pick up the scattered threads of her mistress's knitting.

Lord Cashel certainly did not like the look of things. There was a determination in Fanny's eye, as she made her parting speech, which upset him rather, and which threw considerable difficulties in the way of Lord Kilcullen's wooing. To be sure, time would do a great deal: but then, there wasn't so much time to spare. He had already taken steps to borrow the thirty thousand pounds, and had, indeed, empowered his son to receive it: he had also pledged himself for the other fifty; and then, after all, that perverse fool of a girl would insist on being in love with that scapegrace, Lord Ballindine! This, however, might wear away, and he would take very good care that she should hear of his misdoings. It would be very odd if, after all, his plans were to be destroyed, and his arrangements disconcerted by his own ward, and niece—especially when he designed so great a match for her!

He could not, however, make himself quite omfortable, though he had great confidence in his own diplomatic resources.

XV

HANDICAP LODGE

LORD BALLINDINE left Grey Abbey, and rode homewards, towards Handicap Lodge, in a melancholy and speculative mood. His first thoughts were all of Harry Wyndham. Frank, as the accepted suitor of his sister, had known him well and intimately, and had liked him much; and the poor young fellow had been much attached to him. He was greatly shocked to hear of his death. It was not yet a month since he had seen him shining in all the new-blown splendour of his cavalry regimentals, and Lord Ballindine was unfeignedly grieved to think how short a time the lad had lived to enjoy them. His thoughts, then, naturally turned to his own position, and the declaration which Lord Cashel had made to him respecting himself. Could it be absolutely true that Fanny had determined to give him up altogether?—After all her willing vows, and assurances of unalterable affection, could she be so cold as to content herself with sending him a formal message, by her uncle, that she did not wish to see him again? Frank argued with himself that it was impossible; he was sure he knew her too well. But still, Lord Cashel would hardly tell him a downright lie, and he had distinctly stated that the rejection came from Miss Wyndham herself.

Then, he began to feel indignant, and spurred his horse, and rode a little faster, and made a few resolutions as to upholding his own dignity. He would run after neither Lord Cashel nor his niece; he would not even ask her to change her mind, since she had been able to bring herself to such a determination as that expressed to him. But he would insist on seeing her; she could not refuse that to him, after what had passed between them, and he would then tell her what he thought of her, and leave her for ever. But no; he would do nothing to vex her, as long as she was grieving for her brother. Poor Harry!—she loved him so dearly! Perhaps, after all, his sudden rejection was, in some manner, occasioned by this sad event, and would be revoked as her sorrow grew less with time. And then, for the first time, the idea shot across his mind, of the wealth Fanny must inherit by her brother's death.

It certainly had a considerable effect on him, for he breathed slow awhile, and was some little time before he could entirely realise the conception that Fanny was now the undoubted owner of a large fortune. 'That is it,' thought he to himself, at last; 'that sordid earl considers that he can now be sure of a higher match for his niece, and Fanny has allowed herself to be persuaded out of her engagement: she has allowed herself to be talked into the belief that it was her duty to give up a poor man like me.' And then, he felt very angry again. 'Heavens!' said he to himself—'is it possible she should be so servile and so mean? Fanny Wyndham, who cared so little for the prosy admonitions of her uncle, a few months since, can she have altered her disposition so completely? Can the possession of her brother's money have made so vile a change in her character? Could she be the same Fanny who had so entirely belonged to him, who had certainly loved him truly once? Perish her money! he had sought her from affection alone; he had truly and fondly loved her; he had determined to cling to her, in spite of the advice of his friends! And then, he found himself deserted and betrayed by her, because circumstances had given her the probable power of making a better match!'

Such were Lord Ballindine's thoughts; and he flattered himself with the reflection that he was a most cruelly used, affectionate, and disinterested lover. He did not, at the moment, remember that it was Fanny's twenty thousand pounds which had first attracted his notice; and that he had for a considerable time wavered, before he made up his mind to part with himself at so low a price. It was not to be expected that he should remember that, just at present; and he rode on, considerably out of humour with all the world except himself.

As he got near to Handicap Lodge, however, the genius of the master-spirit of that classic spot came upon him, and he began to bethink himself that it would be somewhat foolish of him to give up the game just at present. He reflected that a hundred thousand pounds would work a wondrous change and improvement at Kelly's Court—and that, if he was before prepared to marry Fanny Wyndham in opposition to the wishes of her guardian, he should now be doubly determined to do so, even though all Grey Abbey had resolved to the contrary. The last idea in his mind, as he got off his horse at his friend's door was, as to what Dot Blake would think, and say, of the tidings he brought home with him?

It was dark when he reached Handicap Lodge, and, having first asked whether Mr. Blake was in, and heard that he was dressing for dinner, he went to perform the same operation himself. When he came down, full of his budget, and quite ready, as usual, to apply to Dot for advice, he was surprised, and annoyed, to find two other gentlemen in the room, together with Blake. What a bore! to have to make one of a dinner-party of four, and the long protracted rubber of shorts which would follow it, when his mind was so full of other concerns! However, it was not to be avoided.

The guests were, the fat, good-humoured, ready-witted Mat Tierney, and a little Connaught member of Parliament, named Morris, who wore a wig, played a very good rubber of whist, and knew a good deal about selling hunters. He was not very bright, but he told one or two good stories of his own adventures in the world, which he repeated oftener than was approved of by his intimate friends; and he drank his wine plentifully and discreetly—for, if he didn't get a game of cards after consuming a certain quantum, he invariably went to sleep.

There was something in the manner in which the

three greeted him, on entering the room, which showed him that they had been speaking of him and his affairs. Dot was the first to address him.

'Well, Frank, I hope I am to wish you joy. I hope you've made a good morning's work of it?'

Frank looked rather distressed: before he could answer, however, Mat Tierney said,

'Well, Ballindine, upon my soul I congratulate you sincerely, though, of course, you've seen nothing at Grey Abbey but tears and cambric handkerchiefs. I'm very glad, now, that what Kilcullen told me wasn't true. He left Dublin for London yesterday, and I suppose he won't hear of his cousin's death before he gets there.'

'Upon my honour, Lord Ballindine,' said the horse-dealing member, 'you are a lucky fellow. I believe old Wyndham was a regular golden nabob, and I suppose, now, you'll touch the whole of his gatherings.'

Dot and his guests had heard of Harry Wyndham's death, and Fanny's accession of fortune; but they had not heard that she had rejected her lover, and that he had been all but turned out of her guardian's house. Nor did he mean to tell them; but he did not find himself pleasantly situated in having to hear their congratulations and listen to their jokes, while he himself felt that the rumour which he had so emphatically denied to Mat Tierney, only two days since, had turned out to be true.

Not one of the party made the slightest reference to the poor brother from whom Fanny's new fortune had come, except as the lucky means of conveying it to her. There was no regret even pretended for his early death, no sympathy expressed with Fanny's sorrow. And there was, moreover, an evident conviction, in the minds of all the three, that Frank, of course, looked on the accident as a piece of unalloyed good fortune—a splendid windfall in his way, unattended with any disagreeable concomitants. This grated against his feelings, and made him conscious that he was not yet heartless enough to be quite fit for the society in which he found himself.

The party soon went into the dining-room; and Frank at first got a little ease, for Fanny Wyndham seemed to be forgotten in the willing devotion which was paid to Blake's soup; the interest of the fish, also, seemed to be absorbing; and though conversation became more general towards the latter courses, still it was on general subjects, as long as the servants were in the room. But, much to his annoyance, his mistress again came on the tapis, together with the claret.

'You and Kilcullen don't hit it off together—eh, Ballindine?' said Mat.

'We never quarrelled,' answered Frank; 'we never, however, were very intimate.'

'I wonder at that, for you're both fond of the turf. There's a large string of his at Murphy's now, isn't there, Dot?'

'Too many, I believe,' said Blake. 'If you've a mind to be a purchaser, you'll find him a very pleasant fellow—especially if you don't object to his own prices.'

'Faith I'll not trouble him,' said Mat; 'I've two of them already, and a couple on the turf and a couple for the saddle are quite enough to suit me. But what the deuce made him say, so publicly, that your match was off, Ballindine? He couldn't have heard of Wyndham's death at the time, or I should think he was after the money himself.'

'I cannot tell; he certainly had not my authority,' said Frank.

'Nor the lady's either, I hope.'

'You had better ask herself, Tierney; and, if she rejects me, maybe she'll take you.'

'There's a speculation for you,' said Blake; 'you don't think yourself too old yet, I hope, to make your fortune by marriage?—and, if you don't, I'm sure Miss Wyndham can't.'

'I tell you what, Dot, I admire Miss Wyndham

much, and I admire a hundred thousand pounds
more. I don't know anything I admire more than a
hundred thousand pounds, except two; but, upon
my word, I wouldn't take the money and the lady
together.'

'Well, that's kind of him, isn't it, Frank? So,
you've a chance left, yet.'

'Ah! but you forget Morris,' said Tierney; 'and
there's yourself, too. If Ballindine is not to be the
lucky man, I don't see why either of you should
despair.'

'Oh! as for me, I'm the devil. I've a tail, only I
don't wear it, except on state occasions; and I've
horns and hoofs, only people can't see them. But
I don't see why Morris should not succeed: he's the
only one of the four that doesn't own a racehorse,
and that's much in his favour. What do you say,
Morris?'

'I'd have no objection,' said the member; 'except
that I wouldn't like to stand in Lord Ballindine's
way.'

'Oh! he's the soul of good-nature. You wouldn't
take it ill of him, would you, Frank?'

'Not the least,' said Frank, sulkily; for he didn't
like the conversation, and he didn't know how to put
a stop to it.

'Perhaps you wouldn't mind giving him a line of
introduction to Lord Cashel,' said Mat.

'But, Morris,' said Blake, 'I'm afraid your politics
would go against you. A Repealer would never go
down at Grey Abbey.'

'Morris'll never let his politics harm him,' said
Tierney. 'Repeal's a very good thing the other side
of the Shannon; or one might carry it as far as
Conciliation Hall, if one was hard pressed, and near an
election. Were you ever in Conciliation Hall yet,
Morris?'

'No, Mat; but I'm going next Thursday. Will you
go with me?'

'Faith, I will not: but I think you should go; you

ought to do something for your country, for you're
a patriot. I never was a public man.'

'Well, when I can do any good for my country, I'll
go there. Talking of that, I saw O'Connell in town
yesterday, and I never saw him looking so well. The
verdict hasn't disturbed him much. I wonder what
steps the Government will take now? They must be
fairly bothered. I don't think they dare imprison
him.'

'Not dare!' said Blake—'and why not? When
they had courage to indict him, you need not fear but
what they'll dare to go on with a strong hand, now
they have a verdict.'

'I'll tell you what, Dot; if they imprison the whole
set,' said Mat, 'and keep them in prison for twelve
months, every Catholic in Ireland will be a Repealer
by the end of that time.'

'And why shouldn't they all be Repealers?' said
Morris. 'It seems to me that it's just as natural for
us to be Repealers, as it is for you to be the contrary.'

'I won't say they don't dare to put them in prison,'
continued Mat; 'but I will say they'll be great fools
to do it. The Government have so good an excuse
for not doing so: they have such an easy path out of
the hobble. There was just enough difference of
opinion among the judges—just enough irregularity
in the trial, such as the omissions of the names from
the long panel—to enable them to pardon the whole
set with a good grace.'

'If they did,' said Blake, 'the whole high Tory
party in this country—peers and parsons—would be
furious. They'd lose one set of supporters, and
wouldn't gain another. My opinion is, they'll lock
the whole party up in the stone jug—for some time,
at least.'

'Why,' said Tierney, 'their own party could not
quarrel with them for not taking an advantage of a
verdict, as to the legality of which there is so much
difference of opinion even among the judges. I don't
know much about these things, myself; but, as far as

I can understand, they would have all been found guilty of high treason a few years back, and probably have been hung or beheaded; and if they could do that now, the country would be all the quieter. But they can't: the people will have their own way; and if they want the people to go easy, they shouldn't put O'Connell into prison. Rob them all of the glories of martyrdom, and you'd find you'll cut their combs and stop their crowing.'

'It's not so easy to do that now, Mat,' said Morris. 'You'll find that the country will stick to O'Connell, whether he's in prison or out of it;—but Peel will never dare to put him there. They talk of the Penitentiary; but I'll tell you what, if they put him there, the people of Dublin won't leave one stone upon another; they'd have it all down in a night.'

'You forget, Morris, how near Richmond barracks are to the Penitentiary.'

'No, I don't. Not that I think there'll be any row of the kind, for I'll bet a hundred guineas they're never put in prison at all.'

'Done,' said Dot, and his little book was out— 'put that down, Morris, and I'll initial it: a hundred guineas, even, that O'Connell is not in prison within twelve months of this time.'

'Very well: that is, that he's not put there and kept there for six months, in consequence of the verdict just given at the State trials.'

'No, my boy; that's not it. I said nothing about being kept there six months. They're going to try for a writ of error, or what the devil they call it, before the peers. But I'll bet you a cool hundred he is put in prison before twelve months are over, in consequence of the verdict. If he's locked up there for one night, I win. Will you take that?'

'Well, I will,' said Morris; and they both went to work at their little books.

'I was in London,' said Mat, 'during the greater portion of the trial—and it's astonishing what unanimity of opinion there was at the club that the whole set would be acquitted. I heard Howard make a bet, at the Reform Club, that the only man put in prison would be the Attorney-General.'

'He ought to have included the Chief Justice,' said Morris. 'By the bye, Mat, is that Howard the brother of the Honourable and Riverind Augustus?'

'Upon my soul, I don't know whose brother he is. Who is the Riverind Augustus?'

'Morris wants to tell a story, Mat,' said Blake; 'don't spoil him, now.'

'Indeed I don't,' said the member: 'I never told it to any one till I mentioned it to you the other day. It only happened the other day, but it *is* worth telling.'

'Out with it, Morris,' said Mat, 'it isn't very long, is it?—because, if it is, we'll get Dot to give us a little whiskey and hot water first. I'm sick of the claret.'

'Just as you like, Mat,' and Blake rang the bell, and the hot water was brought.

'You know Savarius O'Leary,' said Morris, anxious to tell his story, 'eh, Tierney?'

'What, Savy, with the whiskers?' said Tierney, 'to be sure I do. Who doesn't know Savy?'

'You know him, don't you, Lord Ballindine?' Morris was determined everybody should listen to him.

'Oh yes, I know him; he comes from County Mayo —his property's close to mine; that is, the patch of rocks and cabins—which he has managed to mortgage three times over, and each time for more than its value—which he still calls the O'Leary estate.'

'Well; some time ago—that is, since London began to fill, O'Leary was seen walking down Regent Street, with a parson. How the deuce he'd ever got hold of the parson, or the parson of him, was never explained; but Phil Mahon saw him, and asked him who his friend in the white choker was. "Is it my friend in black, you mane?" says Savy, "thin, my frind was the Honorable and the Riverind Augustus

Howard, the Dane." "Howard the Dane," said
Mahon, "how the duce did any of the Howards
become Danes?" "Ah, bother!" said Savy, "it's
not of thim Danes he is; it's not the Danes of
Shwaden I mane, at all, man; but a rural Dane of
the Church of England."'

Mat Tierney laughed heartily at this, and even
Frank forgot that his dignity had been hurt, and that
he meant to be sulky; and he laughed also: the little
member was delighted with his success, and felt
himself encouraged to persevere.

'Ah, Savy's a queer fellow, if you knew him,' he
continued, turning to Lord Ballindine, 'and, upon
my soul, he's no fool. Oh, if you knew him as well—'

'Didn't you hear Ballindine say he was his next
door neighbour in Mayo?' said Blake, 'or, rather,
next barrack neighbour; for they dispense with doors
in Mayo—eh, Frank? and their houses are all cabins
or barracks.'

'Why, we certainly don't pretend to all the
Apuleian luxuries of Handicap Lodge; but we are
ignorant enough to think ourselves comfortable, and
swinish enough to enjoy our pitiable state.'

'I beg ten thousand pardons, my dear fellow. I
didn't mean to offend your nationality. Castlebar,
we must allow, is a fine provincial city—though
Killala's the Mayo city, I believe; and Claremorris,
which is your own town I think, is, as all admit, a
gem of Paradise: only it's a pity so many of the
houses have been unroofed lately. It adds perhaps
to the picturesque effect, but it must, I should think,
take away from the comfort.'

'Not a house in Claremorris belongs to me,' said
Lord Ballindine, again rather sulky, 'or ever did to
any of my family. I would as soon own Claremorris,
though, as I would Castleblakeney. Your own town
is quite as shattered-looking a place.'

'That's quite true—but I have some hopes that
Castleblakeney will be blotted out of the face of
creation before I come into possession.'

'But I was saying about Savy O'Leary,' again interposed Morris, 'did you ever hear what he did?'

But Blake would not allow his guest the privilege of another story. 'If you encourage Morris,' said he, 'we shall never get our whist,' and with that he rose from the table and walked away into the next room.

They played high. Morris always played high if he could, for he made money by whist. Tierney was not a gambler by profession; but the men he lived among all played, and he, therefore, got into the way of it, and played the game well, for he was obliged to do so in his own defence. Blake was an adept at every thing of the kind; and though the card-table was not the place where his light shone brightest, still he was quite at home at it.

As might be supposed, Lord Ballindine did not fare well among the three. He played with each of them, one after the other, and lost with them all. Blake, to do him justice, did not wish to see his friend's money go into the little member's pocket, and, once or twice, proposed giving up; but Frank did not second the proposal, and Morris was inveterate. The consequence was that, before the table was broken up, Lord Ballindine had lost a sum of money which he could very ill spare, and went to bed in a very unenviable state of mind, in spite of the brilliant prospects on which his friends congratulated him.

XVI

BRIEN BORU

THE next morning, at breakfast, when Frank was alone with Blake, he explained to him how matters really stood at Grey Abbey. He told him how impossible he had found it to insist on seeing Miss Wyndham so soon after her brother's death, and how disgustingly disagreeable, stiff and repulsive the earl had been; and, by degrees, they got to talk of other things, and among them, Frank's present pecuniary miseries.

'There can be no doubt, I suppose,' said Dot, when Frank had consoled himself by anathematising the earl for ten minutes, 'as to the fact of Miss Wyndham's inheriting her brother's fortune?'

'Faith, I don't know; I never thought about her fortune if you'll believe me. I never even remembered that her brother's death would in any way affect her in the way of money, until after I left Grey Abbey.'

'Oh, I can believe you capable of anything in the way of imprudence.'

'Ah, but, Dot, to think of that pompous fool—who sits and caws in that dingy book-room of his, with as much wise self-confidence as an antiquated raven— to think of him insinuating that I had come there looking for Harry Wyndham's money; when, as you know, I was as ignorant of the poor fellow's death as Lord Cashel was himself a week ago. Insolent blackguard! I would never, willingly, speak another word to him, or put my foot inside that infernal door of his, if it were to get ten times all Harry Wyndham's fortune.'

'Then, if I understand you, you now mean to relinquish your claims to Miss Wyndham's hand.'

'No; I don't believe she ever sent the message her uncle gave me. I don't see why I'm to give her up, just because she's got this money.'

'Nor I, Frank, to tell the truth; especially considering how badly you want it yourself. But I don't think quarrelling with the uncle is the surest way to get the niece.'

'But, man, he quarrelled with me.'

'It takes two people to quarrel. If he quarrelled with you, do you be the less willing to come to loggerheads with him.'

'Wouldn't it be the best plan, Dot, to carry her off?'

'She wouldn't go, my boy: rope ladders and post-chaises are out of fashion.'

'But if she's really fond of me—and, upon my honour, I don't believe I'm flattering myself in thinking that she is—why the deuce shouldn't she marry me, *malgré* Lord Cashel? She must be her own mistress in a week or two. By heavens, I cannot stomach that fellow's arrogant assumption of superiority.'

'It will be much more convenient for her to marry you *bon gré* Lord Cashel, whom you may pitch to the devil, in any way you like best, as soon as you have Fanny Wyndham at Kelly's Court. But, till that happy time, take my advice, and submit to the cawing. Rooks and ravens are respectable birds, just because they do look so wise. It's a great thing to look wise; the doing so does an acknowledged fool, like Lord Cashel, very great credit.'

'But what ought I to do? I can't go to the man's house when he told me expressly not to do so.'

'Oh, yes, you can: not immediately, but by and by—in a month or six weeks. I'll tell you what I should do, in your place; and remember, Frank, I'm quite in earnest now, for it's a very different thing playing a game for twenty thousand pounds, which, to you, joined to a wife, would have been a positive irreparable loss, and starting for five or six times that sum, which would give you an income on which you might manage to live.'

'Well, thou sapient counsellor—but, I tell you beforehand, the chances are ten to one I sha'n't follow your plan.'

'Do as you like about that: you sha'n't, at any rate, have me to blame. I would in the first place, assure myself that Fanny inherited her brother's money.'

'There's no doubt about that. Lord Cashel said as much.'

'Make sure of it however. A lawyer'll do that for you, with very little trouble. Then, take your name off the turf at once; it's worth your while to do it now. You may either do it by a *bona fide* sale of the horses, or by running them in some other person's name. Then, watch your opportunity, call at Grey Abbey, when the earl is not at home, and manage to see some of the ladies. If you can't do that, if you can't effect an *entrée*, write to Miss Wyndham; don't be too lachrymose, or supplicatory, in your style, but ask her to give you a plain answer personally, or in her own handwriting.'

'And if she declines the honour?'

'If, as you say and as I believe, she loves, or has loved you, I don't think she'll do so. She'll submit to a little parleying, and then she'll capitulate. But it will be much better that you should see her, if possible, without writing at all.'

'I don't like the idea of calling at Grey Abbey. I wonder whether they'll go to London this season?'

'If they do, you can go after them. The truth is simply this, Ballindine; Miss Wyndham will follow her own fancy in the matter, in spite of her guardian; but, if you make no further advances to her, of course she can make none to you. But I think the game is in your own hand. You haven't the head to play it, or I should consider the stakes as good as won.'

'But then, about these horses, Dot. I wish I could sell them, out and out, at once.'

'You'll find it very difficult to get anything like the value for a horse that's well up for the Derby. You see, a purchaser must make up his mind to so much outlay: there's the purchase-money, and expense of English training, with so remote a chance of any speedy return.'

'But you said you'd advise me to sell them.'

'That's if you can get a purchaser:—or else run them in another name. You may run them in my name, if you like it; but Scott must understand that I've nothing whatever to do with the expense.'

'Would you not buy them yourself, Blake?'

'No. I would not.'

'Why not?'

'If I gave you anything like the value for them, the bargain would not suit me; and if I got them for what they'd be worth to me, you'd think, and other people would say, that I'd robbed you.'

Then followed a lengthened and most intricate discourse on the affairs of the stable. Frank much wanted his friend to take his stud entirely off his hands, but this Dot resolutely refused to do. In the course of conversation, Frank owned that the present state of his funds rendered it almost impracticable for him to incur the expense of sending his favourite, Brien Boru, to win laurels in England. He had lost nearly three hundred pounds the previous evening which his account at his banker's did not enable him to pay; his Dublin agent had declined advancing him more money at present, and his tradesmen were very importunate. In fact, he was in a scrape, and Dot must advise him how to extricate himself from it.

'I'll tell you the truth, Ballindine,' said he; 'as far as I'm concerned myself, I never will lend money, except where I see, as a matter of business, that it is a good speculation to do so. I wouldn't do it for my father.'

'Who asked you?' said Frank, turning very red, and looking very angry.

'You did not, certainly; but I thought you might, and you would have been annoyed when I refused you; now, you have the power of being indignant, instead. However, having said so much, I'll tell you what I think you should do, and what I will do to relieve you, as far as the horses are concerned. Do you go down to Kelly's Court, and remain there quiet for a time. You'll be able to borrow what money you absolutely want down there, if the Dublin fellows actually refuse; but do with as little as you can. The horses shall run in my name for twelve months. If they win, I will divide with you at the end of the year the amount won, after deducting their expenses. If they lose, I will charge you with half the amount lost, including the expenses. Should you not feel inclined, at the end of the year, to repay me this sum, I will then keep the horses, instead, or sell them at Dycer's, if you like it better, and hand you the balance if there be any. What do you say to this?

You will be released from all trouble, annoyance, and expense, and the cattle will, I trust, be in good hands.'

'That is to say, that, for one year, you are to possess one half of whatever value the horses may be?'

'Exactly: we shall be partners for one year.'

'To make that fair,' said Frank, 'you ought to put into the concern three horses, as good and as valuable as my three.'

'Yes; and you ought to bring into the concern half the capital to be expended in their training; and knowledge, experience, and skill in making use of them, equal to mine. No, Frank; you're mistaken if you think that I can afford to give up my time, merely for the purpose of making an arrangement to save you from trouble.'

'Upon my word, Dot,' answered the other, 'you're about the coolest hand I ever met! Did I ask you for your precious time, or anything else? You're always afraid that you're going to be done. Now, you might make a distinction between me and some of your other friends, and remember that I am not in the habit of doing anybody.'

'Why, I own I don't think it very likely that I, or indeed anyone else, should suffer much from you in that way, for your sin is not too much sharpness.'

'Then why do you talk about what you can afford to do?'

'Because it's necessary. I made a proposal which you thought an unfair one. You mayn't believe me, but it is a most positive fact, that my only object in making that proposal was, to benefit you. You will find it difficult to get rid of your horses on any terms; and yet, with the very great stake before you in Miss Wyndham's fortune, it would be foolish in you to think of keeping them; and, on this account, I thought in what manner I could take them from you. If they belong to my stables I shall consider myself bound to run them to the best advantage, and '—

'Well, well—for heaven's sake don't speechify about it.'

'Stop a moment, Frank, and listen, for I must make you understand. I must make you see that I am not taking advantage of your position, and trying to rob my own friend in my own house. I don't care what most people say of me, for in my career I must expect people to lie of me. I must, also, take care of myself. But I do wish you to know, that though I could not disarrange my schemes for you, I would not take you in.'

'Why, Dot—how can you go on so? I only thought I was taking a leaf out of your book, by being careful to make the best bargain I could.'

'Well, as I was saying—I would run the horses to the best advantage—especially Brien, for the Derby: by doing so, my whole book would be upset: I should have to bet all round again—and, very likely, not be able to get the bets I want. I could not do this without a very strong interest in the horse. Besides, you remember that I should have to go over with him to England myself, and that I should be obliged to be in England a great deal at a time when my own business would require me here.'

'My dear fellow,' said Frank, 'you're going on as though it were necessary to defend yourself. I never accused you of anything.'

'Never mind whether you did or no. You understand me now: if it will suit you, you can take my offer, but I should be glad to know at once.'

While this conversation was going on, the two young men had left the house, and sauntered out into Blake's stud-yard. Here were his stables, where he kept such horses as were not actually in the trainer's hands—and a large assortment of aged hunters, celebrated timber-jumpers, brood mares, thoroughbred fillies, cock-tailed colts, and promising foals. They were immediately joined by Blake's stud groom, who came on business intent, to request a few words with his master; which meant that Lord

Ballindine was to retreat, as it was full time for his
friend to proceed to his regular day's work. Blake's
groom was a very different person in appearance,
from the sort of servant in the possession of which
the fashionable owner of two or three horses usually
rejoices. He had no diminutive top boots; no loose
brown breeches, buttoned low beneath the knee; no
elongated waistcoat with capacious pockets; no dandy
coat with remarkably short tail. He was a very ugly
man of about fifty, named John Bottom, dressed
somewhat like a seedy gentleman; but he understood
his business well, and did it; and was sufficiently wise
to know that he served his own pocket best, in the
long run, by being true to his master, and by resisting
the numerous tempting offers which were made to
him by denizens of the turf to play foul with his
master's horses. He was, therefore, a treasure to
Blake; and he knew it, and valued himself accordingly.

'Well, John,' said his master, 'I suppose I must
desert Lord Ballindine again, and obey your summons. Your few words will last nearly till dinner,
I suppose?'

'Why, there is a few things, to be sure, 'll be the
better for being talked over a bit, as his lordship
knows well enough. I wish we'd as crack a nag in
our stables, as his lordship.'

'Maybe we may, some day; one down and another
come on, you know; as the butcher-boy said.'

'At any rate, your horses don't want bottom,'
said Frank.

He—he—he! laughed John, or rather tried to do
so. He had laughed at that joke a thousand times;
and, in the best of humours, he wasn't a merry man.

'Well, Frank,' said Blake, 'the cock has crowed; I
must away. I suppose you'll ride down to Igoe's,
and see Brien: but think of what I've said, and,' he
added, whispering—'remember that I will do the
best I can for the animals, if you put them into my
stables. They shall be made second to nothing, and
shall only and always run to win.'

So, Blake and John Bottom walked off to the box stables and home paddocks.

Frank ordered his horse, and complied with his friend's suggestion, by riding down to Igoe's. He was not in happy spirits as he went; he felt afraid that his hopes, with regard to Fanny, would be blighted; and that, if he persevered in his suit, he would only be harassed, annoyed, and disappointed. He did not see what steps he could take, or how he could manage to see her. It would be impossible for him to go to Grey Abbey, after having been, as he felt, turned out by Lord Cashel. Other things troubled him also. What should he now do with himself? It was true that he could go down to his own house; but everyone at Kelly's Court expected him to bring with him a bride and a fortune; and, instead of that, he would have to own that he had been jilted, and would be reduced to the disagreeable necessity of borrowing money from his own tenants. And then, that awful subject, money—took possession of him. What the deuce was he to do? What a fool he had been, to be seduced on to the turf by such a man as Blake! And then, he expressed a wish to himself that Blake had been—a long way off before he ever saw him. There he was, steward of the Curragh, the owner of the best horse in Ireland, and absolutely without money to enable him to carry on the game till he could properly retreat from it!

Then he was a little unfair upon his friend: he accused him of knowing his position, and wishing to take advantage of it; and, by the time he had got to Igoe's, his mind was certainly not in a very charitable mood towards poor Dot. He had, nevertheless, determined to accept his offer, and to take a last look at the three Milesians.

The people about the stables always made a great fuss with Lord Ballindine, partly because he was one of the stewards, and partly because he was going to run a crack horse for the Derby in England; and though, generally speaking, he did not care much for personal complimentary respect, he usually got chattered and flattered into good humour at Igoe's.

'Well, my lord,' said a sort of foreman, or partner, or managing man, who usually presided over the yard, ' I think we'll be apt to get justice to Ireland on the downs this year. That is, they'll give us nothing but what we takes from 'em by hard fighting, or running, as the case may be.'

'How's Brien looking this morning, Grady?'

'As fresh as a primrose, my lord, and as clear as crystal: he's ready, this moment, to run through any set of three years old as could be put on the Curragh, anyway.'

'I'm afraid you're putting him on too forward.'

'Too forrard, is it, my lord? not a bit. He's a hoss as naturally don't pick up flesh; though he feeds free, too. He's this moment all wind and bottom, though, as one may say, he's got no training. He's niver been sthretched yet. Faith it's thrue I'm telling you, my lord.'

'I know Scott doesn't like getting horses, early in the season, that are too fine—too much drawn up; he thinks they lose power by it, and so they do;—it's the distance that kills them, at the Derby. It's so hard to get a young horse to stay the distance.'

'That's thrue, shure enough, my lord; and there isn't a gentleman this side the wather, anyway, undherstands thim things betther than your lordship.'

'Well, Grady, let's have a look at the young chieftain: he's all right about the lungs, anyway.'

'And feet too, my lord; niver saw a set of claner feet with plates on: and legs too! If you were to canter him down the road, I don't think he'd feel it; not that I'd like to thry, though.'

'Why, he's not yet had much to try them.'

'Faix, he has, my lord: didn't he win the Autumn Produce Stakes?'

'The only thing he ever ran for.'

'Ah, but I tell you, as your lordship knows very well—no one betther—that it's a ticklish thing to

bring a two year old to the post, in anything like
condition—with any running in him at all, and not
hurt his legs.'

'But I think he's all right—eh, Grady?'

'Right?—your lordship knows he's right. I wish
he may be made righter at John Scott's, that's all.
But that's unpossible.'

'Of course, Grady, you think he might be trained
here, as well as at the other side of the water?'

'No, I don't, my lord: quite different. I've none of
thim ideas at all, and never had, thank God. I
knows what we can do, and I knows what they can
do:—breed a hoss in Ireland, train him in the North
of England, and run him in the South; and he'll do
your work for you, and win your money, steady and
shure.'

'And why not run in the North, too?'

'They're too 'cute, my lord: they like to pick up
the crumbs themselves—small blame to thim in that
matther. No; a bright Irish nag, with lots of heart,
like Brien Boru, is the hoss to stand on for the Derby;
where all run fair and fair alike, the best wins;—but
I won't say but he'll be the bether for a little polish-
ing at Johnny Scott's.'

'Besides, Grady, no horse could run immediately
after a sea voyage. Do you remember what a show
we made of Peter Simple at Kilrue?'

'To be shure I does, my lord: besides, they've
proper gallops there, which we haven't—and they've
bether manes of measuring horses:—why, they can
measure a horse to half a pound, and tell his rale pace
on a two-mile course, to a couple of seconds.—Take
the sheets off, Larry, and let his lordship run his hand
over him. He's as bright as a star, isn't he?'

'I think you're getting him too fine. I'm sure
Scott'll say so.'

'Don't mind him, my lord. He's not like one of
those English cats, with jist a dash of speed about
'em, and nothing more—brutes that they put in
training half a dozen times in as many months.

Thim animals pick up a lot of loose, flabby flesh in no time, and loses it in less; and, in course, av' they gets a sweat too much, there's nothin left in 'em; not a hapoth. Brien's a different guess sort of animal from that.'

'Were you going to have him out, Grady?'

'Why, we was not—that is, only just for walking exercise, with his sheets on: but a canter down the half mile slope, and up again by the bushes won't go agin him.'

'Well, saddle him then, and let Pat get up.'

'Yes, my lord'; and Brien was saddled by the two men together, with much care and ceremony, and Pat was put up—'and now, Pat,' continued Grady, 'keep him well in hand down the slope—don't let him out at all at all, till you come to the turn: when you're fairly round the corner, just shake your reins the laste in life, and when you're halfway up the rise, when the lad begins to snort a bit, let him just see the end of the switch—just raise it till it catches his eye; and av' he don't show that he's disposed for running, I'm mistaken. We'll step across to the bushes, my lord, and see him come round.'

Lord Ballindine and the managing man walked across to the bushes accordingly, and Pat did exactly as he was desired. It was a pretty thing to see the beautiful young animal, with his sleek brown coat shining like a lady's curls, arching his neck, and throwing down his head, in his impatience to start. He was the very picture of health and symmetry; when he flung up his head you'd think the blood was running from his nose, his nostrils were so ruddy bright. He cantered off in great impatience, and fretted and fumed because the little fellow on his back would be the master, and not let him have his play—down the slope, and round the corner by the trees. It was beautiful to watch him, his motions were so easy, so graceful. At the turn he answered to the boy's encouragement, and mended his pace, till again he felt the bridle, and then, as the jock barely moved his right arm, he bounded up the rising ground, past the spot where Lord Ballindine and the trainer were standing, and shot away till he was beyond the place where he knew his gallop ordinarily ended. As Grady said, he hadn't yet been stretched; he had never yet tried his own pace, and he had that look so beautiful in a horse when running, of working at his ease, and much within his power.

'He's a beautiful creature,' said Lord Ballindine, as he mournfully reflected that he was about to give up to Dot Blake half the possession of his favourite, and the whole of the nominal title. It was such a pity he should be so hampered; the mere *éclat* of possessing such a horse was so great a pleasure; 'He is a fine creature,' said he, 'and, I am sure, will do well.'

'Your lordship may say that: he'll go precious nigh to astonish the Saxons, I think. I suppose the pick-up at the Derby'll be nigh four thousand this year.'

'I suppose it will—something like that.'

'Well; I would like a nag out of our stables to do the trick on the downs, and av' we does it iver, it'll be now. Mr. Igoe's standing a deal of cash on him. I wonder is Mr. Blake standing much on him, my lord?'

'You'd be precious deep, Grady, if you could find what he's doing in that way.'

'That's thrue for you, my lord; but av' he, or your lordship, wants to get more on, now's the time. I'll lay twenty thousand pounds this moment, that afther he's been a fortnight at Johny Scott's the odds agin him won't be more than ten to one, from that day till the morning he comes out on the downs.'

'I dare say not.'

'I wondher who your lordship'll put up?'

'That must depend on Scott, and what sort of a string he has running. He's nothing, as yet, high in the betting, except Hardicanute.'

'Nothing, my lord; and, take my word for it, that

horse is ownly jist run up for the sake of the betting; that's not his nathural position. Well, Pat, you may take the saddle off. Will your lordship see the mare out to-day?'

'Not to-day, Grady. Let's see, what's the day she runs?'

'The fifteenth of May, my lord. I'm afraid Mr. Watts' Patriot 'll be too much for her; that's av' he'll run kind; but he don't do that always. Well, good morning to your lordship.'

'Good morning, Grady;' and Frank rode back towards Handicap Lodge.

He had a great contest with himself on his road home. He had hated the horses two days since, when he was at Grey Abbey, and had hated himself, for having become their possessor; and now he couldn't bear the thought of parting with them. To be steward of the Curragh—to own the best horse of the year—and to win the Derby, were very pleasant things in themselves; and for what was he going to give over all this glory, pleasure and profit, to another? To please a girl who had rejected him, even jilted him, and to appease an old earl who had already turned him out of his house! No, he wouldn't do it. By the time that he was half a mile from Igoe's stables he had determined that, as the girl was gone it would be a pity to throw the horses after her; he would finish this year on the turf; and then, if Fanny Wyndham was still her own mistress after Christmas, he would again ask her her mind. 'If she's a girl of spirit,' he said to himself—'and nobody knows better than I do that she is, she won't like me the worse for having shown that I'm not to be led by the nose by a pompous old fool like Lord Cashel,' and he rode on, fortifying himself in this resolution, for the second half mile. 'But what the deuce should he do about money?' There was only one more half mile before he was again at Handicap Lodge.—Guinness's people had his title-deeds, and he knew he had twelve hundred a year after paying the interest of the old

incumbrances. They hadn't advanced him much since
he came of age; certainly not above five thousand
pounds; and it surely was very hard he could not get
five or six hundred pounds when he wanted it so
much; it was very hard that he shouldn't be able to
do what he liked with his own, like the Duke of
Newcastle. However, the money must be had: he
must pay Blake and Tierney the balance of what
they had won at whist, and the horse couldn't go
over the water till the wind was raised. If he was
driven very hard he might get something from
Martin Kelly. These unpleasant cogitations brought
him over the third half mile, and he rode through the
gate of Handicap Lodge in a desperate state of
indecision.

'I'll tell you what I'll do, Dot,' he said, when he
met his friend coming in from his morning's work;
'and I'm deuced sorry to do it, for I shall be giving
you the best horse of his year, and something tells
me he'll win the Derby.'

'I suppose "something" means old Jack Igoe, or
that blackguard Grady,' said Dot. 'But as to his
winning, that's as it may be. You know the chances
are sixteen to one he won't.'

'Upon my honour I don't think they are.'

'Will you take twelve to one?'

'Ah! youk now, Dot, I'm not now wanting to bet
on the horse with you. I was only saying that I've
a kind of inward conviction that he will win.'

'My dear Frank,' said the other, 'if men selling
horses could also sell their inward convictions with
them, what a lot of articles of that description there
would be in the market! But what were you going to
say you'd do?'

'I'll tell you what I'll do: I'll agree to your terms
providing you'll pay half the expenses of the horses
since the last race each of them ran. You must see
that would be only fair, supposing the horses belonged to you, equally with me, ever since that time.'

'It would be quite fair, no doubt, if I agreed to it:

it would be quite fair also if I agreed to give you five
hundred pounds; but I will do neither one nor the
other.'

'But look here, Dot—Brien ran for the Autumn
Produce Stakes last October, and won them: since
then he has done nothing to reimburse me for his
expense, nor yet has anything been taken out of him
by running. Surely, if you are to have half the profits,
you should at any rate pay half the expenses?'

'That's very well put, Frank; and if you and I
stood upon equal ground, with an arbiter between
us by whose decision we were bound to abide, and to
whom the settlement of the question was entrusted,
your arguments would, no doubt, be successful,
but—'

'Well—that's the fair way of looking at it.'

'But, as I was going to say, that's not the case.
We are neither of us bound to take any one's decision; and, therefore, any terms which either of us
chooses to accept must be fair. Now I have told you
my terms—the lowest price, if you like to call it so,—
at which I will give your horses the benefit of my
experience, and save you from their immediate
pecuniary pressure; and I will neither take any other
terms, nor will I press these on you.'

'Why, Blake, I'd sooner deal with all the Jews of
Israel——'

'Stop, Frank: one word of abuse, and I'll wash my
hands of the matter altogether.'

'Wash away then, I'll keep the horses, though I
have to sell my hunters and the plate at Kelly's
Court into the bargain.'

'I was going to add—only your energy's far too
great to allow of a slow steady man like me finishing
his sentence—I was going to say that, if you're
pressed for money as you say, and if it will be any
accommodation, I will let you have two hundred and
fifty pounds at five per cent. on the security of the
horses; that is, that you will be charged with that
amount, and the interest, in the final closing of the

account at the end of the year, before the horses are restored to you.'

Had an uninterested observer been standing by he might have seen with half an eye that Blake's coolness was put on, and that his indifference to the bargain was assumed. This offer of the loan was a second bid, when he found the first was likely to be rejected: it was made, too, at the time that he was positively declaring that he would make none but the first offer. Poor Frank!—he was utterly unable to cope with his friend at the weapons with which they were playing, and he was consequently most egregiously plundered. But it was in an affair of horse-flesh, and the sporting world, when it learned the terms on which the horses were transferred from Lord Ballindine's name to that of Mr. Blake, had not a word of censure to utter against the letter. He was pronounced to be very wide awake, and decidedly at the top of his profession; and Lord Ballindine was spoken of, for a week, with considerable pity and contempt.

When Blake mentioned the loan Frank got up, and stood with his back to the fire; then bit his lips, and walked twice up and down the room, with his hands in his pockets, and then he paused, looked out of the window, and attempted to whistle: then he threw himself into an armchair, poked out both his legs as far as he could, ran his fingers through his hair, and set to work hard to make up his mind. But it was no good; in about five minutes he found he could not do it; so he took out his purse, and, extracting half-a-crown, threw it up to the ceiling, saying.

'Well, Dot—head or harp? If you're right, you have them.'

'Harp,' cried Dot.

They both examined the coin. 'They're yours,' said Frank, with much solemnity; 'and now you've got the best horse—yes, I believe the very best horse alive, for nothing.'

'Only half of him, Frank.'

'Well,' said Frank; 'it's done now, I suppose.'

'Oh, of course it is,' said Dot: 'I'll draw out the agreement, and give you a cheque for the money to-night.'

And so he did; and Frank wrote a letter to Igoe, authorizing him to hand over the horses to Mr. Blake's groom, stating that he had sold them—for so ran his agreement with Dot—and desiring that his bill for training, &c., might be forthwith forwarded to Kelly's Court. Poor Frank! he was ashamed to go to take a last look at his dear favourites, and tell his own trainer that he had sold his own horses.

The next morning saw him, with his servant, on the Ballinasloe coach, travelling towards Kelly's Court; and, also, saw Brien Boru, Granuell, and Finn M'Goul led across the downs, from Igoe's stables to Handicap Lodge.

The handsome sheets, hoods, and rollers, in which they had hitherto appeared, and on which the initial B was alone conspicuous, were carefully folded up, and they were henceforth seen in plainer, but as serviceable apparel, labelled W. B.

'Will you give fourteen to one against Brien Boru?' said Viscount Avoca to Lord Tathenham Corner, about ten days after this, at Tattersall's.

'I will,' said Lord Tathenham.

'In hundreds?' said the sharp Irishman.

'Very well,' said Lord Tathenham; and the bet was booked.

'You didn't know, I suppose,' said the successful viscount, 'that Dot Blake has bought Brien Boru?'

'And who the devil's Dot Blake?' said Lord Tathenham.

'Oh! you'll know before May's over,' said the viscount.

XVII

MARTIN KELLY'S COURTSHIP

IT will be remembered that the Tuam attorney,
Daly, dined with Barry Lynch, at Dunmore House,
on the same evening that Martin Kelly reached
home after his Dublin excursion; and that, on that
occasion, a good deal of interesting conversation
took place after dinner. Barry, however, was hardly
amenable to reason at that social hour, and it was not
till the following morning that he became thoroughly
convinced that it would be perfectly impossible for
him to make his sister out a lunatic to the satisfaction of the Chancellor.

He then agreed to abandon the idea, and, in lieu
of it, to indict, or at any rate to threaten to indict,
the widow Kelly and her son for a conspiracy, and
an attempt to inveigle his sister Anty into a disgraceful marriage, with the object of swindling her
out of her property.

'I'll see Moylan, Mr. Lynch,' said Daly; 'and if I can
talk him over, I think we might succeed in frightening
the whole set of them, so far as to prevent the
marriage. Moylan must know that if your sister was
to marry young Kelly, there'd be an end to his agency;
but we must promise him something, Mr. Lynch.'

'Yes; I suppose we must pay him, before we get
anything out of him.'

'No, not before—but he must understand that he
will get something, if he makes himself useful. You
must let me explain to him that if the marriage is
prevented, you will make no objection to his con-
tinuing to act as Miss Lynch's agent; and I might
hint the possibility of his receiving the rents on the
whole property.'

'Hint what you like, Daly, but don't tie me down
to the infernal ruffian. I suppose we can throw him
overboard afterwards, can't we?'

'Why, not altogether, Mr. Lynch. If I make him a
definite promise, I shall expect you to keep to it.'

'Confound him!—but tell me, Daly; what is it he's to do?—and what is it we're to do?'

'Why, Mr. Lynch, it's more than probable, I think, that this plan of Martin Kelly's marrying your sisther may have been talked over between the ould woman, Moylan, and the young man; and if so, that's something like a conspiracy. If I could worm that out of him, I think I'd manage to frighten them.'

'And what the deuce had I better do? You see, there was a bit of a row between us. That is, Anty got frightened when I spoke to her of this rascal, and then she left the house. Couldn't you make her understand that she'd be all right if she'd come to the house again?'

While Barry Lynch had been sleeping off the effects of the punch, Daly had been inquiring into the circumstances under which Anty had left the house, and he had pretty nearly learned the truth; he knew, therefore, how much belief to give to his client's representation.

'I don't think,' said he, 'that your sister will be likely to come back at present; she will probably find herself quieter and easier at the inn. You see, she has been used to a quiet life.'

'But, if she remains there, she can marry that young ruffian any moment she takes it into her head to do so. There's always some rogue of a priest ready to do a job of that sort.'

'Exactly so, Mr. Lynch. Of course your sister can marry whom she pleases, and when she pleases, and neither you nor any one else can prevent her; but still—'

'Then what the devil's the use of my paying you to come here and tell me that?'

'That's your affair: I didn't come without being sent for. But I was going to tell you that, though we can't prevent her from marrying if she pleases, we may make her afraid to do so. You had better write her a kind, affectionate note, regretting what has taken place between you, and promising to give her no molestation of any kind, if she will return to her own house,—and keep a copy of this letter. Then I will see Moylan; and, if I can do anything with him, it will be necessary that you should also see him. You could come over to Tuam, and meet him in my office; and then I will try and force an entrance into the widow's castle, and, if possible, see your sister, and humbug the ould woman into a belief that she has laid herself open to criminal indictment. We might even go so far as to have notices served on them; but, if they snap their fingers at us, we can do nothing further. My advice in that case would be, that you should make the best terms in your power with Martin Kelly.'

'And let the whole thing go! I'd sooner—Why, Daly, I believe you're as bad as Blake! You're afraid of these huxtering thieves!'

'If you go on in that way, Mr. Lynch, you'll get no professional gentleman to act with you. I give you my best advice; if you don't like it, you needn't follow it; but you won't get a solicitor in Connaught to do better for you than what I'm proposing.'

'Confusion!' muttered Barry, and he struck the hot turf in the grate a desperate blow with the tongs which he had in his hands, and sent the sparks and bits of fire flying about the hearth.

'The truth is, you see, your sister's in her full senses; there's the divil a doubt of that; the money's her own, and she can marry whom she pleases. All that we can do is to try and make the Kellys think they have got into a scrape.'

'But this letter—What on earth am I to say to her?'

'I'll just put down what I would say, were I you; and if you like you can copy it.' Daly then wrote the following letter—

'My Dear Anty,

'Before taking other steps, which could not fail of being very disagreeable to you and to others, I wish to point out to you how injudiciously you are acting in leaving your own house; and to try to induce you to do that which will be most beneficial to yourself, and most conducive to your happiness and respectability. If you will return to Dunmore House, I most solemnly promise to leave you unmolested. I much regret that my violence on Thursday should have annoyed you, but I can assure you it was attributable merely to my anxiety on your account. Nothing, however, shall induce me to repeat it. But you must be aware that a little inn is not a fit place for you to be stopping at; and I am obliged to tell you that I have conclusive evidence of a conspiracy having been formed, by the family with whom you are staying, to get possession of your money; and that this conspiracy was entered into very shortly after the contents of my father's will had been made public. I *must* have this fact proved at the Assizes, and the disreputable parties to it punished, unless you will consent, at any rate for a time, to put yourself under the protection of your brother.

'In the meantime pray believe me, dear Anty, in spite of appearances,

'Your affectionate brother,

'BARRY LYNCH.'

It was then agreed that this letter should be copied and signed by Barry, and delivered by Terry on the following morning, which was Sunday. Daly then returned to Tuam, with no warm admiration for his client.

In the meantime the excitement at the inn, arising from Anty's arrival and Martin's return, was gradually subsiding. These two important events, both happening on the same day, sadly upset the domestic economy of Mrs. Kelly's establishment. Sally had indulged in tea almost to stupefaction, and Kattie's elfin locks became more than ordinarily disordered. On the following morning, however, things seemed to fall a little more into their places:

the widow was, as usual, behind her counter; and if her girls did not give her as much assistance as she desired of them, and as much as was usual with them, they were perhaps excusable, for they could not well leave their new guest alone on the day after her coming to them.

Martin went out early to Toneroe; doubtless the necessary labours of the incipient spring required him at the farm—but I believe that if his motives were analysed, he hardly felt himself up to a *tête-à -tête* with his mistress, before he had enjoyed a cool day's consideration of the extraordinary circumstances which had brought her into the inn as his mother's guest. He, moreover, wished to have a little undisturbed conversation with Meg, and to learn from her how Anty might be inclined towards him just at present. So Martin spent his morning among his lambs and his ploughs; and was walking home, towards dusk, tired enough, when he met Barry Lynch, on horseback, that hero having come out, as usual, for his solitary ride, to indulge in useless dreams of the happy times he would have, were his sister only removed from her tribulations in this world. Though Martin had never been on friendly terms with his more ambitious neighbour, there had never, up to this time, been any quarrel between them, and he therefore just muttered 'Good morning, Mr. Lynch,' as he passed him on the road.

Barry said nothing, and did not appear to see him as he passed; but some idea struck him as soon as he had passed, and he pulled in his horse and hallooed out 'Kelly!'—and, as Martin stopped, he added, 'Come here a moment—I want to speak to you.'

'Well, Mr. Barry, what is it?' said the other, returning. Lynch paused, and evidently did not know whether to speak or let it alone. At last he said, 'Never mind—I'll get somebody else to say what I was going to say. But you'd better look sharp what you're about, my lad, or you'll find yourself in a scrape that you don't dream of.'

'And is that all you called me back for?' said
Martin.

'That's all I mean to say to you at present.'

'Well then, Mr. Lynch, I must say you're very
good, and I'm shure I will look sharp enough. But,
to my thinking, d'you know, you want looking
afther yourself a precious dale more than I do,' and
then he turned to proceed homewards, but said, as
he was going—'Have you any message for your
sisther, Mr. Lynch?'

'By—! my young man, I'll make you pay for
what you're doing,' answered Barry.

'I know you'll be glad to hear she's pretty well:
she's coming round from the thratement she got the
other night; though, by all accounts, it's a wondher
she's alive this moment to tell of it.'

Barry did not attempt any further reply, but rode
on, sorry enough that he had commenced the conversation. Martin got home in time for a snug tea
with Anty and his sisters, and succeeded in prevailing
on the three to take each a glass of punch; and,
before Anty went to bed he began to find himself
more at his ease with her, and able to call her by her
Christian name without any disagreeable emotion.
He certainly had a most able coadjutor in Meg. She
made room on the sofa for him between herself and
his mistress, and then contrived that the room should
be barely sufficient, so that Anty was rather closely
hemmed up in one corner: moreover, she made Anty
give her opinion as to Martin's looks after his metro-
politan excursion, and tried hard to make Martin
pay some compliments to Anty's appearance. But
in this she failed, although she gave him numerous
opportunities.

However, they passed the evening very comfortably,—quite sufficiently so to make Anty feel that
the kindly, humble friendship of the inn was
infinitely preferable to the miserable grandeur of
Dunmore House; and it is probable that all the love-
making in the world would not have operated so

strongly in Martin's favour as this feeling. Meg, however, was not satisfied, for as soon as she had seen Jane and Anty into the bedroom she returned to her brother, and lectured him as to his lukewarm manifestations of affection.

'Martin,' said she, returning into the little sitting-room, and carefully shutting the door after her, 'you're the biggest bosthoon of a gandher I ever see, to be losing your opportunities with Anty this way! I b'lieve it's waiting you are for herself to come forward to you. Do you think a young woman don't expect something more from a lover than jist for you to sit by her, and go on all as one as though she was one of your own sisthers? Av' once she gets out of this before the priest has made one of the two of you, mind, I tell you, it'll be all up with you. I wondher, Martin, you haven't got more pluck in you!'

'Oh! bother, Meg. You're thinking of nothing but kissing and slobbhering.—Anty's not the same as you and Jane, and doesn't be all agog for such nonsense!'

'I tell you, Martin, Anty's a woman; and, take my word for it, what another girl likes won't come amiss to her. Besides, why don't you spake to her?'

'Spake?—why, what would you have me spake?'

'Well, Martin, you're a fool. Have you, or have you not, made up your mind to marry Anty?'

'To be shure I will, av' she'll have me.'

'And do you expect her to have you without asking?'

'Shure, you know, didn't I ask her often enough?'

'Ah, but you must do more than jist ask her that way. She'll never make up her mind to go before the priest, unless you say something sthronger to her. Jist tell her, plump out, you're ready and willing, and get the thing done before Lent. What's to hindher you?—shure, you know,' she added, in a whisper, 'you'll not get sich a fortune as Anty's in your way every day. Spake out, man, and don't be afraid of her: take my word she won't like you a bit the worse for a few kisses.'

Martin promised to comply with his sister's advice, and to sound Anty touching their marriage on the following morning after mass.

On the Sunday morning, at breakfast, the widow proposed to Anty that she should go to mass with herself and her daughters; but Anty trembled so violently at the idea of showing herself in public, after her escape from Dunmore House, that the widow did not press her to do so, although afterwards she expressed her disapprobation of Anty's conduct to her own girls.

'I don't see what she has to be afeard of,' said she, 'in going to get mass from her own clergyman in her own chapel. She don't think, I suppose, that Barry Lynch'd dare come in there to pull her out, before the blessed altar, glory be to God.'

'Ah but, mother, you know, she has been so frighted.'

'Frighted, indeed! She'll get over these tantrums, I hope, before Sunday next, or I know where I'll wish her again.'

So Anty was left at home, and the rest of the family went to mass. When the women returned, Meg manœuvred greatly, and, in fine, successfully, that no one should enter the little parlour to interrupt the wooing she intended should take place there. She had no difficulty with Jane, for she told her what her plans were; and though her less energetic sister did not quite agree in the wisdom of her designs, and pronounced an opinion that it would be 'better to let things settle down a bit,' still she did not presume to run counter to Meg's views; but Meg had some work to dispose of her mother. It would not have answered at all, as Meg had very well learned herself, to caution her mother not to interrupt Martin in his love-making, for the widow had no charity for such follies. She certainly expected her daughters to get married, and wished them to be well and speedily settled; but she watched anything like a flirtation on their part as closely as a cat does a mouse. If any young man

were in the house, she'd listen to the fall of his footsteps with the utmost care; and when she had reason
to fear that there was anything like a lengthened
tête-à-tête upstairs, she would steal on the pair, if
possible, unawares, and interrupt, without the least
reserve, any billing and cooing which might be going
on, sending the delinquent daughter to her work, and
giving a glower at the swain, which she expected
might be sufficient to deter him from similar offences
for some little time.

The girls, consequently, were taught to be on the
alert—to steal about on tiptoe, to elude their mother's
watchful ear, to have recourse to a thousand little
methods of deceiving her, and to baffle her with her
own weapons. The mother, if she suspected that any
prohibited frolic was likely to be carried on, at a late
hour, would tell her daughters that she was going to
bed, and would shut herself up for a couple of hours
in her bedroom, and then steal out eavesdropping,
peeping through key-holes and listening at door-
handles; and the daughters, knowing their mother's
practice, would not come forth till the listening and
peeping had been completed, and till they had ascertained, by some infallible means, that the old woman
was between the sheets.

Each party knew the tricks of the other; and yet,
taking it all in all, the widow got on very well with
her children, and everybody said what a good mother
she had been: she was accustomed to use deceit, and
was therefore not disgusted by it in others. Whether
the system of domestic manners which I have described is one likely to induce to sound restraint and
good morals is a question which I will leave to be
discussed by writers on educational points.

However Meg managed it, she did contrive that
her mother should not go near the little parlour this
Sunday morning, and Anty was left alone, to receive
her lover's visit. I regret to say that he was long in
paying it. He loitered about the chapel gates before
he came home; and seemed more than usually willing

to talk to anyone about anything. At last, however, just as Meg was getting furious, he entered the inn.

'Why, Martin, you born ideot—av' she ain't waiting for you this hour and more!'

'Thim that's long waited for is always welcome when they do come,' replied Martin.

'Well—afther all I've done for you! Are you going in now?—cause, av' you don't, I'll go and tell her not to be tasing herself about you. I'll neither be art or part in any such schaming.'

'Schaming, is it, Meg? Faith, it'd be a clever fellow 'd beat you at that,' and, without waiting for his sister's sharp reply, he walked into the little room where Anty was sitting.

'So, Anty, you wouldn't come to mass?' he began.

'Maybe I'll go next Sunday,' said she.

'It's a long time since you missed mass before, I'm thinking.'

'Not since the Sunday afther father's death.'

'It's little you were thinking then how soon you'd be stopping down here with us at the inn.'

'That's thrue for you, Martin, God knows.'

At this point of the conversation Martin stuck fast: he did not know Rosalind's recipe for the difficulty a man feels, when he finds himself gravelled for conversation with his mistress; so he merely scratched his head, and thought hard to find what he'd say next. I doubt whether the conviction, which was then strong on his mind, that Meg was listening at the |keyhole to every word that passed, at all assisted him in the operation. At last, some Muse came to his aid, and he made out another sentence.

'It was very odd my finding you down here, all ready before me, wasn't it?'

''Deed it was: your mother was a very good woman to me that morning, anyhow.'

'And tell me now, Anty, do you like the inn?'

''Deed I do—but it's quare, like.'

'How quare?'

'Why, having Meg and Jane here: I wasn't ever used to anyone to talk to, only just the servants.'

'You'll have plenty always to talk to now—eh, Anty?' and Martin tried a sweet look at his lady love.

'I'm shure I don't know. Av' I'm only left quiet, that's what I most care about.'

'But, Anty, tell me—you don't want always to be what you call quiet?'

'Oh! but I do—why not?'

'But you don't mane, Anty, that you wouldn't like to have some kind of work to do—some occupation, like?'

'Why, I wouldn't like to be idle; but a person needn't be idle because they're quiet.'

'And that's thrue, Anty.' And Martin broke down again.

'There'd be a great crowd in chapel, I suppose?' said Anty.

'There was a great crowd.'

'And what was father Geoghegan preaching about?'

'Well, then, I didn't mind. To tell the truth, Anty, I came out most as soon as the preaching began; only I know he told the boys to pray that the liberathor might be got out of his throubles; and so they should—not that there's much to throuble him, as far as the verdict's concerned.'

'Isn't there then? I thought they made him out guilty?'

'So they did, the false ruffians: but what harum 'll that do? they daren't touch a hair of his head!'

Politics, however, are not a favourable introduction to love-making: so Martin felt, and again gave up the subject, in the hopes that he might find something better. 'What a fool the man is!' thought Meg to herself, at the door—'if I had a lover went on like that, wouldn't I pull his ears!'

Martin got up—walked across the room—looked out of the little window—felt very much ashamed of himself, and, returning, sat himself down on the sofa.

'Anty,' he said, at last, blushing nearly brown as

he spoke; 'were you thinking of what I was spaking to you about before I went to Dublin?'

Anty blushed also, now. 'About what?' she said.

'Why, just about you and me making a match of it. Come, Anty, dear, what's the good of losing time? I've been thinking of little else; and, afther what's been between us, you must have thought the matther over too, though you do let on to be so innocent. Come, Anty, now that you and mother's so thick, there can be nothing against it.'

'But indeed there is, Martin, a great dale against it—though I'm sure it's good of you to be thinking of me. There's so much against it, I think we had betther be of one mind, and give it over at once.'

'And what's to hindher us marrying, Anty, av' yourself is plazed? Av' you and I, and mother are plazed, sorrow a one that I know of has a word to say in the matther.'

'But Barry don't like it!'

'And, afther all, are you going to wait for what Barry likes? You didn't wait for what was plazing to Barry Lynch when you came down here; nor yet did mother when she went up and fetched you down at five in the morning, dreading he'd murdher you outright. And it was thrue for her, for he would, av' he was let, the brute. And are you going to wait for what he likes?'

'Whatever he's done, he's my brother; and there's only the two of us.'

'But it's not that, Anty—don't you know it's not that? Isn't it because you're afraid of him? because he threatened and frightened you? And what on 'arth could he do to harum you av' you was the wife of—of a man who'd, anyway, not let Barry Lynch, or anyone else, come between you and your comfort and aise?'

'But you don't know how wretched I've been since he spoke to me about—about getting myself married: you don't know what I've suffered; and I've a feeling that good would never come of it.'

'And, afther all, are you going to tell me now, that I may jist go my own way? Is that to be your answer, and all I'm to get from you?'

'Don't be angry with me, Martin. I'm maning to do everything for the best.'

'Maning?—what's the good of maning? Anyways, Anty, let me have an answer, for I'll not be making a fool of myself any longer. Somehow, all the boys here, every sowl in Dunmore, has it that you and I is to be married—and now, afther promising me as you did—'

'Oh, I never promised, Martin.'

'It was all one as a promise—and now I'm to be thrown overboard. And why?—because Barry Lynch got dhrunk, and frightened you. Av' I'd seen the ruffian striking you, I think I'd 've been near putting it beyond him to strike another woman iver again.'

'Glory be to God that you wasn't near him that night,' said Anty, crossing herself. 'It was bad enough, but av' the two of you should ever be set fighting along of me, it would kill me outright.'

'But who's talking of fighting, Anty, dear?' and Martin drew a little nearer to her—'who's talking of fighting? I never wish to spake another word to Barry the longest day that ever comes. Av' he'll get out of my way, I'll go bail he'll not find me in his.'

'But he wouldn't get out of your way, nor get out of mine, av' you and I got married: he'd be in our way, and we'd be in his, and nothing could iver come of it but sorrow and misery, and maybe bloodshed.'

'Them's all a woman's fears. Av' you an I were once spliced by the priest, God bless him, Barry wouldn't trouble Dunmore long afther.'

'That's another rason, too. Why should I be dhriving him out of his own house? you know he's a right to the house, as well as I.'

'Who's talking of dhriving him out? Faith, he'd be welcome to stay there long enough for me! He'd go, fast enough, without dhriving, though; you can't say the counthry wouldn't have a good riddhance of

him. But never mind that, Anty: it wasn't about
Barry, one way or the other, I was thinking, when I
first asked you to have me; nor it wasn't about myself altogether, as I could let you know; though, in
course, I'm not saying but that myself's as dear to
myself as another, an' why not? But to tell the
blessed truth, I was thinking av' you too; and that
you'd be happier and asier, let alone betther an'
more respecthable, as an honest man's wife, as I'd
make you, than being mewed up there in dread of
your life, never daring to open your mouth to a
Christian, for fear of your own brother, who niver
did, nor niver will lift a hand to sarve you, though he
wasn't backward to lift it to sthrike you, woman and
sisther though you were. Come, Anty, darlin,' he
added, after a pause, during which he managed to
get his arm behind her back, though he couldn't be
said to have it fairly round her waist—'Get quit of
all these quandaries, and say at once, like an honest
girl, you'll do what I'm asking—and what no living
man can hindher you from or say against it.—Or
else jist fairly say you won't, and I'll have done
with it.'

Anty sat silent, for she didn't like to say she
wouldn't; and she thought of her brother's threats,
and was afraid to say she would. Martin advanced a
little in his proceedings, however, and now succeeded
in getting his arm round her waist—and, having
done so, he wasn't slow in letting her feel its pressure.
She made an attempt, with her hand, to disengage
herself,—certainly not a successful, and, probably,
not a very energetic attempt, when the widow's step
was heard on the stairs. Martin retreated from his
position on the sofa, and Meg from hers outside the
door, and Mrs. Kelly entered the room, with Barry's
letter in her hand, Meg following, to ascertain the
cause of the unfortunate interruption.

XVIII

AN ATTORNEY'S OFFICE IN CONNAUGHT

' ANTY, here's a letter for ye,' began the widow.
'Terry's brought it down from the house, and
says it's from Misther Barry. I b'lieve he was in the
right not to bring it hisself.'

'A letther for me, Mrs. Kelly?—what can he be
writing about? I don't just know whether I ought
to open it or no;' and Anty trembled, as she turned
the epistle over and over again in her hands.

'What for would you not open it? The letther can't
hurt you, girl, whatever the writher might do.'

Thus encouraged, Anty broke the seal, and made
herself acquainted with the contents of the letter
which Daly had dictated; but she then found that
her difficulties had only just commenced. Was she
to send an answer, and if so, what answer? And if
she sent none, what notice ought she to take of it?
The matter was one evidently too weighty to be
settled by her own judgment, so she handed the
letter to be read, first by the widow, and then by
Martin, and lastly by the two girls, who, by this
time, were both in the room.

'Well, the dethermined impudence of that blackguard!' exclaimed Mrs. Kelly. 'Conspiracy!—av'
that don't bang Banagher! What does the man mane
by "conspiracy," eh, Martin?'

'Faith, you must ask himself that, mother; and
then it's ten to one he can't tell you.'

'I suppose,' said Meg, 'he wants to say that we're
all schaming to rob Anty of her money—only he
daren't, for the life of him, spake it out straight
forrard.'

'Or, maybe,' suggested Jane, 'he wants to bring
something agen us like this affair of O'Connell's—
only he'll find, down here, that he an't got Dublin
soft goods to deal wid.'

Then followed a consultation, as to the proper
steps to be taken in the matter.

The widow advised that father Geoghegan should be sent for to indite such a reply as a Christian ill-used woman should send to so base a letter. Meg, who was very hot on the subject, and who had read of some such proceeding in a novel, was for putting up in a blank envelope the letter itself, and returning it to Barry by the hands of Jack, the ostler; at the same time, she declared that 'No surrender' should be her motto. Jane was of opinion that 'Miss Anastasia Lynch's compliments to Mr. Barry Lynch, and she didn't find herself strong enough to move to Dunmore House at present,' would answer all purposes, and be, on the whole, the safest course. While Martin pronounced that 'if Anty would be led by him, she'd just pitch the letter behind the fire an' take no notice of it, good, bad, or indifferent.'

None of these plans pleased Anty, for, as she remarked, 'After all, Barry was her brother, and blood was thickher than wather.' So, after much consultation, pen, ink, and paper were procured, and the following letter was concocted between them, all the soft bits having been great stumbling-blocks, in which, however, Anty's quiet perseverance carried the point, in opposition to the wishes of all the Kellys. The words put in brackets were those peculiarly objected to.

Dunmore Inn. February, 1844.

Dear Barry,

I (am very sorry I) can't come back to the house, at any rate just at present. I am not very sthrong in health, and there are kind female friends about me here, which you know there couldn't be up at the house.'—Anty herself, in the original draft inserted 'ladies,' but the widow's good sense repudiated the term, and insisted on the word 'females': Jane suggested that 'females' did not sound quite respectful alone, and Martin thought that Anty might call them 'female friends,' which was consequently done. —'Besides. there are reasons why I'm quieter here, till things are a little more settled. I will forgive (and forget) all that happened up at the house between us'—'Why, you can't forget it,' said Meg. 'Oh, I could, av' he was kind to me. I'd forget it all in a week av' he was kind to me,' answered Anty—'(and I will do nothing particular without first letting you know).'—They were all loud against this paragraph, but they could not carry their point. 'I must tell you, dear Barry, that you are very much mistaken about the people of this house: they are dear, kind friends to me, and, wherever I am, I must love them to the last day of my life—but indeed I am, and hope you believe so,

Your affectionate sister,

ANASTASIA LYNCH.

When the last paragraph was read over Anty's shoulder, Meg declared she was a dear, dear creature: Jane gave her a big kiss, and began crying; even the widow put the corner of her apron to her eye, and Martin, trying to look manly and unconcerned, declared that he was 'quite shure they all loved her, and they'd be brutes and bastes av' they didn't!'

The letter, as given above, was finally decided on; written, sealed, and despatched by Jack, who was desired to be very particular to deliver it at the front door, with Miss Lynch's love, which was accordingly done. All the care, however, which had been bestowed on it did not make it palatable to Barry, who was alone when he received it, and merely muttered, as he read it, 'Confound her, low-minded slut! friends, indeed! what business has she with friends, except such as I please?—if I'd the choosing of her friends, they'd be a strait waistcoat, and the madhouse doctor. Good Heaven! that half my property—no, but two-thirds of it,—should belong to her!—the stupid, stiff-necked robber!'

These last pleasant epithets had reference to his respected progenitor.

On the same evening, after tea, Martin endeavoured

to make a little further advance with Anty, for he felt that he had been interrupted just as she was coming round; but her nerves were again disordered, and he soon found that if he pressed her now, he should only get a decided negative, which he might find it very difficult to induce her to revoke.

Anty's letter was sent off early on the Monday morning—at least, as early as Barry now ever managed to do anything—to the attorney at Tuam, with strong injunctions that no time was to be lost in taking further steps, and with a request that Daly would again come out to Dunmore. This, however, he did not at present think it expedient to do. So he wrote to Barry, begging him to come into Tuam on the Wednesday, to meet Moylan, whom he, Daly, would, if possible, contrive to see on the intervening day.

'Obstinate puppy!' said Barry to himself—'if he'd had the least pluck in life he'd have broken the will, or at least made the girl out a lunatic. But a Connaught lawyer hasn't half the wit or courage now that he used to have.' However, he wrote a note to Daly, agreeing to his proposal, and promising to be in Tuam at two o'clock on the Wednesday.

On the following day Daly saw Moylan, and had a long conversation with him. The old man held out for a long time, expressing much indignation at being supposed capable of joining in any underhand agreement for transferring Miss Lynch's property to his relatives the Kellys, and declaring that he would make public to every one in Dunmore and Tuam the base manner in which Barry Lynch was treating his sister. Indeed, Moylan kept to his story so long and so firmly that the young attorney was nearly giving him up; but at last he found his weak side.

'Well, Mr. Moylan,' he said, 'then I can only say your own conduct is very disinterested;—and I might even go so far as to say that you appear to me foolishly indifferent to your own concerns. Here's the agency of the whole property going a-begging: the rents, I believe, are about a thousand a-year: you

might be recaving them all by jist a word of your
mouth, and that only telling the blessed truth; and
here, you're going to put the whole thing into the
hands of young Kelly; throwing up even the half of
the business you have got!'

'Who says I'm afther doing any sich thing, Mr.
Daly?'

'Why, Martin Kelly says so. Didn't as many as
four or five persons hear him say, down at Dunmore,
that divil a one of the tenants'd iver pay a haporth
of the November rents to anyone only jist to himself? There was father Geoghegan heard him, an
Doctor Ned Blake.'

'Maybe he'll find his mistake, Mr. Daly.'

'Maybe he will, Mr. Moylan. Maybe we'll put the
whole affair into the courts, and have a regular
recaver over the property, under the Chancellor.
People, though they're ever so respectable in their
way,—and I don't mane to say a word against the
Kellys, Mr. Moylan, for they were always friends of
mine—but people can't be allowed to make a dead
set at a property like this, and have it all their own
way, like the bull in the china-shop. I know there has
been an agreement made, and that, in the eye of the
law, is a conspiracy. I positively know that an agreement has been made to induce Miss Lynch to become
Martin Kelly's wife; and I know the parties to it,
too; and I also know that an active young fellow like
him wouldn't be paying an agent to get in his rents;
and I thought, if Mr. Lynch was willing to appoint
you his agent, as well as his sister's, it might be worth
your while to lend us a hand to settle this affair,
without forcing us to stick people into a witness-box
whom neither I nor Mr. Lynch—'

'But what the d——l can I—'

'Jist hear me out, Mr. Moylan; you see, if they
once knew—the Kellys I mane—that you wouldn't
lend a hand to this piece of iniquity—'

'Which piece of iniquity, Mr. Daly?—for I'm
entirely bothered.'

'Ah, now, Mr. Moylan, none of your fun: this piece of iniquity of theirs, I say; for I can call it no less. If they once knew that you wouldn't help 'em, they'd be obliged to drop it all; the matter'd never have to go into court at all, and you'd jist step into the agency fair and aisy; and, into the bargain, you'd do nothing but an honest man's work.'

The old man broke down, and consented to 'go agin the Kellys,' as he somewhat ambiguously styled his apostasy, provided the agency was absolutely promised to him; and he went away with the understanding that he was to come on the following day and meet Mr. Lynch.

At two o'clock, punctual to the time of his appointment, Moylan was there, and was kept waiting an hour in Daly's little parlour. At the end of this time Barry came in, having invigorated his courage and spirits with a couple of glasses of brandy. Daly had been for some time on the look-out for him, for he wished to say a few words to him in private, and give him his cue before he took him into the room where Moylan was sitting. This could not well be done in the office, for it was crowded. It would, I think, astonish a London attorney in respectable practice, to see the manner in which his brethren towards the west of Ireland get through their work. Daly's office was open to all the world; the front door of the house, of which he rented the ground floor, was never closed, except at night; nor was the door of the office, which opened immediately into the hall.

During the hour that Moylan was waiting in the parlour, Daly was sitting, with his hat on, upon a high stool, with his feet resting on a small counter which ran across the room, smoking a pipe: a boy, about seventeen years of age, Daly's clerk, was filling up numbers of those abominable formulas of legal persecution in which attorneys deal, and was plying his trade as steadily as though no February blasts were blowing in on him through the open door, no sounds of loud and boisterous conversation were

rattling in his ears. The dashing manager of one of
the branch banks in the town was sitting close to the
little stove, and raking out the turf ashes with the
office rule, while describing a drinking-bout that had
taken place on the previous Sunday at Blake's of
Blakemount; he had a cigar in his mouth, and was
searching for a piece of well-kindled turf, wherewith to
light it. A little fat oily shopkeeper in the town, who
called himself a woollen merchant, was standing with
the raised leaf of the counter in his hand, roaring
with laughter at the manager's story. Two frieze
coated farmers, outside the counter, were stretching
across it, and whispering very audibly to Daly some
details of litigation which did not appear very much
to interest him; and a couple of idle blackguards were
leaning against the wall, ready to obey any behest of
the attorney's which might enable them to earn a
sixpence without labour, and listening with all their
ears to the different interesting topics of conversation
which might be broached in the inner office.

'Here's the very man I'm waiting for, at last,' said
Daly, when, from his position on the stool, he saw,
through the two open doors, the bloated red face of
Barry Lynch approaching; and, giving an impulse to
his body by a shove against the wall behind him, he
raised himself on to the counter, and, assisting himself by a pull at the collar of the frieze coat of the
farmer who was in the middle of his story, jumped to
the ground, and met his client at the front door.

'I beg your pardon, Mr. Lynch,' said he as soon as
he had shaken hands with him, 'but will you just
step up to my room a minute, for I want to spake to
you;' and he took him up into his bed-room, for he
hadn't a second sitting-room. 'You'll excuse my
bringing you up here, for the office was full, you see,
and Moylan's in the parlour.'

'The d—l he is! He came round then, did he, eh,
Daly?'

'Oh, I've had a terrible hard game to play with
him. I'd no idea he'd be so tough a customer, or

make such a good fight; but I think I've managed him.'

'There was a regular plan then, eh, Daly? Just as I said. It was a regular planned scheme among them?'

'Wait a moment, and you'll know all about it, at least as much as I know myself; and, to tell the truth, that's devilish little. But, if we manage to break off the match, and get your sister clane out of the inn there, you must give Moylan your agency, at any rate for two or three years.'

'You haven't promised that?'

'But I have, though. We can do nothing without it: it was only when I hinted that, that the old sinner came round.'

'But what the deuce is it he's to do for us, after all?'

'He's to allow us to put him forward as a bugbear, to frighten the Kellys with: that's all, and, if we can manage that, that's enough. But come down now. I only wanted to warn you that, if you think the agency is too high a price to pay for the man's services, whatever they may be, you must make up your mind to dispense with them.'

'Well,' answered Barry, as he followed the attorney downstairs, 'I can't understand what you're about; but I suppose you must be right;' and they went into the little parlour where Moylan was sitting.

Moylan and Barry Lynch had only met once, since the former had been entrusted to receive Anty's rents, on which occasion Moylan had been grossly insulted by her brother. Barry, remembering the meeting, felt very awkward at the idea of entering into amicable conversation with him, and crept in at the door like a whipped dog. Moylan was too old to feel any such compunctions, and consequently made what he intended to be taken as a very complaisant bow to his future patron. He was an ill-made, ugly, stumpy man, about fifty; with a blotched face, straggling sandy hair, and grey shaggy whiskers. He wore a long brown great coat, buttoned up to his chin, and this was the only article of wearing apparel visible upon him: in his hands he twirled a shining new four-and-fourpenny hat.

As soon as their mutual salutations were over, Daly commenced his business.

'There is no doubt in the world, Mr. Lynch,' said he, addressing Barry, 'that a most unfair attempt has been made by this family to get possession of your sister's property—a most shameful attempt, which the law will no doubt recognise as a misdemeanour. But I think we shall be able to stop their game without any law at all, which will save us the annoyance of putting Mr. Moylan here, and other respectable witnesses, on the table. Mr. Moylan says that very soon afther your father's will was made known—'

'Now, Mr. Daly—shure I niver said a word in life at all about the will,' said Moylan, interrupting him.

'No, you did not: I mane, very soon afther you got the agency—'

'Divil a word I said about the agency, either.'

'Well, well; some time ago—he says that, some time ago, he and Martin Kelly were talking over your sister's affairs; I believe the widow was there, too.'

'Ah, now, Mr. Daly—why'd you be putting them words into my mouth? sorrow a word of the kind I iver utthered at all.'

'What the deuce was it you did say, then?'

'Faix, I don't know that I said much, at all.'

'Didn't you say, Mr. Moylan, that Martin Kelly was talking to you about marrying Anty, some six weeks ago?'

'Maybe I did; he was spaking about it.'

'And, if you were in the chair now, before a Jury, wouldn't you swear that there was a schame among them to get Anty Lynch married to Martin Kelly? Come, Mr. Moylan, that's all we want to know: if you can't say as much as that for us now, just that we may let the Kellys know what sort of evidence we could bring against them, if they push us, we must only have you and others summoned, and see what you'll have to say then.'

'Oh, I'd say the truth, Mr. Daly—divil a less—and I'd do as much as that now; but I thought Mr. Lynch was wanting to say something about the property?'

'Not a word then I've to say about it,' said Barry, 'except that I won't let that robber, young Kelly, walk off with it, as long as there's law in the land.'

'Mr. Moylan probably meant about the agency,' observed Daly.

Barry looked considerably puzzled, and turned to the attorney for assistance. 'He manes,' continued Daly, 'that he and the Kellys are good friends, and it wouldn't be any convenience to him just to say anything that wouldn't be pleasing to them, unless we could make him independent of them:—isn't that about the long and the short of it, Mr. Moylan?'

'Indepindent of the Kellys, is it, Mr. Daly?—Faix, thin, I'm teetotally indepindent of them this minute, and mane to continue so, glory be to God. Oh, I'm not afeard to tell the thruth agin ere a Kelly in Galway or Roscommon—and, av' that was all, I don't see why I need have come here this day. When I'm called upon in the rigular way, and has a rigular question put me before the Jury, either at Sessions or 'Sizes, you'll find I'll not be bothered for an answer, and, av' that's all, I b'lieve I may be going,'—and he made a movement towards the door.

'Just as you please, Mr. Moylan,' said Daly; 'and you may be sure that you'll not be long without an opportunity of showing how free you are with your answers. But, as a friend, I tell you you'll be wrong to lave this room till you've had a little more talk with Mr. Lynch and myself. I believe I mentioned to you Mr. Lynch was looking out for someone to act as agent over his portion of the Dunmore property?'

Barry looked as black as thunder, but he said nothing.

'You war, Mr. Daly. Av' I could accommodate Mr. Lynch, I'm shure I'd be happy to undhertake the business.'

'I believe, Mr. Lynch,' said Daly, turning to the other, ' I may go so far as to promise Mr. Moylan the agency of the whole property, provided Miss Lynch is induced to quit the house of the Kellys? Of course, Mr. Moylan, you can see that as long as Miss Lynch is in a position of unfortunate hostility to her brother, the same agent could not act for both; but I think my client is inclined to put his property under your management, providing his sister returns to her own home. I believe I'm stating your wishes, Mr. Lynch.'

'Manage it your own way,' said Barry, 'for I don't see what you're doing. If this man can do anything for me, why, I suppose I must pay him for it; and if so, your plan's as good a way of paying him as another.'

The attorney raised his hat with his hand, and scratched his head: he was afraid that Moylan would have again gone off in a pet at Lynch's brutality, but the old man sat quite quiet. He wouldn't have much minded what was said to him, as long as he secured the agency.

'You see, Mr. Moylan,' continued Daly, 'you can have the agency. Five per cent. upon the rents is what my client—'

'No, Daly—Five per cent.!—I'm shot if I do!' exclaimed Barry.

'I'm gething twenty-five pounds per annum from Miss Anty, for her half, and I wouldn't think of collecting the other for less,' declared Moylan.

And then a long battle followed on this point, which it required all Daly's tact and perseverance to adjust. The old man was pertinacious, and many whispers had to be made into Barry's ear before the matter could be settled. It was, however, at last agreed that notice was to be served on the Kellys, of

Barry Lynch's determination to indict them for a
conspiracy; that Daly was to see the widow, Martin,
and, if possible, Anty, and tell them all that Moylan
was prepared to prove that such a conspiracy had
been formed;—care was also to be taken that copies
of the notices so served should be placed in Anty's
hands. Moylan, in the meantime, agreed to keep out
of the way, and undertook, should he be unfortunate
enough to encounter any of the family of the Kellys,
to brave the matter out by declaring that 'av' he
war brought before the Judge and Jury he couldn't
do more than tell the blessed thruth, and why not?'
In reward for this, he was to be appointed agent over
the entire property the moment that Miss Lynch
left the inn, at which time he was to receive a document, signed by Barry, undertaking to retain him in
the agency for four years certain, or else to pay him
a hundred pounds when it was taken from him.

These terms having been mutually agreed to, and
Barry having, with many oaths, declared that he was
a most shamefully ill-used man, the three separated.
Moylan skulked off to one of his haunts in the town;
Barry went to the bank, to endeavour to get a bill
discounted; and Daly returned to his office, to prepare the notices for the unfortunate widow and her
son.

XIX

MR. DALY VISITS THE DUNMORE INN

DALY let no grass grow under his feet, for early on
the following morning he hired a car, and proceeded to Dunmore, with the notices in his pocket.
His feelings were not very comfortable on his journey,
for he knew that he was going on a bad errand, and he
was not naturally either a heartless or an unscrupulous
man, considering that he was a provincial attorney;
but he was young in business, and poor, and he could
not afford to give up a client. He endeavoured to
persuade himself that it certainly was a wrong thing

for Martin Kelly to marry such a woman as Anty
Lynch, and that Barry had some show of justice on
his side; but he could not succeed. He knew that
Martin was a frank, honourable fellow, and that a
marriage with him would be the very thing most
likely to make Anty happy; and he was certain,
moreover, that, however anxious Martin might naturally be to secure the fortune, he would take no
illegal or even unfair steps to do so. He felt that his
client was a ruffian of the deepest die: that his sole
object was to rob his sister, and that he had no case
which it would be possible even to bring before a
jury. His intention now was, merely to work upon
the timidity and ignorance of Anty and the other
females, and to frighten them with a bugbear in the
shape of a criminal indictment; and Daly felt that
the work he was about was very, very dirty work.
Two or three times on the road, he had all but made
up his mind to tear the letters he had in his pocket,
and to drive at once to Dunmore House, and tell
Barry Lynch that he would do nothing further in the
case. And he would have done so, had he not reflected that he had gone so far with Moylan, that he
could not recede, without leaving it in the old rogue's
power to make the whole matter public.

As he drove down the street of Dunmore, he endeavoured to quiet his conscience, by reflecting that
he might still do much to guard Anty from the ill
effects of her brother's rapacity; and that at any rate
he would not see her property taken from her, though
she might be frightened out of her matrimonial
speculation.

He wanted to see the widow, Martin, and Anty,
and if possible to see them, at first, separately; and
fortune so far favoured him that, as he got off the
car, he saw our hero standing at the inn door.

'Ah! Mr. Daly,' said he, coming up to the car and
shaking hands with the attorney, for Daly put out
his hand to him—'how are you again?—I suppose
you're going up to the house? They say you're

Barry's right hand man now. Were you coming into the inn?'

'Why, I will step in just this minute; but I've a word I want to spake to you first.'

'To me!' said Martin.

'Yes, to you, Martin Kelly: isn't that quare?' and then he gave directions to the driver to put up the horse, and bring the car round again in an hour's time. 'D' you remember my telling you, the day we came into Dunmore on the car together, that I was going up to the house?'

'Faith I do, well; it's not so long since.'

'And do you mind my telling you, I didn't know from Adam what it was for, that Barry Lynch was sending for me?'

'And I remember that, too.'

'And that I tould you, that when I did know I shouldn't tell you?'

'Begad you did, Mr. Daly; thim very words.'

'Why then, Martin, I tould you what wasn't thrue, for I'm come all the way from Tuam, this minute, to tell you all about it.'

Martin turned very red, for he rightly conceived that when an attorney came all the way from Tuam to talk to him, the tidings were not likely to be agreeable.

'And is it about Barry Lynch's business?'

'It is.'

'Then it's schames—there's divil a doubt of that.'

'It is schames, as you say, Martin,' said Daly, slapping him on the shoulder—'fine schames—no less than a wife with four hundred a-year! Wouldn't that be a fine schame?'

''Deed it would, Mr. Daly, av' the wife and the fortune were honestly come by.'

'And isn't it a hundred pities that I must come and upset such a pretty schame as that? But, for all that, it's thrue. I'm sorry for you, Martin, but you must give up Anty Lynch.'

'Give her up, is it? Faith I haven't got her to give up, worse luck.'

'Nor never will, Martin; and that's worse luck again.'

'Well, Mr. Daly, av' that's all you've come to say, you might have saved yourself car-hire. Miss Lynch is nothing to me, mind; how should she be? But av' she war, neither Barry Lynch—who's as big a rogue as there is from this to hisself and back again—nor you, who, I take it, ain't rogue enough to do Barry's work, wouldn't put me off it.'

'Well, Martin; thank 'ee for the compliment. But now, you know what I've come about, and there's no joke in it. Of course I don't want you to tell me anything of your plans; but, as Mr. Lynch's lawyer, I must tell you so much as this of his:—that, if his sister doesn't lave the inn, and honestly assure him that she'll give up her intention of marrying you, he's determined to take proceedings.' He then fumbled in his pocket, and, bringing out the two notices, handed to Martin the one addressed to him. 'Read that, and it'll give you an idea what we're afther. And when I tell you that Moylan owns, and will swear to it too, that he was present when all the plans were made, you'll see that we're not going to sea without wind in our sails.'

'Well—I'm shot av' I know the laist in the world what all this is about!' said Martin, as he stood in the street, reading over the legally-worded letter— '"conspiracy!"—well that'll do, Mr. Daly; go on— "enticing away from her home!"—that's good, when the blackguard nearly knocked the life out of her, and mother brought her down here, from downright charity, and to prevent murdher—"wake intellects!"—well, Mr. Daly, I didn't expect this kind of thing from you: begorra, I thought you were above this!—wake intellects! faith, they're a dale too sthrong, and too good—and too wide awake too, for Barry to get the betther of her that way. Not that I'm in the laist in life surprised at anything he'd do; but I thought that you, Mr. Daly, wouldn't put your hands to such work as that.'

Daly felt the rebuke, and felt it strongly, too; but now that he was embarked in the business, he must put the best face he could upon it. Still it was a moment or two before he could answer the young farmer.

'Why,' he said—'why did you put your hands to such a dirty job as this, Martin?—you were doing well, and not in want—and how could you let any-one persuade you to go and sell yourself to an ugly ould maid, for a few hundred pounds? Don't you know, that if you were married to her this minute, you'd have a lawsuit that'd go near to ruin you before you could get possession of the property?'

'Av' I'm in want of legal advice, Mr. Daly, which thank God, I'm not, nor likely to be—but av' I war, it's not from Barry Lynch's attorney I'd be looking for it.'

'I'd be sorry to see you in want of it, Martin; but if you mane to keep out of the worst kind of law, you'd better have done with Anty Lynch. I'd a dale sooner be drawing up a marriage settlement between you and some pretty girl with five or six hundred pound fortune, than I'd be exposing to the counthry such a mane trick as this you're now afther, of seducing a poor half-witted ould maid, like Anty Lynch, into a disgraceful marriage.'

'Look here, Mr. Daly,' said the other; 'you've hired yourself out to Barry Lynch, and you must do his work, I suppose, whether it's dirthy or clane; and you know yourself, as well as I can tell you, which it's likely to be—'

'That's my concern; lave that to me; you've quite enough to do to mind yourself.'

'But av' he's nothing bether for you to do, than to send you here bally-ragging and calling folks out of their name, he must have a sight more money to spare than I give him credit for; and you must be a dale worse off than your neighbours thought you, to do it for him.'

'That'll do,' said Mr. Daly, knocking at the door

of the inn; 'only, remember, Mr. Kelly, you've now
received notice of the steps which my client feels
himself called upon to take.'

Martin turned to go away, but then, reflecting
that it would be as well not to leave the women by
themselves in the power of the enemy, he also
waited at the door till it was opened by Katty.

'Is Miss Lynch within?' asked Daly.

'Go round to the shop, Katty,' said Martin, 'and
tell mother to come to the door. There's a gentleman
wanting her.'

'It was Miss Lynch I asked for,' said Daly, still
looking to the girl for an answer.

'Do as I bid you, you born ideot, and don't stand
gaping there,' shouted Martin to the girl, who immediately ran off towards the shop.

'I might as well warn you, Mr. Kelly, that, if Miss
Lynch is denied to me, the fact of her being so denied
will be a very sthrong proof against you and your
family. In fact, it amounts to an illegal detention of
her person, in the eye of the law.' Daly said this in
a very low voice, almost a whisper.

'Faith, the law must have quare eyes, av' it makes
anything wrong with a young lady being asked the
question whether or no she wishes to see an attorney,
at eleven in the morning.'

'An attorney!' whispered Meg to Jane and Anty,
at the top of the stairs.

'Heaven and 'arth,' said poor Anty, shaking and
shivering—'what's going to be the matter now?'

'It's young Daly,' said Jane, stretching forward
and peeping down the stairs: 'I can see the curl of
his whiskers.'

By this time the news had reached Mrs. Kelly, in
the shop, 'that a sthrange gentleman war axing for
Miss Anty, but that she warn't to be shown to him on
no account;' so the widow dropped her tobacco
knife, flung off her dirty apron, and, having summoned Jane and Meg to attend to the mercantile
affairs of the establishment—turned into the inn,

and met Mr. Daly and her son still standing at the bottom of the stairs.

The widow curtsied ceremoniously, and wished Mr. Daly good morning, and he was equally civil in his salutation.

'Mr. Daly's going to have us all before the assizes, mother. We'll never get off without the treadmill, any way: it's well av' the whole kit of us don't have to go over the wather at the queen's expense!'

'The Lord be good to us;' said the widow, crossing herself. 'What's the matter, Mr. Daly?'

'Your son's joking, ma'am. I was only asking to see Miss Lynch, on business.'

'Step upstairs, mother, into the big parlour, and don't let's be standing talking here where all the world can hear us.'

'And wilcome, for me, I'm shure'—said the widow, stroking down the front of her dress with the palms of her hands, as she walked upstairs—'and wilcome too for me I'm very shure. I've said or done nothing as I wish to consail, Mr. Daly. Will you be plazed to take a chair?' and the widow sat down herself on a chair in the middle of the room, with her hands folded over each other in her lap, as if she was preparing to answer questions from that time to a very late hour in the evening.

'And now, Mr. Daly—av' you've anything to say to a poor widdy like me, I'm ready.'

'My chief object in calling, Mrs. Kelly, was to see Miss Lynch. Would you oblige me by letting Miss Lynch know that I'm waiting to see her on business.'

'Maybe it's a message from her brother, Mr. Daly?' said Mrs. Kelly.

'You had better go in to Miss Lynch, mother,' said Martin, 'and ask her av' it's pleasing to her to see Mr. Daly. She can see him, in course, av' she likes.'

'I don't see what good 'll come of her seeing him,' rejoined the widow. 'With great respect to you, Mr. Daly, and not maning to say a word agin you, I

don't see how Anty Lynch 'll be the betther for seeing ere an attorney in the counthry.'

'I don't want to frighten you, ma'am,' said Daly;
'but I can assure you, you will put yourself in a very
awkward position if you refuse to allow me to see
Miss Lynch.'

'Ah, mother!' said Martin, 'don't have a word to
say in the matther at all, one way or the other.
Just tell Anty Mr. Daly wishes to see her—let her
come or not, just as she chooses. What's she afeard
of, that she shouldn't hear what anyone has to say
to her?'

The widow seemed to be in great doubt and per-
plexity, and continued whispering with Martin for
some time, during which Daly remained standing
with his back to the fire. At length Martin said,
'Av' you've got another of them notices to give my
mother, Mr. Daly, why don't you do it?'

'Why, to tell you the thruth,' answered the attorney, 'I don't want to throuble your mother unless
it's absolutely necessary; and although I have the
notice ready in my pocket, if I could see Miss Lynch,
I might be spared the disagreeable job of serving it
on her.'

'The Holy Virgin save us!' said the widow; 'an'
what notice is it at all, you're going to serve on a
poor lone woman like me?'

'Be said by me, mother, and fetch Anty in here.
Mr. Daly won't expect, I suppose, but what you
should stay and hear what it is he has to say?'

'Both you and your mother are welcome to hear all
that I have to say to the lady,' said Daly; for he felt
that it would be impossible for him to see Anty alone.

The widow unwillingly got up to fetch her guest.
When she got to the door, she turned round, and
said, 'And is there a notice, as you calls it, to be
sarved on Miss Lynch?'

'Not a line, Mrs. Kelly; not a line, on my honour.
I only want her to hear a few words that I'm commissioned by her brother to say to her.'

'And you're not going to give her any paper—nor nothing of that sort at all?'

'Not a word, Mrs. Kelly.'

'Ah, mother,' said Martin, 'Mr. Daly couldn't hurt her, av' he war wishing, and he's not. Go and bring her in.'

The widow went out, and in a few minutes returned, bringing Anty with her, trembling from head to foot. The poor young woman had not exactly heard what had passed between the attorney and the mother and her son, but she knew very well that his visit had reference to her, and that it was in some way connected with her brother. She had, therefore, been in a great state of alarm since Meg and Jane had left her alone. When Mrs. Kelly came into the little room where she was sitting, and told her that Mr. Daly had come to Dunmore on purpose to see her, her first impulse was to declare that she wouldn't go to him; and had she done so, the widow would not have pressed her. But she hesitated, for she didn't like to refuse to do anything which her friend asked her; and when Mrs. Kelly said, 'Martin says as how the man can't hurt you, Anty, so you'd betther jist hear what it is he has to say,' she felt that she had no loophole of escape, and got up to comply.

'But mind, Anty,' whispered the cautious widow, as her hand was on the parlour door, 'becase this Daly is wanting to speak to you, that's no rason you should be wanting to spake to him; so, if you'll be said by me, you'll jist hould your tongue, and let him say on.'

Fully determined to comply with this prudent advice, Anty followed the old woman, and, curtseying at Daly without looking at him, sat herself down in the middle of the old sofa, with her hands crossed before her.

'Anty,' said Martin, making great haste to speak, before Daly could commence, and then checking himself as he remembered that he shouldn't have ventured on the familiarity of calling her by her

Christian name in Daly's presence—'Miss Lynch, I
mane—as Mr. Daly here has come all the way from
Tuam on purpose to spake to you, it wouldn't perhaps be manners in you to let him go back without
hearing him. But remember, whatever your brother
says, or whatever Mr. Daly says for him—and it's
all one—you're still your own mistress, free to act
and to spake, to come and to go; and that neither the
one nor the other can hurt you, or mother, or me, nor
anybody belonging to us.'

'God knows,' said Daly, 'I want to have no hand
in hurting any of you; but, to tell the truth, Martin,
it would be well for Miss Lynch to have a better
adviser than you, or she may get herself, and, what
she'll think more of, she'll get her friends—maning
you, Mrs. Kelly, and your family—into a heap of
throubles.'

'Oh, God forbid, thin!' exclaimed Anty.

'Niver mind us, Mr. Daly,' said the widow. 'The
Kellys was always able to hould their own; thanks be
to glory.'

'Well, I've said my say, Mr. Daly,' said Martin,
'and now do you say your'n: as for throubles, we've
all enough of thim; but your own must have been
bad, when you undhertook this sort of job for Barry
Lynch.'

'Mind yourself, Martin, as I told you before, and
you'll about have enough to do.—Miss Lynch, I've
been instructed by your brother to draw up an indictment against Mrs. Kelly and Mr. Kelly, charging
them with conspiracy to get possession of your fortune.'

'A what!' shouted the widow, jumping up from
her chair—'to rob Anty Lynch of her fortune! I'd
have you to know, Mr. Daly, I wouldn't demane myself to rob the best gentleman in Connaught, let alone
a poor unprotected young woman, whom I've—'

'Whist, mother—go asy,' said Martin. 'I tould
you that that was what war in the paper he gave me;
he'll give you another, telling you all about it just
this minute.'

'Well, the born ruffian! Does he dare to accuse me of wishing to rob his sister! Now, Mr. Daly, av' the blessed thruth is in you this minute, don't your own heart know who it is, is most likely to rob Anty Lynch?—Isn't it Barry Lynch himself is thrying to rob his own sisther this minute? ay, and he'd murdher her too, only the heart within him isn't sthrong enough.'

'Ah, mother! don't be saying such things,' said Martin; 'what business is that of our'n? Let Barry send what messages he plazes; I tell you it's all moonshine; he can't hurt the hair of your head, nor Anty's neither. Go asy, and let Mr. Daly say what he has to say, and have done with it.'

'It's asy to say "go asy"—but who's to sit still and be tould sich things as that? Rob Anty Lynch indeed!'

'If you'll let me finish what I have to say, Mrs. Kelly, I think you'll find it betther for the whole of us,' said Daly.

'Go on thin, and be quick with it; but don't talk to dacent people about robbers any more. Robbers indeed! they're not far to fitch; and black robbers too, glory be to God.'

'Your brother, Miss Lynch, is determined to bring this matter before a jury at the assizes, for the sake of protecting you and your property.'

'Protecthing Anty Lynch!—is it Barry? The Holy Virgin defind her from sich prothection! a broken head the first moment the dhrink makes his heart sthrong enough to sthrike her!'

'Ah, mother! you're a fool,' exclaimed Martin: 'why can't you let the man go on?—ain't he paid for saying it? Well, Mr. Daly, begorra I pity you, to have such things on your tongue; but go on, go on, and finish it.'

'Your brother conceives this to be his duty,' continued Daly, rather bothered by the manner in which he had to make his communication, 'and it is a duty which he is determined to go through with.'

'Duty!' said the widow, with a twist of her nose, and giving almost a whistle through her lips, in a manner which very plainly declared the contempt she felt for Barry's ideas of duty.

'With this object,' continued Daly, 'I have already handed to Martin Kelly a notice of what your brother means to do; and I have another notice prepared in my pocket for his mother. The next step will be to swear the informations before a magistrate, and get the committals made out; Mrs. Kelly and her son will then have to give bail for their appearance at the assizes.'

'And so we can,' said the widow; 'betther bail than 'ere a Lynch or Daly—not but what the Dalys is respictable—betther bail, any way, than e'er a Lynch in Galway could show, either for sessions or 'sizes, by night or by day, winter or summer.'

'Ah, mother! you don't understhand: he's maning that we're to be tried in the dock, for staling Anty's money.'

'Faix, but that'd be a good joke! Isn't Anty to the fore herself to say who's robbed her? Take an ould woman's advice, Mr. Daly, and go back to Tuam: it ain't so asy to put salt on the tail of a Dunmore bird.'

'And so I will, Mrs. Kelly,' said Daly; 'but you must let me finish what I have to tell Miss Lynch.— This will be a proceeding most disagreeable to your brother's feelings.'

'Failings, indeed!' muttered the widow; 'faix, I b'lieve his chief failing at present's for sthrong dhrink!'

'—But he must go on with it, unless you at once lave the inn, return to your own home, and give him your promise that you will never marry Martin Kelly.'

Anty blushed deep crimson over her whole face at the mention of her contemplated marriage; and, to tell the truth, so did Martin.

'Here is the notice,' said Daly, taking the paper out of his pocket, 'and the matter now rests with yourself. If you'll only tell me that you'll be guided by your brother on this subject, I'll burn the notice at once; and I'll undertake to say that, as far as your property is concerned, your brother will not in the least interfere with you in the management of it.'

'And good rason why, Mr. Daly,' said the widow— 'jist becase he can't.'

'Well, Miss Lynch, am I to tell your brother that you are willing to oblige him in this matter?'

Whatever effect Daly's threats may have had on the widow and her son, they told strongly upon Anty; for she sat now the picture of misery and indecision. At last she said: 'Oh, Lord defend me! what am I to do, Mrs. Kelly?'

'Do?' said Martin; 'why, what should you do— but just wish Mr. Daly good morning, and stay where you are, snug and comfortable?'

'Av' you war to lave this, Anty, and go up to Dunmore House afther all that's been said and done, I'd say Barry was right, and that Ballinasloe Asylum was the fitting place for you,' said the widow.

'The blessed virgin guide and prothect me,' said Anty, 'for I want her guidance this minute. Oh, that the walls of a convent was round me this minute—I wouldn't know what throuble was!'

'And you needn't know anything about throuble,' said Martin, who didn't quite like his mistress's allusion to a convent. 'You don't suppose there's a word of thruth in all this long story of Mr. Daly's?— He knows,—and I'll say it out to his face—he knows Barry don't dare carry on with sich a schame. He knows he's only come here to frighten you out of this, that Barry may have his will on you again.'

'And God forgive him his errand here this day,' said the widow, 'for it was a very bad one.'

'If you will allow me to offer you my advice, Miss Lynch,' said Daly, 'you will put yourself, at any rate for a time, under your brother's protection.'

'She won't do no sich thing,' said the widow. 'What! to be locked into the parlour agin—and be nigh murdhered? holy father!'

'Oh, no,' said Anty, at last, shuddering in horror at the remembrance of the last night she passed in Dunmore House, 'I cannot go back to live with him, but I'll do anything else, av' he'll only lave me, and my kind, kind friends, in pace and quiet.'

'Indeed, and you won't, Anty,' said the widow; 'you'll do nothing for him. Your frinds—that's av' you mane the Kellys—is very able to take care of themselves.'

'If your brother, Miss Lynch, will lave Dunmore House altogether, and let you have it to yourself, will you go and live there, and give him the promise not to marry Martin Kelly?'

'Indeed an' she won't,' said the widow. 'She'll give no promise of the kind. Promise, indeed! what for should she promise Barry Lynch whom she will marry, or whom she won't?'

'Raily, Mrs. Kelly, I think you might let Miss Lynch answer for herself.'

'I wouldn't, for all the world thin, go to live at Dunmore House,' said Anty.

'And you are determined to stay in this inn here?'

'In course she is—that's till she's a snug house of her own,' said the widow.

'Ah, mother!' said Martin, 'what for will you be talking?'

'And you're determined,' repeated Daly, 'to stay here?'

'I am,' faltered Anty.

'Then I have nothing further to do than to hand you this, Mrs. Kelly'—and he offered the notice to the widow, but she refused to touch it, and he consequently put it down on the table. 'But it is my duty to tell you, Miss Lynch, that the gentry of this counthry, before whom you will have to appear, will express very great indignation at your conduct in persevering in placing poor people like the Kellys in so dreadful a predicament, by your wilful and disgraceful obstinacy.'

Poor Anty burst into tears. She had been for some

time past trying to restrain herself, but Daly's last speech, and the horrible idea of the gentry of the country browbeating and frowning at her, completely upset her, and she hid her face on the arm of the sofa, and sobbed aloud.

'Poor people like the Kellys!' shouted the widow, now for the first time really angry with Daly—'not so poor, Mr. Daly, as to do dirthy work for anyone. I wish I could say as much this day for your mother's son! Poor people, indeed! I suppose, now, you wouldn't call Barry Lynch one of your poor people; but in my mind he's the poorest crature living this day in county Galway. Av' you've done now, Mr. Daly, you've my lave to be walking; and the less you let the poor Kellys see of you, from this time out, the betther.'

When Anty's sobs commenced, Martin had gone over to her to comfort her, 'Ah, Anty, dear,' he whispered to her, 'shure you'd not be minding what such a fellow as he'd be saying to you?—shure he's jist paid for all this—he's only sent here by Barry to thry and frighten you,'—but it was of no avail: Daly had succeeded at any rate in making her miserable, and it was past the power of Martin's eloquence to undo what the attorney had done.

'Well, Mr. Daly,' he said, turning round sharply, 'I suppose you have done here now, and the sooner you turn your back on this place the betther—An' you may take this along with you. Av' you think you've frightened my mother or me, you're very much mistaken.'

'Yes,' said Daly, 'I have done now, and I am sorry my business has been so unpleasant. Your mother, Martin, had betther not disregard that notice. Good morning, Miss Lynch: good morning, Mrs. Kelly; good morning, Martin;' and Daly took up his hat, and left the room.

'Good morning to you, Mr. Daly,' said Martin: 'as I've said before, I'm sorry to see you've taken to this line of business.'

As soon as the attorney was gone, both Martin and his mother attempted to console and re-assure poor Anty, but they did not find the task an easy one. 'Oh, Mrs. Kelly,' she said, as soon as she was able to say anything, 'I'm sorry I iver come here, I am: I'm sorry I iver set my foot in the house!'

'Don't say so, Anty, dear,' said the widow. 'What'd you be sorry for—an't it the best place for you?'

'Oh! but to think that I'd bring all these throubles on you! Betther be up there, and bear it all, than bring you and yours into law, and sorrow, and expense. Only I couldn't find the words in my throat to say it, I'd 've tould the man that I'd 've gone back at once. I wish I had—indeed, Mrs. Kelly, I wish I had.'

'Why, Anty,' said Martin, 'you an't fool enough to believe what Daly's been saying? Shure all he's afther is to frighthen you out of this. Never fear: Barry can't hurt us a halfporth, though no doubt he's willing enough, av' he had the way.'

'I wish I was in a convent, this moment,' said Anty. 'Oh! I wish I'd done as father asked me long since. Av' the walls of a convent was around me, I'd niver know what throubles was.'

'No more you shan't now,' said Martin: 'Who's to hurt you? Come, Anty, look up; there's nothing in all this to vex you.'

But neither son nor mother were able to soothe the poor young woman. The very presence of an attorney was awful to her; and all the jargon which Daly had used, of juries, judges, trials, and notices, had sounded terribly in her ears. The very names of such things were to her terrible realities, and she couldn't bring herself to believe that her brother would threaten to make use of such horrible engines of persecution, without having the power to bring them into action. Then, visions of the lunatic asylum, into which he had declared that he would throw her, flitted across her, and made her whole body shiver and shake; and again she remembered the horrid

glare of his eye, the hot breath, and the frightful
form of his visage, on the night when he almost told
her that he would murder her.

Poor Anty had at no time high or enduring spirits,
but such as she had were now completely quelled. A
dreadful feeling of coming evil—a foreboding of
misery, such as will sometimes overwhelm stronger
minds than Anty's, seemed to stifle her; and she
continued sobbing till she fell into hysterics, when
Meg and Jane were summoned to her assistance.
They sat with her for above an hour, doing all that
kindness and affection could suggest; but after a
time Anty told them that she had a cold, sick feeling
within herself, that she felt weak and ill, and that
she'd sooner go to bed. To bed they accordingly took
her; and Sally brought her tea, and Katty lighted a
fire in her room, and Jane read to her an edifying
article from the lives of the Saints, and Meg argued
with her as to the folly of being frightened. But it
was all of no avail; before night, Anty was really ill.
The next morning, the widow was obliged to own to
herself that such was the case. In the afternoon,
Doctor Colligan was called in; and it was many,
many weeks before Anty recovered from the effects
of the attorney's visit.

XX

VERY LIBERAL

WHEN the widow left the parlour, after having
placed her guest in the charge of her daughters,
she summoned her son to follow her down stairs, and
was very careful not to leave behind her the notice
which Daly had placed on the table. As soon as she
found herself behind the shutter of her little desk,
which stood in the shop-window, she commenced
very eagerly spelling it over. The purport of the
notice was, to inform her that Barry Lynch intended
immediately to apply to the magistrates to commit

her and her son, for conspiring together to inveigle
Anty into a marriage; and that the fact of their
having done so would be proved by Mr. Moylan, who
was prepared to swear that he had been present when
the plan had been arranged between them. The reader
is aware that whatever show of truth there might
be for this accusation, as far as Martin and Moylan
himself were concerned, the widow at any rate was
innocent; and he can conceive the good lady's indignation at the idea of her own connection, Moylan,
having been seduced over to the enemy. Though she
had put on a bold front against Daly, and though she
did not quite believe that Barry was in earnest in
taking proceedings against her, still her heart failed
her as she read the legal technicalities of the papers
she held in her hand, and turned to her son for
counsel in considerable tribulation.

'But there must be something in it, I tell you,'
said she. 'Though Barry Lynch, and that limb o' the
divil, young Daly, 'd stick at nothin in the way of lies
and desait, they'd niver go to say all this about
Moylan, unless he'd agree to do their bidding.'

'That's like enough, mother: I dare say Moylan
has been talked over—bought over rather; for he's
not one of them as'd do mischief for nothin.'

'And does the ould robber mane to say that
I—. As I live, I niver as much as mentioned Anty's
name to Moylan, except jist about the agency!'

'I'm shure you didn't, mother.'

'And what is it then he has to say agin us?'

'Jist lies; that's av' he were called on to say anything; but he niver will be. This is all one of Barry's
schames to frighten you, and get Anty turned out of
the inn.'

'Thin Master Barry doesn't know the widdy Kelly,
I can tell him that; for when I puts my hand to a
thing, I mane to pull through wid it. But tell me—
all this'll be costing money, won't it? Attorneys
don't bring thim sort of things about for nothing,'
and she gave a most contemptuous twist to the notice.

'Oh, Barry must pay for that.'

'I doubt that, Martin: he's not fond of paying, the mane, dirthy blackguard. I tell you what, you shouldn't iver have let Daly inside the house: he'll make us pay for the writing o' thim as shure as my name's Mary Kelly: av' he hadn't got into the house, he couldn't've done a halfporth.'

'I tell you, mother, it wouldn't have done not to let him see Anty. They'd have said we'd got her shut up here, and wouldn't let any one come nigh her.'

'Well, Martin, you'll see we'll have to pay for it. This comes of meddling with other folks! I wonder how I was iver fool enough to have fitched her down here!—Good couldn't come of daling with such people as Barry Lynch.'

'But you wouldn't have left her up there to be murdhered?'

'She's nothin' to me, and I don't know as she's iver like to be.'

'May-be not.'

'But, tell me, Martin—was there anything said between you and Moylan about Anty before she come down here?'

'How, anything said, mother?'

'Why, was there any schaming betwixt you?'

'Schaming?—when I want to schame, I'll not go shares with sich a fellow as Moylan.'

'Ah, but was there anything passed about Anty and you getting married? Come now, Martin; I'm in all this throuble along of you, and you shouldn't lave me in the dark. Was you talking to Moylan about Anty and her fortune?'

'Why, thin, I'll jist tell you the whole thruth, as I tould it all before to Mister Frank—that is, Lord Ballindine, up in Dublin; and as I wouldn't mind telling it this minute to Barry, or Daly, or any one else in the three counties. When Moylan got the agency, he come out to me at Toneroe; and afther talking a bit about Anty and her fortune, he let on as how it would be a bright spec for me to marry her, and I won't deny that it was he as first put it into my head. Well, thin, he had schames of his own about keeping the agency, and getting a nice thing out of the property himself, for putting Anty in my way; but I tould him downright I didn't know anything about that; and that 'av iver I did anything in the matter it would be all fair and above board; and that was all the conspiracy I and Moylan had.'

'And enough too, Martin,' said the widow. 'You'll find it's quite enough to get us into throuble. And why wouldn't you tell me what was going on between you?'

'There was nothing going on between us.'

'I say there was;—and to go and invaigle me into your schames without knowing a word about it!—It was a murdhering shame of you—and av' I do have to pay for it, I'll never forgive you.'

'That's right, mother; quarrel with me about it, do. It was I made you bring Anty down here, wasn't it? when I was up in Dublin all the time.'

'But to go and put yourself in the power of sich a fellow as Moylan! I didn't think you were so soft.'

'Ah, bother, mother! Who's put themselves in the power of Moylan?'

'I'll moyle him, and spoil him too, the false black-guard, to turn agin the family—them as has made him! I wondher what he's to get for swearing agin us?'—And then, after a pause, she added in a most pathetic voice—'oh, Martin, to think of being drag-ged away to Galway, before the whole counthry, to be made a conspirather of! I, that always paid my way, before and behind, though only a poor widdy! Who's to mind the shop, I wondher?—I'm shure Meg's not able; and there'll be Mary'll be jist nigh her time, and won't be able to come! Martin, you've been and ruined me with your plots and your marriages! What did you want with a wife, I wondher, and you so well off!—and Mrs. Kelly began wiping her eyes, for she was affected to tears at the prospect of her coming misery.

'Av' you take it so to heart, mother, you'd betther give Anty a hint to be out of this. You heard Daly tell her, that was all Barry wanted.'

Martin knew his mother tolerably well, or he would not have made this proposition. He understood what the real extent of her sorrow was, and how much of her lamentation he was to attribute to her laudable wish to appear a martyr to the wishes and pleasures of her children.

'Turn her out!' replied she, 'no, niver; and I didn't think I'd 've heard you asking me to.'

'I didn't ask you, mother,—only anything'd be betther than downright ruin.'

'I wouldn't demane myself to Barry so much as to wish her out of this now she's here. But it was along of you she came here, and av' I've to pay for all this lawyer work, you oughtn't to see me at a loss. I'm shure I don't know where your sisthers is to look for a pound or two when I'm gone, av' things goes on this way,' and again the widow whimpered.

'Don't let that throuble you, mother: av' there's anything to pay, I won't let it come upon you, any way. But I tell you there'll be nothing more about it.'

Mrs. Kelly was somewhat quieted by her son's guarantee, and, muttering that she couldn't afford to be wasting her mornings in that way, diligently commenced weighing out innumerable three-halfporths of brown sugar, and Martin went about his own business.

Daly left the inn, after his interview with Anty and the Kellys, in anything but a pleasant frame of mind. In the first place, he knew that he had been signally unsuccessful, and that his want of success had been mainly attributable to his having failed to see Anty alone; and, in the next place, he felt more than ever disgusted with his client. He began to reflect, for the first time, that he might, and probably would, irretrievably injure his character by undertaking, as Martin truly called it, such a very low line of business: that, if the matter were persevered in, every

one in Connaught would be sure to hear of Anty's
persecution; and that his own name would be so
mixed up with Lynch's in the transaction as to leave
him no means of escaping the ignominy which was so
justly due to his employer. Beyond these selfish
motives of wishing to withdraw from the business, he
really pitied Anty, and felt a great repugnance at
being the means of adding to her troubles; and he
was aware of the scandalous shame of subjecting her
again to the ill-treatment of such a wretch as her
brother, by threatening proceedings which he knew
could never be taken.

As he got on the car to return to Tuam, he determined that whatever plan he might settle on adopt-
ing, he would have nothing further to do with prose-
cuting or persecuting either Anty or the Kellys. 'I'll
give him the best advice I can about it,' said Daly to
himself; 'and if he don't like it he may do the other
thing. I wouldn't carry on with this game for all he's
worth, and that I believe is not much.' He had
intended to go direct to Dunmore House from the
Kellys, and to have seen Barry, but he would have
had to stop for dinner if he had done so; and though,
generally speaking, not very squeamish in his
society, he did not wish to enjoy another after-dinner
tête-à-tête with him—'It's better to get him over
to Tuam,' thought he, 'and try and make him see
rason when he's sober: nothing's too hot or too bad
for him, when he's mad dhrunk afther dinner.'

Accordingly, Lynch was again summoned to Tuam,
and held a second council in the attorney's little
parlour. Daly commenced by telling him that his
sister had seen him, and had positively refused to
leave the inn, and that the widow and her son had
both listened to the threats of a prosecution unmoved
and undismayed. Barry indulged in his usual volubility of expletives; expressed his fixed intention of
exterminating the Kellys; declared, with many
asseverations, his conviction that his sister was a
lunatic; swore, by everything under, in, and above

the earth, that he would have her shut up in the
Lunatic Asylum in Ballinasloe, in the teeth of the
Lord Chancellor and all the other lawyers in Ireland;
cursed the shades of his father, deeply and copi-
ously; assured Daly that he was only prevented from
recovering his own property by the weakness and
ignorance of his legal advisers, and ended by asking
the attorney's advice as to his future conduct.

'What the d——l, then, am I to do with the confounded ideot?' said he.

'If you'll take my advice, you'll do nothing.'

'What, and let her marry and have that young
blackguard brought up to Dunmore under my very
nose?'

'I'm very much afraid, Mr. Lynch, if you wish to
be quit of Martin Kelly, it is you must lave Dunmore.
You may be shure he won't.'

'Oh, as for that, I've nothing to tie me to Dunmore. I hate the place; I never meant to live there.
If I only saw my sister properly taken care of, and
that it was put out of her power to throw herself
away, I should leave it at once.'

'Between you and me, Mr. Lynch, she will be
taken care of; and as for throwing herself away, she
must judge of that herself. Take my word for it, the
best thing for you to do is to come to terms with
Martin Kelly, and to sell out your property in Dunmore. You'll make much better terms before marriage than you would afther, it stands to rason.'

Barry was half standing, and half sitting on the
small parlour table, and there he remained for a few
minutes, meditating on Daly's most unpleasant proposal. It was a hard pill for him to swallow, and he
couldn't get it down without some convulsive gri-
maces. He bit his under lip, till the blood came
through it, and at last said,

'Why, you've taken this thing up, Daly, as if you
were to be paid by the Kellys instead of by me! I
can't understand it, confound me if I can!'

Daly turned very red at the insinuation. He was

within an ace of seizing Lynch by the collar, and
expelling him in a summary way from his premises,
a feat which he was able to perform; and willing also,
for he was sick of his client; but he thought of it a
second time, and restrained himself.

'Mr. Lynch,' he said, after a moment or two,
'that's the second time you've made an observation
of that kind to me; and I'll tell you what; if your
business was the best in the county, instead of being
as bad a case as was ever put into a lawyer's hands,
I wouldn't stand it from you. If you think you can
let out your passion against me, as you do against
your own people, you'll find your mistake out very
soon; so you'd betther mind what you're saying.'

'Why, what the devil did I say?' said Lynch, half
abashed.

'I'll not repeat it—and you hadn't betther, either.
And now, do you choose to hear my professional
advice, and behave to me as you ought and shall do?
or will you go out of this and look out for another
attorney? To tell you the truth, I'd jist as lieve you'd
take your business to some one else.'

Barry's brow grew very black, and he looked at
Daly as though he would much like to insult him
again if he dared. But he did not dare. He had no
one else to look to for advice or support; he had
utterly estranged from him his father's lawyer; and
though he suspected that Daly was not true to him,
he felt that he could not break with him. He was
obliged, therefore, to swallow his wrath, though it
choked him, and to mutter something in the shape
of an apology.

It was a mutter: Daly heard something about its
being only a joke, and not expecting to be taken up so
d— sharp; and, accepting these sounds as an *amende
honorable*, again renewed his functions as attorney.

'Will you authorise me to see Martin Kelly, and
to treat with him? You'll find it the cheapest thing
you can do; and, more than that, it'll be what nobody
can blame you for.'

'How treat with him?—I owe him nothing—I don't see what I've got to treat with him about. Am I to offer him half the property on condition he'll consent to marry my sister? Is that what you mean?'

'No: that's not what I mean; but it'll come to much the same thing in the end. In the first place, you must withdraw all opposition to Miss Lynch's marriage; indeed, you must give it your direct sanction; and, in the next place, you must make an amicable arrangement with Martin about the division of the property.'

'What—coolly give him all he has the impudence to ask?—throw up the game altogether, and pitch the whole stakes into his lap?—Why, Daly, you—'

'Well, Mr. Lynch, finish your speech,' said Daly, looking him full in the face.

Barry had been on the point of again accusing the attorney of playing false to him, but he paused in time; he caught Daly's eye, and did not dare to finish the sentence which he had begun.

'I can't understand you, I mean,' said he; 'I can't understand what you're after: but go on; may-be you're right, but I can't see, for the life of me. What am I to get by such a plan as that?'

Barry was now cowed and frightened; he had no dram-bottle by him to reassure him, and he became, comparatively speaking, calm and subdued. Indeed, before the interview was over he fell into a pitiably lachrymose tone, and claimed sympathy for the many hardships he had to undergo through the ill-treatment of his family.

'I'll try and explain to you, Mr. Lynch, what you'll get by it. As far as I can understand, your father left about eight hundred a-year between the two— that's you and your sisther; and then there's the house and furniture. Nothing on earth can keep her out of her property, or prevent her from marrying whom she plases. Martin Kelly, who is an honest fellow, though sharp enough, has set his eye on her, and before many weeks you'll find he'll make her his

wife. Undher these circumstances, wouldn't he be
the best tenant you could find for Dunmore? You're
not fond of the place, and will be still less so when
he's your brother-in-law. Lave it altogether, Mr.
Lynch; give him a laise of the whole concern, and
if you'll do that now at once, take my word for it
you'll get more out of Dunmore than iver you will
by staying here, and fighting the matther out.'

'But about the debts, Daly?'

'Why, I suppose the fact is, the debts are all your
own, eh?'

'Well—suppose they are?'

'Exactly so: personal debts of your own. Why,
when you've made some final arrangement about the
property, you must make some other arrangement
with your creditors. But that's quite a separate
affair; you don't expect Martin Kelly to pay your
debts, I suppose?'

'But I might get a sum of money for the good-will,
mightn't I?'

'I don't think Martin's able to put a large sum
down. I'll tell you what I think you might ask; and
what I think he would give, to get your good-will and
consent to the match, and to prevent any further
difficulty. I think he'd become your tenant, for the
whole of your share, at a rent of five-hundred a year;
and maybe he'd give you three hundred pounds for
the furniture and stock, and things about the place.
If so, you should give him a laise of three lives.'

There was a good deal in this proposition that was
pleasing to Barry's mind: five hundred a-year without any trouble in collecting it; the power of living
abroad in the unrestrained indulgence of hotels and
billiard rooms; the probable chance of being able to
retain his income and bilk his creditors; the prospect
of shaking off from himself the consequences of a
connection with the Kellys, and being for ever rid of
Dunmore encumbrances. These things all opened
before his eyes a vista of future idle, uncontrolled
enjoyment, just suited to his taste, and strongly

tempted him at once to close with Daly's offer. But
still, he could hardly bring himself to consent to be
vanquished by his own sister; it was wormwood to
him to think that after all she should be left to the
undisturbed enjoyment of her father's legacy. He
had been brow-beaten by the widow, insulted by
young Kelly, cowed and silenced by the attorney,
whom he had intended to patronise and convert into
a creature of his own: he could however have borne
and put up with all this, if he could only have got his
will of his sister; but to give up to her, who had been
his slave all his life—to own, at last, that he had no
power over her, whom he had always looked upon as
so abject, so mean a thing; to give in, of his own
accord, to the robbery which had been committed
on him by his own father; and to do this, while he
felt convinced as he still did, that a sufficiently unscrupulous attorney could save him from such cruel
disgrace and loss, was a trial to which he could hardly
bring himself to submit, crushed and tamed as he
was.

He still sat on the edge of the parlour table, and
there he remained mute, balancing the pros and cons
of Daly's plan. Daly waited a minute or two for his
answer, and, finding that he said nothing, left him
alone for a time, to make up his mind, telling him
that he would return in about a quarter of an hour.
Barry never moved from his position; it was an
important question he had to settle, and so he felt it,
for he gave up to the subject his undivided attention.
Since his boyhood he had looked forward to a life
of ease, pleasure, and licence, and had longed for his
father's death that he might enjoy it. It seemed now
within his reach; for his means, though reduced,
would still be sufficient for sensual gratification. But,
idle, unprincipled, brutal, castaway wretch as Barry
was, he still felt the degradation of inaction, when
he had such stimulating motives to energy as un-
satisfied rapacity and hatred for his sister: ignorant
as he was of the meaning of the word right, he tried

to persuade himself that it would be wrong in him to yield.

Could he only pluck up sufficient courage to speak his mind to Daly, and frighten him into compliance with his wishes, he still felt that he might be successful—that he might, by some legal tactics, at any rate obtain for himself the management of his sister's property. But this he could not do: he felt that Daly was his master; and though he still thought that he might have triumphed had he come sufficiently prepared, that is, with a considerable quantum of spirits inside him, he knew himself well enough to be aware that he could do nothing without this assistance; and, alas, he could not obtain it there. He had great reliance in the efficacy of whiskey; he would trust much to a large dose of port wine; but with brandy he considered himself invincible.

He sat biting his lip, trying to think, trying to make up his mind, trying to gain sufficient self-composure to finish his interview with Daly with some appearance of resolution and self-confidence, but it was in vain; when the attorney returned, his face still plainly showed that he was utterly unresolved, utterly unable to resolve on anything.

'Well, Mr. Lynch,' said Daly, 'will you let me spake to Kelly about this, or would you rather sleep on the matther?'

Barry gave a long sigh—'Wouldn't he give six hundred, Daly? he'd still have two hundred clear, and think what that'd be for a fellow like him!'

'You must ask him for it yourself then; I'll not propose to him any such thing. Upon my soul, he'll be a great fool to give the five hundred, because he's no occasion to meddle with you in the matther at all, at all. But still I think he may give it; but as for asking for more—at any rate I won't do it; you can do what you like, yourself.'

'And am I to sell the furniture, and everything—horses, cattle, and everything about the place—for three hundred pounds?'

'Not unless you like it, you ain't, Mr. Lynch; but I'll tell you this—if you can do so, and do do so, it'll be the best bargain you ever made:—mind, one-half of it all belongs to your sisther.'

Barry muttered an oath through his ground teeth; he would have liked to scratch the ashes of his father from their resting-place, and wreak his vengeance on them, whenever this degrading fact was named to him.

'But I want the money, Daly,' said he: 'I couldn't get afloat unless I had more than that: I couldn't pay your bill, you know, unless I got a higher figure down than that. Come, Daly, you must do something for me; you must do something, you know, to earn the fees,' and he tried to look facetious, by giving a wretched ghastly grin.

'My bill won't be a long one, Mr. Lynch, and you may be shure I'm trying to make it as short as I can. And as for earning it, whatever you may think, I can assure you I shall never have got money harder. I've now given you my best advice; if your mind's not yet made up, perhaps you'll have the goodness to let me hear from you when it is?' and Daly walked from the fire towards the door, and placed his hand upon the handle of it.

This was a hint which Barry couldn't misunderstand. 'Well, I'll write to you,' he said, and passed through the door. He felt, however, that it was useless to attempt to trust himself to his own judgment, and he turned back, as Daly passed into his office— 'Daly,' he said, 'step out one minute: I won't keep you a second.' The attorney unwillingly lifted up the counter, and came out to him. 'Manage it your own way,' said he; 'do whatever you think best; but you must see that I've been badly used—infernally cruelly treated, and you ought to do the best you can for me. Here am I, giving away, as I may say, my own property to a young shopkeeper, and upon my soul you ought to make him pay something for it; upon my soul you ought, for it's only fair!'

'I've tould you, Mr. Lynch, what I'll propose to Martin Kelly; if you don't think the terms fair, you can propose any others yourself; or you're at liberty to employ any other agent you please.'

Barry sighed again, but he yielded. He felt broken-hearted, and unhappy, and he longed to quit a country so distasteful to him, and relatives and neighbours so ungrateful; he longed in his heart for the sweet, easy haunts of Boulogne, which he had never known, but of which he had heard many a glowing description from congenial spirits whom he knew. He had heard enough of the ways and means of many a leading star in that Elysium, to be aware that, with five hundred a-year, unembarrassed and punctually paid, he might shine as a prince indeed. He would go at once to that happy foreign shore, where the memory of no father would follow him, where the presence of no sister would degrade and irritate him, where billiard-tables were rife, and brandy cheap; where virtue was easy, and restraint unnecessary; where no duties would harass him, no tenants upbraid him, no duns persecute him. There, carefully guarding himself against the schemes of those less fortunate followers of pleasure among whom he would be thrown in his social hours, he would convert every shilling of his income to some purpose of self-enjoyment, and live a life of luxurious abandonment. And he need not be altogether idle, he reflected within himself afterwards, as he was riding home: he felt that he was possessed of sufficient energy and talent to make himself perfectly master of a pack of cards, to be a proficient over a billiard-table, and even to get the upper hand of a box of dice. With such pursuits left to him, he might yet live to be talked of, feared, and wealthy; and Barry's utmost ambition would have carried him no further.

As I said before, he yielded to the attorney, and commissioned him fully to treat with Martin Kelly in the manner proposed by himself. Martin was to give him five hundred a-year for his share of the property, and three hundred pounds for the furniture, &c.; and Barry was to give his sister his written and unconditional assent to her marriage; was to sign any document which might be necessary as to her settlement, and was then to leave Dunmore for ever. Daly made him write an authority for making such a proposal, by which he bound himself to the terms, should they be acceded to by the other party.

'But you must bear in mind,' added Daly, as his client for the second time turned from the door, 'that I don't guarantee that Martin Kelly will accept these terms: it's very likely he may be sharp enough to know that he can manage as well without you as he can with you. You'll remember that, Mr. Lynch.'

'I will—I will, Daly; but look here—if he bites freely—and I think he will, and if you find you could get as much as a thousand out of him, or even eight hundred, you shall have one hundred clear for yourself.'

This was Barry's last piece of diplomacy for that day. Daly vouchsafed him no answer, but returned into his office, and Barry mounted his horse, and returned home not altogether ill-pleased with his prospects, but still regretting that he should have gone about so serious a piece of business, so utterly unprepared.

These regrets rose stronger, when his after-dinner courage returned to him as he sate solitary over his fire. 'I should have had him here,' said he to himself, 'and not gone to that confounded cold hole of his. After all, there's no place for a cock to fight on like his own dunghill; and there's nothing able to carry a fellow well through a tough bit of jobation with a lawyer like a stiff tumbler of brandy punch. It'd have been worth a couple of hundred to me, to have had him out here—impertinent puppy! Well, devil a halfpenny I'll pay him!' This thought was consolatory, and he began again to think of Boulogne.

XXI

LORD BALLINDINE AT HOME

TWO days after the last recorded interview between Lord Ballindine and his friend, Dot Blake,
the former found himself once more sitting down to
dinner with his mother and sisters, the Honourable
Mrs. O'Kelly and the Honourable Misses O'Kelly; at
least such were the titular dignities conferred on them
in County Mayo, though I believe, strictly speaking,
the young ladies had no claim to the appellation.

Mrs. O'Kelly was a very small woman, with no
particularly developed character, and perhaps of no
very general utility. She was fond of her daughters,
and more than fond of her son, partly because he was
so tall and so handsome, and partly because he was
the lord, the head of the family, and the owner of the
house. She was, on the whole, a good-natured person, though perhaps her temper was a little soured by
her husband having, very unfairly, died before he
had given her a right to call herself Lady Ballindine.
She was naturally shy and reserved, and the seclusion
of O'Kelly's Court did not tend to make her less so;
but she felt that the position and rank of her son
required her to be dignified; and consequently, when
in society, she somewhat ridiculously aggravated her
natural timidity with an assumed rigidity of demeanour. She was, however, a good woman, striving,
with small means, to do the best for her family;
prudent and self-denying, and very diligent in looking after the house servants.

Her two daughters had been, at the instance of
their grandfather, the courtier, christened Augusta
and Sophia, after the two Princesses of that name,
and were now called Guss and Sophy: they were both
pretty, good-natured girls—one with dark brown and
the other light brown hair: they both played the harp
badly, sung tolerably, danced well, and were very

fond of nice young men. They both thought Kelly's
Court rather dull; but then they had known nothing
better since they had grown up, and there were some
tolerably nice people not very far off, whom they
occasionally saw: there were the Dillons, of Ballyhaunis, who had three thousand a-year, and spent
six; they were really a delightful family,—three
daughters and four sons, all unmarried, and up to
anything: the sons all hunted, shot, danced, and did
everything that they ought to do—at least in the
eyes of young ladies; though some of their more
coldly prudent acquaintances expressed an opinion
that it would be as well if the three younger would
think of doing something for themselves; but they
looked so manly and handsome when they breakfasted at Kelly's Court on a hunt morning, with their
bright tops, red coats, and hunting-caps, that Guss and
Sophy, and a great many others, thought it would be
a shame to interrupt them in their career. And then,
Ballyhaunis was only eight miles from Kelly's Court;
though they were Irish miles, it is true, and the road
was not patronised by the Grand Jury; but the distance was only eight miles, and there were always
beds for them when they went to dinner at Peter
Dillon's. Then there were the Blakes of Castletown.
To be sure they could give no parties, for they were
both unmarried; but they were none the worse for
that, and they had plenty of horses, and went out
everywhere. And the Blakes of Morristown; they
also were very nice people; only unfortunately, old
Blake was always on his keeping, and couldn't show
himself out of doors except on Sundays, for fear of
the bailiffs. And the Browns of Mount Dillon, and
the Browns of Castle Brown; and General Bourke of
Creamstown. All these families lived within fifteen
or sixteen miles of Kelly's Court, and prevented the
O'Kellys from feeling themselves quite isolated from
the social world. Their nearest neighbours, however,
were the Armstrongs, and of them they saw a great
deal.

The Reverend Joseph Armstrong was rector of
Ballindine, and Mrs. O'Kelly was his parishioner, and
the only Protestant one he had; and, as Mr. Armstrong did not like to see his church quite deserted,
and as Mrs. O'Kelly was, as she flattered herself, a
very fervent Protestant, they were all in all to each
other.

Ballindine was not a good living, and Mr. Armstrong had a very large family; he was, therefore, a
poor man. His children were helpless, uneducated,
and improvident; his wife was nearly worn out with
the labours of bringing them forth and afterwards
catering for them; and a great portion of his own life
was taken up in a hard battle with tradesmen and
tithe-payers, creditors, and debtors. Yet, in spite of
the insufficiency of his two hundred a-year to meet
all or half his wants, Mr. Armstrong was not an
unhappy man. At any moment of social enjoyment
he forgot all his cares and poverty, and was always
the first to laugh, and the last to cease to do so. He
never refused an invitation to dinner, and if he did
not entertain many in his own house, it was his
fortune, and not his heart, that prevented him from
doing so. He could hardly be called a good clergyman, and yet his remissness was not so much his
own fault as that of circumstances. How could a
Protestant rector be a good parish clergyman, with
but one old lady and her daughters, for the exercise
of his clerical energies and talents? He constantly
lauded the zeal of St. Paul for proselytism; but, as
he himself once observed, even St. Paul had never
had to deal with the obstinacy of an Irish Roman
Catholic. He often regretted the want of work, and
grieved that his profession, as far as he saw and had
been instructed, required nothing of him but a short
service on every Sunday morning, and the celebration
of the Eucharist four times a-year; but such were the
facts; and the idleness which this want of work
engendered, and the habits which his poverty induced, had given him a character as a clergyman,

very different from that which the high feelings and strict principles which animated him at his ordination would have seemed to ensure. He was, in fact, a loose, slovenly man, somewhat too fond of his tumbler of punch; a little lax, perhaps, as to clerical discipline, but very staunch as to doctrine. He possessed no industry or energy of any kind; but he was good-natured and charitable, lived on friendly terms with all his neighbours, and was intimate with every one that dwelt within ten miles of him, priest and parson, lord and commoner.

Such was the neighbourhood of Kelly's Court, and among such Lord Ballindine had now made up his mind to remain a while, till circumstances should decide what further steps he should take with regard to Fanny Wyndham. There were a few hunting days left in the season, which he intended to enjoy; and then he must manage to make shift to lull the time with shooting, fishing, farming, and nursing his horses and dogs.

His mother and sisters had heard nothing of the rumour of the quarrel between Frank and Fanny, which Mat Tierney had so openly alluded to at Handicap Lodge; and he was rather put out by their eager questions on the subject. Nothing was said about it till the servant withdrew, after dinner, but the three ladies were too anxious for information to delay their curiosity any longer.

'Well, Frank,' said the elder sister, who was sitting over the fire, close to his left elbow—(he had a bottle of claret at his right)—'well, Frank, do tell us something about Fanny Wyndham; we are so longing to hear; and you never will write, you know.'

'Everybody says it's a brilliant match,' said the mother. 'They say here she's forty thousand pounds: I'm sure I hope she has, Frank.'

'But when is it to be?' said Sophy. 'She's of age now, isn't she? and I thought you were only waiting for that. I'm sure we shall like her; come, Frank, do tell us—when are we to see Lady Ballindine?'

Frank looked rather serious and embarrassed, but did not immediately make any reply.

'You haven't quarrelled, have you, Frank?' said the mother.

'The match isn't off—is it?' said Guss.

'Miss Wyndham has just lost her only brother,' said he; 'he died quite suddenly in London about ten days since; she was very much attached to him.'

'Good gracious, how shocking!' said Sophy.

'I'm sorry,' said Guss.

'Why, Frank,' said their mother, now excited into absolute animation; 'his fortune was more than double hers, wasn't it?—who'll have it now?'

'It was, mother; five times as much as hers, I believe.'

'Gracious powers! and who has it now? Why don't you tell me, Frank?'

'His sister Fanny.'

'Heavens and earth!—I hope you're not going to let her quarrel with you, are you? Has there been anything between you? Have there been any words between you and Lord Cashel? Why don't you tell me, Frank, when you know how anxious I am?'

'If you must know all about it, I have not had any words, as you call them, with Fanny Wyndham; but I have with her guardian. He thinks a hundred and twenty thousand pounds much too great a fortune for a Connaught viscount. However, I don't think so. It will be for time to show what Fanny thinks. Meanwhile, the less said about it the better; remember that, girls, will you?'

'Oh, we will—we won't say a word about it; but she'll never change her mind because of her money, will she?'

'That's what would make me love a man twice the more,' said Guss; 'or at any rate show it twice the stronger.'

'Frank,' said the anxious mother, 'for heaven's sake don't let anything stand between you and Lord Cashel; think what a thing it is you'd lose! Why;

it'd pay all the debts, and leave the property worth twice what it ever was before. If Lord Cashel thinks you ought to give up the hounds, do it at once, Frank; anything rather than quarrel with him. You could get them again, you know, when all's settled.'

'I've given up quite as much as I intend for Lord Cashel.'

'Now, Frank, don't be a fool, or you'll repent it all your life: what does it signify how much you give up to such a man as Lord Cashel? You don't think, do you, that he objects to our being at Kelly's Court? Because I'm sure we wouldn't stay a moment if we thought that.'

'Mother, I wouldn't part with a cur dog out of the place to please Lord Cashel. But if I were to do everything on earth at his beck and will, it would make no difference: he will never let me marry Fanny Wyndham if he can help it; but, thank God, I don't believe he can.'

'I hope not—I hope not. You'll never see half such a fortune again.'

'Well, mother, say nothing about it one way or the other, to anybody. And as you now know how the matter stands, it's no good any of us talking more about it till I've settled what I mean to do myself.'

'I shall hate her,' said Sophy, 'if her getting all her brother's money changes her; but I'm sure it won't.' And so the conversation ended.

Lord Ballindine had not rested in his paternal halls the second night, before he had commenced making arrangements for a hunt breakfast, by way of letting all his friends know that he was again among them. And so missives, in Guss and Sophy's handwriting, were sent round by a bare-legged little boy, to all the Mounts, Towns, and Castles, belonging to the Dillons, Blakes, Bourkes, and Browns of the neighbourhood, to tell them that the dogs would draw the Kelly's Court covers at eleven o'clock on the following Tuesday morning, and that the preparatory breakfast would be on the table at ten. This was welcome

news to the whole neighbourhood. It was only on
the Sunday evening that the sportsmen got the
intimation, and very busy most of them were on the
following Monday to see that their nags and breeches
were all right—fit to work and fit to be seen. The
four Dillons, of Ballyhaunis, gave out to their grooms
a large assortment of pipe-clay and putty-powder.
Bingham Blake, of Castletown, ordered a new set of
girths to his hunting saddle; and his brother Jerry,
who was in no slight degree proud of his legs, but
whose nether trappings were rather the worse from
the constant work of a heavy season, went so far as
to go forth very early on the Monday morning to
excite the Ballinrobe tailor to undertake the almost
impossible task of completing him a pair of doeskin
by the Tuesday morning. The work was done, and
the breeches home at Castletown by eight—though
the doeskin had to be purchased in Tuam, and an
assistant artist taken away from his mother's wake,
to sit up all night over the seams. But then the tailor
owed a small trifle of arrear of rent for his potato-
garden, and his landlord was Jerry Blake's cousin-
german. There's nothing carries one further than a
good connexion, thought both Jerry and the tailor
when the job was finished.

Among the other invitations sent was one to Martin
Kelly,—not exactly worded like the others, for
though Lord Ballindine was perhaps more anxious
to see him than anyone else, Martin had not yet got
quite so high in the ladder of life as to be asked to
breakfast at Kelly's Court. But the fact that Frank
for a moment thought of asking him showed that he
was looking upwards in the world's estimation.
Frank wrote him a note himself, saying that the
hounds would throw off at Kelly's Court, at eleven;
that, if he would ride over, he would be sure to see a
good hunt, and that he, Lord Ballindine, had a few
words to say to him on business, just while the dogs
were being put into the cover. Martin, as usual, had
a good horse which he was disposed to sell, if, as he

said, he got its value; and wrote to say he would wait
on Lord Ballindine at eleven. The truth was, Frank
wanted to borrow money from him.

Another note was sent to the Glebe, requesting the
Rector to come to breakfast, and to look at the hounds
being thrown off. The modest style of the invitation
was considered as due to Mr. Armstrong's clerical
position, but was hardly rendered necessary by his
habits; for though the parson attended such meetings in an old suit of rusty black, and rode an equally
rusty-looking pony, he was always to be seen, at the
end of the day, among those who were left around
the dogs.

On the Tuesday morning there was a good deal of
bustle at Kelly's Court. All the boys about the place
were collected in front of the house, to walk the
gentlemen's horses about while the riders were at
breakfast, and earn a sixpence or a fourpenny bit;
and among them, sitting idly on the big stepping-
stone placed near the door, was Jack the fool, who,
for the day, seemed to have deserted the service of
Barry Lynch.

And now the red-coats flocked up to the door, and
it was laughable to see the knowledge of character
displayed by the gossoons in the selection of their
customers. One or two, who were known to be 'bad
pays,' were allowed to dismount without molestation of any kind, and could not even part with their
steeds till they had come to an absolute bargain as to
the amount of gratuity to be given. Lambert Brown
was one of these unfortunate characters—a younger
brother who had a little, and but a very little money,
and who was determined to keep that. He was a
miserable hanger-on at his brother's house, without
profession or prospects; greedy, stingy, and disagreeable; endowed with a squint, and long lank
light-coloured hair: he was a bad horseman, always
craning and shirking in the field, boasting and lying
after dinner; nevertheless, he was invited and endured—because he was one of the Browns of Mount

Dillon, cousin to the Browns of Castle Brown, nephew to Mrs. Dillon the member's wife, and third cousin of Lord Ballaghaderrin.

He dismounted in the gravel circle before the door, and looked round for someone to take his horse; but none of the urchins would come to him. At last he caught hold of a little ragged boy whom he knew, from his own side of the country, and who had come all the way there, eight long Irish miles, on the chance of earning sixpence and seeing a hunt.

'Here, Patsy, come here, you born little divil,' and he laid hold of the arm of the brat, who was trying to escape from him—'come and hold my horse for me—and I'll not forget you.'

'Shure, yer honer, Mr. Lambert, I can't thin, for I'm afther engaging myself this blessed minute to Mr. Larry Dillon, only he's jist trotted round to the stables to spake a word to Mick Keogh.'

'Don't be lying, you little blackguard; hould the horse, and don't stir out of that.'

'Shure how can I, Mr. Lambert, when I've been and guv my word to Mr. Larry?' and the little fellow put his hands behind him, that he might not be forced to take hold of the reins.

'Don't talk to me, you young imp, but take the horse. I'll not forget you when I come out. What's the matter with you, you fool; d'ye think I'd tell you a lie about it?'

Patsy evidently thought he would; for though he took the horse almost upon compulsion, he whimpered as he did so, and said:

'Shure, Mr. Lambert, would you go and rob a poor boy of his chances?—I come'd all the way from Bally-glass this blessed morning to 'arn a tizzy, and av' I doesn't get it from you this turn, I'll—' But Lambert Brown had gone into the house, and on his return after breakfast he fully justified the lad's suspicion, for he again promised him that he wouldn't forget him, and that he'd see him some day at Mr. Dillon's.

'Well, Lambert Brown,' said the boy, as that worthy gentleman rode off, 'it's you're the raal blackguard—and it's well all the counthry knows you: sorrow be your bed this night; it's little the poor'll grieve for you, when you're stretched, or the rich either, for the matther of that.'

Very different was the reception Bingham Blake got, as he drove up with his tandem and tax-cart: half-a-dozen had kept themselves idle, each in the hope of being the lucky individual to come in for Bingham's shilling.

'Och, Mr. Bingham, shure I'm first,' roared one fellow.

But the first, as he styled himself, was soon knocked down under the wheels of the cart by the others.

'Mr. Blake, thin—Mr. Blake, darlint—doesn't ye remimber the promise you guv me?'

'Mr. Jerry, Mr. Jerry, avick,'—this was addressed to the brother—'spake a word for me; do, yer honour; shure it was I come all the way from Teddy Mahony's with the breeches this morning, God bless 'em, and the fine legs as is in 'em.'

But they were all balked, for Blake had his servant there.

'Get out, you blackguards!' said he, raising his tandem whip, as if to strike them. 'Get out, you robbers! Are you going to take the cart and horses clean away from me? That mare'll settle some of ye, if you make so free with her! she's not a bit too chary of her hind feet. Get out of that, I tell you;' and he lightly struck with the point of his whip the boy who had Lambert Brown's horse.

'Ah, Mr. Bingham,' said the boy, pretending to rub the part very hard, 'you owe me one for that, anyhow, and it's you are the good mark for it, God bless you.'

'Faix,' said another, 'one blow from your honour is worth two promises from Lambert Brown, any way.'

There was a great laugh at this among the ragged crew, for Lambert Brown was still standing on the doorsteps: when he heard this sally, however, he walked in, and the different red-coats and top-boots were not long in crowding after him.

Lord Ballindine received them in the same costume, and very glad they all seemed to see him again. When an Irish gentleman is popular in his neighbourhood, nothing can exceed the real devotion paid to him; and when that gentleman is a master of hounds, and does not require a subscription, he is more than ever so.

'Welcome back, Ballindine—better late than never; but why did you stay away so long?' said General Bourke, an old gentleman with long, thin, flowing grey hairs, waving beneath his broad-brimmed felt hunting-hat. 'You're not getting so fond of the turf, I hope, as to be giving up the field for it? Give me the sport where I can ride my own horse myself; not where I must pay a young rascal for doing it for me, and robbing me into the bargain, most likely.'

'Quite right, General,' said Frank; 'so you see I've given up the Curragh, and come down to the dogs again.'

'Yes, but you've waited too long, man; the dogs have nearly done their work for this year. I'm sorry for it; the last day of the season is the worst day in the year to me. I'm ill for a week after it.'

'Well, General, please the pigs, we'll be in great tune next October. I've as fine a set of puppies to enter as there is in Ireland, let alone Connaught. You must come down, and tell me what you think of them.'

'Next October's all very well for you young fellows, but I'm seventy-eight. I always make up my mind that I'll never turn out another season, and it'll be true for me this year. I'm hunting over sixty years, Ballindine, in these three counties. I ought to have had enough of it by this time, you'll say.'

'I'll bet you ten pounds,' said Bingham Blake, 'that you hunt after eighty.'

'Done with you Bingham,' said the General, and the bet was booked.

General Bourke was an old soldier, who told the truth in saying that he had hunted over the same ground sixty years ago. But he had not been at it ever since, for he had in the meantime seen a great deal of hard active service, and obtained high military reputation. But he had again taken kindly to the national sport of his country, on returning to his own estate at the close of the Peninsular War; and had ever since attended the meets twice a week through every winter, with fewer exceptions than any other member of the hunt. He always wore top-boots—of the ancient cut, with deep painted tops and square toes, drawn tight up over the calf of his leg; a pair of most capacious dark-coloured leather breeches, the origin of which was unknown to any other present member of the hunt, and a red frock coat, very much soiled by weather, water, and wear. The General was a rich man, and therefore always had a horse to suit him. On the present occasion, he was riding a strong brown beast, called Parsimony, that would climb over anything, and creep down the gable end of a house if he were required to do so. He was got by Œconomy; those who know county Mayo know the breed well.

They were now all crowded into the large dining-room at Kelly's Court; about five-and-twenty red-coats, and Mr. Armstrong's rusty black. In spite of his shabby appearance, however, and the fact that the greater number of those around him were Roman Catholics, he seemed to be very popular with the lot; and his opinion on the important subject of its being a scenting morning was asked with as much confidence in his judgment, as though the foxes of the country were peculiarly subject to episcopalian jurisdiction.

'Well, then, Peter,' said he, 'the wind's in the right quarter. Mick says there's a strong dog-fox in the long bit of gorse behind the firs; if he breaks from that he must run towards Ballintubber, and when you're once over the meering into Roscommon, there's not an acre of tilled land, unless a herd's garden, between that and—the deuce knows where all—further than most of you'll like to ride, I take it.'

'How far'll you go yourself, Armstrong? Faith, I believe it's few of the crack nags'll beat the old black pony at a long day.'

'Is it I?' said the Parson, innocently. 'As soon as I've heard the dogs give tongue, and seen them well on their game, I'll go home. I've land ploughing, and I must look after that. But, as I was saying, if the fox breaks well away from the gorse, you'll have the best run you've seen this season; but if he dodges back into the plantation, you'll have enough to do to make him break at all; and when he does, he'll go away towards Ballyhaunis, through as cross a country as ever a horse put a shoe into.'

And having uttered this scientific prediction, which was listened to with the greatest deference by Peter Dillon, the Rev. Joseph Armstrong turned his attention to the ham and tea.

The three ladies were all smiles to meet their guests; Mrs. O'Kelly, dressed in a piece of satin turk, came forward to shake hands with the General, but Sophy and Guss kept their positions, beneath the coffee-pot and tea-urn, at each end of the long table, being very properly of opinion that it was the duty of the younger part of the community to come forward, and make their overtures to them. Bingham Blake, the cynosure on whom the eyes of the beauty of county Mayo were most generally placed, soon found his seat beside Guss, rather to Sophy's mortification; but Sophy was good-natured, and when Peter Dillon placed himself at her right hand, she was quite happy, though Peter's father was still alive, and Bingham's had been dead this many a year and Castletown much in want of a mistress.

'Now, Miss O'Kelly,' said Bingham, 'do let me

manage the coffee-pot; the cream-jug and sugar-tongs will be quite enough for your energies.'

'Indeed and I won't, Mr. Blake; you're a great deal too awkward, and a great deal too hungry. The last hunt-morning you breakfasted here you threw the coffee-grouts into the sugar-basin, when I let you help me.'

'To think of your remembering that!—but I'm improved since then. I've been taking lessons with my old aunt at Castlebar.'

'You don't mean you've really been staying with Lady Sarah?'

'Oh, but I have, though. I was there three days; made tea every night; washed the poodle every morning, and clear-starched her Sunday pelerine, with my own hands on Saturday evening.'

'Oh, what a useful animal! What a husband you'll make, when you're a little more improved!'

'Shan't I? As you're so fond of accomplishments, perhaps you'll take me yourself by-and-by?'

'Why, as you're so useful, maybe I may.'

'Well, Lambert,' said Lord Ballindine, across the table, to the stingy gentleman with the squint, 'are you going to ride hard to-day?'

'I'll go bail I'm not much behind, my lord,' said Lambert; 'if the dogs go, I'll follow.'

'I'll bet you a crown, Lambert,' said his cousin, young Brown of Mount Brown, 'the dogs kill, and you don't see them do it.'

'Oh, that may be, and yet I mayn't be much behind.'

'I'll bet you're not in the next field to them.'

'Maybe you'll not be within ten fields yourself.'

'Come, Lambert, I'll tell you what—we'll ride together, and I'll bet you a crown I pound you before you're over three leaps.'

'Ah, now, take it easy with yourself,' said Lambert; 'there are others ride better than you.'

'But no one better than yourself; is that it, eh?'

'Well, Jerry, how do the new articles fit?' said Nicholas Dillon.

'Pretty well, thank you: they'd be a deal more comfortable though, if you'd pay for them.'

'Did you hear, Miss O'Kelly, what Jerry Blake did yesterday?' said Nicholas Dillon aloud, across the table.

'Indeed, I did not,' said Guss—'but I hope, for the sake of the Blakes in general, he didn't do anything much amiss?'

'I'll tell you then,' continued Nicholas. 'A portion of his ould hunting-dress—I'll not specify what, you know—but a portion, which he'd been wearing since the last election, were too shabby to show: well, he couldn't catch a hedge tailor far or near, only poor lame Andy Oulahan, who was burying his wife, rest her sowl, the very moment Jerry got a howld of him. Well, Jerry was wild that the tailors were so scarce, so he laid his hands on Andy, dragged him away from the corpse and all the illigant enthertainment of the funeral, and never let him out of sight till he'd put on the last button.'

'Oh, Mr. Blake!' said Guss, 'you did not take the man away from his dead wife?'

'Indeed I did not, Miss O'Kelly: Andy 'd no such good chance; his wife's to the fore this day, worse luck for him. It was only his mother he was burying.'

'But you didn't take him away from his mother's funeral?'

'Oh, I did it according to law, you know. I got Bingham to give me a warrant first, before I let the policeman lay a hand on him.'

'Now, General, you've really made no breakfast at all,' said the hospitable hostess: 'do let Guss give you a hot cup of coffee.'

'Not a drop more, Mrs. O'Kelly. I've done more than well; but, if you'll allow me, I'll just take a crust of bread in my pocket.'

'And what would you do that for?—you'll be coming back to lunch, you know.'

'Is it lunch, Mrs. O'Kelly, pray don't think of troubling yourself to have lunch on the table. May-

be we'll be a deal nearer Creamstown than Kelly's
Court at lunch time. But it's quite time we were off.
As for Bingham Blake, from the look of him, he's
going to stay here with your daughter Augusta all
the morning.'

'I believe then he'd much sooner be with the dogs,
General, than losing his time with her.'

'Are you going to move at all, Ballindine,' said the
impatient old sportsman. 'Do you know what time
it is?—it'll be twelve o'clock before you have the
dogs in the cover.'

'Very good time, too, General: men must eat, you
know, and the fox won't stir till we move him. But
come, gentlemen, you seem to be dropping your
knives and forks. Suppose we get into our saddles?'

And again the red-coats sallied out. Bingham gave
Guss a tender squeeze, which she all but returned, as
she bade him take care and not go and kill himself.
Peter Dillon stayed to have a few last words with
Sophy, and to impress upon her his sister Nora's
message, that she and *her* sister were to be sure to
come over on Friday to Ballyhaunis, and spend the
night there.

'We will, if we're let, tell Nora,' said Sophy; 'but
now Frank's at home, we must mind him, you know.'

'Make him bring you over: there'll be a bed for
him; the old house is big enough, heaven knows.'

'Indeed it is. Well, I'll do my best; but tell Nora
to be sure and get the fiddler from Hollymount.
It's so stupid for her to be sitting there at the piano
while we're dancing.'

'I'll manage that; only do you bring Frank to
dance with her,' and another tender squeeze was
given—and Peter hurried out to the horses.

And now they were all gone but the Parson.
'Mrs. O'Kelly,' said he, 'Mrs. Armstrong wants a
favour from you. Poor Minny's very bad with her
throat; she didn't get a wink of sleep last night.'

'Dear me—poor thing. Can I send her anything?'

'If you could let them have a little black currant

jelly, Mrs. Armstrong would be so thankful. She
has so much to think of, and is so weak herself, poor
thing, she hasn't time to make those things.'

'Indeed I will, Mr. Armstrong. I'll send it down
this morning; and a little calf's foot jelly won't hurt
her. It is in the house, and Mrs. Armstrong mightn't
be able to get the feet, you know. Give them my
love, and if I can get out at all to-morrow, I'll go and
see them.'

And so the Parson, having completed his domestic
embassy for the benefit of his sick little girl, followed
the others, keen for the hunt; and the three ladies were
left alone, to see the plate and china put away.

XXII

THE HUNT

THOUGH the majority of those who were in the
habit of hunting with the Kelly's Court hounds
had been at the breakfast, there were still a considerable number of horsemen waiting on the lawn in front
of the house, when Frank and his friends sallied forth.
The dogs were collected round the huntsman, behav-
ing themselves, for the most part, with admirable
propriety; an occasional yelp from a young hound
would now and then prove that the whipper had his
eye on them, and would not allow rambling; but the
old dogs sat demurely on their haunches, waiting the
well-known signal for action. There they sat, as
grave as so many senators, with their large heads
raised, their heavy lips hanging from each side of
their jaws, and their deep, strong chests expanded
so as to show fully their bone, muscle, and breeding.

Among the men who had arrived on the lawn
during breakfast were two who certainly had not
come together, and who had not spoken since they
had been there. They were Martin Kelly and Barry
Lynch. Martin was dressed just as usual, except
that he had on a pair of spurs, but Barry was armed

cap-a-pie. Some time before his father's death he had supplied himself with all the fashionable requisites for the field,—not because he was fond of hunting, for he was not,—but in order to prove himself as much a gentleman as other people. He had been out twice this year, but had felt very miserable, for no one spoke to him, and he had gone home, on both occasions, early in the day; but he had now made up his mind that he would show himself to his old schoolfellow in his new character as an independent country gentleman; and what was more, he was determined that Lord Ballindine should not cut him.

He very soon had an opportunity for effecting his purpose, for the moment that Frank got on his horse, he unintentionally rode close up to him.

'How d'ye do, my lord?—I hope I see your lordship well?' said Barry, with a clumsy attempt at ease and familiarity. 'I'm glad to find your lordship in the field before the season's over.'

'Good morning, Mr. Lynch,' said Frank, and was turning away from him, when, remembering that he must have come from Dunmore, he asked, 'did you see Martin Kelly anywhere?'

'Can't say I did, my lord,' said Barry, and he turned away completely silenced, and out of countenance.

Martin had been talking to the huntsman, and criticizing the hounds. He knew every dog's name, character, and capabilities, and also every horse in Lord Ballindine's stable, and was consequently held in great respect by Mick Keogh and his crew.

And now the business began. 'Mick,' said the lord, 'we'll take them down to the young plantation, and bring them back through the firs and so into the gorse. If the lad's lying there, we must hit him that way.'

'That's thrue for yer honer, my lord;' and he started off with his obedient family.

'You're wrong, Ballindine,' said the Parson; 'for

you'll drive him up into the big plantation, and you'll be all day before you make him break; and ten to one they'll chop him in the cover.'

'Would you put them into the gorse at once then?'

'Take 'em gently through the firs; maybe he's lying out—and down into the gorse, and then, if he's there, he must go away, and into a tip-top country too—miles upon miles of pasture—right away to Ballintubber.'

'That's thrue, too, my lord: let his Rivirence alone for understandhing a fox,' said Mick, with a wink.

The Parson's behests were obeyed. The hounds followed Mick into the plantation, and were followed by two or three of the more eager of the party, who did not object to receiving wet boughs in their faces, or who delighted in riding for half an hour with their heads bowed close down over their saddle-bows. The rest remained with the whipper, outside.

'Stay a moment here, Martin,' said Lord Ballindine. 'They can't get away without our seeing them, and I want to speak a few words to you.'

'And I want particularly to spake to your lordship,' said Martin; 'and there's no fear of the fox! I never knew a fox lie in those firs yet.'

'Nor I either, but you see the Parson would have his way. I suppose, if the priest were out, and he told you to run the dogs through the gooseberry-bushes, you'd do it?'

'I'm blessed if I would, my lord! Every man to his trade. Not but what Mr. Armstrong knows pretty well what he's about.'

'Well but, Martin, I'll tell you what I want of you. I want a little money, without bothering those fellows up in Dublin; and I believe you could let me have it; at any rate, you and your mother together. Those fellows at Guinness's are stiff about it, and I want three hundred pounds, without absolutely telling them that they must give it me. I'd give you my bill for the amount at twelve months, and allow

you six per cent.; but then I want it immediately.
Can you let me have it?'

'Why, my lord,' said Martin, after pausing awhile
and looking very contemplative during the time,
'I certainly have the money; that is, I and mother
together; but—'

'Oh, if you've any doubt about it—or if it puts
you out, don't do it.'

'Divil a doubt on 'arth, my lord; but I'll tell you—
I was just going to ask your lordship's advice about
laying out the same sum in another way, and I don't
think I could raise twice that much.'

'Very well, Martin; if you've anything better to
do with your money, I'm sure I'd be sorry to take
it from you.'

'That's jist it, my lord. I don't think I can do
betther—but I want your advice about it.'

'My advice whether you ought to lend me three
hundred pounds or not! Why, Martin, you're a fool.
I wouldn't ask you to lend it me, if I thought you
oughtn't to lend 'it.'

'Oh—I'm certain sure of that, my lord; but there's
an offer made me, that I'd like to have your lordship's mind about. It's not much to my liking,
though; and I think it'll be betther for me to be
giving you the money,' and then Martin told his
landlord the offer which had been made to him by
Daly, on the part of Barry Lynch. 'You see, my
lord,' he concluded by saying, 'it'd be a great thing
to be shut of Barry entirely out of the counthry, and
to have poor Anty's mind at ase about it, should
she iver live to get betther; but thin, I don't like to
have dailings with the divil, or any one so much of
his colour as Barry Lynch.'

'This is a very grave matter, Martin, and takes
some little time to think about. To tell the truth,
I forgot your matrimonial speculation when I asked
for the money. Though I want the cash, I think you
should keep it in your power to close with Barry:
no, you'd better keep the money by you.'

'After all, the ould woman could let me have it on the security of the house, you know, av I did take up with the offer. So, any way, your lordship needn't be balked about the cash.'

'But is Miss Lynch so very ill, Martin?'

''Deed, and she is, Mr. Frank; very bad intirely. Doctor Colligan was with her three times yestherday.'

'And does Barry take any notice of her now she's ill?'

'Why, not yet he didn't; but then, we kept it from him as much as we could, till it got dangerous like. Mother manes to send Colligan to him to-day, av he thinks she's not betther.'

'If she were to die, Martin, there'd be an end of it all, wouldn't there?'

'Oh, in course there would, my lord'—and then he added, with a sigh, 'I'd be sorry she'd die, for, somehow, I'm very fond of her, quare as it'll seem to you. I'd be very sorry she should die.'

'Of course you would, Martin; and it doesn't seem queer at all.'

'Oh, I wasn't thinking about the money, then, my lord; I was only thinking of Anty herself: you don't know what a good young woman she is—it's anything but herself she's thinking of always.'

'Did she make any will?'

''Deed she didn't, my lord: nor won't, it's my mind.'

'Ah! but she should, after all that you and your mother've gone through. It'd be a thousand pities that wretch Barry got all the property again.'

'He's wilcome to it for the Kellys, av Anty dies. But av she lives he shall niver rob a penny from her. Oh, my lord! we wouldn't put sich a thing as a will into her head, and she so bad, for all the money the ould man their father iver had. But, hark! my lord— that's Gaylass, I know the note well, and she's as true as gould: there's the fox there, just inside the gorse, as the Parson said'—and away they both trotted, to the bottom of the plantation, from whence the cheering sound of the dog's voices came, sharp, sweet, and mellow.

Yes; the Parson was as right as if he had been let into the fox's confidence overnight, and had betrayed it in the morning. Gaylass was hardly in the gorse before she discovered the doomed brute's vicinity, and told of it to the whole canine confraternity. Away from his hiding-place he went, towards the open country, but immediately returned into the covert, for he saw a lot of boys before him, who had assembled with the object of looking at the hunt, but with the very probable effect of spoiling it; for, as much as a fox hates a dog, he fears the human race more, and will run from an urchin with a stick into the jaws of his much more fatal enemy.

'As long as them blackguards is there, a hollering, and a screeching, divil a fox in all Ireland 'd go out of this,' said Mick to his master.

'Ah, boys,' said Frank, riding up, 'if you want to see a hunt, will you keep back!'

'Begorra we will, yer honer,' said one.

'Faix—we wouldn't be afther spiling your honer's divarsion, my lord, on no account,' said another.

'We'll be out o' this althogether, now this blessed minute,' said a third, but still there they remained, each loudly endeavouring to banish the others.

At last, however, the fox saw a fair course before him, and away he went; and with very little start, for the dogs followed him out of the covert almost with a view.

And now the men settled themselves to the work, and began to strive for the pride of place, at least the younger portion of them: for in every field there are two classes of men. Those who go out to get the greatest possible quantity of riding, and those whose object is to get the least. Those who go to work their nags, and those who go to spare them. The former think that the excellence of the hunt depends on the horses; the latter, on the dogs. The former go to act, and the latter to see. And it is very generally

the case that the least active part of the community
know the most about the sport.

They, the less active part above alluded to, know
every high-road and bye-road; they consult the wind,
and calculate that a fox won't run with his nose
against it; they remember this stream and this bog,
and avoid them; they are often at the top of emi-
nences, and only descend when they see which way
the dogs are going; they take short cuts, and lay
themselves out for narrow lanes; they dislike galloping, and eschew leaping; and yet, when a hard-riding
man is bringing up his two hundred guinea hunter,
a minute or two late for the finish, covered with
foam, trembling with his exertion, not a breath left
in him—he'll probably find one of these steady
fellows there before him, mounted on a broken-down
screw, but as cool and as fresh as when he was
brought out of the stable; and what is, perhaps, still
more amazing, at the end of the day, when the hunt
is canvassed after dinner, our dashing friend, who is
in great doubt whether his thoroughbred steeple-
chaser will ever recover his day's work, and who has
been personally administering warm mashes and
bandages before he would venture to take his own
boots off, finds he does not know half as much about
the hunt, or can tell half as correctly where the game
went, as our quiet-going friend, whose hack will probably go out on the following morning under the car,
with the mistress and children. Such a one was Parson Armstrong; and when Lord Ballindine and most
of the others went away after the hounds, he coolly
turned round in a different direction, crept through
a broken wall into a peasant's garden, and over
a dunghill, by the cabin door into a road, and then
trotted along as demurely and leisurely as though he
were going to bury an old woman in the next parish.

Frank was, generally speaking, as good-natured
a man as is often met, but even he got excited and
irritable when hunting his own pack. All masters
of hounds do. Some one was always too forward,

another too near the dogs, a third interfering with the servants, and a fourth making too much noise.

'Confound it, Peter,' he said, when they had gone over a field or two, and the dogs missed the scent for a moment, 'I thought at any rate you knew better than to cross the dogs that way.'

'Who crossed the dogs?' said the other—'what nonsense you're talking: why I wasn't out of the potato-field till they were nearly all at the next wall.'

'Well, it may be nonsense,' continued Frank; 'but when I see a man riding right through the hounds, and they hunting, I call that crossing them.'

'Hoicks! tally'—hollowed some one—'there's Graceful has it again—well done, Granger! Faith, Frank, that's a good dog! if he's not first, he's always second.'

'Now, gentlemen, steady, for heaven's sake. Do let the dogs settle to their work before you're a-top of them. Upon my soul, Nicholas Brown, it's ridiculous to see you!'

'It'd be a good thing if he were half as much in a hurry to get to heaven,' said Bingham Blake.

'Thank'ee,' said Nicholas; 'go to heaven yourself. I'm well enough where I am.'

And now they were off again. In the next field the whole pack caught a view of the fox just as he was stealing out; and after him they went, with their noses well above the ground, their voices loud and clear, and in one bevy.

Away they went: the game was strong; the scent was good; the ground was soft, but not too soft; and a magnificent hunt they had; but there were some misfortunes shortly after getting away. Barry Lynch, wishing, in his ignorance, to lead and show himself off, and not knowing how—scurrying along among the dogs, and bothered at every leap, had given great offence to Lord Ballindine. But, not wishing to speak severely to a man whom he would not under any circumstances address in a friendly way, he talked at him, and endeavoured to bring him to order

by blowing up others in his hearing. But this was
thrown away on Barry, and he continued his career
in a most disgusting manner; scrambling through
gaps together with the dogs, crossing other men
without the slightest reserve, annoying every one,
and evidently pluming himself on his performance.
Frank's brow was getting blacker and blacker. Jerry
Blake and young Brown were greatly amusing themselves at the exhibition, and every now and then
gave him a word or two of encouragement, praising
his mare, telling how well he got over that last fence,
and bidding him mind and keep well forward. This
was all new to Barry, and he really began to feel
himself in his element;—if it hadn't been for those
abominable walls, he would have enjoyed himself.
But this was too good to last, and before very long
he made a *faux pas*, which brought down on him in
a torrent the bottled-up wrath of the viscount.

They had been galloping across a large, unbroken
sheep-walk, which exactly suited Barry's taste, and
he had got well forward towards the hounds. Frank
was behind, expostulating with Jerry Blake and the
others for encouraging him, when the dogs came to
a small stone wall about two feet and a half high.
In this there was a broken gap, through which many
of them crept. Barry also saw this happy escape
from the grand difficulty of jumping, and, ignorant
that if he rode the gap at all, he should let the hounds
go first, made for it right among them, in spite of
Frank's voice, now raised loudly to caution him.
The horse the man rode knew his business better
than himself, and tried to spare the dogs which were
under his feet; but, in getting out, he made a slight
spring, and came down on the haunches of a favourite
young hound called 'Goneaway'; he broke the leg
close to the socket, and the poor beast most loudly
told his complaint.

This was too much to be borne, and Frank rode up
red with passion; and a lot of others, including the
whipper, soon followed.

'He has killed the dog!' said he. 'Did you ever see such a clumsy, ignorant fool? Mr. Lynch, if you'd do me the honour to stay away another day, and amuse yourself in any other way, I should be much obliged.'

'It wasn't my fault then,' said Barry.

'Do you mean to give me the lie, sir?' replied Frank.

'The dog got under the horse's feet. How was I to help it?'

There was a universal titter at this, which made Barry wish himself at home again, with his brandy-bottle.

'Ah! sir,' said Frank; 'you're as fit to ride a hunt as you are to do anything else which gentlemen usually do. May I trouble you to make yourself scarce? Your horse, I see, can't carry you much farther, and if you'll take my advice, you'll go home, before you're ridden over yourself. Well, Martin, is the bone broken?'

Martin had got off his horse, and was kneeling down beside the poor hurt brute. 'Indeed it is, my lord, in two places. You'd better let Tony kill him; he has an awful sprain in the back, as well; he'll niver put a foot to the ground again.'

'By heavens, that's too bad! isn't it Bingham? He was, out and out, the finest puppy we entered last year.'

'What can you expect,' said Bingham, 'when such fellows as that come into a field? He's as much business here as a cow in a drawing-room.'

'But what can we do?—one can't turn him off the land; if he chooses to come, he must.'

'Why, yes,' said Bingham, 'if he will come he must. But then, if he insists on doing so, he may be horsewhipped; he may be ridden over; he may be kicked; and he may be told that he's a low, vulgar, paltry scoundrel; and, if he repeats his visits, that's the treatment he'll probably receive.'

Barry was close to both the speakers, and of course heard, and was intended to hear, every word that

was said. He contented himself, however, with
muttering certain inaudible defiances, and was seen
and heard of no more that day.

The hunt was continued, and the fox was killed;
but Frank and those with him saw but little more
of it. However, as soon as directions were given for
the death of poor Goneaway, they went on, and
received a very satisfactory account of the proceedings from those who had seen the finish. As usual,
the Parson was among the number, and he gave
them a most detailed history, not only of the fox's
proceedings during the day, but also of all the
reasons which actuated the animal, in every different
turn he took.

. 'I declare, Armstrong,' said Peter Dillon, 'I think
you were a fox yourself, once! Do you remember
anything about it?'

'What a run he would give!' said Jerry; 'the best
pack that was ever kennelled wouldn't have a chance
with him.'

'Who was that old chap,' said Nicholas Dillon,
showing off his classical learning, 'who said that
dead animals always became something else?—may-
be it's only in the course of nature for a dead fox to
become a live parson.'

'Exactly: you've hit it,' said Armstrong; 'and, in
the same way, the moment the breath is out of a
goose it becomes an idle squireen, and, generally
speaking, a younger brother.'

'Put that in your pipe and smoke it, Nick,' said
Jerry; 'and take care how you meddle with the
Church again.'

'Who saw anything of Lambert Brown?' said
another; 'I left him bogged below there at Gurtna-
screenagh, and all he could do, the old grey horse
wouldn't move a leg to get out for him.'

'Oh, he's there still,' said Nicholas. 'He was
trying to follow me, and I took him there on purpose.
It's not deep, and he'll do no hurt: he'll keep as well
there, as anywhere else.'

'Nonsense, Dillon!' said the General—'you'll make his brother really angry, if you go on that way. If the man's a fool, leave him in his folly, but don't be playing tricks on him. You'll only get yourself into a quarrel with the family.'

'And how shall we manage about the money, my lord?' said Martin, as he drew near the point at which he would separate from the rest, to ride towards Dunmore. 'I've been thinking about it, and there's no doubt about having it for you on Friday, av that'll suit.'

'That brother-in-law of yours is a most unmitigated blackguard, isn't he, Martin?' said Frank, who was thinking more about poor Goneaway than the money.

'He isn't no brother-in-law of mine yet, and probably niver will be, for I'm afeard poor Anty'll go. But av he iver is, he'll soon take himself out of the counthry, and be no more throuble to your lordship or any of us.'

'But to think of his riding right a-top of the poor brute, and then saying that the dog got under his horse's feet! Why, he's a fool as well as a knave. Was he ever out before?'

'Well, then, I believe he was, twice this year; though I didn't see him myself.'

'Then I hope this'll be the last time: three times is quite enough for such a fellow as that.'

'I don't think he'll be apt to show again afther what you and Mr. Bingham said to him. Well, shure, Mr. Bingham was very hard on him!'

'Serve him right; nothing's too bad for him.'

'Oh, that's thrue for you, my lord: I don't pity him one bit. But about the money, and this job of my own. Av it wasn't asking too much, it'd be a great thing av your lordship 'd see Daly.'

It was then settled that Lord Ballindine should ride over to Dunmore on the following Friday, and if circumstances seemed to render it advisable, that he and Martin should go on together to the attorney as Tuam.

XXIII

DOCTOR COLLIGAN

DOCTOR COLLIGAN, the Galen of Dunmore, though a practitioner of most unprepossessing appearance and demeanour, was neither ignorant nor careless. Though for many years he had courted the public in vain, his neighbours had at last learned to know and appreciate him; and, at the time of Anty's illness, the inhabitants of three parishes trusted their corporeal ailments to his care, with comfort to themselves and profit to him. Nevertheless, there were many things about Doctor Colligan not calculated to inspire either respect or confidence. He always seemed a little afraid of his patient, and very much afraid of his patient's friends: he was always dreading the appearance at Dunmore of one of those young rivals, who had lately established themselves at Tuam on one side, and Hollymount on the other; and, to prevent so fatal a circumstance, was continually trying to be civil and obliging to his customers. He would not put on a blister, or order a black dose, without consulting with the lady of the house, and asking permission of the patient, and consequently had always an air of doubt and indecision. Then, he was excessively dirty in his person and practice: he carried a considerable territory beneath his nails; smelt equally strongly of the laboratory and the stable; would wipe his hands on the patient's sheets, and wherever he went left horrid marks of his whereabouts: he was very fond of good eating and much drinking, and would neglect the best customer that ever was sick, when tempted by the fascination of a game of loo. He was certainly a bad family-man; for though he worked hard for the support of his wife and children, he was little among them, paid them no attention, and felt no scruple in assuring Mrs. C. that he had been obliged to remain up all night with that dreadful Mrs. Jones, whose children were always so tedious; or that Mr. Blake was so bad after his accident that he could not leave him for a moment; when, to tell the truth, the Doctor had passed the night with the cards in his hands, and a tumbler of punch beside him.

He was a tall, thick-set, heavy man, with short black curly hair; was a little bald at the top of his head; and looked always as though he had shaved himself the day before yesterday, and had not washed since. His face was good-natured, but heavy and unintellectual. He was ignorant of everything but his profession, and the odds on the card-table or the race-course. But to give him his due, on these subjects he was not ignorant; and this was now so generally known that, in dangerous cases, Doctor Colligan had been sent for, many, many miles.

This was the man who attended poor Anty in her illness, and he did as much for her as could be done; but it was a bad case, and Doctor Colligan thought it would be fatal. She had intermittent fever, and was occasionally delirious; but it was her great debility between the attacks which he considered so dangerous.

On the morning after the hunt, he told Martin that he greatly feared she would go off, from exhaustion, in a few days, and that it would be wise to let Barry know the state in which his sister was. There was a consultation on the subject between the two and Martin's mother, in which it was agreed that the Doctor should go up to Dunmore House, and tell Barry exactly the state of affairs.

'And good news it'll be for him,' said Mrs. Kelly; 'the best he heard since the ould man died. Av he had his will of her, she'd niver rise from the bed where she's stretched. But, glory be to God, there's a providence over all, and maybe she'll live yet to give him the go-by.'

'How you talk, mother,' said Martin; 'and what's the use? Whatever he wishes won't harum her; and maybe, now she's dying, his heart'll be softened to her. Any way, don't let him have to say she died here, without his hearing a word how bad she was.'

'Maybe he'd be afther saying we murdhered her for her money,' said the widow, with a shudder.

'He can hardly complain of that, when he'll be getting all the money himself. But, however, it's much betther, all ways, that Doctor Colligan should see him.'

'You know, Mrs. Kelly,' said the Doctor, 'as a matter of course he'll be asking to see his sister.'

'You wouldn't have him come in here to her, would you?—Faix, Doctor Colligan, it'll be her death outright at once av he does.'

'It'd not be nathural, to refuse to let him see her,' said the Doctor; 'and I don't think it would do any harm: but I'll be guided by you, Mrs. Kelly, in what I say to him.'

'Besides,' said Martin, 'I know Anty would wish to see him: he is her brother; and there's only the two of 'em.'

'Between you be it,' said the widow; 'I tell you I don't like it. You neither of you know Barry Lynch, as well as I do; he'd smother her av it come into his head.'

'Ah, mother, nonsense now; hould your tongue; you don't know what you're saying.'

'Well; didn't he try to do as bad before?'

'It wouldn't do, I tell you,' continued Martin, 'not to let him see her; that is, av Anty wishes it.'

It ended in the widow being sent into Anty's room, to ask her whether she had any message to send to her brother. The poor girl knew how ill she was, and expected her death; and when the widow told her that Doctor Colligan was going to call on her brother, she said that she hoped she should see Barry once more before all was over.

'Mother,' said Martin, as soon as the Doctor's back was turned, 'you'll get yourself in a scrape av you go on saying such things as that about folk before strangers.'

'Is it about Barry?'

'Yes; about Barry. How do you know Colligan won't be repating all them things to him?'

'Let him, and wilcome. Shure wouldn't I say as much to Barry Lynch himself? What do I care for the blagguard?—only this, I wish I'd niver heard his name, or seen his foot over the sill of the door. I'm sorry I iver heard the name of the Lynches in Dunmore.'

'You're not regretting the throuble Anty is to you, mother?'

'Regretting?—I don't know what you mane by regretting. I don't know is it regretting to be slaving as much and more for her than I would for my own, and no chance of getting as much as thanks for it.'

'You'll be rewarded hereafther, mother; shure won't it all go for charity?'

'I'm not so shure of that,' said the widow. 'It was your schaming to get her money brought her here, and, like a poor wake woman, as I was, I fell into it; and now we've all the throuble and the expinse, and the time lost, and afther all, Barry'll be getting everything when she's gone. You'll see, Martin; we'll have the wake, and the funeral, and the docthor and all, on us—mind my words else. Och musha, musha! what'll I do at all? Faix, forty pounds won't clear what this turn is like to come to; an' all from your dirthy undherhand schaming ways.'

In truth, the widow was perplexed in her inmost soul about Anty; torn and tortured by doubts and anxieties. Her real love of Anty and true charity was in state of battle with her parsimony; and then, avarice was strong within her; and utter, uncontrolled hatred of Barry still stronger. But, opposed to these was dread of some unforeseen evil—some tremendous law proceedings: she had a half-formed idea that she was doing what she had no right to do, and that she might some day be walked off to Galway assizes. Then again, she had an absurd pride about it, which often made her declare that she'd never be beat by such a 'scum of the 'arth' as Barry Lynch, and that she'd fight it out with him if it cost her a hundred pounds; though no one understood what the battle was which she was to fight.

Just before Anty's illness had become so serious, Daly called, and had succeeded in reconciling both Martin and the widow to himself; but he had not quite made them agree to his proposal. The widow, indeed, was much averse to it. She wouldn't deal with such a Greek as Barry, even in the acceptance of a boon. When she found him willing to compromise, she became more than ever averse to any friendly terms; but now the whole ground was slipping from under her feet. Anty was dying: she would have had her trouble for nothing; and that hated Barry would gain his point, and the whole of his sister's property, in triumph.

Twenty times the idea of a will had come into her mind, and how comfortable it would be if Anty would leave her property, or at any rate a portion of it, to Martin. But though the thoughts of such a delightful arrangement kept her in a continual whirlwind of anxiety, she never hinted at the subject to Anty. As she said to herself, 'a Kelly wouldn't demane herself to ask a brass penny from a Lynch.' She didn't even speak to her daughters about it, though the continual twitter she was in made them aware that there was some unusual burthen on her mind.

It was not only to the Kellys that the idea occurred that Anty in her illness might make a will. The thoughts of such a catastrophe had robbed Barry of half the pleasure which the rumours of his sister's dangerous position had given him. He had not received any direct intimation of Anty's state, but had heard through the servants that she was ill— very ill—dangerously—'not expected,' as the country people call it; and each fresh rumour gave him new hopes, and new life. He now spurned all idea of connexion with Martin; he would trample on the

Kellys for thinking of such a thing: he would show Daly, when in the plenitude of his wealth and power, how he despised the lukewarmness and timidity of his councils. These and other delightful visions were floating through his imagination; when, all of a sudden, like a blow, like a thunderbolt, the idea of *a will* fell as it were upon him with a ton weight. His heart sunk low within him; he became white, and his jaw dropped. After all, there were victory and triumph, plunder and wealth, *his* wealth, in the very hands of his enemies! Of course the Kellys would force her to make a will, if she didn't do it of her own accord; if not, they'd forge one. There was some comfort in that thought: he could at any rate contest the will, and swear that it was a forgery.

He swallowed a dram, and went off, almost weeping to Daly.

'Oh, Mr. Daly, poor Anty's dying: did you hear, Mr. Daly—she's all but gone?' Yes; Daly had been sorry to hear that Miss Lynch was very ill. 'What shall I do,' continued Barry, 'if they say that she's left a will?'

'Go and hear it read. Or, if you don't like to do that yourself, stay away, and let me hear it.'

'But they'll forge one! They'll make out what they please, and when she's dying, they'll make her put her name to it; or they'll only just put the pen in her hand, when she's not knowing what she's doing. They'd do anything now, Daly, to get the money they've been fighting for so hard.'

'It's my belief,' answered the attorney, 'that the Kellys not only won't do anything dishonest, but that they won't even take any unfair advantage of you. But at any rate you can do nothing. You must wait patiently; you, at any rate, can take no steps till she's dead.'

'But couldn't she make a will in my favour? I know she'd do it if I asked her—if I asked her now—now she's going off, you know. I'm sure she'd do it. Don't you think she would?'

'You're safer, I think, to let it alone,' said Daly, who could hardly control the ineffable disgust he felt.

'I don't know that,' continued Barry. 'She's weak, and 'll do what she's asked: besides, *they'll* make her do it. Fancy if, when she's gone, I find I have to share everything with those people!' And he struck his forehead and pushed the hair off his perspiring face, as he literally shook with despair. 'I must see her, Daly. I'm quite sure she'll make a will if I beg her; they can't hinder me seeing my own, only, dying sister; can they, Daly? And when I'm once there, I'll sit with her, and watch till it's all over. I'm sure, now she's ill, I'd do anything for her.'

Daly said nothing, though Barry paused for him to reply. 'Only about the form,' continued he, 'I wouldn't know what to put. By heavens, Daly! you must come with me. You can be up at the house, and I can have you down at a minute's warning.' Daly utterly declined, but Barry continued to press him. 'But you must, Daly; I tell you I know I'm right. I know her so well—she'll do it at once for the sake —for the sake of—You know she is my own sister, and all that—and she thinks so much of that kind of thing. I'll tell you what, Daly; upon my honour and soul,' and he repeated the words in a most solemn tone, 'if you'll draw the will, and she signs it, so that I come in for the whole thing—and I know she will—I'll make over fifty—ay, seventy pounds a year for you for ever and ever. I will, as I live.'

The interview ended by the attorney turning Barry Lynch into the street, and assuring him that if he ever came into his office again, on any business whatsoever, he would unscrupulously kick him out. So ended, also, the connexion between the two; for Daly never got a farthing for his labour. Indeed, after all that had taken place, he thought it as well not to trouble his *ci-devant* client with a bill. Barry went home, and of course got drunk.

When Doctor Colligan called on Lynch, he found that he was not at home. He was at that very moment at Tuam, with the attorney. The doctor repeated his visit later in the afternoon, but Barry had still not returned, and he therefore left word that he would call early after breakfast the following morning. He did so; and, after waiting half an hour in the dining-room, Barry, only half awake and half dressed, and still half drunk, came down to him.

The doctor, with a long face, delivered his message, and explained to him the state in which his sister was lying; assured him that everything in the power of medicine had been and should be done; that, nevertheless, he feared the chance of recovery was remote; and ended by informing him that Miss Lynch was aware of her danger, and had expressed a wish to see him before it might be too late. Could he make it convenient to come over just now—in half an hour—or say an hour?—said the doctor, looking at the red face and unfinished toilet of the dis-tressed brother.

Barry at first scarcely knew what reply to give. On his return from Tuam, he had determined that he would at any rate make his way into his sister's room, and, as he thought to himself, see what would come of it. In his after-dinner courage he had further determined, that he would treat the widow and her family with a very high hand, if they dared to make objection to his seeing his sister; but now, when the friendly overture came from Anty herself, and was brought by one of the Kelly faction, he felt himself a little confounded, as though he rather dreaded the interview, and would wish to put it off for a day or two.

'Oh, yes—certainly, Doctor Colligan; to be sure— that is—tell me, doctor, is she really so bad?'

'Indeed, Mr. Lynch, she is very weak.'

'But, doctor, you don't think there is any chance —I mean, there isn't any danger, is there, that she'd go off at once?'

'Why, no, I don't think there is; indeed, I have no doubt she will hold out a fortnight yet.'

'Then, perhaps, doctor, I'd better put it off till to-morrow; I'll tell you why: there's a person I wish—'

'Why, Mr. Lynch, to-day would be better. The fever's periodical, you see, and will be on her again to-morrow—'

'I beg your pardon, Doctor Colligan,' said Barry, of a sudden remembering to be civil,—'but you'll take a glass of wine?'

'Not a drop, thank ye, of anything.'

'Oh, but you will;' and Barry rang the bell and had the wine brought. 'And you expect she'll have another attack to-morrow?'

'That's a matter of course, Mr. Lynch; the fever'll come on her again to-morrow. Every attack leaves her weaker and weaker, and we fear she'll go off, before it leaves her altogether.'

'Poor thing!' said Barry, contemplatively.

'We had her head shaved,' said the doctor.

'Did you, indeed!' answered Barry. 'She was my favourite sister, Doctor Colligan—that is, I had no other.'

'I believe not,' said Doctor Colligan, looking sympathetic.

'Take another glass of wine, doctor?—now do,' and he poured out another bumper.

'Thank'ee, Mr. Lynch, thank'ee; not a drop more. And you'll be over in an hour then? I'd better go and tell her, that she may be prepared, you know,' and the doctor returned to the sick room of his patient.

Barry remained standing in the parlour, looking at the glasses and the decanter, as though he were speculating on the manner in which they had been fabricated. 'She may recover, after all,' thought he to himself. 'She's as strong as a horse—I know her better than they do. I know she'll recover, and then what shall I do? Stand to the offer Daly made to Kelly, I suppose!' And then he sat down close to the table, with his elbow on it, and his chin resting on

his hand; and there he remained, full of thought. To
tell the truth, Barry Lynch had never thought more
intensely than he did during those ten minutes.
At last he jumped up suddenly, as though surprised
at what had been passing within himself; he looked
hastily at the door and at the window, as though to
see that he had not been watched, and then went upstairs to dress himself, preparatory to his visit to the
inn.

XXIV

ANTY LYNCH'S BED-SIDE.——SCENE THE FIRST

ANTY had borne her illness with that patience
and endurance which were so particularly in-
herent in her nature. She had never complained;
and had received the untiring attentions and care of
her two young friends, with a warmth of affection
and gratitude which astonished them, accustomed as
they had been in every little illness to give and receive that tender care with which sickness is treated
in affectionate families. When ill, they felt they had
a right to be petulant, and to complain; to exact, and
to be attended to: they had been used to it from
each other, and thought it an incidental part of the
business. But Anty had hitherto had no one to
nurse her, and she looked on Meg and Jane as kind
ministering angels, emulous as they were to relieve her
wants and ease her sufferings.

Her thin face had become thinner, and was very
pale; her head had been shaved close, and there was
nothing between the broad white border of her nightcap and her clammy brow and wan cheek. But illness was more becoming to Anty than health; it gave
her a melancholy and beautiful expression of resignation, which, under ordinary circumstances, was wanting to her features, though not to her character. Her
eyes were brighter than they usually were, and her
complexion was clear, colourless, and transparent.
I do not mean to say that Anty in her illness was
beautiful, but she was no longer plain; and even to

the young Kellys, whose feelings and sympathies cannot be supposed to have been of the highest order, she became an object of the most intense interest, and the warmest affection.

'Well, doctor,' she said, as Doctor Colligan crept into her room, after the termination of his embassy to Barry; 'will he come?'

'Oh, of course he will; why wouldn't he, and you wishing it? He'll be here in an hour, Miss Lynch. He wasn't just ready to come over with me.'

'I'm glad of that,' said Anty, who felt that she had to collect her thoughts before she saw him; and then, after a moment, she added, 'Can't I take my medicine now, doctor?'

'Just before he comes you'd better have it, I think. One of the girls will step up and give it you when he's below. He'll want to speak a word or so to Mrs. Kelly before he comes up.'

'Spake to me, docthor!' said the widow, alarmed. 'What'll he be spaking to me about? Faix. I had spaking enough with him last time he was here.'

'You'd better just see him, Mrs. Kelly,' whispered the doctor. 'You'll find him quiet enough, now; just take him fair and asy; keep him down-stairs a moment, while Jane gives her the medicine. She'd better take it just before he goes to her, and don't let him stay long, whatever you do. I'll be back before the evening's over; not that I think that she'll want me to see her, but I'll just drop in.'

'Are you going, doctor?' said Anty, as he stepped up to the bed. He told her he was. 'You've told Mrs. Kelly, haven't you, that I'm to see Barry alone?'

'Why, I didn't say so,' said the doctor, looking at the widow; 'but I suppose there'll be no harm—eh, Mrs. Kelly?'

'You must let me see him alone, dear Mrs. Kelly!'

'If Doctor Colligan thinks you ought, Anty dear, I wouldn't stay in the room myself for worlds.'

'But you won't keep him here long, Miss Lynch— eh? And you won't excite yourself?—indeed, you

mustn't. You'll allow them fifteen minutes, Mrs.
Kelly, not more, and then you'll come up;' and with
these cautions, the doctor withdrew.

'I wish he was come and gone,' said the widow to
her elder daughter. 'Well; av I'd known all what
was to follow, I'd niver have got out of my warm bed
to go and fetch Anty Lynch down here that cowld
morning! Well, I'll be wise another time. Live and
larn, they say, and it's thrue, too.'

'But, mother, you ain't wishing poor Anty wasn't
here?'

'Indeed, but I do; everything to give and nothin'
to get—that's not the way I have managed to live.
But it's not that altogether, neither. I'm not be-
grudging Anty anything for herself; but that I'd be
dhriven to let that blagguard of a brother of hers into
the house, and that as a frind like, is what I didn't
think I'd ever have put upon me!'

Barry made his appearance about an hour after
the time at which they had begun to expect him; and
as soon as Meg saw him, one of them flew up-stairs,
to tell Anty and give her her tonic. Barry had made
himself quite a dandy to do honour to the occasion
of paying probably a parting visit to his sister, whom
he had driven out of her own house to die at the inn.
He had on his new blue frock-coat, and a buff waistcoat with gilt buttons, over which his watch-chain was
gracefully arranged. His pantaloons were strapped
down very tightly over his polished boots; a shining
new silk hat was on one side of his head; and in his
hand he was dangling an ebony cane. In spite, however, of all these gaudy trappings, he could not muster
up an easy air; and, as he knocked, he had that look
proverbially attributed to dogs who are going to be
hung.

Sally opened the door for him, and the widow, who
had come out from the shop, made him a low courtesy
in the passage.

'Oh—ah—yes—Mrs. Kelly, I believe?' said Barry.

'Yes, Mr. Lynch, that's my name; glory be to God!'

'My sister, Miss Lynch, is still staying here, I believe?'

'Why, drat it, man; wasn't Dr. Colligan with you less than an hour ago, telling you you must come here, av you wanted to see her?'

'You'll oblige me by sending up the servant to tell Miss Lynch I'm here.'

'Walk up here a minute, and I'll do that errand for you myself.—Well,' continued she, muttering to herself—'for him to ax av she war staying here, as though he didn't know it! There niver was his ditto for desait, maneness and divilry!'

A minute or two after the widow had left him, Barry found himself by his sister's bed-side, but never had he found himself in a position for which he was less fitted, or which was less easy to him. He assumed, however, a long and solemn face, and crawling up to the bed-side, told his sister, in a whining voice, that he was very glad to see her.

'Sit down, Barry, sit down,' said Anty, stretching out her thin pale hand, and taking hold of her brother's

Barry did as he was told, and sat down. 'I'm so glad to see you, Barry,' said she: 'I'm so very glad to see you once more—' and then after a pause, 'and it'll be the last time, Barry, for I'm dying.'

Barry told her he didn't think she was, for he didn't know when he'd seen her looking better.

'Yes, I am, Barry: Doctor Colligan has said as much; and I should know it well enough myself, even if he'd never said a word. We're friends now, are we not?—Everything's forgiven and forgotten, isn't it, Barry?'

Anty had still hold of her brother's hand, and seemed desirous to keep it. He sat on the edge of his chair, with his knees tucked in against the bed, the very picture of discomfort, both of body and mind.

'Oh, of course it is, Anty,' said he; 'forgive and forget; that was always my motto. I'm sure I never bore any malice—indeed I never was so sorry as when you went away, and—'

'Ah, Barry,' said Anty; 'it was better I went then; maybe it's all better as it is. When the priest has been with me and given me comfort, I won't fear to die. But there are other things, Barry, I want to spake to you about.'

'If there's anything I can do, I'm sure I'd do it: if there's anything at all you wish done.—Would you like to come up to the house again?'

'Oh no, Barry, not for worlds.'

'Why, perhaps, just at present, you are too weak to move; only wouldn't it be more comfortable for you to be in your own house? These people here are all very well, I dare say, but they must be a great bother to you, eh?—so interested, you know, in everything they do.'

'Ah! Barry, you don't know them.'

Barry remembered that he would be on the wrong tack to abuse the Kellys. 'I'm sure they're very nice people,' said he; 'indeed I always thought so, and said so—but they're not like your own flesh and blood, are they, Anty?—and why shouldn't you come up and be—'

'No, Barry,' said she; 'I'll not do that; as they're so very, very kind as to let me stay here, I'll remain till—till God takes me to himself. But they're not my flesh and blood'—and she turned round and looked affectionately in the face of her brother—'there are only the two of us left now; and soon, very soon you'll be all alone.' Barry felt very uncomfortable, and wished the interview was over: he tried to say something, but failed, and Anty went on—'when that time comes, will you remember what I say to you now?—When you're all alone, Barry; when there's nothing left to trouble you or put you out— will you think then of the last time you ever saw your sister, and—'

'Oh, Anty, sure I'll be seeing you again!'

'No, Barry, never again. This is the last time we

shall ever meet, and think how much we ought to be to each other! We've neither of us father or mother, husband or wife.—When I'm gone you'll be alone: will you think of me then—and will you remember, remember every day—what I say to you now?'

'Indeed I will, Anty. I'll do anything, everything you'd have me. Is there anything you'd wish me to give to any person?'

'Barry,' she continued, 'no good ever came of my father's will.'—Barry almost jumped off his chair as he heard his sister's words, so much did they startle him; but he said nothing.—'The money has done me no good, but the loss of it has blackened your heart, and turned your blood to gall against me. Yes, Barry—yes—don't speak now, let me go on ;— the old man brought you up to look for it, and, alas, he taught you to look for nothing else ; it has not been your fault, and I'm not blaming you—I'm not maning to blame you, my own brother, for you are my own '—and she turned round in the bed and shed tears upon his hand, and kissed it.—'But gold, and land, will never make you happy,—no, not all the gold of England, nor all the land the old kings ever had could make you happy, av the heart was bad within you. You'll have it all now, Barry, or mostly all. You'll have what you think the old man wronged you of ; you'll have it with no one to provide for but yourself, with no one to trouble you, no one to thwart you. But oh, Barry, av it's in your heart that that can make you happy—there's nothing before you but misery—and death—and hell.'—Barry shook like a child in the clutches of its master—'Yes, Barry ; misery and death, and all the tortures of the damned. It's to save you from this, my own brother, to try and turn your heart from that foul love of money, that your sister is now speaking to you from her grave.—Oh, Barry! try and cure it. Learn to give to others, and you'll enjoy what you have yourself.—Learn to love others, and then you'll know what it is to be loved yourself. Try, try to soften that hard heart. Marry at once, Barry, at once, before you're older and worse to cure; and you'll have children, and love them; and when you feel, as feel you must, that the money is clinging round your soul, fling it from you, and think of the last words your sister said to you.'

The sweat was now running down the cheeks of the wretched man, for the mixed rebuke and prayer of his sister had come home to him, and touched him; but it was neither with pity, with remorse, nor penitence. No; in that foul heart there was no room, even for remorse; but he trembled with fear as he listened to her words, and, falling on his knees, swore to her that he would do just as she would have him.

'If I could but think,' continued she, 'that you would remember what I am saying—'

'Oh, I will, Anty: I will—indeed, indeed, I will!'

'If I could believe so, Barry—I'd die happy and in comfort, for I love you better than anything on earth;' and again she pressed his hot red hand— 'but oh, brother! I feel for you:—you never kneel before the altar of God—you've no priest to move the weight of sin from your soul—and how heavy that must be! Do you remember, Barry; it's but a week or two ago and you threatened to kill me for the sake of our father's money? you wanted to put me in a mad-house; you tried to make me mad with fear and cruelty; me, your sister; and I never harmed or crossed you. God is now doing what you threatened; a kind, good God is now taking me to himself, and you will get what you so longed for without more sin on your conscience; but it'll never bless you, av you've still the same wishes in your heart, the same love of gold—the same hatred of a fellow-creature.'

'Oh, Anty!' sobbed out Barry, who was now absolutely in tears, 'I was drunk that night; I was indeed, or I'd never have said or done what I did.'

'And how often are you so, Barry?—isn't it so with you every night? That's another thing; for my sake, for your own sake—for God's sake, give up the

dhrink. It's killing you from day to day, and hour to
hour. I see it in your eyes, and smell it in your
breath, and hear it in your voice; it's that that makes
your heart so black:—it's that that gives you over,
body and soul, to the devil. I would not have said a
word about that night to hurt you now; and, dear
Barry, I wouldn't have said such words as these to
you at all, but that I shall never speak to you again.
And oh! I pray that you'll remember them. You're
idle now, always:—don't continue so; earn your
money, and it will be a blessing to you and to others.
But in idleness, and drunkenness, and wickedness, it
will only lead you quicker to the devil.'

Barry reiterated his promises; he would take the
pledge; he would work at the farm; he would marry
and have a family; he would not care the least for
money; he would pay his debts; he would go to
church, or chapel, if Anty liked it better; at any rate,
he'd say his prayers; he would remember every word
she had said to the last day of his life; he promised
everything or anything, as though his future existence depended on his appeasing his dying sister. But
during the whole time, his chief wish, his longing
desire, was to finish the interview, and get out of that
horrid room. He felt that he was mastered and
cowed by the creature whom he had so despised, and
he could not account for the feeling. Why did he not
dare to answer her? She had told him he would have
her money: she had said it would come to him as a
matter of course; and it was not the dread of losing
that which prevented his saying a word in his own
defence. No; she had really frightened him: she had
made him really feel that he was a low, wretched,
wicked creature, and he longed to escape from her,
that he might recover his composure.

'I have but little more to say to you, Barry,' she
continued, 'and that little is about the property.
You will have it all, but a small sum of money—'

Here Anty was interrupted by a knock at the door,
and the entrance of the widow. She came to say that

the quarter of an hour allowed by the doctor had been long exceeded, and that really Mr. Barry ought to take his leave, as so much talking would be bad for Anty.

This was quite a god-send for Barry, who was only anxious to be off; but Anty begged for a respite.

'One five minutes longer, dear Mrs. Kelly,' said she, 'and I shall have done; only five minutes—I'm much stronger now, and really it won't hurt me.'

'Well, then—mind, only five minutes,' said the widow, and again left them alone.

'You don't know, Barry—you can never know how good that woman has been to me; indeed all of them —and all for nothing. They've asked nothing of me, and now that they know I'm dying, I'm sure they expect nothing from me. She has enough; but I wish to leave something to Martin, and the girls;' and a slight pale blush covered her wan cheeks and forehead as she mentioned Martin's name. 'I will leave him five hundred pounds, and them the same between them. It will be nothing to you, Barry, out of the whole; but see and pay it at once, will you?' and she looked kindly into his face.

He promised vehemently that he would, and told her not to bother herself about a will: they should have the money as certainly as if twenty wills were made. To give Barry his due, at that moment, he meant to be as good as his word. Anty, however, told him that she would make a will; that she would send for a lawyer, and have the matter properly settled.

'And now,' she said, 'dear Barry, may God Almighty bless you—may He guide you and preserve you; and may He, above all, take from you that horrid love of the world's gold and wealth. Good bye,' and she raised herself up in her bed—'good bye, for the last time, my own dear brother; and try to remember what I've said to you this day. Kiss me before you go, Barry.'

Barry leaned over the bed, and kissed her, and then

crept out of the room, and down the stairs, with the tears streaming down his red cheeks; and skulked across the street to his own house, with his hat slouched over his face, and his handkerchief held across his mouth.

XXV

ANTY LYNCH'S BED-SIDE.——SCENE THE SECOND

ANTY was a good deal exhausted by her interview with her brother, but towards evening she rallied a little, and told Jane, who was sitting with her, that she wanted to say one word in private, to Martin. Jane was rather surprised, for though Martin was in the habit of going into the room every morning to see the invalid, Anty had never before asked for him. However, she went for Martin, and found him.

'Martin,' said she; 'Anty wants to see you alone, in private.'

'Me?' said Martin, turning a little red. 'Do you know what it's about?'

'She didn't say a word, only she wanted to see you alone; but I'm thinking it's something about her brother; he was with her a long long time this morning, and went away more like a dead man than a live one. But come, don't keep her waiting; and, whatever you do, don't stay long; every word she spakes is killing her.'

Martin followed his sister into the sick-room, and, gently taking Anty's offered hand, asked her in a whisper, what he could do for her. Jane went out; and, to do her justice sat herself down at a distance from the door, though she was in a painful state of curiosity as to what was being said within.

'You're all too good to me, Martin,' said Anty; 'you'll spoil me, between you, minding every word I say so quick.'

Martin assured her again, in a whisper, that anything and everything they could do for her was only a pleasure.

'Don't mind whispering,' said Anty; 'spake out; your voice won't hurt me. I love to hear your voices, they're all so kind and good. But Martin, I've business you must do for me, and that at once, for I feel within me that I'll soon be gone from this.'

'We hope not, Anty; but it's all with God now— isn't it? No one knows that betther than yourself.'

'Oh yes, I do know that; and I feel it is His pleasure that it should be so, and I don't fear to die. A few weeks back the thoughts of death, when they came upon me, nearly killed me; but that feeling's all gone now.'

Martin did not know what answer to make; he again told her he hoped she would soon get better. It is a difficult task to talk properly to a dying person about death, and Martin felt that he was quite incompetent to do so.

'But,' she continued, after a little, 'there's still much that I want to do,—that I ought to do. In the first place, I must make my will.'

Martin was again puzzled. This was another subject on which he felt himself equally unwilling to speak; he could not advise her not to make one; and he certainly would not advise her to do so.

'Your will, Anty?—there's time enough for that; you'll be sthronger you know, in a day or two. Doctor Colligan says so—and then we'll talk about it.'

'I hope there is time enough, Martin; but there isn't more than enough; it's not much that I'll have to say—'

'Were you spaking to Barry about it this morning?'

'Oh, I was. I told him what I'd do: he'll have the property now, mostly all as one as av the ould man had left it to him. It would have been betther so, eh Martin?' Anty never doubted her lover's disinterestedness; at this moment she suspected him of no dirty longing after her money, and she did him only justice. When he came into her room he had no thoughts of inheriting anything from her. Had he

been sure that by asking he could have induced her
to make a will in his favour, he would not have done
so. But still his heart sunk a little within him when
he heard her declare that she was going to leave
everything back to her brother. It was, however,
only for a moment; he remembered his honest determination firmly and resolutely to protect their joint
property against any of her brother's attempts,
should he ever marry her; but in no degree to strive
or even hanker after it, unless it became his own in
a fair, straightforward manner.

'Well, Anty; I think you're right,' said he. 'But
wouldn't it all go to Barry, nathurally, without your
bothering yourself about a will, and you so wake.'

'In course it would, at laist I suppose so; but
Martin,' and she smiled faintly as she looked up into
his face, 'I want the two dear, dear girls, and I want
yourself to have some little thing to remember me
by; and your dear kind mother,—she doesn't want
money, but if I ask her to take a few of the silver
things in the house, I'm sure she'll keep them for my
sake. Oh, Martin! I do love you all so very—so very
much!' and the warm tears streamed down her cheeks.

Martin's eyes were affected, too: he made a
desperate struggle to repress the weakness, but he
could not succeed, and was obliged to own it by
rubbing his eyes with the sleeve of his coat. 'And
I'm shure, Anty,' said he, 'we all love you; any one
must love you who knew you.' And then he paused:
he was trying to say something of his own true
personal regard for her, but he hardly knew how to
express it. 'We all love you as though you were one
of ourselves—and so you are—it's all the same—at
any rate it is to me.'

'And I would have been one of you, had I lived.
I can talk to you more about it now, Martin, than I
ever could before, because I know I feel I am dying.'

'But you mustn't talk, Anty; it wakens you, and
you've had too much talking already this day.'

'It does me good, Martin, and I must say what I

have to say to you. I mayn't be able again. Had it
plazed God I should have lived, I would have prayed
for nothing higher or betther than to be one of such
a family as yourselves. Had I been——had I been'——
and now Anty blushed again, and she also found a
difficulty in expressing herself; but she soon got over
it, and continued, 'had I been permitted to marry
you, Martin, I think I would have been a good wife
to you. I am very, very sure I would have been an
affectionate one.'

'I'm shure you would——I'm shure you would,
Anty. God send you may still: av you war only once
well again there's nothing now to hindher us.'

'You forget Barry,' Anty said, with a shudder.
'But it doesn't matther talking of that now'——
Martin was on the point of telling her that Barry had
agreed, under certain conditions, to their marriage:
but, on second thoughts, he felt it would be useless to
do so; and Anty continued,

'I would have done all I could, Martin. I would
have loved you fondly and truly. I would have liked
what you liked, and, av I could, I would 've made
your home quiet and happy. Your mother should
have been my mother, and your sisthers my sisthers.'

'So they are now, Anty——so they are now, my own,
own Anty——they love you as much as though they
were.'

'God Almighty bless them for their goodness, and
you too, Martin. I cannot tell you, I niver could tell
you, how I've valued your honest thrue love, for I
know you have loved me honestly and thruly; but
I've always been afraid to spake to you. I've sometimes thought you must despise me, I've been· so
wake and cowardly.'

'Despise you, Anty?——how could I despise you,
when I've always loved you?'

'But now, Martin, about poor Barry——for he is poor.
I've sometimes thought, as I've been lying here the
long long hours awake, that, feeling to you as I do, I
ought to be laving you what the ould man left to me.'

'I'd be sorry you did, Anty. I'll not be saying but what I thought of that when I first looked for you, but it was never to take it from you, but to share it with you, and make you happy with it.'

'I know it, Martin: I always knew it and felt it.'

'And now, av it's God's will that you should go from us, I'd rather Barry had the money than us. We've enough, the Lord be praised; and I wouldn't for worlds it should be said that it war for that we brought you among us; nor for all County Galway would I lave it to Barry to say, that when you were here, sick, and wake, and dying, we put a pen into your hand to make you sign a will to rob him of what should by rights be his.'

'That's it, dear Martin; it wouldn't bless you if you had it; it can bless no one who looks to it alone for a blessing. It wouldn't make you happy—it would make you miserable, av people said you had that which you ought not to have. Besides, I love my poor brother; he is my brother, my only real relation; we've lived all our lives together; and though he isn't what he should be, the fault is not all his own, I should not sleep in my grave, av I died with his curse upon me; as I should, av he found, when I am gone, that I'd willed the property all away. I've told him he'd have it all—nearly all; and I've begged him, prayed to him, from my dying bed, to mend his ways; to try and be something betther in the world than what I fear he's like to be. I think he minded what I said when he was here, for death-bed words have a solemn sound to the most worldly; but when I'm gone he'll be all alone, there'll be no one to look afther him. Nobody loves him—no one even likes him; no one will live with him but those who mane to rob him; and he will be robbed, and plundered, and desaved, when he thinks he's robbing and desaving others.' Anty paused, more for breath than for a reply, but Martin felt that he must say something.

'Indeed, Anty, I fear he'll hardly come to good.

He dhrinks too much, by all accounts; besides, he's idle, and the honest feeling isn't in him.'

'It's thrue, dear Martin; it's too thrue. Will you do me a great great favour, Martin'—and she rose up a little and turned her moist clear eye full upon him—'will you show your thrue love to your poor Anty, by a rale lasting kindness, but one that'll be giving you much much throuble and pain? Afther I'm dead and gone—long long after I'm in my cold grave, will you do that for me, Martin?'

'Indeed I will, Anty,' said Martin, rather astonished, but with a look of solemn assurance; 'anything that I can do, I will: you needn't dread my not remembering, but I fear it isn't much that I can do for you.'

'Will you always think and spake of Barry—will you always act to him and by him, and for him, not as a man whom you know and dislike, but as my brother—your own Anty's only brother?—Whatever he does, will you thry to make him do betther? Whatever troubles he's in, will you lend him your hand? Come what come may to him, will you be his frind? He has no frind now. When I'm gone, will you be a frind to him?'

Martin was much confounded. 'He won't let me be his frind,' he said; 'he looks down on us and despises us; he thinks himself too high to be befrinded by us. Besides, of all Dunmore he hates us most.'

'He won't when he finds you haven't got the property from him: but frindship doesn't depend on letting—rale frindship doesn't. I don't want you to be dhrinking, and ating, and going about with him. God forbid!—you're too good for that. But when you find he wants a frind, come forward, and thry and make him do something for himself. You can't but come together; you'll be the executhor in the will; won't you, Martin? and then he'll meet you about the property; he can't help it, and you must meet then as frinds. And keep that up. If he insults you, forgive it for my sake; if he's fractious and

annoying, put up with it for my sake ; for my sake thry
to make him like you, and thry to make others like
him.' Martin felt that this would be impossible, but
he didn't say so—'No one respects him now, but
all respect you. I see it in people's eyes and manners,
without hearing what they say. Av you spake well
of him—at any rate kindly of him, people won't
turn themselves so against him. Will you do all this,
for my sake?'

Martin solemnly promised that, as far as he could,
he would do so; that, at any rate as far as himself
was concerned, he would never quarrel with him.

'You'll have very, very much to forgive,' continued Anty; 'but then it's so swect to forgive; and
he's had no fond mother like you; he has not been
taught any duties, any virtues, as you have. He has
only been taught that money is the thing to love,
and that he should worship nothing but that. Martin,
for my sake, will you look on him as a brother?—a
wicked, bad, castaway brother; but still as a brother,
to be forgiven, and, if possible, redeemed?'

'As I hope for glory in Heaven, I will,' said Martin;
'but I think he'll go far from this; I think he'll quit
Dunmore.'

'Maybe he will; perhaps it's betther he should;
but he'll lave his name behind him. Don't be too
hard on that, and don't let others; and even av he
does go, it'll not be long before he'll want a frind,
and I don't know anywhere he can go that he's likely
to find one. Wherever he may go, or whatever he
may do, you won't forget he was my brother; will
you, Martin? You won't forget he was your own
Anty's only brother.'

Martin again gave her his solemn word that he
would, to the best of his ability, act as a friend and
brother to Barry.

'And now about the will.' Martin again endeavoured to dissuade her from thinking about a will
just at present.

'Ah! but my heart's set upon it,' she said; 'I

shouldn't be happy unless I did it, and I'm sure
you don't want to make me unhappy, now. You
must get me some lawyer here, Martin; I'm afraid
you're not lawyer enough for that yourself.'

'Indeed I'm not, Anty; it's a trade I know little
about.'

'Well; you must get me a lawyer; not to-morrow,
for I know I shan't be well enough; but I hope I shall
next day, and you may tell him just what to put in
it. I've no secrets from you.' And she told him exactly what she had before told her brother. 'That'll
not hurt him,' she continued; 'and I'd like to think
you and the dear girls should accept something
from me.'

Martin then agreed to go to Daly. He was on good
terms with them all now, since making the last offer
to them respecting the property; besides, as Martin
said, 'he knew no other lawyer, and, as the will was
so decidedly in Barry's favour, who was so proper to
make it as Barry's own lawyer?'

'Good-bye now, Martin,' said Anty; 'we shall be
desperately scolded for talking so long; but it was on
my mind to say it all, and I'm betther now it's all
over.'

'Good night, dear Anty,' said Martin, 'I'll be seeing you to-morrow.'

'Every day, I hope, Martin, till it's all over. God
bless you, God bless you all—and you above all.
You don't know, Martin—at laist you didn't know all
along, how well, how thruly I've loved you. Good
night,' and Martin left the room, as Barry had done,
in tears. But he had no feeling within him of which
he had cause to be ashamed. He was ashamed, and
tried to hide his face, for he was not accustomed to be
seen with the tears running down his cheeks; but
still he had within him a strong sensation of gratified
pride, as he reflected that he was the object of the
warmest affection to so sweet a creature as Anty
Lynch.

'Well, Martin—what was it she wanted?' said

his mother, as she met him at the bottom of the stairs.

'I couldn't tell you now, mother,' said he; 'but av there was iver an angel on 'arth, it's Anty Lynch.' And saying so, he pushed open the door and escaped into the street.

'I wondher what she's been about now?' said the widow, speculating to herself—'well, av she does lave it away from Barry, who can say but what she has a right to do as she likes with her own?—and who's done the most for her, I'd like to know?'—and pleasant prospects of her son's enjoying an independence flitted before her mind's eye. 'But thin,' she continued, talking to herself, 'I wouldn't have it said in Dunmore that a Kelly demaned hisself to rob a Lynch, not for twice all Sim Lynch ever had. Well— we'll see; but no good 'll ever come of meddling with them people. Jane, Jane,' she called out, at the top of her voice, 'are you niver coming down, and letting me out of this?—bad manners to you.'

Jane answered, in the same voice, from the parlour upstairs, 'Shure, mother, ain't I getting Anty her tay?'

'Drat Anty and her tay!—Well, shure, I'm railly bothered now wid them Lynches!—Well, glory be to God, there's an end to everything—not that I'm wishing her anywhere but where she is; she's welcome, for Mary Kelly.'

XXVI

LOVE'S AMBASSADOR

TWO days after the hunt in which poor Goneaway was killed by Barry's horse, Ballindine received the following letter from his friend Dot Blake.

Limmer's Hotel, 27th March, 1844.
Dear Frank,

I and Brien, and Bottom, crossed over last Friday night, and, thanks to the God of storms, were allowed to get quietly through it. The young chieftain didn't like being boxed on the quay a bit too well; the rattling of the chains upset him, and the fellows there are so infernally noisy and awkward, that I wonder he was ever got on board. It's difficult to make an Irishman handy, but it's the very devil to make him quiet. There were four at his head, and three at his tail, two at the wheel, turning, and one up aloft, hallooing like a demon in the air; and when Master Brien showed a little aversion to this comic performance, they were going to drag him into the box *bon gré, mal gré*, till Bottom interposed and saved the men and the horse from destroying each other.

We got safe to Middleham on Saturday night, the greatest part of the way by rail. Scott has a splendid string of horses. These English fellows do their work in tiptop style, only they think more of spending money than they do of making it. I waited to see him out on Monday, when he'd got a trot, and he was as bright as though he'd never left the Curragh. Scott says he's a little too fine; but you know of course he must find some fault. To give Igoe his due, he could not be in better condition, and Scott was obliged to own that, *considering where he came from*, he was very well. I came on here on Tuesday, and have taken thirteen wherever I could get it, and thought the money safe. I have got a good deal on, and won't budge till I do it at six to one; and I'm sure I'll bring him to that. I think he'll rise quickly, as he wants so little training, and as his qualities must be at once known now he's in Scott's stables; so if you mean to put any more on you had better do it at once.

So much for the stables. I left the other two at home, but have one of my own string here, as maybe I'll pick up a match: and now I wish to let you know a report that I heard this morning—at least a secret, which bids fair to become a report. It is said that Kilcullen is to marry F—— W——, and that he has already paid Heaven only knows how many thousand pounds of debt with her money; that the old earl has arranged it all, and that the beautiful heiress has

reluctantly agreed to be made a viscountess. I'm
very far from saying that I believe this; but it may
suit you to know that I heard the arrangement
mentioned before two other persons, one of whom
was Morris;—strange enough this, as he was one of
the set at Handicap Lodge when you told them that
the match with yourself was still on. I have no doubt
the plan would suit father and son; you best know
how far the lady may have been likely to accede. At
any rate, my dear Frank, if you'll take my advice,
you'll not sit quiet till she does marry some one.
You can't expect she'll wear the willow for you very
long, if you do nothing yourself. Write to her by
post, and write to the earl by the same post, saying
you have done so. Tell her in the sweetest way you
can, that you cannot live without seeing her, and
getting your *congé*, if *congé* it is to be, from her own
dear lips; and tell him, in as few words, as you please,
that you mean to do yourself the honour of knocking
at his door on such and such a day—and do it.

By the bye, Kilcullen certainly returns to Ireland
immediately. There's been the devil's own smash
among him and the Jews. He has certainly been
dividing money among them; but not near enough,
by all accounts, to satisfy the half of them. For the
sake of your reputation, if not of your pocket, don't
let him walk off with the hundred and thirty thousand pounds. They say it's not a penny less.

Very faithfully yours,
W. BLAKE.

Shall I do anything for you here about Brien?
I think I might still get you eleven to one, but let
me hear at once.

As Frank read the first portion of this epistle, his
affection for his poor dear favourite nag returned in
full force, and he felt all the pangs of remorse for
having parted with him; but when he came to the
latter part, to Lord Kilcullen's name, and the
initials by which his own Fanny was designated, he

forgot all about horse and owner; became totally
regardless of thirteen, eleven, and six to one, and read
on hastily to the end; read it all again—then closed
the letter, and put it in his pocket, and remained for
a considerable time in silent contemplation, trying to
make up his mind what he would do.

Nobody was with him as he opened his post-bag,
which he took from the messenger as the boy was
coming up to the house; he therefore read his letter
alone, on the lawn, and he continued pacing up and
down before the house with a most perturbed air, for
half an hour.

Kilcullen going to marry Fanny Wyndham! So,
that was the cause of Lord Cashel's singular be-
haviour—his incivility, and refusal to allow Frank
to see his ward. 'What! to have arranged it all in
twenty-four hours,' thought Frank to himself; 'to
have made over his ward's money to his son, before
her brother, from whom she inherited it, was in his
grave: to determine at once to reject an accepted
suitor for the sake of closing on the poor girl's
money—and without the slightest regard for her
happiness, without a thought for her welfare! And
then, such lies,' said the viscount, aloud, striking his
heel into the grass in his angry impetuosity; 'such
base, cruel lies!—to say that she had authorised him,
when he couldn't have dared to make such a proposal to her, and her brother but two days dead.
Well; I took him for a stiff-necked pompous fool,
but I never thought him such an avaricious knave.'
And Fanny, too,—could Fanny have agreed, so soon,
to give her hand to another? She could not have
transferred her heart. His own dear, fond Fanny!
A short time ago they had been all in all to each
other; and now so completely estranged as they
were! However, Dot was right; up to this time
Fanny might be quite true to him; indeed, there was
not ground even for doubting her, for it was evident
that no reliance was to be placed in Lord Cashel's
asseverations. But still he could not expect that she

should continue to consider herself engaged, if she
remained totally neglected by her lover. He must do
something, and that at once; but there was very
great difficulty in deciding what that something was
to be. It was easy enough for Dot to say, first write,
and then go. If he were to write, what security was
there that his letter would be allowed to reach
Fanny? and if he went, how much less chance was
there that he would be allowed to see her. And then,
again to be turned out of the house! again informed,
by that pompous scheming earl, that his visits there
were not desired. Or, worse still, not to be admitted;
to be driven from the door by a footman who would
well know for what he came! No; come what come
might, he would never again go to Grey Abbey; at
least not unless he was specially and courteously
invited thither by the owner; and then it should only
be to marry his ward, and take her from the odious
place, never to return again.

'The impudent impostor!' continued Frank to
himself; 'to pretend to suspect me, when he was
himself hatching his dirty, mercenary, heartless
schemes!'

But still the same question recurred,—what was to
be done? Venting his wrath on Lord Cashel would
not get him out of the difficulty: going was out of the
question; writing was of little use. Could he not
send somebody else? Some one who could not be
refused admittance to Fanny, and who might at any
rate learn what her wishes and feelings were? He did
not like making love by deputy; but still, in his
present dilemma, he could think of nothing better.
But whom was he to send? Bingham Blake was a
man of character, and would not make a fool of
himself; but he was too young; he would not be able
to make his way to Fanny. No—a young unmarried
man would not do.—Mat Tierney?—he was afraid
of no one, and always cool and collected; but then,
Mat was in London; besides, he was a sort of friend
of Kilcullen's. General Bourke? No one could refuse

an *entrée* to his venerable grey hairs, and polished manner; besides, his standing in the world was so good, so unexceptionable; but then the chances were he would not go on such an errand; he was too old to be asked to take such a troublesome service; and besides, if asked, it was very probable he would say that he considered Lord Cashel entitled to his ward's obedience. The rector—the Rev. Joseph Armstrong? He must be the man: there was, at any rate, respectability in his profession; and he had sufficient worldly tact not easily to be thrust aside from his object: the difficulty would be, whether he had a coat sufficiently decent to appear in at Grey Abbey.

After mature consideration he made up his mind that the parson should be his ambassador. He would sooner have confided in Bingham Blake, but an unmarried man would not do. No; the parson must be the man. Frank was, unfortunately, but little disposed to act in any case without advice, and in his anxiety to consult some one as to consulting the parson, returned into the house, to make a clear breast of it to his mother. He found her in the breakfast-room with the two girls, and the three were holding council deep.

'Oh, here's Frank,' said Sophy; 'we'd better tell him all about it at once—and he'll tell us which she'd like best.'

'We didn't mean to tell you,' said Guss; 'but I and Sophy are going to work two sofas for the drawing-room—in Berlin wool, you know: they'll be very handsome—everybody has them now, you know; they have a splendid pair at Ballyhaunis which Nora and her cousin worked.'

'But we want to know what pattern would suit Fanny's taste,' said Sophy.

'Well; you can't know that,' said Frank rather pettishly, 'so you'd better please yourselves.'

'Oh, but you must know what she likes,' continued Guss; 'I'm for this,' and she displayed a pattern showing forth two gorgeous macaws—each with plumage of the brightest colours. 'The colours are so bright, and the feathers will work in so well.'

'I don't like anything in worsted-work but flowers,' said Sophy; 'Nora Dillon says she saw two most beautiful wreaths at that shop in Grafton Street, both hanging from bars, you know; and that would be so much prettier. I'm sure Fanny would like flowers best; wouldn't she now, Frank?—Mamma thinks the common cross-bar patterns are nicer for furniture.'

'Indeed I do, my dear,' said Mrs. O'Kelly; 'and you see them much more common now in well-furnished drawing-rooms. But still I'd much sooner have them just what Fanny would like best. Surely, Frank, you must have heard her speak about worsted-work?'

All this completely disconcerted Frank, and made him very much out of love with his own plan of consulting his mother. He gave the trio some not very encouraging answer as to their good-natured intentions towards his drawing-room, and again left them alone. 'Well; there's nothing for it but to send the parson; I don't think he'll make a fool of himself, but then I know he'll look so shabby. However, here goes,' and he mounted his nag, and rode off to Ballindine glebe.

The glebe-house was about a couple of miles from Kelly's Court, and it was about half-past four when Lord Ballindine got there. He knocked at the door, which was wide open, though it was yet only the last day of March, and was told by a remarkably slatternly maid-servant, that her master was 'jist afther dinner;' that he was stepped out, but was about the place, and could be 'fetched in at oncet;'—and would his honor walk in? And so Lord Ballindine was shown into the rectory drawing-room on one side of the passage (alias hall), while the attendant of all work went to announce his arrival in the rectory dining-room on the other side. Here Mrs. Armstrong was sitting among her numerous progeny, securing the débris of the dinner from their rapacious paws, and endeavouring to make two very unruly boys consume the portions of fat which had been supplied to them with, as they loudly declared, an unfairly insufficient quantum of lean. As the girl was good-natured enough to leave both doors wide open, Frank had the full advantage of the conversation.

'Now, Greg,' said the mother, 'if you leave your meat that way I'll have it put by for you, and you shall have nothing but potatoes till it's ate.'

'Why, mother, it's nothing but tallow; look here; you gave me all the outside part.'

'I'll tell your dada, and see what he'll say, if you call the meat tallow; and you're just as bad, Joe; worse if anything—gracious me, here's waste! well, I'll lock it up for you, and you shall both of you eat it to-morrow, before you have a bit of anything else.'

Then followed a desperate fit of coughing.

'My poor Minny!' said the mother, 'you're just as bad as ever. Why would you go out on the wet grass?—Is there none of the black currant jam left?'

'No, mother,' coughed Minny, 'not a bit.'

'Greg ate it all,' peached Sarah, an elder sister; 'I told him not, but he would.'

'Greg, I'll have you flogged, and you never shall come from school again. What's that you're saying, Mary?'

'There's a jintleman in the drawing-room as is axing afther masther.'

'Gentleman—what gentleman?' asked the lady.

'Sorrow a know I know, ma'am!' said Mary, who was a new importation—'only, he's a dark, sightly jintleman, as come on a horse.'

'And did you send for the master?'

'I did, ma'am; I was out in the yard, and bad Patsy go look for him.'

'It's Nicholas Dillon, I'll bet twopence,' said Greg, jumping up to rush into the other room: 'he's come about the black colt, I know.'

'Stay where you are, Greg; and don't go in there

with your dirty face and fingers;' and, after speculating a little longer, the lady went into the drawing-room herself; though, to tell the truth, her own face and fingers were hardly in a state suitable for receiving company.

Mrs. Armstrong marched into the drawing-room with something of a stately air, to meet the strange gentleman, and there she found her old friend Lord Ballindine. Whoever called at the rectory, and at whatever hour the visit might be made, poor Mrs. Armstrong was sure to apologise for the confusion in which she was found. She had always just got rid of a servant, and could not get another that suited her; or there was some other commonplace reason for her being discovered *en déshabille*. However, she managed to talk to Frank for a minute or two with tolerable volubility, till her eyes happening to dwell on her own hands, which were certainly not as white as a lady's should be, she became a little uncomfortable and embarrassed—tried to hide them in her drapery—then remembered that she had on her morning slippers, which were rather the worse for wear; and, feeling too much ashamed of her *tout ensemble* to remain, hurried out of the room, saying that she would go and see where Armstrong could possibly have got himself to. She did not appear again to Lord Ballindine.

Poor Mrs. Armstrong!—though she looked so little like one, she had been brought up as a lady, carefully and delicately; and her lot was the more miserable, for she knew how lamentable were her present deficiencies. When she married a poor curate, having, herself, only a few hundred pounds' fortune, she had made up her mind to a life of comparative poverty; but she had meant even in her poverty to be decent, respectable, and lady-like. Weak health, nine children, an improvident husband, and an income so lamentably ill-suited to her wants, had however been too much for her, and she had degenerated into a slatternly, idle scold.

In a short time the parson came in from his farm, rusty and muddy—rusty, from his clerical dress; muddy from his farming occupations; and Lord Ballindine went into the business of his embassy. He remembered, however, how plainly he had heard the threats about the uneaten fat, and not wishing the household to hear all he had to say respecting Fanny Wyndham, he took the parson out into the road before the house, and, walking up and down, unfolded his proposal.

Mr. Armstrong expressed extreme surprise at the nature of the mission on which he was to be sent; secondly at the necessity of such a mission at all; and thirdly, lastly, and chiefly, at the enormous amount of the heiress's fortune, to lose which he declared would be an unpardonable sin on Lord Ballindine's part. He seemed to be not at all surprised that Lord Cashel should wish to secure so much money in his own family; nor did he at all participate in the unmeasured reprobation with which Frank loaded the worthy earl's name. One hundred and thirty thousand pounds would justify anything, and he thought of his nine poor children, his poor wife, his poor home, his poor two hundred a-year, and his poor self. He calculated that so very rich a lady would most probably have some interest in the Church, which she could not but exercise in his favour, if he were instrumental in getting her married; and he determined to go. Then the difficult question as to the wardrobe occurred to him. Besides, he had no money for the road. Those, however, were minor evils to be got over, and he expressed himself willing to undertake the embassy.

'But, my dear Ballindine; what is it I'm to do?' said he. 'Of course you know, I'd do anything for you, as of course I ought—anything that ought to be done; but what is it exactly you wish me to say?'

'You see, Armstrong, that pettifogging schemer told me he didn't wish me to come to his house again, and I wouldn't, even for Fanny Wyndham, force

myself into any man's house. He would not let me
see her when I was there, and I could not press it,
because her brother was only just dead; so I'm
obliged to take her refusal second hand. Now I don't
believe she ever sent the message he gave me. I
think he has made her believe that I'm deserting and
ill-treating her; and in this way she may be piqued
and tormented into marrying Kilcullen.'

'I see it now: upon my word then Lord Cashel
knows how to play his cards! But if I go to Grey
Abbey I can't see her without seeing him.'

'Of course not—but I'm coming to that. You see,
I have no reason to doubt Fanny's love; she has
assured me of it a thousand times. I wouldn't say so
to you even, as it looks like boasting, only it's so
necessary you should know how the land lies; besides,
everybody knew it; all the world knew we were
engaged.'

'Oh, boasting—it's no boasting at all: it would be
very little good my going to Grey Abbey, if she had
not told you so.'

'Well, I think that if you were to see Lord Cashel
and tell him, in your own quiet way, who you are;
that you are rector of Ballindine, and my especial
friend; and that you had come all the way from
County Mayo especially to see Miss Wyndham, that
you might hear from herself whatever message she
had to send to me—if you were to do this, I don't
think he would dare to prevent you from seeing her.'

'If he did, of course I would put it to him that you,
who were so long received as Miss Wyndham's accepted swain, were at least entitled to so much consideration at her hands; and that I must demand so
much on your behalf, wouldn't that be it, eh?'

'Exactly. I see you understand it, as if you'd been
at it all your life; only don't call me her swain.'

'Well, I'll think of another word—her beau.'

'For Heaven's sake, no!—that's ten times worse.'

'Well, her lover?'

'That's at any rate English: but say, her accepted

husband—that'll be true and plain: if you do that I think you will manage to see her, and then—'

'Well, then—for that'll be the difficult part.'

'Oh, when you see her, one simple word will do: Fanny Wyndham loves plain dealing. Merely tell her that Lord Ballindine has not changed his mind; and that he wishes to know from herself, by the mouth of a friend whom he can trust, whether she has changed hers. If she tells you that she has, I would not follow her farther though she were twice as rich as Crœsus. I'm not hunting her for her money; but I am determined that Lord Cashel shall not make us both miserable by forcing her into a marriage with his *roué* of a son.'

'Well, Ballindine, I'll go; but mind, you must not blame me if I fail. I'll do the best I can for you.'

'Of course I won't. When will you be able to start?'

'Why, I suppose there's no immediate hurry?' said the parson, remembering that the new suit of clothes must be procured.

'Oh, but there is. Kilcullen will be there at once; and considering how long it is since I saw Fanny— three months, I believe—no time should be lost.'

'How long is her brother dead?'

'Oh, a month—or very near it.'

'Well, I'll go Monday fortnight; that'll do, won't it?'

It was at last agreed that the parson was to start for Grey Abbey on the Monday week following; that he was to mention to no one where he was going; that he was to tell his wife that he was going on business he was not allowed to talk about;—she would be a very meek woman if she rested satisfied with that!—and that he was to present himself at Grey Abbey on the following Wednesday.

'And now,' said the parson, with some little hesitation, 'my difficulty commences. We country rectors are never rich; but when we've nine children, Ballindine, it's rare to find us with money in our pockets.

You must advance me a little cash for the emergencies of the road.'

'My dear fellow! Of course the expense must be my own. I'll send you down a note between this and then; I haven't enough about me now. Or, stay —I'll give you a cheque,' and he turned into the house, and wrote him a cheque for twenty pounds.

That'll get the coat into the bargain, thought the rector, as he rather uncomfortably shuffled the bit of paper into his pocket. He had still a gentleman's dislike to be paid for his services. But then, Necessity—how stern she is! He literally could not have gone without it.

XXVII

MR. LYNCH'S LAST RESOURCE

ON the following morning Lord Ballindine as he had appointed to do, drove over to Dunmore, to settle with Martin about the money, and, if necessary, to go with him to the attorney's office in Tuam. Martin had as yet given Daly no answer respecting Barry Lynch's last proposal; and though poor Anty's health made it hardly necessary that any answer should be given, still Lord Ballindine had promised to see the attorney, if Martin thought it necessary.

The family were all in great confusion that morning, for Anty was very bad—worse than she had ever been. She was in a paroxysm of fever, was raving in delirium, and in such a state that Martin and his sister were occasionally obliged to hold her in bed. Sally, the old servant, had been in the room for a considerable time during the morning, standing at the foot of the bed with a big tea-pot in her hand, and begging in a whining voice, from time to time, that 'Miss Anty, God bless her, might get a dhrink of tay!' But, as she had been of no other service, and as the widow thought it as well that she should not hear what Anty said in her raving, she had been desired to go down-stairs, and was sitting over the fire. She had fixed the big tea-pot among the embers, and held a slop-bowl of tea in her lap, discoursing to Nelly, who with her hair somewhat more than ordinarily dishevelled, in token of grief for Anty's illness, was seated on a low stool, nursing a candle-stick.

'Well, Nelly,' said the prophetic Sally, boding evil in her anger—for, considering how long she had been in the family, she had thought herself entitled to hear Anty's ravings; 'mind, I tell you, good won't come of this. The Virgin prothect us from all harum!— it niver war lucky to have sthrangers dying in the house.'

'But shure Miss Anty's no stranger.'

'Faix thin, her words must be sthrange enough when the likes o' me wouldn't be let hear 'em. Not but what I did hear, as how could I help it? There'll be no good come of it. Who's to be axed to the wake, I'd like to know.'

'Axed to the wake, is it? Why, shure, won't there be rashions of ating and lashings of dhrinking? The misthress isn't the woman to spare, and sich a frind as Miss Anty dead in the house. Let 'em ax whom they like.'

'You're a fool, Nelly—Ax whom they like!— that's asy said. Is they to ax Barry Lynch, or is they to let it alone, and put the sisther into the sod without a word said to him about it? God be betwixt us and all evil'—and she took a long pull at the slop-bowl; and, as the liquid flowed down her throat, she gradually threw back her head till the top of her mop cap was flattened against the side of the wide fire-place, and the bowl was turned bottom upwards, so that the half-melted brown sugar might trickle into her mouth. She then gave a long sigh, and repeated that difficult question—'Who is they to ax to the wake?'

It was too much for Nelly to answer: she re-echoed the sigh, and more closely embraced the candlestick.

'Besides, Nelly, who'll have the money when she's

gone?—and she's nigh that already, the Blessed Virgin guide and prothect her. Who'll get all her money?'

'Why; won't Mr. Martin? Sure, an't they as good as man and wife—all as one?'

'That's it; they'll be fighting and tearing, and tatthering about that money, the two young men will, you'll see. There'll be lawyering, an' magisthrate's work—an' factions—an' fighthins at fairs; an' thin, as in course the Lynches can't hould their own agin the Kellys, there'll be undherhand blows, an' blood, an' murdher!—you'll see else.'

'Glory be to God,' involuntarily prayed Nelly, at the thoughts suggested by Sally's powerful eloquence.

'There will, I tell ye,' continued Sally, again draining the tea-pot into the bowl. 'Sorrow a lie I'm telling you;' and then, in a low whisper across the fire, 'didn't I see jist now Miss Anty ketch a hould of Misther Martin, as though she'd niver let him go agin, and bid him for dear mercy's sake have a care of Barry Lynch?—Shure I knowed what that meant. And thin, didn't he thry and do for herself with his own hands? Didn't Biddy say she'd swear she heard him say he'd do it?—and av he wouldn't boggle about his own sisther, it's little he'd mind what he'd do to an out an out inemy like Misther Martin.'

'Warn't that a knock at the hall-door, Sally?'

'Run and see, girl; may-be it's the docthor back again; only mostly he don't mind knocking much.'

Nelly went to the door, and opened it to Lord Ballindine, who had left his gig in charge of his servant. He asked for Martin, who in a short time, joined him in the parlour.

'This is a dangerous place for your lordship, now,' said he: 'the fever is so bad in the house. Thank God, nobody seems to have taken it yet, but there's no knowing.'

'Is she still so bad, Martin?'

'Worse than iver, a dale worse; I don't think it'll last long, now: another bout such as this last 'll about

finish it. But I won't keep your lordship. I've
managed about the money;'—and the necessary
writing was gone through, and the cash was handed
to Lord Ballindine.

'You've given over all thoughts then, about
Lynch's offer—eh, Martin?—I suppose you've done
with all that, now?'

'Quite done with it, my lord; and done with for-
tune-hunting too. I've seen enough this last time
back to cure me altogether—at laist, I hope so.'

'She doesn't mean to make any will, then?'

'Why, she wishes to make one, but I doubt
whether she'll ever be able;' and then Martin gave
his landlord an account of all that Anty had said
about her will, her wishes as to the property, her
desire to leave something to him (Martin) and his
sisters: and last he repeated the strong injunctions
which Anty had given him respecting her poor brother,
and her assurance, so full of affection, that had she
lived she would have done her best to make him
happy as her husband.

Lord Ballindine was greatly affected; he warmly
shook hands with Martin, told him how highly he
thought of his conduct, and begged him to take care
that Anty had the gratification of making her will as
she had desired to do. 'The fact,' Lord Ballindine
said, ' of your being named in the will as her executor
will give you more control over Barry than anything
else could do.' He then proposed at once to go, himself, to Tuam, and explain to Daly what it was Miss
Lynch wished him to do. This Lord Ballindine did,
and the next day the will was completed.

For a week or ten days Anty remained in much the
same condition. After each attack of fever it was
expected that she would perish from weakness and
exhaustion; but she still held on, and then the fever
abated, and Doctor Colligan thought that it was
possible she might recover: she was, however, so
dreadfully emaciated and worn out, there was so
little vitality left in her, that he would not encourage

more than the faintest hope. Anty herself was too
weak either to hope or fear;—and the women of the
family, who from continual attendance knew how
very near to death she was, would hardly allow themselves to think that she could recover.

There were two persons, however, who from the
moment of her amendment felt an inward sure conviction of her convalescence. They were Martin and
Barry. To the former this feeling was of course one
of unalloyed delight. He went over to Kelly's Court,
and spoke there of his betrothed as though she were
already sitting up and eating mutton chops; was
congratulated by the young ladies on his approaching
nuptials, and sauntered round the Kelly's Court
shrubberies with Frank, talking over his future
prospects; asking advice about this and that, and
propounding the pros and cons on that difficult question, whether he would live at Dunmore, or build a
house at Toneroe for himself and Anty. With Barry,
however, the feeling was very different: he was again
going to have his property wrenched from him; he
was again to suffer the pangs he had endured, when
first he learned the purport of his father's will; after
clutching the fruit for which he had striven, as even
he himself felt, so basely, it was again to be torn from
him so cruelly.

He had been horribly anxious for a termination to
Anty's sufferings; horribly impatient to feel himself
possessor of the whole. From day to day, and sometimes two or three times a day, he had seen Dr.
Colligan, and inquired how things were going on: he
had especially enjoined that worthy man to come up
after his morning call at the inn, and get a glass of
sherry at Dunmore House; and the doctor had very
generally done so. For some time Barry endeavoured
to throw the veil of brotherly regard over the true
source of his anxiety; but the veil was much too thin to
hide what it hardly covered, and Barry, as he got intimate with the doctor, all but withdrew it altogether.
When Barry would say, 'Well, doctor, how is she

to-day?' and then remark, in answer to the doctor's statement that she was very bad—'Well, I suppose it can't last much longer; but it's very tedious, isn't it, poor thing?' it was plain enough that the brother was not longing for the sister's recovery. And then he would go a little further, and remark that 'if the poor thing was to go, it would be better for all she went at once,' and expressed an opinion that he was rather ill-treated by being kept so very long in suspense.

Doctor Colligan ought to have been shocked at this; and so he was, at first, to a certain extent, but he was not a man of a very high tone of feeling. He had so often heard of heirs to estates longing for the death of the proprietors of them; he had so often seen relatives callous and indifferent at the loss of those who ought to have been dear to them; it seemed so natural to him that Barry should want the estate, that he gradually got accustomed to his impatient inquiries, and listened to, and answered them, without disgust. He fell too into a kind of intimacy with Barry; he liked his daily glass, or three or four glasses, of sherry; and besides, it was a good thing for him to stand well in a professional point of view with a man who had the best house in the village, and who would soon have eight hundred a-year.

If Barry showed his impatience and discontent as long as the daily bulletins told him that Anty was still alive, though dying, it may easily be imagined that he did not hide his displeasure when he first heard that she was alive and better. His brow grew very black, his cheeks flushed, the drops of sweat stood on his forehead, and he said, speaking through his closed teeth, 'D—— it, doctor, you don't mean to tell me she's recovering now?'

'I don't say, Mr. Lynch, whether she is or no; but it's certain the fever has left her. She's very weak, very weak indeed; I never knew a person to be alive and have less life in 'em; but the fever has left her and there certainly is hope.'

'Hope!' said Barry—'why, you told me she couldn't live!'

'I don't say she will, Mr. Lynch, but I say she may. Of course we must do what we can for her,' and the doctor took his sherry and went his way.

How horrible then was the state of Barry's mind! For a time he was absolutely stupified with despair; he stood fixed on the spot where the doctor had left him, realising, bringing home to himself, the tidings which he had heard. His sister to rise again, as though it were from the dead, to push him off his stool! Was he to fall again into that horrid low abyss in which even the Tuam attorney had scorned him; in which he had even invited that odious huxter's son to marry his sister and live in his house? What! was he again to be reduced to poverty, to want, to despair, by her whom he so hated? Could nothing be done?—Something must be done—she should not be, could not be allowed to leave that bed of sickness alive. 'There must be an end of her,' he muttered through his teeth, 'or she'll drive me mad!' And then he thought how easily he might have smothered her, as she lay there clasping his hand, with no one but themselves in the room; and as the thought crossed his brain his eyes nearly started from his head, the sweat ran down his face, he clutched the money in his trousers' pocket till the coin left an impression on his flesh, and he gnashed his teeth till his jaws ached with his own violence. But then, in that sick-room, he had been afraid of her; he could not have touched her then for the wealth of the Bank of England!—but now!

The devil sat within him, and revelled with full dominion over his soul: there was then no feeling left akin to humanity to give him one chance of escape; there was no glimmer of pity, no shadow of remorse, no sparkle of love, even though of a degraded kind; no hesitation in the will for crime, which might yet, by God's grace, lead to its eschewal: all there was black, foul, and deadly, ready for the devil's deadliest work. Murder crouched there, ready to spring, yet afraid;—cowardly, but too thirsty after blood to heed its own fears. Theft,—low, pilfering, petti-fogging, theft; avarice, lust, and impotent, scalding hatred. Controlled by these the black blood rushed quick to and from his heart, filling him with sensual desires below the passions of a brute, but denying him one feeling or one appetite for aught that was good or even human.

Again the next morning the doctor was questioned with intense anxiety; 'Was she going?—was she drooping?—had yesterday's horrid doubts raised only a false alarm?' It was utterly beyond Barry's power to make any attempt at concealment, even of the most shallow kind. 'Well, doctor, is she dying yet?' was the brutal question he put.

'She is, if anything, rather stronger;' answered the doctor, shuddering involuntarily at the open expression of Barry's atrocious wish, and yet taking his glass of wine.

'The devil she is!' muttered Barry, throwing him-self into an arm-chair. He sat there some little time, and the doctor also sat down, said nothing, but continued sipping his wine.

'In the name of mercy, what must I do?' said Barry, speaking more to himself than to the other.

'Why, you've enough, Mr. Lynch, without hers; you can do well enough without it.'

'Enough! Would you think you had enough if you were robbed of more than half of all you have. Half, indeed,' he shouted—'I may say all, at once. I don't believe there's a man in Ireland would bear it. Nor will I.'

Again there was a silence; but still, somehow, Colligan seemed to stay longer than usual. Every now and then Barry would for a moment look full in his face, and almost instantly drop his eyes again. He was trying to mature future plans; bringing into shape thoughts which had occurred to him, in a wild way at different times; proposing to himself schemes,

with which his brain had been long loaded, but which
he had never resolved on,—which he had never made
palpable and definite. One thing he found sure and
certain; on one point he was able to become determined: he could not do it alone; he must have an
assistant; he must buy some one's aid; and again he
looked at Colligan, and again his eyes fell. There was
no encouragement there, but there was no discour-
agement. Why did he stay there so long? Why did
he so slowly sip that third glass of wine? Was he
waiting to be asked? was he ready, willing, to be
bought? There must be something in his thoughts—
he must have some reason for sitting there so long,
and so silent, without speaking a word, or taking his
eyes off the fire.

Barry had all but made up his mind to ask the aid
he wanted; but he felt that he was not prepared to
do so—that he should soon quiver and shake, that
he could not then carry it through. He felt that he
wanted spirit to undertake his own part in the business, much less to inspire another with the will to
assist him in it. At last he rose abruptly from his
chair, and said,

'Will you dine with me to-day, Colligan?—I'm so
down in the mouth, so deucedly hipped, it will be
a charity.'

'Well,' said Colligan, ' I don't care if I do. I must
go down to your sister in the evening, and I shall be
near her here.'

'Yes, of course; you'll be near her here, as you say:
come at six, then. By the bye, couldn't you go to
Anty first, so that we won't be disturbed over our
punch?'

'I must see her the last thing,—about nine, but
I can look up again afterwards, for a minute or so.
I don't stay long with her now: it's better not.'

'Well, then, you'll be here at six?'

'Yes, six sharp;' and at last the doctor got up and
went away.

It was odd that Doctor Colligan should have sat

thus long; it showed a great want of character and
of good feeling in him. He should never have become
intimate, or even have put up with a man expressing
such wishes as those which so often fell from Barry's
lips. But he was entirely innocent of the thoughts
which Barry attributed to him. It had never even
occurred to him that Barry, bad as he was, would
wish to murder his sister. No; bad, heedless, sensual
as Doctor Colligan might be, Barry was a thousand
fathoms deeper in iniquity than he.

As soon as he had left the room the other uttered
a long, deep sigh. It was a great relief to him to be
alone: he could now collect his thoughts, mature his
plans, and finally determine. He took his usual
remedy in his difficulties, a glass of brandy; and,
going out into the garden, walked up and down the
gravel walk almost unconsciously, for above an hour.

Yes: he would do it. He would not be a coward.
The thing had been done a thousand times before.
Hadn't he heard of it over and over again? Besides,
Colligan's manner was an assurance to him that he
would not boggle at such a job. But then, of course,
he must be paid—and Barry began to calculate how
much he must offer for the service; and, when the
service should be performed, how he might avoid the
fulfilment of his portion of the bargain.

He went in and ordered the dinner; filled the spirit
decanters, opened a couple of bottles of wine, and
then walked out again. In giving his orders, and
doing the various little things with which he had
to keep himself employed, everybody, and everything seemed strange to him. He hardly knew what
he was about, and felt almost as though he were in
a dream. He had quite made up his mind as to what
he would do; his resolution was fixed to carry it
through but:—still there was the but,—how was he
to open it to Doctor Colligan? He walked up and
down the gravel path for a long time, thinking of
this; or rather trying to think of it, for his thoughts
would fly away to all manner of other subjects, and

he continually found himself harping upon some
trifle, connected with Anty, but wholly irrespective
of her death; some little thing that she had done for
him, or ought to have done; something she had said
a long time ago, and which he had never thought of
till now; something she had worn, and which at the
time he did not even know that he had observed;
and as often as he found his mind thus wandering,
he would start off at a quicker pace, and again
endeavour to lay out a line of conduct for the
evening.

At last, however, he came to the conclusion that
it would be better to trust to the chapter of chances:
there was one thing, or rather two things, he could
certainly do: he could make the doctor half drunk
before he opened on the subject, and he would take
care to be in the same state himself. So he walked
in and sat still before the fire, for the two long remaining hours, which intervened before the clock
struck six.

It was about noon when the doctor left him, and
during those six long solitary hours no one feeling of
remorse had entered his breast. He had often
doubted, hesitated as to the practicability of his
present plan, but not once had he made the faintest
effort to overcome the wish to have the deed done.
There was not one moment in which he would not
most willingly have had his sister's blood upon his
hands, upon his brain, upon his soul; could he have
willed and accomplished her death, without making
himself liable to the penalties of the law.

At length Doctor Colligan came, and Barry made
a great effort to appear unconcerned and in good
humour.

'And how is she now, doctor?' he said, as they sat
down to table.

'Is it Anty?—why, you know I didn't mean to
see her since I was here this morning, till nine
o'clock.'

'Oh, true; so you were saying. I forgot. Well, will

you take a glass of wine?'—and Barry filled his own glass quite full.

He drank his wine at dinner like a glutton, who had only a short time allowed him, and wished during that time to swallow as much as possible; and he tried to hurry his companion in the same manner. But the doctor didn't choose to have wine forced down his throat; he wished to enjoy himself, and remonstrated against Barry's violent hospitality.

At last, dinner was over; the things were taken away, they both drew their chairs over the fire, and began the business of the evening—the making and consumption of punch. Barry had determined to begin upon the subject which lay so near his heart, at eight o'clock. He had thought it better to fix an exact hour, and had calculated that the whole matter might be completed before Colligan went over to the inn. He kept continually looking at his watch, and gulping down his drink, and thinking over and over again how he would begin the conversation.

'You're very comfortable here, Lynch,' said the doctor, stretching his long legs before the fire, and putting his dirty boots upon the fender.

'Yes, indeed,' said Barry, not knowing what the other was saying.

'All you want's a wife, and you'd have as warm a house as there is in Galway. You'll be marrying soon, I suppose?'

'Well, I wouldn't wonder if I did. You don't take your punch; there's brandy there, if you like it better than whiskey.'

'This is very good, thank you—couldn't be better. You haven't much land in your own hands, have you?'

'Why, no—I don't think I have. What's that you're saying?—land?—No, not much: if there's a thing I hate, it's farming.'

'Well, upon my word you're wrong. I don't see what else a gentleman has to do in the country. I wish to goodness I could give up the gallipots and farm a few acres of my own land. There's nothing

I wish so much as to get a bit of land: indeed, I've been looking out for it, but it's so difficult to get.'

Up to this, Barry had hardly listened to what the doctor had been saying; but now he was all attention. 'So that is to be his price,' thought he to himself; 'he'll cost me dear, but I suppose he must have it.'

Barry looked at his watch: it was near eight o'clock, but he seemed to feel that all he had drank had had no effect on him: it had not given him the usual pluck; it had not given him the feeling of reckless assurance, which he mistook for courage and capacity.

'If you've a mind to be a tenant of mine, Colligan, I'll keep a look out for you. The land's crowded now, but there's a lot of them cottier devils I mean to send to the right about. They do the estate no good, and I hate the sight of them. But you know how the property's placed, and while Anty's in this wretched state, of course I can do nothing.'

'Will you bear it in mind though, Lynch? When a bit of land does fall into your hands, I should be glad to be your tenant. I'm quite in earnest, and should take it as a great favour.'

'I'll not forget it;' and then he remained silent for a minute. What an opportunity this was for him to lose! Colligan so evidently wished to be bribed—so clearly showed what the price was which was to purchase him. But still he could not ask the fatal question.

Again he sat silent for a while, till he looked at his watch, and found it was a quarter past eight. 'Never fear,' he said, referring to the farm; 'you shall have it, and it shall not be the worst land on the estate that I'll give you, you may be sure; for, upon my soul, I have a great regard for you; I have indeed.'

The doctor thanked him for his good opinion.

'Oh! I'm not blarneying you; upon my soul I'm not; that's not the way with me at all; and when you know me better you'll say so,— and you may be sure you shall have the farm by Michaelmas.' And then, in a voice which he tried to make as unconcerned as possible, he continued: 'By the bye, Colligan, when do you think this affair of Anty's *will* be over? It's the devil and all for a man not to know when he'll be his own master.'

'Oh, you mustn't calculate on your sister's property at all now,' said the other, in an altered voice. 'I tell you it's very probable she may recover.'

This again silenced Barry, and he let the time go by, till the doctor took up his hat, to go down to his patient.

'You'll not be long, I suppose?' said Barry.

'Well, it's getting late,' said Colligan, 'and I don't think I'll be coming back to-night.'

'Oh, but you will; indeed, you must. You promised you would, you know, and I want to hear how she goes on.'

'Well, I'll just come up, but I won't stay, for I promised Mrs. Colligan to be home early.' This was always the doctor's excuse when he wished to get away. He never allowed his domestic promises to draw him home when there was anything to induce him to stay abroad; but, to tell the truth, he was getting rather sick of his companion. The doctor took his hat, and went to his patient.

'He'll not be above ten minutes or at any rate a quarter of an hour,' thought Barry, 'and then I must do it. How he sucked it all in about the farm!— that's the trap, certainly.' And he stood leaning with his back against the mantel-piece, and his coat-laps hanging over his arm, waiting for and yet fearing, the moment of the doctor's return. It seemed an age since he went. Barry looked at his watch almost every minute; it was twenty minutes past nine, five-and-twenty — thirty — forty — three quarters of an hour—'By Heaven!' said he, 'the man is not coming! he is going to desert me—and I shall be ruined! Why the deuce didn't I speak out when the man was here!'

At last his ear caught the sound of the doctor's heavy foot on the gravel outside the door, and immediately afterwards the door bell was rung. Barry hastily poured out a glass of raw spirits and swallowed it; he then threw himself into his chair, and Doctor Colligan again entered the room.

'What a time you've been, Colligan! Why I thought you weren't coming all night. Now, Terry, some hot water, and mind you look sharp about it. Well, how's Anty to-night?'

'Weak, very weak; but mending, I think. The disease won't kill her now; the only thing is whether the cure will.'

'Well, doctor, you can't expect me to be very anxious about it: unfortunately, we had never any reason to be proud of Anty, and it would be humbug in me to pretend that I wish she should recover, to rob me of what you know I've every right to consider my own.' Terry brought the hot water in, and left the room.

'Well, I can't say you do appear very anxious about it. I'll just swallow one dandy of punch, and then I'll get home. I'm later now than I meant to be.'

'Nonsense, man. The idea of your being in a hurry, when everybody knows that a doctor can never tell how long he may be kept in a sick-room! But come now, tell the truth; put yourself in my condition, and do you mean to say you'd be very anxious that Anty should recover?—Would you like your own sister to rise from her death-bed to rob you of everything you have? For, by Heaven! it is robbery—nothing less. She's so stiff-necked that there's no making any arrangement with her. I've tried everything, fair means and foul, and nothing'll do but she must go and marry that low young Kelly—so immeasurably beneath her, you know, and of course only scheming for her money. Put yourself in my place, I say; and tell me fairly what your own wishes would be?'

'I was always fond of my brothers and sisters,'

answered the doctor; 'and we couldn't well rob each other, for none of us had a penny to lose.'

'That's a different thing, but just supposing you were exactly in my shoes at this moment, do you mean to tell me that you'd be glad she should get well?—that you'd be glad she should be able to deprive you of your property, disgrace your family, drive you from your own home, and make your life miserable for ever after?'

'Upon my soul I can't say; but good night now, you're getting excited, and I've finished my drop of punch.'

'Ah! nonsense, man, sit down. I've something in earnest I want to say to you,' and Barry got up and prevented the doctor from leaving the room. Colligan had gone so far as to put on his hat and great coat, and now sat down again without taking them off.

'You and I, Colligan, are men of the world, and too wide awake for all the old woman's nonsense people talk. What can I, or what could you in my place, care for a half-cracked old maid like Anty, who's better dead than alive, for her own sake and everybody's else; unless it is some scheming ruffian like young Kelly there, who wants to make money by her?'

'I'm not asking you to care for her; only, if those are your ideas, it's as well not to talk about them for appearance sake.'

'Appearance sake! There's nothing makes me so sick, as for two men like you and me, who know what's what, to be talking about appearance sake, like two confounded parsons, whose business it is to humbug everybody, and themselves into the bargain. I'll tell you what: had my father—bad luck to him for an old rogue,—not made such a will as he did, I'd 've treated Anty as well as any parson of 'em all would treat an old maid of a sister; but I'm not going to have her put over my head this way. Come, doctor, confound all humbug. I say it openly to you—to please me, Anty must never come out of that bed alive.'

'As if your wishes could make any difference. If it is to be so, she'll die, poor creature, without your saying so much about it; but may-be, and it's very likely too, she'll be alive and strong, after the two of us are under the sod.'

'Well; if it must be so, it must; but what I wanted to say to you is this: while you were away, I was thinking about what you said of the farm—of being a tenant of mine, you know.'

'We can talk about that another time,' said the doctor, who began to feel an excessive wish to be out of the house.

'There's no time like the present, when I've got it in my mind; and, if you'll wait, I can settle it all for you to-night. I was telling you that I hate farming, and so I do. There are thirty or five-and-thirty acres of land about the house, and lying round to the back of the town; you shall take them off my hands, and welcome.'

This was too good an offer to be resisted, and Colligan said he would take the land, with many thanks, if the rent any way suited him.

'We'll not quarrel about that, you may be sure, Colligan,' continued Barry; 'and as I said fifty acres at first—it was fifty acres I think you were saying you wished for—I'll not baulk you, and go back from my own word.'

'What you have yourself, round the house, 'll be enough; only I'm thinking the rent 'll be too high.'

'It shall not; it shall be low enough; and, as I was saying, you shall have the remainder, at the same price, immediately after Michaelmas, as soon as ever those devils are ejected.'

'Well;' said Colligan, who was now really interested, 'what's the figure?'

Barry had been looking stedfastly at the fire during the whole conversation, up to this: playing with the poker, and knocking the coals about. He was longing to look into the other's face, but he did not dare. Now, however, was his time; it was now or never: he took one furtive glance at the doctor, and saw that he was really anxious on the subject—that his attention was fixed.

'The figure,' said he; 'the figure should not trouble you if you had no one but me to deal with. But there'll be Anty, confound her, putting her fist into this and every other plan of mine!'

'I'd better deal with the agent, I'm thinking,' said Colligan; 'so, good night.'

'You'll find you'd a deal better be dealing with me: you'll never find an easier fellow to deal with, or one who'll put a better thing in your way.'

Colligan again sat down. He couldn't quite make Barry out: he suspected he was planning some iniquity, but he couldn't tell what; and he remained silent, looking full into the other's face till he should go on. Barry winced under the look, and hesitated; but at last he screwed himself up to the point, and said,

'One word, between two friends, is as good as a thousand. If Anty dies of this bout, you shall have the fifty acres, with a lease for perpetuity, at sixpence an acre. Come, that's not a high figure, I think.'

'What?' said Colligan, apparently not under-standing him, 'a lease for perpetuity at how much an acre?'

'Sixpence—a penny—a pepper-corn—just any-thing you please. But it's all on Anty's dying. While she's alive I can do nothing for the best friend I have.'

'By the Almighty above us,' said the doctor, al-most in a whisper, 'I believe the wretched man means me to murder her—his own sister!'

'Murder?—Who talked or said a word of murder?' said Barry, with a hoarse and croaking voice—'isn't she dying as she is?—and isn't she better dead than alive? It's only just not taking so much trouble to keep the life in her; you're so exceeding clever, you know!'—and he made a ghastly attempt at smiling. 'With any other doctor she'd have been

dead long since: leave her to herself a little, and the
farm's your own; and I'm sure there'll 've been
nothing at all like murder between us.'

'By Heavens, he does!'—and Colligan rose quickly
from his seat—'he means to have her murdered, and
thinks to make me do the deed! Why, you vile,
thieving, murdering reptile!' and as he spoke the
doctor seized him by the throat, and shook him
violently in his strong grasp—'who told you I was
a fit person for such a plan? who told you to come
to me for such a deed? who told you I would sell my
soul for your paltry land?'—and he continued
grasping Barry's throat till he was black in the face,
and nearly choked. 'Merciful Heaven! that I should
have sat here, and listened to such a scheme! Take
care of yourself,' said he; and he threw him violently
backwards over the chairs—'if you're to be found in
Connaught to-morrow, or in Ireland the next day,
I'll hang you!'—and so saying, he hurried out of the
room, and went home.

'Well,' thought he, on his road: 'I have heard of
such men as that before, and I believe that when
I was young I read of such: but I never expected to
meet so black a villain! What had I better do?—If
I go and swear an information before a magistrate
there'll be nothing but my word and his. Besides,
he said nothing that the law could take hold of.
And yet I oughtn't to let it pass: at any rate I'll
sleep on it.' And so he did; but it was not for a long
time, for the recollection of Barry's hideous proposal
kept him awake.

Barry lay sprawling among the chairs till the
sound of the hall door closing told him that his
guest had gone, when he slowly picked himself up,
and sat down upon the sofa. Colligan's last words
were ringing in his ear—'If you're found in Ireland
the next day, I'll hang you.'—Hang him!—and had
he really given any one the power to speak to him in
such language as that? After all, what had he said?
—He had not even whispered a word of murder; he

had only made an offer of what he would do if Anty should die: besides, no one but themselves had heard even that; and then his thoughts went off to another train. 'Who'd have thought,' he said to himself 'the man was such a fool! He meant it, at first, as well as I did myself. I'm sure he did. He'd never have caught as he did about the farm else, only he got afraid—the confounded fool! As for hanging, I'll let him know; it's just as easy for me to tell a story, I suppose, as it is for him.' And then Barry, too, dragged himself up to bed, and cursed himself to sleep. His waking thoughts, however, were miserable enough.

XXVIII

FANNY WYNDHAM REBELS

WE will now return to Grey Abbey, Lord Cashel, and that unhappy love-sick heiress, his ward, Fanny Wyndham. Affairs there had taken no turn to give increased comfort either to the earl or to his niece, during the month which succeeded the news of young Harry Wyndham's death.

The former still adhered, with fixed pertinacity of purpose, to the matrimonial arrangement which he had made with his son. Circumstances, indeed, rendered it even much more necessary in the earl's eyes than it had appeared to be when he first contemplated this scheme for releasing himself from his son's pecuniary difficulties. He had, as the reader will remember, advanced a very large sum of money to Lord Kilcullen, to be repaid out of Fanny Wyndham's fortune. This money Lord Kilcullen had certainly appropriated in the manner intended by his father, but it had anything but the effect of quieting the creditors. The payments were sufficiently large to make the whole hungry crew hear that his lordship was paying his debts, but not at all sufficient to satisfy their craving. Indeed, nearly the whole went in liquidation of turf engagements, and gambling debts. The Jews, money-lenders, and

tradesmen merely heard that money was going from
Lord Kilcullen's pocket; but with all their exertions
they got very little of it themselves.

Consequently, claims of all kinds—bills, duns, re-
monstrances and threats, poured in not only upon
the son but also upon the father. The latter, it is
true, was not in his own person liable for one penny
of them, nor could he well, on his own score, be said
to be an embarrassed man; but he was not the less
uneasy. He had determined if possible to extricate
his son once more, and as a preliminary step had himself already raised a large sum of money which it would
much trouble him to pay; and he moreover, as he
frequently said to Lord Kilcullen, would not and
could not pay another penny for the same purpose,
until he saw a tolerably sure prospect of being repaid
out of his ward's fortune.

He was therefore painfully anxious on the subject;
anxious not only that the matter should be arranged,
but that it should be done at once. It was plain that
Lord Kilcullen could not remain in London, for he
would be arrested; the same thing would happen at
Grey Abbey, if he were to remain there long without
settling his affairs; and if he were once to escape his
creditors by going abroad, there would be no such
thing as getting him back again. Lord Cashel saw
no good reason why there should be any delay;
Harry Wyndham was dead above a month, and
Fanny was evidently grieving more for the loss of
her lover than that of her brother; she naturally
felt alone in the world—and, as Lord Cashel thought,
one young viscount would be just as good as another.
The advantages, too, were much in favour of his
son; he would one day be an earl, and possess Grey
Abbey. So great an accession of grandeur, dignity,
and rank could not but be, as the earl considered,
very delightful to a sensible girl like his ward. The
marriage, of course, needn't be much hurried; four
or five months' time would do for that; he was only
anxious that they should be engaged—that Lord

Kilcullen should be absolutely accepted—Lord Ballindine finally rejected.

The earl certainly felt some scruples of conscience at the sacrifice he was making of his ward, and stronger still respecting his ward's fortune; but he appeased them with the reflection that if his son were a gambler, a *roué*, and a scamp, Lord Ballindine was probably just as bad; and that if the latter were to spend all Fanny's money there would be no chance of redemption; whereas he could at any rate settle on his wife a jointure, which would be a full compensation for the loss of her fortune, should she outlive her husband and father-in-law. Besides, he looked on Lord Kilcullen's faults as a father is generally inclined to look on those of a son, whom he had not entirely given up—whom he is still striving to redeem.   He called his iniquitous vices, follies—his licentiousness, love of pleasure—his unprincipled expenditure and extravagance, a want of the knowledge of what money was: and his worst sin of all, because the one least likely to be abandoned, his positive, unyielding damning selfishness, he called 'fashion'—the fashion of the young men of the day.

Poor Lord Cashel! he wished to be honest to his ward; and yet to save his son, and his own pocket at the same time, at her expense: he wished to be, in his own estimation, high-minded, honourable, and disinterested, and yet he could not resist the temptation to be generous to his own flesh and blood at the expense of another.   The contest within him made him miserable; but the devil and mammon were too strong for him, particularly coming as they did, half hidden beneath the gloss of parental affection. There was little of the Roman about the earl, and he could not condemn his own son; so he fumed and fretted, and twisted himself about in the easy chair in his dingy book-room, and passed long hours in trying to persuade himself that it was for Fanny's advantage that he was going to make her Lady Kilcullen.

He might have saved himself all his anxiety. Fanny Wyndham had much too strong a mind— much too marked a character of her own, to be made Lady Anything by Lord Anybody. Lord Cashel might possibly prevent her from marrying Frank, especially as she had been weak enough, through ill-founded pique and anger, to lend him her name for dismissing him; but neither he nor anyone else could make her accept one man, while she loved another, and while that other was unmarried.

Since the interview between Fanny and her uncle and aunt, which has been recorded, she had been nearly as uncomfortable as Lord Cashel, and she had, to a certain extent, made the whole household as much so as herself. Not that there was anything of the kill-joy character in Fanny's composition; but that the natural disposition of Grey Abbey and all belonging to it was to be dull, solemn, slow, and respectable. Fanny alone had ever given any life to the place, or made the house tolerable; and her secession to the ranks of the sombre crew was therefore the more remarked. If Fanny moped, all Grey Abbey might figuratively be said to hang down its head. Lady Cashel was, in every sense of the words, continually wrapped up in wools and worsteds. The earl was always equally ponderous, and the specific gravity of Lady Selina could not be calculated. It was beyond the power of figures, even in algebraic denominations, to describe her moral weight.

And now Fanny did mope, and Grey Abbey was triste indeed. Griffiths in my lady's boudoir rolled and unrolled those huge white bundles of mysterious fleecy hosiery with more than usually slow and un- broken perseverance. My lady herself bewailed the fermentation among the jam-pots with a voice that did more than whine, it was almost funereal. As my lord went from breakfast-room to book-room, from book-room to dressing-room, and from dressing-room to dining-room, his footsteps creaked with a sound more deadly than that of a death-watch. The book-

room itself had caught a darker gloom; the backs of
the books seemed to have lost their gilding, and the
mahogany furniture its French polish. There, like
a god, Lord Cashel sate alone, throned amid clouds
of awful dulness, ruling the world of nothingness
around by the silent solemnity of his inertia.

Lady Selina was always useful, but with a solid,
slow activity, a dignified intensity of heavy perseverance, which made her perhaps more intolerable than
her father. She was like some old coaches which we
remember—very sure, very respectable; but so tedious, so monotonous, so heavy in their motion, that
a man with a spark of mercury in his composition
would prefer any danger from a faster vehicle to
their horrid, weary, murderous, slow security. Lady
Selina from day to day performed her duties in
a most uncompromising manner; she knew what was
due to her position, and from it, and exacted and
performed accordingly with a stiff, steady propriety
which made her an awful if not a hateful creature.
One of her daily duties, and one for the performance
of which she had unfortunately ample opportunity,
was the consolation of Fanny under her troubles.
Poor Fanny! how great an aggravation was this to
her other miseries! For a considerable time Lady
Selina had known nothing of the true cause of
Fanny's gloom; for though the two cousins were
good friends, as far as Lady Selina was capable of
admitting so human a frailty as friendship, still
Fanny could not bring herself to make a confidante
of her. Her kind, stupid, unpretending old aunt was
a much better person to talk to, even though she did
arch her eyebrows, and shake her head when Lord
Ballindine's name was mentioned, and assure her
niece that though she had always liked him herself, he
could not be good for much, because Lord Kilcullen
had said so. But Fanny could not well dissemble;
she was tormented by Lady Selina's condolements,
and recommendations of Gibbon, her encomiums on
industry, and anathemas against idleness; she was

so often reminded that weeping would not bring back her brother, nor inactive reflection make his fate less certain, that at last she made her monitor understand that it was about Lord Ballindine's fate that she was anxious, and that it was his coming back which might be effected by weeping—or other measures.

Lady Selina was shocked by such feminine, girlish weakness, such want of dignity and character, such forgetfulness, as she said to Fanny, of what was due to her own position. Lady Selina was herself unmarried, and not likely to marry; and why had she maintained her virgin state, and foregone the blessings of love and matrimony? Because, as she often said to herself, and occasionally said to Fanny, she would not step down from the lofty pedestal on which it had pleased fortune and birth to place her.

She learned, however, by degrees, to forgive, though she couldn't approve, Fanny's weakness; she remembered that it was a very different thing to be an earl's niece and an earl's daughter, and that the same conduct could not be expected from Fanny Wyndham and Lady Selina Grey.

The two were sitting together, in one of the Grey Abbey drawing-rooms, about the middle of April. Fanny had that morning again been talking to her guardian on the subject nearest to her heart, and had nearly distracted him by begging him to take steps to make Frank understand that a renewal of his visits at Grey Abbey would not be ill received. Lord Cashel at first tried to frighten her out of her project by silence, frowns, and looks: but not finding himself successful, he commenced a long oration, in which he broke down, or rather, which he had to cut up into sundry short speeches; in which he endeavoured to make it appear that Lord Ballindine's expulsion had originated with Fanny herself, and that, banished or not banished, the less Fanny had to do with him the better. His ward, however, declared, in rather a tempestuous manner, that if she

could not see him at Grey Abbey she would see him
elsewhere; and his lordship was obliged to capitulate
by promising that if Frank were unmarried in twelve
months' time, and Fanny should then still be of the
same mind, he would consent to the match and use
his influence to bring it about. This by no means
satisfied Fanny, but it was all that the earl would say,
and she had now to consider whether she would
accept those terms or act for herself. Had she had
any idea what steps she could with propriety take in
opposition to the earl, she would have withdrawn
herself and her fortune from his house and hands,
without any scruples of conscience. But what was
she to do? She couldn't write to her lover and ask
him to come back to her!—Whither could she go?
She couldn't well set up house for herself.

Lady Selina was bending over her writing-desk,
and penning most decorous notes, with a precision of
calligraphy which it was painful to witness. She was
writing orders to Dublin tradesmen, and each order
might have been printed in the Complete Letter-
Writer, as a specimen of the manner in which young
ladies should address such correspondents. Fanny
had a volume of French poetry in her hand, but had
it been Greek prose it would have given her equal
occupation and amusement. It had been in her
hands half-an-hour, and she had not read a line.

'Fanny,' said Lady Selina, raising up her thin red
spiral tresses from her desk, and speaking in a firm,
decided tone, as if well assured of the importance of
the question she was going to put; 'don't you want
some things from Ellis's?'

'From where, Selina?' said Fanny, slightly starting.

'From Ellis's,' repeated Lady Selina.

'Oh, the man in Grafton Street.—No, thank you.'
And Fanny returned to her thoughts.

'Surely you do, Fanny,' said her ladyship. 'I'm
sure you want black crape; you were saying so on
Friday last.'

'Was I?—Yes; I think I do. It'll do another time, Selina; never mind now.'

'You had better have it in the parcel he will send to-morrow; if you'll give me the pattern and tell me how much you want, I'll write for it.'

'Thank you, Selina. You're very kind, but I won't mind it to-day.'

'How very foolish of you, Fanny; you know you want it, and then you'll be annoyed about it. You'd better let me order it with the other things.'

'Very well, dear: order it then for me.'

'How much will you want? you must send the pattern too, you know.'

'Indeed, Selina, I don't care about having it at all; I can do very well without it, so don't mind troubling yourself.'

'How very ridiculous, Fanny! You know you want black crape—and you must get it from Ellis's.' Lady Selina paused for a reply, and then added, in a voice of sorrowful rebuke, 'It's to save yourself the trouble of sending Jane for the pattern.'

'Well, Selina, perhaps it is. Don't bother me about it now, there's a dear. I'll be more myself by-and-by; but indeed, indeed, I'm neither well nor happy now.'

'Not well, Fanny! What ails you?'

'Oh, nothing ails me; that is, nothing in the doctor's way. I didn't mean I was ill.'

'You said you weren't well; and people usually mean by that, that they are ill.'

'But I didn't mean it,' said Fanny, becoming almost irritated, 'I only meant—' and she paused and did not finish her sentence.

Lady Selina wiped her pen, in her scarlet embroidered pen-wiper, closed the lid of her patent inkstand, folded a piece of blotting-paper over the note she was writing, pushed back the ruddy ringlets from her contemplative forehead, gave a slight sigh, and turned herself towards her cousin, with the purpose of commencing a vigorous lecture and cross-examination, by which she hoped to exorcise the spirit of lamentation from Fanny's breast, and restore her to a healthful activity in the performance of this world's duties. Fanny felt what was coming; she could not fly; so she closed her book and her eyes, and prepared herself for endurance.

'Fanny,' said Lady Selina, in a voice which was intended to be both severe and sorrowful, 'you are giving way to very foolish feelings in a very foolish way; you are preparing great unhappiness for yourself, and allowing your mind to waste itself in uncontrolled sorrow in a manner—in a manner which cannot but be ruinously injurious. My dear Fanny, why don't you do something?—why don't you occupy yourself? You've given up your work; you've given up your music; you've given up everything in the shape of reading; how long, Fanny, will you go on in this sad manner?' Lady Selina paused, but, as Fanny did not immediately reply, she continued her speech— 'I've begged you to go on with your reading, because nothing but mental employment will restore your mind to its proper tone. I'm sure I've brought you the second volume of Gibbon twenty times, but I don't believe you've read a chapter this month back. How long will you allow yourself to go on in this sad manner?'

'Not long, Selina. As you say, I'm sad enough.'

'But is it becoming in you, Fanny, to grieve in this way for a man whom you yourself rejected because he was unworthy of you?'

'Selina, I've told you before that such was not the case. I believe him to be perfectly worthy of me, and of any one much my superior too.'

'But you did reject him, Fanny: you bade papa tell him to discontinue his visits—didn't you?'

Fanny felt that her cousin was taking an unfair advantage in throwing thus in her teeth her own momentary folly in having been partly persuaded, partly piqued, into quarrelling with her lover; and she resented it as such. 'If I did,' she said, somewhat angrily, 'it does not make my grief any lighter, to know that I brought it on myself.'

'No, Fanny; but it should show you that the loss for which you grieve is past recovery. Sorrow, for which there is no cure, should cease to be grieved for, at any rate openly. If Lord Ballindine were to die you would not allow his death to doom you to perpetual sighs, and perpetual inactivity. No; you'd then know that grief was hopeless, and you'd recover.'

'But Lord Ballindine is not dead,' said Fanny.

'Ah! that's just the point,' continued her ladyship; 'he should be dead to you; to you he should now be just the same as though he were in his grave. You loved him some time since, and accepted him; but you found your love misplaced,—unreturned, or at any rate coldly returned. Though you loved him, you passed a deliberate judgment on him, and wisely rejected him. Having done so, his name should not be on your lips; his form and figure should be forgotten. No thoughts of him should sully your mind, no love for him should be permitted to rest in your heart; it should be rooted out, whatever the exertion may cost you.'

'Selina, I believe you have no heart yourself.'

'Perhaps as much as yourself, Fanny. I've heard of some people who were said to be all heart; I flatter myself I am not one of them. I trust I have some mind, to regulate my heart; and some conscience, to prevent my sacrificing my duties for the sake of my heart.'

'If you knew,' said Fanny, 'the meaning of what love was, you'd know that it cannot be given up in a moment, as you suppose; rooted out, as you choose to call it. But, to tell you the truth, Selina, I don't choose to root it out. I gave my word to Frank not twelve months since, and that with the consent of every one belonging to me. I owned that I loved him, and solemnly assured him I would always do so. I cannot, and I ought not, and I will not break my word. You would think of nothing but what you call your own dignity; I will not give up my own happiness, and, I firmly believe his, too, for anything so empty.'

'Don't be angry with me, Fanny,' said Lady Selina; 'my regard for your dignity arises only from my affection for you. I should be sorry to see you lessen yourself in the eyes of those around you. You must remember that you cannot act as another girl might, whose position was less exalted. Miss O'Joscelyn might cry for her lost lover till she got him back again, or got another; and no one would be the wiser, and she would not be the worse; but you cannot do that. Rank and station are in themselves benefits; but they require more rigid conduct, much more control over the feelings than is necessary in a humbler position. You should always remember, Fanny, that much is expected from those to whom much is given.'

'And I'm to be miserable all my life because I'm not a parson's daughter, like Miss O'Joscelyn!'

'God forbid, Fanny! If you'd employ your time, engage your mind, and cease to think of Lord Ballindine, you'd soon cease to be miserable. Yes; though you might never again feel the happiness of loving, you might still be far from miserable.'

'But I can't cease to think of him, Selina;—I won't even try.'

'Then, Fanny, I truly pity you.'

'No, Selina; it's I that pity you,' said Fanny, roused to energy as different thoughts crowded to her mind. 'You, who think more of your position as an earl's daughter—an aristocrat, than of your nature as a woman! Thank Heaven, I'm not a queen, to be driven to have other feelings than those of my sex. I do love Lord Ballindine, and if I had the power to cease to do so this moment, I'd sooner drown myself than exercise it.'

'Then why were you weak enough to reject him?'

'Because I was a weak, wretched, foolish girl. I said it in a moment of passion, and my uncle acted

on it at once, without giving me one minute for
reflection—without allowing me one short hour to
look into my own heart, and find how I was deceiving
myself in thinking that I ought to part from him. I
told Lord Cashel in the morning that I would give
him up; and before I had time to think of what I had
said, he had been here, and had been turned out of
the house. Oh, Selina! it was very, very cruel in your
father to take me at my word so shortly!' And Fanny
hid her face in her handkerchief, and burst into tears.

'That's unfair, Fanny; it couldn't be cruel in him
to do for you that which he would have done for his
own daughter. He thought, and thinks, that Lord
Ballindine would not make you happy.'

'Why should he think so?—he'd no business to
think so,' sobbed Fanny through her tears.

'Who could have a business to think for you, if not
your guardian?'

'Why didn't he think so then, before he encouraged
me to receive him? It was because Frank wouldn't
do just what he was bid; it was because he wouldn't
become stiff, and solemn, and grave like—like—'
Fanny was going to make a comparison that would
not have been flattering either to Lady Selina or to
her father, but she did not quite forget herself, and
stopped short without expressing the likeness. 'Had
he spoken against him at first, I would have obeyed;
but I will not destroy myself now for his prejudices.'
And Fanny buried her face among the pillows of the
sofa, and sobbed aloud.

Lady Selina walked over to the sofa, and stood at
the head of it bending over her cousin. She wished
to say something to soothe and comfort her, but
did not know how; there was nothing soothing or
comforting in her nature, nothing soft in her voice;
her manner was repulsive, and almost unfeeling; and
yet she was not unfeeling. She loved Fanny as warmly
as she was capable of loving; she would have made
almost any personal sacrifice to save her cousin from
grief; she would, were it possible, have borne her

sorrows herself; but she could not unbend; she could not sit down by Fanny's side, and, taking her hand, say soft and soothing things; she could not make her grief easier by expressing hope for the future or consolation for the past. She would have felt that she was compromising truth by giving hope, and dignity by uttering consolation for the loss of that which she considered better lost than retained. Lady Selina's only recipe was endurance and occupation. And at any rate, she practised what she preached; she was never idle, and she never complained.

As she saw Fanny's grief, and heard her sobs, she at first thought that in mercy she should now give up the subject of the conversation; but then she reflected that such mercy might be the greatest cruelty, and that the truest kindness would be to prove to Fanny the hopelessness of her passion.

'But, Fanny,' she said, when the other's tears were a little subsided, 'it's no use either saying or thinking impossibilities. What are you to do? You surely will not willingly continue to indulge a hopeless passion?'

'Selina, you'll drive me mad, if you go on! Let me have my own way.'

'But, Fanny, if your own way's a bad way? Surely you won't refuse to listen to reason? You must know that what I say is only from my affection. I want you to look before you; I want you to summon courage to look forward; and then I'm sure your common sense will tell you that Lord Ballindine can never be anything to you.'

'Look here, Selina,' and Fanny rose, and wiped her eyes, and somewhat composed her ruffled hair, which she shook back from her face and forehead, as she endeavoured to repress the palpitation which had followed her tears; 'I have looked forward, and I have determined what I mean to do. It was your father who brought me to this, by forcing me into a childish quarrel with the man I love. I have implored him, almost on my knees, to invite Lord

Ballindine again to Grey Abbey: he has refused to do
so, at any rate for twelve months—'

'And has he consented to ask him at the end of
twelve months?' asked Selina, much astonished,
and, to tell the truth, considerably shocked at this
instance of what she considered her father's weakness.

'He might as well have said twelve years,' replied
Fanny. 'How can I, how can any one, suppose that
he should remain single for my sake for twelve
months, after being repelled without a cause, or without a word of explanation; without even seeing me;
—turned out of the house, and insulted in every
way? No; whatever he might do, I will not wait
twelve months. I'll ask Lord Cashel once again, and
then—' Fanny paused for a moment, to consider in
what words she would finish her declaration.

'Well, Fanny,' said Selina, waiting with eager
expectation for Fanny's final declaration; for she
expected to hear her say that she would drown herself, or lock herself up for ever, or do something
equally absurd.

'Then,' continued Fanny,—and a deep blush
covered her face as she spoke, 'I will write to Lord
Ballindine, and tell him that I am still his own if he
chooses to take me.'

'Oh, Fanny! do not say such a horrid thing.
Write to a man, and beg him to accept you? No,
Fanny; I know you too well, at any rate, to believe
that you'll do that.'

'Indeed, indeed, I will.'

'Then you'll disgrace yourself for ever. Oh,
Fanny! though my heart were breaking, though I
knew I were dying for very love, I'd sooner have it
break, I'd sooner die at once, than disgrace my sex
by becoming a suppliant to a man.'

'Disgrace, Selina!—and am I not now disgraced?
Have I not given him my solemn word? Have I not
pledged myself to him as his wife? Have I not
sworn to him a hundred times that my heart was all
his own? Have I not suffered those caresses which

would have been disgraceful had I not looked on myself as almost already his bride? And is it no disgrace, after that, to break my word?—to throw him
aside like a glove that wouldn't fit?—to treat him as
as servant that wouldn't suit me?—to send him a
contemptuous message to be gone?—and so, to forget him, that I might lay myself out for the addresses
and admiration of another? Could any conduct be
worse than that?—any disgrace deeper? Oh, Selina!
I shudder as I think of it. Could I ever bring my lips
to own affection for another, without being overwhelmed with shame and disgrace? And then, that
the world should say that I had accepted, and rejoiced in his love when I was poor, and rejected it
with scorn when I was rich! No; I would sooner—
ten thousand times sooner my uncle should do it for
me! but if he will not write to Frank, I will. And
though my hand will shake, and my face will be
flushed as I do so, I shall never think that I have
disgraced myself.'

'And if, Fanny—if, after that he refuses you?'

Fanny was still standing, and she remained so for
a moment or two, meditating her reply, and then she
answered:—

'Should he do so, then I have the alternative which
you say you would prefer; then I will endeavour to
look forward to a broken heart, and death, without a
complaint and without tears. Then, Selina,' and she
tried to smile through the tears which were again
running down her cheeks, 'I'll come to you, and
endeavour to borrow your stoic endurance, and
patient industry;' and, as she said so, she walked to
the door and escaped, before Lady Selina had time
to reply.

XXIX

THE COUNTESS OF CASHEL IN TROUBLE

AFTER considerable negotiation between the father and the son, the time was fixed for Lord Kilcullen's arrival at Grey Abbey. The earl tried much to accelerate it, and the viscount was equally anxious to stave off the evil day; but at last it was arranged that, on the 3rd of April, he was to make his appearance, and that he should commence his wooing as soon as possible after that day.

When this was absolutely fixed, Lord Cashel paid a visit to his countess, in her boudoir, to inform her of the circumstance, and prepare her for the expected guest. He did not, however, say a word of the purport of his son's visit. He had, at one time, thought of telling the old lady all about it, and bespeaking her influence with Fanny for the furtherance of his plan; but, on reconsideration, he reflected that his wife was not the person to be trusted with any intrigue. So he merely told her that Lord Kilcullen would be at Grey Abbey in five days; that he would probably remain at home a long time; that, as he was giving up his London vices and extravagances, and going to reside at Grey Abbey, he wished that the house should be made as pleasant for him as possible; that a set of friends, relatives, and acquaintances should be asked to come and stay there; and, in short, that Lord Kilcullen, having been a truly prodigal son, should have a fatted calf prepared for his arrival.

All this flurried and rejoiced, terrified and excited my lady exceedingly. In the first place it was so truly delightful that her son should turn good and proper, and careful and decorous, just at the right time of life; so exactly the thing that ought to happen. Of course young noblemen were extravagant, and wicked, and lascivious, habitual breakers of the commandments, and self-idolators; it was their nature. In Lady Cashel's thoughts on the education of young men, these evils were ranked with the measles and hooping cough; it was well that they should be gone through and be done with early in life. She had a kind of hazy idea that an opera-dancer and a gambling club were indispensable in fitting a young aristocrat for his future career; and I doubt whether she would not have agreed to the expediency of inoculating a son of hers with these ailments in a mild degree—vaccinating him as it were with dissipation, in order that he might not catch the disease late in life in a violent and fatal form. She had not therefore made herself unhappy about her son for a few years after his first entrance on a life in London, but latterly she had begun to be a little uneasy. Tidings of the great amount of his debts reached even her ears; and, moreover, it was nearly time that he should reform and settle down. During the last twelve months she had remarked fully twelve times, to Griffiths, that she wondered when Kilcullen would marry?—and she had even twice asked her husband, whether he didn't think that such a circumstance would be advantageous. She was therefore much rejoiced to hear that her son was coming to live at home. But then, why was it so sudden? It was quite proper that the house should be made a little gay for his reception; that he shouldn't be expected to spend his evenings with no other society than that of his father and mother, his sister and his cousin; but how was she to get the house ready for the people, and the people ready for the house, at so very short a notice?—What trouble, also, it would be to her!—Neither she nor Griffiths would know another moment's rest; besides,—and the thought nearly drove her into hysterics,—where was she to get a new cook?

However, she promised her husband to do her best. She received from him a list of people to be invited, and, merely stipulating that she shouldn't be required to ask any one except the parson of the parish under a week, undertook to make the place as bearable as possible to so fastidious and *distingué* a person as her own son.

Her first confidante was, of course, Griffiths; and, with her assistance, the wool and the worsted, and the knitting-needles, the unfinished vallances and interminable yards of fringe, were put up and rolled out of the way; and it was then agreed that a council should be held, to which her ladyship proposed to invite Lady Selina and Fanny. Griffiths, however, advanced an opinion that the latter was at present too lack-a-daisical to be of any use in such a matter, and strengthened her argument by asserting that Miss Wyndham had of late been quite mumchance. Lady Cashel was at first rather inclined to insist on her niece being called to the council, but Griffiths's cloquence was too strong, and her judgment too undoubted; so Fanny was left undisturbed, and Lady Selina alone summoned to join the aged female senators of Grey Abbey.

'Selina,' said her ladyship, as soon as her daughter was seated on the sofa opposite to her mother's easy chair, while Griffiths, having shut the door, had, according to custom, sat herself down on her own soft-bottomed chair, on the further side of the little table that always stood at the countess's right hand. 'Selina, what do you think your father tells me?'

Lady Selina couldn't think, and declined guessing; for, as she remarked, guessing was a loss of time, and she never guessed right.

'Adolphus is coming home on Tuesday.'

'Adolphus! why it's not a month since he was here.'

'And he's not coming only for a visit; he's coming to stay here; from what your father says, I suppose he'll stay here the greater part of the summer.'

'What, stay at Grey Abbey all May and June?' said Lady Selina, evidently discrediting so unlikely a story, and thinking it all but impossible that her brother should immure himself at Grey Abbey during the London season.

'It's true, my lady,' said Griffiths, oracularly; as if her word were necessary to place the countess's statement beyond doubt.

'Yes,' continued Lady Cashel; 'and he has given up all his establishment in London—his horses, and clubs, and the opera, and all that. He'll go into Parliament, I dare say, now, for the county; at any rate he's coming to live at home here for the summer.'

'And has he sold all his horses?' asked Lady Selina.

'If he's not done it, he's doing it,' said the countess. 'I declare I'm delighted with him; it shows such proper feeling. I always knew he would; I was sure that when the time came for doing it, Adolphus would not forget what was due to himself and to his family.'

'If what you say is true, mamma, he's going to be married.'

'That's just what I was thinking, my lady,' said Griffiths. 'When her ladyship first told me all about it, —how his lordship was coming down to live regular and decorous among his own people, and that he was turning his back upon his pleasures and iniquities, thinks I to myself there'll be wedding favours coming soon to Grey Abbey.'

'If it is so, Selina, your father didn't say anything to me about it,' said the countess, somewhat additionally flustered by the importance of the last suggestion; 'and if he'd even guessed such a thing, I'm sure he'd have mentioned it.'

'It mightn't be quite fixed, you know, mamma: but if Adolphus is doing as you say, you may be sure he's either engaged, or thinking of becoming so.'

'Well, my dear, I'm sure I wish it may be so; only I own I'd like to know, because it makes a difference, as to the people he'd like to meet, you know. I'm sure nothing would delight me so much as to receive Adolphus's wife. Of course she'd always be welcome to lie in here—indeed it'd be the fittest place. But we should be dreadfully put about, eh, Griffiths?'

'Why, we should, my lady; but, to my mind, this would be the only most proper place for my lord's heir to be born in. If the mother and child couldn't have the best of minding here, where could they?'

'Of course, Griffiths; and we wouldn't mind the trouble, on such an occasion. I think the south room would be the best, because of the dressing-room being such a good size, and neither of the fireplaces smoking, you know.'

'Well, I don't doubt but it would, my lady; only the blue room is nearer to your ladyship here, and in course your ladyship would choose to be in and out.'

And visions of caudle cups, cradles, and monthly nurses, floated over Lady Cashel's brain, and gave her a kind of dreamy feel that the world was going to begin again with her.

'But, mamma, is Adolphus really to be here on Tuesday?' said Lady Selina, recalling the two old women from their attendance on the unborn, to the necessities of the present generation.

'Indeed he is, my dear, and that's what I sent for you for. Your papa wishes to have a good deal of company here to meet your brother; and indeed it's only reasonable, for of course this place would be very dull for him, if there was nobody here but our-selves—and he's always used to see so many people; but the worst is, it's all to be done at once, and you know there'll be so much to be got through before we'll be ready for a house full of company,—things to be got from Dublin, and the people to be asked. And then, Selina,' and her ladyship almost wept as the latter came to her great final difficulty—'What are we to do about a cook?—Richards'll never do; Griffiths says she won't even do for ourselves, as it is.'

'Indeed she won't, my lady; it was only impudence in her coming to such a place at all.—She'd never be able to send a dinner up for eighteen or twenty.'

'What are we to do, Griffiths? What can have become of all the cooks?—I'm sure there used to be cooks enough when I was first married.'

'Well, my lady, I think they must be all gone to
England, those that are any good; but I don't know
what's come to the servants altogether; as your ladyship says, they're quite altered for the worse since we
were young.'

'But, mamma,' said Lady Selina, 'you're not
going to ask people here just immediately, are you?'

'Directly, my dear; your papa wishes it done at
once. We're to have a dinner-party this day week—
that'll be Thursday; and we'll get as many of the
people as we can to stay afterwards; and we'll get
the O'Joscelyns to come on Wednesday, just to make
the table look not quite so bare, and I want you to
write the notes at once. There'll be a great many
things to be got from Dublin too.'

'It's very soon after poor Harry Wyndham's
death, to be receiving company,' said Lady Selina,
solemnly. 'Really, mamma, I don't think it will be
treating Fanny well to be asking all these people so
soon. The O'Joscelyns, or the Fitzgeralds, are all
very well—just our own near neighbours; but don't
you think, mamma, it's rather too soon to be asking
a house-full of strange people?'

'Well, my love, I was thinking so, and I mentioned
it to your father; but he said that poor Harry had
been dead a month now—and that's true, you know
—and that people don't think so much now about
those kind of things as they used to; and that's true
too, I believe.'

'Indeed you may say that, my lady,' interposed
Griffiths. 'I remember when bombazines used to be
worn three full months for an uncle or cousin, and
now they're hardly ever worn at all for the like,
except in cases where the brother or sister of him or
her as is dead may be stopping in the house, and then
only for a month: and they were always worn the
full six months for a brother or sister, and sometimes
the twelve months round. Your aunt, Lady Charlotte,
my lady, wore hers the full twelve months, when your
uncle, Lord Frederick, was shot by Sir Patrick

O'Donnel; and now they very seldom, never, I may say, wear them the six months!—Indeed, I think mourning is going out altogether; and I'm very sorry for it, for it's a very decent, proper sort of thing; at least, such was always my humble opinion, my lady.'

'Well; but what I was saying is,' continued the countess, 'that what would be thought strange a few years ago, isn't thought at all so now; and though I'm sure, Selina, I wouldn't like to do anything that looked unkind to Fanny, I really don't see how we can help it, as your father makes such a point of it.'

'I can't say I think it's right, mamma, for I don't. But if you and papa do, of course I've nothing further to say.'

'Well, my love, I don't know that I do exactly think it's right; and I'm sure it's not my wish to be having people, especially when I don't know where on earth to turn for a cook. But what can we do, my dear? Adolphus wouldn't stay the third night here, I'm sure, if there was nobody to amuse him; and you wouldn't have him turned out of the house, would you?'

'*I* have him turned out, mamma? God forbid! I'd sooner he should be here than anywhere, for here he must be out of harm's way; but still I think that if he comes to a house of mourning, he might, for a short time, submit to put up with its decent tranquillity.'

'Selina,' said the mother, pettishly, 'I really thought you'd help me when I've so much to trouble and vex me—and not make any fresh difficulties. How can I help it?—If your father says the people are to come, I can't say I won't let them in. I hope you won't make Fanny think I'm doing it from disrespect to her. I'm sure I wouldn't have a soul here for a twelvemonth, on my own account.'

'I'm sure Miss Wyndham won't think any such thing, my lady,' said Griffiths; 'will she, Lady Selina?—Indeed, I don't think she'll matter it one **pin.**'

'Indeed, Selina, I don't think she will,' said the

countess; and then she half whispered to her
daughter. 'Poor Fanny! it's not about her brother
she's grieving; it's that horrid man, Ballindine. She
sent him away, and now she wants to have him back.
I really think a little company will be the best thing
to bring her to herself again.' There was a little
degree of humbug in this whisper, for her ladyship
meant her daughter to understand that she wouldn't
speak aloud about Fanny's love-affair before Griffiths;
and yet she had spent many a half hour talking to
her factotum on that very subject. Indeed, what
subject was there of any interest to Lady Cashel on
which she did not talk to Griffiths!

'Well, mamma,' said Lady Selina, dutifully, 'I'll
not say another word about it; only let me know
what you want me to do, and I'll do it. Who is it you
mean to ask?'

'Why, first of all, there's the Fitzgeralds: your
father thinks that Lord and Lady George would
come for a week or so, and you know the girls have
been long talking of coming to Grey Abbey—these
two years I believe, and more.'

'The girls will come, I dare say, mamma; though
I don't exactly think they're the sort of people who
will amuse Adolphus; but I don't think Lord George
or Lady George will sleep away from home. We can
ask them, however; Mountains is only five miles from
here, and I'm sure they'll go back after dinner.'

'Well, my dear, if they will, they must, and I can't
help it; only I must say it'll be very ill-natured of
them. I'm sure it's a long time since they were
asked to stay here.'

'As you say, mamma, at any rate we can ask
them. And who comes next?'

'Why your father has put down the Swinburn
people next; though I'm sure I don't know how they
are to come so far.'

'Why, mamma, the colonel is a martyr to the
gout!'

'Yes, my lady,' said Griffiths, 'and Mrs. Ellison is

worse again, with rheumatics. There would be nothing to do, the whole time, but nurse the two of them.'

'Never mind, Griffiths; you'll not have to nurse them, so you needn't be so ill-natured.'

'Me, ill-natured, my lady? I'm sure I begs pardon, but I didn't mean nothing ill-natured; besides, Mrs. Ellison was always a very nice lady to me, and I'm sure I'd be happy to nurse her, if she wanted it; only that, as in duty bound, I've your ladyship to look to first, and so couldn't spare time very well for nursing any one.'

'Of course you couldn't, Griffiths; but, Selina, at any rate you must ask the Ellisons: your papa thinks a great deal about the colonel—he has so much influence in the county, and Adolphus will very likely stand, now. Your papa and the colonel were members together for the county more than forty years since.'

'Well, mamma, I'll write Mrs. Ellison. Shall I say for a week or ten days?'

'Say for ten days or a fortnight, and then perhaps they'll stay a week. Then there's the Bishop of Maryborough, and Mrs. Moore. I'm sure Adolphus will be glad to meet the bishop, for it was he that christened him.'

'Very well, mamma, I'll write to Mrs. Moore. I suppose the bishop is in Dublin at present?'

'Yes, my dear, I believe so. There can't be anything to prevent their coming.'

'Only that he's the managing man on the Education Board, and he's giving up his time very much to that at present. I dare say he'll come, but he won't stay long.'

'Well, Selina, if he won't, I can't help it; and I'm sure, now I think about the cook, I don't see how we're to expect anybody to stay. What am I to do, Griffiths, about that horrid woman?'

'I'll tell you what I was thinking, my lady; only I don't know whether your ladyship would like it,

either, and if you didn't you could easily get rid of
him when all these people are gone.'

'Get rid of who?'

'I was going to say, my lady—if your ladyship
would consent to have a man cook for a time, just to
try.'

'Then I never will, Griffiths: there'd be no peace in
the house with him!'

'Well, your ladyship knows best, in course; only
if you thought well of trying it, of course you needn't
keep the man; and I know there's Murray in Dublin,
that was cook so many years to old Lord Galway.
I know he's to be heard of at the hotel in Grafton
Street.

'I can't bear the thoughts of a man cook, Griffiths:
I'd sooner have three women cooks, and I'm sure
one's enough to plague anybody.'

'But none's worse, my lady,' said Griffiths.

'You needn't tell me that. I wonder, Selina, if I
were to write to my sister, whether she could send
me over anything that would answer?'

'What, from London, my lady?' answered
Griffiths—'You'd find a London woman cook sent
over in that way twice worse than any man: she'd be
all airs and graces. If your ladyship thought well of
thinking about Murray, Richards would do very well
under him: she's a decent poor creature, poor woman
—only she certainly is not a cook that'd suit for such
a house as this; and it was only impudence her
thinking to attempt it.'

'But, mamma,' said Lady Selina, 'do let me know
to whom I am to write, and then you and Griffiths
can settle about the cook afterwards; the time is so
very short that I ought not to lose a post.'

The poor countess threw herself back in her easy
chair, the picture of despair. Oh, how much preferable were rolls of worsted and yards of netting, to the
toils and turmoil of preparing for, and entertaining
company! She was already nearly overcome by the
former: she didn't dare to look forward to the miseries

of the latter. She already began to feel the ill effects of her son's reformation, and to wish that it had been postponed just for a month or two, till she was a little more settled.

'Well, mamma,' said Lady Selina, as undisturbed and calm as ever, and as resolved to do her duty without flinching, 'shall we go on?'

The countess groaned and sighed—'There's the list there, Selina, which your father put down in pencil. You know the people as well as I do: just ask them all—'

'But, mamma, I'm not to ask them all to stay here:—I suppose some are only to come to dinner?—the O'Joscelyns, and the Parchments?'

'Ask the O'Joscelyns for Wednesday and Thursday: the girls might as well stay and sleep here. But what's the good of writing to them?—can't you drive over to the Parsonage and settle it all there?—you do nothing but make difficulties, Selina, and my head's racking.'

Lady Selina sate silent for a short time, conning the list, and endeavouring to see her way through the labyrinth of difficulties which was before her, without further trouble to her mother; while the countess leaned back, with her eyes closed, and her hands placed on the arms of her chair, as though she were endeavouring to get some repose, after the labour she had gone through. Her daughter, however, again disturbed her.

'Mamma,' she said, trying by the solemnity of her tone to impress her mother with the absolute necessity she was under of again appealing to her upon the subject, 'what *are* we to do about young men?'

'About young men, my dear?'

'Yes, mamma: there'll be a house-full of young ladies—there's the Fitzgeralds—and Lady Louisa Pratt—and Miss Ellison—and the three O'Joscelyns—and not a single young man, except Mr. O'Joscelyn's curate!'

'Well, my dear, I'm sure Mr. Hill's a very nice young man'.

'So he is, mamma; a very good young man; but
he won't do to amuse such a quantity of girls. If
there were only one or two he'd do very well; besides,
I'm sure Adolphus won't like it.'

'Why; won't he talk to the young ladies?—I'm
sure he was always fond of ladies' society.'

'I tell you, mamma, it won't do. There'll be the
bishop and two other clergymen, and old Colonel
Ellison, who has always got the gout, and Lord
George, if he comes—and I'm sure he wont. If you
want to make a pleasant party for Adolphus, you
must get some young men; besides, you can't ask
all those girls, and have nobody to dance with them
or talk to them.'

'I'm sure, my dear, I don't know what you're to do.
I don't know any young men except Mr. Hill; and
there's that young Mr. Grundy, who lives in Dublin.
I promised his aunt to be civil to him: can't you ask
him down?'

'He was here before, mamma, and I don't think he
liked it. I'm sure we didn't. He didn't speak a word
the whole day he was here. He's not at all the
person to suit Adolphus.'

'Then, my dear, you *must* go to your papa, and ask
him: it's quite clear I can't make young men. I
remember, years ago, there always used to be too
many of them, and I don't know where they're all
gone to. At any rate, when they do come, there'll be
nothing for them to eat,' and Lady Cashel again fell
back upon her deficiencies in the kitchen establishment.

Lady Selina saw that nothing more could be obtained from her mother, no further intelligence as
regarded the embryo party. The whole burden was
to lie on her shoulders, and very heavy she felt it.
As far as concerned herself, she had no particular
wish for one kind of guest more than another: it was
not for herself that she wanted young men; she knew
that at any rate there were none within reach whom
she could condescend to notice save as her father's

guests; there could be no one there whose presence could be to her of any interest: the gouty colonel, and the worthy bishop, would be as agreeable to her as any other men that would now be likely to visit Grey Abbey. But Lady Selina felt a real desire that others in the house might be happy while there. She was no flirt herself, nor had she ever been; it was not in her nature to be so. But though she herself might be contented to twaddle with old men, she knew that other girls would not. Yet it was not that she herself had no inward wish for that admiration which is desired by nearly every woman, or that she thought a married state was an unenviable one. No; she could have loved and loved truly, and could have devoted herself most scrupulously to the duties of a wife; but she had vainly and foolishly built up for herself a pedestal, and there she had placed herself; nor would she come down to stand on common earth, though Apollo had enticed her, unless he came with the coronet of a peer upon his brow.

She left her mother's boudoir, went down into the drawing-room, and there she wrote her notes of invitation, and her orders to the tradesmen; and then she went to her father, and consulted him on the difficult subject of young men. She suggested the Newbridge Barracks, where the dragoons were; and the Curragh, where perhaps some stray denizen of pleasure might be found, neither too bad for Grey Abbey, nor too good to be acceptable to Lord Kilcullen; and at last it was decided that a certain Captain Cokely, and Mat Tierney, should be asked. They were both acquaintances of Adolphus; and though Mat was not a young man, he was not very old, and was usually very gay.

So that matter was settled, and the invitations were sent off. The countess overcame her difficulty by consenting that Murray the man cook should be hired for a given time, with the distinct understanding that he was to take himself off with the rest of the guests, and so great was her ladyship's sense

of the importance of the negotiation, that she absolutely despatched Griffiths to Dublin to arrange it,
though thereby she was left two whole days in
solitary misery at Grey Abbey; and had to go to bed,
and get up, she really hardly knew how, with such
assistance as Lady Selina's maid could give her.

When these things were all arranged, Selina told
her cousin that Adolphus was coming home, and that
a house full of company had been asked to meet him.
She was afraid that Fanny would be annoyed and
offended at being forced to go into company so soon
after her brother's death, but such was not the case.
She felt, herself, that her poor brother was not the
cause of the grief that was near her heart; and she
would not pretend what she didn't really feel.

'You were quite right, Selina,' she said, smiling,
'about the things you said yesterday I should
want from Dublin: now, I shall want them; and, as
I wouldn't accept of your good-natured offer, I must
take the trouble of writing myself.'

'If you like it, Fanny, I'll write for you,' said
Selina.

'Oh no, I'm not quite so idle as that'—and she
also began her preparations for the expected festivi-
ties. Little did either of them think that she, Fanny
Wyndham, was the sole cause of all the trouble
which the household and neighbourhood were to
undergo:—the fatigue of the countess; Griffiths's
journey; the arrival of the dread man cook; Richards's
indignation at being made subordinate to such
authority; the bishop's desertion of the Education
Board; the colonel's dangerous and precipitate consumption of colchicum; the quarrel between Lord
and Lady George as to staying or not staying; the
new dresses of the Miss O'Joscelyns, which their
worthy father could so ill afford; and, above all, the
confusion, misery, rage, and astonishment which
attended Lord Kilcullen's unexpected retreat from
London, in the middle of the summer. And all in
vain!

How proud and satisfied Lord Ballindine might have been, had he been able to see all this, and could he have known how futile was every effort Lord Cashel could make to drive from Fanny Wyndham's heart the love she felt for him.

The invitations, however, were, generally speaking, accepted. The bishop and his wife would be most happy; the colonel would come if the gout would possibly allow; Lady George wrote a note to say they would be very happy to stay a few days, and Lord George wrote another soon after to say he was sorry, but that they must return the same evening. The O'Joscelyns would be delighted; Mat Tierney would be very proud; Captain Cokely would do himself the honour; and, last but not least, Mr. Murray would preside below stairs—for a serious consideration.

What a pity so much trouble should have been taken! They might all have stayed at home; for Fanny Wyndham will never become Lady Kilcullen.

XXX

LORD KILCULLEN OBEYS HIS FATHER

ON the appointed day, or rather on the night of the appointed day, Lord Kilcullen reached Grey Abbey; for it was about eleven o'clock when his travelling-phaëton rattled up to the door. He had been expected to dinner at seven, and the first attempts of Murray in the kitchens of Grey Abbey had been kept waiting for him till half-past eight; but in vain. At that hour the earl, black with ill-humour, ordered dinner; and remarked that he considered it criminal in any man to make an appointment, who was not sufficiently attached to veracity to keep it.

The evening was passed in moody silence. The countess was disappointed, for she always contrived to persuade herself that she was very anxious to see her son. Lady Selina was really vexed, and began to have her doubts as to her brother's coming at all: what was to be done, if it turned out that all the company had been invited for nothing? As to Fanny, though very indifferent to the subject of her cousin's coming, she was not at all in a state of mind to dissipate the sullenness which prevailed. The ladies went to bed early, the countess grumbling at her lot, in not being allowed to see her son, and her daughter and niece marching off with their respective candlesticks in solemn silence. The earl retired to his book-room soon afterwards; but he had not yet sat down, when the quick rattle of the wheels was heard upon the gravel before the house.

Lord Cashel walked out into the hall, prepared to meet his son in a befitting manner; that is, with a dignified austerity that could not fail to convey a rebuke even to his hardened heart. But he was balked in his purpose, for he found that Lord Kilcullen was not alone; Mat Tierney had come down with him. Kilcullen had met his friend in Dublin, and on learning that he also was bound for Grey Abbey on the day but one following, had persuaded him to accelerate his visit, had waited for him, and brought him down in his own carriage. The truth was, that Lord Kilcullen had thought that the shades of Grey Abbey would be too much for him, without some genial spirit to enlighten them: he was delighted to find that Mat Tierney was to be there, and was rejoiced to be able to convey him with him, as a sort of protection from his father's eloquence for the first two days of the visit.

'Lord Kilcullen, your mother and I—' began the father, intent on at once commenting on the iniquity of the late arrival; when he saw the figure of a very stout gentleman, amply wrapped up in travelling habiliments, follow his son into the inner hall.

'Tierney, my lord,' said the son, 'was good enough to come down with me. I found that he intended to be here to-morrow, and I told him you and my mother would be delighted to see him to-day instead.'

The earl shook Mr. Tierney's hand, and told him how very welcome he was at all times, and especially at present—unexpected pleasures were always the most agreeable; and then the earl bustled about, and ordered supper and wine, and fussed about the bedrooms, and performed the necessary rites of hospitality, and then went to bed, without having made one solemn speech to his son. So far, Lord Kilcullen had been successful in his manœuvre; and he trusted that by making judicious use of Mat Tierney, he might be able to stave off the evil hour for at any rate a couple of days.

But he was mistaken. Lord Cashel was now too much in earnest to be put off his purpose; he had been made too painfully aware that his son's position was desperate, and that he must at once be saved by a desperate effort, or given over to utter ruin. And, to tell the truth, so heavy were the new debts of which he heard from day to day, so insurmountable seemed the difficulties, that he all but repented that he had not left him to his fate. The attempt, however, must again be made; he was there, in the house, and could not be turned out; but Lord Cashel determined that at any rate no time should be lost.

The two new arrivals made their appearance the next morning, greatly to Lady Cashel's delight; she was perfectly satisfied with her son's apology, and delighted to find that at any rate one of her expected guests would not fail her in her need. The breakfast went over pleasantly enough, and Kilcullen was asking Mat to accompany him into the stables, to see what novelties they should find there, when Lord Cashel spoiled the arrangement by saying,

'Could you spare me half-an-hour in the bookroom first, Kilcullen?'

This request, of course, could not be refused; and the father and son walked off, leaving Mat Tierney to the charity of the ladies.

There was much less of flippant overbearing impudence now, about Lord Kilcullen, much less of arrogance and insult from the son towards the father, than there had been in the previous interview which has been recorded. He seemed to be somewhat in dread, to be cowed, and ill at ease; he tried, however, to asume his usual manner, and followed his father into the book-room with an affected air of in-difference, which very ill concealed his real feelings.

'Kilcullen,' began the earl, 'I was very sorry to see Tierney with you last night. It would have been much better that we should have been alone to-gether, at any rate for one morning. I suppose you are aware that there is a great deal to be talked over between us?'

'I suppose there is,' said the son; 'but I couldn't well help bringing the man, when he told me he was coming here.'

'He didn't ask you to bring him, I suppose?—but we will not talk about that. Will you do me the favour to inform me what your present plans are?'

'My present plans, my lord? Indeed, I've no plans!—It's a long time since I had a plan of my own. I am, however, prepared to acquiesce entirely in any which you may propose. I have come quite prepared to throw at Miss Wyndham's feet myself—and my fortune.'

'And do you expect her to accept you?'

'You said she would, my lord: so I have taken that for granted. I, at any rate, will ask her; if she refuses me, your lordship will perhaps be able to persuade her to a measure so evidently beneficial to all parties.'

'The persuading must be with yourself; but if you suppose you can carry her with a high hand, without giving yourself the trouble to try to please her, you are very much mistaken. If you think she'll accept you merely because you ask her, you might save yourself the trouble, and as well return to London at once.'

'Just as you please, my lord; but I thought I came in obedience to your express wishes.'

'So you did; but, to tell you the truth—your manner in coming is very different from what I would wish it to be. Your—'

'Did you want me to crawl here on my hands and knees?'

'I wanted you to come, Kilcullen, with some sense of what you owe to those who are endeavouring to rescue you from ruin: with some feeling of, at any rate, sorrow for the mad extravagance of your past career. Instead of that, you come gay, reckless, and unconcerned as ever; you pick up the first jovial companion you meet, and with him disturb the house at a most unseasonable hour. You are totally regardless of the appointments you make; and plainly show, that as you come here solely for your own pleasure, you consider it needless to consult my wishes or my comfort. Are you aware that you kept your mother and myself two hours waiting for dinner yesterday?'

The pathos with which Lord Cashel terminated his speech—and it was one the thrilling effect of which he intended to be overwhelming—almost restored Lord Kilcullen to his accustomed effrontery.

'My lord,' he said, 'I did not consider myself of sufficient importance to have delayed your dinner ten minutes.'

'I have always endeavoured, Kilcullen, to show the same respect to you in my house, which my father showed to me in his; but you do not allow me the opportunity. But let that pass; we have more important things to speak of. When last we were here together why did you not tell me the whole truth?'

'What truth, my lord?'

'About your debts, Kilcullen: why did you conceal from me their full amount? Why, at any rate, did you take pains to make me think them so much less than they really are?'

'Conceal, my lord?—that is hardly fair, considering that I told you expressly I could not give you any idea what was the amount I owed. I concealed nothing; if you deceived yourself, the fault was not mine.'

'You could not but have known that the claims against you were much larger than I supposed them to be—double, I suppose. Good heaven!—why in ten years more, at this rate, you would more than consume the fee simple of the whole property! What can I say to you, Kilcullen, to make you look on your own conduct in the proper light?'

'I think you have said enough for the purpose; you have told me to marry, and I have consented to do so.'

'Do you think, Kilcullen, you have spent the last eight years in a way which it can please a father to contemplate? Do you think I can look back on your conduct with satisfaction or content? And yet you have no regret to express for the past—no promises to make for the future. I fear it is all in vain. I fear that what I am doing—what I am striving to do, is now all in vain. I fear it is hopeless to attempt to recall you from the horrid, reckless, wicked mode of life you have adopted.' The sombre mantle of expostulatory eloquence had now descended on the earl, and he continued, turning full upon his victim, and raising and lowering his voice with monotonous propriety.—' I fear it is to no good purpose that I am subjecting your mother and myself to privation, restraint, and inconvenience; that I am straining every nerve to place you again in a position of re-spectability, a position suitable to my fortune and your own rank. I am endeavouring to retrieve the desperate extravagance—the—I must say—though I do not wish to hurt your feelings, yet I must say, disgraceful ruin of your past career. And how do you help me? what regret do you show? what promises of amendment do you afford? You drive up to my hall-door at midnight with your boon companion; you disturb the whole household at most unseasonable hours, and subject my family to the same disreputable irregularity in which you have

yourself so long indulged. Can such doings, Kilcullen, give me any hopes for the future? Can—'

'My lord—I am extremely sorry for the dinner:
what can I say more? And as for Mat Tierney, he is
your own guest—or her ladyship's—not mine. It is
my misfortune to have come in the same carriage
with him, but that is the extent of my offence.'

'Well, Kilcullen; if you think your conduct has
always been such as it ought to be, it is of little use
for me to bring up arguments to the contrary.'

'I don't think so, my lord. What can I say more?
I have done those things which I ought not to have
done. Were I to confess my transgressions for the
hour together, I could not say more; except that
I have left undone the things which I ought to have
done. Or, do you want me to beat my breast and
tear my hair?'

'I want you, Lord Kilcullen, to show some sense
of decency—some filial respect.'

'Well, my lord, here I am, prepared to marry
a wife of your own choosing, and to set about the
business this morning, if you please. I thought you
would have called that decent, filial, and respectable.'

The earl could hardly gainsay this; but still he
could not bring himself to give over so soon the
unusual pleasure of blowing up his only son. It was
so long since Lord Kilcullen had been regularly in
his power, and it might never occur again. So he
returned from consideration of the future to a further
retrospect on the past.

'You certainly have played your cards most
foolishly; you have thrown away your money—
rather, I should say, my money, in a manner which
nothing can excuse or palliate. You might have
made the turf a source of gratifying amusement;
your income was amply sufficient to enable you to
do so; but you have possessed so little self-control,
so little judgment, so little discrimination, that you
have allowed yourself to be plundered by every

blackleg, and robbed by every—everybody in short, who chose to rob you. The same thing has been the case in all your other amusements and pursuits—'

'Well, my lord, I confess it all; isn't that enough?'

'Enough, Kilcullen!' said the earl, in a voice of horrified astonishment, 'how enough?—how can anything be enough after such a course—so wild, so mad, so ruinous!'

'For Heaven's sake, my lord, finish the list of my iniquities, or you'll make me feel that I am utterly unfit to become my cousin's husband.'

'I fear you are—indeed I fear you are. Are the horses disposed of yet, Kilcullen?'

'Indeed they are not, my lord; nor can I dispose of them. There is more owing for them than they are worth; you may say they belong to the trainer now.'

'Is the establishment in Curzon Street broken up?'

'To tell the truth, not exactly; but I've no thoughts of returning there. I'm still under rent for the house.'

The cross-examination was continued for a considerable time—till the earl had literally nothing more to say, and Lord Kilcullen was so irritated that he told his father he would not stand it any longer. Then they went into money affairs, and the earl spoke despondingly about ten thousands and twenty thousands, and the viscount somewhat flippantly of fifty thousands and sixty thousands; and this was continued till the earl felt that his son was too deep in the mire to be pulled out, and the son thought that, deep as he was there, it would be better to remain and wallow in it than undergo so disagreeable a process as that to which his father subjected him in extricating him from it. It was settled, however, that Mr. Jervis, Lord Cashel's agent, should receive full authority to deal summarily in all matters respecting the horses and their trainers, the house in Curzon Street, and its inhabitants, and all other

appendages and sources of expense which Lord Kilcullen had left behind him; and that he, Kilcullen,
should at once commence his siege upon his cousin's
fortune. And on this point the son bargained that,
as it would be essentially necessary that his spirits
should be light and easy, he was not, during the
operation, to be subjected to any of his father's
book-room conversations: for this he stipulated as an
absolute *sine quâ non* in the negotiation, and the
clause was at last agreed to, though not without
much difficulty.

Both father and son seemed to think that the offer
should be made at once. Lord Cashel really feared
that his son would be arrested at Grey Abbey, and he
was determined to pay nothing further for him, unless he felt secure of Fanny's fortune; and whatever
were Lord Kilcullen's hopes and fears as to his future
lot, he was determined not to remain long in suspense,
as far as his projected marriage was concerned. He
was determined to do his best to accomplish it, for
he would have done anything to get the command
of ready money; if he was not successful, at any rate
he need not remain in the purgatory of Grey Abbey.
The Queen's Bench would be preferable to that.
He was not, however, very doubtful; he felt but
little confidence in the constancy of any woman's
affection, and a great deal in his own powers of
fascination: he had always been successful in his
appeals to ladies' hearts, and did not doubt of
being so now, when the object of his adoration must,
as he thought, be so dreadfully in want of some
excitement, something to interest her. Any fool
might have her now, thought he, and she can't have
any violent objection to being Lady Kilcullen for the
present, and Lady Cashel in due time. He felt, however, something like remorse at the arrangement to
which he was a party; it was not that he was about
to make a beautiful creature, his own cousin,
miserable for life, by uniting her to a spendthrift,
a *roué*, and a gambler—such was the natural lot of

women in the higher ranks of life—but he felt that
he was robbing her of her money. He would have
thought it to be no disgrace to carry her off had
another person been her guardian. She would then
have had fair play, and it would be the guardian's
fault if her fortune were not secure. But she had no
friend now to protect her: it was her guardian himself who was betraying her to ruin.

However, the money must be had, and Lord
Kilcullen was not long in quieting his conscience.

'Tierney,' said Kilcullen, meeting his friend after
his escape from the book-room; 'you are not troubled
with a father now, I believe;—do you recollect
whether you ever had one?'

'Well, I can't say I remember just at present,'
said Mat; 'but I believe I had a sort of one, once.'

'I'm a more dutiful son than you,' said the other;
'I never can forget mine. I have no doubt an alli-
gator on the banks of the Nile is a fearful creature:—
a shark when one's bathing, or a jungle tiger when
one's out shooting, ought, I'm sure, to be avoided; but
no creature yet created, however hungry, or however savage, can equal in ferocity a governor who
has to shell out his cash! I've no wish for a *tête-à-tête*
with any bloody-minded monster; but I'd sooner
meet a starved hyena, single-handed in the desert,
than be shut up for another hour with my Lord
Cashel in that room of his on the right-hand side of
the hall. If you hear of my having beat a retreat
from Grey Abbey, without giving you or any one
else warning of my intention, you will know that
I have lacked courage to comply with a second
summons to those gloomy realms. If I receive
another invite such as that I got this morning, I am
off.'

Lady Cashel's guests came on the day appointed;
the carriages were driven up, one after another, in
quick succession, about an hour before dinner-time;
and, as her ladyship's mind became easy on the score
of disappointments, it was somewhat troubled as to

the multitude of people to be fed and entertained.
Murray had not yet forgiven the injury inflicted on
him when the family dinner was kept waiting for
Lord Kilcullen, and Richards was still pouting at her
own degraded position. The countess had spent the
morning pretending to make arrangements, which
were in fact all settled by Griffiths; and when she
commenced the operation of dressing herself, she
declared she was so utterly exhausted by what she
had gone through during the last week, as to be
entirely unfit to entertain her company. Poor dear
Lady Cashel! Was she so ignorant of her own nature
as to suppose it possible that she should ever entertain anybody?

However, a glass of wine, and some mysterious
drops, and a little paint; a good deal of coaxing, the
sight of her diamonds, and of a large puce-coloured
turban, somewhat revivified her; and she was in her
drawing-room in due time, supported by Lady Selina
and Fanny, ready to receive her visitors as soon as
they should descend from their respective rooms.

Lady Cashel had already welcomed Lord George,
and shaken hands with the bishop: and was now
deep in turnips and ten-pound freeholders with the
gouty colonel, who had hobbled into the room on
a pair of crutches, and was accommodated with two
easy chairs in a corner—one for himself, and the
other for his feet.

'Now, my dear Lady George,' said the countess,
'you must not think of returning to Mountains to-
night: indeed, we made sure of you and Lord George
for a week.'

'My dear Lady Cashel, it's impossible; indeed, we
wished it of all things, and tried it every way: but
we couldn't manage it; Lord George has so much to
do: there's the Sessions to-morrow at Dunlavin, and
he has promised to meet Sir Glenmalure Aubrey,
about a road, or a river, or a bridge—I forget which
it is; and they must attend to those things, you
know, or the tenants couldn't get their corn to

market. But you don't know how sorry we are, and
such a charming set you have got here!'

'Well, I know it's no use pressing you; but I can't
tell you how vexed I am, for I counted on you, above
all, and Adolphus will be so sorry. You know Lord
Kilcullen's come home, Lady George?'

'Yes; I was very glad to hear we were to meet
him.'

'Oh, yes! He's come to stay here some time,
I believe; he's got quite fond of Grey Abbey lately.
He and his father get on so well together, it's quite
a delight to me.'

'Oh, it must be, I'm sure,' said Lady George; and
the countess sidled off to the bishop's fat wife.

'Well, this is very kind of you and the bishop, to
come at so short a notice: indeed I hardly dared
expect it. I know he has so much to do in Dublin
with those horrid boards and things.'

'He is busy there, to be sure, Lady Cashel; but he
couldn't deny himself the pleasure of coming to
Grey Abbey; he thinks so very much of the earl.
Indeed, he'd contrive to be able to come here, when
he couldn't think of going anywhere else.'

'I'm sure Lord Cashel feels how kind he is; and so
do I, and so does Adolphus. Lord Kilcullen will be
delighted to meet you and the bishop.'

The bishop's wife assured the countess that
nothing on earth, at the present moment, would
give the bishop so much pleasure as meeting Lord
Kilcullen.

'You know the bishop christened him, don't you?'
said Lady Cashel.

'No! did he though?' said the bishop's wife; 'how
very interesting!'

'Isn't it? And Adolphus longs to meet him. He's
so fond of everything that's high-minded and
talented, Adolphus is: a little sarcastic perhaps—
I don't mind saying so to you; but that's only to
inferior sort of people—not talented, you know:
some people are stupid, and Adolphus can't bear that.'

'Indeed they are, my lady. I was dining last week at Mrs. Prijean's, in Merrion Square; you know Mrs. Prijean?'

'I think I met her at Carton, four years ago.'

'Well, she is very heavy: what do you think, Lady Cashel, she—'

'Adolphus can't bear people of that sort, but he'll be delighted with the bishop: it's so delightful, his having christened him. Adolphus means to live a good deal here now. Indeed, he and his father have so much in common that they can't get on very well apart, and I really hope he and the bishop'll see a good deal of each other;' and the countess left the bishop's wife and sat herself down by old Mrs. Ellison.

'My dear Mrs. Ellison, I am so delighted to see you once again at Grey Abbey; it's such ages since you were here!'

'Indeed it is, Lady Cashel, a very long time; but the poor colonel suffers so much, it's rarely he's fit to be moved; and, indeed, I'm not much better myself. I was not able to move my left shoulder from a week before Christmas-day till a few days since!'

'You don't say so! Rheumatism, I suppose?'

'Oh, yes—all rheumatism: no one knows what I suffer.'

'And what do you use for it?'

'Oh, there's nothing any use. I know the very nature of rheumatism now, I've had it so long—and it minds nothing at all: there's no preventing it, and no curing it. It's like a bad husband, Lady Cashel; the best way is to put up with it.'

'And how is the dear colonel, Mrs. Ellison?'

'Why, he was just able to come here, and that was all; but he was dying to see Lord Cashel. He thinks the ministers'll be shaken about this business of O'Connell's; and if so, that there'll be a general election, and then what'll they do about the county?'

'I'm sure Lord Cashel wanted to see the colonel

on that very subject; so does Adolphus—Lord Kilcullen, you know. I never meddle with those things;
but I really think Adolphus is thinking of going into
Parliament. You know he's living here at present:
his father's views and his own are so exactly the
same on all those sort of things, that it's quite
delightful. He's taking a deal of interest about
the county lately, is Adolphus, and about Grey
Abbey too: he's just the same his father used to
be, and that kind of thing is so pleasant, isn't it,
Mrs. Ellison?'

Mrs. Ellison said it was, and at the same moment
groaned, for her shoulder gave her a twinge.

The subject of these eulogiums, in the meantime,
did not make his appearance till immediately before
dinner was announced, and certainly did not evince
very strongly the delight which his mother had
assured her friends he would feel at meeting them,
for he paid but very little attention to any one but
Mat Tierney and his cousin Fanny; he shook hands
with all the old gentlemen, bowed to all the old
ladies, and nodded at the young ones. But if he
really felt that strong desire, which his mother had
imputed to him, of opening his heart to the bishop
and the colonel respecting things temporal and
spiritual, he certainly very successfully suppressed
his anxiety.

He had, during the last two or three days, applied
himself to the task of ingratiating himself with
Fanny. He well knew how to suit himself to different
characters, and to make himself agreeable when he
pleased; and Fanny, though she had never much
admired her dissipated cousin, certainly found his
conversation a relief after the usual oppressive
tedium of Grey Abbey society.

He had not begun by making love to her, or
expressing admiration, or by doing or saying anything which could at all lead her to suspect his
purpose, or put her on her guard. He had certainly
been much more attentive to her, much more inti-

mate with her, than he usually had been in his flying
visits to Grey Abbey; but then he was now making
his first appearance as a reformed rake; and besides,
he was her first cousin, and she therefore felt no
inclination to repel his advances.

He was obliged, in performance of a domestic
duty, to walk out to dinner with one of Lady
George's daughters, but he contrived to sit next to
Fanny—and, much to his father's satisfaction, talked
to her during the whole ceremony.

'And where have you hidden yourself all the
morning, Fanny,' said he, 'that nobody has seen
anything of you since breakfast?'

'Whither have *you* taken yourself all the day,
rather, that you had not a moment to come and look
after us? The Miss O'Joscelyns have been expecting
you to ride with them, walk with them, talk with
them, and play *la grace* with them. They didn't give
up the sticks till it was quite dark, in the hope of you
and Mr. Tierney making your appearance.'

'Well, Fanny, don't tell my mother, and I'll tell
you the truth:—promise now.'

'Oh, I'm no tell-tale.'

'Well then,' and he whispered into her ear—'I was
running away from the Miss O'Joscelyns.'

'But that won't do at all; don't you know they
were asked here for your especial edification and
amusement?'

'Oh, I know they were. So were the bishop, and
the colonel, and Lord George, and their respective
wives, and Mr. Hill. My dear mamma asked them
all here for my amusement; but, you know, one
man may lead a horse to water—a hundred can't
make him drink. I cannot, cannot drink of the Miss
O'Joscelyns, and the Bishop of Maryborough.'

'For shame, Adolphus! you ought at any rate to
do something to amuse them.'

'Amuse them! My dear Fanny, who ever heard of
amusing a bishop? But it's very easy to find fault;
what have you done, yourself, for their amusement?'

'I didn't run away from them; though, had I done
so, there would have been more excuse for me than
for you.'

'So there would, Fanny,' said Kilcullen, feeling
that she had alluded to her brother's death; 'and I'm
very, very sorry all these people are here to bore you
at such a time, and doubly sorry that they should
have been asked on my account. They mistake me
greatly, here. They know that I've thought Grey
Abbey dull, and have avoided it; and now that I've
determined to get over the feeling, because I think
it right to do so, they make it ten times more unbearable than ever, for my gratification! It's like
giving a child physic mixed in sugar; the sugar's sure
to be the nastiest part of the dose. Indeed I have
no dislike to Grey Abbey at present; though I own
I have no taste for the sugar in which my kind
mother has tried to conceal its proper flavour.'

'Well, make the best of it; they'll all be gone in
ten days.'

'Ten days! Are they to stay ten days? Will you
tell me, Fanny, what was the object in asking Mat
Tierney to meet such a party?'

'To help you to amuse the young ladies.'

'Gracious heavens! Does Lady Cashel really expect Mat Tierney to play *la grace* with the Miss
O'Joscelyns?—Well, the time will come to an end,
I suppose. But in truth I'm more sorry for you than
for any one. It was very ill-judged, their getting
such a crowd to bore you at such a time,' and Lord
Kilcullen contrived to give his voice a tone of tender
solicitude.

'Kilcullen,' said the earl, across the table, 'you
don't hear the bishop. His lordship is asking you to
drink wine with him.'

'I shall be most proud of the honour,' said the son,
and bobbed his head at the bishop across the table.

Fanny was on the point of saying something
respecting her brother to Lord Kilcullen, which
would have created a kind of confidence between

them, but the bishop's glass of wine broke it off, and from that time Lord Kilcullen was forced by his father into a general conversation with his guests.

In the evening there was music and singing. The Miss O'Joscelyns, and Miss Fitzgeralds, and Mr. Hill, performed: even Mat Tierney condescended to amuse the company by singing the 'Coronation', first begging the bishop to excuse the peculiar allusions to the 'clargy', contained in one of the verses; and then Fanny was asked to sing. She had again become silent, dull, and unhappy, was brooding over her miseries and disappointments, and she declined. Lord Kilcullen was behind her chair, and when they pressed her, he whispered to her, 'Don't sing for them, Fanny; it's a shame that they should tease you at such a time; I wonder how my mother can have been so thoughtless.'

Fanny persisted in declining to sing—and Lord Kilcullen again sat down beside her. 'Don't trouble yourself about them, Fanny,' said he, 'they're just fit to sing to each other; it's very good work for them.'

'I should think it very good work, as you call it, for myself, too, another time; only I'm hardly in singing humour at present, and, therefore, obliged to you for your assistance and protection.'

'Your most devoted knight as long as this fearful invasion lasts!—your Amadis de Gaul—your Bertrand du Guesclin! And no paladin of old ever attempted to defend a damsel from more formidable foes.'

'Indeed, Adolphus, I don't think them so formidable. Many of them are my own friends.'

'Is Mrs. Ellison your own friend?—or Mrs. Moore?'

'Not exactly those two, in particular.'

'Who then? Is it Miss Judith O'Joscelyn? or is the Reverend Mr. Hill one of those to whom you give that sweetest of all names?'

'Yes; to both of them. It was only this morning I had a long tête-à-tête—'

'What, with Mr. Hill?'

'No, not with Mr. Hill—though it wouldn't be the first even with him, but with Judith O'Joscelyn. I lent her a pattern for worsted work.'

'And does that make her your friend? Do you give your friendship so easily?'

'You forget that I've known her for years.'

'Well, now, I've not. I've seen her about three times in my life, and spoken two words to her perhaps twice; and yet I'll describe her character to you; and if you can say that the description is incorrect, I will permit you to call her your friend.'

'Well, let's hear the character.'

'It wouldn't be kind in me, though, to laugh at your *friend*.

'Oh, she's not so especially and particularly my friend that you need mind that.'

'Then you'll promise not to be angry?'

'Oh no, I won't be angry.'

'Well, then; she has two passions: they are for worsted and hymn-books. She has a moral objection to waltzing. Theoretically she disapproves of flirtations: she encourages correspondence between young ladies; always crosses her letters, and never finished one for the last ten years without expressing entire resignation to the will of God,—as if she couldn't be resigned without so often saying so. She speaks to her confidential friends of young men as a very worthless, insignificant race of beings; she is, however, prepared to take the very first that may be unfortunate enough to come in her way; she has no ideas of her own, but is quick enough at borrowing those of other people; she considers herself a profound theologian; dotes on a converted papist, and looks on a Puseyite as something one shade blacker than the devil. Now isn't that sufficiently like for a portrait?'

'It's the portrait of a set, I fear, rather than an individual. I don't know that it's particularly like Miss O'Joscelyn, except as to the worsted and hymn-books.'

'What, not as to the waltzing, resignation, and worthless young men? Come, are they not exactly her traits? Does she waltz?'

'No, she does not.'

'And haven't you heard her express a moral objection to it?'

'Well, I believe I have.'

'Did you ever get a letter from her, or see a letter of hers?'

'I don't remember; yes, I did once, a long time ago.'

'And wasn't she very resigned in it?'

'Well, I declare I believe she was; and it's very proper too; people ought to be resigned.'

'Oh, of course. And now doesn't she love a convert and hate a Puseyite?'

'All Irish clergyman's daughters do that.'

'Well, Fanny, you can't say but that it was a good portrait; and after that, will you pretend to say you call Miss O'Joscelyn your friend?'

'Not my very friend of friends; but, as friends go, she's as good as most others.'

'And who is the friend of friends, Fanny?'

'Come, you're not my father confessor. I'm not to tell you all. If I told you that, you'd make another portrait.'

'I'm sure I couldn't draw a disparaging picture of anybody you would really call your friend. But indeed I pity you, living among so many such people. There can be nobody here who understands you.'

'Oh, I'm not very unintelligible.'

'Much more so than Miss O'Joscelyn. I shouldn't wish to have to draw your portrait.'

'Pray don't; if it were frightful I should think you uncivil; and if you made it handsome, I should know you were flattering. Besides, you don't know enough of me to tell me my character.'

'I think I do; but I'll study it a little more before I put it on the canvass. Some likenesses are very hard to catch.'

Fanny felt, when she went to bed, that she had
spent a pleasanter evening than she usually did, and
that it was a much less nuisance to talk to her cousin
Adolphus than to either his father, mother, or sister;
and as she sat before her fire, while her maid was
brushing her hair, she began to think that she had
mistaken his character, and that he couldn't be the
hard, sensual, selfish man for which she had taken
him. Her ideas naturally fell back to Frank and her
love, her difficulties and sorrows; and, before she
went to sleep, she had almost taught herself to think
that she might make Lord Kilcullen the means of
bringing Lord Ballindine back to Grey Abbey.

She had, to be sure, been told that her cousin had
spoken ill of Frank; that it was he who had been
foremost in decrying Lord Ballindine's folly and
extravagance; but she had never heard him do so;
she had only heard of it through Lord Cashel; and
she quite ceased to believe anything her guardian
might say respecting her discarded lover. At any
rate she would try. Some step she was determined to
take about Lord Ballindine; and, if her cousin
refused to act like a cousin and a friend, she would
only be exactly where she was before.

XXXI

THE TWO FRIENDS

THE next three days passed slowly and tediously
for most of the guests assembled at Grey Abbey.
Captain Cokely, and a Mr. Battersby, came over from
Newbridge barracks, but they did not add much to
the general enjoyment of the party, though their
arrival was hailed with delight by some of the young
ladies. At any rate they made the rooms look less
forlorn in the evenings, and made it worth the girls'
while to put on their best bibs and tuckers.

'But what's the use of it at all?' said Matilda
Fitzgerald to little Letty O'Joscelyn, when she had
spent three-quarters of an hour in adjusting her

curls, and setting her flounces properly, on the evening before the arrival of the two cavalry officers; 'not
a soul to look at us but a crusty old colonel, a musty
old bishop, and a fusty old beau!'

'Who's the old beau?' said Letty.

'Why, that Mr. Tierney. I can't conceive how
Lady Cashel can have asked us to meet such a set,'
and Matilda descended, pouting, and out of humour.

But on the next day she went through her work
much more willingly, if not more carefully.

'That Captain Cokely's a very nice fellow,' said
Matilda; 'the best of that Newbridge set, out and
out.'

'Well now, I really think he's not so nice as Mr.
Battersby,' said Letty. 'I'm sure he's not so good-
looking.'

'Oh, Battersby's only a boy. After all, Letty, I
don't know whether I like officers so much better
than other men,'—and she twisted her neck round
to get a look at her back in the pier-glass, and gave
her dress a little pull just above her bustle.

'I'm sure I do,' said Letty; 'they've so much more
to say for themselves, and they're so much smarter.'

'Why, yes, they are smarter,' said Matilda; 'and
there's nothing on earth so dowdy as an old black
coat. But, then, officers are always going away: you
no sooner get to know one or two of a set, and to feel
that one of them is really a darling fellow, but there,
they are off—to Jamaica, China, Hounslow barracks,
or somewhere; and then it's all to do over again.'

'Well, I do wish they wouldn't move them about
quite so much.'

'But let's go down. I think I'll do now, won't I?'
and they descended, to begin the evening campaign.

'Wasn't Miss Wyndham engaged to some one?'
said old Mrs. Ellison to Mrs. Moore. 'I'm sure some
one told me so.'

'Oh, yes, she was,' said Mrs. Moore; 'the affair
was settled, and everything arranged; but the man
was very poor, and a gambler,—Lord Ballindine: he

has the name of a property down in Mayo somewhere; but when she got all her brother's money, Lord Cashel thought it a pity to sacrifice it,—so he got her out of the scrape. A very good thing for the poor girl, for they say he's a desperate scamp.'

'Well, I declare I think,' said Mrs. Ellison, 'she'll not have far to look for another.'

'What, you think there's something between her and Lord Kilcullen?' said Mrs. Moore.

'It*looks like it, at any rate, don't it?' said Mrs. Ellison.

'Well, I really think it does,' said Mrs. Moore; 'I'm sure I'd be very glad of it. I know he wants money desperately, and it would be such a capital thing for the earl.'

'At any rate, the lady does not look a bit un-willing,' said Mrs. Ellison. 'I suppose she's fond of rakish young men. You say Lord Ballindine was of that set; and I'm sure Lord Kilcullen's the same, —he has the reputation, at any rate. They say he and his father never speak, except just in public, to avoid the show of the thing.'

And the two old ladies set to work to a good dish of scandal.

'Miss Wyndham's an exceedingly fine girl,' said Captain Cokely to Mat Tierney, as they were playing a game of piquet in the little drawing-room.

'Yes,' said Mat; 'and she's a hundred thousand exceedingly fine charms too, independently of her fine face.'

'So I hear,' said Cokely; 'but I only believe half of what I hear about those things.'

'She has more than that; I know it.'

'Has she though? Faith, do you know I think Kilcullen has a mind to keep it in the family. He's very soft on her, and she's just as sweet to him. I shouldn't be surprised if he were to marry now, and turn steady.'

'Not at all; there are two reasons against it. In the first place, he's too much dipped for even Fanny's

fortune to be any good to him; and secondly, she's
engaged.'

'What, to Ballindine?' said Cokely.

'Exactly so,' said Mat.

'Ah, my dear fellow, that's all off long since. I
heard Kilcullen say so myself. I'll back Kilcullen to
marry her against Ballindine for a hundred pounds.'

'Done,' said Mat; and the bet was booked.

The same evening, Tierney wrote to Dot Blake,
and said in a postscript, 'I know you care for
Ballindine; so do I, but I don't write to him. If he
really wants to secure his turtle-dove, he should see
that she doesn't get bagged in his absence. Kilcullen
is here, and I tell you he's a keen sportsman. They
say it's quite up with him in London, and I should be
sorry she were sacrificed: she seems a nice girl.'

Lord Kilcullen had ample opportunities of for-
warding his intimacy with Fanny, and he did not
neglect them. To give him his due, he played his
cards as well as his father could wish him. He first of
all overcame the dislike with which she was prepared
to regard him; he then interested her about himself;
and, before he had been a week at Grey Abbey, she
felt that she had a sort of cousinly affection for him.
He got her to talk with a degree of interest about
himself; and when he could do that, there was no
wonder that Tierney should have fears for his friend's
interests. Not that there was any real occasion for
them. Fanny Wyndham was not the girl to be
talked out of, or into, a real passion, by anyone.

'Now, tell me the truth, Fanny,' said Kilcullen, as
they were sitting over the fire together in the library,
one dark afternoon, before they went to dress for
dinner; 'hadn't you been taught to look on me as a
kind of ogre—a monster of iniquity, who spoke nothing but oaths, and did nothing but sin?'

'Not exactly that: but I won't say I thought you
were exactly just what you ought to be.'

'But didn't you think I was exactly what I ought
not to have been? Didn't you imagine, now, that

I habitually sat up all night, gambling, and drinking buckets of champagne and brandy-and-water? And that I lay in bed all day, devising iniquity in my dreams? Come now, tell the truth, and shame the devil; if I am the devil, I know people have made me out to be.'

'Why, really, Adolphus, I never calculated how your days and nights were spent. But if I am to tell the truth, I fear some of them might have been passed to better advantage.'

'Which of us, Fanny, mightn't, with truth, say the same of ourselves?'

'Of course, none of us,' said Fanny; 'don't think I'm judging you; you asked me the question,—and I suppose you wanted an answer.'

'I did; I wanted a true one—for though you may never have given yourself much trouble to form an opinion about me, I am anxious that you should do so now. I don't want to trouble you with what is done and past; I don't want to make it appear that I have not been thoughtless and imprudent—wicked and iniquitous, if you are fond of strong terms; neither do I want to trouble you with confessing all my improprieties, that I may regularly receive absolution. But I do wish you to believe that I have done nothing which should exclude me from your future good opinion; from your friendship and esteem.'

'I am not of an unforgiving temperament, even had you done anything for me to forgive: but I am not aware that you have.'

'No; nothing for you to forgive, in the light of an offence to yourself; but much, perhaps, to prevent your being willing to regard me as a personal friend. We're not only first cousins, Fanny, but are placed more closely together than cousins usually are. You have neither father nor mother; now, also, you have no brother,' and he took her hands in his own as he said so. 'Who should be a brother to you, if I am not? who, at any rate, should you look on as a friend, if not on me? Nobody could be better, I believe, than Selina ; but she is stiff, and cold—unlike you in everything. I should be so happy if I could be the friend—the friend of friends you spoke of the other evening; if I could fill the place which must be empty near your heart. I can never be this to you, if you believe that anything in my past life has been really disgraceful. It is for this reason that I want to know what you truly think of me. I won't deny that I am anxious you should think well of me:—well, at any rate for the present, and the future, and charitably as regards the past.'

Fanny had been taken much by surprise by the turn her cousin had given to the conversation ; and was so much affected, that, before he had finished, she was in tears. She had taken her hand out of his, to put her handkerchief to her eyes, and as she did not immediately answer, he continued:

' I shall probably be much here for some time to come—such, at least, are my present plans ; and I hope that while I am, we shall become friends: not such friends, Fanny, as you and Judith O'Joscelyn— friends only of circumstance, who have neither tastes, habits, or feelings in common—friends whose friendship consists in living in the same parish, and meeting each other once or twice a week ; but friends in reality—friends in confidence—friends in mutual dependence—friends in love—friends, dear Fanny, as cousins situated as we are should be to each other.'

Fanny's heart was very full, for she felt how much, how desperately, she wanted such a friend as Kilcullen described. How delightful it would be to have such a friend, and to find him in her own cousin! The whole family, hitherto, were so cold to her—so uncongenial. The earl she absolutely disliked ; she loved her aunt, but it was only because she was her aunt—she couldn't like her ; and though she loved Lady Selina, and, to a degree, admired her, it was like loving a marble figure. There was more true feeling in what Kilcullen had now said to her, than in all that had fallen from the whole family for the

four years she had lived at Grey Abbey, and she
could not therefore but close on the offer of his
affection.

'Shall we be such friends, then?' said he; 'or,
after all, am I too bad? Have I too much of the
taint of the wicked world to be the friend of so pure
a creature as you?'

'Oh no, Adolphus; I'm sure I never thought so,'
said she. 'I never judged you, and indeed I am not
disposed to do so now. I'm too much in want of
kindness to reject yours,—even were I disposed to do
so, which I am not.'

'Then, Fanny, we are to be friends—true, loving,
trusting friends?'

'Oh, yes!' said Fanny. 'I am really, truly grateful
for your affection and kindness. I know how precious
they are, and I will value them accordingly.'

Again Lord Kilcullen took her hand, and pressed
it in his; and then he kissed it, and told her she was
his own dear cousin Fanny; and then recommended
her to go and dress, which she did. He sat himself
down for a quarter of an hour, ruminating, and then
also went off to dress; but, during that quarter of an
hour, very different ideas passed through his mind,
than such as those who knew him best would have
given him credit for.

In the first place, he thought that he really began
to feel an affection for his cousin Fanny, and to
speculate whether it were absolutely within the
verge of possibility that he should marry her—
retrieve his circumstances—treat her well, and live
happily for the rest of his life as a respectable
nobleman.

For two or three minutes the illusion remained, till
it was banished by retrospection. It was certainly
possible that he should marry her: it was his full
intention to do so: but as to retrieving his circumstances and treating her well!—the first was absolutely impossible—the other nearly so; and as to his
living happily at Grey Abbey as a family man, he

yawned as he felt how impossible it would be that he should spend a month in such a way, let alone a life. But then Fanny Wyndham was so beautiful, so lively, so affectionate, so exactly what a cousin and a wife ought to be: he could not bear to think that all his protestations of friendship and love had been hypocritical; that he could only look upon her as a gudgeon, and himself as a bigger fish, determined to swallow her! Yet such must be his views regarding her. He departed to dress, absolutely troubled in his conscience.

And what were Fanny's thoughts about her cousin? She was much surprised and gratified, but at the same time somewhat flustered and overwhelmed, by the warmth and novelty of his affection. However, she never for a moment doubted his truth towards her, or had the slightest suspicion of his real object. Her chief thought was whether she could induce him to be a mediator for her, between Lord Cashel and Lord Ballindine.

During the next two days he spoke to her a good deal about her brother—of whom, by-the-bye, he had really known nothing. He contrived, however, to praise him as a young man of much spirit and great promise; then he spoke of her own large fortune, asked her what her wishes were about its investment, and told her how happy he would be to express those wishes at once to Lord Cashel, and to see that they were carried out. Once or twice she had gradually attempted to lead the conversation to Lord Ballindine, but Kilcullen was too crafty, and had prevented her; and she had not yet sufficient courage to tell him at once what was so near her heart.

'Fanny,' said Lady Selina, one morning, about a week after the general arrival of the company at Grey Abbey, and when some of them had taken their departure, 'I am very glad to see you have recovered your spirits: I know you have made a great effort, and I appreciate and admire it.'

'Indeed, Selina, I fear you are admiring me too soon. I own I have been amused this week past, and, to a certain degree, pleased; but I fear you'll find I shall relapse. There's been no radical reform; my thoughts are all in the same direction as they were.'

'But the great trial in this world is to behave well and becomingly in spite of oppressive thoughts: and it always takes a struggle to do that, and that struggle you've made. I hope it may lead you to feel that you may be contented and in comfort without having everything which you think necessary to your happiness. I'm sure I looked forward to this week as one of unmixed trouble and torment; but I was very wrong to do so. It has given me a great deal of unmixed satisfaction.'

'I'm very glad of that, Selina, but what was it? I'm sure it could not have come from poor Mrs. Ellison, or the bishop's wife; and you seemed to me to spend all your time in talking to them. Virtue, they say, is its own reward: I don't know what other satisfaction you can have had from them.'

'In the first place, it has given me great pleasure to see that you were able to exert yourself in company, and that the crowd of people did not annoy you: but I have chiefly been delighted by seeing that you and Adolphus are such good friends. You must think, Fanny, that I am anxious about an only brother—especially when we have all had so much cause to be anxious about him; and don't you think it must be a delight to me to find that he is able to take pleasure in your society? I should be doubly pleased, doubly delighted, if I could please him myself. But I have not the vivacity to amuse him.'

'What nonsense, Selina! Don't say that.'

'But it's true, Fanny; I have not; and Grey Abbey has become distasteful to him because we are all sedate, steady people. Perhaps some would call us dull, and heavy; and I have grieved that it should be so, though I cannot alter my nature; but you are so much the contrary—there is so much in your character like his own, before he became fond of the world, that I feel he can become attached to and fond of you; and I am delighted to see that he thinks so himself. What do you think of him, now that you have seen more of him than you ever did before?'

'Indeed,' said Fanny, 'I like him very much.'

'He is very clever, isn't he? He might have been anything if he had given himself fair play. He seems to have taken greatly to you.'

'Oh yes; we are great friends:' and then Fanny paused—'so great friends,' she continued, looking somewhat gravely in Lady Selina's face, 'that I mean to ask the greatest favour of him that I could ask of anyone: one I am sure I little dreamed I should ever ask of him.'

'What is it, Fanny? Is it a secret?'

'Indeed it is, Selina; but it's a secret I will tell you. I mean to tell him all I feel about Lord Ballindine, and I mean to ask him to see him for me. Adolphus has offered to be a brother to me, and I mean to take him at his word.'

Lady Selina turned very pale, and looked very grave as she replied,

'That is not giving him a brother's work, Fanny. A brother should protect you from importunity and insult, from injury and wrong; and that, I am sure, Adolphus would do: but no brother would consent to offer your hand to a man who had neglected you and been refused, and who, in all probability, would now reject you with scorn if he has the opportunity—or if not that, will take you for your money's sake. That, Fanny, is not a brother's work; and it is an embassy which I am sure Adolphus will not undertake. If you take my advice you will not ask him.'

As Lady Selina finished speaking she walked to the door, as if determined to hear no reply from her cousin; but, as she was leaving the room, she fancied that she heard her sobbing, and her heart softened, and she again turned towards her and said, 'God knows, Fanny, I do not wish to be severe or ill-

natured to you; I would do anything for your comfort and happiness, but I cannot bear to think that
you should '—Lady Selina was puzzled for a word to
express her meaning—' that you should forget yourself,' and she attempted to put her arm round
Fanny's waist.

But she was mistaken; Fanny was not sobbing,
but was angry; and what Selina now said about her
forgetting herself, did not make her less so.

'No,' she said, withdrawing herself from her
cousin's embrace and standing erect, while her
bosom was swelling with indignation: 'I want no
affection from you, Selina, that is accompanied by
so much disapprobation. You don't wish to be
severe, only you say that I am likely to forget
myself. Forget myself!' and Fanny threw back her
beautiful head, and clenched her little fists by her
side: 'The other day you said "disgrace myself", and
I bore it calmly then; but I will not any longer bear
such imputations. I tell you plainly, Selina, I will
not forget myself, nor will I be forgotten. Nor will
I submit to whatever fate cold, unfeeling people may
doom me, merely because I am a woman and alone.
I will not give up Lord Ballindine, if I have to walk
to his door and tell him so. And were I to do so, I
should never think that I had forgotten myself.'

'Listen to me, Fanny,' said Selina.

'Wait a moment,' continued Fanny, 'I have
listened enough: it is my turn to speak now. For one
thing I have to thank you: you have dispelled the
idea that I could look for help to anyone in this
family. I will not ask your brother to do anything
for me which you think so disgraceful. I will not
subject him to the scorn with which you choose to
think my love will be treated by him who loved me so
well. That you should dare to tell me that he who
did so much for my love should now scorn it!—Oh,
Selina, that I may live to forget that you said those
words!' and Fanny, for a moment, put her handkerchief to her eyes—but it was but for a moment.

'However,' she continued, 'I will now act for myself. As you think I might forget myself, I tell you I will do it in no clandestine way. I will write to Lord Ballindine, and I will show my letter to my uncle. The whole house shall read it if they please. I will tell Lord Ballindine all the truth—and if Lord Cashel turns me from his house, I shall probably find some friend to receive me, who may still believe that I have not forgotten myself.' And Fanny Wyndham sailed out of the room.

Lady Selina, when she saw that she was gone, sat down on the sofa and took her book. She tried to make herself believe that she was going to read; but it was no use: the tears dimmed her eyes, and she put the book down.

The same evening the countess sent for Selina into her boudoir, and, with a fidgety mixture of delight and surprise, told her that she had a wonderful piece of good news to communicate to her.

'I declare, my dear,' she said, 'it's the most delightful thing I've heard for years and years; and it's just exactly what I had planned myself, only I never told anybody. Dear me; it makes me so happy!'

'What is it, mamma?'

'Your papa has been talking to me since dinner, my love, and he tells me Adolphus is going to marry Fanny Wyndham.'

'Going to marry whom?' said Lady Selina, almost with a shout.

'Fanny, I say: it's the most delightful match in the world: it's just what ought to be done. I suppose they won't have the wedding before summer; though May is a very nice month. Let me see; it only wants three weeks to May.'

'Mamma, what are you talking about?—you're dreaming.'

'Dreaming, my dear? I'm not dreaming at all: it's a fact. Who'd've thought of all this happening so soon, out of this party, which gave us so much trouble! However, I knew your father was right. I said all along that he was in the right to ask the people.'

'Mamma,' said Lady Selina, gravely, 'listen to me: calmly now, and attentively. I don't know what papa has told you; but I tell you Fanny does not dream of marrying Adolphus. He has never asked her, and if he did she would never accept him. Fanny is more than ever in love with Lord Ballindine.'

The countess opened her eyes wide, and looked up into her daughter's face, but said nothing.

'Tell me, mamma, as nearly as you can recollect, what it is papa has said to you, that, if possible, we may prevent mischief and misery. Papa couldn't have said that Fanny had accepted Adolphus?'

'He didn't say exactly that, my dear; but he said that it was his wish they should be married; that Adolphus was very eager for it, and that Fanny had received his attentions and admiration with evident pleasure and satisfaction. And so she has, my dear; you couldn't but have seen that yourself.'

'Well, mamma, what else did papa say?'

'Why, he said just what I'm telling you: that I wasn't to be surprised if we were called on to be ready for the wedding at a short notice; or at any rate to be ready to congratulate Fanny. He certainly didn't say she had accepted him. But he said he had no doubt about it; and I'm sure, from what was going on last week, I couldn't have any doubt either. But he told me not to speak to anyone about it yet; particularly not to Fanny; only, my dear, I couldn't help, you know, talking it over with you;' and the countess leaned back in her chair, very much exhausted with the history she had narrated.

'Now, mamma, listen to me. It is not many hours since Fanny told me she was unalterably determined to throw herself at Lord Ballindine's feet.'

'Goodness gracious me, how shocking!' said the countess.

'She even said that she would ask Adolphus to be

the means of bringing Lord Ballindine back to Grey Abbey.'

'Lord have mercy!' said the countess.

'I only tell you this, mamma, to show you how impossible it is that papa should be right.'

'What are we to do, my dear? Oh, dear, there'll be such a piece of work! What a nasty thing Fanny is. I'm sure she's been making love to Adolphus all the week!'

'No, mamma, she has not. Don't be unfair to Fanny. If there is anyone in fault it is Adolphus; but, as you say, what shall we do to prevent further misunderstanding? I think I had better tell papa the whole.'

And so she did, on the following morning. But she was too late; she did not do it till after Lord Kilcullen had offered and had been refused.

XXXII

HOW LORD KILCULLEN FARES IN HIS WOOING

ABOUT twelve o'clock the same night, Lord Kilcullen and Mat Tierney were playing billiards, and were just finishing their last game: the bed-candles were lighted ready for them, and Tierney was on the point of making the final hazard.

'So you're determined to go to-morrow, Mat?' said Kilcullen.

'Oh, yes, I'll go to-morrow: your mother'll take me for a second Paddy Rea, else,' said Mat.

'Who the deuce was Paddy Rea?'

'Didn't you ever hear of Paddy Rea?—Michael French of Clare Abbey—he's dead now, but he was alive enough at the time I'm telling you of, and kept the best house in county Clare—well, he was coming down on the Limerick coach, and met a deuced pleasant, good-looking, talkative sort of a fellow a-top of it. They dined and got a tumbler of punch together at Roscrea; and when French got down at

Bird Hill, he told his acquaintance that if he ever
found himself anywhere near Ennis, he'd be glad to
see him at Clare Abbey. He was a hospitable sort
of a fellow, and had got into a kind of way of saying
the same thing to everybody, without meaning anything except to be civil—just as I'd wish a man good
morning. Well, French thought no more about the
man, whose name he didn't even know; but about
a fortnight afterwards, a hack car from Ennis made
its appearance at Clare Abbey, and the talkative
traveller, and a small portmanteau, had soon found
their way into the hall. French was a good deal
annoyed, for he had some fashionables in the house,
but he couldn't turn the man out; so he asked his
name, and introduced Paddy Rea to the company.
How long do you think he stayed at Clare Abbey?'

'Heaven only knows!—Three months.'

'Seventeen years!' said Mat. 'They did everything to turn him out, and couldn't do it. It killed
old French; and at last his son pulled the house down,
and Paddy Rea went then, because there wasn't a
roof to cover him. Now I don't want to drive your
father to pull down this house, so I'll go to-morrow.'

'The place is so ugly, that if you could make him
do so, it would be an advantage; but I'm afraid the
plan wouldn't succeed, so I won't press you. But if
you go, I shan't remain long. If it was to save my
life and theirs, I can't get up small talk for the rector
and his curate.'

'Well, good night,' said Mat; and the two turned
off towards their bed-rooms.

As they passed from the billiard-room through the
hall, Lord Cashel shuffled out of his room, in his
slippers and dressing-gown.

'Kilcullen,' said he, with a great deal of unconcerned good humour affected in his tone, 'just give
me one moment—I've a word to say to you. Good-
night, Mr. Tierney, good-night; I'm sorry to hear
we're to lose you to-morrow.'

Lord Kilcullen shrugged his shoulders, winked at

his friend and then turned round and followed his
father.

'It's only one word, Kilcullen,' said the father,
who was afraid of angering or irritating his son, now
that he thought he was in so fair a way to obtain the
heiress and her fortune. 'I'll not detain you half a
minute;' and then he said in a whisper, 'take my
advice, Kilcullen, and strike when the iron's hot.'

'I don't quite understand you, my lord,' said his
son, affecting ignorance of his father's meaning.

'I mean, you can't stand better than you do with
Fanny: you've certainly played your cards admirably, and she's a charming girl, a very charming girl,
and I long to know that she's your own. Take my
advice and ask her at once.'

'My lord,' said the dutiful son, 'if I'm to carry on
this affair, I must be allowed to do it in my own way.
You, I dare say, have more experience than I can
boast, and if you choose to make the proposal yourself to Miss Wyndham on my behalf, I shall be
delighted to leave the matter in your hands; but in
that case, I shall choose to be absent from Grey
Abbey. If you wish me to do it, you must let me do
it when I please and how I please.'

'Oh, certainly, certainly, Kilcullen,' said the earl;
'I only want to point out that I think you'll gain
nothing by delay.'

'Very well, my lord. Good night.' And Lord
Kilcullen went to bed, and the father shuffled back
to his study. He had had three different letters that
day from Lord Kilcullen's creditors, all threatening
immediate arrest unless he would make himself
responsible for his son's debts. No wonder that he
was in a hurry, poor man!

And Lord Kilcullen, though he had spoken so
coolly on the subject, and had snubbed his father,
was equally in a hurry. He also received letters, and
threats, and warnings, and understood, even better
than his father did, the perils which awaited him.
He knew that he couldn't remain at Grey Abbey

another week; that in a day or two it wouldn't be safe for him to leave the house; and that his only chance was at once to obtain the promise of his cousin's hand, and then betake himself to some place of security, till he could make her fortune available.

When Fanny came into the breakfast-room next morning, he asked her to walk with him in the demesne after breakfast. During the whole of the previous evening she had sat silent and alone, pretending to read, although he had made two or three efforts to engage her in conversation. She could not, however, refuse to walk with him, nor could she quite forgive herself for wishing to do so. She felt that her sudden attachment for him was damped by what had passed between her and Lady Selina; but she knew, at the same time, that she was very unreasonable for quarrelling with one cousin for what another had said. She accepted his invitation, and shortly after breakfast went upstairs to get ready. It was a fine, bright, April morning, though the air was cold, and the ground somewhat damp; so she put on her boa and strong boots, and sallied forth with Lord Kilcullen; not exactly in a good humour, but still feeling that she could not justly be out of humour with him. At the same moment, Lady Selina knocked at her father's door, with the intention of explaining to him how impossible it was that Fanny should be persuaded to marry her brother. Poor Lord Cashel! his life, at that time, was certainly not a happy one.

The two cousins walked some way, nearly in silence. Fanny felt very little inclined to talk, and even Kilcullen, with all his knowledge of womankind —with all his assurance, had some difficulty in commencing what he had to get said and done that morning.

'So Grey Abbey will once more sink into its accustomed dulness,' said he. 'Cokely went yesterday, and Tierney and the Ellisons go to-day. Don't you dread it, Fanny?'

'Oh, I'm used to it: besides, I'm one of the com-
ponent elements of the dulness, you know. I'm a
portion of the thing itself: it's you that must feel it.'

'*I* feel it? I suppose I shall. But, as I told you
before, the physic to me was not nearly so nauseous
as the sugar. I'm at any rate glad to get rid of such
sweetmeats as the bishop and Mrs. Ellison;' and they
were both silent again for a while.

'But you're not a portion of the heaviness of Grey
Abbey, Fanny,' said he, referring to what she had
said. 'You're not an element of its dulness. I don't
say this in flattery—I trust nothing so vile as flattery
will ever take place between us; but you know yourself that your nature is intended for other things;
that you were not born to pass your life in such a
house as this, without society, without excitement,
without something to fill your mind. Fanny, you
can't be happy here, at Grey Abbey.'

Happy! thought Fanny to herself. No, indeed,
I'm not happy! She didn't say so, however; and
Kilcullen, after a little while, went on speaking.

'I'm sure you can't be comfortable here. You
don't feel it, I dare say, so intolerable as I do; but
still you have been out enough, enough in the world,
to feel strongly the everlasting do-nothingness of this
horrid place. I wonder what possesses my father,
that he does not go to London—for your sake if for no
one else's. It's not just of him to coop you up here.'

'Indeed it is, Adolphus,' said she. 'You mistake my
character. I'm not at all anxious for London parties
and gaiety. Stupid as you may think me, I'm quite
as well contented to stay here as I should be to go to
London.'

'Do you mean me to believe,' said Kilcullen, with
a gentle laugh, 'that you are contented to live and
die in single blessedness at Grey Abbey?—that your
ambition does not soar higher than the interchange
of worsted-work patterns with Miss O'Joscelyn?'

'I did not say so, Adolphus.'

'What is your ambition then? what kind and

style of life would you choose to live? Come,
Fanny, I wish I could get you to talk with me about
yourself. I wish I could teach you to believe how
anxious I am that your future life should be happy
and contented, and at the same time splendid and
noble, as it should be. I'm sure you must have
ambition. I have studied Lavater well enough to
know that such a head and face as yours never belonged to a mind that could satisfy itself with
worsted-work.'

'You are very severe on the poor worsted-work.'

'But am I not in the right?'

'Decidedly not. Lavater, and my head and face,
have misled you.'

'Nonsense, Fanny. Do you mean to tell me that
you have no aspiration for a kind of life different
from this you are leading?—If so, I am much disappointed in you; much, very much astray in my
judgment of your character.' Then he walked on a
few yards, looking on the ground, and said, 'Come,
Fanny, I am talking very earnestly to you, and you
answer me only in joke. You don't think me impertinent, do you, to talk about yourself?'

'Impertinent, Adolphus—of course I don't.'

'Why won't you talk to me then, in the spirit in
which I am talking to you? If you knew, Fanny, how
interested I am about you, how anxious that you
should be happy, how confidently I look forward to
the distinguished position I expect you to fill—if
you could guess how proud I mean to be of you, when
you are the cynosure of all eyes—the admired of all
admirers—admired not more for your beauty than
your talent—if I could make you believe, Fanny,
how much I expect from you, and how fully I trust
that my expectations will be realised, you would not,
at any rate, answer me lightly.'

'Adolphus,' said Fanny, 'I thought there was to be
no flattering between us?'

'And do you think I would flatter you? Do you
think I would stoop to flatter you? Oh! Fanny, you

don't understand me yet; you don't at all understand, how thoroughly from the heart I'm speaking—how much in earnest I am; and, so far from flattering you, I am quite as anxious to find fault with you as I am to praise you, could I feel that I had liberty to do so.'

'Pray do,' said Fanny: 'anything but flattery; for a friend never flatters.'

But Kilcullen had intended to flatter his fair cousin, and he had been successful. She was gratified and pleased by his warmth of affection. 'Pray do,' repeated Fanny; 'I have more faults than virtues to be told of, and so I'm afraid you'll find out, when you know me better.'

'To begin, then,' said Kilcullen, 'are you not wrong—but no, Fanny, I will not torment you now with a catalogue of faults. I did not ask you to come out with me for that object. You are now in grief for the death of poor Harry'—Fanny blushed as she reflected how much more poignant a sorrow weighed upon her heart—'and are therefore unable to exert yourself; but, as soon as you are able—when you have recovered from this severe blow, I trust you will not be content to loiter and dawdle away your existence at Grey Abbey.'

'Not the whole of it,' said Fanny.

'None of it,' replied her cousin. 'Every month, every day, should have its purpose. My father has got into a dull, heartless, apathetic mode of life, which suits my mother and Selina, but which will never suit you. Grey Abbey is like the Dead Sea, of which the waters are always bitter as well as stagnant. It makes me miserable, dearest Fanny, to see you stifled in such a pool. Your beauty, talents, and energies—your disposition to enjoy life, and power of making it enjoyable for others, are all thrown away. Oh, Fanny, if I could rescue you from this!'

'You are inventing imaginary evils,' said she; 'at any rate they are not palpable to my eyes.'

'That's it; that's just what I fear,' said the other, 'that time, habit, and endurance may teach you to think that nothing further is to be looked for in this world than vegetation at Grey Abbey, or some other place of the kind, to which you may be transplanted. I want to wake you from such a torpor; to save you from such ignominy. I wish to restore you to the world.'

'There's time enough, Adolphus; you'll see me yet the gayest of the gay at Almack's.'

'Ah! but to please me, Fanny, it must be as one of the leaders, not one of the led.'

'Oh, that'll be in years to come: in twenty years' time; when I come forth glorious in a jewelled turban, and yards upon yards of yellow satin—fat, fair, and forty. I've certainly no ambition to be one of the leaders yet.'

Lord Kilcullen walked on silent for a considerable time, during which Fanny went on talking about London, Almack's, and the miserable life of lady patronesses, till at last she also became silent, and began thinking of Lord Ballindine. She had, some little time since, fully made up her mind to open her heart to Lord Kilcullen about him, and she had as fully determined not to do so after what Selina had said upon the subject; but now she again wavered. His manner was so kind and affectionate, his interest in her future happiness appeared to be so true and unaffected: at any rate he would not speak harshly or cruelly to her, if she convinced him how completely her happiness depended on her being reconciled to Lord Ballindine. She had all but brought herself to the point; she had almost determined to tell him everything, when he stopped rather abruptly, and said,

'I also am leaving Grey Abbey again, Fanny.'

'Leaving Grey Abbey?' said Fanny. 'You told me the other day you were going to live here,'

'So I intended; so I do intend; but still I must leave it for a while. I'm going about business, and

I don't know how long I may be away. I go on Saturday.'

'I hope, Adolphus, you haven't quarrelled with your father,' said she.

'Oh, no,' said he: 'it is on his advice that I am going. I believe there is no fear of our quarrelling now. I should rather say I trust there is none. He not only approves of my going, but approves of what I am about to do before I go.'

'And what is that?'

'I had not intended, Fanny, to say what I have to say to you for some time, for I feel that different circumstances make it premature. But I cannot bring myself to leave you without doing so;' and again he paused and walked on a little way in silence —'and yet,' he continued, 'I hardly know how to utter what I wish to say; or rather what I would wish to have said, were it not that I dread so much the answer you may make me. Stop, Fanny, stop a moment; the seat is quite dry; sit down one moment.'

Fanny sat down in a little alcove which they had reached, considerably embarrassed and surprised. She had not, however, the most remote idea of what he was about to say to her. Had any other man in the world, almost, spoken to her in the same language, she would have expected an offer; but from the way in which she had always regarded her cousin, both heretofore, when she hardly knew him, and now, when she was on such affectionate terms with him, she would as soon have thought of receiving an offer from Lord Cashel as from his son.

'Fanny,' he said,' I told you before that I have my father's warmest and most entire approval for what I am now going to do. Should I be successful in what I ask, he will be delighted; but I have no words to tell you what my own feelings will be. Fanny, dearest Fanny,' and he sat down close beside her— 'I love you better—ah! how much better, than all the world holds beside. Dearest, dearest Fanny, will you, can you, return my love?'

'Adolphus,' said Fanny, rising suddenly from her seat, more for the sake of turning round so as to look at him, than with the object of getting from him, 'Adolphus, you are joking with me.'

'No, by heavens then,' said he, following her, and catching her hand; 'no man in Ireland is this moment more in earnest: no man more anxiously, painfully in earnest. Oh, Fanny! why should you suppose that I am not so? How can you think I would joke on such a subject? No: hear me,' he said, interrupting her, as she prepared to answer him, 'hear me out, and then you will know how truly I am in earnest.'

'No, not a word further!' almost shrieked Fanny —'Not a word more, Adolphus—not a syllable; at any rate till you have heard me. Oh, you have made me so miserable!' and Fanny burst into tears.

' I have spoken too suddenly to you, Fanny; I should have given you more time—I should have waited till—'

'No, no, no,' said Fanny, 'it is not that—but yes; what you say is true: had you waited but one hour— but ten minutes—I should have told you that which would for ever have prevented all this. I should have told you, Adolphus, how dearly, how unutterably I love another.' And Fanny again sat down, hid her face in her handkerchief against the corner of the summer-house, and sobbed and cried as though she were broken-hearted: during which time Kilcullen stood by, rather perplexed as to what he was to say next, and beginning to be very doubtful as to his ultimate success.

'Dear Fanny!' he said, 'for both our sakes, pray try to be collected: all my future happiness is at this moment at stake. I did not bring you here to listen to what I have told you, without having become too painfully sure that your hand, your heart, your love, are necessary to my happiness. All my hopes are now at stake; but I would not, if I could, secure my own happiness at the expense of yours. Pray believe me, Fanny, when I say that I love you completely, unalterably, devotedly: it is necessary now for my

own sake that I should say as much as that. Having
told you so much of my own heart, let me hear what
you wish to tell me of yours. Oh, that I might have
the most distant gleam of hope, that it would ever
return the love which fills my own!'

'It cannot, Adolphus—it never can,' said she, still
trying to hide her tears. 'Oh, why should this bitter
misery have been added!' She then rose quickly
from her seat, wiped her eyes, and, pushing back her
hair, continued, 'I will no longer continue to live
such a life as I have done—miserable to myself, and
the cause of misery to others. Adolphus,—I love
Lord Ballindine. I love him with, I believe, as true
and devoted a love as woman ever felt for a man. I
valued, appreciated, gloried in your friendship; but
I can never return your love. My heart is wholly,
utterly, given away; and I would not for worlds receive it back, till I learn from his own mouth that he
has ceased to love me.'

'Oh, Fanny! my poor Fanny!' said Kilcullen; 'if
such is the case, you are really to be pitied. If this
be true, your condition is nearly as unhappy as my
own.'

'I am unhappy, very unhappy in your love,' said
Fanny, drawing herself up proudly; 'but not unhappy in my own. My misery is that I should be the
cause of trouble and unhappiness to others. I have
nothing to regret in my own choice.'

'You are harsh, Fanny. It may be well that you
should be decided, but it cannot become you also to
be unfeeling. I have offered to you all that a man
can offer; my name, my fortune, my life, my heart;
though you may refuse me, you have no right to be
offended with me.'

'Oh, Adolphus!' said she, now in her turn offering
him her hand: 'pray forgive me: pray do not be
angry. Heaven knows I feel no offence: and how
strongly, how sincerely, I feel the compliment you
have offered me. But I want you to see how vain it
would be in me to leave you—leave you in any doubt.

I only spoke as I did to show you I could not think twice, when my heart was given to one whom I so entirely love, respect—and—and approve.'

Lord Kilcullen's face became thoughtful, and his brow grew black: he stood for some time irresolute what to say or do.

'Let us walk on, Fanny, for this is cold and damp,' he said, at last.

'Let us go back to the house, then.'

'As you like, Fanny. Oh, how painful all this is! how doubly-painful to know that my own love is hopeless, and that yours is no less so. Did you not refuse Lord Ballindine?'

'If I did, is it not sufficient that I tell you I love him? If he were gone past all redemption, you would not have me encourage you while I love another?'

'I never dreamed of this! What, Fanny, what are your hopes? what is it you wish or intend? Supposing me, as I wish I were, fathoms deep below the earth, what would you do? You cannot marry Lord Ballindine.'

'Then I will marry no one,' said Fanny, striving hard to suppress her tears, and barely succeeding.

'Good heavens!' exclaimed Kilcullen; 'what an infatuation is this!'—and then again he walked on silent a little way. 'Have you told any one of this, Fanny?—do they know of it at Grey Abbey? Come, Fanny, speak to me: forget, if you will, that I would be your lover: remember me only as your cousin and your friend, and speak to me openly. Do they know that you have repented of the refusal you gave Lord Ballindine?'

'They all know that I love him: your father, your mother, and Selina.'

'You don't say my father?'

'Yes,' said Fanny, stopping on the path, and speaking with energy, as she confronted her cousin. 'Yes, Lord Cashel. He, above all others, knows it. I have told him so almost on my knees. I have im

plored him, as a child may implore her father, to
bring back to me the only man I ever loved. I have
besought him not to sacrifice me. Oh! how I have
implored him to spare me the dreadful punishment
of my own folly—wretchedness rather—in rejecting
the man I loved. But he has not listened to me; he
will never listen to me, and I will never ask again.
He shall find that I am not a tree or a stone, to be
planted or placed as he chooses. I will not again be
subjected to what I have to-day suffered. I will not
—I will not—' But Fanny was out of breath; and
could not complete the catalogue of what she would
not do.

'And did you intend to tell me all this, had I not
spoken to you as I have done?' said Kilcullen.

'I did,' said she. 'I was on the point of telling you
everything: twice I had intended to do so. I intended to implore you, as you loved me as your
cousin, to use your exertions to reconcile my uncle
and Lord Ballindine—and now instead of that—'

'You find I love you too well myself?'

'Oh, forget, Adolphus, forget that the words ever
passed your lips. You have not loved me long, and
therefore will not continue to love me, when you
know I never can be yours: forget your short-lived
love; won't you, Adolphus?'—and she put her
clasped hands upon his breast—'forget,—let us both
forget that the words were ever spoken. Be still my
cousin, my friend, my brother; and we shall still
both be happy.'

Different feelings were disturbing Lord Kilcullen's
breast—different from each other, and some of them
very different from those which usually found a place
there. He had sought Fanny's hand not only with
most sordid, but also with most dishonest views: he
not only intended to marry her for her fortune, but
also to rob her of her money; to defraud her, that he
might enable himself once more to enter the world of
pleasure, with the slight encumbrance of a wretched
wife. But, in carrying out his plan, he had disturbed

it by his own weakness: he had absolutely allowed
himself to fall in love with his cousin; and when, as
he had just done, he offered her his hand, he was
quite as anxious that she should accept him for her
own sake as for that of her money. He had taught
himself to believe that she would accept him, and
many misgivings had haunted him as to the ruined
state to which he should bring her as his wife. But
these feelings, though strong enough to disturb him,
were not strong enough to make him pause: he tried
to persuade himself that he could yet make her
happy, and hurried on to the consummation of his
hopes. He now felt strongly tempted to act a
generous part; to give her up, and to bring Lord
Ballindine back to her feet; to deserve at any rate
well of her, and leave all other things to chance.
But Lord Kilcullen was not accustomed to make
such sacrifices: he had never learned to disregard
himself; and again and again he turned it over in his
mind—'how could he get her fortune?—was there
any way left in which he might be successful?'

'This is child's play, Fanny,' he said. 'You may
reject me: to that I have nothing further to say, for
I am but an indifferent wooer; but you can never
marry Lord Ballindine.'

'Oh, Adolphus, for mercy's sake don't say so!'

'But I do say so, Fanny. God knows, not to
wound you, or for any unworthy purpose, but because it is so. He was your lover, and you sent him
away; you cannot whistle him back as you would
a dog.'

Fanny made no answer to this, but walked on
towards the house, anxious to find herself alone in
her own room, that she might compose her mind and
think over all that she had heard and said; nor did Lord
Kilcullen renew the conversation till he got to the
house. He could not determine what to do. Under
other circumstances it might, he felt, have been wise
for him to wait till time had weakened Fanny's
regret for her lost lover; but in his case this was

impracticable; if he waited anywhere it would be in the Queen's Bench. And yet, he could not but feel that, at present, it was hopeless for him to push his suit.

They reached the steps together, and as he opened the front door, Fanny turned round to wish him good morning, as she was hurrying in; but he stopped her, and said,

'One word more, Fanny, before we part. You must not refuse me; nor must we part in this way. Step in here; I will not keep you a minute;' and he took her into a room off the hall—'Do not let us be children, Fanny; do not let us deceive each other, or ourselves: do not let us persist in being irrational if we ourselves see that we are so;' and he paused for a reply.

'Well, Adolphus?' was all she said.

'If I could avoid it,' continued he, 'I would not hurt your feelings; but you must see, you must know, that you cannot marry Lord Ballindine.'—Fanny, who was now sitting, bit her lips and clenched her hands, but she said nothing. 'If this is so—if you feel that so far your fate is fixed, are you mad enough to give yourself up to a vain and wicked passion—for wicked it will be? Will you not rather strive to forget him who has forgotten you?'

'That is not true,' interposed Fanny.

'His conduct, unfortunately, proves that it is too true,' continued Kilcullen. 'He has forgotten you, and you cannot blame him that he should do so, now that you have rejected him; but he neglected you even before you did so. Is it wise, is it decorous, is it maidenly in you, to indulge any longer in so vain a passion? Think of this, Fanny. As to myself, Heaven knows with what perfect truth, with what true love, I offered you, this morning, all that a man can offer: how ardently I hoped for an answer different from that you have now given me. You cannot give me your heart now; love cannot, at a moment, be transferred. But think, Fanny, think whether it is not better for you to accept an offer which your friends will all approve, and which I trust will never make you unhappy, than to give yourself up to a lasting regret,—to tears, misery, and grief.'

'And would you take my hand without my heart?' said she.

'Not for worlds,' replied the other, 'were I not certain that your heart would follow your hand. Whoever may be your husband, you will love him. But ask my mother, talk to her, ask her advice; she at any rate will only tell you that which must be best for your own happiness. Go to her, Fanny; if her advice be different from mine, I will not say a word farther to urge my suit.'

'I will go to no one,' said Fanny, rising. 'I have gone to too many with a piteous story on my lips. I have no friend, now, in this house. I had still hoped to find one in you, but that hope is over. I am, of course, proud of the honour your declaration has conveyed; but I should be wicked indeed if I did not make you perfectly understand that it is one which I cannot accept. Whatever may be your views, your ideas, I will never marry unless I thoroughly love, and feel that I am thoroughly loved by my future husband. Had you not made this ill-timed declaration—had you not even persisted in repeating it after I had opened my whole heart to you, I could have loved and cherished you as a brother; under no circumstances could I ever have accepted you as a husband. Good morning.' And she left him alone, feeling that he could have but little chance of success, should he again renew the attempt.

He did not see her again till dinner-time, when she appeared silent and reserved, but still collected and at her ease; nor did he speak to her at dinner or during the evening, till the moment the ladies were retiring for the night. He then came up to her as she was standing alone turning over some things on a side-table, and said, 'Fanny, I probably leave Grey

Abbey to-morrow. I will say good bye to you to-night.'

'Good bye, Adolphus; may we both be happier when next we meet,' said she.

'My happiness, I fear, is doubtful: but I will not speak of that now. If I can do anything for yours before I go, I will. Fanny, I will ask my father to invite Lord Ballindine here. He has been anxious that we should be married: when I tell him that that is impossible, he may perhaps be induced to do so.'

'Do that,' said Fanny, 'and you will be a friend to me. Do that, and you will be more than a brother to me.'

'I will; and in doing so I shall crush every hope that I have had left in me.'

'Do not say so, Adolphus:—do not—'

'You'll understand what I mean in a short time. I cannot explain everything to you now. But this will I do; I will make Lord Cashel understand that we never can be more to each other than we are now, and I will advise him to seek a reconciliation with Lord Ballindine. And now, good bye,' and he held out his hand.

'But I shall see you to-morrow.'

'Probably not; and if you do, it will be but for a moment, when I shall have other adieux to make.'

'Good bye, then, Adolphus; and may God bless you; and may we yet live to have many happy days together,' and she shook hands with him, and went to her room.

XXXIII

LORD KILCULLEN MAKES ANOTHER VISIT TO THE BOOK-ROOM

LORD CASHEL'S plans were certainly not lucky. It was not that sufficient care was not used in laying them, nor sufficient caution displayed in maturing them. He passed his time in care and caution; he spared no pains in seeing that the whole machinery was right; he was indefatigable in

deliberation, diligent in manœuvring, constant in attention. But, somehow, he was unlucky; his schemes
were never successful. In the present instance he
was peculiarly unfortunate, for everything went
wrong with him. He had got rid of an obnoxious
lover, he had coaxed over his son, he had spent an
immensity of money, he had undergone worlds of
trouble and self-restraint;—and then, when he really
began to think that his ward's fortune would com-
pensate him for this, his own family came to him, one
after another, to assure him that he was completely
mistaken—that it was utterly impossible—that such
a thing as a family marriage between the two cousins
could never take place, and indeed, ought not to be
thought of.

Lady Selina gave him the first check. On the morning on which Lord Kilcullen made his offer, she paid
her father a solemn visit in his book-room, and told
him exactly what she had before told her mother;
assured him that Fanny could not be induced, at any
rate at present, to receive her cousin as her lover;·
whispered to him, with unfeigned sorrow and shame,
that Fanny was still madly in love with Lord Ballindine; and begged him to induce her brother to postpone his offer, at any rate for some months.

'I hate Lord Ballindine's very name,' said the
earl, petulant with irritation.

'We none of us approve of him, papa: we don't
think of supposing that he could now be a fitting
husband for Fanny, or that they could possibly ever
be married. Of course it's not to be thought of. But
if you would advise Adolphus not to be premature,
he might, in the end, be more successful.'

'Kilcullen has made his own bed and he must lie
in it; I won't interfere between them,' said the angry
father.

'But if you were only to recommend delay,' suggested the daughter; 'a few months' delay; think
how short a time Harry Wyndham has been dead!'

Lord Cashel knew that delay was death in this

case, so he pished, and hummed, and hawed; quite lost the dignity on which he piqued himself, and ended by declaring that he would not interfere; that they might do as they liked; that young people would not be guided, and that he would not make himself unhappy about them. And so, Lady Selina, crestfallen and disappointed, went away.

Then, Lady Cashel, reflecting on what her daughter had told her, and yet anxious that the marriage should, if possible, take place at some time or other, sent Griffiths down to her lord, with a message—'Would his lordship be kind enough to step up-stairs to her ladyship?' Lord Cashel went up, and again had all the difficulties of the case opened out before him.

'But you see,' said her ladyship, 'poor Fanny—she's become so unreasonable—I don't know what's come to her—I'm sure I do everything I can to make her happy: but I suppose if she don't like to marry, nobody can make her.'

'Make her?—who's talking of making her?' said the earl.

'No, of course not,' continued the countess; 'that's just what Selina says; no one can make her do anything, she's got so obstinate, of late: but it's all that horrid Lord Ballindine, and those odious horses. I'm sure I don't know what business gentlemen have to have horses at all; there's never any good comes of it. There's Adolphus—he's had the good sense to get rid of his, and yet Fanny's so foolish, she'd sooner have that other horrid man—and I'm sure he's not half so good-looking, nor a quarter so agreeable as Adolphus.'

All these encomiums on his son, and animadversions on Lord Ballindine, were not calculated to put the earl into a good humour; he was heartily sick of the subject; thoroughly repented that he had not allowed his son to ruin himself in his own way; detested the very name of Lord Ballindine; and felt no very strong affection for his poor innocent ward. He accordingly made his wife nearly the same answer he had made his daughter, and left her anything but comforted by the visit.

It was about eleven o'clock on the same evening, that Lord Kilcullen, after parting with Fanny, opened the book-room door. He had been quite sincere in what he had told her. He had made up his mind entirely to give over all hopes of marrying her himself, and to tell his father that the field was again open for Lord Ballindine, as far as he was concerned.

There is no doubt that he would not have been noble enough to do this, had he thought he had himself any chance of being successful; but still there was something chivalrous in his resolve, something magnanimous in his determination to do all he could for the happiness of her he really loved, when everything in his own prospects was gloomy, dark, and desperate. As he entered his father's room, feeling that it would probably be very long before he should be closeted with him again, he determined that he would not quietly bear reproaches, and even felt a source of satisfaction in the prospect of telling his father that their joint plans were overturned—their schemes completely at an end.

'I'm disturbing you, my lord, I'm afraid,' said the son, walking into the room, not at all with the manner of one who had any hesitation at causing the disturbance.

'Who's that?' said the earl—'Adolphus?—no— yes. That is, I'm just going to bed; what is it you want?' The earl had been dozing after all the vexations of the day.

'To tell the truth, my lord, I've a good deal that I wish to say: will it trouble you to listen to me?'

'Won't to-morrow morning do?'

'I shall leave Grey Abbey early to-morrow, my lord; immediately after breakfast.'

'Good heavens, Kilcullen! what do you mean? You're not going to run off to London again?'

'A little farther than that, I'm afraid, will be necessary,' said the son. 'I have offered to Miss

Wyndham—have been refused—and, having finished my business at Grey Abbey, your lordship will probably think that in leaving it I shall be acting with discretion.'

'You have offered to Fanny and been refused!'

'Indeed I have; finally and peremptorily refused. Not only that: I have pledged my word to my cousin that I will never renew my suit.'

The earl sat speechless in his chair—so much worse was this catastrophe even than his expectations. Lord Kilcullen continued.

'I hope, at any rate, you are satisfied with me. I have not only implicitly obeyed your directions, but I have done everything in my power to accomplish what you wished. Had my marriage with my cousin been a project of my own, I could not have done more for its accomplishment. Miss Wyndham's affections are engaged; and she will never, I am sure, marry one man while she loves another.'

'Loves another—psha!' roared the earl. 'Is this to be the end of it all? After your promises to me—after your engagement! After such an engagement, sir, you come to me and talk about a girl loving another? Loving another! Will her loving another pay your debts?'

'Exactly the reverse, my lord,' said the son. 'I fear it will materially postpone their payment.'

'Well, sir,' said the earl. He did not exactly know how to commence the thunder of indignation with which he intended to annihilate his son, for certainly Kilcullen had done the best in his power to complete the bargain. But still the storm could not be stayed, unreasonable as it might be for the earl to be tempestuous on the occasion. 'Well, sir,' and he stood up from his chair, to face his victim, who was still standing—and, thrusting his hands into his trowsers' pockets, frowned awfully—'Well, sir; am I to be any further favoured with your plans?'

'I have none, my lord,' said Kilcullen; 'I am again ready to listen to yours.'

'My plans?—I have no further plans to offer for you. You are ruined, utterly ruined: you have done your best to ruin me and your mother; I have pointed out to you, I arranged for you, the only way in which your affairs could be redeemed; I made every thing easy for you.'

'No, my lord: you could not make it easy for me to get my cousin's love.'

'Don't contradict me, sir. I say I did. I made every thing straight and easy for you: and now you come to me with a whining story about a girl's love! What's her love to me, sir? Where am I to get my thirty thousand pounds, sir?—and my note of hand is passed for as much more, at this time twelve-month! Where am I to raise that, sir? Do you remember that you have engaged to repay me these sums?—do you remember that, or have such trifles escaped your recollection?'

'I remember perfectly well, my lord, that if I married my cousin, you were to repay yourself those sums out of her fortune. But I also remember, and so must you, that I beforehand warned you that I thought she would refuse me.'

'Refuse you,' said the earl, with a contortion of his nose and lips intended to convey unutterable scorn; 'of course she refused you, when you asked her as a child would ask for an apple, or a cake! What else could you expect?'

'I hardly think your lordship knows—'

'Don't you hardly think?—then I do know; and know well too. I know you have deceived me, grossly deceived me—induced me to give you money—to incur debts, with which I never would have burdened myself had I not believed you were sincere in your promise. But you have deceived me, sir—taken me in; for by heaven it's no better!—it's no better than downright swindling—and that from a son to his father! But it's for the last time; not a penny more do you get from me: you can ruin the property; indeed, I believe you have; but, for your mother's and sister's sake, I'll keep till I die what little you have left me.'

Lord Cashel had worked himself up into a perfect frenzy, and was stamping about the room as he uttered this speech; but, as he came to the end of it, he threw himself into his chair again, and buried his face in his hands.

Lord Kilcullen was standing with his back resting against the mantel-piece, with a look of feigned indifference on his face, which he tried hard to maintain. But his brow became clouded, and he bit his lips when his father accused him of swindling; and he was just about to break forth into a torrent of recrimination, when Lord Cashel turned off into a pathetic strain, and Kilcullen thought it better to leave him there.

'What I'm to do, I don't know; what I am to do, I do not know!' said the earl, beating the table with one hand, and hiding his face with the other. 'Sixty thousand pounds in one year; and that after so many drains!—And there's only my own life—there's only my own life!'—and then there was a pause for four or five minutes, during which Lord Kilcullen took snuff, poked the fire, and then picked up a newspaper, as though he were going to read it. This last was too much for the father, and he again roared out, 'Well, sir, what are you standing there for? If you've nothing else to say; why don't you go? I've done with you—you can not get more out of me, I promise you!'

'I've a good deal to say before I go, my lord,' said Kilcullen. 'I was waiting till you were disposed to listen to me. I've a good deal to say, indeed, which you must hear; and I trust, therefore, you will endeavour to be cool, whatever your opinions may be about my conduct.'

'Cool?—no, sir, I will not be cool. You're too cool yourself!'

'Cool enough for both, you think, my lord.'

'Kilcullen,' said the earl, 'you've neither heart nor principle: you have done your worst to ruin me, and now you come to insult me in my own room. Say what you want to say, and then leave me.'

'As to insulting language, my lord, I think you need not complain, when you remember that you have just called me a swindler, because I have been unable to accomplish your wish and my own, by marrying my cousin. However, I will let that pass. I have done the best I could to gain that object. I did more than either of us thought it possible that I should do, when I consented to attempt it. I offered her my hand, and assured her of my affection, without falsehood or hypocrisy. My bargain was that I should offer to her. I have done more than that, for I have loved her. I have, however, been refused, and in such a manner as to convince me that it would be useless for me to renew my suit. If your lordship will allow me to advise you on such a subject, I would suggest that you make no further objection to Fanny's union with Lord Ballindine. For marry him she certainly will.'

'What, sir?' again shouted Lord Cashel.

'I trust Fanny will receive no further annoyance on the subject. She has convinced me that her own mind is thoroughly made up; and she is not the person to change her mind on such a subject.'

'And haven't you enough on hand in your own troubles, but what you must lecture me about my ward?—Is it for that you have come to torment me at this hour? Had not you better at once become her guardian yourself, sir, and manage the matter in your own way?'

'I promised Fanny I would say as much to you. I will not again mention her name unless you press me to do so.'

'That's very kind,' said the earl.

'And now, about myself. I think your lordship will agree with me that it is better that I should at once leave Grey Abbey, when I tell you that, if I remain here, I shall certainly be arrested before the week is over, if I am found outside the house. I do

not wish to have bailiffs knocking at your lordship's
door, and your servants instructed to deny me.'

'Upon my soul, you are too good.'

'At any rate,' said Kilcullen, 'you'll agree with me
that this is no place for me to remain in.'

'You're quite at liberty to go,' said the earl.
'You were never very ceremonious with regard to
me; pray don't begin to be so now. Pray go—to-
night if you like. Your mother's heart will be broken,
that's all.'

'I trust my mother will be able to copy your lordship's indifference.'

'Indifference! *Is* sixty thousand pounds in one
year, and more than double within three or four,
indifference? I have paid too much to be indifferent.
But it is hopeless to pay more. I have no hope for
you; you are ruined, and I couldn't redeem you even
if I would. I could not set you free and tell you to
begin again, even were it wise to do so; and therefore
I tell you to go. And now, good night; I have not
another word to say to you,' and the earl got up as if
to leave the room.

'Stop, my lord, you must listen to me,' said
Kilcullen.

'Not a word further. I have heard enough;' and
he put out the candles on the book-room table, having lighted a bed candle which he held in his hand.

'Pardon me, my lord,' continued the son, standing
just before his father, so as to prevent his leaving the
room; 'pardon me, but you must listen to what I
have to say.'

'Not another word—not another word. Leave the
door, sir, or I will ring for the servants to open it.'

'Do so,' said Kilcullen, 'and they also shall hear
what I have to say. I am going to leave you to-
morrow, perhaps for ever; and you will not listen to
the last word I wish to speak to you?'

'I'll stay five minutes,' said the earl, taking out his
watch, 'and then I'll go; and if you attempt again
to stop me, I'll ring the bell for the servants.'

'Thank you, my lord, for the five minutes; it will be time enough. I purpose leaving Grey Abbey to-morrow, and I shall probably be in France in three days' time. When there, I trust I shall cease to trouble you; but I cannot, indeed I will not go, without funds to last me till I can make some arrangement. Your lordship must give me five hundred pounds. I have not the means even of carrying myself from hence to Calais.'

'Not one penny. Not one penny—if it were to save you from the gaol to-morrow! This is too bad!' and the earl again walked to the door, against which Lord Kilcullen leaned his back. 'By Heaven, sir, I'll raise the house if you think to frighten me by violence!'

'I'll use no violence, but you must hear the alternative: if you please it, the whole house shall hear it too. If you persist in refusing the small sum I now ask—'

'I will not give you one penny to save you from gaol. Is that plain?'

'Perfectly plain, and very easy to believe. But you will give more than a penny; you would even give more than I ask, to save yourself from the annoyance you will have to undergo.'

'Not on any account will I give you one single farthing.'

'Very well. Then I have only to tell you what I must do. Of course, I shall remain here. You cannot turn me out of your house, or refuse me a seat at your table.'

'By Heavens, though, I both can and will!'

'You cannot, my lord. If you think of it, you'll find you cannot, without much disagreeable trouble. An eldest son would be a very difficult tenant to eject summarily: and of my own accord I will not go without the money I ask.'

'By heavens, this exceeds all I ever heard. Would you rob your own father?'

'I will not rob him, but I'll remain in his house. The sheriff's officers, doubtless, will hang about the doors, and be rather troublesome before the windows; but I shall not be the first Irish gentleman that has remained at home upon his keeping. And, like other Irish gentlemen, I will do so rather than fall into the hands of these myrmidons. I have no wish to annoy you; I shall be most sorry to do so; most sorry to subject my mother to the misery which must attend the continual attempts which will be made to arrest me; but I will not put my head into the lion's jaw.'

'This is the return for what I have done for him!' ejaculated the earl, in his misery. 'Unfortunate reprobate! unfortunate reprobate!—that I should be driven to wish that he was in gaol!'

'Your wishing so won't put me there, my lord. If it would I should not be weak enough to ask you for this money. Do you mean to comply with my request?'

'I do not, sir: not a penny shall you have—not one farthing more shall you get from me.'

'Then good night, my lord. I grieve that I should have to undergo a siege in your lordship's house, more especially as it is likely to be a long one. In a week's time there will be a '*ne exeat*' issued against me, and then it will be too late for me to think of France.' And so saying, the son retired to his own room, and left the father to consider what he had better do in his distress.

Lord Cashel was dreadfully embarrassed. What Lord Kilcullen said was perfectly true; an eldest son was a most difficult tenant to eject; and then, the ignominy of having his heir arrested in his own house, or detained there by bailiffs lurking round the premises! He could not determine whether it would be more painful to keep his son, or to give him up. If he did the latter, he would be driven to effect it by a most disagreeable process. He would have to assist the officers of the law in their duty, and to authorise them to force the doors locked by his son. The prospect, either way, was horrid. He would willingly give the five hundred pounds to be rid of his heir,

were it not for his word's sake, or rather his pride's
sake. He had said he would not, and, as he walked
up and down the room he buttoned up his breeches
pocket, and tried to resolve that, come what come
might, he would not expedite his son's departure by
the outlay of one shilling.

The candles had been put out, and the gloom of the
room was only lightened by a single bed-room taper,
which, as it stood near the door, only served to
render palpable the darkness of the further end of
the chamber. For half an hour Lord Cashel walked
to and fro, anxious, wretched, and in doubt, instead
of going to his room. How he wished that Lord
Ballindine had married his ward, and taken her off
six months since!—all this trouble would not then
have come upon him. And as he thought of the
thirty thousand pounds that he had spent, and the
thirty thousand more that he must spend, he hurried
on with such rapidity that in the darkness he struck
his shin violently against some heavy piece of furniture, and, limping back to the candlestick, swore
through his teeth—'No, not a penny, were it to save
him from perdition! I'll see the sheriff's officer. I'll
see the sheriff himself, and tell him that every door in
the house—every closet—every cellar, shall be open
to him. My house shall enable no one to defy the
law.' And, with this noble resolve, to which, by the
bye, the blow on his shin greatly contributed, Lord
Cashel went to bed, and the house was at rest.

About nine o'clock on the following morning Lord
Kilcullen was still in bed, but awake. His servant
had been ordered to bring him hot water, and he was
seriously thinking of getting up, and facing the
troubles of the day, when a very timid knock at the
door announced to him that some stranger was
approaching. He adjusted his nightcap, brought the
bed-clothes up close to his neck, and on giving the
usual answer to a knock at the door, saw a large cap
introduce itself, the head belonging to which seemed
afraid to follow.

'Who's that?' he called out.

'It's me, my lord,' said the head, gradually following the cap. 'Griffiths, my lord.'

'Well?'

'Lady Selina, my lord; her ladyship bids me give your lordship her love, and would you see her ladyship for five minutes before you get up?'

Lord Kilcullen having assented to this proposal, the cap and head retired. A second knock at the door was soon given, and Lady Selina entered the room, with a little bit of paper in her hand.

'Good morning, Adolphus,' said the sister.

'Good morning, Selina,' said the brother. 'It must be something very particular, which brings you here at this hour.'

'It is indeed, something very particular. I have been with papa this morning, Adolphus: he has told me of the interview between you last night.'

'Well.'

'Oh, Adolphus! he is very angry—he's—'

'So am I, Selina. I am very angry, too;—so we're quits. We laid a plan together, and we both failed, and each blames the other; so you need not tell me anything further about his anger. Did he send any message to me?'

'He did. He told me I might give you this, if I would undertake that you left Grey Abbey to-day:' and Lady Selina held up, but did not give him, the bit of paper.

'What a dolt he is.'

'Oh, Adolphus!' said Selina, 'don't speak so of your father.'

'So he is: how on earth can you undertake that I shall leave the house?'

'I can ask you to give me your word that you will do so; and I can take back the check if you refuse,' said Lady Selina, conceiving it utterly impossible that one of her own family could break his word.

'Well, Selina, I'll answer you fairly. If that bit of

paper is a check for five hundred pounds, I will leave this place in two hours. If it is not—'

'It is,' said Selina. 'It is a check for five hundred pounds, and I may then give it to you?'

'I thought as much,' said Lord Kilcullen; 'I thought he'd alter his mind. Yes, you may give it me, and tell my father I'll dine in London to-morrow evening.'

'He says, Adolphus, he'll not see you before you go.'

'Well, there's comfort in that, anyhow.'

'Oh, Adolphus! how can you speak in that manner now?—how can you speak in that wicked, thoughtless, reckless manner?' said his sister.

'Because I'm a wicked, thoughtless, reckless man, I suppose. I didn't mean to vex you, Selina; but my father is so pompous, so absurd, and so tedious. In the whole of this affair I have endeavoured to do exactly as he would have me; and he is more angry with me now, because his plan has failed, than he ever was before, for any of my past misdoings.—But let me get up now, there's a good girl; for I've no time to lose.'

'Will you see your mother before you go, Adolphus?'

'Why, no; it'll be no use—only tormenting her. Tell her something, you know; anything that won't vex her.'

'But I cannot tell her anything about you that will not vex her.'

'Well, then, say what will vex her least. Tell her—tell her. Oh, you know what to tell her, and I'm sure I don't.'

'And Fanny: will you see her again?'

'No,' said Kilcullen. 'I have bid her good bye. But give her my kindest love, and tell her that I did what I told her I would do.'

'She told me what took place between you yesterday.'

'Why, Selina, everybody tells you everything!

And now, I'll tell you something. If you care for your cousin's happiness, do not attempt to raise difficulties between her and Lord Ballindine. And now, I must say good bye to you. I'll have my breakfast up here, and go directly down to the yard. Good bye, Selina; when I'm settled I'll write to you, and tell you where I am.'

'Good bye, Adolphus; God bless you, and enable you yet to retrieve your course. I'm afraid it is a bad one;' and she stooped down and kissed her brother.

He was as good as his word. In two hours' time he had left Grey Abbey. He dined that day in Dublin, the next in London, and the third in Boulogne; and the sub-sheriff of County Kildare in vain issued half-a-dozen writs for his capture.

XXXIV

THE DOCTOR MAKES A CLEAN BREAST OF IT

WE will now return for a while to Dunmore, and settle the affairs of the Kellys and Lynches, which we left in rather a precarious state.

Barry's attempt on Doctor Colligan's virtue was very unsuccessful, for Anty continued to mend under the treatment of that uncouth but safe son of Galen. As Colligan told her brother, the fever had left her, though for some time it was doubtful whether she had strength to recover from its effects. This, however, she did gradually; and, about a fortnight after the dinner at Dunmore House, the doctor told Mrs. Kelly and Martin that his patient was out of danger.

Martin had for some time made up his mind that Anty was to live for many years in the character of Mrs. Martin, and could not therefore be said to be much affected by the communication. But if he was not, his mother was. She had made up her mind that Anty was to die; that she was to pay for the doctor—the wake, and the funeral, and that she would have a hardship and grievance to boast of, and a subject of self-commendation to enlarge on, which would have

lasted her till her death; and she consequently felt
something like disappointment at being ordered to
administer to Anty a mutton chop and a glass of
sherry every day at one o'clock. Not that the widow
was less assiduous, or less attentive to Anty's wants
now that she was convalescent; but she certainly had
not so much personal satisfaction, as when she was
able to speak despondingly of her patient to all her
gossips.

'Poor cratur!' she used to say—'it's all up with
her now; the Lord be praised for all his mercies. She's
all as one as gone, glory be to God and the Blessed
Virgin. Shure no good ever come of ill-got money;—
not that she was iver to blame. Thank the Lord, av'
I have a penny saved at all, it was honestly come by;
not that I shall have when this is done and paid for,
not a stifle; (stiver Mrs. Kelly probably meant)—but
what's that!' and she snapped her fingers to show
that the world's gear was all dross in her estimation.
—'She shall be dacently sthretched, though she is a
Lynch, and a Kelly has to pay for it. Whisper, neighbour; in two years' time there'll not be one penny left
on another of all the dirthy money Sim Lynch
scraped together out of the gutthers.'

There was a degree of triumph in these lamenta-
tions, a tone of self-satisfied assurance in the truth of
her melancholy predictions, which showed that the
widow was not ill at ease with herself. When Anty
was declared out of danger, her joy was expressed
with much more moderation.

'Yes, thin,' she said to Father Pat Geoghegan,
'poor thing, she's rallying a bit. The docthor says
maybe she'll not go this time; but he's much in dread
of a re-claps—'

'Relapse, Mrs. Kelly, I suppose?'

'Well, relapse, av' you will, Father Pat—relapse
or reclaps, it's pretty much the same I'm thinking;
for she'd niver get through another bout. God send
we may be well out of the hobble this day twelve-
month. Martin's my own son, and ain't above

industhrying, as his father and mother did afore him, and I won't say a word agin him; but he's brought more throuble on me with them Lynches than iver I knew before. What has a lone woman like me, Father Pat, to do wid sthrangers like them? jist to turn their backs on me when I ain't no furder use, and to be gitting the hights of insolence and abuse, as I did from that blagguard Barry. He'd betther keep his toe in his pump and go asy, or he'll wake to a sore morning yet, some day.'

Doctor Colligan, also, was in trouble from his connection with the Lynches: not that he had any dissatisfaction at the recovery of his patient, for he rejoiced at it, both on her account and his own. He had strongly that feeling of self-applause, which must always be enjoyed by a doctor who brings a patient safely through a dangerous illness. But Barry's iniquitous proposal to him weighed heavy on his conscience. It was now a week since it had been made, and he had spoken of it to no one. He had thought much and frequently of what he ought to do; whether he should publicly charge Lynch with the fact; whether he should tell it confidentially to some friend whom he could trust; or whether—by far the easiest alternative, he should keep it in his own bosom, and avoid the man in future as he would an incarnation of the devil. It preyed much upon his spirits, for he lived in fear of Barry Lynch—in fear lest he should determine to have the first word, and, in his own defence, accuse him (Colligan) of the very iniquity which he had himself committed. Nothing, the doctor felt, would be too bad or too false for Barry Lynch; nothing could be more damnable than the proposal he had made; and yet it would be impossible to convict him, impossible to punish him. He would, of course, deny the truth of the accusation, and probably return the charge on his accuser. And yet Colligan felt that he would be compromising the matter, if he did not mention it to some one; and that he would outrage his own feelings if he did not express his horror at the murder which he had been asked to commit.

For one week these feelings quite destroyed poor Colligan's peace of mind; during the second, he determined to make a clean breast of it; and, on the first day of the third week, after turning in his mind twenty different people—Martin Kelly—young Daly —the widow—the parish priest—the parish parson— the nearest stipendiary magistrate—and a brother doctor in Tuam, he at last determined on going to Lord Ballindine, as being both a magistrate and a friend of the Kellys. Doctor Colligan himself was not at all acquainted with Lord Ballindine: he attended none of the family, who extensively patronised his rival, and he had never been inside Kelly's Court house. He felt, therefore, considerable embarrassment at his mission; but he made up his mind to go, and, manfully setting himself in his antique rickety gig, started early enough, to catch Lord Ballindine, as he thought, before he left the house after breakfast.

Lord Ballindine had spent the last week or ten days restlessly enough. Armstrong, his clerical ambassador, had not yet started on his mission to Grey Abbey, and innumerable difficulties seemed to arise to prevent his doing so. First of all, the black cloth was to be purchased, and a tailor, sufficiently adept for making up the new suit, was to be caught. This was a·work of some time; for though there is in the West of Ireland a very general complaint of the stagnation of trade, trade itself is never so stagnant as are the tradesmen, when work is to be done; and it is useless for a poor wight to think of getting his coat or his boots, till such time as absolute want shall have driven the artisan to look for the price of his job—unless some private and underhand influence be used, as was done in the case of Jerry Blake's new leather breeches.

This cause of delay was, however, not mentioned to Lord Ballindine; but when it was well got over,

and a neighbouring parson procured to preach on the
next Sunday to Mrs. O'Kelly and the three policemen
who attended Ballindine Church, Mrs. Armstrong
broke her thumb with the rolling-pin while making a
beef pudding for the family dinner, and her husband's
departure was again retarded. And then, on the next
Sunday, the neighbouring parson could not leave his
own policemen, and the two spinsters, who usually
formed his audience.

All this tormented Lord Ballindine, and he was
really thinking of giving up the idea of sending Mr.
Armstrong altogether, when he received the following letter from his friend Dot Blake.

Limmer's Hotel. April, 1847.

Dear Frank,

One cries out, 'what are you at?' the other,
'what are you after?' Every one is saying what a
fool you are! Kilcullen is at Grey Abbey, with the
evident intention of superseding you in possession of
Miss W——, and, what is much more to his taste, as it
would be to mine, of her fortune. Mr. T. has written
to me *from Grey Abbey*, where he has been staying:
he is a good-hearted fellow, and remembers how
warmly you contradicted the report that your match
was broken off. For heaven's sake, follow up your
warmth of denial with some show of positive action,
a little less cool than your present quiescence, or you
cannot expect that any amount of love should be
strong enough to prevent your affianced from resenting your conduct. I am doubly anxious; quite as
anxious that Kilcullen, whom I detest, should not
get young Wyndham's money, as I am that you
should. He is utterly, *utterly* smashed. If he got
double the amount of Fanny Wyndham's cash, it
could not keep him above water for more than a year
or so; and then she must go down with him. I am
sure the old fool, his father, does not half know the
amount of his son's liabilities, or he could not be
heartless enough to consent to sacrifice the poor girl

as she will be sacrificed, if Kilcullen gets her. I am not usually very anxious about other people's concerns; but I do feel anxious about this matter. I want to have a respectable house in the country, in which I can show my face when I grow a little older, and be allowed to sip my glass of claret, and talk about my horses, in spite of my iniquitous propensities—and I expect to be allowed to do so at Kelly's Court. But, if you let Miss Wyndham slip through your fingers, you won't have a house over your head in a few years' time, much less a shelter to offer a friend. For God's sake, start for Grey Abbey at once. Why, man alive, the ogre can't eat you!

The whole town is in the devil of a ferment about Brien. Of course you heard the rumour, last week, of his heels being cracked? Some of the knowing boys want to get out of the trap they are in; and, despairing of bringing the horse down in the betting by fair means, got a boy out of Scott's stables to swear to the fact. I went down at once to Yorkshire, and published a letter in *Bell's Life* last Saturday, stating that he is all right. This you have probably seen. You will be astonished to hear it, but I believe Lord Tattenham Corner got the report spread. For heaven's sake don't mention this, particularly not as coming from me. They say that if Brien does the trick, he will lose more than he has made these three years, and I believe he will. He is nominally at 4 to 1; but you can't get 4 to anything like a figure from a safe party.

For heaven's sake go to Grey Abbey, and at once.

Always faithfully,

W. BLAKE.

This letter naturally increased Lord Ballindine's uneasiness, and he wrote a note to Mr. Armstrong, informing him that he would not trouble him to go at all, unless he could start the next day. Indeed, that he should then go himself, if Mr. Armstrong did not do so.

This did not suit Mr. Armstrong. He had made up his mind to go; he could not well return the twenty pounds he had received, nor did he wish to forego the advantage which might arise from the trip. So he told his wife to be very careful about her thumb, made up his mind to leave the three policemen for once without spiritual food, and wrote to Lord Ballindine to say that he would be with him the next morning, immediately after breakfast, on his road to catch the mail-coach at Ballyglass.

He was as good as his word, or rather better; for he breakfasted at Kelly's Court, and induced Lord Ballindine to get into his own gig, and drive him as far as the mail-coach road.

'But you'll be four or five hours too soon,' said Frank; 'the coach doesn't pass Ballyglass till three.'

'I want to see those cattle of Rutledge's. I'll stay there, and maybe get a bit of luncheon; it's not a bad thing to be provided for the road.'

'I'll tell you what, though,' said Frank. 'I want to go to Tuam, so you might as well get the coach there; and if there's time to spare, you can pay your respects to the bishop.'

It was all the same to Mr. Armstrong, and the two therefore started for Tuam together. They had not, however, got above half way down the avenue, when they saw another gig coming towards them; and, after sundry speculations as to whom it might contain, Mr. Armstrong pronounced the driver to be 'that dirty gallipot, Colligan.'

It was Colligan; and, as the two gigs met in the narrow road, the dirty gallipot took off his hat, and was very sorry to trouble Lord Ballindine, but had a few words to say to him on very important and pressing business.

Lord Ballindine touched his hat, and intimated that he was ready to listen, but gave no signs of getting out of his gig.

'My lord,' said Colligan, 'it's particularly important, and if you could, as a magistrate, spare me five minutes.'

'Oh, certainly, Mr. Colligan,' said Frank; 'that is, I'm rather hurried—I may say very much hurried just at present. But still—I suppose there's no objection to Mr. Armstrong hearing what you have to say?'

'Why, my lord,' said Colligan, 'I don't know. Your lordship can judge yourself afterwards; but I'd rather—'

'Oh, I'll get down,' said the parson. 'I'll just take a walk among the trees: I suppose the doctor won't be long?'

'If you wouldn't mind getting into my buggy, and letting me into his lordship's gig, you could be following us on, Mr. Armstrong,' suggested Colligan.

This suggestion was complied with. The parson and the doctor changed places; and the latter, awkwardly enough, but with perfect truth, whispered his tale into Lord Ballindine's ear.

At first, Frank had been annoyed at the interruption; but, as he learned the cause of it, he gave his full attention to the matter, and only interrupted the narrator by exclamations of horror and disgust.

When Doctor Colligan had finished, Lord Ballindine insisted on repeating the whole affair to Mr. Armstrong. 'I could not take upon myself,' said he, 'to advise you what to do; much less to tell you what you should do. There is only one thing clear; you cannot let things rest as they are. Armstrong is a man of the world, and will know what to do; you cannot object to talking the matter over with him.'

Colligan consented: and Armstrong, having been summoned, drove the doctor's buggy up alongside of Lord Ballindine's gig.

'Armstrong,' said Frank, 'I have just heard the most horrid story that ever came to my ears. That wretch, Barry Lynch, has tried to induce Doctor Colligan to poison his sister!'

'What!' shouted Armstrong; 'to poison his sister?'

'Gently, Mr. Armstrong; pray don't speak so loud, or it'll be all through the country in no time.'

'Poison his sister!' repeated Armstrong. 'Oh, it'll hang him! There's no doubt it'll hang him! Of course you'll take the doctor's information?'

'But the doctor hasn't tendered me any information,' said Frank, stopping his horse, so that Armstrong was able to get close up to his elbow.

'But I presume it is his intention to do so?' said the parson.

'I should choose to have another magistrate present then,' said Frank. 'Really, Doctor Colligan, I think the best thing you can do is to come before myself and the stipendiary magistrate ·at Tuam. We shall be sure to find Brew at home to-day.'

'But, my lord,' said Colligan, 'I really had no intention of doing that. I have no witnesses. I can prove nothing. Indeed, I can't say he ever asked me to do the deed: he didn't say anything I could charge him with as a crime: he only offered me the farm *if* his sister should die. But I knew what he meant; there was no mistaking it: I saw it in his eye.'

'And what did you do, Doctor Colligan, at the time?' said the parson.

'I hardly remember,' said the doctor; 'I was so flurried. But I know I knocked him down, and then I rushed out of the room. I believe I threatened I'd have him hung.'

'But you did knock him down?'

'Oh, I did. He was sprawling on the ground when I left him.'

'You're quite sure you knocked him down?' repeated the parson.

'The divil a doubt on earth about that!' replied Colligan. 'I tell you, when I left the room he was on his back among the chairs.'

'And you did not hear a word from him since?'

'Not a word.'

'Then there can't be any mistake about it, my lord,' said Armstrong. 'If he did not feel that his life was in the doctor's hands, he would not put up with being knocked down. And I'll tell you what's more, —if you tax him with the murder, he'll deny it and defy you; but tax him with having been knocked down, and he'll swear his foot slipped, or that he'd have done as much for the doctor if he hadn't run away. And then ask him why the doctor knocked him down?—you'll have him on the hip so.'

'There's something in that,' said Frank; 'but the question is, what is Doctor Colligan to do? He says he can't swear any information on which a magistrate could commit him.'

'Unless he does, my lord,' said Armstrong, 'I don't think you should listen to him at all; at least, not as a magistrate.'

'Well, Doctor Colligan, what do you say?'

'I don't know what to say, my lord. I came to your lordship for advice, both as a magistrate and as a friend of the young man who is to marry Lynch's sister. Of course, if you cannot advise me, I will go away again.'

'You won't come before me and Mr. Brew, then?'

'I don't say I won't,' said Colligan; 'but I don't see the use. I'm not able to prove anything.'

'I'll tell you what, Ballindine,' said the parson; 'only I don't know whether it mayn't be tampering with justice—suppose we were to go to this hell-hound, you and I together, and, telling him what we know, give him his option to stand his trial or quit the country? Take my word for it, he'd go; and that would be the best way to be rid of him. He'd leave his sister in peace and quiet then, to enjoy her fortune.'

'That's true,' said Frank; 'and it would be a great thing to rid the country of him. Do you remember the way he rode a-top of that poor bitch of mine the other day—Goneaway, you know; the best bitch in the pack?'

'Indeed I do,' said the parson; 'but for all that, she wasn't the best bitch in the pack: she hadn't half the nose of Gaylass.'

'But, as I was saying, Armstrong, it would be a great thing to rid the country of Barry Lynch.'

'Indeed it would.'

'And there'd be nothing then to prevent young Kelly marrying Anty at once.'

'Make him give his consent in writing before you let him go,' said Armstrong.

'I'll tell you what, Doctor Colligan,' said Frank; 'do you get into your own gig, and follow us on, and I'll talk the matter over with Mr. Armstrong.'

The doctor again returned to his buggy, and the parson to his own seat, and Lord Ballindine drove off at a pace which made it difficult enough for Doctor Colligan to keep him in sight.

'I don't know how far we can trust that apothecary,' said Frank to his friend.

'He's an honest man, I believe,' said Armstrong, 'though he's a dirty, drunken blackguard.'

'Maybe he was drunk this evening, at Lynch's?'

'I was wrong to call him a drunkard. I believe he doesn't get drunk, though he's always drinking. But you may take my word for it, what he's telling you now is as true as gospel. If he was telling a lie from malice, he'd be louder, and more urgent about it: you see he's half afraid to speak, as it is. He would not have come near you at all, only his conscience makes him afraid to keep the matter to himself. You may take my word for it, Ballindine, Barry Lynch did propose to him to murder his sister. Indeed, it doesn't surprise me. He is so utterly worthless.'

'But murder, Armstrong! downright murder; of the worst kind; studied—premeditated. He must have been thinking of it, and planning it, for days. A man may be worthless, and yet not such a wretch as that would make him. Can you really think he meant Colligan to murder his sister?'

'I can, and do think so,' said the parson. 'The temptation was great: he had been waiting for his sister's death; and he could not bring himself to bear disappointment. I do not think he could do it with his own hand, for he is a coward; but I can quite believe that he could instigate another person to do it.'

'Then I'd hang him. I wouldn't raise my hand to save him from the rope!'

'Nor would I: but we can't hang him. We can do nothing to him, if he defies us; but, if he's well handled, we can drive him from the country.'

The lord and the parson talked the matter over till they reached Dunmore, and agreed that they would go, with Colligan, to Barry Lynch; tell him of the charge which was brought against him, and give him his option of standing his trial, or of leaving the country, under a written promise that he would never return to it. In this case, he was also to write a note to Anty, signifying his consent that she should marry Martin Kelly, and also execute some deed by which all control over the property should be taken out of his own hands; and that he should agree to receive his income, whatever it might be, through the hands of an agent.

There were sundry matters connected with the subject, which were rather difficult of arrangement. In the first place, Frank was obliged, very unwillingly, to consent that Mr. Armstrong should remain, at any rate one day longer, in the country. It was, however, at last settled that he should return that night and sleep at Kelly's Court. Then Lord Ballindine insisted that they should tell young Kelly what they were about, before they went to Barry's house, as it would be necessary to consult him as to the disposition he would wish to have made of the property. Armstrong was strongly against this measure,—but it was, at last, decided on; and then they had to induce Colligan to go with them. He much wished them to manage the business without him. He had had quite enough of Dunmore House; and, in spite of the valiant manner in which he had knocked its owner down the last time he was there,

seemed now quite afraid to face him. But Mr. Armstrong informed him that he must go on now, as he
had said so much, and at last frightened him into an
unwilling compliance.

The three of them went up into the little parlour of
the inn, and summoned Martin to the conference,
and various were the conjectures made by the family
as to the nature of the business which brought three
such persons to the inn together. But the widow
settled them all by asserting that 'a Kelly needn't
be afeared, thank God, to see his own landlord in his
own house, nor though he brought an attorney wid
him as well as a parson and a docther.' And so,
Martin was sent for, and soon heard the horrid story.
Not long after he had joined them, the four sallied
out together, and Meg remarked that something very
bad was going to happen, for the lord never passed
her before without a kind word or a nod; and now he
took no more notice of her than if it had been only
Sally herself that met him on the stairs.

XXXV

MR. LYNCH BIDS FAREWELL TO DUNMORE

POOR Martin was dreadfully shocked; and not
only shocked, but grieved and astonished. He
had never thought well of his intended brother-in-
law, but he had not judged him so severely as Mr.
Armstrong had done. He listened to all Lord Ballindine said to him, and agreed as to the propriety of the
measures he proposed. But there was nothing of
elation about him at the downfall of the man whom
he could not but look on as his enemy: indeed, he was
not only subdued and modest in his demeanour, but
he appeared so reserved that he could hardly be got
to express any interest in the steps which were to be
taken respecting the property. It was only when
Lord Ballindine pointed out to him that it was his
duty to guard Anty's interests, that he would consent
to go to Dunmore House with them, and to state,

when called upon to do so, what measures he would
wish to have adopted with regard to the property.

'Suppose he denies himself to us?' said Frank, as
the four walked across the street together, to the
great astonishment of the whole population.

'If he's in the house, I'll go bail we won't go away
without seeing him,' said the parson. 'Will he be at
home, Kelly, do you think?'

'Indeed he will, Mr. Armstrong,' said Martin; 'he'll
be in bed and asleep. He's never out of bed, I believe,
much before one or two in the day. It's a bad life
he's leading since the ould man died.'

'You may say that,' said the doctor:—'cursing
and drinking; drinking and cursing; nothing else.
You'll find him curse at you dreadful, Mr. Armstrong,
I'm afraid.'

'I can bear that, doctor; it's part of my own trade,
you know; but I think we'll find him quiet enough.
I think you'll find the difficulty is to make him
speak at all. You'd better be spokesman, my lord,
as you're a magistrate.'

'No, Armstrong, I will not. You're much more
able, and more fitting: if it's necessary for me to act
as a magistrate, I'll do so—but at first we'll leave
him to you.'

'Very well,' said the parson; 'and I'll do my best.
But I'll tell you what I am afraid of: if we find him in
bed we must wait for him, and when the servant
tells him who we are, and mentions the doctor's name
along with yours, my lord, he'll guess what we're
come about, and he'll be out of the window, or into
the cellar, and then there'd be no catching him without the police. We must make our way up into his
bed-room.'

'I don't think we could well do that,' said the
doctor.

'No, Armstrong,' said Lord Ballindine. 'I don't
think we ought to force ourselves upstairs: we might
as well tell all the servants what we'd come about.'

'And so we must,' said Armstrong, 'if it's necessary. The more determined we are—in fact, the rougher we are with him, the more likely we are to bring him on his knees. I tell you, you must have no scruples in dealing with such a fellow; but leave him to me;' and so saying, the parson gave a thundering rap at the hall door, and in about one minute repeated it, which brought Biddy running to the door without shoes or stockings, with her hair streaming behind her head, and, in her hand, the comb with which she had been disentangling it.

'Is your master at home?' said Armstrong.

'Begorra, he is,' said the girl out of breath. 'That is, he's not up yet, nor awake, yer honer,' and she held the door in her hand, as though this answer was final.

'But I want to see him on especial and immediate business,' said the parson, pushing back the door and the girl together, and walking into the hall. 'I must see him at once. Mr. Lynch will excuse me: we've known each other a long time.'

'Begorra, I don't know,' said the girl, 'only he's in bed and fast. Couldn't yer honer call agin about four or five o'clock? That's the time the masther's most fittest to be talking to the likes of yer honer.'

'These gentlemen could not wait,' said the parson.

'Shure the docther there, and Mr. Martin, knows well enough I'm not telling you a bit of a lie, Misther Armstrong,' said the girl.

'I know you're not, my good girl; I know you're not telling a lie but, nevertheless, I must see Mr. Lynch. Just step up and wake him, and tell him I'm waiting to say two words to him.'

'Faix, yer honer, he's very bitther intirely, when he's waked this early. But in course I'll be led by yer honers. I'll say then, that the lord, and Parson Armstrong, and the docther, and Mr. Martin, is waiting to spake two words to him. Is that it?'

'That'll do as well as anything,' said Armstrong; and then, when the girl went upstairs, he continued, 'You see she knew us all, and of course will tell him

who we are; but I'll not let him escape, for I'll go up
with her,' and, as the girl slowly opened her master's
bedroom door, Mr. Armstrong stood close outside it
in the passage.

After considerable efforts, Biddy succeeded in
awaking her master sufficiently to make him understand that Lord Ballindine, and Doctor Colligan
were downstairs, and that Parson Armstrong was
just outside the bedroom door. The poor girl tried
hard to communicate her tidings in such a whisper as
would be inaudible to the parson; but this was impossible, for Barry only swore at her, and asked her
'what the d— she meant by jabbering there in that
manner?' When, however, he did comprehend who
his visitors were, and where they were, he gnashed
his teeth and clenched his fist at the poor girl, in sign
of his anger against her for having admitted so un-
welcome a party; but he was too frightened to speak.

Mr. Armstrong soon put an end to this dumb show,
by walking into the bedroom, when the girl escaped,
and he shut the door. Barry sat up in his bed, rubbed
his eyes, and stared at him, but he said nothing.

'Mr. Lynch,' said the parson, 'I had better at once
explain the circumstances which have induced me to
make so very strange a visit.'

'Confounded strange, I must say! to come up to a
man's room in this way, and him in bed!'

'Doctor Colligan is downstairs—'

'D— Doctor Colligan! He's at his lies again, I
suppose? Much I care for Doctor Colligan.'

'Doctor Colligan is downstairs,' continued Mr.
Armstrong, 'and Lord Ballindine, who, you are
aware, is a magistrate. They wish to speak to you,
Mr. Lynch, and that at once.'

'I suppose they can wait till a man's dressed?'

'That depends on how long you're dressing, Mr.
Lynch.'

'Upon my word, this is cool enough, in a man's
own house!' said Barry. 'Well, you don't expect me
to get up while you're there, I suppose?'

'Indeed I do, Mr. Lynch: never mind me; just wash and dress yourself as though I wasn't here. I'll wait here till we go down together.'

'I'm d—d if I do,' said Barry. 'I'll not stir while you remain there!' and he threw himself back in the bed, and wrapped the bedclothes round him.

'Very well,' said Mr. Armstrong; and then going out on to the landing-place, called out over the banisters—'Doctor—Doctor Colligan! tell his lordship Mr. Lynch objects to a private interview: he had better just step down to the Court-house, and issue his warrant. You might as well tell Constable Nelligan to be in the way.'

'D—n!' exclaimed Barry, sitting bolt upright in his bed. 'Who says I object to see anybody? Mr. Armstrong, what do you go and say that for?' Mr. Armstrong returned into the room. 'It's not true. I only want to have my bedroom to myself, while I get up.'

'For once in the way, Mr. Lynch, you must manage to get up although your privacy be intruded on. To tell you the plain truth, I will not leave you till you come downstairs with me, unless it be in the custody of a policeman. If you will quietly dress and come downstairs with me, I trust we may be saved the necessity of troubling the police at all.'

Barry, at last, gave way, and, gradually extricating himself from the bedclothes, put his feet down on the floor, and remained sitting on the side of his bed. He leaned his head down on his hands, and groaned inwardly; for he was very sick, and the fumes of last night's punch still disturbed his brain. His stockings and drawers were on; for Terry, when he put him to bed, considered it only waste of time to pull them off, for 'shure wouldn't they have jist to go on agin the next morning?'

'Don't be particular, Mr. Lynch: never mind washing or shaving till we're gone. We won't keep you long, I hope.'

'You're very kind, I must say,' said Barry. 'I

suppose you won't object to my having a bottle
of soda water?'—and he gave a terrible tug at
the bell.

'Not at all—nor a glass of brandy in it, if you like
it. Indeed, Mr. Lynch, I think that, just at present,
it will be the better thing for you.'

Barry got his bottle of soda water, and swallowed
about two glasses of whiskey in it, for brandy was
beginning to be scarce with him; and then commenced his toilet. He took Parson Armstrong's hint,
and wasn't very particular about it. He huddled
on his clothes, smoothed his hair with his brush, and
muttering something about it's being their own fault,
descended into the parlour, followed by Mr. Armstrong. He made a kind of bow to Lord Ballindine;
took no notice of Martin, but, turning round sharp on
the doctor, said:

'Of all the false ruffians, I ever met, Colligan,—
by heavens, you're the worst! There's one comfort,
no man in Dunmore will believe a word you say.'
He then threw himself back into the easy chair, and
said, 'Well, gentlemen—well, my lord—here I am.
You can't say I'm ashamed to show my face, though
I must say your visit is not made in the genteelest
manner.'

'Mr. Lynch,' said the parson, 'do you remember
the night Doctor Colligan knocked you down in this
room? In this room, wasn't it, doctor?'

'Yes; in this room,' said the doctor, rather *sotto
voce.*

'Do you remember the circumstance, Mr. Lynch?'

'It's a lie!' said Barry.

'No it's not,' said the parson. 'If you forget it, I
can call in the servant to remember so much as that
for me; but you'll find it better, Mr. Lynch, to let
us finish this business among ourselves. Come, think
about it. I'm sure you remember being knocked
down by the doctor.'

'I remember a scrimmage there was between us.
I don't care what the girl says, she didn't see it.

Colligan, I suppose, has given her half-a-crown, and
she'd swear anything for that.'

'Well, you remember the night of the scrimmage?'

'I do: Colligan got drunk here one night. He
wanted me to give him a farm, and said cursed queer
things about my sister. I hardly know what he said;
but I know I had to turn him out of the house, and
there was a scrimmage between us.'

'I see you're so far prepared, Mr. Lynch: now, I'll
tell you my version of the story.—Martin Kelly, just
see that the door is shut. You endeavoured to bribe
Doctor Colligan to murder your own sister.'

'It's a most infernal lie!' said Barry. 'Where's
your evidence?—where's your evidence? What's
the good of your all coming here with such a story as
that? Where's your evidence?'

'You'd better be quiet, Mr. Lynch, or we'll adjourn
at once from here to the open Court-house.'

'Adjourn when you like; it's all one to me. Who'll
believe such a drunken ruffian as that Colligan, I'd
like to know? Such a story as that!'

'My lord,' said Armstrong, 'I'm afraid we must go
on with this business at the Court-house. Martin,
I believe I must trouble you to go down to the police
barrack.' And the whole party, except Barry, rose
from their seats.

'What the devil are you going to drag me down to
the Court-house for, gentlemen?' said he. 'I'll give
you any satisfaction, but you can't expect I'll own
to such a lie as this about my sister. I suppose my
word's as good as Colligan's, gentlemen? I suppose
my character as a Protestant gentleman stands
higher than his—a dirty Papist apothecary. He
tells one story; I tell another; only he's got the
first word of me, that's all. I suppose, gentlemen,
I'm not to be condemned on the word of such a man
as that?'

'I think, Mr. Lynch,' said Armstrong, 'if you'll
listen to me, you'll save yourself and us a great deal
of trouble. You asked me who my witness was: my

witness is in this house. I would not charge you with
so horrid, so damnable a crime, had I not thoroughly
convinced myself you were guilty—now, do hold your
tongue, Mr. Lynch, or I will have you down to the
Court-house. We all know you are guilty, you know
it yourself—'

'I'm—' began Barry.

'Stop, Mr. Lynch; not one word till I've done; or
what I have to say, shall be said in public. We all
know you are guilty, but we probably mayn't be
able to prove it—'

'No, I should think not!' shouted Barry.

'We mayn't be able to prove it in such a way as to
enable a jury to hang you, or, upon my word, I
wouldn't interfere to prevent it: the law should have
its course. I'd hang you with as little respite as I
would a dog.'

Barry grinned horribly at this suggestion, but said
nothing, and the parson continued:

'It is not the want of evidence that stands in the
way of so desirable a proceeding, but that Doctor
Colligan, thoroughly disgusted and shocked at the
iniquity of your proposal—'

'Oh, go on, Mr. Armstrong!—go on; I see you are
determined to have it all your own way, but my
turn'll come soon.'

'I say that Doctor Colligan interrupted you before
you fully committed yourself.'

'Fully committed myself, indeed! Why, Colligan
knows well enough, that when he got up in such a
fluster, there'd not been a word at all said about
Anty.'

'Hadn't there, Mr. Lynch?—just now you said you
turned the doctor out of your house for speaking
about your sister. You're only committing yourself.
I say, therefore, the evidence, though quite strong
enough to put you into the dock as a murderer in
intention, might not be sufficient to induce a jury to
find you guilty. But guilty you would be esteemed
in the mind of every man, woman, and child in this

county: guilty of the wilful, deliberate murder of your own sister.'

'By heavens I'll not stand this!' exclaimed Barry. —'I'll not stand this! I didn't do it, Mr. Armstrong. I didn't do it. He's a liar, Lord Ballindine: upon my sacred word and honour as a gentleman, he's a liar. Why do you believe him, when you won't believe me? Ain't I a Protestant, Mr. Armstrong, and ain't you a Protestant clergyman? Don't you know that such men as he will tell any lie; will do any dirty job? On my sacred word of honour as a gentleman, Lord Ballindine, he offered to poison Anty, on condition he got the farm round the house for nothing!— He knows it's true, and why should you believe him sooner than me, Mr. Armstrong?'

Barry had got up from his seat, and was walking up and down the room, now standing opposite Lord Ballindine, and appealing to him, and then doing the same thing to Mr. Armstrong. He was a horrid figure: he had no collar round his neck, and his handkerchief was put on in such a way as to look like a hangman's knot: his face was blotched, and red, and greasy, for he had neither shaved nor washed himself since his last night's debauch; he had neither waistcoat nor braces on, and his trousers fell on his hips; his long hair hung over his eyes, which were bleared and bloodshot; he was suffering dreadfully from terror, and an intense anxiety to shift the guilt from himself to Doctor Colligan. He was a most pitiable object— so wretched, so unmanned, so low in the scale of creation. Lord Ballindine did pity his misery, and suggested to Mr. Armstrong whether by any possibility there could be any mistake in the matter— whether it was possible Doctor Colligan could have mistaken Lynch's object?—The poor wretch jumped at this loop-hole, and doubly condemned himself by doing so.

'He did, then,' said Barry; 'he must have done so. As I hope for heaven, Lord Ballindine, I never had the idea of getting him to—to do anything to Anty.

I wouldn't have done it for worlds—indeed I wouldn't. There must be some mistake, indeed there must. He'd been drinking, Mr. Armstrong—drinking a good deal that night—isn't that true, Doctor Colligan? Come, man, speak the truth—don't go and try and hang a fellow out of mistake! His lordship sees it's all a mistake, and of course he's the best able to judge of the lot here; a magistrate, and a nobleman and all. I know you won't see me wronged, Lord Ballindine, I know you won't. I give you my sacred word of honour as a gentleman, it all came from mistake when we were both drunk, or nearly drunk. Come, Doctor Colligan, speak man—isn't that the truth? I tell you, Mr. Armstrong, Lord Ballindine's in the right of it. There is some mistake in all this.'

'As sure as the Lord's in heaven,' said the doctor, now becoming a little uneasy at the idea that Lord Ballindine should think he had told so strange a story without proper foundation—'as sure as the Lord's in heaven, he offered me the farm for a reward, should I manage to prevent his sister's recovery.'

'What do you think, Mr. Armstrong?' said Lord Ballindine.

'Think!' said the parson—'There's no possibility of thinking at all. The truth becomes clearer every moment. Why, you wretched creature, it's not ten minutes since you yourself accused Doctor Colligan of offering to murder your sister! According to your own showing, therefore, there was a deliberate conversation between you; and your own evasion now would prove which of you were the murderer, were any additional proof wanted. But it is not. Barry Lynch, as sure as you now stand in the presence of your Creator, whose name you so constantly blaspheme, you endeavoured to instigate that man to murder your own sister.'

'Oh, Lord Ballindine!—oh, Lord Ballindine!' shrieked Barry, in his agony, 'don't desert me! pray,

pray don't desert me! I didn't do it—I never thought
of doing it. We were at school together, weren't we?
—And you won't see me put upon this way. You
mayn't think much of me in other things, but you
won't believe that a school-fellow of your own ever—
ever—ever—' Barry couldn't bring himself to use
the words with which his sentence should be finished,
and so he flung himself back into his armchair and
burst into tears.

'You appeal to me, Mr. Lynch,' said Lord Ballindine, 'and I must say I most firmly believe you to be
guilty. My only doubt is whether you should not at
once be committed for trial at the next assizes.'

'Oh, my G—!' exclaimed Barry, and for some time
he continued blaspheming most horribly—swearing
that there was a conspiracy against him—accusing
Mr. Armstrong, in the most bitter terms, of joining
with Doctor Colligan and Martin Kelly to rob and
murder him.

'Now, Mr. Lynch,' continued the parson, as soon
as the unfortunate man would listen to him, 'as I
before told you, I am in doubt—we are all in doubt—
whether or not a jury would hang you; and we think
that we shall do more good to the community by
getting you out of the way, than by letting you
loose again after a trial which will only serve to
let everyone know how great a wretch there is in
the county. We will, therefore, give you your option
either to stand your trial, or to leave the country at
once—and for ever.'

'And my property?—what's to become of my
property?' said Barry.

'Your property's safe, Mr. Lynch; we can't touch
that. We're not prescribing any punishment to you.
We fear, indeed we know, you're beyond the reach
of the law, or we shouldn't make the proposal.'
Barry breathed freely again as he heard this avowal.
'But you're not beyond the reach of public opinion—
of public execration—of general hatred, and of a
general curse. For your sister's sake—for the sake of

Martin Kelly, who is going to marry the sister whom
you wished to murder, and not for your own sake,
you shall be allowed to leave the country without
this public brand being put upon your name. If you
remain, no one shall speak to you but as to a man
who would have murdered his sister: murder shall be
everlastingly muttered in your ears; nor will your
going then avail you, for your character shall go
with you, and the very blackguards with whom you
delight to assort, shall avoid you as being too bad
even for their society. Go now, Mr. Lynch—go at
once;—leave your sister to happiness which you cannot prevent; and she at least shall know nothing of
your iniquity, and you shall enjoy the proceeds of
your property anywhere you will—anywhere, that
is, but in Ireland. Do you agree to this?'

'I'm an innocent man, Mr. Armstrong. I am indeed.'

'Very well,' said the parson, 'then we may as well
go away, and leave you to your fate. Come, Lord
Ballindine, we can have nothing further to say,' and
they again all rose from their seats.

'Stop, Mr. Armstrong; stop,' said Barry.

'Well,' said the parson; for Barry repressed the
words which were in his mouth, when he found that
his visitors did stop as he desired them.

'Well, Mr. Lynch, what have you further to say.'

'Indeed I am not guilty.' Mr. Armstrong put on his
hat and rushed to the door—'but—' continued Barry.

'I will have no "buts," Mr. Lynch; will you at
once and unconditionally agree to the terms I have
proposed?'

'I don't want to live in the country,' said Barry;
'the country's nothing to me.'

'You will go then, immediately?' said the parson.

'As soon as I have arranged about the property, I
will,' said Barry.

'That won't do,' said the parson. 'You must go at
once, and leave your property to the care of others.
You must leave Dunmore *to-day*, for ever.'

'To-day!' shouted Barry.

'Yes, to-day. You can easily get as far as Roscommon. You have your own horse and car. And, what is more, before you go, you must write to your sister, telling her that you have made up your mind to leave the country, and expressing your consent to her marrying whom she pleases.'

'I can't go to-day,' said Barry, sulkily. 'Who's to receive my rents? who'll send me my money?— besides—besides. Oh, come—that's nonsense. I ain't going to be turned out in that style.'

'You ain't in earnest, are you, about his going to-day?' whispered Frank to the parson.

'I am, and you'll find he'll go, too,' said Armstrong. 'It must be to-day—this very day, Mr. Lynch. Martin Kelly will manage for you about the property.'

'Or you can send for Mr. Daly, to meet you at Roscommon,' suggested Martin.

'Thank you for nothing,' said Barry; 'you'd better wait till you're spoken to. I don't know what business you have here at all.'

'The business that all honest men have to look after all rogues,' said Mr. Armstrong. 'Come, Mr. Lynch, you'd better make up your mind to prepare for your journey.'

'Well, I won't—and there's an end of it,' said Barry. 'It's all nonsense. You can't do anything to me: you said so yourself. I'm not going to be made a fool of that way—I'm not going to give up my property and everything.'

'Don't you know, Mr. Lynch,' said the parson, 'that if you are kept in jail till April next, as will be your fate if you persist in staying at Dunmore to-night, your creditors will do much more damage to your property, than your own immediate absence will do? If Mr. Daly is your lawyer, send for him, as Martin Kelly suggests. I'm not afraid that he will recommend you to remain in the country, even should you dare to tell him of the horrid accusation which is brought against you. But at any rate make up your mind, for if you do stay in Dunmore to-night it shall be in the Bridewell, and your next move shall be to Galway.'

Barry sat silent for a while, trying to think. The parson was like an incubus upon him, which he was totally unable to shake off. He knew neither how to resist nor how to give way. Misty ideas got into his head of escaping to his bed-room and blowing his own brains out. Different schemes of retaliation and revenge flitted before him, but he could decide on nothing. There he sat, silent, stupidly gazing at nothing, while Lord Ballindine and Mr. Armstrong stood whispering over the fire.

'I'm afraid we're in the wrong: I really think we are,' said Frank.

'We must go through with it now, any way,' said the parson. 'Come, Mr. Lynch, I will give you five minutes more, and then I go;' and he pulled out his watch, and stood with his back to the fire, looking at it. Lord Ballindine walked to the window, and Martin Kelly and Doctor Colligan sat in distant parts of the room, with long faces, silent and solemn, breathing heavily. How long those five minutes appeared to them, and how short to Barry! The time was not long enough to enable him to come to any decision: at the end of the five minutes he was still gazing vacantly before him: he was still turning over in his brain, one after another, the same crowd of undigested schemes.

'The time is out, Mr. Lynch: will you go?' said the parson.

'I've no money,' hoarsely croaked Barry.

'If that's the only difficulty, we'll raise money for him,' said Frank.

'I'll advance him money,' said Martin.

'Do you mean you've no money at all?' said the parson.

'Don't you hear me say so?' said Barry.

'And you'll go if you get money—say ten pounds?' said the parson.

'Ten pounds! I can go nowhere with ten pounds. You know that well enough.'

'I'll give him twenty-five,' said Martin. 'I'm sure his sister'll do that for him.'

'Say fifty,' said Barry, 'and I'm off at once.'

'I haven't got it,' said Martin.

'No,' said the parson; 'I'll not see you bribed to go: take the twenty-five—that will last you till you make arrangements about your property. We are not going to pay you for going, Mr. Lynch.'

'You seem very anxious about it, any way.'

'I *am* anxious about it,' rejoined the parson. 'I am anxious to save your sister from knowing what it was that her brother wished to accomplish.'

Barry scowled at him as though he would like, if possible, to try his hand at murdering him; but he did not answer him again. Arrangements were at last made for Barry's departure, and off he went, that very day—not to Roscommon, but to Tuam; and there, at the instigation of Martin, Daly the attorney took upon himself the division and temporary management of the property. From thence, with Martin's, or rather with his sister's twenty-five pounds in his pocket, he started to that Elysium for which he had for some time so ardently longed, and soon landed at Boulogne, regardless alike of his sister, his future brother, Lord Ballindine, or Mr. Armstrong. The parson had found it quite impossible to carry out one point on which he had insisted. He could not induce Barry Lynch to write to his sister: no, not a line; not a word. Had it been to save him from hanging he could hardly have induced himself to write those common words, '*dear sister*'.

'Oh! you can tell her what you like,' said he. 'It's you're making me go away at once in this manner. Tell her whatever confounded lies you like; tell her I'm gone because I didn't choose to stay and see her make a fool of herself—and that's the truth, too. If it wasn't for that I wouldn't move a step for any of you.'

He went, however, as I have before said, and troubled the people of Dunmore no longer, nor shall he again trouble us.

'Oh! but Martin, what nonsense!' said the widow, coaxingly to her son, that night before she went to bed. 'The lord wouldn't be going up there just to wish him good bye—and Parson Armstrong too. What the dickens could they be at there so long? Come, Martin—you're safe with me, you know; tell us something about it now.'

'Nonsense, mother; I've nothing to tell: Barry Lynch has left the place for good and all, that's all about it.'

'God bless the back of him, thin; he'd my lave for going long since. But you might be telling us what made him be starting this way all of a heap.'

'Don't you know, mother, he was head and ears in debt?'

'Don't tell me,' said the widow. 'Parson Armstrong's not a sheriff's officer, that he should be looking after folks in debt.'

'No, mother, he's not, that I know of; but he don't like, for all that, to see his tithes walking out of the country.'

'Don't be coming over me that way, Martin. Barry Lynch, nor his father before him, never held any land in Ballindine parish.'

'Didn't they—well thin, you know more than I, mother, so it's no use my telling you,' and Martin walked off to bed.

'I'll even you, yet, my lad,' said she, 'close as you are; you see else. Wait awhile, till the money's wanting, and then let's see who'll know all about it!' And the widow slapped herself powerfully on that part where her pocket depended, in sign of the great confidence she had in the strength of her purse.

'Did I manage that well?' said the parson, as Lord Ballindine drove him home to Kelly's Court, as soon as the long interview was over. 'If I can do as well at Grey Abbey, you'll employ me again, I think!'

'Upon my word, then, Armstrong,' said Frank, 'I never was in such hot water as I have been all this day: and, now it's over, to tell you the truth, I'm sorry we interfered. We did what we had no possible right to do.'

'Nonsense, man. You don't suppose I'd have dreamed of letting him off, if the law could have touched him? But it couldn't. No magistrates in the county could have committed him; for he had done, and, as far as I can judge, had said, literally nothing. It's true we know what he intended; but a score of magistrates could have done nothing with him: as it is, we've got him out of the country: he'll never come back again.'

'What I mean is, we had no business to drive him out of the country with threats.'

'Oh, Ballindine, that's nonsense. One can keep no common terms with such a blackguard as that. However, it's done now; and I must say I think it was well done.'

'There's no doubt of your talent in the matter, Armstrong: upon my soul I never saw anything so cool. What a wretch—what an absolute fiend the fellow is!'

'Bad enough,' said the parson. 'I've seen bad men before, but I think he's the worst I ever saw. What'll Mrs. O'Kelly say of my coming in this way, without notice?'

The parson enjoyed his claret at Kelly's Court that evening, after his hard day's work, and the next morning he started for Grey Abbey.

XXXVI

MR. ARMSTRONG VISITS GREY ABBEY ON A DELICATE MISSION

LORD CASHEL certainly felt a considerable degree of relief when his daughter told him that Lord Kilcullen had left the house, and was on his way to Dublin, though he had been forced to pay so dearly for the satisfaction, had had to falsify his solemn assurance that he would not give his son another penny, and to break through his resolution of acting the Roman father. He consoled himself with the idea that he had been actuated by affection for his profligate son; but such had not been the case. Could he have handed him over to the sheriff's officer silently and secretly, he would have done so; but his pride could not endure the reflection that all the world should know that bailiffs had forced an entry into Grey Abbey.

He closely questioned Lady Selina, with regard to all that had passed between her and her brother.

'Did he say anything?' at last he said—'did he say anything about—about Fanny?'

'Not much, papa; but what he did say, he said with kindness and affection,' replied her ladyship, glad to repeat anything in favour of her brother.

'Affection—pooh!' said the earl. 'He has no affection; no affection for any one; he has no affection even for 'me.—What did he say about her, Selina?'

'He seemed to wish she should marry Lord Ballindine.'

'She may marry whom she pleases, now,' said the earl. 'I wash my hands of her. I have done my best to prevent what I thought a disgraceful match for her—'

'It would not have been disgraceful, papa, had she married him six months ago.'

'A gambler and a *roué*!' said the earl, forgetting, it is to be supposed, for the moment, his own son's character. 'She'll marry him now, I suppose, and repent at her leisure. I'll give myself no further trouble about it.'

The earl thought upon the subject, however, a good deal; and before Mr. Armstrong's arrival he had all but made up his mind that he must again swallow his word, and ask his ward's lover back to his house. He had at any rate become assured that if he did not do so, some one else would do it for him.

Mr. Armstrong was, happily, possessed of a considerable stock of self-confidence, and during his first day's journey, felt no want of it with regard to the delicate mission with which he was entrusted. But when he had deposited his carpet-bag at the little hotel at Kilcullen bridge, and found himself seated on a hack car, and proceeding to Grey Abbey, he began to feel that he had rather a difficult part to play; and by the time that the house was in sight, he felt himself completely puzzled as to the manner in which he should open his negotiation.

He had, however, desired the man to drive to the house, and he could not well stop the car in the middle of the demesne, to mature his plans; and when he was at the door he could not stay there without applying for admission. So he got his cardcase in his hand, and rang the bell. After a due interval, which to the parson did not seem a bit too long, the heavy-looking, powdered footman appeared, and announced that Lord Cashel was at home; and, in another minute Mr. Armstrong found himself in the book-room.

It was the morning after Lord Kilcullen's departure, and Lord Cashel was still anything but comfortable. Her ladyship had been bothering him about the poor boy, as she called her son, now that she learned he was in distress; and had been beseeching him to increase his allowance. The earl had not told his wife the extent of their son's pecuniary delinquencies, and consequently she was greatly dismayed when her husband very solemnly said,

'My lady, Lord Kilcullen has no longer any allowance from me.'

'Good gracious!' screamed her ladyship; 'no allowance?—how is the poor boy to live?'

'That I really cannot tell. I cannot even guess; but, let him live how he may, I will not absolutely ruin myself for his sake.'

The interview was not a comfortable one, either to the father or mother. Lady Cashel cried a great deal, and was very strongly of opinion that her son would die of cold and starvation: 'How could he get shelter or food, any more than a common person, if he had no allowance? Mightn't he, at any rate, come back, and live at Grey Abbey?—That wouldn't cost his father anything.' And then the countess remembered how she had praised her son to Mrs. Ellison, and the bishop's wife; and she cried worse than ever, and was obliged to be left to Griffiths and her drops.

This happened on the evening of Lord Kilcullen's departure, and on the next morning her ladyship did not appear at breakfast. She was weak and nervous, and had her tea in her own sitting-room. There was no one sitting at breakfast but the earl, Fanny, and Lady Selina, and they were all alike, stiff, cold, and silent. The earl felt as if he were not at home even in his own breakfast-parlour; he felt afraid of his ward, as though he were conscious that she knew how he had intended to injure her: and, as soon as he had swallowed his eggs, he muttered something which was inaudible to both the girls, and retreated to his private den.

He had not been there long before the servant brought in our friend's name. 'The Rev. George Armstrong', written on a plain card. The parson had not put the name of his parish, fearing that the earl, knowing from whence he came, might guess his business, and decline seeing him. As it was, no difficulty was made, and the parson soon found himself *tête-à-tête* with the earl.

'I have taken the liberty of calling on you, Lord Cashel,' said Mr. Armstrong, having accepted the offer of a chair, 'on a rather delicate mission.'

The earl bowed, and rubbed his hands, and felt more comfortable than he had done for the last week. He liked delicate missions coming to him, for he flattered himself that he knew how to receive them in a delicate manner; he liked, also, displaying his dignity to strangers, for he felt that strangers stood rather in awe of him: he also felt, though he did not own it to himself, that his manner was not so effective with people who had known him some time.

'I may say, a very delicate mission,' said the parson; 'and one I would not have undertaken had I not known your lordship's character for candour and honesty.'

Lord Cashel again bowed and rubbed his hands.

'I am, my lord, a friend of Lord Ballindine; and as such I have taken the liberty of calling on your lordship.'

'A friend of Lord Ballindine?' said the earl, arching his eyebrows, and assuming a look of great surprise.

'A very old friend, my lord; the clergyman of his parish, and for many years an intimate friend of his father. I have known Lord Ballindine since he was a child.'

'Lord Ballindine is lucky in having such a friend: few young men now, I am sorry to say, care much for their father's friends. Is there anything, Mr. Armstrong, in which I can assist either you or his lordship?'

'My lord,' said the parson, 'I need not tell you that before I took the perhaps unwarrantable liberty of troubling you, I was made acquainted with Lord Ballindine's engagement with your ward, and with the manner in which that engagement was broken off.'

'And your object is, Mr. Armstrong—?'

'My object is to remove, if possible, the un-

fortunate misunderstanding between your lordship
and my friend.'

'Misunderstanding, Mr. Armstrong?—There was
no misunderstanding between us. I really think we
perfectly understood each other. Lord Ballindine
was engaged to my ward; his engagement, however,
being contingent on his adoption of a certain line of
conduct. This line of conduct his lordship did not
adopt; perhaps, he used a wise discretion; however,
I thought not. I thought the mode of life which he
pursued—'

'But—'

'Pardon me a moment, Mr. Armstrong, and I shall
have said all which appears to me to be necessary on
the occasion; perhaps more than is necessary; more
probably than I should have allowed myself to say,
had not Lord Ballindine sent as his ambassador the
clergyman of his parish and the friend of his father,'
and Lord Cashel again bowed and rubbed his hands.
'I thought, Mr. Armstrong, that your young friend
appeared wedded to a style of life quite incompatible
with his income—with his own income as a single man,
and the income which he would have possessed had
he married my ward. I thought that their marriage
would only lead to poverty and distress, and I felt
that I was only doing my duty to my ward in expressing this opinion to her. I found that she was
herself of the same opinion; that she feared a union
with Lord Ballindine would not ensure happiness
either to him or to herself. His habits were too
evidently those of extravagance, and hers had not
been such as to render a life of privation anything
but a life of misery.'

'I had thought—'

'One moment more, Mr. Armstrong, and I shall
have done. After mature consideration, Miss Wyndham commissioned me to express her sentiments,—
and I must say they fully coincided with my own,—
to Lord Ballindine, and to explain to him, that she
found herself obliged to—to—to retrace the steps

which she had taken in the matter. I did this in a manner as little painful to Lord Ballindine as I was able. It is difficult, Mr. Armstrong, to make a disagreeable communication palatable; it is very difficult to persuade a young man who is in love, to give up the object of his idolatry; but I trust Lord Ballindine will do me the justice to own that, on the occasion alluded to, I said nothing unnecessarily harsh—nothing calculated to harass his feelings. I appreciate and esteem Lord Ballindine's good qualities, and I much regretted that prudence forbad me to sanction the near alliance he was anxious to do me the honour of making with me.'

Lord Cashel finished his harangue, and felt once more on good terms with himself. He by no means intended offering any further vehement resistance to his ward's marriage. He was, indeed, rejoiced to have an opportunity of giving way decently. But he could not resist the temptation of explaining his conduct, and making a speech.

'My lord,' said the parson, 'what you tell me is only a repetition of what I heard from my young friend.'

'I am glad to hear it. I trust, then, I may have the pleasure of feeling that Lord Ballindine attributes to me no personal unkindness?'

'Not in the least, Lord Cashel; very far from it. Though Lord Ballindine may not be—may not hitherto have been, free from the follies of his age, he has had quite sense enough to appreciate your lordship's conduct.'

'I endeavoured, at any rate, that it should be such as to render me liable to no just imputation of fickleness or cruelty.'

'No one would for a moment accuse your lordship of either. It is my knowledge of your lordship's character in this particular which has induced me to undertake the task of begging you to reconsider the subject. Lord Ballindine has, you are aware, sold his race-horses.'

'I had heard so, Mr. Armstrong; though, perhaps, not on good authority.'

'He has; and is now living among his own tenantry and friends at Kelly's Court. He is passionately, devotedly attached to your ward, Lord Cashel; and with a young man's vanity he still thinks that she may not be quite indifferent to him.'

'It was at her own instance, Mr. Armstrong, that his suit was rejected.

'I am well aware of that, my lord. But ladies, you know, do sometimes mistake their own feelings. Miss Wyndham must have been attached to my friend, or she would not have received him as her lover. Will you, my lord, allow me to see Miss Wyndham? If she still expresses indifference to Lord Ballindine, I will assure her that she shall be no further persecuted by his suit. If such be not the case, surely prudence need not further interfere to prevent a marriage desired by both the persons most concerned. Lord Ballindine is not now a spendthrift, whatever he may formerly have been; and Miss Wyndham's princely fortune, though it alone would never have induced my friend to seek her hand, will make the match all that it should be. You will not object, my lord, to my seeing Miss Wyndham?'

'Mr. Armstrong—really—you must be aware such a request is rather unusual.'

'So are the circumstances,' replied the parson. 'They also are unusual. I do not doubt Miss Wyndham's wisdom in rejecting Lord Ballindíne, when, as you say, he appeared to be wedded to a life of extravagance. I have no doubt she put a violent restraint on her own feelings; exercised, in fact, a self-denial which shows a very high tone of character, and should elicit nothing but admiration; but circumstances are much altered.'

Lord Cashel continued to raise objections to the parson's request, though it was, throughout the interview, his intention to accede to it. At last, he gave up the point, with much grace, and in such a manner as he thought should entitle him to the eternal gratitude of his ward, Lord Ballindine, and the parson. He consequently rang the bell, and desired the servant to give his compliments to Miss Wyndham and tell her that the Rev. Mr. Armstrong wished to see her, alone, upon business of importance.

Mr. Armstrong felt that his success was much greater than he had had any reason to expect, from Lord Ballindine's description of his last visit at Grey Abbey. He had, in fact, overcome the only difficulty. If Miss Wyndham really disliked his friend, and objected to the marriage, Mr. Armstrong was well aware that he had only to return, and tell his friend so in the best way he could. If, however, she still had a true regard for him, if she were the Fanny Wyndham Ballindine had described her to be, if she had ever really been devoted to him, if she had at all a wish in her heart to see him again at her feet, the parson felt that he would have good news to send back to Kelly's Court; and that he would have done the lovers a service which they never could forget.

'At any rate, Mr. Armstrong,' said Lord Cashel, as the parson was bowing himself backwards out of the room, 'you will join our family circle while you are in the neighbourhood. Whatever may be the success of your mission—and I assure you I hope it may be such as will be gratifying to you, I am happy to make the acquaintance of any friend of Lord Ballindine's, when Lord Ballindine chooses his friends so well.' (This was meant as a slap at Dot Blake.) 'You will give me leave to send down to the town for your luggage.' Mr. Armstrong made no objection to this proposal, and the luggage was sent for.

The powder-haired servant again took him in tow, and ushered him out of the book-room, across the hall through the billiard-room, and into the library; gave him a chair, and then brought him a newspaper, giving him to understand that Miss Wyndham would soon be with him.

The parson took the paper in his hands, but he did

not trouble himself much with the contents of it. What was he to say to Miss Wyndham?—how was he to commence? He had never gone love-making for another in his life; and now, at his advanced age, it really did come rather strange to him. And then he began to think whether she were short or tall, dark or fair, stout or slender. It certainly was very odd, but, in all their conversations on the subject, Lord Ballindine had never given him any description of his inamorata. Mr. Armstrong, however, had not much time to make up his mind on any of these points, for the door opened, and Miss Wyndham entered.

She was dressed in black, for she was, of course, still in mourning for her brother; but, in spite of her sable habiliments, she startled the parson by the brilliance of her beauty. There was a quiet dignity of demeanour natural to Fanny Wyndham; a well-balanced pose, and a grace of motion, which saved her from ever looking awkward or confused. She never appeared to lose her self-possession. Though never arrogant, she seemed always to know what was due to herself. No insignificant puppy could ever have attempted to flirt with her.

When summoned by the servant to meet a strange clergyman alone in the library, at the request of Lord Cashel, she felt that his visit must have some reference to her lover; indeed, her thoughts for the last few days had run on little else. She had made up her mind to talk to her cousin about him; then, her cousin had matured that determination by making love to her himself: then, she had talked to him of Lord Ballindine, and he had promised to talk to his father on the same subject; and she had since been endeavouring to bring herself to make one other last appeal to her uncle's feelings. Her mind was therefore, full of Lord Ballindine, when she walked into the library. But her face was no tell-tale; her gait and demeanour were as dignified as though she had no anxious love within her heart—no one grand

desire, to disturb the even current of her blood. She
bowed her beautiful head to Mr. Armstrong as she
walked into the room, and, sitting down herself,
begged him to take a chair.

The parson had by no means made up his mind as
to what he was to say to the young lady, so he shut
his eyes, and rushed at once into the middle of his
subject. 'Miss Wyndham,' he said, ' I have come a
long way to call on you, at the request of a friend of
yours—a very dear and old friend of mine—at the
request of Lord Ballindine.'

Fanny's countenance became deeply suffused at
her lover's name, but the parson did not observe it;
indeed he hardly ventured to look in her face. She
merely said, in a voice which seemed to him to be
anything but promising, 'Well, sir?' The truth was,
she did not know what to say. Had she dared, she
would have fallen on her knees before her lover's
friend, and sworn to him how well she loved him.

'When Lord Ballindine was last at Grey Abbey,
Miss Wyndham, he had not the honour of an interview with you.'

'No, sir,' said Fanny. Her voice, look, and manner
were still sedate and courtly; her heart, however,
was beating so violently that she hardly knew what
she said.

'Circumstances, I believe, prevented it,' said the
parson. 'My friend, however, received, through
Lord Cashel, a message from you, which—which—
which has been very fatal to his happiness.'

Fanny tried to say something, but she was not
able.

'The very decided tone in which your uncle then
spoke to him, has made Lord Ballindine feel that
any further visit to Grey Abbey on his own part
would be an intrusion.'

'I never—' said Fanny, 'I never—'

'You never authorised so harsh a message, you
would say. It is not the harshness of the language,
but the certainty of the fact, that has destroyed my

friend's happiness. If such were to be the case—if it were absolutely necessary that the engagement between you and Lord Ballindine should be broken off, the more decided the manner in which it were done, the better. Lord Ballindine now wishes—I am a bad messenger in such a case as this, Miss Wyndham: it is, perhaps, better to tell you at once a plain tale. Frank has desired me to tell you that he loves you well and truly; that he cannot believe you are indifferent to him; that your vows, to him so precious, are still ringing in his ears; that he is, as far as his heart is concerned, unchanged; and he has commissioned me to ascertain from yourself, whether you—have really changed your mind since he last had the pleasure of seeing you.' The parson waited a moment for an answer, and then added, 'Lord Ballindine by no means wishes to persecute you on the subject; nor would I do so, if he did wish it. You have only to tell me that you do not intend to renew your acquaintance with Lord Ballindine, and I will leave Grey Abbey.' Fanny still remained silent. 'Say the one word "go", Miss Wyndham, and you need not pain yourself by any further speech. I will at once be gone.'

Fanny strove hard to keep her composure, and to make some fitting reply to Mr. Armstrong, but she was unable. Her heart was too full; she was too happy. She had, openly, and in spite of rebuke, avowed her love to her uncle, her aunt, to Lady Selina, and her cousin. But she could not bring herself to confess it to Mr. Armstrong. At last she said:

'I am much obliged to you for your kindness, Mr. Armstrong. Perhaps I owe it to Lord Ballindine to—to . . . I will ask my uncle, sir, to write to him.'

'I shall write to Lord Ballindine this evening, Miss Wyndham; will you intrust me with no message? I came from him, to see you, with no other purpose. I must give him some news: I must tell him I have seen you. May I tell him not to despair?'

'Tell him—tell him—' said Fanny,—and she

paused to make up her mind as to the words of her message,—'tell him to come himself.' And, hurrying from the room, she left the parson alone, to meditate on the singular success of his mission. He stood for about half an hour, thinking over what had occurred, and rejoicing greatly in his mind that he had undertaken the business. 'What fools men are about women!' he said at last, to himself. 'They know their nature so well when they are thinking and speaking of them with reference to others; but as soon as a man is in love with one himself, he is cowed! He thinks the nature of one woman is different from that of all others, and he is afraid to act on his general knowledge. Well; I might as well write to him! for, thank God, I can send him good news'—and he rang the bell, and asked if his bag had come. It had, and was in his bed-room. 'Could the servant get him pen, ink, and paper?' The servant did so; and, within two hours of his entering the doors of Grey Abbey, he was informing his friend of the success of his mission.

XXXVII

VENI; VIDI; VICI

THE two following letters for Lord Ballindine were sent off, in the Grey Abbey post-bag, on the evening of the day on which Mr. Armstrong had arrived there. They were from Mr. Armstrong and Lord Cashel. That from the former was first opened.

Grey Abbey, April, 1844.

Dear Frank,

You will own I have not lost much time. I only left Kelly's Court the day before yesterday, and I am already able to send you good news. I have seen Lord Cashel, and found him anything but uncourteous. I have also seen Miss Wyndham, and though she said but little to me, that little was just

what you would have wished her to say. She bade
me tell you to come yourself. In obedience to her
commands, I do hereby require you to pack yourself
up, and proceed forthwith to Grey Abbey. His lordship has signified to me that it is his intention, in
his own and Lady Cashel's name, to request the
renewed pleasure of an immediate, and, he hopes, a
prolonged visit from your lordship. You will not,
my dear Frank, I am sure, be such a fool as to allow
your dislike to such an empty butter-firkin as this
earl, to stand in the way of your love or your fortune. You can't expect Miss Wyndham to go to you,
so pocket your resentment like a sensible fellow, and
accept Lord Cashel's invitation as though there had
been no difference between you.

I have also received an invite, and intend staying
here a day or two. I can't say that, judging from the
master of the house, I think that a prolonged sojourn would be very agreeable. I have, as yet, seen
none of the ladies, except my embryo Lady Ballin-
di ie.

I think I have done my business a little in the *veni
vidi vici* style. What has effected the change in Lord
Cashel's views, I need not trouble myself to guess.
You will soon learn all about it from Miss Wyndham.

I will not, in a letter, express my admiration, &c.,
&c., &c. But I will proclaim in Connaught, on my
return, that so worthy a bride was never yet brought
down to the far west. Lord Cashel will, of course,
have some pet bishop or dean to marry you; but,
after what has passed, I shall certainly demand the
privilege of christening the heir.

Believe me, dear Frank,
Your affectionate friend,
GEORGE ARMSTRONG.

Lord Cashel's letter was as follows. It cost his lordship three hours to compose, and was twice copied.
I trust, therefore, it is a fair specimen of what a
nobleman ought to write on such an occasion.

Grey Abbey, April, 1844.

My dear lord,

Circumstances, to which I rejoice that I need not now more particularly allude, made your last visit at my house a disagreeable one to both of us. The necessity under which I then laboured, of communicating to your lordship a decision which was likely to be inimical to your happiness, but to form which my duty imperatively directed me, was a source of most serious inquietude to my mind. I now rejoice that that decision was so painful to you —has been so lastingly painful; as I trust I may measure your gratification at a renewal of your connection with my family, by the acuteness of the sufferings which an interruption of that connexion has occasioned you.

I have, I can assure you, my lord, received much pleasure from the visit of your very estimable friend, the Reverend Mr. Armstrong; and it is no slight addition to my gratification on this occasion, to find your most intimate friendship so well bestowed. I have had much unreserved conversation to-day with Mr. Armstrong, and I am led by him to believe that I may be able to induce you to give Lady Cashel and myself the pleasure of your company at Grey Abbey. We shall be truly delighted to see your lordship, and we sincerely hope that the attractions of Grey Abbey may be such as to induce you to prolong your visit for some time.

Perhaps it might be unnecessary for me now more explicitly to allude to my ward; but still, I cannot but think that a short but candid explanation of the line of conduct I have thought it my duty to adopt, may prevent any disagreeable feeling between us, should you, as I sincerely trust you will, do us the pleasure of joining our family circle. I must own, my dear lord, that, a few months since, I feared you were wedded to the expensive pleasures of the turf.—Your acceptance of the office of Steward at the

Curragh meetings confirmed the reports which reached me from various quarters. My ward's fortune was then not very considerable; and, actuated by an uncle's affection for his niece as well as a guardian's caution for his ward, I conceived it my duty to ascertain whether a withdrawal from the engagement in contemplation between Miss Wyndham and yourself would be detrimental to her happiness. I found that my ward's views agreed with my own. She thought her own fortune insufficient, seeing that your habits were then expensive: and, perhaps, not truly knowing the intensity of her own affection, she coincided in my views. You are acquainted with the result. These causes have operated in inducing me to hope that I may still welcome you by the hand as my dear niece's husband. Her fortune is very greatly increased; your character is—I will not say altered—is now fixed and established. And, lastly and chiefly, I find—I blush, my lord, to tell a lady's secret—that my ward's happiness still depends on you.

I am sure, my dear lord, I need not say more. We shall be delighted to see you at your earliest convenience. We wish that you could have come to us before your friend left, but I regret to learn from him that his parochial duties preclude the possibility of his staying with us beyond Thursday.

I shall anxiously wait for your reply. In the meantime I beg to assure you, with the joint kind remembrances of all our party, that I am,

Most faithfully yours,
Cashel.

Mr. Armstrong descended to the drawing-room, before dinner, looking most respectable, with a stiff white tie and the new suit expressly prepared for the occasion. He was introduced to Lady Cashel and Lady Selina as a valued friend of Lord Ballindine, and was received, by the former at least, in a most flattering manner. Lady Selina had hardly recon-

ciled herself to the return of Lord Ballindine. It was
from no envy at her cousin's happiness; she was
really too high-minded, and too falsely proud, also,
to envy any one. But it was the harsh conviction of her
mind, that no duties should be disregarded, and that
all duties were disagreeable: she was always opposed
to the doing of anything which appeared to be the
especial wish of the person consulting her; because it
would be agreeable, she judged that it would be
wrong. She was most sincerely anxious for her poor
dependents, but she tormented them most cruelly.
When Biddy Finn wished to marry, Lady Selina told
her it was her duty to put a restraint on her inclina-
tions; and ultimately prevented her, though there
was no objection on earth to Tony Mara; and when
the widow Cullen wanted to open a little shop for
soap and candles, having eight pounds ten shillings
left to stock it, after the wake and funeral were over,
Lady Selina told the widow it was her duty to restrain her inclination, and she did so; and the eight
pounds ten shillings drifted away in quarters of tea,
and most probably, half noggins of whiskey.

In the same way, she could not bring herself to
think that Fanny was doing right, in following the
bent of her dearest wishes—in marrying this man
she loved so truly. She was weak; she was giving way
to temptation; she was going back from her word;
she was, she said, giving up her claim to that high
standard of feminine character, which it should be the
proudest boast of a woman to maintain.

It was in vain that her mother argued the point
with her in her own way. 'But why shouldn't she
marry him, my dear,' said the countess, 'when they
love each other—and now there's plenty of money
and all that; and your papa thinks it's all right? I
declare I can't see the harm of it.'

'I don't say there's harm, mother,' said Lady
Selina; 'not absolute harm; but there's weakness.
She had ceased to esteem Lord Ballindine.'

'Ah, but, my dear, she very soon began to esteem

him again. Poor dear! she didn't know how well she loved him.'

'She ought to have known, mamma—to have known well, before she rejected him; but, having rejected him, no power on earth should have induced her to name him, or even to think of him again. She should have been dead to him; and he should have been the same as dead to her.'

'Well, I don't know,' said the countess; 'but I'm sure I shall be delighted to see anybody happy in the house again, and I always liked Lord Ballindine myself. There was never any trouble about his dinners or anything.'

And Lady Cashel *was* delighted. The grief she had felt at the abrupt termination of all her hopes with regard to her son had been too much for her; she had been unable even to mind her worsted-work, and Griffiths had failed to comfort her; but from the moment that her husband had told her, with many hems and haws, that Mr. Armstrong had arrived to repeat Lord Ballindine's proposal, and that he had come to consult her about again asking his lordship to Grey Abbey, she became happy and light-hearted; and, before Griffiths had left her for the night, she had commenced her consultations as to the preparations for the wedding.

XXXVIII

WAIT TILL I TELL YOU

THERE was no one at dinner that first evening, but Mr. Armstrong, and the family circle; and the parson certainly felt it dull enough. Fanny, naturally, was rather silent; Lady Selina did not talk a great deal; the countess reiterated, twenty times, the pleasure she had in seeing him at Grey Abbey, and asked one or two questions as to the quantity of flannel it took to make petticoats for the old women in his parish; but, to make up the rest, Lord Cashel talked incessantly. He wished to show every attention to his guest, and he crammed him with ecclesiastical conversation, till Mr. Armstrong felt that, poor as he was, and much as his family wanted the sun of lordly favour, he would not give up his little living down in Connaught, where, at any rate, he could do as he pleased, to be domestic chaplain to Lord Cashel, with a salary of a thousand a-year.

The next morning was worse, and the whole of the long day was insufferable. He endeavoured to escape from his noble friend into the demesne, where he might have explored the fox coverts, and ascertained something of the sporting capabilities of the country; but Lord Cashel would not leave him alone for an instant; and he had not only to endure the earl's tediousness, but also had to assume a demeanour which was not at all congenial to his feelings. Lord Cashel would talk Church and ultra-Protestantism to him, and descanted on the abominations of the National system, and the glories of Sunday-schools. Now, Mr. Armstrong had no leaning to popery, and had nothing to say against Sunday schools; but he had not one in his own parish, in which, by the bye, he was the father of all the Protestant children to be found there—without the slightest slur upon his reputation be it said. Lord Cashel totally mistook his character, and Mr. Armstrong did not know how to set him right; and at five o'clock he went to dress, more tired than he ever had been after hunting all day, and then riding home twelve miles on a wet, dark night, with a lame horse.

To do honour to her guest Lady Cashel asked Mr. O'Joscelyn, the rector, together with his wife and daughters, to dine there on the second day; and Mr. Armstrong, though somewhat afraid of brother clergymen, was delighted to hear that they were coming. Anything was better than another *tête-à-tête* with the ponderous earl. There were no other neighbours near enough to Grey Abbey to be asked on so short a notice; but the rector, his wife, and their daughters, entered the dining-room punctually at half-past six.

The character and feelings of Mr. O'Joscelyn were exactly those which the earl had attributed to Mr. Armstrong. He had been an Orangeman, and was a most ultra and even furious Protestant. He was, by principle, a charitable man to his neighbours; but he hated popery, and he carried the feeling to such a length, that he almost hated Papists. He had not, generally speaking, a bad opinion of human nature; but he would not have considered his life or property safe in the hands of any Roman Catholic. He pitied the ignorance of the heathen, the credulity of the Mahommedan, the desolateness of the Jew, even the infidelity of the atheist; but he execrated, abhorred, and abominated the Church of Rome. 'Anathema Maranatha; get thee from me, thou child of Satan— —go out into utter darkness, thou worker of iniquity —into everlasting lakes of fiery brimstone, thou doer of the devil's work—thou false prophet—thou ravenous wolf!' Such was the language of his soul, at the sight of a priest; such would have been the language of his tongue, had not, as he thought, evil legislators given a licence to falsehood in his unhappy country, and rendered it impossible for a true Churchman openly to declare the whole truth.

But though Mr. O'Joscelyn did not absolutely give utterance to such imprecations as these against the wolves who, as he thought, destroyed the lambs of his flock,—or rather, turned his sheep into foxes,— yet he by no means concealed his opinion, or hid his light under a bushel. He spent his life—an eager, anxious, hard-working life, in denouncing the scarlet woman of Babylon and all her abominations; and he did so in season and out of season: in town and in country; in public and in private; from his own pulpit, and at other people's tables; in highways and byways; both to friends—who only partly agreed with him, and to strangers, who did not agree with him at all. He totally disregarded the feelings of his auditors; he would make use of the same language to persons who might in all probability be Romanists, as he did to those whom he knew to be Protestants. He was a most zealous and conscientious, but a most indiscreet servant of his Master. He made many enemies, but few converts. He rarely convinced his opponents, but often disgusted his own party. He had been a constant speaker at public meetings; an orator at the Rotunda, and, on one occasion, at Exeter Hall. But even his own friends, the ultra Protestants, found that he did the cause more harm than good, and his public exhibitions had been as much as possible discouraged. Apart from his fanatical enthusiasm, he was a good man, of pure life, and simple habits; and rejoiced exceedingly, that, in the midst of the laxity in religious opinions which so generally disfigured the age, his wife and his children were equally eager and equally zealous with himself in the service of their Great Master.

A beneficed clergyman from the most benighted, that is, most Papistical portion of Connaught, would be sure, thought Mr. O'Joscelyn, to have a fellow-feeling with him; to sympathise with his wailings, and to have similar woes to communicate.

'How many Protestants have you?' said he to Mr. Armstrong, in the drawing-room, a few minutes after they had been introduced to each other. 'I had two hundred and seventy in the parish on New Year's day; and since that we've had two births, and a very proper Church of England police-serjeant has been sent here, in place of a horrid Papist. We've a great gain in Serjeant Woody, my lord.'

'In one way we certainly have, Mr. O'Joscelyn,' said the earl. 'I wish all the police force were Protestants; I think they would be much more effective. But Serjeant Carroll was a very good man; you know he was removed from hence on his promotion.'

'I know he was, my lord—just to please the priests —just because he was a Papist. Do you think there

was a single thing done, or a word said at Petty
Sessions, but what Father Flannery knew all about
it?—Yes, every word. When did the police ever take
any of Father Flannery's own people?'

'Didn't Serjeant Carroll take that horrible man
Leary, that robbed the old widow that lived under
the bridge?' said the countess.

'True, my lady, he did,' said Mr. O'Joscelyn; 'but
you'll find, if you inquire, that Leary hadn't paid the
priest his dues, nor yet his brother. How a Protestant
government can reconcile it to their conscience—how
they can sleep at night, after pandering to the priests
as they daily do, I cannot conceive. How many
Protestants did you say you have, Mr. Armstrong?'

'We're not very strong down in the West, Mr.
O'Joscelyn,' said the other parson. 'There are
usually two or three in the Kelly's Court pew. The
vicarage pew musters pretty well, for Mrs. Armstrong
and five of the children are always there. Then there
are usually two policemen, and the clerk; though, by
the bye, he doesn't belong to the parish. I borrowed
him from Claremorris.'

Mr. O'Joscelyn gave a look of horror and astonishment.

'I can, however, make a boast, which perhaps you
cannot, Mr. Joscelyn: all my parishioners are usually
to be seen in church, and if one is absent I'm able to
miss him.'

'It must paralyse your efforts, preaching to such
congregation,' said the other.

'Do not disparage my congregation,' said Mr.
Armstrong, laughing; 'they are friendly and neigh-
bourly, if not important in point of numbers; and,
if I wanted to fill my church, the Roman Catholics
think so well of me, that they'd flock in crowds there
if I asked them; and the priest would show them the
way—for any special occasion, I mean; if the bishop
came to see me, or anything of that kind.'

Mr. O'Joscelyn was struck dumb; and, indeed, he
would have had no time to answer if the power of

speech had been left to him, for the servant announced dinner.

The conversation was a little more general during dinner-time, but after dinner the parish clergyman returned to another branch of his favourite subject. Perhaps, he thought that Mr. Armstrong was himself not very orthodox; or, perhaps, that it was useless to enlarge on the abominations of Babylon to a Protestant peer and a Protestant parson; but, on this occasion, he occupied himself with the temporal iniquities of the Roman Catholics. The trial of O'Connell and his fellow-prisoners had come to an end, and he and they, with one exception, had just commenced their period of imprisonment. The one exception was a clergyman, who had been acquitted. He had in some way been connected with Mr. O'Joscelyn's parish; and, as the parish priest and most of his flock were hot Repealers, there was a good deal of excitement on the occasion,—rejoicings at the priest's acquittal, and howlings, yellings, and murmurings at the condemnation of the others.

'We've fallen on frightful days, Mr. Armstrong,' said Mr. O'Joscelyn: 'frightful, lawless, dangerous days.'

'We must take them as we find them, Mr. O'Joscelyn.'

'Doubtless, Mr. Armstrong, doubtless; and I acknowledge His infinite wisdom, who, for His own purposes, now allows sedition to rear her head unchecked, and falsehood to sit in the high places. They are indeed dangerous days, when the sympathy of government is always with the evil doers, and the religion of the state is deserted by the crown.'

'Why, God bless me! Mr. O'Joscelyn!—the queen hasn't turned Papist, and the Repealers are all in prison, or soon will be there.'

'I don't mean the queen. I believe she is very good. I believe she is a sincere Protestant, God bless her;' and Mr. O'Joscelyn, in his loyalty, drank a glass of port wine; 'but I mean her advisers. They do not dare protect the Protestant faith: they do not dare secure the tranquillity of the country.'

'Are not O'Connell and the whole set under conviction at this moment? I'm no politician myself, but the only question seems to be, whether they haven't gone a step too far?'

'Why did they let that priest escape them?' said Mr. O'Joscelyn.

'I suppose he was not guilty;' said Mr. Armstrong; 'at any rate, you had a staunch Protestant jury.'

'I tell you the priests are at the head of it all. O'Connell would be nothing without them; he is only their creature. The truth is, the government did not dare to frame an indictment that would really lead to the punishment of a priest. The government is truckling to the false hierarchy of Rome. Look at Oxford,—a Jesuitical seminary, devoted to the secret propagation of Romish falsehood.—Go into the churches of England, and watch their bowings, their genuflexions, their crosses and their candles; see the demeanour of their apostate clergy; look into their private oratories; see their red-lettered prayer-books, their crucifixes, and images; and then, can you doubt that the most dreadful of all prophecies is about to be accomplished?'

'But I have not been into their closets, Mr. O'Joscelyn, nor yet into their churches lately, and therefore I have not seen these things; nor have I seen anybody who has. Have you seen crucifixes in the rooms of Church of England clergymen? or candles on the altar-steps of English churches?'

'God forbid that I should willingly go where such things are to be seen; but of the fearful fact there is, unfortunately, no doubt. And then, as to the state of the country, we have nothing round us but anarchy and misrule: my life, Mr. Armstrong, has not been safe any day this week past.'

'Good Heaven, Mr. O'Joscelyn—your life not safe! I thought you were as quiet here, in Kildare, as we are in Mayo.'

'Wait till I tell you, Mr. Armstrong: you know this priest, whom they have let loose to utter more sedition?—He was coadjutor to the priest in this parish.'

'Was he? The people are not attacking you, I suppose, because he's let loose?'

'Wait till I tell you. No; the people are mad because O'Connell and his myrmidons are to be locked up; and, mingled with their fury on this head are their insane rejoicings at the escape of this priest. They are, therefore,—or were, till Saturday last, howling for joy and for grief at the same time. Oh! such horrid howls, Mr. Armstrong. I declare, Mr. Armstrong, I have trembled for my children this week past.'

The earl, who well knew Mr. O'Joscelyn, and the nature of his grievances, had heard all these atrocities before; and, not being very excited by their interest, had continued sipping his claret in silence till he began to doze; and, by the time the worthy parson had got to the climax of his misery, the nobleman was fast asleep.

'You don't mean that the people made any attack on the parsonage?' said Mr. Armstrong.

'Wait till I tell you, Mr. Armstrong,' replied the other. 'On Thursday morning last they all heard that O'Connell was a convicted felon.'

'Conspirator, I believe? Mr. O'Joscelyn.'

'Conspiracy is felony, Mr. Armstrong—and that their priest had been let loose. It was soon evident that no work was to be done that day. They assembled about the roads in groups; at the chapel-door; at Priest Flannery's house; at the teetotal reading-room as they call it, where the people drink cordial made of whiskey, and disturb the neighbourhood with cracked horns; and we heard that a public demonstration was to be made.'

'Was it a demonstration of joy or of grief?'

'Both, Mr. Armstrong! it was mixed. They were to shout and dance for joy about Father Tyrrel; and howl and curse for grief about O'Connell; and they did shout and howl with a vengeance. All Thursday, you would have thought that a legion of devils had been let loose into Kilcullen.'

'But did they commit any personal outrages, Mr. O'Joscelyn?'

'Wait till I tell you. I soon saw how the case was going to be, and I determined to be prepared. I armed myself, Mr. Armstrong; and so did Mrs. O'Joscelyn. Mrs. O'Joscelyn is a most determined woman—a woman of great spirit; we were resolved to protect our daughters and our infants from ill-usage, as long as God should leave us the power to do so. We both armed ourselves with pistols, and I can assure you that, as far as ammunition goes, we were prepared to give them a hot reception.'

'Dear me! This must have been very unpleasant to Mrs. O'Joscelyn.'

'Oh, she's a woman of great nerve, Mr. Armstrong. Mary is a woman of very great nerve. I can assure you we shall never forget that Thursday night. About seven in the evening it got darkish, but the horrid yells of the wild creatures had never ceased for one half-hour; and, a little after seven, twenty different bon-fires illuminated the parish. There were bonfires on every side of us: huge masses of blazing turf were to be seen scattered through the whole country.'

'Did they burn any thing except the turf, Mr. O'Joscelyn?'

'Wait till I tell you, Mr. Armstrong. I shall never forget that night; we neither of us once lay down; no, not for a moment. About eight, the children were put to bed; but with their clothes and shoes on, for there was no knowing at what moment and in how sudden a way the poor innocents might be called up. My daughters behaved admirably; they remained quite quiet in the drawing-room till about eleven, when we had evening worship, and then they retired to rest. Their mother, however, insisted that they should not take off their petticoats or stockings. At about one, we went to the hall-door: it was then bright moonlight—but the flames of the surrounding fires overpowered the moon. The whole horizon was one glare of light.'

'But were not the police about, Mr. O'Joscelyn?'

'Oh, they were about, to be sure, poor men; but what could they do? The government now licenses every outrage.'

'But what *did* the people do? said Mr. Armstrong.

'Wait till I tell you. They remained up all night; and so did we, you may be sure. Mary did not rise from her chair once that night without a pistol in her hand. We heard the sounds of their voices continually, close to the parsonage gate; we could see them in the road, from the windows—crowds of them —men, women and children; and still they continued shouting. The next morning they were a little more quiet, but still the parish was disturbed: nobody was at work, and men and women stood collected together in the roads. But as soon as it was dusk, the shoutings and the bonfires began again; and again did I and Mrs. O'Joscelyn prepare for a night of anxious watching. We sat up all Friday night, Mr. Armstrong.'

'With the pistols again?'

'Indeed we did; and lucky for us that we did so. Had they not known that we were prepared, I am convinced the house would have been attacked. Our daughters sat with us this night, and we were so far used to the state of disturbance, that we were able to have a little supper.'

'You must have wanted that, I think.'

'Indeed we did. About four in the morning, I dropped asleep on the sofa; but Mary never closed her eyes.'

'Did they come into the garden at all, or near the house?'

'No, they did not. And I am very thankful they refrained from doing so, for I determined to act promptly, Mr. Armstrong, and so was Mary—that is, Mrs. O'Joscelyn. We were both determined to fire, if we found our premises invaded. Thank God! the miscreants did not come within the gate.'

'You did not suffer much, then, except the anxiety, Mr. O'Joscelyn?'

'God was very merciful, and protected us; but who can feel safe, living in such times, and among such a people? And it all springs from Rome; the scarlet woman is now in her full power, and in her full deformity. She was smitten down for a while, but has now risen again. For a while the right foot of truth was on her neck; for a while she lay prostrated before the strength of those, who by God's grace, had prevailed against her. But the latter prophecies which had been revealed to us, are now about to be accomplished. It is well for those who comprehend the signs of the coming time.'

'Suppose we join the ladies,' said the earl, awakened by the sudden lull in Mr. O'Joscelyn's voice. 'But won't you take a glass of Madeira first, Mr. Armstrong?'

Mr. Armstrong took his glass of Madeira, and then went to the ladies; and the next morning, left Grey Abbey, for his own parish. Well; thought he to himself, as he was driven through the park, in the earl's gig, I'm very glad I came here, for Frank's sake. I've smoothed his way to matrimony and a fortune. But I don't know anything which would induce me to stay a week at Grey Abbey. The earl is bad—nearly unbearable; but the parson!—I'd sooner by half be a Roman myself, than think so badly of my neighbours as he does. Many a time since has he told in Connaught, how Mr. O'Joscelyn, and Mary, his wife, sat up two nights running, armed to the teeth, to protect themselves from the noisy Repealers of Kilcullen.

Mr. Armstrong arrived safely at his parsonage, and the next morning he rode over to Kelly's Court. But Lord Ballindine was not there. He had started for Grey Abbey almost immediately on receiving the two letters which we have given, and he and his friend had passed each other on the road.

XXXIX

IT NEVER RAINS BUT IT POURS

WHEN Frank had read his two letters from Grey Abbey, he was in such a state of excitement as to be unable properly to decide what he would immediately do. His first idea was to gallop to Tuam, as fast as his best horse would carry him; to take four horses there, and not to stop one moment till he found himself at Grey Abbey: but a little consideration showed him that this would not do. He would not find horses ready for him on the road; he must take some clothes with him; and it would be only becoming in him to give the earl some notice of his approach. So he at last made up his mind to postpone his departure for a few hours.

He was, however, too much overcome with joy to be able to do anything rationally. His anger against the earl totally evaporated; indeed, he only thought of him now as a man who had a house in which he could meet his love. He rushed into the drawing-room, where his mother and sisters were sitting, and, with the two letters open in his hand, proclaimed his intention of leaving home that day.

'Goodness gracious, Frank! and where are you going?' said Mrs. O'Kelly.

'To Grey Abbey.'

'No!' said Augusta, jumping up from her chair.

'I am so glad!' shouted Sophy, throwing down her portion of the worsted-work sofa.

'You have made up your difference, then, with Miss Wyndham?' said the anxious mother. 'I am so glad! My own dear, good, sensible Frank!'

'I never had any difference with Fanny,' said he. 'I was not able to explain all about it, nor can I now: it was a crotchet of the earl's—only some nonsense; however, I'm off now—I can't wait a day, for I mean to write to say I shall be at Grey Abbey the day after to-morrow, and I must go by Dublin. I shall be off

in a couple of hours; so, for Heaven's sake, Sophy,
look sharp and put up my things.'

The girls both bustled out of the room, and Frank
was following them, but his mother called him back.
'When is it to be, Frank? Come tell me something
about it. I never asked any questions when I thought
the subject was a painful one.'

'God bless you, mother, you never did. But I can
tell you nothing—only the stupid old earl has begged
me to go there at once. Fanny must settle the time
herself: there'll be settlements, and lawyer's work.'

'That's true, my love. A hundred thousand
pounds in ready cash does want looking after. But
look here, my dear; Fanny is of age, isn't she?'

'She is, mother.'

'Well now, Frank, take my advice; they'll want
to tie up her money in all manner of ways, so as to
make it of the least possible use to you, or to her
either. They always do; they're never contented unless they lock up a girl's money, so that neither she
nor her husband can spend the principal or the interest. Don't let them do it, Frank. Of course she
will be led by you, let them settle whatever is fair on
her; but don't let them bother the money so that
you can't pay off the debts. It'll be a grand thing,
Frank, to redeem the property.'

Frank hemmed and hawed, and said he'd consult
his lawyer in Dublin before the settlements were
signed; but declared that he was not going to marry
Fanny Wyndham for her money.

'That's all very well, Frank,' said the mother; 'but
you know you could not marry her without the money,
and mind, it's now or never. Think what a thing
it would be to have the property unencumbered!'

The son hurried away to throw himself at the feet
of his mistress, and the mother remained in her drawing-room, thinking with delight on the renovated
grandeur of the family, and of the decided lead which
the O'Kellys would again be able to take in Connaught.

Fanny's joy was quite equal to that of her lover, but it was not shown quite so openly. Her aunt congratulated her most warmly; kissed her twenty times; called her her own dear, darling niece, and promised her to love her husband, and to make him a purse if she could get Griffiths to teach her that new stitch; it looked so easy she was sure she could learn it, and it wouldn't tease her eyes. Lady Selina also wished her joy; but she did it very coldly, though very sensibly.

'Believe me, my dear Fanny, I am glad you should have the wish of your heart. There were obstacles to your union with Lord Ballindine, which appeared to be insurmountable, and I therefore attempted to wean you from your love. I hope he will prove worthy of that love, and that you may never have cause to repent of your devotion to him. You are going greatly to increase your cares and troubles; may God give you strength to bear them, and wisdom to turn them to advantage!'

The earl made a very long speech to her, in which there were but few pauses, and not one full stop. Fanny was not now inclined to quarrel with him; and he quite satisfied himself that his conduct, throughout, towards his ward, had been dignified, prudent, consistent, and disinterested.

These speeches and congratulations all occurred during the period of Mr. Armstrong's visit, and Fanny heard nothing more about her lover, till the third morning after that gentleman's departure; the earl announced then, on entering the breakfast-room, that he had that morning received a communication from Lord Ballindine, and that his lordship intended reaching Grey Abbey that day in time for dinner.

Fanny felt herself blush, but she said nothing; Lady Selina regretted that he had had a very wet day yesterday, and hoped he would have a fine day to-day; and Lady Cashel was overcome at the reflection that she had no one to meet him at dinner, and that she had not yet suited herself with a cook.

'Dear me,' exclaimed her ladyship; 'I wish we'd got this letter yesterday; no one knows now, beforehand, when people are coming. I'm sure it usen't to be so. I shall be so glad to see Lord Ballindine; you know, Fanny, he was always a great favourite of mine. Do you think, Selina, the O'Joscelyns would mind coming again without any notice? I'm sure I don't know—I would not for the world treat Lord Ballindine shabbily; but what can I do, my dear?'

'I think, my lady, we may dispense with any ceremony now, with Lord Ballindine,' said the earl. 'He will, I am sure, be delighted to be received merely as one of the family. You need not mind asking the O'Joscelyns to-day.'

'Do you think not? Well, that's a great comfort: besides, Lord Ballindine never was particular. But still, Fanny, had I known he was coming so soon, I would have had Murray down from Dublin again at once, for Mrs. Richards is not a good cook.'

During the remainder of the morning, Fanny was certainly very happy; but she was very uneasy. She hardly knew how to meet Lord Ballindine. She felt that she had treated him badly, though she had never ceased to love him dearly; and she also thought she owed him much for his constancy. It was so good of him to send his friend to her—and one to whom her uncle could not refuse admission; and then she thought she had treated Mr. Armstrong haughtily and unkindly. She had never thanked him for all the trouble he had taken; she had never told him how very happy he had made her; but she would do so at some future time, when he should be an honoured and a valued guest in her own and her husband's house.

But how should she receive her lover? Would they allow her to be alone with him, if only for a moment, at their first meeting? Oh! how she longed for a confidante! but she could not make a confidante of her cousin. Twice she went down to the drawing-room, with the intention of talking of her love; but

Lady Selina looked so rigid, and spoke so rigidly, that she could not do it. She said such common-place things, and spoke of Lord Ballindine exactly as she would of any other visitor who might have been coming to the house. She did not confine herself to his eating and drinking, as her mother did; but she said, he'd find the house very dull, she was afraid— especially as the shooting was all over, and the hunting very nearly so; that he would, however, probably be a good deal at the Curragh races.

Fanny knew that her cousin did not mean to be unkind; but there was no sympathy in her: she could not talk to her of the only subject which occupied her thoughts; so she retreated to her own room, and endeavoured to compose herself. As the afternoon drew on, she began to wish that he was not coming till to-morrow. She became very anxious; she must see him, somewhere, before she dressed for dinner; and she would not, could not, bring herself to go down into the drawing-room, and shake hands with him, when he came, before her uncle, her aunt, and her cousin.

She was still pondering on the subject, when, about four o'clock in the afternoon, she got a message from her aunt, desiring her to go to her in her boudoir.

'That'll do, Griffiths,' said the countess, as Fanny entered her room; 'you can come up when I ring. Sit down, Fanny; sit down, my dear. I was thinking Lord Ballindine will soon be here.'

'I suppose he will, aunt. In his letter to Lord Cashel, he said he'd be here before dinner.'

'I'm sure he'll be here soon. Dear me; I'm so glad it's all made up between you. I'm sure, Fanny, I hope, and think, and believe, you'll be very, very happy.'

'Dear aunt'—and Fanny kissed Lady Cashel. A word of kindness to her then seemed invaluable.

'It was so very proper in Lord Ballindine to give up his horses, and all that sort of thing,' said the

countess; 'I'm sure I always said he'd turn out just
what he should be; and he is so good-tempered. I
suppose, dear, you'll go abroad the first thing?'

'I haven't thought of that yet, aunt,' said Fanny,
trying to smile.

'Oh, of course you will; you'll go to the Rhine, and
Switzerland, and Como, and Rome, and those sort of
places. It'll be very nice: we went there—your uncle
and I—and it was delightful; only I used to be very
tired. It wasn't then we went to Rome though. I
remember now it was after Adolphus was born.
Poor Adolphus!' and her ladyship sighed, as her
thoughts went back to the miseries of her eldest
born. 'But I'll tell you why I sent for you, my dear:
you know, I must go downstairs to receive Lord
Ballindine, and tell him how glad I am that he's
come back; and I'm sure I am very glad that he's
coming; and your uncle will be there. But I was
thinking you'd perhaps sooner see him first alone.
You'll be a little flurried, my dear,—that's natural;
so, if you like, you can remain up here, my dear, in
my room, quiet and comfortable, by yourself; and
Griffiths shall show Lord Ballindine upstairs, as soon
as he leaves the drawing-room.'

'How very, very kind of you, dear aunt!' said
Fanny, relieved from her most dreadful difficulty. And
so it was arranged. Lady Cashel went down into the
drawing-room to await her guest, and Fanny brought
her book into her aunt's boudoir, and pretended she
would read till Lord Ballindine disturbed her.

I need hardly say that she did not read much.
She sat there over her aunt's fire, waiting to catch
the sound of the wheels on the gravel at the front
door. At one moment she would think that he was
never coming—the time appeared to be so long; and
then again, when she heard any sound which might
be that of his approach, she would again wish to
have a few minutes more to herself.

At length, however, she certainly did hear him.
There was the quick rattle of the chaise over the

gravel, becoming quicker and quicker, till the vehicle
stopped with that kind of plunge which is made by
no other animal than a post-horse, and by him only
at his arrival at the end of a stage. Then the steps
were let down with a crash—she would not go to the
window, or she might have seen him; she longed to
do so, but it appeared so undignified. She sat quite
still in her chair; but she heard his quick step at the
hall door; she was sure—she could have sworn to his
step—and then she heard the untying of cords, and
pulling down of luggage. Lord Ballindine was again
in the house, and the dearest wish of her heart was
accomplished.

She felt that she was trembling. She had not yet
made up her mind how she would receive him—what
she would first say to him—and certainly she had no
time to do so now. She got up, and looked in her
aunt's pier-glass. It was more a movement of in-
stinct than one of premeditation; but she thought
she had never seen herself look so wretchedly. She
had, however, but little time, either for regret or
improvement on that score, for there were footsteps
in the corridor. He couldn't have stayed a moment
to speak to anyone downstairs—however, there he
certainly was; she heard Griffiths' voice in the passage, 'This way, my lord—in my lady's boudoir;'
and then the door opened, and in a moment she was
in her lover's arms.

'My own Fanny!—once more my own!'

'Oh, Frank! dear Frank!'

Lord Ballindine was only ten minutes late in
coming down to dinner, and Miss Wyndham not
about half an hour, which should be considered as
showing great moderation on her part. For, of
course, Frank kept her talking a great deal longer
than he should have done; and then she not only had
to dress, but to go through many processes with her
eyes, to obliterate the trace of tears. She was, however, successful, for she looked very beautiful when
she came down, and so dignified, so composed, so

quiet in her happiness, and yet so very happy in her
quietness. Fanny was anything but a hypocrite;
she had hardly a taint of hypocrisy in her composition, but her looks seldom betrayed her feelings.
There was a majesty of beauty about her, a look of
serenity in her demeanour, which in public made her
appear superior to all emotion.

Frank seemed to be much less at his ease. He attempted to chat easily with the countess, and to
listen pleasantly to the would-be witticisms of the
earl; but he was not comfortable, he did not amalga-
mate well with the family; had there been a larger
party, he could have talked all dinner-time to his
love; but, as it was, he hardly spoke a word to her
during the ceremony, and indeed, but few during the
evening. He did sit next to her on the sofa, to be
sure, and watched the lace she was working; but he
could not talk unreservedly to her, when old Lady
Cashel was sitting close to him on the other side, and
Lady Selina on a chair immediately opposite. And
then, it is impossible to talk to one's mistress, in an
ordinary voice, on ordinary subjects, when one has
not seen her for some months. A lover is never so
badly off as in a family party: a *tête-à-tête*, or a large
assembly, are what suit him best: he is equally at his
ease in either; but he is completely out of his element
in a family party. After all, Lady Cashel was right;
it would have been much better to have asked the
O'Joscelyns.

The next morning, Frank underwent a desperate
interview in the book-room. His head was dizzy
before Lord Cashel had finished half of what he had
to say. He commenced by pointing out with what
perfect uprightness and wisdom he had himself acted
with regard to his ward; and Lord Ballindine did not
care to be at the trouble of contradicting him. He
then went to the subject of settlements, and money
matters: professed that he had most unbounded
confidence in his young friend's liberality, integrity,
and good feeling; that he would be glad to listen,

and, he had no doubt, to accede to any proposals
made by him: that he was quite sure Lord Ballindine
would make no proposal which was not liberal, fair,
and most proper; and he said a great deal more of the
kind, and then himself proposed to arrange his
ward's fortune in such a way as to put it quite beyond her future husband's control. On this subject,
however, Frank rather nonplussed the earl by
proposing nothing, and agreeing to nothing; but
simply saying that he would leave the whole matter
in the hands of the lawyers.

'Quite right, my lord, quite right,' said Lord
Cashel, 'my men of business, Green and Grogram,
will manage all that. They know all about Fanny's
property; they can draw out the settlements, and
Grogram can bring them here, and we can execute
them: that'll be the simplest way.'

'I'll write to Mr. Cummings, then, and tell him to
wait on Messrs. Green and Grogram. Cummings is a
very proper man: he was recommended to me by
Guinness.'

'Oh, ah—yes; your attorney, you mean?' said the
earl. 'Why, yes, that will be quite proper, too. Of
course Mr. Cummings will see the necessity of absolutely securing Miss Wyndham's fortune.'

Nothing further, however, was said between them
on the subject; and the settlements, whatever was
their purport, were drawn out without any visible
interference on the part of Lord Ballindine. But Mr.
Grogram, the attorney, on his first visit to Grey
Abbey on the subject, had no difficulty in learning
that Miss Wyndham was determined to have a will
of her own in the disposition of her own money.

Fanny told her lover the whole episode of Lord
Kilcullen's offer to her; but she told it in such a way
as to redound rather to her cousin's credit than otherwise. She had learned to love him as a cousin and
a friend, and his ill-timed proposal to her had not
destroyed the feeling. A woman can rarely be really
offended at the expression of love, unless it be from

some one unfitted to match with her, either in rank or age. Besides, Fanny thought that Lord Kilcullen had behaved generously to her when she so violently repudiated his love: she believed that it had been sincere; she had not even to herself accused him of meanness or treachery; and she spoke of him as one to be pitied, liked, and regarded; not as one to be execrated and avoided.

And then she confessed to Frank all her fears respecting himself; how her heart would have broken, had he taken her own rash word as final, and so deserted her. She told him that she had never ceased to love him, for a day; not even on that day when, in her foolish spleen, she had told her uncle she was willing to break off the match; she owned to him all her troubles, all her doubts; how she had made up her mind to write to him, but had not dared to do so, lest his answer should be such as would kill her at once. And then she prayed to be forgiven for her falseness; for having consented, even for a moment, to forget the solemn vows she had so often repeated to him.

Frank stopped her again and again in her sweet confessions, and swore the blame was only his. He anathematised himself, his horses, and his friends, for having caused a moment's uneasiness to her; but she insisted on receiving his forgiveness, and he was obliged to say that he forgave her. With all his follies, and all his weakness, Lord Ballindine was not of an unforgiving temperament: he was too happy to be angry with any one, now. He forgave even Lord Cashel; and, had he seen Lord Kilcullen, he would have been willing to give him his hand as to a brother.

Frank spent two or three delightful weeks, basking in the sunshine of Fanny's love, and Lord Cashel's favour. Nothing could be more obsequiously civil than the earl's demeanour, now that the matter was decided. Every thing was to be done just as Lord Ballindine liked; his taste was to be consulted in every thing; the earl even proposed different visits

to the Curragh; asked after the whereabouts of
Fin M'Coul and Brien Boru; and condescended
pleasantly to inquire whether Dot Blake was pros-
pering as usual with his favourite amusement.

At length, the day was fixed for the marriage. It
was to be in the pleasant, sweet-smelling, grateful
month of May,—the end of May; and Lord and Lady
Ballindine were then to start for a summer tour, as
the countess had proposed, to see the Rhine, and
Switzerland, and Rome, and those sort of places.
And now, invitations were sent, far and wide, to
relatives and friends. Lord Cashel had determined
that the wedding should be a great concern. The
ruin of his son was to be forgotten in the marriage of
his niece. The bishop of Maryborough was to come
and marry them; the Ellisons were to come again,
and the Fitzgeralds: a Duchess was secured, though
duchesses are scarce in Ireland; and great exertions
were made to get at a royal Prince, who was commanding the forces in the west. But the royal Prince
did not see why he should put himself to so much
trouble, and he therefore sent to say that he was very
sorry, but the peculiar features of the time made it
quite impossible for him to leave his command, even
on so great a temptation; and a paragraph consequently found its way into the papers, very laudatory
of his Royal Highness's military energy and attention. Mrs. O'Kelly and her daughters received a very
warm invitation, which they were delighted to
accept. Sophy and Augusta were in the seventh
heaven of happiness, for they were to form a portion
of the fair bevy of bridesmaids appointed to attend
Fanny Wyndham to the altar. Frank rather pished
and poohed at all these preparations of grandeur; he
felt that when the ceremony took place he would look
like the ornamental calf in the middle of it; but, on
the whole, he bore his martyrdom patiently. Four
spanking bays, and a new chariot ordered from
Hutton's, on the occasion, would soon carry him
away from the worst part of it.

Lord Cashel was in the midst of his glory: he had got an occupation and he delighted in it. Lady Selina performed her portion of the work with exemplary patience and attention. She wrote all the orders to the tradesmen, and all the invitations; she even condescended to give advice to Fanny about her dress; and to Griffiths, about the arrangement of the rooms and tables. But poor Lady Cashel worked the hardest of all,—her troubles had no end. Had she known what she was about to encounter, when she undertook the task of superintending the arrangements for her niece's wedding, she would never have attempted it: she would never have entered into negotiations with that treacherous Murray—that man cook in Dublin—but have allowed Mrs. Richards to have done her best,—or her worst,—in her own simple way, in spite of the Duchess and the Bishop, and the hopes of a royal Prince indulged in by Lord Cashel. She did not dare to say as much to her husband, but she confessed to Griffiths that she was delighted when she heard His Royal Highness would not come. She was sure his coming would not make dear Fanny a bit happier, and she really would not have known what to do with him after the married people were gone.

Frank received two letters from Dot Blake during his stay at Grey Abbey. In the former he warmly congratulated him on his approaching nuptials, and strongly commended him on his success in having arranged matters. 'You never could have forgiven yourself,' he said, 'had you allowed Miss Wyndham's splendid fortune to slip through your hands. I knew you were not the man to make a vain boast of a girl's love, and I was therefore sure that you might rely on her affection. I only feared you might let the matter go too far. You know I strongly advised you not to marry twenty thousand pounds. I am as strongly of opinion that you would be a fool to neglect to marry six times as much. You see I still confine myself to the money part of the business, as

though the lady herself were of no value. I don't
think so, however; only I know *you* never would have
lived happily without an easy fortune.' And then he
spoke of Brien Boru, and informed Lord Ballindine
that that now celebrated nag was at the head of the
list of the Derby horses; that it was all but impossible
to get any odds against him at all;—that the whole
betting world were talking of nothing else; that three
conspiracies had been detected, the object of which was
to make him safe—that is, to make him very unsafe
to his friends; that Scott's foreman had been offered
two thousand to dose him; and that Scott himself
slept in the stable with him every night, to prevent
anything like false play.

The second letter was written by Dot, at Epsom,
on the 4th of May, thirty minutes after the great
race had been run. It was very short; and shall
therefore be given entire.

Epsom, Derby Day,
Race just over.

God bless you, my dear boy—Brien has done the
trick, and done it well! Butler rode him beautifully,
but he did not want any riding; he's the kindest
beast ever had a saddle on. The stakes are close on
four thousand pounds: your share will do well to pay
the posters, &c., for yourself and my lady, on your
wedding trip. I win well—very well; but I doubt the
settling. We shall have awful faces at the corner
next week. You'll probably have heard all about it
by express before you get this.

In greatest haste, yours,
W. BLAKE.

The next week, the following paragraph appeared
in 'Bell's Life in London.'

'It never rains but it pours. It appears pretty
certain, now, that Brien Boru is not the property of
the gentleman in whose name he has run; but that he
is owned by a certain noble lord, well known on the

Irish turf, who has lately, however, been devoting his time to pursuits more pleasant and more profitable than the cares of the stable—pleasant and profitable as it doubtless must be to win the best race of the year. The pick-up on the Derby is about four thousand pounds, and Brien Boru is certainly the best horse of his year. But Lord Ballindine's matrimonial pick-up is, we are told, a clear quarter of a million; and those who are good judges declare that no more beautiful woman than the future Lady Ballindine will have graced the English Court for many a long year. His lordship, on the whole, is not doing badly.'

Lord Cashel, also, congratulated Frank on his success on the turf, in spite of the very decided opinion he had expressed on the subject, when he was endeavouring to throw him on one side.

'My dear Ballindine,' he said, 'I wish you joy with all my heart: a most magnificent animal, I'm told, is Brien, and still partly your own property, you say. Well; it's a great triumph to beat those English lads on their own ground, isn't it? And thorough Irish blood, too!—thorough Irish blood! He has the "Paddy Whack" strain in him, through the dam—the very best blood in Ireland. You know, my mare "Dignity", that won the Oaks in '29, was by "Chanticleer", out of "Floribel", by "Paddy Whack." You say you mean to give up the turf, and you know I've done so, too. But, if you ever do change your mind—should you ever run horses again—take my advice, and stick to the "Paddy Whack" strain. There's no beating the real "Paddy Whack" blood.'

On the 21st of May, 1844, Lord Ballindine and Fanny Wyndham were married. The bishop 'turned 'em off iligant,' as a wag said in the servants' hall. There was a long account of the affair in the 'Morning Post' of the day; there were eight bridesmaids, all of whom, it was afterwards remarked, were themselves married within two years of the time; an omen which was presumed to promise much continued happiness to Lord and Lady Ballindine, and all belonging to them.

Murray, the man cook, did come down from Dublin, just in time; but he behaved very badly. He got quite drunk on the morning of the wedding. He, however, gave Richards an opportunity of immortalising herself. She behaved, on the trying occasion, so well, that she is now confirmed in her situation; and Lady Cashel has solemnly declared that she will never again, on any account, be persuaded to allow a man cook to enter the house.

Lady Selina—she would not officiate as one of the bridesmaids—is still unmarried; but her temper is not thereby soured, nor her life embittered. She is active, energetic, and good as ever: and, as ever, cold, hard, harsh, and dignified. Lord Kilcullen has hardly been heard of since his departure from Grey Abbey. It is known that he is living at Baden, but no one knows on what. His father never mentions his name; his mother sometimes talks of 'poor Adolphus;' but if he were dead and buried he could not give less trouble to the people of Grey Abbey.

No change has occurred, or is likely to take place, in the earl himself—nor is any desirable. How could he change for the better? How could he bear his honours with more dignity, or grace his high position with more decorum? Every year since the marriage of his niece, he has sent Lord and Lady Ballindine an invitation to Grey Abbey; but there has always been some insuperable impediment to the visit. A child had just been born, or was just going to be born; or Mrs. O'Kelly was ill; or one of the Miss O'Kellys was going to be married. It was very unfortunate, but Lord and Lady Ballindine were never able to get as far as Grey Abbey.

Great improvements have been effected at Kelly's Court. Old buildings have been pulled down, and additions built up; a great many thousand young trees have been planted, and some miles of new roads and walks constructed. The place has quite an altered appearance; and, though Connaught is still Connaught, and County Mayo is the poorest part of it, Lady Ballindine does not find Kelly's Court unbearable. She has three children already, and doubtless will have many more. Her nursery, therefore, prevents her from being tormented by the weariness of the far west.

Lord Ballindine himself is very happy. He still has the hounds, and maintains, in the three counties round him, the sporting pre-eminence, which has for so many years belonged to his family. But he has no race-horses. His friend, Dot, purchased the lot of them out and out, soon after the famous Derby; and a very good bargain, for himself, he is said to have made. He is still intimate with Lord Ballindine, and always spends a fortnight with him at Kelly's Court during the hunting-season.

Sophy O'Kelly married a Blake, and Augusta married a Dillon; and, as they both live within ten miles of Kelly's Court, and their husbands are related to all the Blakes and all the Dillons; and as Ballindine himself is the head of all the Kellys, there is a rather strong clan of them. About five-and-twenty cousins muster together in red coats and top-boots, every Tuesday and Friday during the hunting-season. It would hardly be wise, in that country, to quarrel with a Kelly, a Dillon, or a Blake.

XL

CONCLUSION

WE must now return to Dunmore, and say a few parting words of the Kellys and Anty Lynch; and then our task will be finished.

It will be remembered that that demon of Dunmore, Barry Lynch, has been made to vanish: like Lord Kilcullen, he has gone abroad; he has settled himself at an hotel at Boulogne, and is determined to enjoy himself. Arrangements have been made about the property, certainly not very satisfactory to Barry, because they are such as make it necessary for him to pay his own debts; but they still leave him sufficient to allow of his indulging in every vice congenial to his taste; and, if he doesn't get fleeced by cleverer rogues than himself—which, however, will probably be the case—he will have quite enough to last him till he has drunk himself to death.

After his departure, there was nothing to delay Anty's marriage, but her own rather slow recovery. She has no other relatives to ask, no other friends to consult. Now that Barry was gone she was entirely her own mistress, and was quite willing to give up her dominion over herself to Martin Kelly. She had, however, been greatly shaken; not by illness only, but by fear also—her fears of Barry and for Barry. She still dreamed while asleep, and thought while awake, of that horrid night when he crept up to her room and swore that he would murder her. This, and what she had suffered since, had greatly weakened her, and it was some time before Doctor Colligan would pronounce her convalescent. At last, however, the difficulties were overcome; all arrangements were completed. Anty was well; the property was settled; Martin was impatient; and the day was fixed.

There was no bishop, no duchess, no man-cook, at the wedding-party given on the occasion by Mrs. Kelly; nevertheless, it was, in its way, quite as grand an affair as that given by the countess. The widow opened her heart, and opened her house. Her great enemy, Barry Lynch, was gone—clean beaten out of the field—thoroughly vanquished; as far as Ireland was concerned, annihilated; and therefore, any one else in the three counties was welcome to share her hospitality. Oh, the excess of delight the widow experienced in speaking of Barry to one of her gossips, as the 'poor misfortunate crature!' Daly, the attorney, was especially invited, and he came. Moylan also was asked, but he stayed away. Doctor Colligan was there, in great feather; had it not been for him, there would probably have been no wedding at all. It would have been a great thing if

Lord Ballindine could have been got to grace the party, though only for ten minutes; but he was at that time in Switzerland with his own bride, so he could not possibly do so.

'Well, ma'am,' said Mrs. Costelloe, the grocer's wife, from Tuam, an old friend of the widow, who had got into a corner with her to have a little chat, and drink half-a-pint of porter before the ceremony, —'and I'm shure I wish you joy of the marriage. Faix, I'm tould it's nigh to five hundred a-year, Miss Anty has, may God bless and incrase it! Well, Martin has his own luck; but he desarves it, he desarves it.'

'I don't know so much about luck thin, Mrs. Costelloe,' said the widow, who still professed to think that her son gave quite as much as he got, in marrying Anty Lynch; 'I don't know so much about luck: Martin was very well as he was; his poor father didn't lave him that way that he need be looking to a wife for mains, the Lord be praised.'

'And that's thrue, too, Mrs. Kelly,' said the other; 'but Miss Anty's fortune ain't a bad step to a young man, neither. Why, there won't be a young gintleman within tin—no, not within forty miles, more respectable than Martin Kelly; that is, regarding mains.'

'And you needn't stop there, Ma'am, neither; you may say the very same regarding characther, too— and family, too, glory be to the Virgin. I'd like to know where some of their ancesthers wor, when the Kellys of ould wor ruling the whole counthry?'

'Thrue for you, my dear; I'd like to know, indeed: there's nothing, afther all, like blood, and a good characther. But is it thrue, Mrs. Kelly, that Martin will live up in the big house yonder?'

'Where should a man live thin, Mrs. Costelloe, when he gets married, but jist in his own house? Why for should he not live there?'

'That's thrue agin, to be shure: but yet, only to think—Martin living in ould Sim Lynch's big house! I wondther what ould Sim would say, hisself, av he could only come back and see it!'

'I'll tell you what he'd say thin, av he tould the thruth; he'd say there was an honest man living there, which wor niver the case as long as any of his own breed was in it—barring Anty, I main; she's honest and thrue, the Lord be good to her, the poor thing. But the porter's not to your liking, Mrs. Costelloe—you're not tasting it at all this morning.'

No one could have been more humble and meek than was Anty herself, in the midst of her happiness. She had no idea of taking on herself the airs of a fine lady, or the importance of an heiress; she had no wish to be thought a lady; she had no wish for other friends than those of her husband, and his family. She had never heard of her brother's last horrible proposal to Doctor Colligan, and of the manner in which his consent to her marriage had been obtained; nor did Martin intend that she should hear it. She had merely been told that her brother had found that it was for his advantage to leave the neighbour-hood altogether; that he had given up all claim to the house; and that his income was to be sent to him by a person appointed in the neighbourhood to receive it. Anty, however, before signing her own settlement, was particularly careful that nothing should be done, injurious to her brother's interest, and that no unfair advantage should be taken of his absence.

Martin, too, was quiet enough on the occasion. It was arranged that he and his wife, and at any rate one of his sisters, should live at Dunmore House; and that he should keep in his own hands the farm near Dunmore, which old Sim had held, as well as his own farm at Toneroe. But, to tell the truth, Martin felt rather ashamed of his grandeur. He would much have preferred building a nice snug little house of his own, on the land he held under Lord Ballindine; but he was told that he would be a fool to build a house on another man's ground, when he had a very good one ready built on his own. He gave way to such good advice, but he did not feel at all happy at the idea; and, when going up to the house, always felt an inclination to shirk in at the back-way.

But, though neither the widow nor Martin triumphed aloud at their worldly prosperity, the two girls made up for their quiescence. They were full of nothing else; their brother's fine house—Anty's great fortune; their wealth, prosperity, and future station and happiness, gave them subjects of delightful conversation among their friends. Meg, moreover, boasted that it was all her own doing; that it was she who had made up the match; that Martin would never have thought of it but for her,—nor Anty either, for the matter of that.

'And will your mother be staying down at the shop always, the same as iver?' said Matilda Nolan, the daughter of the innkeeper at Tuam.

''Deed she says so, then,' said Jane, in a tone of disappointment; for her mother's pertinacity in adhering to the counter was, at present, the one misery of her life.

'And which of you will be staying here along with her, dears?' said Matilda. 'She'll be wanting one of you to be with her, any ways.'

'Oh, turn about, I suppose,' said Jane.

'She'll not get much of my company, any way,' said Meg. 'I've had enough of the nasty place, and now Martin has a dacent house to put over our heads, and mainly through my mains I may say, I don't see why I'm to be mewing myself up in such a hole as this. There's room for her up in Dunmore House, and wilcome, too; let her come up there. Av she mains to demain herself by sticking down here, she may stay by herself for me.'

'But you'll take your turn, Meg?' said Jane.

'It'll be a very little turn, then,' said Meg; 'I'm sick of the nasty ould place; fancy coming down here, Matilda, to the tobacco and sugar, after living up there a month or so, with everything nice and comfortable! And it's only mother's whims, for she don't want the shop. Anty begged and prayed of her for to come and live at Dunmore House for good and all; but no; she says she'll never live in any one's house that isn't her own.'

'I'm not so, any way,' said Jane; 'I'd be glad enough to live in another person's house av I liked it.'

'I'll go bail you would, my dear,' said Matilda; 'willing enough—especially John Dolan's.'

'Oh! av I iver live in that it'll be partly my own, you know; and may-be a girl might do worse.'

'That's thrue, dear,' said Matilda; 'but John Dolan's not so soft as to take any girl just as she stands. What does your mother say about the money part of the business?'

And so the two friends put their heads together, to arrange another wedding, if possible.

Martin and Anty did not go to visit Switzerland, or Rome, as soon as they were married; but they took a bathing-lodge at Renvill, near Galway, and with much difficulty, persuaded Mrs. Kelly to allow both her daughters to accompany them. And very merry they all were. Anty soon became a different creature from what she ever had been: she learned to be happy and gay; to laugh and enjoy the sunshine of the world. She had always been kind to others, and now she had round her those who were kind and affectionate to her. Her manner of life was completely changed: indeed, life itself was an altered thing to her. It was so new to her to have friends; to be loved; to be one of a family who regarded and looked up to her. She hardly knew herself in her new happiness.

They returned to Dunmore in the early autumn, and took up their residence at Sim Lynch's big house, as had been arranged. Martin was very shy about it: it was long before he talked about it as his house, or his ground, or his farm; and it was long before he could find himself quite at home in his own parlour.

Many attempts were made to induce the widow to give up the inn, and shift her quarters to the big house, but in vain. She declared that, ould as she

was, she wouldn't think of making herself throuble-
some to young folks; who, may-be, afther a bit,
would a dail sooner have her room than her company:
that she had always been misthress, and mostly
masther too, in her own house, glory be to God; and
that she meant to be so still; and that, poor as the
place was, she meant to call it her own. She didn't
think herself at all fit company for people who lived
in grand houses, and had their own demesnes, and
gardens, and the rest of it; she had always lived
where money was to be made, and she didn't see the
sense of going, in her old age, to a place where the
only work would be how to spend it. Some folks
would find it was a dail asier to scatther it than it
wor to put it together. All this she said and a great
deal more, which had her character not been known,
would have led people to believe that her son was a
spendthrift, and that he and Anty were commencing life in an expensive way, and without
means. But then, the widow Kelly *was* known, and
her speeches were only taken at their value.

She so far relaxed, however, that she spent every
Sunday at the house; on which occasions she invariably dressed herself with all the grandeur she was
able to display, and passed the whole afternoon
sitting on a sofa, with her hands before her, trying to
look as became a lady enjoying herself in a fine
drawing-room. Her Sundays were certainly not the
comfort to her, which they had been when spent at
the inn; but they made her enjoy, with a keener
relish, the feeling of perfect sovereignty when she
returned to her own domains.

I have nothing further to tell of Mr. and Mrs. Kelly.
I believe Doctor Colligan has been once called in on an
interesting occasion, if not twice; so it is likely that
Dunmore House will not be left without an heir.

I have also learned, on inquiry, that Margaret and
Jane Kelly have both arranged their own affairs to
their own satisfaction.

THE END

READ MORE IN PENGUIN

In every corner of the world, on every subject under the sun, Penguin represents quality and variety – the very best in publishing today.

For complete information about books available from Penguin – including Puffins, Penguin Classics and Arkana – and how to order them, write to us at the appropriate address below. Please note that for copyright reasons the selection of books varies from country to country.

In the United Kingdom: Please write to *Dept. JC, Penguin Books Ltd, FREEPOST, West Drayton, Middlesex UB7 OBR*

If you have any difficulty in obtaining a title, please send your order with the correct money, plus ten per cent for postage and packaging, to *PO Box No. 11, West Drayton, Middlesex UB7 OBR*

In the United States: Please write to *Penguin USA Inc., 375 Hudson Street, New York, NY 10014*

In Canada: Please write to *Penguin Books Canada Ltd, 10 Alcorn Avenue, Suite 300, Toronto, Ontario M4V 3B2*

In Australia: Please write to *Penguin Books Australia Ltd, 487 Maroondah Highway, Ringwood, Victoria 3134*

In New Zealand: Please write to *Penguin Books (NZ) Ltd, 182–190 Wairau Road, Private Bag, Takapuna, Auckland 9*

In India: Please write to *Penguin Books India Pvt Ltd, 706 Eros Apartments, 56 Nehru Place, New Delhi 110 019*

In the Netherlands: Please write to *Penguin Books Netherlands B.V., Keizersgracht 231 NL–1016 DV Amsterdam*

In Germany: Please write to *Penguin Books Deutschland GmbH, Friedrichstrasse 10–12, W–6000 Frankfurt/Main 1*

In Spain: Please write to *Penguin Books S. A., C. San Bernardo 117–6° E–28015 Madrid*

In Italy: Please write to *Penguin Italia s.r.l., Via Felice Casati 20, I–20124 Milano*

In France: Please write to *Penguin France S. A., 17 rue Lejeune, F–31000 Toulouse*

In Japan: Please write to *Penguin Books Japan, Ishikiribashi Building, 2–5–4, Suido, Tokyo 112*

In Greece: Please write to *Penguin Hellas Ltd, Dimocritou 3, GR–106 71 Athens*

In South Africa: Please write to *Longman Penguin Southern Africa (Pty) Ltd, Private Bag X08, Bertsham 2013*

READ MORE IN PENGUIN

CHARLES DICKENS – A SELECTION

The Old Curiosity Shop
Edited by Angus Easson with an Introduction by Malcolm Andrews

Described as a 'tragedy of sorrows', *The Old Curiosity Shop* tells of 'Little Nell' uprooted from a secure and innocent childhood and cast into a world where evil takes many shapes, the most fascinating of which is the stunted, lecherous Quilp. He is Nell's tormentor and destroyer, and it is his demonic energy that dominates the book.

Nicholas Nickleby
Edited with an Introduction by Michael Slater

The work of a young man at the height of his powers, *Nicholas Nickleby* will remain one of the touchstones of the English comic novel. Around his central story of Nicholas Nickleby and the misfortunes of his family, Dickens weaves a great gallery of comic types.

David Copperfield
Edited by Trevor Blount

Written in the form of an autobiography, it tells the story of David Copperfield, growing to maturity in the affairs of the world and the affairs of the heart – his success as an artist arising out of his sufferings and out of the lessons he derives from life.

Oliver Twist
Edited by Peter Fairclough with an Introduction by Angus Wilson

Scathing in its exposure of contemporary cruelties, always exciting, and clothed in an unforgettable atmosphere of mystery and pervasive evil, Dickens's second novel was a huge popular success, its major characters – Fagin, Bill Sykes, and the Artful Dodger – now creatures of myth.

READ MORE IN PENGUIN

CHARLES DICKENS – A SELECTION

Bleak House
Edited by Norman Page with an Introduction by J. Hillis Miller

At the Court of Chancery the interminable suit of Jarndyce and Jarndyce becomes the centre of a web of relationships at all levels, from Sir Leicester Dedlock to Jo the crossing-sweeper, and a metaphor for the decay and corruption at the heart of English society.

A Tale of Two Cities
Edited by George Woodcock

This stirring tale of resurrection, renunciation and revolution is one of Dickens's best and most popular novels and the embodiment of his own passions, fears and forebodings; the revolution which engulfs the characters symbolizes his own psychological revolution, both as man and artist.

Martin Chuzzlewit
Edited by P. N. Furbank

The story of an inheritance, *Martin Chuzzlewit* relates the contrasting destinies of two descendants of the brothers Chuzzlewit, both born and bred to the same heritage of selfishness, showing how one, Martin, by good fortune escapes and how the other, Jonas, does not – only to reap a fatal harvest.

The Mystery of Edwin Drood
Edited by Arthur J. Cox with an Introduction by Angus Wilson

The Mystery of Edwin Drood is even more of a mystery than Dickens himself intended, for he died before completing it. As intriguing as the central plot are the startling innovations in Dickens's work and the troubled elements lurking within the novel: a dark opium underworld and the uneasy and violent fantasies of its inhabitants.

THE PENGUIN TROLLOPE

1. The Macdermots of Ballycloran (1847)
2. The Kellys and the O'Kellys: Or Landlords and Tenants (1848)
3. La Vendée: An Historical Romance (1850)
4. The Warden (1855)
5. Barchester Towers (1857)
6. The Three Clerks (1858)
7. Doctor Thorne (1858)
8. The Bertrams (1859)
9. Castle Richmond (1860)
10. Framley Parsonage (1861)
11. Tale of All Countries: First Series (1861)
12. Orley Farm (1862)
13. The Struggles of Brown, Jones and Robinson: By One of the Firm (1862)
14. Tales of All Countries: Second Series (1863)
15. Rachel Ray (1863)
16. The Small House at Allington (1864)
17. Can You Forgive Her? (1865)
18. Miss Mackenzie (1865)
19. The Belton Estate (1866)
20. Nina Balatka (1867)
21. The Last Chronicle of Barset (1867)
22. The Claverings (1867)
23. Lotta Schmidt and Other Stories (1867)
24. Linda Tressel (1868)
25. Phineas Finn: The Irish Member (1869)
26. He Knew He Was Right (1869)

THE PENGUIN TROLLOPE

27. The Vicar of Bullhampton (1870)
28. An Editor's Tales (1870)
29. Sir Harry Hotspur of Humblethwaite (1871)
30. Ralph the Heir (1871)
31. The Golden Lion of Granpère (1872)
32. The Eustace Diamonds (1873)
33. Phineas Redux (1874)
34. Lady Anna (1874)
35. Harry Heathcote of Gangoil: A Tale of Australian Bush Life (1874)
36. The Way We Live Now (1875)
37. The Prime Minister (1876)
38. The American Senator (1877)
39. Is He Popenjoy? (1878)
40. An Eye for an Eye (1879)
41. John Caldigate (1879)
42. Cousin Henry (1879)
43. The Duke's Children (1880)
44. Dr Wortle's School (1881)
45. Ayala's Angel (1881)
46. Why Frau Frohmann Raised Her Prices and Other Stories (1882)
47. Kept in the Dark (1882)
48. Marion Fay (1882)
49. The Fixed Period (1882)
50. Mr Scarborough's Family (1883)
51. The Landleaguers (1883)
52. An Old Man's Love (1884)
53. An Autobiography (1883)